Windup

More by Brooke Shaffer

The Timekeeper Chronicles

The Chivalrous Welshman
Time to Kill
Tick Tock
Windup
Stopwatch (Summer 2019)

Windup
Book Three of The Chivalrous Welshman
The Timekeeper Chronicles

Brooke Shaffer

Black Bear Publishing

Published in Michigan by Black Bear Publishing.

ISBN:
    Hardcover: 978-0-9991392-6-4
    Softcover: 978-0-9991392-8-8
    eBook: 978-0-9991392-7-1

A re you sure you want to do this, Walt?" Cory James asked as he punched out, grabbed a final cup of coffee, and walked out of the precinct. "Kids are a lot of work on their own; bringing one in who's eight years old and already has or had a family, that's a whole new ballgame. Like, that goes beyond left field; you're out of the park."

"If I wasn't sure, I wouldn't be here," Walter told him. "It's just something I have to do."

"So is this for the kid, or for you?"

Walter opened the car door and paused. "For both of us."

Cory sighed. "Walt, I'm your partner and your friend, and you know I'll stand by you, but you do know that I will tell you the honest truth if I don't think it's good for him. The welfare of the kid is what I'm concerned about."

"I know, and I would be hurt if you did anything less than tell me the truth. But whether it's you and your wife having your first, or me taking him in, kids aren't like new cars or new houses. You're never 'ready' for them. You have them or you don't; there is no middle ground."

The younger officer still looked unsure, but he nodded. "Well, I know I'm not going to talk you out of it, and I won't try. But if you need anything, just give me a holler. And above all, put the kid first."

"I always do."

With that, Walter started the car and left the precinct. He was scared spitless, actually. He'd had to fight to the death just to be able to foster Tommen, as if he were committing some great crime by not being married and living in a cute little neighborhood with a picket fence and a dog. Literally, that was what he'd had to compete against. The only reason he'd managed to win was the hospital psychiatrist suggesting Tommen might adjust better if he were an only child and not bombarded by siblings ranging in age from six months to thirteen years. Once he'd calmed down and his psychosis subsided—meaning, once he accepted some disjointed reality where he hadn't walked through a Time Portal and jumped a hundred and fifty years into the future—then he could be reevaluated and sent to a better family.

Walter was determined to keep Tommen, no matter what the cost. He was the only one who understood Tommen, where he was from, what he was seeing, his whole experience. He could help him, really help him, rather than just brush it off as psychosis or autism or something stupid like that. He was a good kid; his pa had told him so before he went looking for him. Walter was determined to keep his word to find Tommen. He would just have to add a clause in there about raising him, too.

He arrived at the hospital and sat in the parking lot for a few minutes, trying to gather his nerves. He was terrified; there was no other way to say it. He'd been nervous before when Victoria was born, but back then, he'd hardly cared for more than a few hours or days before he was back to drinking to cope with it, telling himself he was celebrating when really he was running and hiding. This time, he was facing everything completely sober.

He'd picked up a few things for Tommen, some clothes and a backpack to put them in. Everything was rather plain; the boy had no concept of TV, movies, or animation, so all the shirts and backpacks with the animated movie or comic book characters on them would mean nothing. He grabbed the backpack and took it in with him.

"Today's the day," Dina greeted as he walked in. "Are you excited?"

"Nervous as hell," he admitted.

"Well, know that he's nervous, too. Scared out of his mind almost. The doc will write a script for anti-anxiety meds, probably

Ritalin."

"He's eight years old."

"And running almost a hundred and fifty beats per minute just sitting down. It's not fair, but he needs to calm down. I don't envy you, Walter."

Walter said nothing to that, just put on a good face as he entered Tommen's room. He'd healed well from his accident, not the least thanks to Walter who had done a little speeding up of the healing process during their visits. According to all the nurses, Tommen seemed to prefer him, and that had been another factor in why he'd won the case to foster him.

"Are you ready to get out of here and go home?" Walter asked, pulling up a chair.

Tommen nodded.

"All right. Let's get some proper clothes on you, and let's go home."

Chapter One
On Cochleas

Tommen was glad that Micaiah was driving, because he knew that if he'd been in the driver's seat, they probably would have landed in a ditch somewhere, as distracted as he was.

Finally, his dad was coming home from the hospital. It was difficult to believe that hardly ten days ago, Tommen had been taken hostage by the renegade Timekeeper Rifun, seeking to use him to get to Walter in order that he would give up the corrupt bureaucrat Lily to save him. Tommen closed his eyes and could effortlessly bring to mind standing there in the shipping yard, Rifun's gun pressed against his head, Walter hardly ten yards away trying to do his best to bring everyone home and haul Rifun and his associates off to jail.

But not everyone had gone home. Even before they'd gotten to the standoff, Rifun had murdered seven police officers. When all was said and done, nine officers had died, three had been maimed to the point of never returning to the force, and the rest were on suicide watch pending psychological evaluation.

It was difficult to gauge where Walter fell on that spectrum. He'd gotten separated from the rest of the group, cornered by Rifun and an alien called a Borelian, whose very touch was a death sentence. Shot with poison bullets and left to die, he'd made it to the ER and gotten into surgery, but the poison was already working, and he lapsed into a coma with only about a week to live.

Tommen, not one to give up, had gone to the Hands of Time, seeking help. Not only did they refuse to help him, but he managed to start a civil war because of it. But one of the Hands took pity on him and told him where to find a cure that, by all accounts, did not exist.

He'd ended up traipsing across a blazing hot desert, getting in a fight with the world's ugliest cat, traipsing through a jungle, getting in a fight with the world's ugliest bear-slash-komodo dragon, free-climbing a rock wall, dislocating his hand, losing all but a fraction of the antidote he'd collected, and escaping by the skin of his teeth. And that wasn't even considering the chase through the Wheel that ensued.

When he returned, he got the antidote to Walter, and within twenty-four hours, his dad was awake and talking, almost as if he hadn't been on the verge of death.

That had been three days ago. The doctors insisted on keeping him for several more days, despite his apparent miracle recovery, or perhaps because of it. They did scans and ran tests, always doing something, trying to figure out what had pulled him back from the brink. Ultimately, they'd found nothing to explain it, and, since he hadn't relapsed or shown any other signs of imminent medical danger, they were forced to release him.

But that wasn't to say he was going to be out dancing anytime soon. He'd still been shot three times. While it was normally possible for Walter to Band his injuries and recover from them faster, he was unable to do so with these injuries. His best guess had been some kind of residual effect of the Borelian poison, that even as it was immune to Time, so his injuries would be also.

"Got everything?" Micaiah asked as he pulled into a parking spot. Behind them, Micah, Micaiah's younger twin brother, cruised past to find a spot in the lot. The idea was that Tommen would drive Walter home, but since he didn't have his full license yet, he still needed to catch a ride.

"Huh? Oh, um, I think so," Tommen said, perusing through the bag. That was another thing. Between multiple close-range gunshots, one set directly next to his head as close as it could get, and a number of very loud animal sounds, he'd lost part of his hearing, to the point where as soon as Walter was checked out, Tommen would be checking in to see the audiologist.

"We'll be over a little later to make sure he's settled in and make sure you don't need help or anything," the elder Durvin twin told him as they got out of the car. "Take it easy on him, Tommen; he's as shaken as you are."

At first, Tommen figured he was referring to his dad's near-death experience, which could very well have been part or a majority of it. Then he also considered that there was probably a part of Walter that still felt the shame of his dishonesty, or his perceived dishonesty, that he'd never told Tommen about just how closely related they were. Not only was Walter his adopted father, but his biological uncle as well.

The last few days, despite Tommen forgiving him completely, he could honestly say that he looked at his dad just a little differently. Not just as dad, but as uncle, too. It was a strange sensation. Family. A real, living relative, a connection to his old life, someone who could answer so many questions about his old life, his pa and their family.

Walter, for the most part, seemed to carry on as normally as could be expected, but there were times when Tommen could see, not only the relief of finally sharing his secret, but also the fear of being rejected as a father. He blamed himself for a lot of things, wondering if things might have been different if Tommen had known, if he would have stayed out of trouble more or gotten in even deeper; wondering if things in the warehouse really would have turned out differently if he'd spilled as Rifun had wanted.

And there was a moment, too, during one of those conversations, when Tommen felt another sensation: equality. He loved his dad and respected him, but he almost felt a shift in their relationship, as if he'd finally been elevated from just a child who happened to be growing up, to an adult who was able to function on his own. Maybe it was just him. Maybe it was still too soon to tell. Hell, his dad hadn't even left the hospital yet.

The hospital was busy, as was to be expected on New Year's Day. If people hadn't gotten drunk and done stupid things to land themselves in the hospital, their families were constantly in and out, bringing cards and flowers and gifts and trying to make a bad holiday better. Tommen had considered it, then figured that his dad wasn't even really a card, flowers, or gift kind of person. Just getting out of the hospital and back home to sleep in his own recliner, er, bed, would be enough for him.

Tommen got to the elevator just as it was closing, someone putting their hand out to stop the door and let him on. He thanked them briefly and bounced on his toes as the box began moving.

"Stop twitching, you're making me nervous," a lady chuckled.

"Sorry," Tommen said meekly, forcing himself to stop bouncing and settle instead for anxious toe-curling in the ends of his shoes. "My dad's coming home today."

"That's good. I'm happy for you."

The polite thing to do probably would have been to reciprocate the unasked question, ask her who she was visiting, what happened, did they have a nice Christmas, wish them well, and so on and so forth. Unfortunately, or maybe fortunately in his case, elevators didn't give a lot of opportunities for small talk. So he waited out the awkward four seconds between her statement and his stop.

He shot out of the elevator with the speed of a bullet and the flexibility of water, weaving his way around doctors, nurses, assorted hospital staff, patients, and patients' families, slipping into his dad's room with minimal hindrance.

"Little early, aren't we?" Walter asked from his bed.

Before he could do much more than look around for the remote, Tommen was at his bedside, holding down the button until the head of the bed was up almost as far as it could go.

"You seem very certain they're going to let me leave."

"Aren't they?" Tommen's heart skipped a beat.

His dad chuckled softly. "Of course they are. They have no reason to keep me, and I think with me being so restless now, they'll be glad to get rid of me."

"Are you chasing nurses again?"

"Absolutely. None of them can hope to withstand my winning wobble. They want to run, but they just can't."

He was referring to the gunshot wound to his right thigh. It had severed the artery and screwed up the major muscle groups, but thankfully missed the femur. He was supposed to use a cane or walker or even a wheelchair until it healed, but his stubborn determination to walk took over just as soon as the doctor wasn't looking. He couldn't even use a cane or a walker well seeing how his right arm was in a box sling from another gunshot wound that had cracked his shoulder blade, almost splitting it up the middle. His left arm might have been in the same predicament had he woken up from surgery like he was supposed to have. That bullet had cracked his sternum, ricocheted, and taken a chip off his other shoulder blade. Other than essentially grinding down the sharp edges into more rounded ones, there was little they could do for him, and he was told simply not to exert himself to any more pain than about the equivalent of a paper cut.

At first he'd thought it silly, until he'd tried to pull up his blankets at night or reach any farther than his hip. So it was that Tommen had to help him into his clothes, everything from his boxers to his jacket.

"While you're working and whatnot, I will be figuring out a way to do this by myself," Walter assured him as he weakly fumbled with his belt and pulled it just a little tighter than it used to be and clicked it in.

"I don't mind," Tommen said. "It's the right thing to do. And it's only temporary."

His dad let out a breath and sat down on the bed. He looked at Tommen. "You know what I saw this morning out the window?"

"A car accident?"

Walter grinned and shook his head. "Good guess, but no. Two eagles and a sunrise."

He nodded slowly, and Tommen stared at him, not sure how to respond. Only when his dad's expression started to waver did he shift his stance and fold his arms. "Are you joking?"

Walter cracked up laughing for a second or two, then was

forced to stop, cringing in pain. When the agony had passed, he was still smiling as he looked at his son. "I'm not dying, Tommen. You're right, it's only temporary, but what you have seen cannot be unseen. And I would just as soon not show it off any more than I have to."

Other than a few jokes between men as Tommen helped him dress, he was more likely referring to any number of scars that covered his body, injuries sustained long before his introduction to Time, injuries inflicted upon him by angry drunks with glass bottles or angry villagers with shotguns. The three new ones he'd gained from Rifun were nothing new or truly surprising, just a few more to add to the rest.

As Tommen was helping his dad put his socks and shoes on, the doctor walked in. He was a friendly enough person, Tommen figured, though he seemed a little more intent on testing Walter for his unusual miracle cure than congratulating him on recovering at all and getting him home.

"Thought you'd sneak out on us while we weren't looking, huh?" the doctor began amiably.

"Your backs would have to be turned for quite a while for me to make that kind of getaway," Walter told him, casting a knowing glance at Tommen who turned his head so the doctor wouldn't see him smile.

"Well, I thought I would come by to wish you good luck and happy new year." He tore a script note off his pad and handed it to Walter. "One is for the pain, two as needed but not more than six in a day. The other is a muscle relaxer since you said your thigh would sometimes feel very tight."

"Like a charliehorse, yes."

"The relaxers should help. One as needed, not to exceed four in a day. And if you feel like they're not being effective, come back and we'll take a look, make sure nothing's going on either in the wound or neurologically." The doctor paused and nodded, half to himself. "Other than that, definitely take it easy. You're good to go home, but everything is still in its earliest stages of healing."

"What should I be looking for to, like, call an ambulance or bring him back?" Tommen cut in.

"Any change in his behavior, lethargy, pain that won't go away, signs of infection, excessive bruising, bleeding, that sort of thing. And as always, do not hesitate to call. If you even think you have a question or concern, get a hold of me or one of the other doctors. Better to be on the safe side than go through all of this again."

"I couldn't agree more," Walter said.

"Like I said, take it easy. A little pain is good, but do not exert yourself. No lifting, running, and I would wait on the driving, too."

"Well, there go my drag racing plans."

The doctor smiled. "Do you have any questions now while I'm standing here? I don't want to send you home if you don't feel comfortable."

Comfort had very little to do with it, and he'd been asking that question for the last two days. As usual, neither of them really had anything, and the doctor handed over a thick set of papers, the staple in the corner straining to hold them together.

"Home and work instructions, which I will let you look over at your leisure. Rachel will get you checked out at the desk. Other than that, happy new year, and I am very happy to see you walking out of here."

"You and me both," Walter said.

The doctor nodded once and finally left the room. Tommen looked at his dad expectantly.

"Well, I'm ready to get out of here," Walter decided.

Tommen helped his dad get his shoes on, no small feat considering the man had virtually no strength left in him after the coma, not to mention his thigh injury stealing what little strength he had in reserve. But the shoes went on easily enough, and Tommen positioned himself to help his dad off the bed.

Not that he expected to be utilized in such a way. His dad still had his pride, after all, and after three days of being chastised by nurses for sneaking off to the bathroom on his own, Tommen figured he could get up and down well enough.

Walking was another matter altogether, however. The room offered a number of handholds and lean-tos that he'd been able to use, but there would be no such conveniences once they got out into the hallway. Well, technically there were, but there wouldn't be any in the parking lot or at home. So while Walter made it to the door with much limping and plodding along, he was then forced to choose between Tommen and an assist.

"You okay?" Tommen wondered after a few seconds of his dad staring at the door.

"I seem to be losing more and more of my dignity each day," Walter replied thoughtfully. "Lend me your arm for now; I'm probably going to have to break down and get a cane or some stupid thing before we actually get out of here."

Tommen came on his dad's left side, offering an arm and helping him out into the chaos that was the larger hospital. For a minute, his dad seemed stunned by the people and activity going on.

"A little busier than I remember," he said.

"Well, home should be quieter," Tommen told him.

"Should." Walter started ahead, gimping toward the desk. "But first we have your appointment to take care of."

Right. His appointment. The one where he would be tested and scanned and officially told that he had hearing loss and was going to need hearing aids. It was a terrible thing that, while he dreaded going to the appointment, he was also looking forward to it. He'd grown more used to his hearing loss, but he knew that he read lips and body language as much as he heard voices. Many sounds, the ones that weren't lost to him on the higher end of the audible spectrum, were muted and fuzzy.

"Checking out?" the receptionist asked.

"Finally," Walter told her.

"All right, well, it will take a few days for your insurance to be billed because of the weekend and holidays and all that. And your prescriptions have been forwarded to the pharmacy for you to pick up on your way out. I'm also showing that you should have a follow-up with your regular doctor in about one week and then again two weeks after that."

"Sounds like what the doctor was telling me."

Tommen let them haggle and negotiate over dates and times, not that there was a lot to do. Wasn't like his dad was going to be returning to work first thing Monday morning; the only schedule that needed to be worked around was Tommen's school and work schedule. Theoretically, Walter could be driving himself to the second appointment, if not the first, depending on how far he wanted to push his luck.

"Great," the receptionist said, bringing Tommen back to the present. "I'll get everything sent over to him, and his office will confirm with you. But you are good to go from here. Congratulations and happy new year. Do you need help getting to your vehicle?"

"Not going out to the car yet, but thanks for the offer," Walter informed her, taking Tommen on one side and slowly limping away.

They made it to the elevator easily enough, going first to the ground floor where the pharmacy was so Walter could fill his prescriptions before heading to the second floor.

Intensive Care was busy, and the ER was even busier. Stepping onto the second floor was like a breath of fresh air, a break from the busyness. This was where the more low-key treatments were done. Optometry—or was that ophthalmology?—audiology, physical therapy. The place where people made appointments, coming for a predetermined purpose, not walking in and panicking because they didn't understand what was going to happen, or what was supposed to happen.

Down one hallway, a man no older than thirty was limping along on a prosthetic leg, using a walker and being guided by a therapist. Elsewhere, a child was experimenting with new specialized glasses, constantly taking them off and putting them back on. Tommen guessed the floor was probably a lot busier on regular days. They made their way through the maze of maps and signs to a set of large, frosted glass double doors reading Audiology.

"Good afternoon," the receptionist greeted. "What can I do for you?"

Her voice was soft, but not in the calm, reassuring manner that might have been expected. More likely, her voice was soft because if it got any louder, she would be shouting, probably over the unfairness of having to work a holiday. Tommen bet she wouldn't be complaining about the paycheck that came her way because of it, but whatever.

"He's got an audiology appointment," Walter said, indicating Tommen. "Tommen Forbes."

Tommen didn't miss the momentary bewildered expression that crossed the receptionist's face. She'd probably been fully prepared to direct Walter to physical therapy, only to be side-swiped by the sixteen year old standing next to him who had the real appointment.

"Yes, I have him right here," the receptionist said after a second or two. "If you want to take a seat, I'll let the doctor know you're here."

"Busy day?" Tommen asked, trying to find some humor.

"Busier than you might expect. A lot of people have the day off, but usually that doesn't mean anything because so does everyone else. Having the doctor in today means people can get in on their schedule to see him."

Again, her words said one thing, but her tone and body language said another. She probably had any number of things she would have rathered been doing, but instead got stuck sitting behind a desk.

Still, she disappeared into the office while Tommen and his dad headed for the seats along one wall. Walter more collapsed than sat, leaning back and closing his eyes.

"You okay?" Tommen wondered.

"That's a lot of walking," his dad replied.

Any other time, Walter would not only have been able to do all that walking around the hospital, he would have been able to take the stairs instead of the elevator, too, and not even break a sweat. Tommen hoped that his strength and stamina would return with time, but there was no telling what side effects he would suffer because of Isthim's poison.

"Is there anything you want to do or anywhere you want to go before we go home?" Tommen asked conversationally.

"No," Walter said. "I just want to go home, have a nice home-cooked meal, and be able to sleep in my own bed."

"Yeah, so do I."

Tommen hadn't realized it—or maybe he had, but it just seemed unimportant until now—but he hadn't slept in his own bed just as long as Walter hadn't been in his own bed; he'd been staying with the twins. Had it really been that long since either of them had been home? The house would need some cleaning. Worse, the refrigerator would need some cleaning.

"So how have you been coping since you lost your hearing?" Walter asked as Tommen reached for a magazine.

Tommen felt his cheeks burn hot. "Okay, I guess. I mean, I can hold a conversation just fine in a quiet room—"

"Making out sounds and hearing them as they are, are two different things." Walter still hadn't opened his eyes.

Tommen chewed his lip and let out a slow breath. "I can hear what you're saying. I know what you're saying. In a quiet room, I don't really notice a difference. But anything louder than this and it goes downhill fast. Micaiah tried to help, and it improved a little, but it's not likely I'll ever recover my full hearing. And that's why we're here."

"How'd you do on your trip?"

With nothing else to do besides sit in a hospital room for two days, Walter had managed to weasel every last little detail that Tommen could recall about his adventures with Sifura, from the oasis and the feast and the harvesting and getting drunk, to the skimmer and the desert, to the D'Bok and the warrior duel and the jungle, to the mountain and the antidote and the animal d'bok, to S'Bal's treachery and the ensuing chase in the Wheel.

In the end, they'd decided that if they ever found themselves discussing the thing in public, outside of a Band, they would simply refer to the whole thing as "Tommen's trip." What kind of trip that was, was up for speculation, but people did a lot of traveling over the holidays after all.

"If not for the translator, I probably wouldn't have survived," Tommen answered slowly. "And I don't mean language barrier, but I would have been so far in the dark on cultural and social cues and niceties that..." He drew his finger across his neck. "Without that translator, I basically heard nothing but the din of voices."

Even as he spoke, Walter opened his eyes and nudged him. Tommen looked up to see the doctor standing not far away, folder in hand. Case and point, the doctor had probably called his name, and he hadn't known.

"How are we doing today, guys?" the doctor asked amiably. He was not an old man, but probably pretty close to retirement, with graying hair and wrinkled features.

"Better all the time," Walter told him. "Or at least I am. Hopefully you can help him get to that point too."

"I will certainly try. I'm Dr. Polski by the way."

"Walter Forbes. My son, Tommen. How long have you been in practice, Dr. Polski?"

"I've been in practice for about forty years now, actually. My family and I just recently moved from California where I did almost fifteen years."

"What brings you here?"

"Family, mostly. This room right here."

They entered a little exam room. Walter found a seat in the corner while Tommen assumed the spinning stool and the doctor brought out his luxury office chair.

"So, Tommen, can you tell me when you started experiencing hearing loss or what triggered it?"

"I had a gun go off next to my ear. Literally, like, right next to it. .45 revolver. There were some other gunshot incidents, but that one...I couldn't hear anything for about ten minutes, and it wasn't until the next morning that I could really say I got anything back, or enough to be really useful and not shout at everyone."

"When did this happen?"

"December 23rd."

"How has your hearing been since? I noticed you didn't respond when I called your name."

Tommen shrugged. "It has its good days and bad days. In a quiet room, I do okay. Once you start adding noise, it goes downhill pretty fast."

"And sitting here, in a quiet room in close proximity, can you describe it?"

"I can hear you; I can understand you. But I know that most computers whine and make noise if they're running. Your computer over there on the desk is running, but if I didn't see it, I wouldn't know it was there."

"Okay. That's a good description, actually. So what I'm going to do is take a peek inside your ears and look for physical damage, then start out with a standard hearing test, similar to the one you probably got when you were in grade school; that will tell me where you're at, and then we'll decide how to proceed. Sound good?" He looked first at Tommen, then at Walter.

"Sounds okay to me," Walter told him.

Tommen shrugged. "Gotta do what you gotta do."

"All right, so come over this way and we'll get started."

Tommen scooted himself over to another table set up perpendicular to the desk with the computer, this one with some unknown machine that looked like it walked straight out of 1985. He remained on his stool while Polski rummaged around in a drawer for a true old-school doctor housecall bag.

"Sit very still, Tommen," he ordered, flicking on a little light and looking in his ear.

Polski did whatever looking and poking and prodding he

needed to do, first in one ear, then the other, then back to the first ear, then back to the other, back and forth probably three times before putting his stuff away and going around to the other side of the table to face him.

"I didn't see any structural damage to your ear, which is a good thing," Polski reported.

"So then why am I half-deaf?" Tommen asked.

Polski reached for an ear model sitting next to the computer. He took several pieces and parts off. "Everyone knows the eardrum, and for as much care as people take in protecting that, it's a tough little bugger. What people forget about is the cochlea, here. Inside are millions of tiny little hairs — technically fibers, but we'll call them hairs — that receive sound waves from the ear drum and send them to the brain to be interpreted. These little hairs, however, can both degrade naturally over time or they can be broken. The more hairs you have, the better you are able to perceive and interpret sound. Otherwise, there are sound waves going in, but no hairs to catch those waves and send them to your brain."

"And there's nothing you can do? There's not like some surgery you can do to, I don't know, replace or replant or something?"

"In some cases of extreme or even complete hearing loss, there are some implants that can be used to bypass the inner ear completely and send information directly to the brain. However, this is considered a last-resort option even in those cases."

"So what happens to me, then?"

"Well, first I'm going to test your hearing, figure out your range, your highs and lows of frequency perception." He handed Tommen a pair of headphones that were almost as old as the machine they were attached to. "We're going to start off in broad increments. You are either going to hear it or you won't. Hold your hands up like this, and give me either left, right, or both as you hear the tones."

Tommen hadn't done anything like this since he entered school in third grade. The tests themselves were normally conducted in second grade, but because he had been new to the school and had no similar records to give them, he'd had to take the tests before they would let him into the classroom. He remembered being terrified of the machine, of the sounds, of the magic of technology, but he'd passed with flying colors. Well, the colors that he could see anyway.

So he went through the same motions again, except this time there seemed to be fewer of them. He knew that Polski was sending more tones than he was hearing, but he also knew that the doctor would know if he was trying to fake his way through.

Not that he particularly wanted to fake his way through. Whether or not he liked the situation, he needed to be able to hear. It wasn't going to get better, and lying would only hurt him in the long run. Better to swallow his pride and get it over with.

"Tommen?" It was like hearing his name while he was underwater. He looked at the doctor and took off the headphones. "I'm going to change it up now," Polski told him. "This is going to be a little more specific. This time when you tell me which ear, give me a one if you think you hear it, a two if you can hear it but it's unclear, and a three if it is very clear."

And so they went through the same test again, this time with tones at frequencies that were closer together on the spectrum. Tommen was both amazed and terrified of how he could hear one tone very well, the next one okay, and by the fifth one in the sequence, it was gone. He wasn't sure if he was supposed to have heard it or where it fell on the spectrum of normal hearing, and the thought was discomforting. What if it was worse than he thought? What if the doctor wanted to have a more intimate and serious chat about moving forward?

"And we're done," Polski said suddenly.

Tommen took the headphones off and scooted back six inches from the table.

"How bad is it?" he wondered fearfully, searching the man's face for any sign of encouragement or grave concern.

"Well, I don't think it's quite as bad as you're fearing, but let me gather up some numbers and paperwork and we'll have a little sit-down. How about that?"

He apparently meant it as an encouragement, but Tommen felt anything but encouraged. Polski left the room.

"So what do you think?" Walter inquired from his chair. He fumbled with a magazine he'd swiped from the waiting area.

"About what?" Tommen wondered.

"You're the physics whiz, and sound is part of physics. Any ideas?"

At first Tommen thought he was joking, then he realized that his dad was really trying to cheer him up. First it acknowledged his love of physics, then it gave him a puzzle to work through. Rather than just sitting around, his mind swirling in the unknown, it let him try to come up with a known variable to which to compare his experience.

He tried to bring to mind everything he knew about sound and frequencies, the range of normal human hearing. At first, it was a good puzzle to chew on, but when he tried to compare normal hearing to his hearing, what he should and could hear, it was like trying to compare his normal vision with the full spectrum of color.

Eventually he gave up on the puzzle. No sooner had he done that than Polski walked back in with a small stack of papers, printouts, and a couple brochures. He was kind enough to bring the conversation over to Walter rather than try and make Walter move over to one of the desks.

"So, these are your numbers," Polski began. "This is your right ear, which was the worse of the two. Your lowest range, your highest range, all indicating moderate hearing loss. Your left ear, same thing, but with better numbers, showing me only mild to just touching in the moderate hearing loss. Now then, as with any of the senses, it could fluctuate a little bit from day to day, and there is every possibility that, given time, you could recover some of your hearing. Probably not all, but some is better than none. You're only sixteen, so it is possible."

"What do you recommend?" Walter asked, his voice level.

"For his situation, I would say hearing aids. His hearing loss isn't so extreme that I believe any kind of implants or bypass to be necessary at this time. That could change, especially if it gets worse, but there is no reason that simple hearing aids won't help. Most common is a behind-the-ear style. Most people tell me that they are more comfortable and easier to manage than the hearing aids your grandpa used to wear, and with your hair as long as it is, you could cover it up and no one would be the wiser."

Tommen sighed and looked at his dad who nodded once, deferring the decision. "It's your hearing, your call. But you need something for school."

"There's nothing else you can do?" Tommen asked Polski, knowing he sounded whiny.

Polski frowned and shook his head slowly. "Believe me, I wish there were. My sister is deaf. She's what got me into audiology because I was convinced that I could cure her. But the ear, the human body itself, is a little more complicated than that. We have the technology to boost or bypass your hearing, but not to fix it quite like that yet."

He sighed again. "What do I have to do?"

"Well, first I have to make a mold of your ear; all long-term or permanent hearing aids are custom fit, for obvious reasons. If you'd like, however, I can send you home with a trial pair just to get you used to wearing them and how to take care of them. Then, when your pair comes in, you can throw away the trial pair or save it in case something happens to yours."

"I don't want a trial pair," Tommen said.

"Yes, you do," Walter interrupted. He looked at Polski. "How long do they take to come in?"

"On a rush order, I can get them here hopefully by Monday or Tuesday."

"You have school on Monday," Walter told Tommen. He Banded the two of them. "And you still have your review tomorrow."

"If I was able to bring a case before the Hands without hearing aids, I think I can do my review without them, too." It was hard to say whether his remark came from his own stubborn pride, or from his secret that supposed he was going to pass no matter what, at least according to Rifun.

But his dad wouldn't let it go. "You're going to need every advantage you can get for your review."

Walter released the Band and looked at Polski. "He'll take the trial pair. And he'll wear them."

Polski nodded once in such a way that said he was going to send them home with a trial pair and simply let the two of them fight it out. He scribbled something on a piece of paper and stood. "So then, I will get the stuff to make a mold." He handed Tommen a couple small brochures. "I will let you peruse through these for a few minutes." He paused. "And don't be embarrassed about saying what you do or don't like about a hearing aid. I know it's new and it might take a few tries and some discussion, but this is your hearing, and you'll be in this for the long haul. Best to get comfortable now."

The worst part was that he was right.

Tommen glowered at the brochures until the doctor left the room. Then he cautiously opened one and looked through. He'd never realized that hearing aids were such a competitive industry. He always figured that, sure, there were a couple different styles just for different fit preferences, but he'd never imagined that there would be different brands or companies. Most of the differences seemed to be purely about style—or else so small, Tommen would have to have Polski explain the differences and benefits or shortcomings—but a few boasted clearer sound or better crowd noise filtration and such.

"So what are you thinking?" his dad asked after a minute, looking through each brochure as Tommen finished and handed them off.

"I'm thinking this is a lot more complicated than it needs to be," Tommen answered honestly.

"Well, think about what you want."

"What's the insurance cover?"

"Unless you're getting the diamond-studded outlier, don't

worry about the insurance. Better to pay a little more now and have hearing aids that work for ten years, than go for the cheapest pair and be back every two years to get them replaced."

"Do hearing aids last ten years?"

"Honestly, I don't know, but you get my point."

Polski returned then with his ear mold making kit. Tommen sat very still once again, feeling his heart race as first one ear was done, than the other, the sticky plaster-like material being applied to his ears and then carefully peeled off when it was set, similar to when the orthodontist had made molds of his mouth over the years.

"What questions do you have for me about the hearing aids?" Polski wondered once he had the molds carefully packed away.

"Is there really any difference between one and another? Like these two, for instance?" Walter indicated a couple brochures, both behind the ear aids, but two different companies.

"There is some difference," Polski answered. "Generally, cheap is cheap, but expensive doesn't make it the end-all of hearing aids."

"Do you have any recommendations?"

The doctor pulled out a marker. "If I had to pick a top three, based on your needs, I would suggested any of these. This one comes from a brand that is known for durability and long-lasting hearing aids; some will last five, ten years, maybe more. Some people have reported, however, that the quality and clarity of sounds isn't always the greatest. This one boasts the best quality, but there have been complaints of the battery going out before the end of the day, which can be a problem if you're a sunrise to sunset kind of worker. This one is the cheapest and has good sound, but some people will tell you that physically it doesn't hold up; the plastic breaks or the earpiece comes off or something to that effect."

"What about this one?" Tommen asked, showing him one hidden in a corner of a brochure.

"That is an option." Polski ran his tongue over his teeth. "Actually, that's a very good option, why didn't I think of that before?" Beat. "Huh. Yes, that would work, too. Those guys have excellent battery life and good sound quality. They're not the cheapest, but—"

"So what are the drawbacks of it?" Walter cut in. "Is it going to break the first time he drops it?"

"No, nothing like that. However, I have heard that the average lifespan of those ones is about two to three years."

"How often should he be reevaluated for new ones? Does it really matter that much?"

"In children, it doesn't matter much because they are always growing and changing. In adults, it matters more because they've stopped growing and don't want to get new ones every few years. In Tommen's case, three years would probably be good enough because he is still growing but not at an exorbitant rate, and by the time they start to go, he'll have a better idea of what works and what doesn't."

"Sounds good to me. What about you?" Walter looked at Tommen.

He let out a breath. "I guess if I need 'em, I need 'em."

"It'll work," Walter told the doctor.

"Excellent. I will get all of this prepared and sent off, rush order so you can have them for school. Cary will take care of you guys at the desk and get you a trial pair to take home."

Chapter Two
The Return

It felt like forever before they got out of the hospital, between Walter breaking down and buying a cane so he didn't have to rely on Tommen, and his general pedestrian movements even with said cane. After watching several people slip and slide across the parking lot, Tommen thought it was a good idea to drive up instead of forcing his dad to brave the icy asphalt. Walter readily agreed.

"You're sure you're okay to drive in this?" his dad asked as he maneuvered his way into the front seat. "It's not exactly sunshine and rainbows."

"I'm fine," Tommen told him, hoping he sounded more confident than he felt. Another storm was moving in and poised to squat down right over them for a few days. Even now, the wind was picking up, and the visibility was dropping. As they pulled out of the hospital into regular traffic, Tommen could feel the slickness of the roads and knew it was only going to get worse. He tried not to clench his fists on the wheel and drive white-knuckled, but he sorely felt like it. Confidence, that was it. If he was able to brave a blazing desert and poisonous jungle, then driving through his neighborhood ought to be a piece of cake.

"You doing okay over there?" Tommen wondered as he saw, in his peripheral vision, his dad shift position for the tenth time.

"Just imagining my recliner," Walter told him, forcing a laugh.

Thankfully, it wasn't far from the hospital to home, though it felt like a long time since either of them had been there. It wasn't until they pulled off onto their road that he realized that the driveway wouldn't be plowed, so there was probably no way that they were going to get into the garage.

"I see that house finally sold," Walter said suddenly.

Tommen's first instinct was to look, but he caught himself with enough time to Band first. He looked around his dad at a house that had been for sale for at least a year. Two-story, blue-gray vinyl siding—at least as far as Tommen was concerned—new windows, new roof. Late afternoon with the gathering darkness and impending storm, all activity outside had ceased, soon to be erased by the snows. But the lights were on inside, and Tommen saw a number of boxes stacked high and scattered about.

"Cool," Tommen said finally, putting his hands back on the wheel and releasing the Band. He wasn't too concerned about the house selling or not selling, only that it was something different from when he'd left.

"Maybe they'll have kids you'll meet at school."

Tommen stole a glance at his dad who looked awfully uncomfortable in the passenger seat, reclined though it was. Walter opened one eye and looked at him. "I haven't forgotten that you lost your best friends."

Yeah. That. Varad had left on the last flight out of the country, eleven-fifty p.m. on December 31st, destination India. Eric was still in the area and occasionally showed up in school, but after the whole Time debacle where they'd been intentionally exposed, he'd wanted nothing more to do with Tommen. Well, Varad had wanted nothing more to do with him. Eric was prickly and good enough to be civil, at least until someone showed him how to control his new Time abilities. But both of them had felt a deep sense of betrayal, as if Tommen had been holding out on them, been dishonest in some way. Maybe he had been dishonest, but, as their experience only proved, for good reason.

"Maybe," Tommen conceded diplomatically, "but unlikely."

Walter let out a breath, and Tommen looked at him again. His dad had lost some of his best friends, too. Seven out of eight members of Bravo team, which was only supposed to have been backup, plus Ian Dorn and Renee Elhart from the Alpha team had also been killed.

The last Bravo team member was said to not be seriously wounded physically, but the psychological scars would all but guarantee his retirement from the police force. Norm Waters had suffered a traumatic brain injury and actually been in a room just down the hall from Walter in ICU, except he didn't have any kids to run off across the galaxy to find a cure for his impending vegetable state. Sean Tanner, single dad of three young kids, had taken a bullet to the spine which paralyzed him about midback. He could breathe and eat, but he had no core muscle control and could not sit up by himself. The rest of the team had sustained minor injuries, anything from scratches and scrapes to a broken wrist or twisted ankle.

Tommen knew the officers shared a special band of brothers kind of mentality, but he also knew that his dad would bear the brunt of the grief. He'd not only been part of the team, but he'd been leading it. Not only had he been leading it, but he'd fully understood what they'd been up against. He would doubt himself constantly over it. What if he'd set his men up differently? What if he'd done something different? What if his judgment had been too clouded by the fact that his son was in the mix? Would anything have changed? Would any of those men still be alive or able to work again?

For as much as Tommen wanted to tell his dad it was okay and he did everything he could, he knew it would only fall on deaf ears. Walter would probably smile and thank him for the support, but it would mean a lot more coming from his brothers in blue. As it was, Steggmann hadn't been around to see Walter since the day Tommen gave him the antidote, and that probably worried his dad the most, that there was some sinister reason why he hadn't been in. Maybe he was fired or going to be more diplomatically released. Maybe there was some media shit storm saying Walter had gotten them all killed, and Steggmann was working hard to clean it up and make things look as good as possible.

Again, Tommen knew it wasn't true, but his dad would only believe it coming from the horse's mouth. So they drove the rest of the way in silence, not that it was a terribly long way, but the snows and winds had picked up and with the brakes and tires on the car in question, Tommen wasn't going to push his luck.

"Micaiah told me you walked all the way from his house to the hospital in weather like this, but in the middle of the night," Walter said.

"Well, I walked part of the way." Tommen felt his cheeks grow warm. "I hitchhiked the rest."

Walter let out a breath and shook his head. "I'm gone for a week and look at all the dangerous things you go out and get yourself into. Clearly I'm going to have to stick around a little longer and make sure you don't do anything else stupid."

"Yes, please do. Clearly I am only a young, dumb teenager who needs his dad to stick around and tell me more about life."

"Young, maybe. But I think you've done a lot of growing up."

"Maybe next time you want to teach me a lesson, though, let me spend a night in jail or something. Dying is a little extreme. Deal?"

Walter chuckled. "Okay, deal."

Surprisingly enough, when they arrived home, the driveway had been recently plowed, and Tommen was able to plod the old Cadillac up the slope into the garage, the brakes making their familiar squeak as they ground to a halt. Immediately, he jumped out and went to turn on the light before rushing around to the other side of the car and stooping to help his dad who was fumbling his way out of the passenger seat.

"I can get it," Walter said, even as he stumbled out, catching himself and gritting his teeth in pain as he landed on his right leg.

"You okay?" Tommen wondered.

"Fine. Go in, and make sure the furnace is on. Last thing I want to do tonight is freeze to death."

Fair enough, Tommen figured, and not too far from the truth. But the moment he stepped through the door into the house, he was greeted with a gentle warm breeze. His dad normally turned down the thermostat when they would both be gone for a while, had probably turned it down the morning he left to negotiate for his release, except it was easily above sixty-five degrees. Tommen turned down the thermostat until the furnace shut off, then went to help his dad who was slowly and thoughtfully making his way up the two steps from the garage to the tiny kitchen.

"I think at this point, the more you try to help, the worse it will be for both of us," Walter told him.

Worst part was, he was right. The kitchen was so tiny, even one of them had a hard time getting through on a normal day. The washer and dryer were nestled into a small alcove but still stuck out, and the fridge couldn't be opened if someone was sitting at the table where a breakfast plate couldn't even share the space with a folded morning newspaper. The cabinets were flaking paint in such an array of color it was almost psychedelic.

Not that the living room was much better by way of decor, the 60's dying a horrible, slow death, refusing to let go of the metallic wallpaper, retro UFO and Elvis posters, shag rugs, and paisley furniture. But it was the most open room in the house, the only one Walter could comfortably walk through, straight to his recliner where he collapsed more than sat.

"I've been waiting for this for two days," he said, sighing. He opened his eyes and looked around. "Damn, this place needs a good renovation. Maybe while I'm off."

"If you're off work because of your injuries, I don't think you'll be doing much painting or floor replacement or whatever you decide to do," Tommen told him, folding his arms.

"Maybe not, but I know a couple fine young men who might be willing to help. And, really, the biggest project would be the floor. I don't have to do the floors right now. A little paint and some new furniture and decor goes a long way."

"Well, it would help."

"What color do you think would work well?"

Tommen almost wanted to say green, a nice, rich, dark green, forest green. In his mind, he could just picture it, a full, rich color that was shadowy and mysterious while providing a calming ambiance.

Problem was, he knew he would never see it. It would be blue or gray. The loss of the gift of color tugged at him, but he refused to indulge it. *Don't let Rifun win.*

"I don't know," he answered at last. "It's either going to be yellow or blue to me."

"Maybe green. Dark green, that way it provides a nice, calming color without messing too much with you."

"I don't think anything could mess with me more than the paisley," Tommen told him.

"True enough for anyone, I guess." Walter sighed. "Your pa was color-blind, too, you know."

"I know. That was how they figured out I was color-blind and not crazy. Ma said she had the same problems getting me to bring her things of specific colors as my pa."

"Our pa—your grandpa—had it, too. He always said there was something strange about his pa, too, but I don't really know. Before that is anyone's guess, I suppose."

Tommen studied his dad for a minute. Uncle. Uncle Dad. It was like looking at a new man, or looking at a man who was now free to be himself without fear or shame. How many times had he wanted to tell Tommen something but held back out of fear of rejection?

And how would have Tommen responded, honestly? If one day after school, when he was twelve, Walter just walked up to him and said, "By the way, I'm your biological uncle; your pa was my younger brother," how would that have gone over? Not very well, in all reality, and Tommen probably would have rejected him as both uncle and dad at that moment. Not that Tommen wanted his dad to have to go to such extreme lengths to share his secrets, but there had to be a better way than dying.

"Obviously you don't have it," he said, figuring his response was a little late in the conversation.

Walter chuckled. "There's more than one type of color-blindness, Tommen; red-green is just the most common."

"So which do you have?"

"Protonomaly. I have a hard time distinguishing red."

"Why didn't you ever tell me?"

"Is it that important? I can physically see red, pure red, as long as it's not set against anything else besides black or white, but I can guess well enough at pink, orange and purple in order to pass a color vision test at work."

"Oh."

How desperately Tommen wanted to tell Walter about Rifun, or about his gift anyway. How he wanted to try to describe the wonders of the color spectrum, how his eyes had exploded with color like one's nose might explode from the succulent smells of a restaurant with wonderful food. He'd finally seen red, green, and all the colors in between, orange, purple, pink, so wonderful to behold. Now that he knew his dad couldn't see red, he longed to be able to not only describe it, but show him, even though he knew it would be fruitless; his dad just said he could see pure red by itself. But to share such joy with him, the feeling of not having any problems distinguishing any color...it was almost worth risking Rifun's revenge, assuming he was as omniscient as he seemed to think he was.

"So are there any other genetic disorders I should know about?" Tommen wondered, meaning it as more of a joke while secretly being terrified of the answer.

"None that I know of. Our pa and grandpa and grandpa's pa all had lung problems, but they were avid smokers. Pipes and cigars, one or the other was always in their mouths."

"What am I supposed to tell people now? I mean, I can't just keep all of this to myself."

"I don't know what you're going to tell them, but if you figure it out, let me know because we're going to have to get our stories straight. Obviously I never told any of the guys at the precinct that you're secretly my nephew, so we have to be in cahoots about this."

Tommen gasped loudly, feigning shock. "Why, Homicide Detective Forbes, are you talking about conspiracy here?"

"Maybe I am, but who are you going to tell?"

No one who hasn't already tried to kill you for it. "Fair enough. I'll think of something, I'm sure."

"And while you're thinking hard about that, why don't you start thinking hard about something for dinner?"

"You hungry?"

"Hospital food leaves much to be desired, especially when it's supposed to be low-carb, sodium-free, cholesterol-free, fat-free, and whatever else."

"Right, so, one New York strip coming up."

"I wouldn't go that far; I don't think my system's quite up for that yet."

"I'll look and see what we have."

But as Tommen headed for the kitchen, his stomach started twisting in knots. Ten days of neglect, the fridge was going to be disgusting; he just knew it. The cheese was going to be moldy; the meat would have turned; the fruits and vegetables would be rotten; the leftovers would look like a science experiment gone wrong. He was almost ready to be sick just thinking about it.

When he opened the refrigerator door, however, he was not a little surprised. Not only was there no moldy cheese, rancid meat, rotten vegetables, or suspicious containers of leftovers, but it was fully stocked with fresh food. The cheese was cleanly packaged, the meat fresh, vegetables bright and not wilted, and no leftovers to be found. It was like a before and after photos between what his imagination had conjured up and what his eyes were actually seeing.

Next Tommen went to the cupboards. Once, he'd expected them to be full of spiders and mice, but when he opened them, he found fresh boxes of pasta, biscuit and pancake mix, canned foods, cake mixes, all neatly arranged in cupboards that probably hadn't been cleaned so thoroughly in over ten years.

"Micah and Micaiah were here!" Tommen called out.

"I don't doubt that!" Walter shouted back.

"Did you know?" Tommen grabbed a box of pasta and set it out on the counter.

"I had my suspicions. The driveway was plowed, the house was warm, and my recliner wasn't covered in an inch of dust, so I figured either someone had been sitting my chair, or they came by and cleaned before we came home."

Was it really so surprising? Not only was Walter the District Captain and the twins his Lieutenants, but he was a good friend, and they would do anything for him. Case and point, they'd showed up at the shipping yard and tried to help, only to be foiled themselves.

"How does pasta sound?" Tommen asked.

"Light on the sauce," his dad answered after a moment of consideration.

"I think they brought over a box of crackers, and I know they brought cheese."

"No, no, pasta is fine."

Tommen found a freshly-scrubbed saucepan and started the water boiling, smiling to himself as he brought to mind his promise that for at least a month he wasn't going to eat jerky or trail mix. Spaghetti would do very nicely. As he was thinking this, he happened to glance out into the living room where his dad was up out of his recliner, gimping along toward the hallway.

"Where are you going?" Tommen asked, striding purposefully out to meet him.

Walter raised a brow. "Well, Nurse, if you must know, I'm going to the bathroom. You want to stand there and help me wipe my ass?"

Tommen took a step back. "Um, no."

"That's what I thought."

Walter's eyes glittered with amusement even as Tommen felt his cheeks turn red, and he slunk off back to the kitchen where the pasta was on the verge of boiling over from under the lid. He took a breath as he stirred the noodles. His dad wasn't helpless. It was a scary experience, but he was home now and on the mend. True, he couldn't do everything, but he couldn't do nothing either. From the scars on his body, this wasn't his first rodeo with injuries or pain. And he had his pride and dignity to maintain, too, and Tommen knew he would have to be respectful of that.

Spaghetti wasn't a difficult meal, but Tommen found himself wondering how his dad was going to get along when he went back to work and school. Strictly speaking, he, Tommen, wasn't back to work or school until Monday, and it was only Wednesday, but if Walter wasn't able to Band his injuries and recover from them even a little faster, it was going to be a long, hard recovery.

No, no, no. Walter was a big boy; he could handle himself. He knew his limits, and he could respect them.

Yeah, and pigs might fly. People did a lot of stupid shit in the name of pride and dignity. Tommen got into stupid fights over a code of chivalry that most people had only ever read about in books, never mind even loosely believed in.

Tommen got out a couple of bowls as his dad slowly gimped out of the bathroom and headed for his recliner.

"You want to add your own sauce or have me do it?" Tommen asked.

Walter paused in his tracks and thought a second before turning and trudging toward the kitchen. Tommen had known it was a dumb question even as the words left his mouth. The man had been shot, had suffered trauma to both shoulders blades, and Tommen was asking him to add his own sauce to his spaghetti. It didn't sound like much, but the human body is an intricate thing, and when something isn't right, suddenly you realize just how valuable each piece is.

"You pour, and I'll tell you when," Walter said.

Tommen did so, doling out each bowl according to the diner's requirements and following his dad back out to the living room. Once Walter was seated and reasonably comfortable in his recliner, Tommen handed him his bowl then went to the sofa to start on his own.

"My first real meal in, realistically, about three days, but almost two weeks," Walter said, taking a bite and, if his expression was any indication, loving it. "It has salt, sugar, and carbs."

"Maybe I ought to open my own restaurant," Tommen chuckled. "Call it Tommen's Fresh From the Hospital Buffet."

"No kidding."

Tommen shifted in his seat. "So, I've been meaning to ask..."

"Yes...?" Walter's tone suggested as much fear as curiosity.

"*Ydych chi'n siarad Cymraeg? Ych chi'n cofio hi o gwbl?*" (Do you speak Welsh? Do you remember it at all?)

His dad's expression went from fear to relief to amusement. "*Beth oeddet ti'n meddwl bod fe'i dewisais fel fy iath yn yr Olwyn?*" (What did you think I chose as my translator language in the Wheel?)

"But, all that time as a kid...when I would go on and on and had such a hard time with English...you played the fool."

"I always knew what you were saying, Tommen. But my reasoning was always the same: better to make a clean break and a clean start. Everyone spoke English. Had we lived as isolated as you had with your family, we might have gotten away with it, but in the middle of the big city, you had to assimilate and assimilate fast. It wasn't fair and I hated doing it, but it was necessary."

"And all those old recipes..."

"I didn't learn much from my parents, but I did learn some things. Cooking was probably the only real thing I was good at, other than fighting or drinking."

Tommen studied him as he chowed down on his spaghetti. "I can't imagine you ever fighting or drinking, at least, not like that."

His dad sighed. "Believe me, Tommen, if I had been fighting Rifun in that warehouse and not Isthim, you probably would have seen a part of me I hope you never will. It's something that's buried and gone, and I intend to leave it that way."

His words were a dismissal, and Tommen backed off. The secret was revealed, but the truth would come slowly. His dad had lived a much longer life than him, and while he was open to the idea of bringing his skeletons out of the closet, there was no need to open the door in a rush and get buried by them.

"Are you done?" Tommen asked after a bit, when both had

finished their meals and sat in silent contemplation.

"Hm? Yes, thank you." Walter handed Tommen his bowl. "Thank you for cooking."

"It was nothing. Just trying to help as much as I can before I go back to school."

"I think I'll be all right by then."

Tommen had his doubts, but he kept silent on them as he took the dishes to the sink and started the water. As he did so, he reflected how ordinary washing dishes felt. Before, he might have whined or done it grudgingly, but now it was just water, soap, scrub, rinse, done. No muss, no fuss. Ordinary.

He'd just put the last dishes away in the cupboard when there was a knock at the door. Tommen looked outside through the kitchen window before going to the door to find their neighbor from across the street, Mrs. Carver. She bore a large casserole dish.

"Mrs. Carver," Tommen acknowledged.

"Tommen, hi," Mrs. Carver greeted cheerily. "We heard all the terrible things that happened, but when we saw that you guys were home—both of you—I guess I just wanted to bring you a little something to say welcome home. And if you need anything, you can always let us know."

"Oh, thank you." Tommen took the dish which was much heavier than it looked. "I'll be sure to wash it and return it as soon as possible."

"No rush, dear. How is your dad?"

"Resting. It's been a trying couple of weeks."

"I bet it has. Well, like I said, if you need anything, you just let us know."

"We will, thank you."

Then there was that awkward pause at the end of an awkward conversation. Tommen wanted her to leave; she wanted to be invited in. In the end, neither was quite sure of the appropriate dismissal. Eventually, the cold got to her, and she turned toward home. Tommen turned and fumbled the dish inside to set it on the counter.

"Who was that?" Walter wondered.

"Mrs. Carver." Tommen peeked under the tin foil. "Looks like tuna casserole."

"Guess I won't have to rely on you for food."

"Thought you liked my cooking."

Walter didn't get a chance to respond before there was another knock at the door. He chuckled. "She bringing dessert, too?"

"Must be."

But the person who stood on the porch now made Tommen stop short, and even the other guy looked surprised.

"Doctor Polski."

"Tommen," Polski stated, bewildered.

"What are you doing here?"

"What's going on now?" Walter grunted, shuffling his way to the door. He was just as surprised as the rest of them when he got there. Still, he managed a step back. "Well, if you're going to stand there a while, you might as well come in and keep the warm air in."

"Thank you." The doctor stepped inside. "I promise, I'm not stalking you. I didn't even think about it when I saw your address on your file, that you live on the same street as me. See, we just moved in down the road. We've been kind of making the rounds and introducing ourselves to all the neighbors, but this house was always empty. One of the other neighbors told us that the owner was a police officer who'd been shot and was in the hospital. Tonight, my wife had another neighbor over for dinner—she's huge on entertaining—who said that the officer, you obviously, had just gotten home tonight. So I figured I would come and introduce myself and offer you my appreciation for your line of work and say that if you needed anything, here we are, happy to help. Us or our kids or grandkids."

"You're very kind," Walter replied, sounding exhausted from the otherwise one-sided conversation.

"As I said, I don't stalk my patients, though your order did go through I will say."

"That's good...I guess," Tommen said awkwardly.

"It is. But I didn't come here to bore you with that. So." Polski glanced at Walter. "Welcome home. Thank you for your service and your line of work. Get well soon. And if you need anything, just let me or my wife know. It's a little dark for her comforts which is why she didn't come with me, but she's just a lover of people. Helps them out like stray cats."

"Thank you." Walter was trying to be sincere, and some part of him deep down probably was, but Tommen could hear and see the strain. He'd gotten out of the hospital, gotten something to eat, now he was ready to just sleep it all off and start fresh in the morning. Tommen felt the same way.

Polski left, but over the course of an hour, several more neighbors came to the door, offering everything from well wishes to desserts and baked goods to a bouquet of flowers. And as always, each neighbor departed with an offer of, "If you ever need anything..." As the clock ticked by and neighbors came and went, Walter was joking about seeing just how helpful the neighbors were really feeling and wondering if he could rope each one into some chore that would eventually get the house remodeled.

"I don't think that would work the way you want it to," Tommen said, getting up to lock the door and start turning off lights.

"Why not?" Walter wondered from his recliner where he sat with his eyes closed, just about on the verge of sleep.

"You might be able to get a few roped into it, but word would get around, and they'd figure out your plan. Besides, I don't think you'll be down and out quite that long."

"Just because I can't Band my own wounds doesn't mean I can't Band those who would be working on the house. We'll have it done in a day."

Tommen shook his head. "No, I think not. Besides, you don't even have the floors or paint picked out yet."

"Don't I? You think I don't think about remodeling all the time?"

"Then why haven't you?"

Walter barked a laugh and painstakingly got up from his recliner. "Yeah, I have some funds stashed away or I could cash in my turns, but even if I did that, when would I have the time? More than just the remodel itself, when in the world would I ever get to enjoy it?"

Tommen raised a brow. "Any time you came home and didn't have to look at Elvis or paisley power?"

Walter ran his tongue over his teeth, making his mustache bulge. "What's wrong with Elvis?"

"Elvis is great," Tommen told him. "But you don't need three posters of him."

"Hey, I got those autographed by the king himself." He sighed. "But I suppose this place could use a little TLC while I'm here."

"Well, don't worry about it right now; you're tired."

"So are you, and we both have a big day tomorrow."

Tommen opened his mouth to say more but there was a knock at the door. He glanced at his dad who sighed.

"Lights out," Walter said under his breath.

"I'll make them go away," Tommen promised.

But when he got to the door, he didn't find a well-meaning brownnosing neighbor; instead he found the twins.

"Oh, good, you're still awake," Micah said as the brothers invited themselves in.

"Barely," Tommen grumbled.

But they'd already crossed the tiny house and intercepted Walter who grudgingly returned to his recliner to entertain them.

"Unhappy captains are not a good way to get promoted," Walter informed them grumpily.

"Good thing we're not looking for a promotion," Micaiah replied with a smirk. "We're here to discuss Tommen's review tomorrow."

Tommen stifled a groan. He didn't even want to think about that; he had enough to worry about. It might not have been so bad except for that whole part about starting a civil war the last time he went before the Hands, plus Rifun's little deal to pass him and so put him under the madman's power. Couldn't he have just a normal day this week? Something that didn't involve him risking his life, his father dying, impending war, and being stalked by a terrorist? For as much as he complained about it at work sometimes, there was something to be said for boredom.

"What's there to discuss?" Walter was saying as Tommen joined them in the living room.

"Walt, there is no way you're going to be able to open a portal to the Wheel," Micah told him honestly.

"Then I guess you'll have to do it for me." He went on before either twin could say something. "I'm not dying anymore, and barring any recurring catastrophes, I am expected to be there for his review."

"You think you can even make it through the portal?"

"What choice do I have?"

Seriously, *one* day. Just *one* day where someone wasn't dying or in danger of dying. Was that really too much to ask?

"Send a message, and ask for a reschedule," Micaiah proposed. "Get it after the elections, that way you are...more healed than you are now, and maybe Tommen will be out of danger."

"If Cassius is planning to seize control of the Hands, our better bet is to do this before the elections," Walter pointed out.

"January 13th then," Micah offered. "Give yourself another week and a half to heal."

"His review is tomorrow. We're going tomorrow."

Micaiah sighed and pinched the bridge of his nose. "Fine. Get it over and done with. I get it."

"It's not fun that these wounds can't be Banded, but these are the cards I have; let me figure out how to play them."

"What do you mean?" Tommen wondered.

"Nothing," Micaiah answered too quickly. "What matters now is that you are ready for your review."

"I don't know what more I can do to prepare myself."

"You know your stuff?" Micah asked.

"I think I do. I mean, I can Band really well. I can Predict and Band others—"

"They won't ask you to do that," Micaiah told him. "And don't offer it up. Play the idiot, but do your best, if that makes sense."

It made more sense than Tommen thought it should have. *Don't give the Hands anything they didn't ask for. Volunteer no information and demonstrate no skills; do exactly as you're told and no more. Maybe don't even do that. Don't be the straight A+ 4.0 kid that gets noticed. Be the B to A- kid with the 3.4, a good student but not someone who is going to have everyone keeping an eye on him.* It was great in high school to be that kind of superstar, but it only spelled danger in the Time industry. Lily had done that once, and look at everything that came out of that, and Tommen had a feeling they weren't done feeling the effects of her stardom.

"I understand," Tommen answered finally.

"Good. Once you're officially an Apprentice, we can start training you more and bringing you in on more stuff, but first we have to make it that far."

"You really think it's going to be that hard?"

"There's been a huge increase in Runner activity lately," Micah said. "And it's not just the usual petty theft. People have been getting hurt."

Walter chuckled. "When the Powers That Be descend into chaos, the bottom feeders ascend into power."

"Yeah, and we're the unfortunate souls caught in the middle," Micaiah scoffed. "It might not be so bad if Cassius weren't human, if he were part of some Openly Engaged civilization or something. Or if Tommen hadn't incited civil war."

Tommen bristled. "Hey, I was just going by the plan that you guys came up with."

"We know." Micah's tone said that the comment had been meant as a joke, not because it was funny, but because they needed the humor. "Believe us, we're not exactly in the Hands' good graces either right now."

Tommen had an awful thought then. Rifun had only promised him safe passage; he'd said nothing about his dad or the twins. He mentally scolded himself. Stupid! Trying to save his father and when it came right down to the wire, he was still thinking only about himself. He should have included Walter, Micah, and Micaiah in that deal. Safe passage to and from the Wheel, the elections, wherever they needed to go, without being harassed, arrested, detained, or whatever by the Grandfathers or the Hands. But it was too late for that now. He just had to hope that it was sort of a given. After all, Walter had to be present for Tommen's review, so that kind of brought him in under the umbrella of protection, right? And if the twins were needed to open and close the portal, they should be safe, too, right?

He had his doubts.

"What time is the review?" Micah was inquiring.

"Three-eleven a.m.," Walter replied grouchily.

"And it's nine-thirty now," Micaiah mused. "Well, looks like we'll be spending the night for a bit. You guys go ahead and go to bed, do whatever you have to do. Get some sleep. We'll stay up and Band you when the time comes. What time do you want to be up?"

Tommen glanced at his dad who was studying him.

"Two," Walter answered at last. "The review is meant to be a formal, professional event, and he'll need time to get ready. Means shower, shave, brushed hair, brushed teeth, good clothes. And while they do provide food, you'll need a good breakfast, too."

So was he going to a review, a test of skill that could determine his fate in the grand scheme of Time and Timekeeping, or a job interview? In a way, he supposed it was a little of both. Essentially, he was having to convince the Hands why he was still a good candidate for a Timekeeper, why he should be allowed to stay and move up in the industry. He just had to do this by demonstrating both knowledge and skill.

"Well, don't let us ruin your evening," Micaiah was saying, leaning back on the couch. "Carry on with whatever you were doing."

Normally Tommen didn't have a problem getting ready for bed and getting to sleep, but it was a little disconcerting having someone around waiting for him to do just that. Even more disconcerting was the knowledge that they would be watching him sleep at some point, and influencing his sleep. And then there was that part about having to wake up at some ungodly hour to get ready for a huge review.

At the same time, it was relaxing to finally walk back into his own room and lay down on his own bed again. He didn't have empty boxes and packages around him, but all the familiar comforts: dressers, stereo, TV, posters, everything that made the room his. And regardless of everything that had been going on for the last almost month, all the fear and all the tension melted away in the first five minutes that he lay in bed. He might have cried a little, there in the darkness; he didn't know. But he was content. He was home. And before he even realized what was happening, he was asleep.

Chapter Three
Tension

I t was a strange sensation, to be able to stuff eight hours or more of sleep into only a few hours. Tommen figured he'd slept well enough, though the last remnants of some bad dream or nightmare still clung to his groggy consciousness as he was shaken awake. He came around slowly, somewhat confused, half-expecting that he was having to get ready for school. Then he recalled that it was time for his review.

"Wake up, sleepyhead," his dad said, backlit by the light in the hall. "Micaiah and Micah are making breakfast; you need to jump in the shower."

"Okay, I'm coming," Tommen mumbled, fighting his way out of his blankets.

Walter headed for the door at a determined, yet still slow, pace. "Pretend like you're getting married, and prepare for that. This is almost as important and nerve-wracking."

"Gee, thanks for the pep talk."

"Shower, shave, the works!"

Tommen rubbed his face, noting how he seemed to have gone from barely managing wispy peach fuzz to his father's grizzly beard, seemingly overnight. But such was the way of things. Despite getting a full night's sleep, he still stumbled his way to the bathroom, wondering if his dad actually believed that emphasizing the importance of the shower and shave would actually help. He thought he did a pretty good job most days; was his dad saying he didn't?

Prepare for the review like preparing for a wedding. Given the state of things, that was not the most comforting or exciting of thoughts. If he had to pick a more appropriate analogy, he might go for something more along the lines of, "Pretend like you're going to court, but not as a spectator. Pretend like you're on trial for murder, and you don't want to look like the schlob in every mugshot ever."

Ironically, Tommen wasn't on trial for murder; he was on trial for saving someone's life, his dad's life, his Captain's life. Earth-side, he would be applauded, interviewed by news outlets for being such a selfless sixteen year old. Time-side, he was accused of starting a war, and he'd had to make a deal with a terrorist to ensure that he wouldn't be arrested on the spot and taken to have his clock broken before being deposited back on Earth as a drooling idiot.

He toweled himself dry and looked at himself in the mirror. He'd tried extra hard to scrub every inch and even used some extra soap, and he'd shaved twice just to be sure, but he didn't think he looked any cleaner than on normal days. Well, it was no skin off his back to scrub a little harder for just this occasion.

"Tommen?" His dad knocked on the door.

"Yeah?" he replied, wondering if Walter was going to remind him to clean his ears or pluck some nose hairs or something.

"Don't get into your good clothes until after breakfast; I don't want them getting ruined."

"Got it."

He hadn't brought them in with him anyway because he'd had the same thoughts. As he was pulling on his underclothes, he was forced to wonder if his dad was on edge because he felt as if he'd lost time and was having to play catch-up, or if he really was that nervous about the review. It would make sense that Tommen's performance reflected on him as a mentor, but if Tommen was already breaking into Apprentice-level abilities, he shouldn't have anything to worry about in that department. Was he really afraid of the repercussions of his little adventures to find a cure for the Borelian poison? How would it affect him since he'd kind of been in a coma during the whole thing?

The whole house smelled like a five-star luxury restaurant

when Tommen finally stepped out of the bathroom and he was reminded of the breakfast they'd had Christmas morning, a regular three-course meal that was enough to feed five people each. When he got out to the kitchen, he found biscuits and gravy, omelets stuffed to overflowing, pancakes, even oatmeal. Every inch of counter space was covered in food, or the pans and utensils needed to prepare it.

"*Oh, math, tá tú anseo,*" Micah said, grabbing a plate and dishing a little bit of everything onto it. (Oh, good, you're here.)

"*Hai rŵan, dim o'n tramor defnydd 'na am yma,*" Tommen told him, grinning as he took the plate and headed to the living room where his dad was already in his recliner, just mopping up the last bit of syrup with the last bit of pancake. (Hey now, none of that foreign stuff around here.)

"No coffee for you then," Micaiah answered.

"Did you bring it?" Tommen looked up hopefully, remembering the glorious taste of the coffee the twins kept stashed in their kitchen. Premium stuff, that. He'd almost hated to give it away to the D'Bok, knowing they would probably never cherish it as much as a human would.

"No. Last thing you need is caffeine."

"But if the test is as rigorous as you say it is, why not?"

"Caffeine will do you no favors, Tommen," Walter answered. "Better to go on your own energy, your own power."

Tommen was no athlete, that much was for damn sure—even if his adventures halfway across the universe had beaten some of the weakness out of him—but he'd seen more than half the players on any given sports team at school walking around with coffee or energy drinks or both, on practice days and on game days. Supposedly it was really bad, but the way he saw it, if they were going to be out there playing hard anyway, what did it matter? It was like the difference between Joe Schmo who ate McDonald's every day, weighed two-eighty and had two heart attacks under his belt, and any number of Olympic athletes who could only get sufficient caloric intake by eating McDonald's and still maintain a healthy weight and muscle tone.

But he wasn't going to press the matter. Whether they'd brought the coffee or not, he wasn't getting any, so he had to make his plans based on that reality and not what he wished he could have. Wishes, fantasies, and realities, and the only thing that mattered right now was the reality.

He finished his breakfast and took the empty plate out to the twins who were busy doing dishes.

"Better hurry up," Micaiah told him. "Almost time to go."

Tommen nodded and headed to his room to pick out his clothes. The pants were easy enough, but he always had a hard time with the shirts. If they weren't blue, they were yellow. Supposedly it didn't matter because his pants were black anyway, and most times he hadn't cared. But now that he had seen the full color spectrum — or the one humans were capable of seeing — he had his doubts about his clothes. Was that yellow, or was it actually red? Could it be green? Maybe a color in between, like orange or purple. And what about his ties, few though he had? They were all dark in the background, but what about the ones that had little designs on them? Would they match correctly? Would he look properly coordinated, or like a dumb, color-blind sixteen year old? He kept little pins on the sleeves to mark the colors, but still, what did he know?

Only because of the emphasis that his dad placed on looking nice for this particular event did he call him in and ask for help, thinking it ironic that he was red-green colorblind, and his dad was red colorblind. So it could still turn out disastrously. Talk about the blind leading the blind?

"Do the twins know you're red color-blind?" Tommen wondered as his dad helped him pick out what he assured him was a green dress shirt and appropriately matching tie.

"Oh yes," Walter answered. "And it's not color-blind, it's only color-deficient. If anyone cares to pay attention, they tend to notice when you avoid certain things, like colors. You never think about them until you lose them."

"So you weren't always color-blind? Is that possible?"

"No, I have been, but there are certain lines of work where color can be very important. Try to avoid those situations, and people notice."

"How come I never noticed?"

"I don't know. I'm not you." Walter headed for the door. "Ten minutes."

So Tommen simply put up a Band and got dressed at his own pace, taking time to brush out his hair—not quite long enough for a decent ponytail—and even dig out a little bottle of rarely-used cologne. He stood in front of the mirror, wondering just how much appearances would matter once he got before the Hands. Would it have made a difference when he petitioned them the first time? Then, with a last check to be sure all was in order, just as if he was going to a wedding or going to court, he left his bedroom.

His dad was barely five steps in front of him as he released the Band.

"Ready," Tommen said.

Walter turned and looked him up and down. "Looking sharp." He looked Tommen in the eye and raised a brow, his mustache twitching. "Are your hearing aids in?"

Tommen's heart sank. "But—"

"Tommen, you have them for a reason. They may not be 'yours,' and they may not be the most comfortable, but we had a deal. I wasn't going to force you to wear them yesterday, but you had to wear them today. Believe me, I know you're not a dress-up kind of person, but if I didn't think it mattered, I wouldn't make you do it. Same goes for those hearing aids. Now." He made a circling motion with his hand. "In."

Tommen knew it was for his own good, and he knew it could only help him at this point. As he looked at the tiny devices sitting there on the charging stand on his dresser, he felt as though he stood at the edge of a cliff and peered over the edge into darkness. Whether or not they were his, as soon as he claimed them, admitted his need for help and that he would never again be whole, there was no going back. He would always need hearing aids. He would always need some sort of accommodation.

But claim them he did, trying to fit them exactly as Polski had done in the office. That first time, he'd been astonished at how much his hearing had changed, how all the sharpness of sound came back to him, how he could hear nuances in conversation and small sounds just around the office.

It should have made him want to keep them in, but he'd taken them out before they even got to the car. He'd begged off, saying that they were uncomfortable and that he wanted to go back and forth, hear the difference. It was amazing and yet terrifying, his excuse not too far from the truth. He'd come to terms with his hearing loss when he was halfway across the universe; he'd never expected that he would also have to come to terms with getting his hearing back, as if it had all been some little game or test, the hearing aids his prize.

He fit them as best he could and went back out to the living room, listening to the footsteps and the shuffles and the low voices and the drip of the kitchen faucet, all the little things that had been taken from him.

His dad and the twins stood in the living room, speaking softly. And maybe that was the most discomforting thing about the hearing aids; like the translators in the Wheel, he only heard, but his ability to locate sounds was all but gone. He could vaguely tell in front, behind, left and right, but he couldn't tell whether someone was talking to him from one corner of the room or another, only that they were talking.

"Ready?" Walter asked.

"I guess." Tommen shrugged.

"You look very handsome," Micah told him. "I'm sure you'll turn heads."

Which heads those were, Tommen didn't care to find out, at least not the hard way. He wasn't sure why dressing up was so important anyway, considering that most, if not all, alien species wouldn't care one way or another. Get cleaned up and don't look like a beer-drinking bum, sure, but dress as if he were going to his own wedding? A stretch, in his opinion.

The twins opened the portal to the Wheel, a dimensional tear that would allow them to step through into the hub of the Time industry. It was hard enough to open a portal, and the walk through was no picnic either. Tommen took a breath and a step. For the split-second it took to walk from Earth into the Wheel, he felt like the air had been sucked from his lungs and all his limbs were being pulled every which way so that when he finally made it through, he collapsed on jellied legs, unable to push himself up for his jellied arms. Nevertheless, he got out of the way enough for the rest of them to get through.

Micaiah came through first, fighting the wishful collapse in order to turn and wait for Walter who all but fell through into his arms. Walter grunted as Micaiah caught and gently lowered him to the ground.

"You okay?" the elder twin asked after a moment.

Walter huffed out a breath. "I think I might be...ah, damn it." He pulled at his shirt collar. "It's not bad."

"Pull some stitches?" Tommen wondered.

"Yeah, but they've been coming out anyway. Barely more than a paper cut."

"Let me look," Micaiah ordered, undoing the top couple buttons of Walter's shirt and poking around for a minute or two. "Good news is, you'll live."

"Well, I figured that much, Mom. Want to kiss it, too?"

"You all right?" Micah asked, recovering from his trip through the portal and unsteadily joining their little group.

"Fine," Walter told him. "Just pulled out a stitch or two."

"Ouch. Should we, I don't know, like, get some gauze or something? I mean, you don't want to be walking around in here with open wounds."

That was the problem with the Wheel being the end-all hub of the Time industry. Intergalactic germs and stuff. Tommen had been exposed to a number of interstellar viruses and illnesses. Some he fought off, others Walter had to find and buy a cure or treatment.

"I think I'll be okay." Walter grabbed his cane and stood with Micaiah's help. "Besides, we don't have a lot of time to waste. This is one appointment we can't afford to be late for, Tommen especially."

Even if there was every possibility that no matter how early or late they arrived, he would still be made to wait long enough that he would begin to long for his bed again, tell himself he could have gotten another hour or two of sleep. He had a sneaking suspicion that the Hands did that on purpose, just to make him squirm.

The going was slow, but his dad was determined to go it alone as they made their way to the front of the portal room. The first thing that Tommen noticed was that there weren't any Grandfather guards posted at the door, and no one assaulted them as they approached the translator dispenser. His dad and the twins got their translators easy enough, but he hesitated.

"I...how do I do this now?" Tommen asked sheepishly. He couldn't wear a hearing aid and a translator.

"Like this," his dad told him calmly. "Take out one of your hearing aids." When Tommen did so, he pressed a button on the side of the dispenser. "Now hold it in your palm, out like this."

Tommen did so, and it was kind of like doing a price check at the grocery store. He jumped as the dispenser took its usual sample of flesh, not much different than a diabetic taking a sugar sample. After a moment, the dispenser spit out the usual collar that went around the neck as well as a small USB-type object, except it appeared to port directly into the hearing aid.

"It works just how it looks," his dad explained.

And so it did. Tommen adjusted the translator settings so he could speak and hear in Welsh, surprised at just how well the adaptation to the hearing aid worked. Once he was satisfied with the adjustments, they started off through the Wheel.

It was busier than before, but not as busy as it normally should have been. At the very least it should have been enough to separate a small child from his mother and make him cry. As it was, Tommen had seen worse crowds on Black Friday. He didn't miss, however, the way it also made his dad and the twins uneasy. This close to an election, it should have been more packed than the Super Bowl on Black Friday with Elvis reincarnate performing at halftime. Being officers, the twins and his dad should have been mobbed by all the political Chihuahuas, barking up a storm about one candidate or another, trying to persuade thinking and buy votes. And they all should have been on high alert for pickpockets, thieves, and Runners, all looking to make a quick buck.

But there was nothing of the sort. Well, not nothing, but far less than there ought to have been. Tommen wasn't sure what was worse, the impending wrath of the Hands and the Grandfathers, or their mysterious silence. To go from normal operations to militaristic lockdown and now having no guards at all, it was more than a little unnerving. Tommen wondered if Rifun and Cassius were watching them, waiting, tracking their every move. He tried to pass it off as paranoia and concentrate on his review, but it was difficult when he knew that there was every chance that his review was rigged.

"I don't like this," Walter said, finally putting words to everyone's thoughts. "It's not as crowded as it should be, and everyone seems too on edge. I would say it's the elections, except the elections seem to be conspicuously absent."

"I was thinking the same thing," Micaiah agreed. "Thousands of alien races from all across the universe and this place is practically a ghost town, relatively speaking."

"What happened here?"

It was not a rhetorical question. Tommen had spared no detail of his adventures to find the cure and heal his did, but that had all been done through a single lens. While he'd been off gallivanting on the other side of the universe, Micaiah and Micah had been keeping an eye on things at home, and it had been much more than just the bakery.

"Tommen's proposal was supposed to be the last case of the

day," Micaiah told him. Tommen noticed that he not only spoke in English, but he had stopped and had removed his translator, making motions like there was something wrong with it. Walter did the same thing with Micah's and Tommen's help.

"According to Sifura, some of the Hands remained in the deliberation chamber to speak secretly," the elder twin went on. "Some wanted to go after Isthim anyway. Others wanted to go straight for the Borelians. She left before they spotted her. Some time later, once Micah and I were recovered enough to return to the Wheel to see the fallout, we found that the Hands were beginning to divide into factions. They're all greedy, and they all have different ideas about how to go about satisfying—or at least adding to—their greed."

"The Grandfathers immediately went on the offense," Micah continued. "They branded Tommen a traitor, a Runner to be pursued and punished."

"And that's where S'Bal comes in," Tommen said.

"And your fiasco with Assim," his dad mused unhappily. "So far we've made it through unmolested."

"The Hands intervened after Assim was arrested," Micaiah said. "They said all the hysteria was bad for business, that the fear was driving away customers to the black markets."

"So if we're going to be apprehended, it's going to be in a dark alley where no one will ever think to look for us. Excellent. What do we know about the factions?"

"Not much. This close to the elections, everything is up in the air. The alliances that the Hands make today might not be there tomorrow."

Tommen bit his tongue. Even if he'd wanted to risk telling them about Rifun, he wasn't going to do it on his home field. But when was there going to be a good time to do it? Would there ever be? Well, first thing, he had to pass his review. If Rifun had rigged the system, better to eat the cake before biting the hand that gave it to him. Was that a good analogy? He brooded on it for a second before deciding it was.

"You think Tommen will be able to make it through his review, given his wanted status?" Micah wondered as they all replaced their translators and kept walking.

"One thing the Hands are good at is dull tradition, especially with introductions and formalities," Walter chuckled. "He'll make it through his review. It's after that I'm more concerned with."

"What? Like me not passing and having my clock broken or something?" Tommen asked.

"Something like that, yes."

It was not a comforting thought as they continued through the Wheel toward the Coliseum, also known as the Sanctum of the Hands. There was no universal language used in the Wheel, but there were a number of symbols marked around portals guiding people to various areas of the Wheel. A symbol for the marketplaces, a symbol for the Archives, a symbol for the Coliseum. The only thing that was remotely related to a fleshed-out writing system was numerical and mathematical notation, used for everything from basic math, such as in the marketplaces and the currency of turns, to the calendar used in the Wheel, as much of a mind-fuck as the Wheel itself given that no matter how much time passed in the Wheel, it would always be the same time when they returned home as when they left.

They found the Coliseum easily enough, its symbol being something like compass points. And it truly was a Coliseum. Not just a coliseum, but *the* Coliseum as it must have been in its glorious Roman days. Or so it appeared. On closer inspection, the whole structure looked more like it was built of glass or windows, then spray painted with some kind of faux texture to make it took like aging stone. Even the metal floor had the appeared of old cobblestone streets. They were in an alternate man-made dimension surrounded by endless information and power and technology, and they were walking through the streets of Ancient Rome. What—the—hell?

There were few entrances into the Coliseum, and even these were all real doors and real arches. No portals here as the whole place was blanketed by some kind of Time-inhibiting force field or something. Timekeepers could not Band, Harvesters could not Harvest, and even Time Capsules would refuse to open here. Tommen was stripped of all his abilities, even his enhanced perception of Time, the seconds and milliseconds as they crept by, all dull, invisible.

He followed his dad through one of the entrance arches, glancing at the barely-visible guards, hidden in little pocket dimensions, ready to jump out at a moment's notice.

Then they were in the outer track, as wide as a football field and probably thirty feet tall. Everything was still stone, or the appearance of stone, with doors on the inner wall. The smaller doors led to rooms of various uses, from janitor closets and break rooms to petitioning rooms like the one Tommen had waited in before going to see a candidate-judge in another room behind the larger doors. The candidate-judges oversaw the cases in a preliminary hearing, where they were either settled quickly or assigned to go before the Hands.

The Hands were placed in the very center of the Coliseum, in the Seat of the Hands, a gladiator-style arena sculpted from solid marble, or so it seemed. While there was an access from the inner track, there were also two enormous—about fifty by fifty feet—iron gates that led directly from the Seat to the outer track.

It was hard to believe Tommen had been here barely two weeks ago, begging the Hands to give him the antidote to save his dying father. Not only had they rejected him, but he'd given them the ammunition to start a civil war. Lovely.

"Good luck," Micah said as they approached one of the smaller doors.

"You're not coming with us?" Tommen wondered.

"We can't," Micaiah told him. "Mentor and probie only. We'll see you when you get back."

"So what will you be doing?"

"Better if you didn't worry about that and instead focused on your review. Good luck."

"Thanks a lot," Walter said sincerely. "We'll see you in a

while."

Micaiah did an imaginary tip of the hat as the twins turned and left.

"A while?" Tommen wondered as he opened the door and followed his dad inside. "How long is a while?"

"As long as the Hands deem necessary."

That was not the answer he'd been hoping for. He could handle "an hour" or "six hours" or even "all day" because that at least put things into a timeline that could be counted and completed. "As long as is necessary" was subject to all manner of unknowns. It was like taking one of those tests that got easier or harder depending on how well you're doing so far, continuing as long as you still have a chance at passing. As a freshman, Tommen had been made to take a similar test before going into Spanish, a placement test of sorts. Needless to say, he didn't make it very far.

He didn't relish the idea of doing something similar with his review. Banding was exhausting, and he didn't like the migraines that came with too much Banding, even if he had built up the fortitude with his trek across the desert. He knew his stuff, or so he thought, and paranoidly feared that such a test might be a way of seeing if the twins had given him any secret information that a normal probie wasn't supposed to know, giving them any excuse to arrest him.

But they entered the room, as his dad had stated earlier, unmolested. It wasn't the same as the other petitioning room that resembled an airport layover with dozens of people just milling around. This was more like what he'd expected the first time, like the DMV. Two secretaries called each person in line in turn, spoke to them for a bit, then sent them to wait in a common area where, at a certain point, another secretary would retrieve the next person in line.

"One thing the Wheel could really use is some proper chairs," Walter said, leaning heavily on his cane. Tommen could see the back of his neck was wet with sweat.

"Are you okay?" Tommen wondered.

"Oh, sure. I'll be sitting around for a while anyway, so I

shouldn't be complaining."

Before either could say more, they were called up to speak with a secretary, a tall, slender thing, like a literal bean pole.

"Walter Forbes, Timekeeper Captain, Quadrant One, Parsec Eleven, Sector Five, System Four, Planet Thirty-Eight, Region Four, District Four. Tommen Forbes, Probationary Timekeeper, here for his review to become an Apprentice."

"You've been here before, Captain, you know how this works." It was more of an observation than a friendly talking point, as none of the Coliseum secretaries seemed to have any life in them. "You have to the best of your abilities trained your charge in the material he needs to learn in order to not only pass his review but become an effective Timekeeper?"

"I have," Walter confirmed.

"And you have conveyed the rigor of this review in accordance with the policies?"

"I have."

"Your charge understands that he will be taxed physically, mentally, and emotionally, to the limits of your species? And he is in optimal health to complete this review?"

"He is."

Tommen didn't like where this conversation was going. It was like signing a waiver in order to go bungee jumping or something, except instead of being able to just assume abstract risks and skip over the fine print, the team leader or instructor was telling the class all about the cool ways this one guy's rope broke and he splatted all over the canyon floor.

"Tommen Forbes, you understand that upon completion of this review, should you pass, you will be responsible for all actions relating to your Timekeeping training, abilities, and the usage of those abilities, in order to uphold the Laws of Time and protect the Hands that govern them? If you do not agree to these terms, it is advised you leave now."

Translation: You complete this, we own you. For life. This is a military contract, but we're not taking just four years at a time, we're taking you for ever. Like, forever for ever. We will have you under a microscope. Serve us or cross us, but we are going to be a monkey on your back for the rest of your puny life which will only get longer and longer the more and more you use Time.

Was it like a bad drug deal or some kind of blackmail or ponze scheme or what? There was just something inherently not right about all of this, the way it was worded, the way it was delivered. Something about it put Tommen in mind of being Mirandized. There were no Grandfathers present, so why did he feel like he was about to be arrested and taken to the Judgment Wing?

"No, I do," Tommen said finally. "I do, I agree. I'll do it. Let's do this."

"Very well. You may wait."

So they went over to the common area where about ten more pairs of masters and apprentices of varying levels waited around. Some spoke quietly while others appeared to engage in some kind of prayer or yoga or other calming exercise. Every so often, a secretary entered the room and took one of the pairs.

"Why do they take them in pairs?" Tommen wondered quietly as his dad found a giant block of something to sit on and relax—stone or some such thing.

"They take them to another waiting room on the inner track," his dad answered, leaning back as far as he dared with his eyes closed. "There we will wait until they come and retrieve you."

"So you're just going to be sitting there waiting for me?"

"Yes."

"Did you bring like a book or something? I mean, if it's going to be a while..."

"Don't worry about me, Tommen. Rest and focus on your review."

"How am I supposed to do that if I don't know what's coming?"

"You know what's coming. Unlike other things and recent

goings on, reviews are fairly straightforward. And to make the leap from probie to Apprentice, especially with your experience and your breakthroughs, I have faith in you."

At least one of them did, Tommen thought as he sat next to his father on the block.

"Just remember that no matter what happens, it all stays silent," Walter told him after a moment. "I can know nothing of what goes on. What happens to you is your business."

Tommen nodded mechanically, out of acknowledgment, not because he agreed with it, especially knowing what he did about Rifun's hand in the whole thing. He sighed. "So does that go both ways?"

"I am not permitted to tell you about any of my reviews either."

"No, I mean, about everything?"

Walter opened his eyes. "What do you mean?"

Tommen shrugged. "I've told you a lot about what happened while you were in the hospital and stuff. But even after telling me that I'm your nephew, you still haven't told me about you. I mean, you never did before, but, that was before."

Walter let out a breath. "Guess it just became habit, not telling you anything. And you have to realize you're not the only one trying to process it. Difference is, I know what I've been living with, I know my lie." He groaned as he sat up. "When we get home, then we'll talk. I don't think you'll be wanting to leave your bed for a few days, so it'll give us plenty of time. Fair?"

After a moment, Tommen nodded. "Fair."

Not much later, a secretary came to retrieve them, taking them out of the waiting room and into the inner track, or the middle track, really, seeing how there was still the very center track around the Seat. It was slow-going as Walter fought for every step, limping far more noticeably than he had been an hour ago. The secretary took them to a room reminisce of the one Tommen had waited in before going to present his case before the lower courts, but he did not leave immediately.

"Captain Walter Forbes," the secretary said.

"Yes?" Walter wondered, standing to speak to the secretary, though his expression was strained as he wanted nothing more than to just sit down.

"It is my understanding that you have been injured. Do you require medical attention?"

"No, I require rest. Something I will get plenty of waiting here in this room, thank you."

Despite his sharp tone, the secretary did not take offense, making some motion that Tommen assumed to be deference, before changing the subject. "This is to be your waiting room. Here you will wait between parts of your review. Food and drink will be delivered as desired. The review itself is to remain only with the one being reviewed and may not be shared with anyone. Violation of this rule is grounds for immediate clock breaking. Do you have any questions?"

"No, thank you," Walter replied after a second.

"A secretary will retrieve you in due time."

With that, the secretary left, closing the door behind him, leaving Tommen alone with his dad.

"Last chance for any questions or uncertainties," Walter said.

"I don't know," Tommen sighed. "I mean, there's been so much going on, I don't know what I'm supposed to know and what I'm supposed to not know. What if they pull a trick question on me and it gets you or Micaiah or Micah in trouble?"

"I'm sure there are things you're not supposed to know. And I'm sure that most probies know things they're not supposed to know because they're not really supposed to know anything beyond Banding and basic Time. I'm also sure that you don't know enough of anything you're not supposed to know about to get me or the twins in trouble."

"How do you know?"

"What could you know that much about? Your case was your case, so you're going to know things about that. Cassius and Rifun kidnapped you, so you could have learned any number of things from them, crackpot though it may be. The rest is conspiracy and theory and a number of things that are truth today that could be not truth tomorrow."

"But the twins told me things."

"I'm sure Rifun told you things, too. And in your search for a cure, I'm sure Sifura may have told you things. And you probably read things in the Archives, even if you didn't understand it. Point is, don't worry. Go back to the basics. What did you learn when you were ten, twelve years old? If you get nervous about a question, think it might be a trick question to get someone in trouble, pull from that. Okay?"

Tommen let out a breath. Simple things. He was only a probationary and all he knew was Banding and basic Time. He nodded. "Okay."

"It'll be all right, Tommen. I'll be right there with you."

Chapter Four
A Test of Knowledge

Tommen played with his watch, the one his dad had gotten him for Christmas, the one he'd taken with him halfway across the universe. Of its many functions, it could take the local time anywhere in the universe and still always give him the current time back home on Earth. It could also change its shape and appearance, anything from an impressive Rolex, to the casual wristwatch, to, as he'd discovered on Sifura's world, simple beaded bracelets. He wore it as such now in order to minimize suspicion that he was carrying anything "illegal" into his review. He wasn't sure if there was a way that they could detect the watch as it was or if it was truly invisible, or if they just didn't care. Any other day he might have enjoyed the thought of sneaking something into a high-stakes review, kind of James Bond-ish. But his adventures had made him tired of the action and adventure and intrigue. What he really wanted was a normal Tuesday.

He couldn't say how much time had passed since being taken into the little waiting room, enough for his dad to quiz him on a few things, give him a little pep talk, and subsequently fall asleep, leaving Tommen alone with his thoughts, which were divided between general test anxiety and all the anxiety that came with being threatened by a terrorist and potentially starting a war.

I should have been allowed to sleep in, Tommen thought grudgingly. *Probably an hour or more has passed and I'm still not in my review.*

He briefly entertained the idea that maybe this was part of his review, that the Hands were watching him, or a secretary was watching him and reporting to the Hands. Was he a dutiful student, sitting patiently at the feet of his mentor and diligently asking questions? Was he insubordinate toward his mentor? Or was he just nervous and lazy, sitting in the middle of an empty room, doing nothing? Maybe it was part of his psychological review, to see what he and his mentor discussed when they thought they weren't being watched.

The sound of the inner door opening was like a gunshot, loud and sudden, making Tommen jump and jolting Walter awake. Tommen took a breath to calm himself, rubbing his face and telling himself that he was relieved; his test was finally beginning. But it was partially a lie. His review was more like one of those things you want to get over with but can't bear to begin.

No surprise, it was the same bat secretary who'd escorted him to his case before the Hands. The creepy bat gave no indication at all of recognition as it opened its mouth slightly at first, enough to use its echolocation, then more in order to speak.

"Tommen Forbes, probationary Timekeeper, you are here for your review," the Bat stated.

Tommen stood from his cross-legged position, feeling his muscles protest and knees pop. "I am."

"Follow me."

"Good luck," Walter said as Tommen stiffly followed the bat out of the room.

Where the outer and center tracks were reminisce of Ancient Rome, the Coliseum, old cobblestone streets and amazing ancient architecture, the inner track was more like a medieval dungeon, something out of the Dark Ages, where a man could be snatched from his home from some perceived crime against the Crown, locked up and left to rot in a cold stone cell with only the rats for company. At least this dungeon had sconces to provide some light, but the general mood was less than comforting.

Oddly enough, Tommen found his attitude toward the dungeon-like feel had changed since the last time. Last time, it was simply a creepy dungeon. This time, he found himself in mind of his dad. He didn't have all the details, but he knew he'd spent time in prison. And not a modern prison, but an old Welsh prison, where daily meals were considered too generous for the inmates. Walter slept with a night light, and Tommen had always assumed it was because of his work as a cop; he didn't like not being able to see. What if his fear of the dark came from prison and his dungeon cell? What did his dad think of this dungeon-like track? What did he see when he went before the Hands?

It was a strange thing to think about, and Tommen was so engrossed in his thoughts, he nearly ran into the Bat when it stopped at the gate of the tunnel leading to the Seat. Before, the Bat had simply opened the gate and said a few cryptic words to send him in. Now he stopped and did not immediately open the gate.

"Your review begins now," the Bat said. "It does not end until the Hands have rendered judgment. You are not to discuss any part of the review with anyone who is not present, including your mentor. Do you understand?"

"I understand," Tommen confirmed, trying to sound confident and serious.

The Bat opened the gate, not with a button or anything high-tech, but with sheer brute force, turning the wheel which tightened the chain and dragged the gate upwards, but all without a sound.

"When you are ready," the Bat said.

"I'm ready," Tommen told him, even though it was more for his own benefit.

"Then may the stars shine bright when the moon hides its face."

Tommen wasn't sure how to take the Bat's words even as he found himself thwarted again at coming up with a really cool, really cryptic parting message. He dismissed it as a cultural good luck or farewell, even if his spine had a hard time agreeing with him. He looked at the Bat one last time as if searching for some hidden meaning, hidden message, some silent warning or code to help him out, but he found nothing but an ugly, leathery, bat-like face.

He turned and walked down the tunnel, trying to hold his head high and keep his back straight. He fingered his watch again, though he made sure to keep his hands separate once he passed out of the tunnel into the Seat of the Hands.

As before, he was awestruck by the magnitude of brilliance in architecture, the cut marble, the carvings, the way the light bathed everything in a faint golden glow. Walking in, he'd almost expected to see tens of thousands of Ancient Roman citizens, cheering and talking and laughing. Well, strictly speaking, that might not have been the best thing seeing how that probably meant he was about to get thrown to the lions. Which he certainly felt like right now.

The design of the Seat was such that the person who walked in ended up walking away from the Hands as they approached the appointed spot on the floor, a way for the Hands to see their prey before their prey saw them. Tommen obediently walked away from the Hands toward the designated spot, but he did not stand there and gawk at the architecture like he had the last time. As soon as his foot hit the symbol of the Hands etched into the floor, he turned — executing a military turn that would probably earn him fifty push-ups — and faced the Hands.

"Tommen Forbes, probationary Timekeeper, you approach the Hands today for your review, your intentions to advance to the rank of Apprentice Timekeeper," the Zero Hour stated. "Is this correct?"

"It is correct," Tommen confirmed.

"Do you believe that you have studied diligently under your mentor, have acquired the necessary knowledge, have learned all the necessary skills, and have achieved the necessary mental fortitude needed to not only pass your review but continue your training as an Apprentice Timekeeper and beyond?"

"I do so believe."

Tommen wasn't sure if his responses were one hundred percent what they were looking for, but he made sure to keep things as formal as he could. *Answer swiftly, politely, and never give them more than they ask for.*

"Your review will consist of three parts. The first part is a test of knowledge, to be sure that you understand the basics of Time and how it works. The second part is a test of skill, to be sure that you have a solid foundation for the skills you will be learning in the future. The third part is a psychological evaluation, to be sure that you are fit to wield Time and uphold the Laws. Do you understand this?"

"I understand."

Part one: Oral exam, to make sure I can talk the talk. Part two: Demonstrations, to make sure I can walk the walk. Part three: Psych eval, so you can check me out and make sure I wasn't completely bullshitting you the entire time and make sure that I'm on your side and not a threat to you.

Tommen was forced to wonder if Rifun really did have a hand in this review. He looked at the Zero Hour but he got no help in determining whether it was the true Zero Hour or Cassius as the False Zero Hour. The acoustics in the room didn't help much either.

"You are not to discuss your review with anyone, even your mentor," the Zero Hour continued. "Do you understand this?"

"I understand."

"The review does not conclude until we have rendered judgment and deemed you worthy of advancement or not. Do you understand this?"

"I understand."

Good grief, it was like signing a release form. *Yes, I understand what I am about to do is dangerous and no one here is liable for anything I do out of my own stupidity, and I agree to hold harmless and release indemnification and blah, blah, blah the organization, and I also promise I won't copy, send, or transmit the work in any form, or turn my music player into a nuclear weapon. Sign here, here, here, initial here, sign here in blood, and we'll pick up your firstborn at the side door.*

"Commence now the first part of the Apprentice Timekeeper review for Tommen Forbes."

Tommen's heart involuntarily leapt into his throat. And it wasn't a startled jump, like when the Bat had opened the door of the waiting room. This was like a full pole vault going for Olympic gold. This was it. He was in his review. At the end of the day, he would either be an Apprentice Timekeeper or a drooling idiot.

"The first part of the review is a test of knowledge. It is an oral exam only. Each of the Hands of Time will pose a question. You will have one Base Minute to begin to answer the question. At the end of the Base Minute, if you have not begun to answer the question, you will forfeit the question. At any time in your answer, you may simply state, 'Unknown' and the test will move on, and you will forfeit the question."

The Zero Hour went on a little more with rules and procedures, but what caught Tommen's attention was his mention that each of the Hands would pose a question. Did that mean that all fifty-one Hands were present? That would mean Sifura had to be up there somewhere. So she had survived whatever S'Bal had done to her. Relief washed over Tommen, and he almost didn't notice that the Zero Hour had stopped speaking; he was lucky to have caught the last "Do you understand this?"

Tommen dipped his head respectfully, even if he had missed the last few bits and pieces. They were probably important. He probably should have been paying more attention to them. But he hadn't. Still, he gave no indication of that as he replied, "I understand."

"Very good. Let's begin."

The Zero Hour did not begin the questioning, as Tommen might have expected; he wasn't even sure if there was any rhyme or reason to the order in which the questions were asked or if the Hands just blurted out questions as they felt like it. Although, he had a sneaking suspicion that after so many reviews, they probably had some kind of system down.

"Name all of the Hands of Time," the first Hand said.

If Tommen hadn't done just that two weeks ago when he was trying to butter them up with overly-pompous formalities, he would probably have been a lot more nervous than he was; indeed, he probably wasn't as nervous as he should have been as he began rattling off the various titles. Some were easy to remember, like the Hand of the Timekeepers or the Hand of Scientifically Advancing but Unengaged Civilizations. Others he remembered only because they were, at first glance, somewhat puzzling, like the Hand of Flora and the Hand of Fauna and the Hand of Rocks and Pebbles. Hey, apparently it was a huge thing on some worlds, the plants and animals and rocks and stuff. Some Hand titles he had to scratch and scrape his memory for, trying to remember his time before, rattling all of them off. Like the Hand of Longevity, representing races with exceptionally long lifespans. Similarly, there was the Hand of the Winking, races with exceptionally short lifespans. Humans fell under the Hand of the Modest Time, pretty much the catch-all of races who lived between fifty and two hundred and fifty years, give or take.

Eventually, though, he got through them all. The Hands did not give him feedback on whether he'd done well or not, and he managed to pull some subconscious memory of the Zero Hour saying he would receive no feedback at all; it was simply pass or fail.

"Name the ranks of the Timekeepers, starting with yourself," the second Hand said.

Well, he was a probationary, the lowest of the low. In children who were accidentally exposed, such as himself, training could not begin until age thirteen, for reasons pretty much summed up as mental and physical maturity. Tommen had been trained earlier because of the threat to his life by Tyler Freeman. The Hands hadn't been happy about it and had come down hard on his dad for it, and he knew they were expecting nothing less than perfection from him because of it.

Generally speaking, an exposed adult could advance at his leisure, though Tommen had heard that it was a minimum of one year between advancements.

After probationary, there were the customary Apprentice, Journeyman, and Master ranks, and they concluded the ranks of the average Timekeeper. After that, they started getting into the officers.

Lieutenants who served under a District Captain, like Micah and Micaiah to Walter, and Walter answered to a Regional Manager who reported to the Gatekeeper of the planet. From there were the Wardens, the Dominion Timekeepers, and finally the Hand of the Timekeepers.

"Name the ranks of the Harvesters," was the next question.

Other than the usual probie to Master ranks, the Harvesters worked a little differently. It was possible to advance from the Master rank without becoming an officer. Actually, the Assistants, Physicians, Surgeons, and Doctorate Harvesters were not considered officers at all even though they correlated roughly to the Lieutenants, Captains, Managers, and Gatekeepers of the Timekeepers. Harvesters did not become officer until they hit Intervention level, and that was like a Warden Timekeeper, which made a Triage Harvester like a Dominion Timekeeper.

Tommen had heard that advancing through Harvester ranks was much more difficult than advancing through Timekeeper ranks, like the difference between eight years of medical school and two years of police academy. He'd also heard it said that Lily, though she was only technically a Master Harvester, was also a kind of upset to the system, rich enough and talented enough to run circles around some Doctorate Harvesters.

"Name the ranks of the Merchants."

While Merchants may reside in a certain District or Region, their ranks were not bound to those areas. Instead, Merchants operated independently of planetary or galactic restrictions, working and advancing almost solely within Time, within the Wheel. Their ranks also weren't linear. Instead of a ladder, they worked more on a spider web. Once a Merchant got through all the basic ranks, he could choose to become a Negotiator and study a particular discipline within the Merchant circles. The actual Merchant-ranked Merchants oversaw the training of new Merchants as well as the lower marketplaces; Auctioneers oversaw both the auctions and the intermediate marketplaces; Investors pretty much oversaw the entire

Time economy and worked very closely with the Hands. Some said too closely, but Tommen did not say this out loud.

"What is a Scout?"

Exactly what I want to be.

Scouts did not have a hierarchy, more of a pecking order. Their job was to go out to all the unexplored, untouched planets and, well, explore them, touch them. They were charged with bringing new worlds, new races into the Time industry. Sometimes it worked, and they were able to successfully mark up planetary regions and districts and bring new, engaged races into the fold. Sometimes a race, no matter how advanced or how much they might profit, just refused Time, and involvement was limited to accidental exposures. Other times, the Scouts deemed it too dangerous or culturally devastating. Probably that was how Sifura's world was Scouted.

Ultimately, Scouts answered only to the Hand of the Scouts, and that Hand sent them on their various missions to the different worlds, gave them their pay, and kept them out of the public eye. The Scouts were not well-liked, considered by some to be "legal Runners."

Tommen had always wondered what it took to be a Scout. Supposedly, any Time Agent could become one, but whether Scouting was more like a last chance before prison kind of job or something where they approached those they deemed worthy, he wasn't sure, and he was still too afraid to ask either his dad or the twins.

"What is the Wheel of Time?"

It was the hub of the Time industry, a mind-fuck of obscenely advanced technology that, when it felt like it, sometimes devolved into Victorian libraries or Roman Coliseums. Tommen didn't word it exactly like that, but it was what he was thinking. He hadn't seen the Judgment Wing yet or the Arena, but somehow he was expecting the former to be kind of like maybe the Wizard of Oz's great hall or something. And the latter he anticipated either like a mini-Coliseum or like a shooting range.

"What is the role of the secretaries?"

What did the secretaries do? Fuck, what didn't they do? Some were charged with janitorial cleanup, others with more building maintenance, still others like Geek Squad kind of computer systems tech support. There was no less than an army of linguistic secretaries, their sole purpose being to keep the translator language interpretation systems up-to-date, plus a subset of secretaries to keep the translator hardware up-to-date, for example, adapting human translators to be compatible with hearing aids. There were the Archive secretaries, those who knew the Archives like the grocery store and made sure everything was in its proper place, and a second set of Archive secretaries who took all of a specific set of information and coded it so as to be "fluid" as Micaiah had described it, able to be translated into any and every language available in the Wheel. Then there were the secretaries in the Food Court who made sure that food was available to all races, sustenance of every kind, whatever kind was required. And there were the secretaries in all parts of the Coliseum, the Judgment Wing, the Arena, and probably places Tommen didn't even realize existed yet.

Of course, there was also the secondary role of the secretaries, that is, to keep an eye on everything and report on everything; Tommen had little doubt that there was some sort of hierarchy among the secretaries and information just kept getting passed up and up to the Hand of the Secretaries who compiled it all and shared it with the rest of the Hands. But he said none of this out loud; better to let them think that he found the secretaries innocent and unthreatening.

It was sort of the way the questions worked, too, he found. Unless he was rattling off ranks or a specified list of information, the questions seemed simple enough, but the answers proved to be tough. For example, What is the nature of the calendar used in the Wheel? Well, it was a calendar, designed to keep track of time and the days as they passed in the Wheel. And yet, it didn't fully capture the fourth dimension of how that calendar worked, so linear, and yet able to remain a fixed point from wherever a Time Agent stepped through. How could time advance in the Wheel, yet not advance at home, but when time advanced at home it advanced in the Wheel, and yet there was a way to convert the dates back and forth so appointments like this one didn't get missed? Tommen liked physics, but that went way over his head.

And then there was the one about describing the role of a Hand. The role of a Hand changed depending on which group he was representing. But was that right? Should it change depending on the group, or should it always be to act in the best interest of that group so the work was pretty much equal no matter which office one occupied? The twins had said that most often, a person would land in an office they were qualified to handle, so a human was probably not likely to land as the Hand of Flora. But what if, through some weird mishap, they did? Did their job change? What was their role as an inexperienced Hand?

There was also a question about the role of a probie, in any discipline. Was it an effective role? Was it worth keeping, or should any new Time Agent go straight into Apprenticeship? On the one hand, probies didn't have much power so they were pretty useless beyond simple party tricks, and it took up a lot of extra time on the part of the mentors, but it did a good job of weeding out those who would become Runners. It also kept those like Eric and Varad safe, those who had been exposed but had no wish to continue training of any sort.

As the test wore on and the questions stacked up, Tommen discovered that they became less and less about straight knowledge, naming ranks and titles, and more about thoughts, opinions, feelings, and ethics. It was as if they were already preparing for the psychological evaluation, as if they were going to take these answers and stack them up against whatever happened in the third part of the review. If he was consistent, then he was safe and on their side and fit to continue his training. If he was inconsistent or blatantly contradictory, then he was a danger, potentially a Runner, and shouldn't continue his training. The twins had said that it was next to impossible to bullshit his way through the psych eval, so what did that mean for him now?

He'd tried to keep a count of the questions but lost it somewhere around fifteen when they began to turn. He'd tried to keep an ear out for Sifura's voice just to know that she was all right, but the acoustics made it difficult to judge her voice any different from most any other voice. He'd tried to always be confident and straight-forward, to project his voice and answer clearly, but the wearing questions and wearing on of time made him slouch and speak less confidently. Perhaps the only thing he had going for him was that he'd so far managed to answer every question. He hadn't had an Unknown or a time-limit expire on him yet.

Secretly, he hoped they would ask him about the test itself, if he thought it was effective. Then he might have suggested that they do it progressively, in exactly the style of test he hated but figured would be very beneficial right now. Save time by making the questions progressively more difficult, but once the candidate reaches a point where they're so awful they can't pass or so awesome they can't fail, just stop the test. Send them on their way. Obviously they know a thing or two, or they know nothing. It's not like a final exam to end all exams; they'll be doing a hell of a lot more training in the days and years to come. They will learn.

But they never did ask him what he thought of the test, and he bore them no ill will for it. It was probably planned that way. First, they probably didn't care. Second, they probably didn't want to listen to candidates whine about the test. They had a system that had worked just fine for hundreds of years, refined to as perfect as it was going to be, and it was going to stay that way for a few more centuries.

Tommen's relief came when finally the Zero Hour stood. He was tired and sweating, his feet were killing him, and he had a headache, whether from the questioning or the lighting he didn't know, but he was ready to be done. At the very least, he hoped he was almost done. There was supposed to be a break between parts of the review, wasn't there?

"Tommen Forbes, your final question," the Zero Hour said.

Tommen let out a level breath, willing himself not to slouch or hang his head or do anything to indicate he was anything more than a bit weary. Not tired, certainly not exhausted, just a bit weary.

"What is Time?"

Fuck. My. Life.

What is Time? What is Time? Might as well as me to describe the universe and give two examples. Might as well ask a religious person to describe God. Might as well ask a blind man to describe the color red. And any of those things would be easier than this question. Time is time. It's cause and effect. It's before and after and during. It's tense and mood and aspect, perfect and progressive. It's manipulable, it's fast and slow and you can bend it and play with it and it's kind of a big ball that's all wibbly-wobbly. It's timey-wimey...stuff. It's Banding and Harvesting, it's life and death. It's...Time.

Tommen sighed. He didn't let out a breath or try to keep himself composed now, but mentally gave up, heaved a great sigh, and said, "Unknown."

The Zero Hour studied him for a moment before dipping his head.

"Thus concludes the first test of the Apprentice Timekeeper review for Tommen Forbes. Thank you for your time and thoughtful consideration of all your answers. You have performed admirably and are a credit to yourself and your mentor. You will now return to the waiting room to await the commencement of part two, the test of skill. Food and drink will be brought for you."

"Thank you," Tommen replied, hoping it was the right thing to say. Funny thing, how he wasn't even sure whether common courtesies were appropriate here.

The Hands stood then, and Tommen headed for the tunnel as the gate opened, the Bat secretary heaving mightily on the wheel that turned silent chains. When he was through, rather than let the gate slam shut, the Bat carefully let the wheel turn back so the only sound was that of the gate gently touching the ground.

"I will now return you to the waiting room with your mentor.

Remember that you are not to speak of anything that transpired during your review," the Bat told him.

"I remember," Tommen confirmed, trying to recover some of his confidence but feeling like he was trying to get a firm grip on jello and it just kept slipping through his fingers.

He followed the Bat through the dungeon, around the inner track to a particular door which the Bat opened. At first, Tommen didn't see his dad, but once he stepped inside, he saw that he'd moved to a different spot in the room. Tommen entered the room and the Bat shut the door heavily behind him.

"So, how do you think you did?" Walter asked. He sat on the long stone bench seat, trying to relax but looking mightily uncomfortable and not a little in pain.

Tommen shrugged, opening his mouth but catching himself before he started talking about it. Not allowed to talk about his review? Like, forever for ever? This was going to be harder than he thought. Eventually he said only, "Good, I guess."

"You look better than I did after my first test."

That sparked a dormant thought in Tommen's mind, something he'd mulled over on his way to the test. "What do you think about when you walk through the inner track?"

His dad blinked. "What do you mean?"

"You said you did time in prison, an old-school prison. The track in there isn't exactly the yellow brick road."

Walter's gaze turned stony and suspicious, but Tommen also caught a glimpse of fear and uncertainty. After a moment he replied, "We agreed that we'd talk once we were back home and you were recovering."

Tommen frowned and looked away. "Sorry."

As promised, food and drink was delivered. Apparently, someone had been taking notes because it was the same meal that he'd had the last time, a cheeseburger with all the fixing, fries, and a strawberry milkshake, almost as if they'd come straight out of a diner from the fifties.

"Well, lucky you," Walter teased as he mused over his tiny plate of fruit, cheese, and cold cuts.

"I wasn't expecting this," Tommen admitted, taking a bite of the burger. "Last time I got fruit."

"They go by the last thing you ordered, if it's available."

"And last time you got fruit, cheese, and cold cuts?"

"Well, they forgot the wine, but yes. Of course, I haven't been in the Coliseum in some time. Last time, I think...yes, I'm pretty sure it was when I brought you when you were ten. They didn't like me very well after that, so I decided to keep my distance. No, wait, I would have had to have been here when you formally started training. You didn't come with me, but I had to let them know that you were officially of an age to begin your training, even if you'd already begun and were already quite adept."

Tommen nodded as he sucked down some of his shake. "Is there anything you can tell me about the skill test?"

Walter rubbed his eyes and groaned. "It's different for each rank, obviously, and it's been a long time since I was a probie. I really don't remember. But I think that with you breaking into Predict and External Banding and whatnot, you shouldn't have any trouble."

"The knowledge test was...different from what I thought it would be."

"Well, it's not like the tests you take at school, that's for sure."

In a way, Tommen was almost sorry for that. The open-ended questions, the ethical questions, they'd caught him off-guard, but now that he was sitting down and thinking about it, he found that he kind of enjoyed them. It wasn't just about knowing the information, but knowing why he knew it, know what he felt about it and why he felt that way, understanding how he worked so he could understand how he learned and what things would be like going forward in his training.

Of course, in that same reflection, he also saw how it was almost certain that the Hands would be using those answers from the knowledge test and stacking them against whatever happened in the psych evaluation. The knowledge test, he had time to think and compose his words, whereas it sounded like the psych test would be almost purely reflexive.

"You look contemplative," his dad observed. "Anything you can share?"

"Question," Tommen said. "Is there actually a third part of the test, or is it somehow comprised of elements from the first two parts?"

The look in Walter's eyes told Tommen that he'd touched on something deep, something secret, something that couldn't be said in present company but they would probably discuss later. But all that came out of his mouth was, "Oh yes, there is very much a third part of the test. The psychological evaluation follows very closely on the heels of the skill test. It's unlikely you'll be able to get food or rest between those parts, so take what you can get now."

Tommen took the hint and said nothing more as he scarfed down his burger, fries, and shake, fully expecting the Bat to return and cart him off to the second part of his review.

"How long did the first part actually take?" Tommen wondered before his dad could relax and probably drift off again.

Walter looked thoughtful. "Not entirely sure, but I'd guess about two, two and a half hours."

"Two and a half hours?!"

Was it really so unbelievable? Fifty-one Hands, one question each, figure at least two minutes per question, plus some of the questions required more than two minutes. And then his dad might also be counting everything from the walking to and from and all the introductions, formalities, and other bullshit they had to go through. So it was entirely possible that he'd been gone for two hours or more, and that was only the first part of his review. At this rate, he was going to be here all day.

"Is the second part likely to take as long?" Tommen wondered cautiously.

His dad chuckled. "Second part is a skill test. Banding, Fast and Slow and all manner of specific ratios. How long do you think it will take?"

Chapter Five
A Test of Skill

Tommen wasn't sure whether it was conniving or coincidence that the door opened again just as he was drifting off to sleep. He felt as though he'd been waiting for hours, long enough that his stomach had grown hungry again, and that was saying something given the meal he'd eaten. As the Bat opened the door and roused him from his near-slumber, he was grateful that the Bat was blind, and it didn't matter that he looked and felt slightly rumpled.

"Tommen Forbes, you are required now for the second part of your review," the Bat told him formally.

Got nowhere else to be, he thought ruefully, glancing at his dad who sat with his eyes closed; the jury was out on whether he was truly asleep, but he made no movement as Tommen quietly left the room, following the Bat.

"So if you're the night secretary, who's the day secretary?" Tommen inquired conversationally.

The Bat did not answer, but Tommen didn't miss the twitch of his ear, though whether that was a simple acknowledgment of the question or some nervous tic, he couldn't say. That was the thing about dealing with aliens; he really couldn't apply the same kind of human psychology and body language and hope to be right.

Tommen ran his tongue over his teeth. "Okay, so...the first part of the review. Done and over with, sure, but will I ever actually know my honest score? Like, not just the pass-fail, but, you know, forty out of fifty right, ninety percent, any of that?"

"Such things are not recorded," the Bat replied. "Only whether you passed or failed."

He found that hard to believe, actually. In a system that esteemed record-keeping and formalities and all that sort of precision time-wasting, why would they not keep records of things like that? Sure, SATs and other high-end test results were little more than a sliding scale of numbers, but someone, somewhere had the actual physical records of the individual questions and answers that determined those sliding numbers. In the inefficient Earth-side system, Tommen could see where they might shred those files. But in the Wheel, where everything was digital and there was no less than an army of secretaries at the Hands' disposal, there was no reason that he shouldn't be able to research his honest score. Maybe he would ask his dad when he was all finished.

That train of thought saw him all the way to the gate where the Bat effortlessly started cranking the wheel to tighten the chains and lift the gate.

"How heavy is that gate?" Tommen wondered. "What does it take to actually, like, turn the wheel and open it?"

"It is heavy, and it requires strength," the Bat replied obviously.

Tommen couldn't quite tell if he was just being stiff, or if the Bat was growing annoyed at his persistent questions. He only talked because he was nervous. He figured he shouldn't have been, since the second part, the skill test, was the only part he was truly confident about. Oral exams could bring out trick questions, psychological exams could do more harm than good. But skill tests were all about raw power and talent. He knew his stuff, and he was ready for this.

The gate opened and the Bat looked at him through blind, golden eyes. "The second part of your review awaits. I will remind you that you are not to speak of any part of your review to anyone."

"Thank you for the reminder," Tommen replied as graciously as he could. *Because I had totally forgotten about that in the last few hours of sitting in an empty room staring at a blank wall.* "I'll see you when I'm done."

The Bat said nothing to that, just waited for him to enter the tunnel, which he did after only half a second's hesitation. That was the thing about skill tests and doing a demonstration in front of a bunch of people who not only hate you but are far more powerful than you. In order for him to be able to demo his skills, they would have to drop whatever Time-dampening field they had in the Seat. But that would allow them to use their Time abilities too, whatever they were. So in the midst of all that skill testing and raw power, however it was done, they could inflict some serious injuries on him out of sadistic glee, then claim him inept and fail him.

Even as he thought about it, walking through the tunnel, he found the point where it was like walking through one of those beaded curtains from the 60's (after all, who would know more about ugly 60's decor?). As he passed through the invisible curtain, he felt his sense of Time coming back to him, sharpening like a fine knife, focusing like when he'd put his hearing aids in. Everything came back to him in a rush.

But there was another feeling with that, like something else piggybacking with the sense of Time. It was a feeling he knew all too well, that is, the prey sense, a rabbit being stalked by a wolf, a mouse hunted by a cat. He knew he was always under observation here, but this was far more intimate, as if the shadows themselves watched him. It was a clear, unadulterated message from the Hands, a threat even: We're giving you your sense of Time back in order to complete this part of your review, but make no mistake, you are in our domain, so don't try anything smart.

Tommen had no intention of trying anything, smart or not. He'd managed to get through the first part of his review, and he would get through the second part the same way. *Don't give them anything they don't ask for. You're just a dumb probie trying to make Apprentice, nothing more.*

So he strode into the Seat of the Hands, heading directly for the symbol etched into the floor, keeping his back obediently turned to the shrouded figures high above him. He did not walk with the same air about him as before; he did not want to appear arrogant. But he walked purposefully, trying to make it look as if the first part hadn't gotten him down and he was ready for the second part. Confidence, that was the word. Part one was the warm-up and now he was ready for the game, bring it on.

For what felt like forever, he and the Hands stared at each other. Had they moved at all since he left from the first part of his review? Did they take a break, go to the water cooler to joke and bullshit about the idiot probie who thought he was all that and a bag of bricks? Did they hear petitions and cases in between? Who decided these things anyway? Did the Hands just walk into work and a personal assistant secretary handed them their agenda for the day? Was it strictly a first-come first-serve basis? Or was there some sort of order and finesse to go along with it?

Strange, Tommen thought, the things you think of when you're under pressure. He was nervous, sure, had talked the Bat's ear off in the track, and now his thoughts were taken more by what the Hands did in their free time in the Wheel.

Then the Zero Hour stood, and Tommen had another thought. Was it possible for the Hands to change shrouds while they were in the Wheel? What if Sifura had been systematically dispatched and Cassius had slipped into her role so as to keep fifty-one Hands? All wore shrouds, so no one would really notice. Plus, then he could both have a Zero Hour who wasn't him and still keep an eye on Tommen's review.

It was a stomach-churning idea, one that he couldn't get away from even as the Zero Hour—whichever one it was—started speaking.

"Tommen Forbes, probationary Timekeeper in the middle of his review to become an Apprentice Timekeeper, are you ready to begin the second part of your review?"

"I am ready," Tommen replied, hoping he sounded confident with an appropriate amount of nervousness. *Stroke their egos just a little, make them think they're still in control. Because, well, they are. Play the whipped dog, get thrown a bone, and be forgotten.*

"The second part of the review is a test of skill, and this test will also be done in two parts." *This could get really bad really fast.* "The first test is a standing test. You will be asked to create Bands with specific parameters which will not exceed the reasonable limits expected of a probationary Timekeeper." *Yup, gotta throw that little footnote in there.* "If we the Hands are satisfied with the results of the standing test, then we will move on to the second test, that is, the reflexive test where you must create Bands reflexively in a variety of scenarios."

There was a time in third grade gym class when the teacher decided to do a short three-day unit on reflexes with a hint of peripheral vision. The first day had been more of a play day as the class was shown and told about all the little reflexes of the body, well, most of them: the knee, the eyes, and so on. And when they weren't exploring those, they were identifying colors and people using only their peripheral vision.

For everyone else, it was great fun. Tommen did not adapt half as well. His first obstacle was trying to figure out what everyone was saying and what the teacher wanted them to do. His English had improved, but big words—because "reflexively" is still a big word to a third grader whose first language isn't English—still confused him. After that, he somehow confused exploring reflexes with pressure points, something Teo had taught him, and not in a kindly manner. After he made four of his classmates cry, the teacher took him aside to explain in simpler terms what they were supposed to be doing.

Once he finally got the gist of the assignment, he spent the next three days only compounding his lack of athletic ability in any scenario. Thankfully, he hadn't been the only one down on his luck during the assignment. In the end, the teacher finally conceded that reflexes were reflexive for a reason. They were, well, reflexes. They couldn't exactly be taught the same way that any concentrated effort could be taught. And so, with a few more bruises and scratches than what they started out the week with, the class moved on to soccer. Because if there was a God, He was intent on making Tommen's life hell.

And it was starting to feel that way again, as soon as the Zero Hour said "reflexive test." This was not going to end well. There was no way it could end well. Sure, he might be able to squeak by because the probie test was supposed to be easy and whatnot, but if there was going to be some kind of reflexive test in every skill portion of every review, he wasn't going to make it to Journeyman. He was going to be an Apprentice forever, assuming he even made it that far.

Was this how Timekeepers became Runners before they were even skilled enough to be Apprentices or Journeymen? Did they fail the skill test and then run off, determined not to have their clocks broken? That they would rather live the life of an outlaw than take that kind of pain and punishment, was it all because of this damn test?

Tommen felt the sweat snaking down his neck and back. *Relax, Tommen. The test hasn't even started yet. It could be nothing. Maybe it's more from their little bag of psychological goodies, something they can hold against you later. Don't give them any more than they ask for. Be strong and complete the fucking test.*

"The test will end when we the Hands are satisfied with your performance," the Zero Hour was saying. "Do you have any questions before we begin the test?"

What does it take to satisfy you that I'm completely inept at this? Is it going to be a bunch of little tests or one big one? Do I get bonus points if I go above and beyond what you ask of me? How suspicious will you be if you realize that I've already broken into Apprentice training? Is it possible to tell if and when I use Predict? Is that considered cheating or a disqualifier? What if I accidentally do an External Band? Is that a disqualifier or do I get brownie points? Are you going to tell me if I pass or fail, or is it more of a, "If you're still alive and have your clock intact, you've passed," sort of thing?

But none of this passed Tommen's lips as he looked up at the Hands, fifty-one shrouded figures poised and ready to chop his head off or break the lock. "No, I have no questions."

The Zero Hand regarded him. "Commence now the first test

of the second portion of the Apprentice Timekeeper review for Tommen Forbes."

Then the Zero Hour sat, and Tommen got the sense that he—or she or it or whatever—ended all the tests. As he sat, another Hand stood, a huge thing, probably as wide as it was tall.

"Fast Band, hour:minute," it commanded.

That was kind of the nice thing about Bands, they were done in ratios. Non-specific ratios, such as hour:minute, defaulted to one. So a Fast Band, which by itself meant that he would be moving faster than the Base Time around him, with such a ratio ultimately meant that spending one hour in the Fast Band was the equivalent of spending one minute in Base Time.

Creating any Band was little more than an effort of will. When properly trained, it was more like an intentional sigh than an involuntary yawn as someone who was untrained. It was simply taking the Time that was around him and bending it, forming it in such a way that he could make it anywhere from two minutes:one minute to day:second. Tommen threw up a Fast Band, trying to keep it as tight and narrow as he could going into it before refining it, like carefully blowing bubbles from a bubble wand, trying to make the biggest bubble possible before it burst.

Of course, any analogy would be inadequate, and they all sounded better in his head anyway, he figured. Best not say them aloud or focus on them too much and lose sight of his Band which he had successfully built around him to the specified Time.

Then he had another thought. He seemed to be having a lot of those today. Would they actually keep him in this Band for a whole hour? It would be a minute to them, but would he have to sit here for an hour just to prove himself? What if they asked him to do something like day:hour? Would he have to sit in his Band for a whole day?

Even as he thought it, he felt a tug at his Band, like someone poking his bubble. Sufficient to prove the bubble analogy tenuous at best, it was also possible to tighten and strengthen a Band so other Timekeepers couldn't break into it, like blowing bubbles made of brick instead of soap. It was also possible to completely break into a Band, commandeer it, manipulate it, destroy it. Rifun had shredded Walter's Bands as he tried to escape the bullets. Similarly, Tommen had pushed into the wake of Rifun's Band and then into the Band itself as he tracked him and Cassius from the museum. He hadn't been strong enough to do anything more than that, to his dismay.

And then the Band was ripped from him. It was as if the air had not just been sucked from his lungs but vacuumed out completely, and Tommen involuntarily doubled over and began coughing and gasping for breath. He tried to recover quickly, but at the same time he wanted to milk it for all it was worth, gain as much strength back as he could.

When he finally looked up, another Hand was standing.

"Slow Band, twenty minutes:four hours," it ordered.

Slow Band meant he would be slipping into a Time slower than Base Time, so everything else would appear to be going very fast. The ratio set wasn't too bad, really, but Slow Bands were used much more infrequently than Fast Bands. Supposedly some races used them almost exclusively, but humans were not one of those races. Humans relied too much on speed and, yes, reflexes. Given the choice, most humans would rather go faster to beat something, for example a speeding bullet moving perpendicular to their position and intended direction, than slow down and let it go by.

So Tommen took his Fast Band and turned it inside out, watched as everything around him seemed to speed up, like an old VHS tape gone wild. Not that the Hands were especially mobile, but in the Band it was funny to watch them wiggle around as they shifted positions and generally tried to get comfortable, as any species does when it is forced to sit or stand in one place for any length of time.

He felt the prod a split-second before his Band was ripped open. Despite his best effort to steel himself against it and not go down like a total weakling, he again was left coughing and gasping for air. Whoever was cutting into his Bands was either under orders to make it as uncomfortable and even as painful as possible, or else they derived a certain sadistic glee from watching him double over in pain. Given the crowd, he guessed it was a little of both.

He'd barely looked up to see the Hand before another order was being issued.

"Fast Band, six hours:forty-two minutes."

It was impossible to say what drove the Hands to pick the ratios they did, whether they were some predetermined ratios that calculations and experiments had long ago deemed the best with which to test probationary Timekeepers, or if there was some unknown cultural significance to the Hands in Time or the numbers themselves, or if they only had to make the gap wider, or if it was truly completely random.

Still, Tommen obeyed, having to pull in just a bit tighter and work a little more to bring in the Band at precisely six hours to forty-two minutes. Default ratios were almost second-nature, with solid numbers close behind, but once the numbers started getting specific, then that took a little more effort.

The third time his Band was broken into, not only did he have difficulty breathing, but a headache started in the back of his head. It would only get worse with each Band, he knew. He wondered if all species had this problem or just humans. Then he wondered if the Hands intentionally exploited it, and whether there was a real reason or just for the fun of it.

He didn't even get to look up before another command was issued.

"Slow Band, eight minutes:ten hours."

He obeyed, though he could feel his mind slogging along like an unwilling puppy trying to give a four-paw stop. He might have compared it to a goat doing a four-hoof stop, but as it was, his mind was still easy to drag along, unwilling though it was. Depending on how much more he had to do, that puppy would soon turn into a very large, very cranky, and very unwilling billy goat.

Barely three seconds into the Band, it was torn away from him. Thankfully, this time it was done a little more gently, and he was at least able to catch his breath before being issued yet another command.

"Fast Band, six hours:fifteen minutes."

And so it went, back and forth, alternating Fast and Slow Bands with greater and greater ratio gaps until he was making a Fast Band of day:minute and a Slow Band of minute:day. It was kind of like being bounced around on a trampoline, always going a little higher and yet always going a little farther down into the...trampoline? Fuck. Nope, not going to work. Maybe like watching wave physics, a little splash on one end of a tub made a bigger splash at the other end and back and forth it went until you got a tsunami. Yeah, little better.

Of course, on the third plane of that was the headache that had turned into a migraine so that he could barely see straight, and he had to turn down the hearing aids because every word was like a shout. Was there going to be a break between the two tests or was it just going to be one after another? Were there even any formalities or indications of when one ended and another began, or was it going to be a surprise, hence the "reflexive" part of the test?

He wasn't sure if he was supposed to be relieved or scared when the Zero Hour finally stood. Either the test was over, or there was still one whopper of a Band he had to make.

"Begin with a Fast Band, day:second. Slide into a Slow Band of second:day."

Slide? Like just take a Fast Band and make it into a Slow Band kind of slide? Like, take his socks and turn them inside out sort of thing? It sounded easy enough, in theory. In practice, though, his experience was limited to making a single Band, adjusting it, then, if he had to switch between Fast and Slow, dropping the Band and making a new one. Where did this sliding business come into play?

Still, he did his best to obey as he threw up a Fast Band, narrowing it and drawing it in tighter, looking for the day:second ratio, something he could normally do very easily, but between the migraine and his general exhaustion, he might as well have been asked to pick between the red wire and the yellow wire.

He found the ratio he was looking for and paused for a second, hoping it would be seen as showing that he'd completed part one before moving into part two. He could slowly loosen the Band easily enough, but it was the threshold between Fast and Slow that was going to be tricky, to reach Base Time and not drop the Band as he moved into Slow Time.

It was kind of like sliding down a steep, rocky hiking trail, knowing there were no good steps to be had; the only thing he could do was try to outsmart gravity by leaning into the mountain face without falling on his ass and sliding down the trail. Or snowplowing down a ski run on a snowboard. Lean too far forward and take a less than graceful tumble down the slope; lean too far back and land on his ass.

He'd held pretty extreme Fast Bands and pretty extreme Slow Bands, and that had been tough. But that was nothing compared to trying to hold onto a Band that was essentially the same as Base Time. That was like trying to fish with his bare hands, and not just fish, but eels. Electric eels, at that.

His slide into Slow Time was less like a slide and more like that ungraceful stomping around when you get going running down a hill too fast and you don't have enough runway to properly slow yourself down so you end up thumping like an idiot and risk falling on your face, even more so when you have to go and climb up the next hill right away. As he searched for his second:day ratio, he almost felt like a rubber band, poised, ready to strike, ready to be launched back into the Fast Band.

Then the rubber band was cut, his Band was gone, and he collapsed to the floor, gasping, coughing, spitting, head pounding like a drum, eyes pulsing, ears ringing and thundering with the blood of his racing heart. There was no sense in trying to play the strong man now; he stayed there on the floor for as long as he could, longing to curl up into a ball and go to sleep. No one made a move to force him to stand, and he stood in his own time, on legs that felt little better than jello. The light in the Seat was far too bright and he was just about ready to take his hearing aids out and suffer the muffle.

"And so concludes the first part of the second portion of the review," the Zero Hour said formally. "You have performed admirably and may take the second test. Are you ready?"

No. I want to go home and go to bed and pretend like none of this ever happened. I just want to wake up, be told that I passed the test and I can start my Apprentice training.

"I am ready."

His words sounded like they belonged to his twelve year old self when he'd hit puberty and his voice began changing.

The Zero Hour was still standing and spoke again.

"The second part of the test is a test of reflexes. As you do not yet possess the skills to perform Outside Bands, this test will be brief." *And the crumbs of mercy fall from God's table.* "For this test, you must use Fast and Slow Bands in order to defend yourself. Do you have any questions before we begin?"

"Defend myself from what?" Tommen wondered warily.

The cryptic and villainous thing to say would have been something like, "Well, you're about to find out," or some variation. As it was, the Zero Hour said only, "A variety of projectiles and assailants."

Because that made him feel any better. Projectiles and assailants could be anything from little plastic balls to axes to bullets to Tyler Freeman to...no, he couldn't really think of anything worse than Tyler Freeman. Well, a case could be made for Rifun or Cassius, but there was a deep-rooted psychological fear of Tyler that just made the senior bully that little bit worse and—

He hit the ground just as something huge and gray came at him from the side, having a momentary revelation that he was supposed to be Banding in order to prove himself. He also found himself a little miffed that the Zero Hour hadn't announced the beginning of the test. At the same time, reflexes were reflexes; they couldn't just be announced and anticipated and forced.

Slowly he stood, throwing up a Band just in time as the huge thing came at him again from the other side. Once he was safely inside the Band, he looked.

He was surprised to find the Bat was his assailant. At the same time, who else would they use?

Up close, the Bat was even bigger and scarier than he was in the dungeon track. In the dungeon, it was dark, and he was dark. He was just a bat, and he used his wings as his secretary shroud. Out there, he was not out of place; he was in his domain so he was comfortable and relaxed.

In the Seat, however, he was something entirely different. The ugliness factor reminded Tommen of the xur on Sifura's home world, even if there was no resemblance. The Bat was, truly, a bat-like creature. Humanoid, he was about seven and a half feet tall and walked on two legs that ended in large, three-toed, taloned feet. Tommen could easily envision him sleeping upside down from the roof of a cave. He had proportionally longer arms than a normal human with four fingers on each hand, each one more talon than finger. His face was more human than bat, though he had true-to-form vampire fangs snarling at him. His ears, however, were bat-like, long, slender things that reached up from a normal human ear position, probably a good six inches above his head. Up close, Tommen could also see he was covered in a velvety layer of peach fuzz.

But it was his wings that gave him the real fear factor. Normally used as his cloak, they were easy to overlook, but unfurled, they commanded attention. Each leathery pinion was probably six feet tall, not including the claw at the joint which added another four to six inches. Had they been completely extended, they each might have been ten feet wide or more, not including another claw at the end, again adding four to six inches.

Remembering himself, Tommen got to the side of the Bat, his attention taken by the long tail streaming out behind him. It was easily three feet long and ended in some kind of tuft that looked more like a barnacle than fur.

Tommen released the Band, fully expecting the Bat to go sailing past where he'd been only a moment before. He was quite unprepared, however, for the Bat to turn and make another go at him, as if he hadn't Banded at all, as if the Bat had been completely prepared for him.

Again, Tommen Banded, effectively stopping the Bat in his tracks. Was he actually supposed to fight the Bat, like, lay hands on him? Or was this strictly defense? Would the Bat actually hurt him? Well, if Tommen didn't Band properly and get out of the way, sheer size and physics said he could do some damage. But was he trying to hurt him, or was he just using his menace to motivate Tommen to fight?

The uncertainty cost Tommen a blow as he released the Band and the Bat got in a left hook ten times more powerful and stunning than anything Tyler had ever done to him. He stumbled several steps and went to the ground, rolling away as the Bat came after him again, Banding and slipping behind him.

The Bat stood slowly and turned on him. He walked forward, and Tommen stepped back. Then the Bat tried a different tactic, twisting his body and moving his shoulders, using his wings to swipe at Tommen, the claws coming closer to his throat than he felt comfortable with. Was this how Cassius planned to get rid of him? An assassination in the middle of a review? Had such a thing happened before? Would his dad even be suspicious? Well, he would probably be suspicious, but would anything actually be done about it?

Tommen managed to use a few successful Slow Bands to ward off the Bat's wings, switching to a Fast Band once he found himself getting closer to a wall than he wanted to be, again slipping behind the Bat.

How long did he have to fight? Was he supposed to use a set number of Fast and Slow Bands? Was there a time limit? Who decided when he'd shown himself worthy or not? What were the rules, and why had no one told them to him?

The Bat did a sweeping turn, but Tommen had made it almost

to the other side of the Seat. Not that it mattered since the Bat had only to spread his massive wings, rise into the air, and then come at him like a javelin.

In that moment of heart-pounding fear, Tommen's Predict kicked in (because apparently he just hadn't been fearful enough earlier in the fight). And he saw exactly where the Bat was heading. He kept moving backwards, watching the Bat come screaming towards him, a hunter fixed on its prey. Tommen could see his little beady golden eyes and sharp fangs. And when he could make out the peach fuzz on his bald head, Tommen slipped into a Fast Band and stepped out of the way.

In the cartoons, the mouse would stop time and step aside for the cat to go careening into a wall or a fire or a pit of dogs or any other amusing trap. That was the thought that Tommen had in mind when he concocted his little scheme, to get the Bat so fixed on him that he could literally get the ugly bastard to crash into a wall.

The Bat did not do that. Instead, even though there was little more than a foot between the Bat and the wall he was clearly aiming for, as soon as Tommen released the Band, the Bat turned so sharply it probably would have put any dancer to shame. It basically defied the laws of physics for an object of that mass and velocity to be able to bank and turn like that. He didn't even touch the wall, to push off or anything, just simply made a turn.

As Tommen dropped his guard for a split-second, just trying to take it all in, he didn't quite process that the Bat had not only turned, but turned in his direction. The Bat crashed into him like a bowling ball into pins, sending Tommen sprawling to the ground most ungracefully. He lay there on his stomach, coughing and groaning as he picked himself up, fully expecting the Bat to take advantage of him and come in for another attack, but none came. Instead, as Tommen pulled himself into a sitting position, the Bat landed probably fifteen feet away and folded his wings around him again in his customary cloak. He did not look at Tommen at all, instead choosing to look only at the Hands, or their direction anyway.

"Stand, Tommen Forbes," the Zero Hour commanded.

Tommen did so slowly, knowing he was going to feel every ache and pain in the morning. His dad and the twins were right about the review being the equivalent of a serious ass-kicking, and he wasn't going to want to leave his bed for a few days. Fuck. He could already feel his eye and cheek swelling where the bastard had gotten in that lucky left hook.

"Thank you, Bat, you are dismissed," the Zero Hour said, looking at the Bat who dipped his head once, turned like any ordinary person and stalked off toward the gate. Wait, so if he was the one who opened the gate, how did it stay open for him while he was in here fighting?

There was little time to ponder as the Zero Hour continued to speak. "The purpose of the test was to assess your ability to act on instinct, to Band as reflexively as throwing up an arm to protect yourself, and to be able to think on your feet and incorporate Time and Banding in such a way as you demonstrated there at the end."

"I apologize, Lord Zero Hour," Tommen said. "I might have done so sooner but I was unsure of the rules, if I was allowed or...supposed to try to actually fight him or touch him in any way."

"Your apology is noted, however, if such was a concern, you should have asked beforehand."

He might have replied that they had not told him he was to be fighting the Bat, but when he thought about it, they did say there would be assailants, and there weren't too many different ways to interpret that one. So this time it was his own damn fault. Oh well. As promised, it had been a brief fight in all reality, lasting hardly more than five minutes. At the same time, it might as well have been an eternity. He was already tired from the oral exam, exhausted from the first part of the skill test, and now he'd been beaten half to death in a fight against a giant bat.

At this point, he just wanted to go home and go to bed. He didn't mind the oral exam, but he'd had enough of the fighting. If he'd had to do this much longer, he probably would have said fuck Time, too. It was fun for party tricks, but at this point, it had caused him nothing but grief. Maybe that was how Runners were made; they liked the party tricks but screw the rest of it.

Only one more part of the review, he told himself. *Psych evals might not be fun, but they are generally pretty calm endeavors.*

"Thus concludes the second part of the Apprentice Timekeeper review for Tommen Forbes," the Zero Hour decided. All the Hands stood. "The third part of the review, the psychological exam, will commence shortly. You will be returned to your waiting room where food and drink will be provided to you."

No words had ever sounded sweeter than "food" and "drink," especially when they were being provided free of charge. Off to one side, he saw the gate opening. With the second part of the review officially closed, he turned and made a beeline for it. Well, only if the bee was drunk. His legs alternated between jello and lead as he stumbled through the tunnel and into the dungeon track where the Bat was waiting for him and closed the gate with the same slow, methodical motions as always.

"So how does the gate stay open while you're in there?" Tommen inquired.

"It is held," the Bat replied.

"I didn't hurt you at all, did I?"

"You never touched me."

Tommen knew he hadn't touched him. Really, he was fishing for some kind of friendliness, some kind of bro shit like, "Hey, did you see that when I totally decked you?" Okay, so people didn't normally say that after an ass-kicking, but he wanted something. He would even take an apology, something along the lines of, "Sorry I totally bashed your face in" or "I didn't hurt you too bad when I drove you into the ground, did I?"

But he got nothing. And, really, he hadn't expected anything, if he wanted to be honest. The Bat was the Bat. He'd seen it all, well, heard it all, done it all. Who knew how many times a day he had to do this? For him, it was just part of the job. At least it probably provided a nice break in his day from just opening and closing the gate and escorting people here and there for one reason or another.

They reached the waiting room and the Bat opened the door. Tommen stepped in and stopped.

"Where's my dad?" he asked, turning around.

"I know not of whom you speak," the Bat said.

"My mentor, the man who was with me? He's my dad, too, and I want to know where he is."

"Your mentor was removed earlier in order to receive medical attention."

"Is he okay? Can I see him?"

"You are not to leave until your review is complete."

"But is he okay? Like, did he collapse or what happened?"

"I am unfamiliar with the physiology of your race; I do not know what happened nor his ailments. But you are to remain here until your review is complete. Afterwards, you may receive directions to the medical facility."

Tommen paced angrily a couple times. "If anything happens to him while I'm in here, will I at least know? Will someone come and tell me?"

"You are to remain here until the completion of your review."

With that, the Bat closed the door.

Tommen reached the door in two strides, then stopped. First, he'd just had his ass handed to him by that thing, and that was probably with the Bat showing some pretty severe restraint. Second, his dad would never forgive him if he somehow forfeited his exam because of some hot-headed stupidity.

He took a breath and went to sit down, telling himself that his dad would be fine. If it was anything physical, the Wheel did have doctors who could repair the damage or whatever was wrong. If it was the Borelian poison making a comeback, then the twins could always return to Earth, grab a little bit of the antidote, and deliver it to him. It worked once, it would work again, problem solved. There was no need to get all worked up about it. And maybe it hadn't been something all that bad; maybe it had been some observation of an overly-cautious secretary who had him removed for safety reasons.

He scratched that last one; none of the secretaries around here were overly-cautious about anything, it seemed like. Most of them just seemed bored. But there was no reason to assume the worst yet. His dad had been in a lot of pain lately, and maybe his injured leg just finally gave out. Maybe he was out to get pain meds and a support brace and he would be back soon enough.

Tommen mulled it over, trying to weigh the likelihood of each scenario and coming up with only uncertainties. Finally he sighed, gave up, closed his eyes, and took a breath. He needed to remain calm. He was heading into the final part of his review, and he didn't need to fuck it up now. He didn't just go through an interrogation and a pit fight for nothing; he would show his dad that he could do things without him holding his hand all the time. So Tommen took a calming breath, sat down, and waited.

Chapter Six
A Test of Will

Theoretically, there wasn't supposed to be a whole lot of time between parts of the review. If the first time was any indication, Tommen might have come to expect that the second time wouldn't be much different. He didn't like not being able to Band or feel Time while in the Wheel, but there was something to be said for not having to perceive every second as it ticked by. At the same time, what he wouldn't give for the ability to Slow Band, even a little bit, to pass the time just a tiny bit faster.

There was, too, also theoretically, supposed to be some sort of food coming his way. No one had thought to take his order, so he guessed that if and when it did come, it would either be the same burger, fries, and shake he'd had the last two times, or else some kind of fruit or cold cut platter. Not that it mattered since no one had come by anyway for any reason.

He tried to pass the time productively, working through his schoolwork orally, dreading the amount of catch-up work he had to do since he'd been missing for two weeks. English he didn't care much about, Art wasn't exactly difficult, and Web Programming could be done anywhere he had Internet access. But Economics was a little more in-depth than he could brush off, especially the investment projects they were working on, and AP Physics was his thing; it was challenging and engaging and a hell of a lot of work to miss for two weeks.

When that failed to amuse him, he went over the various recipes used in the bakery, the cookies, the cakes, the brownies, the bread, anything and everything he could recall, even if he had to make up a few forgotten things. Only once he realized that not working for almost a month basically meant zero paycheck did he stop thinking about that and try to think about other things, like getting a car and an apartment, which eventually turned into a mental debate over whether or not he wanted to go that route or a slightly...different route.

Being a Scout had always held an appeal, once he'd understood what it was. Scouts were the real Trekkies, going where no one had gone before, seeking out new life and new civilizations. Sure, the end goal was trying to bring them into Time, but Scouts were the pioneers, the ones who braved the open oceans to find the New World, who braved the West to bring civilization to all peoples, who risked life and limb just to see what was out there. That sounded like a pretty good package deal to him.

At the same time, it also meant that he would be on his own with no backup, no one to save his ass from ferocious beasts or poisonous plants or angry headhunters. If something went wrong, just poof! Off the radar. Oh well, there goes another one.

So maybe he ought to do some Earth-side traveling first, to get a feel for the concept of traveling alone in a strange land before embarking on a voyage on a much larger, intergalactic scale. Maybe he ought to be an exchange student, in high school or college; he could do it. He spoke Irish, so he could get along fine in an Irish college (there were Irish colleges that spoke Irish...right?). Maybe there was a Welsh college he could go to and he could explore the land of his ancestors. Or he could go somewhere completely different like China or India or South Africa, just plop down in the middle of someplace that was totally foreign to him.

He sighed and rubbed his face. His dad would have a fit if he ever told him any of that. Walter had always made it clear that he disapproved of Tommen wanting to become a Scout, and his general attitude suggested that being a foreign exchange student wasn't going to go over well either. Tommen had always assumed it just came from being a single parent with only one child. Now that he understood a little more of the story, he could understand where his dad was coming from. But honestly, he wasn't going to be a little kid forever. What about if and when he made Journeyman, when he was required to go out and do some training with other Timekeepers in the District? Was his dad going to forbid him then? Well, not likely since District Four was pretty much entirely in the United States.

Sighing, Tommen stood and did a few laps of the room. Someone out there had a screwy sense of time when it came to "it shouldn't be long between the parts of the test." He'd thought the first wait was bad; this was almost intolerable. Had they forgotten him? Was this part of the test, to see how he reacted to being kept waiting? Where was his food? Was his dad okay?

As he sat down, he shivered. Someone had also apparently turned down the thermostat. Maybe it was a cost-saving thing, turning down the heating in unused rooms or before they cleared out for the night. After all, who knew how much it cost to keep the Wheel running day-in and day-out? Just the wage expenses had to be terrible. The secretary salaries alone were probably through the roof, and Tommen had been told on more than one occasion that they weren't the lowly housekeepers and janitors that he might assume them to be; being a secretary, while difficult and demanding, was a position of honor and power. They probably made well above the minimum wage, if the Wheel had a minimum wage.

Tommen let out a breath. *Just be patient. Either they're waiting for you to break or they're going on some kind of set time limit. They don't like your review any more than you do and they want to get it over with just as fast as you do. Maybe they take petition cases between parts of your review and they went long in deliberation. Deliberation in your case went for three hours, so you might have been keeping some other poor sap waiting and wondering, too.*

That line of thought only lasted about five minutes, but he couldn't even be sure of that. Without his sense of Time, his guess at the passage of time was as good as anyone else's he figured. He could count the seconds and might have made a hazardous guess as to five or ten minutes, but it was all up in the air. As far as he was concerned, he could have been waiting one hour or three hours.

Then another thought entered his mind; what if, somehow, this was how his clock got broken? Maybe it wasn't always a quick touch from a Borelian; maybe they could somehow harness the gaseous side effects and channel it into the waiting room. What if he'd failed his review and this was how they got him to submit to his punishment? They would never be able to take him kicking and screaming, but tell him to be patient and wait for the next part of his review, well, that he would do.

Some part of him said he was being paranoid. The other part said it was only paranoia until it was true.

His relief came when the door finally opened, but it lasted only a moment until he realized that it wasn't the Bat coming to retrieve him. Rather, it was Rifun. He carried a tray of food—the same cheeseburger, fries, and shake as before—and set it down on the floor. Then he went to a spot on the bench a short distance away from Tommen and sat, leaning forward, hands clasped together as well as they could be, looking around the room.

"Nice place you got here," he observed conversationally, as if they were actually sitting in a nice little house or apartment. He looked at Tommen and pointed to the tray of food. "You going to eat that?"

"What?" The word came out before Tommen could think up some witty reply. Fuck, he sounded like an idiot.

"The food," Rifun repeated. "If you're not going to eat it, I will, at least while it's hot; I'm starving."

"Are you really here?"

"Pick up that food and find out. If I'm not real, that's not real."

Tommen was pretty sure that somewhere in the universe, there was technology that could make the food real while the man not. In some fantasy world, shape-shifters came to mind. In reality, drugs or some other trick of the eye could be used. Maybe his clock hadn't been broken, but that didn't mean they hadn't pumped drugs into the room. Just where had his dad gone?

Either way, he picked up the food and took it in hand. Looked and smelled just like the real thing. Tasted like the real thing, too. But for as hungry as he had been, he seemed to have lost his appetite.

"You going to finish that?" Rifun asked after a minute or two.

Tommen sighed but pushed the tray down to him. Rifun took the food and started in on it greedily.

"I'd ask how you got in here, but I think I can guess," Tommen said.

"Oh? Do tell." Rifun sucked down the strawberry shake which Tommen wished he'd kept. Oh well, he could get another one later.

"Sure. Cassius let you in."

"Why do you say that?"

"He's the False Zero Hour. He can wield all the power of the Zero Hour with none of the repercussions."

"Well, there is that." Rifun shrugged as he conceded the point. "But Cassius doesn't much care for the boring politics."

"No, but there have to be fifty-one Hands, and if he had Sifura dispatched, then he could masquerade as an ordinary Hand in order to make up the difference. Plus, if it came down to it, he would have to be the one to make sure I passed my review."

"And why is that?"

"Because if I don't, you lose your bargaining chip with my dad and the twins, you lose your control over me, and you lose your latest and greatest Akari-protege, which I suspect is your biggest loss here."

Rifun nodded thoughtfully. "You make a good point there."

"So what are you doing here?"

"What do you mean?"

"Well, the first time we met, you tried to kill me and then have me killed. The second time, you kidnapped me and tried to kill me yourself. The third time, you threatened me and we struck a bargain under duress."

"You will notice a trend here, Tommen, that each time we meet, it is a friendlier and friendlier encounter. Therefore, I am merely extending that trend."

"I have a hard time believing you're just here for a social call."

"So what are you expecting from me this time?"

"Well, given the circumstances, I would expect you to say that you've somehow harmed my dad again which is why he was taken out for medical treatment, and if I want to see him alive after my review, I have to do something for you."

"Not a bad theory. Incorrect, but I commend your sleuthing skills."

"So it comes back to my original question: why are you here?"

"To check up on you, to see how your review is going. Yes, I may have threatened you a little, but I still made you my pupil, and I try to be concerned for the well-being of those whom I mentor."

"And you expect me to just, what, forgive you for threatening me, taking my hearing and almost murdering my father?"

"As I recall, you also took two of my fingers."

"Others, not me. And even if we're trading fingers for hearing, you still tried to kill my dad."

Rifun chuckled. "Your dad."

"My uncle," Tommen said severely. "Yeah, he told me. But he's my dad as far as I'm concerned."

"And you are concerned. Concerned enough to enter into an agreement with me."

"Under duress. Doesn't count."

"Maybe in an American court of law, but that doesn't bode well for you here, which is where it matters. I mean, it might have mattered at one point, but you said it yourself; Cassius controls everything. Here, in Time, he is Big Brother."

"I think the word you're looking for is Hitler. Or Stalin."

"You know it's funny how in the presidential elections, there are always those who proclaim, 'He's not my president.' Tell me, Tommen, do you think that makes the president any less powerful? Is a man who says that somehow immune from the laws governing the rest of the citizens? You listen to me, Tommen. As long as Cassius is in power, you're safe from prosecution."

"As long as I do what you say."

"With Cassius in power, you can continue to train under your dad and be the shining example of a Timekeeper he always wanted you to be. Similarly, you can also train under me without fear of prosecution. If, however, Cassius were somehow removed from power or if you dared to cross me, Daddy can't protect you from everything, and he can only die once to save you."

Tommen studied him, trying to find any giveaway, but coming up empty-handed. "What have you done to him?"

Rifun grinned. "Why, not a thing."

"Fine. What do you want from me?"

"Like I said, I have made you my pupil and so I try to be concerned for the welfare of said pupils. This was nothing more than checking in on you during a difficult review to see how you're faring. And to politely remind you of where you stand, in the event that you started getting any cute ideas about crossing me. I'm glad you and your dad are reunited and doing well, but don't start thinking that it somehow makes you invincible and that you can concoct a scheme behind my back. Remember, I am always watching."

"You're not a god. You can't be in all places, and you certainly can't know all things."

Rifun frowned, the same frown he'd gotten when Tommen pursued him into his getaway boat. It was a frown that spoke of irritation, as if he'd put up with a child's antics for long enough and now he was going to end them swiftly and severely. A rock formed in Tommen's stomach, and he could honestly say he was afraid of what the man would do to him. *Way to go, Tommen, you opened your big mouth again.*

"That sounds like rebellion," Rifun said in a cold tone. "Really, I'm not surprised. You haven't begun your training yet so you don't fully understand what it is to be more than an ordinary Timekeeper. But I don't like rebellion, and if I am to be a good teacher, I have to instill some good discipline into my pupils. I had hoped that my little demonstration last time might have been enough to keep you in line until your training begins, but alas, you are a tough one. Humans are such a forgetful species. So allow me to remind you."

Tommen steeled himself, tried to mentally prepare for the water that would inexplicably fill his lungs, driving him to the floor in writhing, drowning agony. But as he prepared himself for that, he left himself vulnerable to Rifun's real attack.

He couldn't explain quite how he knew; maybe it was a change inside him, but his hearing was suddenly gone. It wasn't as if the hearing aids had failed, but as if his hearing itself was gone, completely, in both ears. He didn't even have internal hearing so he could hear through his skull when he himself made sounds. Everything was completely gone.

"What did you do to me?" he demanded, but he knew he would sound weak. He couldn't hear himself, even through his skull. The stunning revelation and ensuing fear seemed to cause him to forget how to talk, and he knew he sounded like an idiot, like a person whose mouth is not only numb, like after having some dental work done, but drunk on top of that, and having a stroke. With a lisp, because he couldn't think of any other terrible and descriptive things to add.

Rifun answered; Tommen could see his lips moving. But no sound reached him. He strained to read lips, but Rifun was probably speaking French or Malagasy or some other language he'd gained in his wanderings, leaving Tommen high and dry.

Was Rifun going to reverse it before Tommen left for the next part of his review? Was it going to wear off in time? Or was part of his "punishment" that he enter the third part of his review completely helpless, an idiot before the Hands so that the only way he could pass was by Cassius' interference? Or maybe it was permanent, a lasting punishment so Tommen could never "forget" who had the greater power.

Fear coursed through Tommen as he desperately tried to recall if there were any Time Agents anywhere in the world who were deaf or disabled. As far as he knew, most or all of them were fully functional human beings. Statistically, one of them had to be deaf. Other races might have deaf Time Agents or just be biologically "deaf" and have no concept of sound. Surely the Hands would have some kind of accommodation for it. Wouldn't they?

Tommen's hands shot to his ears as they popped painfully, as if another gunshot had gone off just beside them. As he cowered, Rifun moved to side down beside him and spoke.

"The Lord gives, and the Lord takes away. Imagine what happens when a less than perfect human being is given that sort of power. It's classical conditioning, Tommen. Eventually, you will learn what gets you rewarded, like being able to cure your color-blindness, and what gets you punished, like losing your hearing or mysteriously drowning. Now then, is there anything you'd like to say to me? Something that starts with 'I'm' and ends with 'sorry'?"

Tommen's ears were still ringing and ached like he had some kind of infection. Still, he looked at Rifun and said, "Go to hell."

Rifun chuckled and stood, entirely unconcerned. "One day soon, Tommen, we will shape that strength and insolence of yours into the power to wield the Akari."

Your hate gives you focus, makes you stronger, was all Tommen heard, and he laughed stupidly. Humor under stress, the best medicine. Rifun apparently took it as some sort of concession for he shifted his stance into a relaxed pose.

"To wield Time, Time must be given to him. To wield the Akari, the Akari must be within him. What am I?"

Thankfully he did not appear to be interested in an answer as he turned and made for the door, opening it and slipping out without another word, leaving Tommen alone in the room.

"Tommen Forbes."

Tommen jumped and looked up to see the Bat standing in the doorway.

"You saw him, right?" Tommen demanded.

"Your father is still receiving medical care—"

"No, not him. Rifun. Rifun Ndolo. He left like two seconds ago."

Even as he said it, Tommen realized it was a stupid thing to say. The Bat was blind and anything he might have echolocated might not have registered as Rifun, but some secretary or something.

"The track has been empty as I have been approaching," the Bat informed him. "It is time for the final part of your review."

Had he imagined the whole thing? Was it a hallucination, a way for the Hands to get information out of him regarding Rifun, maybe a way to figure out where his loyalties lay?

Groaning, he stood and followed the Bat out into the track, feeling as though he'd just taken another ass-kicking. His head was pounding, and his ears ached deep into his skull. The quiet of the dungeon track helped to quell things for the time being, but the acoustics inside the Seat were going to kill him, he just knew it.

He said nothing as they reached the gate and the Bat began turning the wheel to open it, the light shining at the end of the tunnel. Had Tommen really once walked in there with his head held high, thinking he was going to ace this like any other test because he thought he had experience or some shit? Experience seemed to have very little to do with this. It was like using his trek through the desert and the jungle and the mountain climbing as some sort of super physical workout training, and then having to go and take a test on horse jumping.

Still, it was the final part of his review and he would see it through. Psych evals weren't fun, but he supposed they were necessary, and at the least, they were usually pretty boring.

As he neared the end of the tunnel, the light grew dimmer until he found himself stepping into an almost pitch-black room. He could barely see his hand in front of his face, never mind where he was supposed to go. The best he knew, the symbol was straight ahead, so he kept walking, dragging his feet just a little so he would be able to find the symbol.

He paused as his shadow suddenly leapt out in front of him. It wasn't huge, as if someone had turned on a spotlight behind him, but he had a shadow and he could see himself. What he couldn't see, however, was the stadium beyond. It was as if the entire Seat had vanished into murky blackness.

"Tommen."

Tommen whirled at the sound of his dad's voice. About fifty feet away from him, in a pool of light, Walter stood, leaning heavily on his cane and not looking well at all. In the time it took Tommen to register that, his dad went to his knees, grunting in pain.

"Dad!"

Tommen started off at a desperate sprint, his mind flickering with images of fleeing across the Red Desert, trying to make it to the jungle before the xur reached them.

"Ah-ah-ah! Stop right there."

Tommen slowed to a walk, but he did not stop, though he kept his head on a swivel, looking around for Rifun who had spoken. Only when Rifun stepped into the light did Tommen actually come to a halt. Rifun was holding the same wooden grip revolver he'd used to deafen Tommen and shoot his dad the first time.

"I thought I was being led to my review," Tommen said weakly. *You know, you really need to work on your epic one-liners and openings because so far, well, you aren't winning any Oscars, let's put it that way.*

"And that's where the fun comes in," Rifun said. "Because now you get to decide whether this is really happening. See, on the one hand, if this is real, and part of your review, the Hands are going to expect you to try and engage me, defend your Captain, yes, but stop a dangerous Runner. The catch is, then your dad dies. If you run, he dies. And if you plead for your dad's life and do as I say, well, that doesn't look very good to the Hands, does it?"

"And if it's not real or not part of my review?"

"Then what do you have to lose?"

Only my sanity because then I still have to watch you murder my dad.

Tommen sighed. "You know what? It doesn't matter if it's real or not."

"Oh? And how is that?"

"Have you ever heard of something called death ground?"

Rifun grinned. "I've heard many iterations of that term. What does it mean to you?"

Tommen walked toward him, slowly, trying to seem like a badass, but getting nowhere on that front he was sure. "It's a police term. When a man has nothing left to lose and his life no longer matters to him. He might be drunk, he might be high, he might be angry, he might be depressed, but whatever the case, not only does his own life not matter, but no one else's does either. And if he's going down, he's going to take as many people down with him as he can."

"Ah, so you're trying to be all noble and chivalrous and say that if I shoot your dad, you'll be forced onto death ground, and you'll have no choice but to try and take me down. Is that all?"

Rifun spoke as though he were speaking to a child, trying to cut into Tommen's ego. But Tommen wasn't having it.

"That's right," he confirmed.

"So cute. I'm sure your father is so proud of you. He's taught you so well."

"You know what else he's taught me a great deal about?"

"What's that?"

"Distraction."

Before he was even finished with the first syllable, Tommen's hand flashed out and struck Rifun's wrist, moving the revolver harmlessly away from Walter's head, even as Rifun pulled the trigger.

Now they were on even ground. With the Time-shield in place, Rifun could no more use his high and mighty Warden abilities as Tommen could use his probationary abilities, meager though they were. And Tommen was a fighter who didn't give up easily. There was no one to stop him this time, and Layman wasn't here to lecture him about fighting either. There was just him and Rifun.

Well, the words sounded more noble in his head, even if they proved largely untrue. After knocking the gun away from his dad's head, Tommen managed to get in a lucky uppercut to Rifun's jaw before the man with the long hair got his act together and came back with a full facial blow from the hand with the gun. Tommen stumbled a step but recovered quickly enough that he managed to get inside Rifun's range of motion. His initial intention had been to body-blow him and drive him to the ground, but Rifun proved to be more solid than first appearances gave him credit for. Tommen did little more than a rough bear hug which was quickly thwarted when Rifun grabbed him by the hair and pulled his head back.

"I will give you credit for determination and dedication," Rifun chuckled darkly. "You know, there's a saying, 'Get your heart over the bar and your body will follow.' Unfortunately, I don't think that person had a grasp of physics. Your heart was all for taking me down, but big beats small every time."

At the angle Rifun was holding his head, Tommen could not easily reply; he was happy just to be able to breathe.

"You remember the warehouse, don't you? Of course, how could you forget? Tell me, do you still have nightmares about it? Do you ever wonder if that warehouse will do to you what Beaumaris Gaol did to your dad? You're young so you might yet recover from it. But just in case, let's go back there, shall we?"

Tommen jerked against Rifun's grip, but Rifun held him fast, reaching up and gently removing the hearing aids from his ears, stuffing them in his pocket. Despite the relative quiet of the space, Tommen could still feel his hearing diminish as the acoustics of the Seat changed, dulled, muffled.

"Now then, we're going to play a little game," Rifun whispered in his ear. He began walking, dragging Tommen along with him, one hand in his hair, another pinioning his arm and shoulder. They headed into the darkness that was the Seat so Tommen had no idea where they were in relation to the nearest wall or the gate or anything. The best relative location he was able to judge was when they turned around and the pool of light where his dad still knelt seemed so small, like an entire football field away. Just how big was the Seat? Tommen tried to recall, but he came up blank.

"Now then, you see your dad way down there?" Rifun said, finally releasing his grip on Tommen who nodded. "Run toward him." Tommen looked at him. "Go on. Off you go. We can't play if you don't run." When he didn't move, Rifun sighed. "I thought so. I guess we'll need some motivation, now won't we?"

The last words were said loudly. At the other end of the Seat, or where Walter knelt, now Cassius himself stepped into the pool of light. He didn't waste time on pretty wooden grips or old-fashioned revolvers; he went straight for the Springfield 1911, mil-spec .45. He put it to the back of Walter's head.

Without thinking, Tommen took off running, every muscle screaming at him to slow down before he hurt himself, his mind screaming at him that he was being foolishly manipulated.

Even as he thought it, he heard the gunshot behind him. Well, he knew enough that in real life, the pain came before the noise. If you heard the shot, it wasn't meant for you. He also knew that a moving target was harder to hit, or hit lethally. And, given his past experience, he was willing to bet that Rifun wouldn't shoot his partner in crime. So Tommen broke into a serpentine pattern, keeping Cassius as the center line, noting how Rifun suddenly seemed to stop shooting at him, or less frequently anyway.

But Tommen was no athlete, and he could feel his body start to give out on him as even the adrenaline wore off. Still at least forty yards away, he could see the expression on Cassius' face, a mixture of amusement at watching Tommen run and fight for every step, and irritation that he'd managed to thwart part of the game. *That's right, fuckers, my dad's a cop and he's taught me a few things.*

His sprint slowed to a jog, and his breaths came in ragged gasps. He wasn't going to be a moving target for much longer. And even so, did he really expect Cassius to just give up and go home when he got there? This was about manipulation, being toyed with, two cats batting him around like a lost mouse.

He couldn't stop. He couldn't go forward. He certainly couldn't go back. He was stuck, even as he continued to run toward Cassius who still had his gun at the back of Walter's head.

It's not real, Tommen realized. *My dad might be injured, but he's not helpless, and he's not stupid. He would be fighting back, trying to help me, doing something. He wouldn't just be kneeling there waiting to be executed.*

Taking as big a breath as he could manage, he pushed himself for the final sprint. Hopefully the really, truly, final sprint, closing the gap as quick as he could, no longer worrying about serpentine or any of that. He made a beeline straight for Cassius, straight for that smirking face and twisted grin.

Cassius' expression never changed, even as Tommen came within twenty yards, then ten.

And suddenly he was flying, but not at Cassius. He was soaring backwards through the air. Then came the pain. Then came the thunder. And there went his ability to breathe. He felt something wet begin to soak his clothes just below the breastline on his left side.

Have I been shot? Was I wrong about this all being fake?

He landed hard, slamming his head into the marble, feeling a crack and more wet and sticky blood soak his hair and snake down his neck. He couldn't remember if he blacked out as he tumbled head over ass for several yards before coming to a sticky, crunchy, breathless stop. The best he was able to do was roll onto his side and spit blood. In the darkness of the Seat, it was impossible to tell what was natural darkness and what was the darkness of the Eternal Sleep calling him.

Don't let go, he told himself. *Stay awake. If Walter got medical care, you will, too. Close your eyes and act dead if you have to, but don't fall asleep. Oh, who am I kidding? I've just been shot by the guy who tears people's throats out for fun. There's no coming back from that.*

The light gradually came up in the Seat, but not by much, enough that Tommen could see Cassius standing over him. He couldn't remember seeing him approach. Had Cassius just been that sneaky, or was he going in and out of consciousness? As if that was a tough question.

"Your devotion to your dad is admirable," Cassius told him. "It's too bad your devotion to the Time industry is not. It is the judgment of the Hands and the Zero Hour that you are unfit to become an Apprentice Timekeeper and pursue your Timekeeping education. You will be taken to have your clock broken and then released back to Earth where you will live out the rest of your days apart from Time. Furthermore, it is also the judgment of the Hands that you be punished for inciting violence and unrest against Time and the Hands." He shoved his gun back into his holster and looked elsewhere. "He's all yours."

He stepped back and Tommen struggled to lift his head, feeling nauseous and dizzy, but seeing now that half a dozen black-clad Grandfathers were walking toward him.

"No, no, no." His mind was screaming and his muscles weakly contracted in fear, but all that came out was a pitiful, incomprehensible moan. "No, I'm only a probie. Let me go, I'll never use my Time abilities again, I promise."

"Were you only a probie, we as the Hands might consider it," Cassius told him, even his voice smirking. "But you openly tried to turn the Hands and the Grandfathers against each other, and that we can't let go unpunished."

"I was just trying to save my dad."

"Is one life really worth civil war?"

Tommen managed a glare. "Yes."

Now Cassius paused in his smirking long enough to frown and run his tongue over his teeth. "Noble sentiment. You truly are the Chivalrous Welshman. I'll make sure that gets added as a footnote to your file."

Tommen wanted to say more, but the only thing he was able to do was groan. Worse, it was a groan of pleasure. The Grandfathers knelt around him in a circle. They were still shrouded, but it didn't take a genius to know one of them was a white Borelian. He moaned again as the white Borelian touched him. His moan turned to an involuntary scream as a second Borelian touched him and his pleasure quickly became the most painful erection and ejaculation of his life, enough to make him scream again and black out momentarily. Then another Borelian touched him and he went suddenly blind. As he opened his mouth, his vision came back, but when he closed his eyes, it was as if he held his breath.

Then he was assaulted by a number of different ailments, so many it took him a second to figure out what was doing what, or maybe that was the migraine that just suddenly exploded in his head. First he was hot, then he was cold. His joints hurt, his muscles hurt, he was feeling a whole textbook full of emotions yet he couldn't say why. He was at once very sad that he'd failed his review and failed his dad and, basically, failed at life and doomed to continue failing at life. Then he was extremely happy, finally it was all over, no more Time or Runners or extra training or double-life to hide. As soon as that came, it was gone, replaced by boiling rage. *Fuck you, Rifun. Fuck you, Cassius. Fuck you fuck you fuck you, fuck you for ruining my life, destroying my hearing, shooting my dad, and everything else that I can say "fuck you" for.* That quickly gave way to jealousy. Micah and Micaiah had each other, but he had no one. Yeah, his dad was great, but sometimes he wished he had Teo with him, a big brother that he could share secrets with and get into mischief with. Fuck you, twins.

As that all came to pass in only a second or two, Tommen suddenly became very disoriented. He might have said it was the head wound except it wasn't a spatial disorientation, but a temporal one. With Time, he was sharply aware of the passage of time, each second as it ticked by, feeling Time like a river around him. In places like the Coliseum, that sense was rendered dull, normal like everyone else. Aware of time and yet having little more than a passive awareness of its existence in everyday life. Now, though, it was as if he couldn't count the seconds if he really wanted to. In fact, he found the concept of seconds and time very confusing. It was like he'd been spinning in circles his whole life and now he was finally coming off the track. Sure, he would be disoriented for a while, but eventually he would be free.

Damn, he had to work on his analogies.

Then it hit him.

"This isn't real." He still sounded like a drunk person with a lisp having a stroke after being numbed up for a dental procedure, but as he formed the words, it was just like becoming aware of Borelian side effects. Once he realized they were there, he could overcome them. Basic perception of Time came back to him; he could count off seconds if he wanted to and everything seemed very orderly.

"This isn't real," he said again.

Now it wasn't just the sense of time that came back to him, but the emotional assault abated and his thoughts came back into focus. More than that, the aches and pains in his bones and muscles subsided. He was left feeling terribly weak, but it was like pushing back layers of blankets, or digging his way out of being buried in sand.

"None of this is real."

His head was still achy, but he managed to sit up. The Grandfathers stood and took an uncertain step back. Tommen was about to go to stand but a wave of nausea found him first and he vomited once, twice. He momentarily questioned whether this was real or not; he wouldn't be throwing up if it wasn't real, would he? And what about the blood? But he had the element of surprise against the Grandfathers and Cassius right now. What he planned to do with that element, he wasn't entirely sure.

He got to his hands and knees first, trying to beat down another wave of nausea when he saw Cassius' shadow spill over him. Taking a breath, Tommen got one knee up in a kneeling position, then he got his other foot under him and he stood shakily. He wobbled and waved but he resisted the urge to reach out and use Cassius as a balancing point.

"This isn't real," Tommen told him, breathless as if he'd just run ten miles with a pack of rabid dogs behind him.

"Not real?" Cassius said. "You think this isn't real?"

"Of course it's not. For one, you're not in your shroud, and the Hands and the Wheel are too divided to just let you walk around freely. Second, there's a procedure for the reviews. Regardless of whether I pass or fail, the Hands—all the Hands—have to honor that procedure. What the Grandfathers do to me is their business, but the Hands have rules and procedures and ungodly long and complicated formalities to observe. Included in that is—"

Had Tommen been in better shape overall, he might have screamed as Cassius jammed two fingers into the bullet hole in his left side. As it was, his breath caught and he let it out awkwardly in something that resembled a tight moan as if he'd been kicked in the balls but didn't want to cry out shrilly.

"You think that's not real?" Cassius hissed. He grabbed the back of Tommen's head where he'd cracked it open, pulling on the hair around the wound. Now Tommen whimpered. "Or that? Is that real enough for you?"

Tommen took a few breaths, noting how it no longer hurt him, or not as much as it had initially. "I don't know about those. But I know you're not real. You're Calis Cutthroat. You walked up to two women and murdered them without a second thought, then masturbated to celebrate. You told me that yourself. You don't like to humor Rifun in his stupid games, which is why you didn't actually show up to the warehouse, because you thought it was a waste of time. And you were afraid. But here you are, not only playing along with Rifun in his stupid games, but playing hostage-taker. No, when Cassius wants to make a point, he makes a point. And when Cassius wants someone dead, no matter how much he likes the Grandfathers—which I'm thinking isn't much—he never leaves the kill for someone else."

Cassius released Tommen's hair and took a step back. "Look at you, the little criminal profiler. Going to work for the FBI, are you?"

"No. You're just too stupid to be original."

"Big mouth for a little brat. You're right. Rifun likes his games too much, and he likes showing off his Akari abilities a little too much too. And like you said, when Cassius makes a point, Cassius makes a point." He pointed his gun at Tommen. "Now then, how much are you really willing to risk that this is all fake, that you've somehow been drugged, duped or blindsided?"

"Cassius has never used a gun, not really," Tommen went on. "He always uses his knives, because he likes to see his victims up close, watch their expressions so he can see the exact moment when they realize they're going to die and he's the one who killed them."

Cassius fired then. Tommen did not go flying this time. Instead, he merely stood there, staring at Cassius and the smoking gun. For a full three seconds, they both just stood there, staring at each other. Then Tommen felt something hot, wet and sticky soak his clothes and begin to seep down his chest in sticky trickles. He looked down at the red flower blossoming on his chest.

"What is it you say about fighting?" Cassius wondered. "'The best way to win is to be unpredictable, establish a pattern, so that when you need to win, you become unpredictable.'"

Tommen felt himself falling, watching the lights get brighter in the Seat until it was just like normal. He fully anticipated hitting hard marble again, assuming he didn't die before that point, but he was more than confused when the fell into something much softer.

"Whoa, hold on there, kiddo," his dad said, lopsidedly catching him and weakly lowering him to the ground safely. Then he appeared over him, blue eyes, bushy blond mustache and all. "Tommen? Tommen, can you hear me?"

For a long moment, Tommen didn't answer. His body was in too much of a what-the-fuck state to care about anything external at the moment. He'd been shot. He'd been beaten. He'd done more running than he ever wanted to do again in his life. He'd been terrified out of his wits, he'd been ready to have his clock broken, he'd been ready to fucking die. What the hell? As he took inventory, his body could find no evidence of any gunshot wounds, whether fresh or miraculously healed, and while his head hurt like a nuclear migraine, there was no crack and no blood, not even any missing hair where Rifun and Cassius had pulled on it.

He blinked. "Dad?"

Walter closed his eyes and let his head drop as he sighed. "Tommen, thank God. Are you all right?"

Well, he might not have been shot or anything, but the Bat had still beaten his ass, and his body was still pretty well convinced that he'd just run a couple marathons. Gradually, he got his jellied limbs to respond to motion and he lifted his shirt. Totally clean. "I...was shot." He put a hand to the back of his head. "And I hit my head."

Now that he thought about it, he could hear perfectly fine, too, and he touched the hearing aids, still perfectly intact. He closed his eyes and let out a breath. "The fuck happened?"

"You completed the third part of your review, the psychological exam," Walter replied gently.

"I thought psychological exams were supposed to be ink blots and daddy didn't love me enough and stuff?"

His dad chuckled and shook his head. "Not here. Not in the Wheel."

"So did I pass?"

"Do you think you can stand?"

That was actually the last thing Tommen wanted to do at the moment. Really he just wanted to curl up in a ball and take a nice long nap until his body and mind could sort everything out, reset, and be ready for another day. After a moment, though, he nodded and inched his way off his dad's lap onto the floor so he could start getting his limbs sorted out. Hand here, arm there, leg down there, get a foot under him. Ready and push. His first attempt failed miserably and he almost went down on his face. The second time he got his feet under him, but his back protested and he instinctively reached out for support, but Walter took a step out of his reach.

"Sorry, Tommen, I'm not in much better shape than you are; we don't both need to go down."

He had a point, but Tommen was tired, too. Where was his

cane? Did he at least get help getting out of here?

Finally getting his senses back in order somewhat, he looked around and found that all the Hands were assembled, even the Zero Hour. As they were all shrouded, it was impossible to judge facial expressions, and, while body language was normally minimal, sometimes the absence of something was the most notable thing about it. All of the Hands were completely rigid, unmoving. No normal swaying or body movements, no shuffling to find a more comfortable position, nothing; it was as though they were made of cardboard.

"So what did I actually do? What really happened?" Tommen wondered of no one in particular.

"It was a combination of being drugged and a visual field screen," Walter answered softly. "The drug conjures up a hyperrealistic hallucination while the visual field screen reads the activity and projects it into the Seat which allows the Hands to see without being seen as well as reacts to certain elements of your hallucination."

"Wait, so I was on a trip? Like I was seriously on fucking shrooms or something?"

"Watch your language, Tommen, but yes, essentially it was a trip."

Tommen let out a breath and felt his knees almost give out on him. "Dude, I am seriously never smoking weed ever again. Like ever again."

"Glad to hear it. Now hush."

Whatever had immobilized the Hands—whether fear, shock, or awe—it seemed to have worn off and they were a regular crowd of beings again. After a moment or two, the Zero Hour stood.

"Tommen Forbes, you have completed the third and final part of your review. Do you have any questions about it before the review is closed?"

"Why did I see what I saw? Why those images?" Tommen asked.

"The drug pulls base elements from your primal mind and

constructs them in a way that holds significance only to you and to Time, constructed in such a way that there are only two possible outcomes: either you will realize that it is all a hallucination, or you will die within the hallucination."

"When was the drug administered?"

"It was administered while you waited for the third part of your review to begin, while you were in the waiting room."

So Rifun really hadn't been there in the waiting room with him; that had just been part of the hallucination.

"I understand that I am to be judged based on my actions within the hallucination. Do I have anything to fear from the hallucination itself, any repercussions from the Hands or the Grandfathers?"

"The hallucination is a construction of the mind pulling from many elements. Together, they create a fiction. You are judged based on your actions within that fiction, not the fiction itself."

So basically, unless he'd gone over to the dark side and openly conspired with fake-Rifun and fake-Cassius, they weren't going to punish him for having a hallucination that included them. In theory. That wasn't to say they wouldn't watch him a little more closely given the conversation he'd had with fake-Rifun in the waiting room.

"Do all rank reviews include a similar psychological exam?"

"No. The surprise is effective only once. It is used only to sift out any students who may become Runners before they become too powerful in their abilities."

Made sense, but Tommen still wasn't one hundred percent confident in that for himself. Still, he dipped his head, wobbling just a little at the motion. "Thank you, Lord Zero Hour, I have no further questions."

"Thus concludes the third part of the Apprentice Timekeeper review for Tommen Forbes, and so also concludes the Apprentice Timekeeper review for Tommen Forbes. You will now be taken to a recovery room so you may rest from your ordeal. Food and drink will be provided. When your mentor feels you are ready, we will reconvene for the verdict."

"Thank you, Lord Zero Hour, for presiding over my review," Tommen replied formally, mechanically, all the while beating down a yawn.

As he turned to leave, he felt his knees turn to jelly and he was overcome by a wave of vertigo. He barely had time to register this before the floor was suddenly coming at him and he was out.

Chapter Seven
Recovery

Tommen slept.

It was difficult to make out his dream initially, and he thought it might have been some kind of cross between his warehouse nightmare and a new nightmare that had formed from his ordeal in the Seat of the Hands. To think that had all just been a hallucination, like some kind of bad trip. He'd never denied going off occasionally to smoke some weed, but just like the white Borelian had all but scared his porn addiction out of him, he was fairly certain that he would never be able to even look at another drug without thinking of the terror wrought by that ordeal.

And they had the nerve to call it a psychological exam. That was little better than torture. Of course, their defense would be that it was fake, a fiction conjured up only by his mind, assuming they were even worried enough to feel the need to defend themselves. But still, to put him in that situation, just to prove his loyalty. He really was going to end up like Walter, afraid of the dark and having to sleep with a night light.

Even as he thought it, a speck of light appeared in his dream. It didn't do much to illuminate his surroundings, but he found himself moving towards the light. He didn't have control over his dream like he sometimes did, but he at least knew he was in a dream and he knew what was happening.

When the reached the light, he touched it, and suddenly the world exploded into light and color, and not just gold and blue and shades of gray, but real color, from red to purple and every shade in between. He could have cried. He couldn't see in color anymore, but now that he had seen the colors, he could at least dream in them.

At first, everything was merely a blur of color. Gradually, things started to come into focus. When everything was clear and visible, he found himself a little confused by his surroundings. To describe it as a cozy little fairytale cottage situated in a fairytale field at the edge of a fairytale woods was a bit of an understatement. The cottage was not only the adorable little thing found in most children's books that started with "Once upon a time..." but it came complete with the garden of flowers, all of which had happy little faces on them and could talk. Similarly, the field was bright yellow and pink, also with smiling flowers and tall grass. Even the trees of the fairytale forest had sort of Grandmother Willow-style faces on them.

Tommen let out a breath. *I must still be tripping or something.*

He had no idea what to make of his surroundings. They weren't even vaguely familiar, like some caricature of his old home; everything was completely foreign.

As if on cue, a fawn walked out of the forest, entirely unafraid of him. Birds twittered overhead. A white rabbit hopped out from behind a bush.

"Well, when in Wonderland," Tommen said under his breath, approaching the white rabbit.

The rabbit at least was not wearing a dinner jacket or top hat, nor holding a pocketwatch and crying about how he was late for a very important date. In fact, it hardly acknowledged him until he was right next to it, and even then it looked at him, gave him a sniff, and moved off slowly.

Tommen wasn't sure whether he was doing the right thing, assuming there was anything to be done in this trippy dream, but he wasn't going to stand around, that was for sure. Not that he had a whole lot of control over what he did; his mind seemed to be separate from his will here, attached only tenuously.

He followed the rabbit around the garden for a bit before it hopped off into the field where he very nearly lost it, spotting it briefly as it made its way into the forest and finally catching up before it could disappear under a bush. Before it did, it looked behind itself. It spotted Tommen and turned around. Tommen paused in his approach as the rabbit got up on its hind legs, white ears straight up, nose sniffing the air.

Then the rabbit spoke.

"Why are you following me?"

It was a dream about a fairytale cottage in a fairytale field near a fairytale forest; everything had faces and smiles, and Tommen was surprised that the rabbit was talking. Right. Definitely still tripping.

"Um..." Tommen managed lamely.

"It's a fair question," the rabbit told him matter-of-factly. "Why are you following me? You are deliberately seeking me out, and I want to know why."

"Um, I don't know. I...thought you might lead me down a rabbit hole?"

"What for? You're far too big, and there's nothing of interest down there."

"It's kind of a thing, where I'm from. White rabbits lead to good things. Or, interesting things anyway." Because there was every chance Alice had been tripping as hard as he was.

"Oh? Why white rabbits? Why not white dogs or white owls or white mice or white anything else? Or what about brown rabbits or black rabbits? Why white rabbits?"

"I don't know—"

"Do white rabbits somehow hold special powers to make things good or interesting?"

"Uh—"

"What is it about me that you found worthy enough to pursue? Most people where you're from have held a rabbit or have had the opportunity to hold a rabbit. Not everyone has had the privilege of petting a fawn. Why not pet the fawn? And as you can see, everything around here is friendly, so why not go and pet a bear?"

"Because you were the only one around at the time and I guess I just knew that white rabbits led to good things."

"And what good have you found here?"

Well, that was the question, wasn't it? If what the rabbit said was true, why not go and pet a bear? Or the fawn? Or some other thing just to get in some kind of variety?

"What makes you trust the rabbit?" the white rabbit went on. "Is it because I'm adorable and fluffy? Is it because I'm white? Or is it because you think I can do you no harm? Because believe me, I can claw your eyes out just as easily as any bear."

"I don't know, okay?" Tommen cut in hotly. "This is my dream, and I'm pretty sure I'm still just tripping out from whatever I got drugged with. But I sure didn't come here to argue with a stupid white rabbit."

The rabbit laughed then. "Oh, human. How silly you are. And to answer your earlier question, I do have good things down my rabbit hole. I have interesting things, too. But until you know why you're following me, you just won't fit."

"How do I know that I want what you have?"

"Everybody does. And if you looked inside, you can see what I have. But until you know why you want it, you'll never get in."

Tommen rubbed his face. "I'm tripping. I'm absolutely fucking tripping. I dreaming up a place with smiling flowers and talking rabbits."

"Only because you think you are," the rabbit told him haughtily, nodding sharply once. "But it's time to wake up now, Tommen."

Tommen blinked. "Are you throwing me out of my own dream?"

"Of course not," the rabbit said. "Think about it logically. Your body knows it's almost time to wake up, so it is simply using a convenient medium to politely inform you of that fact."

It made sense, and he figured it was better than being rudely awakened by an alarm or some violent physical shaking or something else unpleasant. He sighed. "I am never doing drugs again, at least not knowingly."

"Foreknowledge had little to do with this, I believe," the white rabbit quipped unwantedly.

"Maybe, but I'm not taking any chances from here on out. I'm done with this trip shit."

"Watch your language, Tommen."

The white rabbit spoke, but it was with his dad's voice. The rabbit blinked, then got down on all fours again and disappeared under the bush. Tommen went to the bush with the intent of ripping it up and seeing just what was under it that was supposed to be so darn interesting, but the closer he got, the darker his surroundings became until the forest was all but pitch black. He stared at the bush, barely visible as black against black. With one hand, he cautiously reached out to the bush. Then, just like Sleeping Beauty, when he touched the spiny thorns on its spindly branches, he was out.

Tommen only dreamed of the white rabbit once, but it was the only dream he could recall. He remembered waking up several times in a groggy, semi-conscious state, most often contorted in unusual postures. He couldn't decide whether the positions themselves were painful or if he was sore all over and any position was going to hurt no matter what. By the time he got around to pondering it, consciousness began slipping away from him and he was out again.

After a time, he was able to remember waking up and looking around through tired, blurry eyes for just a moment. A couple times, he felt like he was shaking. No, that wasn't right. It was more violent than just shaking; it was more like a seizure, assuming he could have a full seizure and still be conscious for it—well, almost conscious. He could feel his muscles tightening to the point of tearing themselves apart, then releasing but being unable to relax, all over his body, moving, twisting, seizing, shaking.

Tommen had never really had seizures before. Supposedly he'd had a few when he was in the hospital when he first came through Forbes Cave, but those had been in reaction to various infections he contracted in the hospital, and then he had more seizures in reaction to some of the medications they gave him to combat the infection seizures. But he'd never had any as a result of his smoking or drinking or any other assorted ailments. Probably these came from whatever drug they'd dosed him with in order to make him hallucinate. Probably LSD or some shit. Fuck, but that was a trip. A very, very bad one.

He couldn't say how he knew, but as he wavered between sleep and consciousness, he got the sense that not a lot of time had passed. True, any amount of time could have gone by before he became lucid enough to recognize time at all, but once his mind started coming back to him, he was able to count off five minutes, ten minutes, never more than half an hour.

Not that it made things better necessarily. He would have rathered been fully unconscious getting in some serious z's and wake up refreshed, than be in this awful state of flux where he couldn't rest his body but his mind wasn't together enough to make any use of his consciousness.

Once, he thought he was able to clear his vision enough to make out a small room, white-washed like some kind of futuristic science fiction show, and he was alone on the floor with only a pillow and a sparse blanket for comfort. He remembered feeling appalled; the Wheel was known for being the most advanced in everything in the universe and he was lying alone on the floor? Didn't they have some sort of medical facility where they could monitor his seizures in case they got out of control? Having the best technology was great, but where technology was predictable, people were not. Even when dealing with a homogeneous race like humans, what worked for one person might not work for another. Now multiply that by a couple thousand alien races.

On top of that, where was his dad? He wanted visitors. He wanted to talk to someone. At the very least, he wanted to know what was going on and that everything was going to be okay. He wanted to know he wasn't suffering through all of this for nothing, and he certainly didn't want to be alone. He wanted his dad, but he was okay with the twins, too. Hell, he'd take a nurse if there was one to be found, but he couldn't recall ever seeing a nurse around the place.

His thoughts ended abruptly. Whether he just passed out or had another seizure, he wasn't sure. He only knew that when he came around again, his body hurt like a son of a bitch. He felt as though he had a whole ton of lead just poured over him and then chained down just for good measure. If he really thought about it, he could move his fingers and toes, but even that was exhausting. Oddly enough, while he hurt beyond all words, that level of pain also constituted a type of no-pain, as if his brain had simply given up trying to process and quantify it and just said, "Yup, you're in pain. Deal with it." Like how frostbite really hurts at first, and then it just stops hurting. Sure, that was more because of the damage to the nerves, but it was the same progression of feeling nonetheless.

At one point, Tommen woke up knowing he'd had another seizure. A violent one, if the throbbing was any indication. But at the same time, his mind felt clear. He could think; he could see. His body felt like a lump of pain-flavored jello, but in the way that feels like a completion of something; he was no longer tensed and poised to suddenly launch into another seizure. He was done. It was over with. Whatever trip he'd been on, wherever his mind and body had gone, it was all over now.

He tried to move, was able to wiggle his limbs to make sure they worked, but they weren't going anywhere. The best he managed was first to pick his head up and look around the empty room briefly, then roll over on one side. It was a bad decision as he chose the side where he had been shot, or thought he'd been shot. Had that actually happened? Or was that just more of the drug and the screen reacting and...whatever. Just fuck it. Tommen took a breath, rolled back onto his back, closed his eyes, and was out again.

When he came back around again, the first thing he saw when he opened his eyes was his dad.

"Dad?" he asked, his voice hardly more than a coarse whisper.

"Welcome back," his dad said gently. "How are you feeling?"

"Like shit." He let out a breath. "What happened? Where am I? How did I get here?"

"Well, when we turned to leave the Seat, you collapsed into seizure and had to be carried here. Since then, you've been having seizures and been in and out of consciousness. It's been about seven hours."

"Why did I have seizures?"

"A combination of the drug and the stress that went with it, your hallucination. It's not uncommon; I did the same thing after my Apprentice review. Normally the seizures don't start until after you get to the recovery room, but it's still not uncommon."

"I know I'm not supposed to talk about what happened, but can I ask a question?"

"By all means."

"Was I actually shot? Or was that all the drug? What about the blood and the pain and stuff?"

Walter hesitated and for a second, Tommen was afraid he wouldn't answer. Finally, "I don't know exactly how it works, but the drug itself is what causes the hallucination, whatever you saw. In the Seat, there's some sort of screen—a psychological screen, a neuroelectrical field sort of thing, I don't know—that interacts with your hallucination to essentially augment it. Anything you touched or otherwise encountered in your hallucination, your body would have perceived as if it was really there, everything from smells to textures to, apparently, blood."

"Doesn't a regular drug like LSD do kind of the same thing? Or like shrooms and stuff?"

"Not to the degree that you experienced. A normal Earth-side hallucinogen, you think you're touching something, and you might think you're interacting with something and perceiving it, but ultimately you can just walk right through it. With this, it was the next best thing to real."

"Shit."

"Tommen."

"Hm?"

"I've indulged you for the time being, but watch your language."

Tommen closed his eyes. Yup, that was his dad all right. He sighed. "So my cheeseburger was fake, too?"

"Afraid so."

"How do I know I'm not still hallucinating?"

"Because I told you so. You're out of the Seat, you're out of the review, it's all over with now."

"So what happens now?"

"Well, once you can stand up on your own and walk straight, we'll head back to the waiting room and wait to be called in for the verdict."

"How long will that be?"

"Verdict has already been rendered. Just waiting on you to feel better so we can go back and get a time to go before the Hands." Walter chuckled as Tommen groaned. "One last time. Then we can go and get you a real cheeseburger and go home."

"I'm sick of cheeseburgers. What's the difference between this room and the waiting room? This doesn't look like much of a recovery room."

"Believe me, it's more advanced than even the best Earth-side hospitals. You just don't need a lot of care so you don't get to see the full scope of its capabilities."

"Is this where you were? Or was that just a lie they told me in order to get you out of the room?"

"Probably a lie."

Tommen took another breath. The edge had come off the pain, but he was still exhausted. It took all his effort just to be able to get his hand to his face so he could rub his eyes. His body was tired, but his mind was active and there was no way he was going to be sleeping anytime soon.

"Why can't we talk about the review?" he wondered.

Walter frowned sympathetically. "Something disturbing?"

"Very. I don't like it."

"I know."

"Why do they do that? I mean, it seems like it would be enough to make someone not want to come back."

Walter nodded slowly. "I know. And when we go before the Hands—and I'm confident that they'll rule in your favor—they will actually give you an option to leave Time."

"What, they just trust that I won't use my Banding or anything else?"

His dad chuckled. "No. Tommen, have you never wondered how it was that you weren't able to Band and use your Time abilities for two years before I started your training early?"

Tommen ran his tongue over his teeth, trying to think back to the early years as it related to Time. "No. I guess not." He frowned. "I guess it would have been kind of strange, now that I think about it. I mean, even Eric and Varad said they were accidentally Banding all the time."

"I know, and I had a talk with Micaiah about how he handled it. He just showed Eric how to control it, when really I think he ought to have placed a lock on the Banding."

"I don't get it."

"All it does is suppress someone's ability to use Time. It's not like the Grandfathers where they destroy your innate sense of Time, it just deadens it about to the level where you would normally feel it, the same concept as the dampener in the Coliseum or the Judgment Wing. The suppression is effective to the skill level of the person either being banded or the person banding, if it's a lower rank to a higher rank. What I did to you was basically an absolute suppression; there is nothing you could have done to break it on your own. If I did it to Micaiah let's say, then he could possibly break it if he mustered up enough strength. Similarly, he could do the same thing to me, but it would only be effective unto the abilities befitting a Lieutenant. Anything I know that he doesn't I would still be able to use and possibly break that suppression."

"So then why not have like a Dominion Timekeeper do that to the Runners or those who fail their reviews and stuff? Why destroy someone's life by breaking their clock? It's like giving someone the death penalty for petty theft."

"Because of the Borelians. And that's all I'll say about it." His words were firm and absolute, as if the answer ought to suffice and they weren't going to argue anymore. "Because I said so" kind of answer. But his expression told a different story, one that said that there would be more talk later; they were not truly alone in the room.

"So are there no nurses or doctors here at all?" Tommen wondered, obediently changing the subject.

"There are," his dad replied, "but like I said, there is little that can be done for you except to ride it out."

"Am I okay now? I mean, I hurt and I can barely move, but I don't have to worry about anymore sudden seizures, do I? And it's not likely to be a permanent or ongoing thing, is it?" The last thing he needed was to lose his hearing *and* his mind.

"No, not likely. No one I know has ever had lasting effects, but I can't say that there never have been any."

It was like the disclaimer in the really tiny print at the bottom of most TV drug commercials. Bymenao was guaranteed to cure all headaches as long as you didn't mind the rash, fever, dizziness, weight gain, boils, blisters, bleeding, tumors, and cancerous side effects that all went with it. Oh, and some patients also reported headaches. But you're not likely to have any of those side effects, no sir, because I, the spokesperson, am wearing a white coat with a stethoscope over my shoulders, so you can trust me.

"And overall, I'd say you're looking a lot better," Walter went on. "How do you feel?"

"Like I just went ten rounds with Tyler Freeman," Tommen answered ruefully. "And he won at least nine of them."

"Given your history together, I'd say a ten percent success rate on your end is an improvement."

"Dad!"

Walter's eyes glittered with amusement. He sighed and nodded, looking away for a moment. "You don't know how happy that makes me, that you would still call me dad after what I did."

Tommen shrugged, sighed from the exertion, and managed a smile. "What else would I call you? My pa might be gone, but I still have a dad."

Walter looked away again. Tommen had never seen his dad cry, ever. He mourned the loss of a fellow police officer, but any crying he did was always in private. He did a poor job of covering it up now even as he cleared his throat, pretended to fiddle with his mustache, and finally turned back to Tommen.

"So, you think you can at least sit up?"

Tommen considered it. Such a simple thing had never seemed like such a long process. Bend the legs, bend the back, get his arms under him, push up, scoot back, keep balance, stay up straight and don't fall over, so many tiny elements all coming together just to get from lying down to sitting up. After a moment, he started to bend his legs.

It was not a coordinated effort and his dad could do little to help by way of strength, though he kept Tommen upright the numerous times he threatened to flop over to one side or the other. It seemed like such a difficult task and it took forever it felt like until he was sitting up against the wall.

"How's that feel?" Walter asked. "You feel dizzy at all? Nauseous?"

Tommen shook his head. "No, just...tired. Like I just sat down after running a super marathon or something."

And actually, that was an improvement over the feeling of being encased in lead and covered in chains. Maybe he was getting better. He wasn't sure what his hurry was exactly; nothing was going to happen until he was able to walk himself out of the room. Of course, that was also part of the problem. Nothing was going to happen. Finally awake and sane for all of ten minutes and he was already bored. He ought to be counting his blessings, starting with the fact that he was still alive.

"Food would probably help," he said suddenly. "Especially since I now know that my cheeseburger wasn't real. Is that a common thing?"

His dad shrugged. "I don't know how common it is. Mine had no food involved whatsoever. As for getting food, there's no food now until we leave the Coliseum."

"So I have to get out of here pretty quick then."

Tommen moved to get his legs under him and try to push himself up, but it was like standing up a paralytic and watching them crumble when their legs couldn't take the weight. He wasn't even much able to catch himself well on his hands and knees and he ended up going straight to the floor on his face which began to sting violently. So the fight with the Bat had happened, and that was still a very real facial injury. His dad came beside him and helped get him back to the wall where he sat like a lump of mashed potatoes.

"Relax," Walter told him. "The world and the Wheel isn't going anywhere without you. Remember that even if you slogged your way to the Seat now and got the verdict, we still have to go back through the portal to home. I've rested and recovered and I'm ready for it. How ready are you?"

Not very, if Tommen wanted to admit the truth, and the last thing he needed was to leave the Coliseum as a brand new shiny Apprentice Timekeeper, only to get lost in the mysterious Land In-Between on his way home.

"What have you been doing for seven hours, waiting for me?" he asked.

"Waiting for you," his dad answered. "I might be your mentor, but that doesn't mean I get any kind of entertainment. You got the more exciting part of this gig."

"I think I'd rather take seven hours of boredom over that ever again. What are future reviews like?"

"Journeyman review is strictly a two-parter, knowledge and

skill. The next psychological exam isn't until Master and that's much less traumatic. Otherwise they'd have no Timekeepers left."

Tommen scoffed. "I'll say. Why do they do it?"

"Just like they said, to weed out potential Runners. It doesn't catch all of them, but enough of them."

"Yeah, they kind of missed a couple. Like Cassius and Rifun and all their goons."

"No system is perfect. And just like anyone, they all probably started off as bright, promising students."

An image flashed through Tommen's mind of Rifun telling him what a willful and difficult student he was and how he needed some discipline in his life. Well, not everyone started off as a bright, promising student.

After a few minutes of silence, Tommen got his hands and feet in position. "I'm done with this sitting around thing. I want to get out of here. I want to eat."

This time was no less difficult, but as long as he took it easy and occasionally paused to think about what he was doing, as well as mentally beat his body into submission, he managed to keep his balance and slowly uncurl his body into a standing position. Well, upright position, even if he did end up leaning against the wall anyway.

"How did that feel?" Walter wondered.

"I feel like an animated pile of sludge," Tommen informed him, breathing heavily, eyes closed, taking stock of his body, his bones and muscles and all the nerves sending pain signals all at once to his brain so that he felt everything and nothing. Why did he hurt so bad anyway? Was it from the drug itself? Was it from the seizures? He knew he wasn't much of an athlete, but he was pretty sure he'd done more work when he was running around with Sifura. Maybe it was from sheer stress, the hallucination.

"Don't push yourself too hard if you're not ready," his dad warned as he pushed himself away from the wall.

"Is that doctor's orders?" Tommen asked.

"It's Dad's orders." His tone was not joking.

"If past experience is in any way reliable for future predictions, we're going to be waiting a while in the waiting room anyway. Might as well get there early and get an earlier audience with the Hands."

That was a bit of logic that his dad couldn't argue with, though Tommen could see him grinding his teeth, warring over whether to concede the logic or pull rank and force him to stay. In the end, he frowned and nodded grudgingly, saying, "If you can walk across the room without help and without failing a basic sobriety test, we'll go."

So Tommen did.

Chapter Eight
Verdict

That wasn't to say that the walk from the recovery room back to the waiting room was any sort of walk in the park. Between Tommen and his dad, they were like a pair of little old grannies moving through the grocery store. Walter was battered and frail, and Tommen had only minimal balance. And it wasn't as though it was from anything like nausea or dizziness, just from sheer weakness. He was constantly having to adjust and shift his weight as the strength in his legs wavered from moment to moment. He'd never even been this drunk, even the first time he'd gone out with his friends.

They were not walking along the inner track, so the secretary who escorted them was not the Bat, thankfully. This was more like some kind of bat-snake. By appearance, he or she or it seemed to be able to move very swiftly when need be. While it accommodated Tommen's and Walter's slowness, Tommen could see that it was probably a little frustrated by it. Not that he was any judge of alien expressions. Nevertheless, they reached their destination. Had they not just walked along the middle track, Tommen might have sworn they had never gone anywhere, as similar as the rooms appeared. But the secretary left them there, saying he would inform the Hands they were ready.

Thus started another waiting game, one they were both eager to begin as they collapsed onto the bench. Tommen could have curled up on the bench to take a nap, but as it was, he simply sat next to his dad who reached into his pocket and brought out a little orange prescription bottle. He shook out two pills, took one, and offered the other to Tommen who raised a brow.

135

"I don't have any Ibuprofen or Tylenol on me, but I know you're in pain," he said. "Only offering once."

Tommen hesitated, only because he didn't favor dry swallowing. Ultimately, however, the pain won out, and he accepted the pill, throwing it back and nearly choking on it.

"Just don't tell anyone a cop gave you drugs," his dad said, shoving the bottle back in his pocket.

"Narcotics at that," Tommen said.

"That's okay. One won't kill you, make you high, or get you addicted. Later on, we'll head over to the Food Court and get some real medicine."

That sounded wonderful to Tommen's mind. He was ready to be done with this, done and over with. Give him his results and let him just go home. Although, when he thought about it, this was probably one of the few tests where he was going to learn the results the same day. Even most school tests took a couple days to get back. Sure, that was because there were at least thirty tests to grade, sometimes more, and therefore the proportional time it took was greater, but he was still getting his test back on the same day as he took it. Or at least within the same twenty-four hour period.

It didn't take long for the painkiller to kick in, and while Tommen's limbs still had little strength in them, the pain itself was subsiding. He could barely move, but he could at least do so without screaming agony shooting through his arms and legs and back and everywhere else. When he got up once to stretch a little and walk off the boredom, he found it much easier than when he'd tried to leave the recovery room.

"When did you come down to the recovery room?" he asked. He cut in before his dad had a chance to answer. "For that matter, how did you get into the exam before it was over? Unless..." He blinked and shook his head. "Were you there?" Walter's silence was enough. "You were there. In the Seat while I went through all that shit."

"Tommen."

"But if we're not supposed to talk about it, why were you —?"

"Tommen." Now his tone was more forceful. "If you would relax, I will tell you." Tommen huffed, sat down, and waited. "The rules of the review can get twisted and interpreted multiple ways. Everyone thinks that not talking about the review means not talking about it ever, when in actuality, the official rules state that you are not permitted to speak of it to outsiders or other probationaries. Basically, you can't spoil the test."

"Then why not tell me that? Why let me believe that I could never tell you about what I saw?"

"I wasn't going to let you believe that forever, just until we were home, alone, with no one else around. That way we could speak in peace and quiet, and so you would have time to yourself to process it and work it through. It's a way for the Hands test your loyalty and, for Unengaged races, your ability to keep a secret."

He hated it when Walter made sense.

"Yes, I was there. I was taken out of the room before you came back from the skill test and then quietly escorted in just before you came into the Seat for your psychological exam. The screen in the Seat would allow me to watch without you seeing me. So yes, I saw the whole thing. I saw you talking to Rifun, I saw you facing off against Rifun and Cassius, and I saw you get turned over to the Grandfathers." He must have seen a change in Tommen's expression because his changed also. "Believe me, Tommen, I wished I could step in and save you from that nightmare, but I couldn't. Because it was only your nightmare, and you had to face it alone."

So he hadn't seen the whole thing. And the jury was still out on whether his conversation with Rifun in the waiting room had been real or not. It sure felt real, but after the events and revelations recently, he couldn't be sure of anything.

"You're not shitting me, are you?" Tommen asked, uncaring of his dad's language preferences.

"No. I really was going to tell you when we got home, but you figured it out beforehand, so it doesn't really matter now."

Tommen let out a breath and ran a hand through his hair, his arm flopping down limply to his side.

"We have time," his dad went on. "Do you want to talk about it?"

He sighed and shook his head. "No."

They sat in silence for a while after that. That was the awful thing about the Wheel. Even for its vast expanse of knowledge and technology, for all the secretaries who worked tirelessly to keep translations current, some things would inevitably get lost in translation. Granted, it was stupid that of all things to get lost, it would be the official rules for the testing and reviews, but there would never be a 100% perfect translation rate. And apparently, someone long ago decided that the mistranslation worked better than fixing it. Have the probies believe that they could never speak about their reviews ever at all to anyone, imply some awful punishment if they did, and then let their mentors inform them that it was only half-true. That way they could have a nice heart-to-heart discussion about it later.

Tommen wasn't sure which was scarier, having his dad not only know but to have been in there with him, or to never be able to tell about the terrible things that happened in there. On the one hand, he could feel the pressure of the secret being relieved, knowing that he could talk to his dad. On the other hand, the Hands had seen it, too. So it would never have been just his secret; someone would have always known.

He wasn't sure just how much time had passed, but it didn't seem like nearly as long as any other wait that he'd had in the waiting rooms thus far. When the door finally opened, it wasn't the Bat who stood there, but something...else. At least the Bat could understandably be called a bat. This thing looked like some sort of giraffe-peacock that decided to go full commando in the brushy camo gear. At least, that's what Tommen got out of it. The thing had to bend over to look into the room and Tommen guessed its height to be somewhere between thirteen and sixteen feet.

"Tommen Forbes, the Hands are ready to deliver the verdict of your review," the thing said.

"That's you, kiddo," Walter said, grabbing his cane and hauling himself wearily to his feet.

Tommen followed suit, feeling pretty good until he got out the door and into the inner track. When he got there, he almost stumbled and hit the floor again. The dark, dungeon-esque feel had been replaced by a sort of palace, despite the fact that almost nothing had changed. As he looked around, the only thing that he could definitively say had changed was the lighting. Rather than low-level torches that looked ready to putter out, the lights were now bright, white fire torches that lit up everything, making everything look cheery and friendly despite it being the same white-washed stone as literally everything else in the Coliseum. Despite his dread and distaste for the dungeon, Tommen found that he also dreaded and disliked change, especially such a sharp change. Well, the Bat had said that he was only the night guy. It was only fitting that the day person be the complete opposite of him, like night and day.

Of course the day guy could also outpace them five to one, ten to one at the rate they were going. Somewhere in the back of Tommen's mind, he found a certain satisfaction in keeping the Hands waiting just like the Hands kept them waiting all the time. A misstep and a near-tumble wiped that mental smirk from his mind.

"You okay?" his dad asked.

"The pain went away, but I still feel like I just ran a super marathon," Tommen said through gritted teeth. He was totally fine with his dad being concerned, and he figured that some might be warranted given how bad he felt, but the man didn't need to hover over him like some worried mother hen.

Of course, hadn't he been doing the same thing to Walter? What was it he'd said when they were on their way home? I'm only injured, not helpless. That sounded about right. So maybe it was a little payback, a way of telling Tommen that he was just fine, too, he just needed time to recover. Time was a tool, not medicine.

They reached the tunnel, and that was where Tommen learned that the brushy camo gear was not a fashion statement by the giraffe-peacock; it was literally part of its body. It's sort of wing-talon-appendage-like things were apparently not opposable, or maybe it wasn't strong enough. Either way, the secretary instead used the branches and vines of the brush as fully functional fingers, thumbs, appendages, whatever to take the wheel and turn it to open the gate.

"That was scary," Tommen said before he was smart enough to keep his mouth shut.

The giraffe-peacock commando was apparently as conversational as the Bat because it said nothing, simply waited for them to pass through the gate into the tunnel.

As they approached, Tommen could feel his heart jump into his throat, and his stomach started doing backflips. He swallowed once as he felt sweat start to slide down his neck. He was afraid. Like, he'd been afraid before in the sense of it being a dark, scary tunnel, but this was a new level of fear. This was warehouse-level fear. This was holding his dying dad in his arms kind of fear.

How could he be so afraid of this thing when he'd been through the tunnel before without incident? Sure, only half a dozen times, but could his perceptions really change so much so fast? Maybe it was just because it was so soon after the exam. He would leave here, start his new training, and he wouldn't be back for a while. In that time, he'd probably get over it. He hoped.

On the other hand, the Hands ruled through fear. What better way than to get everyone to experience a horrifying hallucination in the very spot where they would later face their governors, so that every time they went there, they were afraid? If the Hands couldn't make the peasants fear them, create an atmosphere of fear, and blind fear was blanket fear. Was he being paranoid again?

They reached the end of the tunnel and entered the Seat. Tommen's heart was racing, and he was sweating again, but once he saw that all was as it ought to have been, he calmed just a little. The light was bright, the marble was white, the symbol was where it was supposed to be. They approached it slowly, both giving up some speed in hopes for coordination and even a little bit of confidence. But the Hands were not fooled; they knew fear and weakness when they smelled it.

Be a dog, get thrown a bone, and be forgotten. And boy are we ever the dogs, coming in off the streets.

The Hands were all assembled, looking as though they hadn't moved in the seven-plus hours between the end of his exam and the present moment. Was there some sort of assigned seating or did they actually have to sit there for hours and hours on end?

Tommen tried to stand up straight and look presentable, even if he'd long ago given up the facade of cleanliness and organization; he was running on reserve energy, and his give-a-dam had broken quite a while ago. He couldn't say when, possibly when he'd learned that his dad had been watching his hallucination the entire time.

"Tommen Forbes, you have completed the review in order to advance from probationary Timekeeper to full Apprentice Timekeeper status," the Zero Hour said, standing. "How are you feeling?"

The question caught him off-guard, that the Hands or the Zero Hour would care enough to ask. Still, he found his voice and replied, "I am recovering well, thank you." Maybe it was just because he'd collapsed in the Seat itself instead of a more convenient place, like the recovery room, where the Hands didn't have to see.

"Very good."

Maybe he could also hope for a speedy answer instead of having to —

"As to the first part of the review, the oral exam, testing your knowledge of Time — "

Nope. Just a little too much to ask, wasn't it? Gotta go with the formalities. Worse, gotta go with the suspenseful formalities. You can't tell me results and then the details, you have to give me the details before getting to the overall results.

" —Forty-six of fifty-one Hands were satisfied with your performance."

Forty-six out of fifty-one? What the—? Were they going to go through each of the questions, too? Would they tell him what they were dissatisfied with? Would they tell him which questions he got wrong, at least? Were they mad that he hadn't at least attempted the last question, terrible though it was? Should he have tried? Who were the Hands who said nay? Did they have some vendetta against him? Was it him personally, or did his answers offend some of them? Had he unwittingly gone against the Hands and Time in some way with his answers? Or were they just shrewd judges who expected Master answers out of a probationary, who wanted a college-level essay from a third grade writing contest?

But the Zero Hour moved on, not dwelling on the past. There would be no answers for him. He would never know who or why or what happened. It was like taking the SATs or something; he would only get a number, not an answer.

Wasn't he just complaining about how he just wanted the answer and not the details? Of course, that had been back when the answer was a simple pass or fail. Now, he wanted not only the answer, but a detailed explanation of this defamation of character, real or perceived as it may be.

"As to the second part of the review, the first test, the standing skill test, fifty of fifty-one Hands were satisfied with your performance."

Fifty. Out of fifty-one. Who the hell was that last guy? What didn't he like about it? Tommen had endured a growing migraine as his Bands were ripped apart each time, and he'd still always gotten it right. Was it because he hadn't done it fast enough? Was he too good at it and they hated him for it? Was that same guy one of the ones who penalized his oral exam, too? Was he just the eternally shrewd asshole judge whom no performance could satisfy? Was he one of those who could stand before one of the wonders of the world or an original Da Vinci or Picasso and still find fault with it?

"As to the second part of the review, the second test, the moving skill test, thirty-nine of fifty-one Hands were satisfied with your performance."

Thirty-nine out of—well, okay, he supposed he couldn't fault them for that one. Even he wasn't too thrilled with his own performance there. He'd been slow and sloppy, and he probably still had the black and blue marks to remind him of it for the next few days. At the same time, however, it wasn't entirely his fault, despite what the Zero Hour had said about asking the right questions. He hadn't fully understood the rules or what was really expected of him. If he'd known that it was to be treated as a real fight and his only available weapon was Time, that might have made a difference. Then it would have been like fighting Tyler Freeman, but with a more...no-holds-barred kind of attitude.

"As to the third part of the review, the psychological exam, fifty of fifty-one Hands were satisfied with your performance."

Fifty out—who the fuck *was* that guy? Who was that last fucking guy who couldn't appreciate a son sacrificing himself for his father? Did that guy have some kind of daddy issue that made him prejudiced? What were the criteria for the judging? How qualified were they? Was it really possible that it was the same guy across all four categories?

"As to the review overall, forty-six of fifty-one Hands were satisfied with your review. Congratulations, Tommen Forbes, you passed your review. You are now an Apprentice Timekeeper."

Tommen's mind told him to jump for joy. His body said, *don't you dare.* In the end, the most he figured he could safely manage was a sigh of relief and a slight slump, almost toppling when his dad came beside him to give him an awkward half-hug pat on the back sort of thing which he just as awkwardly returned.

"That is, if you choose it."

He looked up at the Zero Hour who continued, "Timekeeping is not an easy task, and many probationaries are frightened by the things they see in the psychological exam, as well as what they encounter at home. Time demands much from those who protect it, and it is not a job all can accomplish. Therefore, it is now that we offer you a chance to safely renounce your Apprenticeship, renounce Time, and walk away back to what may be a normal or abnormal life for your species. Your clock will not be broken, and no ill mention of you will come because of it. Your Timekeeping abilities will be Suppressed. The idea is not that it is something you can come back to at a whim, like a hobby, but to provide a safe way out and to protect you in the future. While Suppression itself is not irreversible, the premise is that it is permanent. If you require, you may be given time to consider the options."

What options? That he go back home, go to school, go to college, marry and have kids, trudge along in the dull drudgery of normal life? Sure, he could do it, but if experience taught him anything, it's that most anyone would give their right leg to have a chance at doing something great. Besides, he'd made a century and a half leap into the future. The life he wanted, he would never have. He would always be the weird kid, the outcast, the stranger, the old-fashioned kook, the Chivalrous Welshman. Well, if he was going to be weird, he wanted it to mean something; he wanted there to be something behind the weirdness, behind the names.

"I thank you for the opportunity, Lord Zero Hour, however, I must decline," Tommen informed them. "My place is in Time, and I believe I have the mental and physical strength needed to carry out my Timekeeping duties."

At least for the time being. Once he got to be of age and perhaps of better training, then he would see about this whole Scouting business. But until then, yes, he would be a good little Timekeeper. Train in the Arena, turn in Runners, and, hopefully, not start any more civil wars, or wars of any kind.

"Your decision has been rendered," the Zero Hour confirmed. "And so, Tommen Forbes, do you promise to uphold the Laws of Time, to defend them and execute them in the pursuit of justice both within the Wheel and without, apprehending those who would seek the use it selfishly or for destructive purposes, no matter where they may hide, and bring order and peace to the area you serve?"

"I do," Tommen swore.

But it was not lost on him how vague some of the terminology was. It was true that anyone and everyone was capable of committing some crime—his dad saw that happen every day—but something about it just screamed at him, saying that those same words were going to be used against him someday. Everything he said could and would be used against him, and he did not have the right to remain silent, nor did he have the right to an attorney. Was he still being paranoid?

"And do you, Walter Forbes, promise to continue to train Tommen Forbes in the respect of a Timekeeper, to uphold the Laws of Time, to defend them and execute them in the pursuit of justice both within the Wheel and without, teaching him of the wonders and dangers of the universe that he may be wise and bring order and peace to the area you serve?"

"I do," Walter swore.

"And so, Tommen Forbes, you are now a full Apprentice Timekeeper. The use of the Arena is available to you with the oversight of your mentor, as well as several sections of the Archives. Per the standards of human Timekeeper training, it is expected that your Apprentice training take approximately two Base Years. There is much to learn until you become a Journeyman. Study well."

"Thank you, Lord Zero Hour, I will," Tommen replied.

"Do you have any further questions before we close and seal this case?"

He racked his brain, trying to think of any that were relevant to the situation. Should he ask about the specific votes in each part of his review? Would that seem pretentious? Would it make him look like a child? He knew a few classmates who practically threw temper tantrums if they didn't score perfectly on every test, quiz, and homework grade; generally he just figured they ought to chill. So maybe he should take some of his own advice. He passed. He obviously had some mistakes here and there. And he couldn't please everyone. No matter why the Hands wore the shrouds, there were still real people and beings under them who all had different experiences and prejudices and could not honestly be expected to rule objectively every single time no matter what. He'd passed his review, and he was an Apprentice now; everything else was moot. And the way things worked, once the case was closed, it was closed. They couldn't just go back and suddenly strip him of his title; it was set in stone.

"No, I have no questions," he told them.

"And so concludes the review of Tommen Forbes, having passed judgment upon it and increasing his rank from probationary to Apprentice Timekeeper," the Zero Hour ruled. "This case is now closed and may not be reopened under similar circumstances. Congratulations, Tommen Forbes."

"Thank you, Lord Zero Hour, and Great Hands, for presiding over my review."

"Tommen Forbes, you are dismissed, and you may leave the Coliseum at your leisure. Walter Forbes, it is requested that you remain behind for a time."

Tommen had turned to leave, but he paused and turned back. He looked at his dad whose expression said this was highly unusual.

"What is this about?" Walter inquired cautiously.

But the Zero Hour did not answer him, simply turned his attention back toward Tommen. "Tommen Forbes, you are dismissed. You are free to leave the Coliseum at your leisure."

It was not a request, but a polite demand to get out. He glanced at his dad who hesitated but nodded once. "Go on, Tommen. I'll be along. It's probably nothing."

Tommen was still unsure, but he nodded and headed for the gate. The Hands didn't break formalities for just "nothing." They didn't do social calls or welfare checks. They weren't going to make nice and ask how he was doing since being attacked by an insane Runner. Hell, Tommen had needed to start a war in order for them to pay attention to his illness. That was probably what this was about. They were going to question him to try and get to Tommen. What did your boy do? Why did he do it? How did he do it? Did you have any part in this? Did your Lieutenants have any part in this?

Would they strip him of his rank? Would they depose him as Captain? They'd just sworn him in as Tommen's mentor, so they couldn't do anything too awful to him. Could they?

The giraffe-peacock was still holding the wheel as he walked through the second gate into the inner track. He still couldn't get over the change in decor, even if the only thing that had really changed was the lighting. He looked at the giraffe-peacock.

"So do I let myself out?" he wondered.

"The fifth door," the thing replied, using a viney tendril to indicate the direction he should go.

"Ah. And what's your name, or how do they call you?"

"I am simply called the Day, as the night secretary is called the Bat."

More appropriate to the surroundings, maybe, but not nearly as descriptive. "Do you have any idea how long they're going to be?"

"I do not."

"Any idea what they're talking about? And don't tell me you don't know, okay, the Bat pretty much admitted that he spies and eavesdrops and knows everything that goes on."

"Even if I did know, it is not your matter and so you do not need to know."

"He's my dad."

"You are permitted to let yourself out. Or I am able also to remove you."

Translation: Get out now before I make you get out.

Tommen hesitated, cast a last glance at the tunnel, then turned and started off. He found the fifth door and slipped through the room to the middle track. Damn, but he was getting tired. Too much shit to handle in one day. Well, his dad and the twins had been right, he was not going to want to leave his bed for a few days. Sleeping was just way too appealing of an idea right now.

Once he got up the energy, he found a secretary to let him through to the outer track where he was almost stunned by the noise and volume of people and creatures. How long had he been alone or almost alone? Normally it wasn't a big deal, but for some reason this was just stunning.

He got outside the Coliseum and paused. Did he wait? Should he look for the twins? Were they here, or had they already gone ahead to the Food Court? Did he have the energy to go looking? Maybe he would just find a quiet place to rest for a bit, just to sit down and relax his back and legs before they gave out on him.

"Hey, Tommen!"

He turned as the twins approached him, all excited and all smiles, almost perfectly synchronous, as happy as if they'd just won the lottery.

"We saw you come out but the crowds were really thick," Micah said. "Obviously you're not being dragged out to have your clock broken. How'd it go?"

Tommen rubbed his face. If his dad was right, and he was understanding him right, he could tell the twins about his trip. But with how happy they were compared to how miserable he felt just thinking about it, he wasn't inclined to tell them just yet. Instead he shrugged and said simply, "I'd rather not talk about it."

"That's fine," Micaiah assured him, mellowing out a little. "But you feel okay otherwise? The psych exam can be a real ass-kicker."

"It was. It definitely was." There was no denying that one. "Yeah, my dad said I collapsed into seizures before I even got out of the Seat after the exam finished. Then it was seven hours or something before I got my mind back."

"Wow," Micah said. "That's a record."

"It is?"

"Yeah, I'm still out of my mind. So is Dumbo here."

He was trying to be humorous and lighten the mood, but at the moment it just sounded corny, and Tommen really wasn't in the mood. Thankfully, Micah seemed to pick up on this because he sighed. "Sorry. I try." He looked around. "Speaking of your dad, where is he?"

"The Hands asked him to stay behind."

The twins glanced at each other.

"You did get promoted, right?" Micaiah wondered cautiously.

Tommen shrugged. "Yeah, I mean, they told me a couple times that I'm an Apprentice now. They did a swearing in thing for both me as an Apprentice and my dad as my mentor, but then they dismissed me and asked him to stay behind. I kind of wondered if I could stay behind or what the problem was, but they told me to get out. Any idea what it could be about?"

"Come on, Tommen, you're not a dumb kid." Micaiah shook his head. "I think we all know what it is they're talking about, but why or what they're saying or any of that, we'll just have to wait until they're done with him."

"I asked the Day how long they might be, and he told me that I could either let myself out or he would forcibly remove me."

"The Day is about as bad-tempered as the Bat," Micah told him. "Personally I'd rather deal with the Bat."

"So we know what they're talking about, but what could they actually do to him? They wouldn't swear him in as my mentor and then go and, I don't know..." Tommen didn't want to think about his dad having his clock broken.

"No, but they could remove him from his command as Captain," Micaiah said, echoing his thoughts. "If they feel that he is unfit to continue his duties."

"Six weeks and he's good, though."

"Yes, but a lot can happen in six weeks," Micah pointed out. "Rifun might try to take advantage of that weakness. The Hands know how to protect their interests, and it is in their interest to have strong leadership, especially in vulnerable areas, as District Four has proven to be."

"But what Captain is going to be able to face a Warden?"

Micah put his hands up. "Not my rules. But you have to admit that there is a point to it."

Tommen sighed. "I know. And it's not just the six weeks. It's more like three or four weeks for the initial recovery and then he might need physical therapy for another few weeks."

"Exactly. But on the bright side, he'll still have his training, he'll still have regular Master Timekeeper duties, he'll still be up for consideration for future Captain positions, and he'll still be able to mentor you. So regardless of whatever happens in there with ranks and promotions and whatever politics are going on, you two are not going to be separated anytime soon. Okay?"

Tommen nodded, even if it was reluctantly. "Okay. It's just...he's a Captain. I don't want to see him removed from that because of something that might have been prevented if they would have given enough of a fuck to send help."

Micaiah grinned. "Always the fighter. Well, we can talk about it when he joins us. In the meantime, why don't we get something to eat? You look like you're starving."

"I feel like I'm starving."

"Then let's go."

So they turned and left the Coliseum, heading for the Food Court.

Chapter Nine
Inconveniences

Walter watched Tommen leave the Seat. They were supposed to meet up with the twins and then head to the Food Court before going home; hopefully they would find each other and he could catch up later. Tommen looked so weary. The reviews were cruel, inhumane even, not that the Hands or anybody else really cared. He would be feeling it for days; he was probably running on pure adrenaline and the desire to just go home and go to bed.

Lord knew that was how Walter himself felt. True, he needed to rest and recover, but sitting in a room for hours on end was a bit much in his opinion. Just as important as resting his leg was using it, keeping the muscles from contracting too much, which they had done in his solitude. Now, as he stood in the Seat, every muscle from groin to knee throbbed. It might not have been so bad except he was limited in how and how much he used his cane since his shoulder movement was still somewhat restricted.

So there he stood with only one good limb to keep him upright and balanced and hardly a second functional limb between the remaining three. At least it was still early morning back home, so they could all go back to bed without difficulty.

As soon as Tommen disappeared through the tunnel, the Zero Hour moved to speak, but Walter beat him to it.

"Why am I here?" he asked.

"That is the question," the Zero Hour answered. "Why are you here but for the actions of your Apprentice and son who defied the ruling of the Hands and incited violence and even war in order to save you?"

"Where I'm from, that's a phenomenon we call 'love.' And greater love has no man that he should lay down his life for another. And he certainly risked his life for me, just as I did for him."

"Such a 'phenomenon' as you call it is not limited to your race. However, there are more issues at stake here than a single instance of love. As such, we now commence the case of the Hands of Time doing an overview, study, and interrogation of Walter Forbes, Captain Timekeeper, Quadrant One, Parsec Eleven, Sector Five, System Four, Planet Thirty-Eight, Region Four, District Four."

"Interrogation? Am I being prosecuted?"

"Not yet. However, as focusing only on the matter of your Apprentice's actions has proved futile, we have decided to go further back in the progression of events to see if we can't find some evidence of wrongdoing, where justice may be served and further crisis avoided."

For Walter as Cop, the proceeding was appalling, barbaric. They were arresting someone and then looking for a crime to charge them with. Basically, walking up to him on the street, arresting him, and then trying to figure out if he'd ever shoplifted, murdered, vandalized someone's home, or taken candy from a baby. There was no crime, there was no investigation, it was a shot in the dark. Yes, he'd made judgments and decisions and arrests based on a hunch before, but at least a crime had been committed first.

And if they really wanted to go back in time and trace the progression of events, they might find out that they were essentially arresting the victim. Like a husband tries to kill his wife, and the cops arrest the wife while she's still lying in the hospital in a coma. Yeah, the husband is a really bad guy, but he's scary so we can't go after him, but we need someone to pay for this.

For Walter who-was-once-a-criminal, he found the proceeding to be oddly familiar. And back then, at least he'd *actually committed a crime!* Whether it was brawling or drunkenness or murder, at least he'd done something to warrant being brought before a judge who was biased, probably bribed, who was going to do a rough, vague interpretation of sketchy witnesses, twisted interrogation, and sentence him to jail before the end of the day. Sometimes before he even got a chance to speak and defend himself, not that it would matter. That was one thing that hadn't changed in a couple centuries: anything you say can and will be used against you.

So he watched the Hands, especially the Zero Hour. It would be either Cassius or the real Zero Hour. Cassius didn't like to play politics and sit in for petitions and cases and reviews, but Tommen's review might have gotten his attention, especially since he knew Walter would be with him.

If that was Cassius, it might be Walter's only chance at actually speaking to him in a setting where violence was unlikely to erupt at any moment. If he could somehow turn the questions around or get him to say or admit to something that only Cassius would say or know, he could theoretically arrest him on the spot. How likely that was, however, was up for debate.

"Very well," Walter said in response to the Zero Hour's words. "As a Timekeeper and local law enforcement, I can appreciate the need to provide justice and closure."

He spoke stiffly. At the very least, if they were having this much trouble and having to go back and search and look under every rock to find something, then Tommen was probably in the clear, or at least out of the direct line of fire. He, Walter, had been pursuing a Runner according to procedure, well, more or less. The only ones who might not be so easily covered were Micah and Micaiah, and yet, all three of them had gone snooping into the Dispersal. Walter let out a breath. This could get very interesting very fast. He would just have to be careful about how he handled it.

"Excellent," the Zero Hour said. "As your Apprentice and son stated, you were wounded by the Runner Rifun who used ammunition poisoned by the Borelian Isthim."

"That is correct," Walter confirmed.

"How did it get to that point? What led you to the confrontation?"

So Walter spent probably half an hour recounting the tale, starting with the first murder. Yes, Tommen found the body. Yes, he was aware that it was very convenient; it was probably planned that way. Yes, they suspected a connection to Lily right from the beginning. Yes, they suspected Time involvement right from the beginning. Not only that, but it was probably more than just the average Runner. Yes, they did have reasonable suspicion to go digging into the Dispersal. No, they found nothing tangible to go on, so they were forced to give up, at least until the second body. Yes, they interviewed Lily again. Yes, mention was made of Julianna, her husband Richard, and Cassius. Yes, there was potentially a connection to Walter, but that was largely irrelevant to the case.

Then there was the break-in and the journal. Yes, they had reason to believe it was the same one kept by Richard. No, they didn't know that at the time the journal was found; the case brought it to light. No, they didn't know or understand what had been in it either locally or in Time, though Rifun and Cassius swore up and down that it was all about the Akari.

"Do you know what the Akari is?" the Zero Hour inquired.

"I know what the legends are," Walter replied. "Said to be something from another dimension that gives certain people the ability to harness certain physical aspects other than Time. Gravity, light, that sort of thing. Also said to enhance a person's ability to use Time, but the exact meaning of that is often disputed."

"You yourself do not believe the Akari exists, however."

"Either it doesn't exist, or if it does, it's not as grand or miraculous as its cult followers seem to think it is."

"Which is why you were willing to trade the journal to Rifun and Cassius."

"As far as I was concerned, they could have their dusty old legends as long as it kept them from killing more innocent people."

Of course, there was the argument that giving them such a—in their eyes—sacred object would only inspire them to kill more innocent people and perhaps commit some act of terror. At the same time, maybe they would be preoccupied for a while trying to make their old legends come to life and leave the rest of the universe alone. It was a gamble, but if he had to do it all over again, Walter figured he would only make sure that Tommen was in a safer position so they wouldn't have to go through those two weeks of hell when he was held captive.

But that was all in the past, and the Zero Hour trudged on in his questioning. So, yes, Walter had traded the journal for the lives of two meager humans. Yes, they had met in the Wheel. Yes, the twins had managed to rally up a force that was supposed to apprehend and arrest Rifun when he came through, but once again, sentiment won out, and that was called off by Micah for the sake of his brother. Yes, Rifun had taken Tommen and held him captive for two weeks. No, Walter didn't know the details of the captivity because he hadn't had a chance to really sit down and talk to him about it; Tommen was still trying to get over it, and Walter wasn't going to rush him into talking about it if he didn't want to.

The more the Zero Hour asked about the cases and the progression of events, the more Walter suspected that it wasn't really about finding someone to take the blame for everything that had happened, whether the true criminal or a scapegoat. He trusted his gut, and his gut told him that Cassius was the one under that shroud, and he was fishing for details of the case. What did they know, what did they do, what were they going to do next, how close were they to him, how worried did he have to be?

"Cassius himself was not present at this confrontation, was he?" the Zero Hour inquired.

"He was not," Walter admitted grudgingly. "Rifun said he had politics to attend to."

"At one point, you did manage to save both Lily Guile and your son."

"Yes."

"What happened?"

"Rifun set his goons on us and, in the chaos, took them again. I pursued them into the warehouse."

"It was reported that your Lieutenants again had a secret Time rallying force that they were planning to bring to your aid once you and Rifun were alone, as they knew you would be eventually. What happened to that rallying force?"

Walter ground his teeth. "Rifun somehow managed to turn the warehouse into a quasi-dimension, similar to the Wheel in respects that it was cut off from the rest of the universe while physically still occupying the same space. No one could get in or out; he had sealed us off."

"At which time he forced you to fight Isthim."

"Yes."

"Can you describe the fight?"

"Less than stellar on my part, but there was no way I could touch her. I couldn't even really get close to her, but you know how Borelians work, especially *vodraks*. Eventually, she got me to the ground and confused enough that by the time everything became clear, Rifun was already standing over me with his gun, loading poisoned bullets into it."

"How many hits did you take?"

"Three." And how they were throbbing. Holy Lord, but he was hurting. He needed to sit down; he needed a painkiller. "Two in the chest, one in the leg. One in the chest and the one in the leg went straight through me, but the third round got lodged in my body which allowed Isthim's poison to enter my blood and put me into a coma."

"At which time your son came to first petition us, basically inciting civil war within the Wheel and inviting war from the Borelians. And when we did not rule in his favor, he defied us and went looking for a cure to the Borelian poison himself."

"Sounds about right."

"And you are aware of his actions?"

"He wouldn't stop talking about it for days after I woke up. It's almost like I was there with him, the way he described his adventure; he's a very good storyteller."

"Captain Walter Forbes, did you speak to him at all, lecture him or discipline him at all about his actions?"

Walter glared at the Zero Hour. "My son risked his life, risked civil war and imprisonment, traveled halfway across the universe on a whim, to find a cure for my ailment. I'm not about to chastise him for stepping on a few toes along the way. I am alive because of what he did. Anything else, whatever politics or unrest that results, is all secondary."

"Do you think yourself above the Laws of Time, Captain?"

"No, I don't. Which is why I continue to put up with this bullshit here. But Time isn't everything. Billions of my people get along just fine every day without it. I'm just glad my son has the ability to prioritize family over job."

The Zero Hour was silent for a moment. Walter tried to gauge Cassius' reaction despite the shroud.

"And you, Captain Forbes, how do you prioritize the elements in your life?"

Translation: How loyal are you? Is this a like-father like-son deal?

"When you state it that way, my son always comes first. If that's what you're asking."

Again, Cassius was silent. Walter met him head-on, but he knew he was at a disadvantage. Regardless of his rank or his merits, when going before the Hands, one always went under threat of death. Walter was obligated to report certain things, things which he knew Cassius was mulling over and trying to figure out how to use against him. But he couldn't not report them, and if he started making accusations that this was the False Zero Hour, Cassius could just pull rank and authority and order him imprisoned and his clock broken, maybe even lock him up in the asylum.

The fact that the Zero Hour didn't press the issue of prioritization further told Walter everything he needed to know about who it was under that shroud.

"Your world is considered Scientifically Advancing and Unengaged, correct?" the Zero Hour inquired.

"It is," Walter confirmed. Although, having seen some of the things just in the common wares marketplace and on the person of numerous alien species, Earth might as well have been in the Stone Age. But supposedly one of the requirements for the "Scientifically Advancing" status was the ability to leave the planet and go among the stars, and apparently the International Space Station and various manned and unmanned ships and probes were enough to qualify.

"This means also that you have decent medicine."

Well, that was a fairly relative statement. In the United States and other first-world countries, sure, cutting-edge, top-notch, unbelievably expensive. At the same time, there were still primitive tribes running around in the Amazon and the African plains who still relied on witch doctors and taboo, who had no concept of running water, who were filmed by humanitarian organizations to disproportionately represent third-world countries as a means to get money.

"Yes, our available medical care is decent."

At the same time, there was also the point that humans didn't seem to be able to focus their medical research efforts on what really mattered. Vaccines were developed for common, bullshit diseases out of fear of getting sick, while real diseases like cancer and diabetes were simply "manageable" instead of "curable." And then there was the whole point about those common diseases mutating and becoming real problems that couldn't be cured.

"But without your son's efforts, you would have died."

That was the Unengaged part of it, yes. There was no way Tommen could have explained to the doctors that he'd been poisoned by an alien, and not been locked up in the psych ward.

"That is correct."

The Zero Hour, Cassius, shifted position. "Here is our current dilemma, Captain Forbes. Borelian poison is supposed to be incurable. By all accounts, you were on the verge of death anyway. A notice was sent out to the other Captain-trained Timekeepers in your District. On Election Day, all officers in your District will be voting for a new Captain."

Walter's first reaction was stunned horror. He was being replaced. They'd written him off as dead and replaced him. It wasn't even the fact that it was happening — he would have written him off as dead, too — it was the fact that he was around to witness it. Normally replacements came at times of death, retirement, or resignation. He wasn't ready to do any of those things.

"But I'm alive," he said weakly. "I'm alive, and I had no intentions of resigning then or now."

"Which is why, upon word of your survival, the Gatekeeper and Regional Manager decided to put it on the ballot, given how close it is to the election, and not simply name a replacement as is standard procedure."

"Why not simply leave me as Captain?"

"Put simply, they were worried for your health. The side effects of surviving Borelian poison are, put in the best terms, unknown. On top of that are the normal physical injuries you have sustained, which might not have mattered so much except that Cassius, Rifun, and the Borelian Isthim are still at large, last seen in your District. If they decided to take advantage of your weakened state, what do you think would happen?"

What do you think would happen? Of the three people you named, I'm looking at one of them right now.

"Well," Walter said, not bothering to hide the smirk in his voice, "I'm sorry that my recovery has caused so much inconvenience for everyone. Given that the election is still some days away, what is the state of things in my District, speaking of management?"

"Until the elections and a new — or continued — Captain is decided, you are only considered Acting Captain. You have full jurisdiction over the other Timekeepers in your District as well as the logistics, but if anything happens, the Manager will step in."

So basically, you'll let me do all the paperwork and the HR and make me feel like I'm the captain of the team, when really I'm not much more than the mail boy. I get to handle all the important documents, but I don't actually get to open them, see them, or do anything about them. I'm the janitor who has his very own monogrammed trash can and toilet brush. I'm the housekeeper cleaning the Oval Office who actually gets to be in the Oval Office, but only under the black stares of Secret Service. I'm the nursing home resident who gets a paper sign on their door with their name on it in crayon. Believe me, Cassius, if I could Band these injuries away, they would have already been healed. As it is, these braces and slings and cane are the only things keeping me from decking you right here.

"And if, for some odd reason, I am not elected Captain of the District, what happens to me?" Walter inquired stiffly.

"Then you simply become a Captain-trained Master," the Zero Hour replied.

The way he said it actually put Walter in mind of a couple of jerk teenagers he'd once overheard while chaperoning a school dance. There had been more in the group, but the big issue was the girl wanting to break up with the guy, and the guy's attitude being something along the lines of how she was privileged to be dating him because he could have any girl he wanted but he picked her so she ought to be grateful and show some respect. Real piece of work that kid. That was kind of how Walter felt right now, talking to the Zero Hour. Like he ought to be grateful that he was even being given the chance to keep the office he'd held for, what, eleven years now, twelve? Longer? Like walking into the precinct and having Steggmann tell him, in the same tone, that he ought to be grateful that he was still a cop because it really could have been a lot worse, as if the whole fiasco was his fault.

"When was I supposed to be notified of this?" was the best rebuttal he could come up with.

"There is no precedent for such a situation. You originally would have been notified immediately, however, with the review of your son so close to hand, we decided to tell you in person."

"No precedent, huh? So you've never had a case where a

Captain or other officer was presumed dead and later proven to be alive?"

The Zero Hour was silent for just the moment that Walter needed to confirm that it truly was Cassius under that shroud; he could feel the glare coming from the shadow. Oh, how he must have wanted to just tear Walter's throat out right there but he couldn't. *Time to play politics, Cassius.*

"None," Cassius replied stiffly. "Especially given the method of your presumed death from which no one has lived to tell the tale. Given that with most appointments there is a gap in coverage of the office, we decided to try and close that gap by having a new Captain appointed and ready upon your death."

The more they spoke, the weaker the arguments seemed to get, and Walter could only conclude that Cassius was delivering a veiled threat. He'd had someone in mind to replace him, a loyal lackey. As far as Walter knew, both the Manager and the Gatekeeper were Timekeepers loyal to the Hands and Time, not necessarily to Cassius.

Point: Walter was set to die. Being good friends or on good terms with the Manager and the Gatekeeper, they are sad to see him go and want to appoint a decent person to replace him.

Point: Cassius doesn't like the most likely pick. He probably threatens them in some way to get them to pick someone who is trained and capable, but also more loyal to Cassius than Time.

Point: Walter makes a miraculous recovery. The Manager and the Gatekeeper feel they don't have to replace him, but Cassius insists, citing the unprecedented recovery, his injuries, the replacement already being set up, and whatever else he can come up with to cast enough doubt and unsettle enough Timekeepers to upset the issue.

Point: The Manager and the Gatekeeper propose a compromise, citing the elections, deciding to put it to a vote, let the officers decide.

He mulled it over, trying to decide the likelihood of the scenario. Alternatively, the Manager and the Gatekeeper could be the ones loyal to Cassius, and the other District Captains, Lieutenants, and assorted Timekeepers were more upset by the supposed pick and pointed to Walter's miraculous recovery, the political pressure forcing it to a vote. He had a harder time believing that one. He knew Paul the Manager well enough, and he figured he knew Cassius well enough. Cassius was crazy, and so were his followers; Paul wasn't crazy. He didn't know Mi Chin all that well, but they were on friendly enough terms, and she didn't seem crazy either.

But in the here and now, Cassius was the Zero Hour, and he had spoken. Walter was only the Acting Captain of District Four and come Election Day, his title would be put to a vote.

"Any further questions or concerns?" Cassius prompted.

Who is your favored pick for Captain and why? How did you threaten the Manager and the Gatekeeper; what led to this being put to a vote? Who are you bribing in order to get votes to swing your way? What does District Four really mean to you? Are there other Districts in the same predicament?

"No," Walter answered at last. "I've learned all I need."

Basically, he had twelve days to figure out who Cassius intended to replace him, and how he was going to stop it, whether by retaining his position as Captain or at least seeing it go to someone who was a good and decent person, not one of Cassius' lackeys.

"Very well. Remember then, that Election Day is in twelve days." More proof that Cassius was the Zero Hour; no non-human would know that. "It is a short period, but you can still get some campaigning done."

If I was interested in campaigning, I'd run for sheriff. "Thank you for the advice; maybe I will."

"And so concludes the case of the Hands of Time doing an overview, study, and interrogation of Walter Forbes, Captain Timekeeper, Quadrant One, Parsec Eleven, Sector Five, System Four, Planet Thirty-Eight, Region Four, District Four. We'll see how this turns out on Election Day."

And just like that, it was over. The Hands all stood and made to leave while the gate to Walter's left started churning open. He hesitated only a moment before forcing his body to move and head for the exit. God Almighty, he was in pain. He'd stiffened right up standing there before the Hands, just about turned into a statue. He felt a little better once he got through the tunnel to the inner track, but it was about the same relief that Ibuprofen might give to someone who just had their leg involuntarily cut off.

"I don't suppose you're willing to tell me what the hell just happened in there?" he asked of the Day as it slowly turned the wheel to lower the gate once more.

"Everything is as exactly as the Hands and the Zero Hour have said," the Day told him.

That might have been true, he thought, but that didn't mean that they'd said absolutely everything. One hundred percent of what they said was true, but they only said three percent of what they knew. Still, there was no use trying to get the Day to talk. Easier to talk to the Buckingham Guard.

"Follow me," the Day said, apparently taking his hesitation for confusion, which Walter was okay with. The odd creature led him a short distance through the inner track to a door that led to a room not unlike every other waiting room in the Coliseum. "Go through here and find a secretary to see you out."

Can I just sit and rest here a while? he wanted to ask. Would anyone know if he did? Would there be any harm in just sitting down for five minutes, just enough to give his leg a rest at least?

No, he decided as he hobbled through the room and let himself out into the middle track. Tommen and the twins were waiting for him in the Food Court, and he'd kept them long enough already. Likely they'd already eaten and were ready to go home. He shared their sentiment.

Eventually he got a secretary to stop long enough to help him and show him a way out to the outer track. It was busy, probably everyone trying to get in their last petitions before the current petitioning session closed. The rest of the Wheel was just as busy. Whatever scare had gone on earlier, as Tommen and others had described, the fear had evidently abated in favor of last-minute election fever. There was a time, once, when officers had to wear various pins to designate their rank and abilities, make them visible at a glance. It had been an absolute nightmare during election years, as various candidates and campaigners and staff members would just swarm the officers, each one making an offer, a promise, a bribe, anything to get a vote. It was like election year paparazzi. The pins were discarded after the last election cycle because of fighting, overcrowding, and because it made the bribery too obvious.

Walter had never missed those pins, and he made his way through the Wheel unmolested.

Chapter Ten
Lunch and Politics

Wavering between tired but awake, and barely functional, Tommen slogged after the twins as they meandered through the Wheel for a short time before finally heading to the Food Court. His stomach flip-flopped between too sick to even think about food, and too hungry to be picky about anything. Sometimes he found himself leaning on one twin or another for support, and other times he could just manage a straight line. So it was that he stumbled more than walked into the Food Court.

"Food Court" was a gentle term to describe the vastness of the area which they stepped into. It was one of many such courts within the Wheel, designed to cater to any and all food and nutritional needs and preferences, from raw meat to cooked meat, plant material, rocks, waste, carrion, and more.

Humans generally found their food in the "cooked" Food Court. With exception of the middle of the court containing the universe's largest salad bar, everything that could be found in the court was cooked in some fashion. Meat, cooked well. Fruits and vegetables, cooked, roasted, grilled, fried and stir fried. Grains, baked and fried. Cheese, smoked and fried. Unless specific orders were given not to cook something, it was cooked.

So Tommen was left with the same dilemma he always faced at the Food Court: what to get. Food was not considered an industry in the Wheel; everything was provided free of charge. Tommen was able to get everything from a small thing of French fries to a full lobster dinner with a side of caviar. Typically he went with his favorite: a cheeseburger with all the fixings with a side of fries and a milkshake. Problem was, he'd had that so many times over the last few hours or days or whatever that he was tired of it. And then there was the whole psychological aspect of it in that he wasn't even sure if the last burger he'd had—the one which Rifun delivered—had been real, so he was a little skeptical about that.

"Don't fall asleep on us now," Micah said, elbowing him in the ribs. "We still have to get you home."

"Isn't there anywhere to sleep in this dump?" Tommen wondered lightly, his sense of humor moving from sensible to slapstick. "Just a quick nap."

"Trust us, Tommen," Micaiah told him. "Once you fall asleep, after all you've been through, you'll be sleeping for a while. There are no 'quick naps'."

"What about the recovery room?"

"Only that, recovery, usually from the drug they gave you. And I might hazard a guess by saying that it probably wasn't a very restful recovery, was it?"

Tommen sighed. "No."

There had been nothing restful whatsoever about lying on the floor alone, contorting in seizures for seven hours as his body tried to dispel whatever fucked up hallucinogen he'd been given.

"The good news is that it's still early in the morning back home," Micah reassured him. "On top of that, you're out of school and we're nice enough to give you the day off work. You'll need all the rest you can get."

The simple fear of how much resting they were expecting him to do was enough to kick him back upright, at least long enough to coherently order some food, a hot dog with all the fixings and a bowl of mac and cheese, complete with a tall glass of milk. One day he might order the lobster dinner; somehow he still felt guilty about getting anything he perceived as being above his social class.

The twins got easy deli sandwiches, the turkey and cheese kind that soccer moms got when they felt guilty about getting drive-thru every other day of the week with the kids. It was a small meal, hardly befitting Micaiah who looked like he needed to consume five thousand calories a day just to get through his workout, but that was just one of the side effects of Timekeeping; all the Banding and speeding up and slowing down Time, plus whatever else they could do, it messed with the body's metabolism until it basically froze. Hunger and thirst were only intermittent, aging slowed considerably—although some suffered from accelerated aging—and about the only thing that remained at least moderately normal was sex drive, but Tommen figured that was more of a guy thing than anything having to do with Time.

"You falling asleep or deep in thought?" Micah's question jerked him from his thoughts.

"No, just thinking," Tommen answered.

"Want to talk about it?"

"Why was I always led to believe that I could never talk about the review to anyone ever at all? I get out and my dad tells me that I can talk about it, but, really, just to him and you guys."

"It's a mental preparedness thing," Micaiah told him. "How prepared are you to keep that big a secret? What's it going to do to you? In all reality, Tommen, your review started the day your dad lifted that Suppression off you and you began your training. And the review never stops. No matter what you do or where you go, as long as you are a Timekeeper, or part of Time at all, you will be watched and scrutinized."

"And pursued, arrested, and charged with starting a civil war."

Micah shrugged. "You win some, you lose some."

"So I guess that means you can't tell me about the Journeyman review or any of that, right?"

"In the same way that if Cai and I ever wanted to become Captains, your dad couldn't tell us about the Captain's review. The only thing we're allowed to do is tell you the general parts of the review. An oral exam, a skill test, that sort of thing."

"There are other types of tests? Beyond the three I just did?"

"Your tests were the three types in their most general sense. Once you advance, you start having multiple skill tests but in different areas. It's not as scary as it sounds, really. Mostly it's just tedious."

"As tedious as what I just went through?"

They turned as Walter approached, food in hand. The doctors at the hospital had told him to take it easy with food; he'd been getting nutrient lines while in a coma, and his body might not react well to a sudden New York strip or a greasy hamburger or spicy foods or anything like that. Normally, Walter balked at such restrictions, but now he appeared to be obeying them, at least partway. He dutifully got himself a salad, but while it started with a bed of fluffy lettuce and cabbage and carrots, it quickly devolved into onions, peppers, cheese, egg, ham, bacon, a variety of fruits and vegetables Tommen could not identify, layered with dressing, and topped with croutons with a light dusting of herbs to finish it all off. Had he been able to sit in a huff, Tommen was fairly certain he would have. As it was, he carefully set his plate on the table before collapsing into a chair, relaxing for a minute before sitting up and starting in ravenously.

"You okay?" Micah wondered cautiously.

"What did the Hands want?" Micaiah asked boldly.

"Well," Walter began around a mouthful of food, "to make a long story short, they wanted to inform me that I have been removed from office, am only Acting Captain of District Four, and that the position is going up for a vote on Election Day."

"Wait, what?" Micah blurted.

Walter nodded gravely. "Their reasoning is that because I was already written off as dead, they wanted to ensure a minimal transition gap, so a replacement was already named. But because of my miraculous recovery, it puts them in a bind, so it's going up for a vote."

"Something's fishy about that," Micaiah said. "The Gatekeeper or the Manager are in charge of appointing Captains; the Hands should have nothing to do with this."

"Who was the replacement?" Tommen wondered.

"The replacement was never officially named." Micaiah spoke to Tommen but his gaze never left Walter. "Paul didn't want to make the announcement until after your death, but it came down to two candidates. Harold Forester, out of Connecticut. Or Leslie Swan from South Carolina."

Walter's expression grew grim and he mulled it over while reluctantly digging into his salad.

"That's a dark look, Walt. What's your theory?" Micah inquired.

"My theory is that Cassius somehow bullied or blackmailed Mi Chin and-or Paul into naming someone who was more loyal to him than Time," he answered thoughtfully. "Problem is, I couldn't tell you if one, both, or neither of those two fit that profile."

"I met Leslie once," Micah offered. "When I took a vacation to Myrtle Beach a few years ago."

"I've met both of them. I trained both of them when they wanted to be Lieutenants."

"So why don't you know if they could be loyal to Cassius?" Tommen asked.

"Because psychopath sympathizers don't just appear overnight. Just like homegrown terrorists, it starts out small, and it usually stays hidden until the last minute. How many terror attacks happen and all the friends, family, neighbors say, 'Oh, he was just a normal guy, we really liked him, our kids played together' and stuff like that?

"On the one hand, Leslie is a raving liberal feminist; you can find her at every protest and rally, and she's been arrested several times. As a more conservative guy, I would point to her. But on that same token, of course I would point to her as Cassius' supporter because I already disagree with her and butt heads with her on just about everything else. Does that make her the culprit or the scapegoat? As a Timekeeper, she's exemplary. Extremely talented, a good mentor to two Apprentices, and she is very good at catching Runners.

"On the other hand, Harold is your average guy, works forty, steady job, goes out to the bar on a Friday night, coaches little league. However, he's also had four Apprentices turn Runner, which is obscene for any Master, and I seriously considered denying him advancement. But his current pupil is almost ready to make Master, so it really might have been a string of bad luck.

"It could be either, could be both, could be neither," Walter concluded. "I don't know."

"What happens if you don't win the election?" Micaiah asked.

"Then I simply go back to being a Captain-trained Master, or so they tell me. I haven't decided how far I believe that; Cassius was the Zero Hour, of that much I am certain."

"So, you lose the vote, Cassius gets a loyal Captain installed in District Four, what does that mean for the rest of us?" Micah wondered.

"It means he has the power to appoint his own Lieutenants, for one," Micaiah reminded him. "So we could all be out of the job."

"Which means we lose all political access to the Wheel and the Hands," Walter concluded. "Short of becoming fabulously wealthy and buying our way into the elections."

"Except we already squandered everything in trying to catch Cassius and Rifun in the first place, plus trying to get help for you. Not to mention that whole bit about the elections being over for another eleven-slash-seventeen years."

"And that leaves us dead in the water," Micah added. "We have to assume that Cassius is going to become Zero Hour, whether by popular vote or by eliminating the competition until there are no other contenders."

"Where does Rifun fit into all of this?" Tommen interrupted. "I mean, he's not a Hand. He's not particularly interested in politics."

"Neither is Cassius," his dad pointed out. "But I find it hard to believe that they would go to all the trouble of making themselves kings and be content to leave the system the way it is. As for what Rifun's exact role is, I can't say for sure."

"I'm not even sure who's actually in charge, between those two," Micah said. "They both seem to be in charge and yet submissive to the orders of the other."

Tommen thought back to his various encounters with one or both of them. Cassius hadn't even been present at the warehouse, leaving Rifun free to do whatever he wanted. And yet, Rifun had made some comment about Cassius complaining that he spent too much time on playing games with them so he had to wrap things up quickly. But on the other hand, Rifun had also said something about just using Cassius until he was no longer useful. All signs pointed to Rifun being the dominant one in the relationship.

Cassius was the front, the scapegoat, as Walter had alluded to Leslie. Cassius was brutal and violent and everyone feared him because his treachery was obvious. But Rifun worked behind the scenes, a nice guy by day, coming off as intelligent and polite, and yet turning out evil little minions by night as he worked behind Cassius' back. His work appeared, for now, to benefit both of them, and yet all the little minions remained loyal to Rifun who could order them to turn on Cassius at a moment's notice, topple him and crown Rifun king as it were.

A rock lodged itself in Tommen's stomach as he suddenly realized the implications of this revelation.

"At any rate, we should prepare for the worst," Micaiah was saying. "Cassius becomes Zero Hour, probably rigs the election to get rid of you, installs a new loyal Captain who appoints equally loyal Lieutenants, leaving us high and dry. What do we do then?"

"We go back to our day jobs," Micah said. "Heads down, work quietly, turn in Runners like normal."

"You really think Cassius would let us get away with that?"

"It's not about Cassius," Tommen said quietly. "He's only the front. This is Rifun's game."

His dad shifted in his seat. "How do you figure?"

Tommen briefly explained his theory.

"That is a very plausible theory, Tommen," Micaiah acknowledged, "but then it just changes the name. You think Rifun would let us get away with that?"

A pile of rocks twisted in Tommen's gut as he swallowed nervously, half-wishing he would suddenly pass out, half-hoping he wouldn't suddenly burst into flames from Rifun's spooky abilities. "I think he would try blackmail."

"He's not taking you again," his dad stated firmly.

"Not against you, Dad." He took a shaky breath. "Against me."

Micaiah fixed him in a stare as he shifted positions. "What are you talking about?"

"He made me promise not to tell under threat of death, but...I can't not tell."

"Tell what?" Walter coaxed.

Tommen hesitated, then figured there was nothing worse that could happen to him. "When Rifun held me captive, he and his goons kept calling me an Akari-bearer. Which, whatever, but you know that. When I came back from my trip with Sifura, I told you how I had to hide out for a while in the Archives, and how I was pursued by the Grandfathers, right?" He continued as his audience nodded stiffly. "Well, when I got back, just before I could leave the house, Rifun stopped me."

"Rifun was in our house?" Micah blurted.

"Yeah, he was. Like I said, he made me promise not to tell, but...Anyway, I thought he was going to kill me or take the antidote, but he told me to go ahead and give it to you." He looked at his dad. "He said it would be the last thing I ever did as a Timekeeper because the Hands were out for my blood. They were going to charge me with inciting violence and war, and, assuming I survived that, they were going to intentionally fail me on my review just to get my clock broken. I wasn't sure what to believe except that between him and Cassius, it was probably true one way or another.

"But then he started again into the Akari and whatnot, said that as an Akari-bearer, he couldn't just waste me in such a way, especially since I was only a probationary. So he decided to cut me a deal."

"What kind of deal?" his dad demanded.

"He would call off the Grandfathers, call off the Hands, and he would ensure that I passed my review. In exchange, some time after my review and the elections and whatnot, he would call on me and he was going to start training me to, I don't know, use the Akari and whatever other mysticism bullsh-crap he went off spouting about. He said that if I didn't obey him, he would kill me, and I wouldn't doubt it if he threatened you guys, too."

For a minute or two, the twins and his dad just stared at him as if he'd grown another head or something. It was Micaiah who spoke first, looking at Walter.

"So it really was always about Tommen. Rifun uses Tommen's review as blackmail, picks up the whole civil war bit as an added bonus, gets him in the door. He gets you deposed as Captain and us as Lieutenants rendering us politically isolated, and he's able to threaten us to blackmail Tommen to get him into his cult."

"Tommen, did Rifun mention Cassius at all when he visited you?" Walter asked.

Tommen shook his head. "Not that time."

"But...?" Micah prompted.

He sighed. "I don't know if it was real or part of my hallucination because it started in the waiting room."

"The hallucinations can't hurt you, but they can be revealing," Micaiah told him. "No harm in telling us."

Tommen had his doubts, but he nodded anyway. "In the waiting room, Rifun brought me my food. He told me, well, the Bat told me, but that's not the point, that my dad had been taken out for medical treatment and would be back once the third part of my review had been complete. But Rifun sat down for a friendly chat anyway. He said he was concerned for the welfare of his students and made a point of checking in on them periodically.

"He also took care to remind me of our bargain and told me that as long as Cassius was in power, I was safe from prosecution by the Hands and the Grandfathers. But if I tried to go behind his back or if Cassius were suddenly removed from power, then, I believe his exact words were, 'Daddy can't protect you from everything, and he can only die once to save you.' "

Walter and the twins glanced uneasily at each other. Again, it was Micaiah who spoke first.

"When you say he reminded you of the bargain, what did he say?"

Tommen shook his head as his heart began pounding. "It wasn't what he said; it's what he did. I don't know how, but when we were talking in the living room, it's like...he drowned me. I can't describe it except that my lungs suddenly filled with water or fluid and I couldn't breathe. I was...drowning. Then he said that he wasn't all bad and that he was going to give me a gift. It took a while, but I realized that he corrected my vision and I could see color, full color. I saw red and green and everything. It's gone now, but...I just..." He shrugged. "And then, in the waiting room, he said he didn't like my insolence, and he was going to have to instill some discipline in me. So he took away my hearing, like, completely took it away, even with the hearing aids. It was just gone. And then it was back. Like I said, I'm not sure about the stuff in the waiting room, if it was real or not, but it was still freaky."

"How did he do these things?" his dad inquired.

"I don't know! I wish I did because then I could correct my vision on my own."

"Have you had any other contact with Rifun?" Micah asked. "Any at all? Signs, warnings, messages, any of that?"

"No." Tommen shook his head. "I mean, the waiting room was the last. After that, I was with my dad in recovery, and then in the Seat getting my promotion—" He scoffed and looked away, disgusted by the thought now. "—and then I was with you two the whole time. He said that the call wouldn't come until after the elections."

"What difference does that make, I wonder?"

"Means they're still afraid to lose," Walter told them. "This isn't a slow take-over, this is an Election Day coup. It's not just about getting Cassius in power, but Captain, Managers, Gatekeepers, all their loyal lackeys in power, and not just on Earth, but across the universe, enough to back them up and create a small, impenetrable force with which they can defend their power."

"Why worry about little old Earth, though?" Tommen wondered.

"You mean you already forgot that you tried to start a civil war?" Micaiah's words were joking but his tone, less so, making the overall effect of the statement difficult to judge. "Let me put it this way, without Cassius, the Hands can prosecute you for civil war and break your clock as a Runner. Without Rifun, Cassius can have you prosecuted for civil war and break your clock as a Runner. Oddly enough, it's the same crime but with different motivations for prosecution."

"So at this point, the only thing standing between me and prosecution is Rifun."

"Yes, basically."

Tommen wasn't sure how he felt about that, actually. Somehow, it all came back to him depending on Rifun to keep him out of harm's way, when Rifun was the one who put him in harm's way to begin with. In all reality, it sounded like the beginnings of Stockholm Syndrome. Maybe, if Rifun and Cassius and their goons had been better captors, those roots would have already taken hold before he could realize it enough to fight back, like Borelian poison side effects. Now that he was beginning to see their ploy, the side effects no longer held sway over him. The only thing that could harm him now was full contact.

"So now that we know about it, what do we do about it?" Micaiah asked.

Walter was silent for a moment as he brooded over the situation, his face a grim mask. Finally he nodded as if coming to a decision. "Nothing."

"Nothing?" Micah wondered. "Walt, I don't know about you, but I don't feel comfortable with turning Tommen over to a psychopath."

"And you think I do?!" Both twins snapped their mouths shut, stunned at Walter's rare display of anger. "Rifun no longer holds my son captive, and yet he holds him at gunpoint still; do you think I somehow forgot that in the middle of the conversation? Because I haven't. And I don't intend on sacrificing anyone to this psychopath's religious idiocy a second time. So we're going to do a little gentler method of hostage negotiation. For now, we know nothing, or we act like it.

"If we plan for the worst-case scenario, Cassius becomes the Zero Hour, and he gets all his loyal lackeys wherever they need to be, which leaves the three of us out of the job and, as you said, politically isolated. But we won't be isolated because Tommen will be close to Rifun. I imagine he's going to take a greater interest in you than he already has."

"Walt, are you talking, like, infiltration?" Micah asked. "Is that a good idea?"

"We have to do something. But at the same time, I won't do it if Tommen doesn't want to." He looked at Tommen whose stomach was worn out from doing backflips but continued to do so anyway. "It's a dangerous thing, like going undercover except you have no experience, no training, very little backup, and you'll be forced to do things you don't want to do, plus you will always be under the gun, especially if Rifun catches you reporting to us. I won't order you to do it, but—"

"I'll do it," Tommen told him. "I'm tired of being under this guy's thumb."

His dad nodded once. "Good man."

"So what's our plan of action?" Micah wondered.

"As I said—" Walter shifted position in his chair. "—nothing. Not until after the elections and, probably, once Rifun contacts Tommen again with whatever arrangements they need to make. Plans are wonderful things, but we can't plan for something this ambiguous or dangerous without a little more information."

Micaiah grunted. "I just hope we don't fall into reactive plans versus proactive plans."

"I know. I understand. I don't like it either, but this is what I have so this is what I work with."

"I have a question," Tommen interrupted.

"What's that?" His dad sounded worn out. Looked it, too.

"Won't this get back to Cassius and Rifun anyway?"

His dad nodded. "It will. And in a way, I'm sort of banking on it." He went on before any of them could ask further questions. "In the meantime, maybe we ought to discuss normal things, like your new Apprenticeship. Rigged or not, you're an Apprentice now."

"Um, okay." It felt strange to just jump from world-ending conspiracy theories and plots and schemes to, essentially, the start of a new job or the new school year or something that now seemed so trivial. Like when he was running around the desert and the jungle with Sifura; all that mattered was saving his dad, and suddenly he was going to be back at school pretending to care about all the vacations his classmates went on, the presents they got, the petty family arguments that happened, and so on and so forth. It just seemed...meaningless.

"As an Apprentice, you'll be training in the Arena, that way it's a little safer, more controlled environment, or as much as it can be," his dad began. "You don't have to worry about scheduling times; I have to be the one to essentially reserve one of the actual grounds in the Arena. However, if you want extra practice or if you happen to be here with either Micah or Micaiah, sometimes you can catch an arena open between official reservations. Obviously, you have to be out when the official reservation comes in, but it's basically some free practice time."

"How long are the reservations for?"

"Forty Base minutes, but believe me, you'll be spending plenty of time in there with the Banding."

"Is there any more fighting or is it just Banding?" Tommen's mind flitted to his battle with the Bat and how woefully unprepared he'd been.

"The Arena is used for any and all aspects of your Apprentice training," Micah told him. "That means everything from Banding to formal knowledge instruction to fighting. Not that Walter won't teach you stuff outside of the Arena, but there really are no guarantees of what you'll learn and when."

"So you don't choose what I learn in any given session in the Arena?" Tommen looked at his dad.

"I do, in the same way that your teachers at school decide what to teach in class. What you need to know is all laid out; how you get there is more or less up to them."

"Oh."

"Which also means that we'll be spending some time in the Archives as well."

"Great."

Because that's where he really wanted to be, stuck in an infinite library for hours on end, knowing that no matter how much time he spent there, everything would be exactly the way he left it once he got home. It was halfway between reassuring and horrifying. That was the awesome thing about being home and living just in Base Time; everything came to an end eventually. English was dull and difficult, but the class always ended eventually, always right on time. Sitting in the Archives was going to be like the Eternal English Class from Hell. At least he wasn't going to have Satan, er, Mrs. Righting, as a teacher.

"What am I going to be learning? Banding, I mean?" Tommen asked.

"You've already learned a few things, or so I hear," his dad replied, giving him a look that he chose to interpret as pride.

"External Banding, Pinpoint Banding, protecting your Bands, and we'll touch on passing off, even though you won't really get to that until you're a Journeyman. Otherwise, we'll work on refining your Bands, reflexive Banding, the properties of a Band and how to manipulate them."

"Sounds like a lot."

"It is," Micaiah told him. "You're going to put in more time at the Arena over the next two years than you will in four years of full-time college. That much I can promise you. And you'll learn more than what he just listed, but those are the big things."

Tommen wasn't sure if his statement was meant to be a warning, a caution, some sort of inside joke where he was laughing hysterically on the inside, or what. He almost wanted to ask about the rigors of Journeyman training, if he was going to be getting his Masters in Time, and by the time he reached Master Timekeeper, he would be getting his PhD. List that on a resume: Employment, Master Timekeeper at the Wheel of Time; Education, PhD in Time Sciences at the Arena, School of Time. Ha!

"So what about, like, Predict or whatever it is? I get what it is, but so far it seems like it comes and goes on its own."

His dad nodded as he finished his food. "That will get refined as well, as will all of the, I call them 'residual abilities' that you pick up along the way."

"Residual abilities?"

"Things that just come with the normal Banding abilities," Micah explained. "Like if you're training really hard to run a marathon, that's your focus, but you might also find that you can also, I don't know, ride a bike better and farther. Both are good, they get you from A to B and are good exercise, but improvement in one just kind of happened because of your strength in the other."

Tommen wondered if having poor ability to make up decent analogies on the spot was inherited or contagious. At the least it was understandable, but it sounded more like something he himself would say.

"Another good thing," his dad went on, "is that Micaiah was telling me that a Journeyman is going to be passing through our area soon. So we'll be able to catch them and maybe pick their brains a bit as far as your training goes."

"That sounds good." He paused. "So does that mean that I'm going to be getting up at one or two or three in the morning to go and train in the Arena or go to the Archives or whatever? Banding or not, that's going to screw up my sleep schedule."

His dad nodded in understanding. "I know. And I'll try to make arrangements so you can train or do research around bedtime. That way, whenever you get tired, we can just go home and go to bed without having to worry too much about other things we have to do. I make no guarantees, and there will be some early mornings or late nights, but that's what I'm going to try for."

That sounded nice, to just be able to go home and go to bed when he got tired. For one, it sure as hell beat getting up at three in the morning and splitting his time asleep. Secondly, it would cut down on the nights he laid awake in bed because his Circadian rhythm was screwed up or he had general insomnia for one reason or another.

Of course, speaking of being tired and going home and going to bed, he was done. The adrenaline had worn off, and the food had gone from a good way to pep him up a bit to, "Oh, wow, that was some good food, and you're not running for your life anymore, and this is a comfy chair. Time for a little siesta for, say, four or five days?" He broke into a yawn.

"Hey now, don't go doing that," Micah said even as he also yawned.

Pretty soon, all four of them were yawning. Other than the sheer contagiousness of yawns, Tommen wasn't sure why the others should be yawning; it wasn't as if they'd just had dozens of Bands ripped apart, followed by having to fight the Bat, and then ending with the most terrifying hallucination anyone's ever seen. Oh, and then there was that bit about having seizures for seven hours.

Tommen yawned again; he was completely spent.

"I think we ought to get you home before you pass out on us," Micaiah said, standing. "Portals aren't fun, but they're even less fun if you try to go through them unconscious."

Any other day, Tommen might have prodded him with questions, wondering what he meant, asking what happened, and coming up with all sorts of ideas in his own mind. But he was too tired for that now; he couldn't even summon up enough fear of what might happen by going through the portal unconscious to motivate him to anything more than a slow, clumsy stand, yawning again and rubbing his eyes.

"Micah, you stay with Tommen," Micaiah ordered. "You okay, Walt?"

Tommen looked up as his dad didn't appear to be in much better shape, physically anyway. His expression was frustrated, eyes determined, but his body was stiff and awkward as he forced it to move. He allowed Micaiah to help him to stand but quickly shrugged him off afterwards.

"I'm only injured; I'm not helpless," he said grouchily, grabbing his cane and forcing himself to walk and maneuver his way out of the chairs.

They were probably quite a pitiful sight as they left the Food Court. Tommen managed to keep his head up and one foot in front of the other at least until they got out of the Food Court. He might have fared better if they were keeping up a fair pace, but with his dad slowing them all down, his body was falling deeper and deeper into exhaustion with each plodding step. By the time they made it to the marketplace hub, he was all but sleeping on Micah's shoulder. Micaiah's stern voice broke him from his drowsy passiveness.

"Micah, get him to the portal room and get him home before he passes out. We'll be along."

The younger twin nodded and walked faster, grabbing Tommen's arm and almost dragging him along. The faster pace kept his mind awake a little better, but there was no adrenaline left to keep his body going, at least not in any sense of the word "coordinated." He bumped into people and things and once ran straight into Micah who'd stopped short.

"You still awake?" Micah asked as they started moving again.

"Just barely," Tommen admitted. "Do all reviews end like this?"

"You'll be okay for your Journeyman review. Master review isn't as bad as Apprentice, but worse than Journeyman. Officer reviews are pretty much where everything goes straight to hell."

So, note to self, never become an officer. Got it.

"Am I just really this exhausted or is this some side effect of whatever drug they gave me?" Tommen wondered as they crossed the threshold into the portal room.

"Well, I'm no chemist and I wouldn't know where to begin to officially answer it, but I'm pretty sure you are just that exhausted. But like your dad said, it's the middle of the night, you don't have school or work tomorrow. You'll sleep for a day or two, and then you'll be fine."

"A day or two?"

The twin shrugged. "Nothing wrong with that. Except for the circumstances of why you're going to be sleeping that long, I'm a little jealous. Here we are."

Micah steered him to the translator dispenser. Tommen fumbled with the hearing aid and disconnected the translator, momentarily thrown off by the change in hearing balance when he removed the hearing aid. Fuck, he still wasn't used to it. He'd gotten used to having shitty hearing, then apparently today gotten used to having the hearing aids in and having normal, balanced hearing. He shook his head and returned the translator. He was tired, he wanted to go home and get some sleep, stop his mind from racing. If he was this exhausted, the last thing he needed was to pass into excitable delirium where he not only still couldn't sleep, but he was going to go insane because of it.

He followed Micah down a row of portals. They moved

slightly slower so Tommen didn't accidentally stumble into some other alien world. Had he not been following Micah, he might have walked right past the portal to home. As expected, nothing had changed; the little living room lamp was on, casting an orange glow over everything, just enough light to see by.

"Are you sure it's safe?" Tommen wondered.

"Safer now than if you suddenly pass out," Micah told him. "Go get some sleep."

Tommen yawned again and rubbed his eyes once more before finally stepping through the portal. There was the momentary vacuum feeling followed by the feel and smell of old shag carpet, its thickness probably the only thing that saved him from knocking himself out on wood or tile. To say nothing of the way his body rejoiced at the feel of something relatively soft beneath him and instantly went into shutdown mode.

But Tommen got his hands and knees under him, crawling away from the portal and making it as far as the couch before turning and sitting down, watching as his dad and the twins came through the portal after him.

"How you feeling, Walt?" Micah asked.

"I'm fine," Walter replied, stiffly limping over to his recliner.

"That might be a dangerous thing. Why don't you head to bed, too? We'll get going home."

"Tommen?" Tommen's eyes flew open as Micaiah knelt in front of him. Had he fallen asleep? How much time had passed? "You okay?"

"Huh? Yeah? I mean, this is just as far as I made it before you guys came through."

"Okay. How about you head off to bed? Can you walk or do you need me to carry you?"

There was a certain appeal at being carried to bed simply because he was exhausted, and there was still that little boy in him who remembered his ma and pa carrying him to bed when he fell asleep at their feet at night. He knew his dad had carried him to bed a time or two. It was nice; it made him feel safe.

But then there was the matter of his pride. He'd just gotten his promotion to Apprentice. He was going to be learning some real tricks of the trade now. He'd endured potentially life-threatening hallucinogens for the amusement of a corrupt government in order to get promoted. The last thing he needed was to be seen as a needy little boy who had to be carried to bed because he was a little tired and couldn't make the last twenty feet from the living room to his bed.

So it was probably that grouchy determination—something that apparently ran in the family—that made Tommen wave off Micaiah and drunkenly get to his feet, or attempt to. Between the couch and Micaiah's strong arms, he eventually got to his feet. Before he could get too far, his dad called to him.

"Tommen."

Grudgingly, he turned. He just wanted to get to sleep. But his dad was standing now. And though he was still wrapped up in splints and bandages and whatever else, his expression was solid as he said, "I'm proud of you. I know what you had to do was hard, and I know you did it alone, but I'm proud of you for doing it anyway."

Tommen managed a tired smile, stifling a yawn. "Thanks, Dad."

He started toward his bedroom, but not very quickly, putting one hand on either wall of the hallway as he made his way. Behind him, he heard his dad announce that he, too, was going to bed, and the twins were going home.

It was done. His review was finally and truly, officially over with. They'd even made it out of the Wheel alive. More than that, his dad was proud of him for going through with it, enduring the horrors that came with the review. He was an Apprentice now, a real Timekeeper, not just a probationary we'll-see-how-it-goes. He was going to get into some real training, more than just constructing Fast and Slow Bands. And somewhere in there, he was going to get out from under Rifun's thumb. Yes, things seemed to be looking up. He was somebody. He was going places and doing things. He was...he was...well, he was going to bed.

    And so he did.

Chapter Eleven
Stoop Talk

Sometimes it felt silly, sleeping with a night light like a fearful child, and yet, on the occasions when Walter sought to break himself of the need, he found that he was, truly, still a fearful child. The shadows created by the night light, those he could handle. The shadows created by the moonlight outside, those terrified him. The noises he heard when the night light was on, those he could identify readily. The noises he heard in the darkness, those he couldn't identify without wondering if he was going insane. Crackling sound? With the night light, it was just the furnace air rustling against the plastic bag in his little trash can. Without the night light, it was the scuffling of a prisoner's feet as a couple of guards hauled someone off, never to be seen or heard from again.

Having witnessed his son's terrifying hallucination, Walter was fairly certain that he would never again be able to even attempt breaking his night light habit. Even with the night light on, he found himself afraid.

The first night after getting home, he'd fallen asleep out of sheer exhaustion. He'd pretty much had all of Thursday to himself while Tommen slept like a brick, not that he'd had tons of plans and things he needed to do that he was able to do. He was almost as bedridden as his kid. Still, he'd tried to be as active as he could, making food for himself, cleaning a kitchen that hadn't been used in at least a week and so didn't need to be cleaned, that sort of thing. He couldn't shovel snow, not that he would want to since there was supposed to be a huge storm rolling in.

So he tried to pass off his insomnia as simply not having done enough during the day to make him tired, and not a recurring fear of the dark compounded by his son's hallucination and other assorted predicaments. The problem was, he knew he was lying to himself, so he still lay awake there in the dark with the night light casting shadows around the room.

Eventually, he gave in and sat up, getting his legs over the edge of the bed, gritting his teeth at the throbbing. It wasn't as bad as it had been in the Wheel, but still very noticeable. He glanced at the script bottles sitting on his nightstand, considering them for a moment before shaking his head as if reassuring himself. He'd get up, take a look around, and go back to bed. Pills would only be taken if he couldn't get back to sleep for the pain.

His first stop was the bathroom, foolishly hoping his insomnia could be cured by one cup of water going in and another going out. Instead, it seemed to have the opposite effect, his body apparently taking the actions as signs to get up and get ready for the day. He sighed and rubbed his eyes. Damn police training. Well, might as well take a look around.

His next stop was his son's room. Tommen normally kept the door cracked. Walter pushed it open a smidge, just enough that the residual light from the night light in his bedroom as well as the one in the bathroom (for reasons more practical than emotional) could give him a look inside without disturbing the sleeping teenager. The teenager with whom he'd fought a hundred small battles, from the girls he dated, to the car he wanted, to going to school and college and work. The teenager who had gone halfway across the universe, risking everything to save him.

The teenager who was now missing from his bed.

Fear immediately clamped down on Walter's throat. Tommen had talked about Rifun, and Rifun found out. Now he'd taken Tommen, and he probably wouldn't be so merciful as last time. And last time hadn't been merciful.

Walter took a calming breath, took a step back, and turned around. Looking at the empty bed would only make him emotional.

He had to look away and think logically.

As he did, he saw another light on, shining at the end of the hallway. Normally, Walter would have gone into full police mode. While his mind went there instantly and he considered going back to get his gun, he knew it would make no difference, not to Rifun. He was going to have to rethink his strategy there, otherwise he was just wasting bullets and potentially getting himself killed again. Although, if this really was just a common thief, guns were a very persuasive deterrent, whether or not he himself was all but crippled at this point.

But then, how likely was it that this was a common thief?

Still, he headed toward the light, keeping his steps as light as possible and keeping an ear out for anything out of the ordinary. Even before he made it to the end of the hall, he knew that the light that was turned on was the light over the oven, something that gave good light to the kitchen without lighting up the living room and half the hall as well, like the main kitchen light or the one over the sink. Other than that, he didn't see any other red flags or hear anything unusual.

Stepping out into the living room, he saw that both it and the kitchen were empty. Maybe it was the cop in him, but he would have even taken signs of a fight over the way everything looked absolutely pristine. At least then he would have something to go on, a crime scene to investigate. Here, there was nothing.

Well, maybe not quite. As he approached the kitchen, he saw signs of some use. The coffee maker was on, but instead of coffee grounds, there were hot chocolate packets in the trash and powder on the counter. So, someone had been here and made hot chocolate. Did he dare hope it was Tommen? Heading out to the breezeway—from a time when houses had breezeways—Walter also saw that a pair of shoes, a coat, and some assorted winter accessories were missing from the overstuffed coat rack.

By now, most of his fear had abated, and he approached the front door with curiosity more than fearful anxiety. Peeking through the window on the door, he saw his son sitting there on the front step, glowing yellow in the porch light, bundled up as if it was the middle of winter, hot chocolate in hand.

Walter opened the door.

"Tommen?" He turned. "What are you doing out here?"

Tommen shrugged. "I couldn't sleep anymore."

Walter stepped through the door and closed it behind him. "That's fine and dandy for making hot chocolate, but what are you doing out here?"

"I don't know. Just glad to finally be home I guess. Just wanted to look around, make sure it's all real."

"Why don't you come inside? There's supposed to be a storm rolling in; I don't want to come back out in the morning and find a Tommen-sicle."

For a second, Walter was almost sure he was going to refuse, but at the last minute, Tommen nodded, got up, and followed him inside to the kitchen.

"Are you going back to bed?" Tommen wondered, stopping in the door to the breezeway, not even bothering with his winter gear as he stared after Walter.

"Where else would I be going?" Walter inquired.

Tommen shrugged. "I don't know. I guess I thought...I don't know."

Walter turned, one hand on his cane, the other on the counter. "What's wrong?"

"I guess I thought that we could talk." Walter knew where this was going. "Neither of us can sleep, and you promised we would."

Well, damn. He had promised that, hadn't he? Not that he wanted to break his promise or keep the truth from his son-slash-nephew, but did it really have to come now? At—he glanced at the clock—four in the morning?

"Now?" was the best he could come up with.

"Why not?" Tommen started taking off his winter clothes and sat down in one of the chairs at the tiny kitchen table that, had there been food involved, was normally only big enough for one person.

Walter sat down, hoping he could disguise his reluctance as pain from his aching leg and shoulders. He'd read about this moment, and he'd heard about it numerous times from fellow officers, other parents at school, even once from a psychologist or psychiatrist or whatever in a court case. That moment when your adopted child wants to know who they are and where they come from, when they want to learn about their family and all the reasons from Way Back When.

Except, in most cases, it was the parents talking about the child. He'd never heard of a case where it was the child talking about the parent. Sure, there were other aspects of it, Tommen learning more about his pa, but this was largely about Walter. He wasn't sure how he felt about this.

"What do you want to know?" Walter asked diplomatically.

"Everything," was Tommen's unsurprising reply. "Who was my pa? Who are you? How did we get here? I mean, it's like something out of a movie, like a slightly skewed Darth Vader kind of moment."

The boy meant well, but English was never his strong suit, and his analogies were never really up to snuff.

"Well..." Walter let out a breath. "Where do I start?"

"You're my pa's older brother," Tommen stated. "I don't remember that he ever mentioned you."

"And I don't blame him. Your first child is supposed to be your pride and joy, spoiled rotten and the envy of all their siblings. But I think that once my—our parents figured out what I was becoming, they wrote me off and started having more kids just so they could disown me.

"No one could ever explain why I was such an angry, violent child. Everyone's heard of the Terrible Two's, but I never seemed to grow out of that. Instead, I just got bigger, angrier, more out of control." Walter took a breath. "There was a sister between me and your pa. Most delicate little thing you've ever seen, but I took it as weakness, and I exploited it. I didn't just tease her, I mocked her publicly. I didn't just pull her pigtails, but I would literally beat my own sister until she was black and blue.

"When your pa came along, our parents did everything they could to keep us apart. They didn't want me beating up on him, but more importantly, they didn't want him turning out like me. But that was no matter, because any chance I got to be away from home, I took it. It didn't matter what I was doing, just going out and exploring, abusing our animals or neighbor animals, or sneaking off into town to join the local street urchin gang, I wanted to be as far away from home as I could. And not a few times the constables would drag me home to my parents and tell them of my latest exploits, usually fighting or stealing. My pa would switch me, and ma would pray for me and beg the church to help, but I didn't care one bit of it. My stripes healed, toughened, until I couldn't feel them anymore, and I laughed at God and how He'd failed to cure me of my insanity. I spent time in jail.

"Thankfully, your pa was the son our parents could be proud of. He was kind and gentle, hard-working and honest. He ran the farm when our pa started getting old, and he protected our ma and sisters whenever I came stumbling home. We fought more than once. I usually won, and I probably could have beaten him more if I didn't get bored of it or otherwise pass out.

"I'm sorry to say I missed your ma and pa's wedding. I was sitting in jail for fighting and public intoxication—again. When I got out and learned that I'd drunk my way through my own brother's wedding, I suppose I had something of a time of sobriety. I left home for a time, went wandering, did some menial work for a bowl of soup or a bed to sleep in. Pitiful, really.

"During my travels, I met a girl. British girl, woman, her name was Paige. Beautiful woman, kind-hearted and loving like my ma, but with a certain spirit that intrigued me. Not in the Hollywood sense that she was a modern woman living in a old-fashioned age, but she had spirit. If you could have met her, you'd understand.

"Her father was a banker in London, hated my guts because I was a country boy. Not only that, but I was an idiot because I didn't know the first thing about farming. Somehow, she convinced him to take me as a sort of banking apprentice, turn a stupid country boy from Wales into a proper British banker."

"That was how you lost your accent," Tommen stated.

Walter shrugged, wincing. "I suppose. At any rate, he apparently learned to like me enough to let me marry his daughter. He didn't want us to leave London, obviously, but I wanted to take my new bride and return home and show my family that I had made something of myself, that I wasn't just the drunkard anymore."

Now he paused, trying to remind himself that it was all in the past and he was only a storyteller. "When I got home, my parents were a little more than skeptical. Thankfully, they seemed to see that I had made something of myself, and they kept stories of my shenanigans to a minimum around Paige so as not to frighten her." He chuckled sadly. "Paige liked my parents well enough, but she would never see them as more than dumb country folk, Welsh folk at that. She was proud of my accomplishments, but sometimes I wondered if she questioned me and whether I would ever be more than a poor Welshman with nice clothes.

"I also learned that my brother, your pa, had left with his wife and young son for America. Land of opportunity, fields of gold and mountains of silver, they were going to settle down and have their happily ever after. I was happy for them, of course, but part of me was also sad that I couldn't see him to show him what I'd done and how I'd changed.

"We returned to London where her father bought us a nice house very close to where he lived. He told me that we would never be business partners, but as long as I was married to his daughter, he was obligated to treat me with some measure of dignity and see that his daughter was well-cared-for. As if I couldn't do that myself, or so I thought.

"About a year after we were married, Paige announced she was pregnant. Normally, that's supposed to be accompanied by congratulations and parties and all sorts of women things that they just kind of shoo the men out of the room and talk and scheme and giggle secretively. There was some of that, but there was a lot of talk about the 'poor child's pedigree' and whether it would be acceptable simply to pass it off as the grandchild of the valiant Mr. Balk. Or maybe they could say it was Paige's child and leave me out of it. Yes, I was a modestly successful banker, but I was still just a Welshman.

"Well, that miffed me quite a bit and so when the men retired to celebrate with cigars—because rich people celebrate twice and then some—I drank a little more than I should have. I don't know what happened, only that I got on Balk's watch list even more after that. The only thing that I cared about at that point was that I didn't land in jail. And I told myself that I did my celebrating, maybe a little too hard, but now I had to focus on my wife and child.

"I did the best I could, lavishing on Paige the way I'd seen other gentlemen do, but it wasn't always the best for our finances. Paige's father got us out of a few tight spots, and while he was constantly remarking about the idiot Welshman who couldn't count his fingers and toes, I noticed that Paige seemed to side with him more and more, as if she regretted marrying me, as if she didn't want to be 'stuck' with a Welshman forever. I once overheard a conversation where her mother made the comment about that's what she got for marrying for love and not power and influence.

"Well, it was a girl. Victoria was her name, a proper British name for a proper British girl from a proper British family. I was barely acknowledged except to keep Victoria from being considered an illegitimate child and shame Paige. But I figured that if by me stepping back and being scorned that my daughter would have a chance at marrying well and living a better life than I could ever hope for, I would do so.

"That resolve only lasted about two weeks, once the awe and admiration died down and real life set in. Princess she might have one day been, but in the moment, she was still a baby. And babies cry and poop and puke, and they don't do it on a very convenient schedule. Paige wanted to take care of her herself—about the only aspect of 'country life' that she found 'charming' but within the month, she'd hired a nanny. But it still wasn't enough, not for me, anyway. To be woken up multiple times a night. For many parents, it's exhausting but endearing. For me, it was enraging, and that was only the start.

"Paige's father disdained me, her mother openly despised me, and even she didn't look at me the same way. She'd become her parents' child and her attitude was more like...she put up with me because her child needed a father, and I was the one she was stuck with.

"So I turned back to drinking. I stayed away from home as often as I could for as long as I could. Every opportunity to leave, I took it. And when I came home, I got violent. At first, it was just breaking things, stuff—lamps, tables, chairs, that sort of thing. The worst part is, I only know this because I would wake up and see the havoc I had wreaked. And I would weep and beg for forgiveness. Paige obliged at first, but even she abandoned me eventually. So I turned on her.

"It would be easy to excuse my actions as just being drunk, but I had devolved back to a point where I didn't need to be drunk to fight. Just having an argument was enough to elicit uncontrollable rage.

"I fully expected Paige's father to come after me. Worse, I expected her mother to come after me. But neither of them ever did. Maybe it was the usual victim mentality—by admitting the problem to her parents, she was acknowledging that she'd been wrong all along. She was as much their prisoner as mine."

Walter paused long enough to look at Tommen's face, as he'd been avoiding it for the past five minutes, instead preferring to look at the window or the microwave or his own hands, wringing nervously on the table. Tommen thought he was cool and suave, but Walter knew that expression as plain as if it was written on his forehead. Horror. Shock and horror. His dad-slash-uncle was admitting to a number of felony charges, most of them stemming from life lessons which Walter himself had threatened to stripe him for.

"The day my hand turned to Victoria was the day Paige finally broke her silence," Walter said at last. "That same night, I went out drinking again, and I ended up in jail. And it wasn't just an overnight or three-day gig, but I stayed there for probably three months, if not longer. My name was well-known, a split between the son-in-law of the prominent Mr. Balk and the idiot Welsh drunkard who not only got in fights, but beat his wife and infant child beyond what was considered 'acceptable' for the time. And the guards had more than their share of fun beating me and asking how well my wife liked it.

"When I was finally released, I learned that Mr. Balk had publicly denounced me, stripped me of all titles, jobs, funds, properties, contacts, associations, possessions, everything but the clothes on my back. And if I got within a hundred yards of him, his family, any of his establishments, I was to be arrested again. On top of that, Paige had divorced me rather quickly and already remarried to another one of her father's associates, this one considered more civil and socially acceptable.

"I was left to beg on the streets of London. Thankfully, the city is large enough that I could get well away from Balk, or his central hub of activity anyway; the man was everywhere. But no matter what, I was a complete failure. I had literally been given the world, or a pretty good piece of it anyway, and I'd lost it because of my own selfish stupidity."

Walter sighed and shook his head. "Some would have us believe that just giving money to the poor and destitute is enough to get them out of their troubles, but it isn't. As long as they have underlying problems and addictions, money means nothing except as a tool to get more of it.

"So I begged for about a year, stealing food and avoiding local law enforcement—"

"Which is how you know all the tricks of the trade," Tommen interrupted smartly, grinning.

Walter managed a small smile of his own. "I guess you could say that. And I avoided Balk as much as I could, too, as much as to stave off his vengeful hand as cut myself off completely from that life. I knew that if I dwelt on it too long, it would only make me sad, then jealous, then angry, and I would do something incredibly stupid. So I went back.

"It took me a few days to figure out what had happened since I had to ask around from some ignoble sources and sift through hearsay and exaggeration. But in the end, the story remained the same: Paige's new husband had been little better than I. When he hit her and Victoria, she went to her parents again, but her parents dismissed it. Her husband was a well-respected business associate and a proper Brit, not some country ruffian. And if he felt that he had to slap her around a bit, well then she ought to learn to stay in line. She had a child now, and that was her responsibility. So it gets worse and worse and one night he goes into a rage and he kills them both. He beat her to death and strangled Victoria because she wouldn't stop crying."

He paused again, telling himself he was only the storyteller now. "I was awful to her, but in some sick sense, somewhere deep down, I still loved her. So I went after him. His money had managed to keep him out of jail for the time being, which only worked to my advantage.

"The night I killed him, I was completely sober. He was having some sort of get-together with his lawyers and his friends, and Mr. Balk of course. I don't know what they were talking about exactly; I didn't care. I murdered all of them.

"When the police found me, I was sitting outside the front door, drinking the finest brandy you've ever known because it was expensive, and revenge is sweet. They took me away with no resistance whatsoever. Originally, they were going to hang me and be done with it. The only thing I can think is that God must have intervened because they decided to send me back to my homeland 'with the rest of the filthy barbarians' and lock me away in Beaumaris Gaol.

"Some protested because at the time, Beaumaris was the

height of prisoner comfort, featuring one meal every day and time outside to see the sunshine if you were good. I didn't deserve such luxuries, not after already doing time for beating my wife and child, but then also turning around and murdering her father and a multitude of his associates. But the gavel came down, and I was shipped back to Wales.

"I don't remember a whole lot about the trip, except that it was long and grueling, especially in the middle of winter. Only about half of us made it to the gaol, not that it was much to behold. The place was enormous and even though the cells were small and dark, they weren't soundproof. And you could hear the other prisoners at night, shouting, crying, screaming when the guards beat them."

"That's why you sleep with a night light," Tommen said.

Walter sighed. "Old World prisons, when they depict them on TV or in movies, are much nicer than they actually were. Cells are small so you can barely lay out flat on the floor to sleep in straw that is old and rotten, full of urine and feces from both prisoner and rats which come at all hours to chew on your fingers and toes, your nose, your ears, any part of exposed flesh. And if your flesh is covered, they'll chew right through your pathetic garments to get to you. The cells are stone so they're merely cold in the summer and like blocks of ice in the winter. You're left alone for long periods of time just in darkness so bad you can't see your hand in front of your face. The rats come; you can hear them. You can hear the guards outside your door, the screaming of the other prisoners, and you wonder if you'll be next. Will they just beat me or will they actually kill me, you wonder. Is this food clean or did they spit in it, urinate in it, put poison in it? And if you get sick or get any kind of infection, you either see what your immune system is made of, or you die. Didn't matter if it was a simple cut or full-blown dysentery, you were all but black-listed, and it was more of a shock if you survived. I spent far too long in that hellhole. So yes, that's why I sleep with a night light."

He tried to judge Tommen's expression, a sort of mix between thoughtfulness, shock, and horror.

"I spent the first part of my imprisonment numb to the world. I looked around, and all I saw was darkness, both literally and figuratively. All my fighting and drinking had only led me into that dark prison where I was going to die. I was a shame to my parents and siblings, my wife and child and in-law family now dead, and anyone who had ever shown even the slightest bit of mercy toward me. I had nothing to show for myself except death and destruction.

"I attempted suicide twice while in prison. First I tried a hunger strike; it wasn't like the guards would care and force me to eat. Just one less meal for them to deliver once I keeled over. But hunger won out on that one; I couldn't take the noise in the darkness. The darkness does things to you, drives you insane. My stomach sounded like a roaring lion or a bear, and in my darkness-induced hunger-exacerbated delirium, I fully expected a lion or a bear to eat me. The second time, I tried to hang myself, but my pitiful garments gave way, and the worst I did was bang up my knees real good. After that, I figured I might at least get an infection and die that way.

"But as I was thinking about that, I also got an idea in my head. If I died, they would have to dispose of my body in some way; outside the cells, the guards wanted to keep clean, and having bodies around would be dirty and infectious, so they had to be taken outside the gaol.

"So I spent several months training my body to act dead, and it wasn't just about being motionless. I had to be able to not breathe fog over glass, and I couldn't let my eyes blink or react to anything. I had to shut my body down completely without actually dying.

"I made sure to give myself a good cut on the hand in order to make it seem as though I got some infection from it. On the day I was ready to try my plan and make a break for it, I simply lay down in my cell, and when meal came calling, I did not react. As long as I was alone, I breathed and blinked, but I kept my body still, enduring rat bites and hoping they didn't bleed too bad, not that I expected the guards to understand such a thing as morbid lividity.

"When the guards came back, I effectively stopped breathing

and blinking, hoping that my racing heart didn't tip them off and my body would be cool against the stone.

"Apparently, I gave them too much credit for caring to examine me any more than kicking me over and putting glass to my mouth to have me breathe on it. They simply shrugged and made some comment about the undertaker coming for me later. Time must have been a relative thing to them because it felt like days before anyone came to get me. At the very least, it was long enough for *rigor mortis* to have come and gone, and I was loaded on a little cart and taken away.

"I waited until we got outside the gaol before I made a move. I surprised the undertaker, and I don't know if I just knocked him out or he had a heart attack, but either way, he went down. His assistant ran, and so did I—in the opposite direction. Beaumaris Gaol is on an island, and it was pretty well protected, but somehow I got across to Wales proper.

"Once on land, the first house I came to, I broke in and stole a set of clothes and a knife, and I changed myself completely, shaving my mustache and beard which had grown out, and I chopped my hair short. Anyone would have been shocked to see the difference. If Mr. Balk had been alive, I don't think even he would have recognized me.

"I ended up spending too much time in one place because the law caught up to me. That was probably the one and only time where I was on the receiving end of a barricaded fugitive situation. I didn't even have any hostages, but my reputation was such that no one was brave enough to approach me.

"In the end, I managed to negotiate that I would return to Beaumaris instead of being shot on the spot. I didn't expect them to keep their promise past the first day, but it was enough to get me out of that particular situation and by nightfall I was back in chains heading for Beaumaris.

"That night, I escaped my chains and made a break for it again under the cover of darkness, this time resolving not to stop until I was truly free and clear."

"How did you escape without them knowing?" Tommen interrupted.

Walter shifted uncomfortably, not sure if he wanted to tell him that little secret. But he figured it was better for him to tell him than have Tommen go and look it up online and find something he wasn't supposed to. "I broke my thumbs. Not these bones here that is the visible thumb, but this bone and this joint here where it connects to the rest of the hand. It'll basically collapse your hand so anything you can't slip your hands through because of that joint, well, now you can. It hurts, though. God Almighty, it hurt, and I was biting my tongue until it bled to keep from crying out, but I did it.

"And I was running again. I managed to stay ahead of them, using every trick I knew with water and flowers and honey and even feces and rotting carrion. As you can probably guess, I didn't get recaptured, but there were some nights when I was sure those hounds were on my trail, and I would get up and I was on the move again.

"I never knew if they really kept up the search or if they just gave up and put out some kind of APB on me, but I kept running for a while, never returning to the same place twice, avoiding civilization as much as I could except for when I really needed to steal food or clothes or tools. Regardless of whatever Hollywood tells you, the life of a fugitive is not romantic, and sometimes there is no noble cause behind it—it's not always that the fugitive has to get out in order to save his woman or prove his innocence and help the authorities catch the real culprit. Sometimes it really is as simple as a very bad and very dangerous man escapes from prison and, as far as anyone is concerned, he needs to be recaptured."

Even as Walter spoke, he was desperately hoping that Tommen was listening and understanding the lessons in the story. *Stop the fighting, it doesn't lead anywhere. Just because you think you're cool or rich doesn't mean you're above the law. If you're going to fall in love, make sure you don't bring your demons with you. Don't expect marriage or a child to solve your problems because those things have enough problems of their own. Are you listening, Tommen?*

"At some point, I decided to go home. I had no one in the world to care for me, and as far as I knew, no one loved me. Not even God could love me. But maybe my mother still would. It took me probably two or three months to make my way back as I had traveled all over the U.K., but eventually I found the road I knew so well.

"My ma was the first one to spot me coming up the road. She didn't seem to recognize me at first, but as soon as she did, she ran. I won't lie, I broke down crying right then. There's no feeling in the world like the one you get when you realize that even your own mother is afraid of you. And by the time I got to the door, or within sight, my pa was there with the gun pointed at me.

"It was probably the longest standoff of my life, or it felt like it. Even though I hadn't been home since I'd brought Paige to meet them, word had gotten back to them of my exploits and my shame. My pa had denounced me and wanted to shoot me on sight in the name of doing the king's justice or some such thing, but my ma, bless her soul, she wouldn't let him. I was still her boy, and even if I should die for my crimes, it wouldn't be at the hands of my pa or any other family member.

"It took some talking and some doing, but eventually we got to the table for a civilized conversation." Walter sighed. "I was tired of the fighting and the drinking and the running. I wasn't going back to prison, that much I knew. Assuming they managed to take me alive, I knew I was just going to kill myself, sitting alone in the darkness, going mad. But I had nowhere to go, no one to turn to. I had no real skills to get me anywhere, and even so, Balk's family or any of his associates and sympathizers would make sure that I went back to prison as soon as my name resurfaced.

" 'America,' my ma told me. 'Follow your brother. He's made a good life for himself. No one knows you there, so you can make something of yourself, too. A new life, a fresh start, one last chance to get it right.'

"And it really would be my last chance. I could pull one prison escape, maybe two, but my luck was running out; that much I knew.

And there are only so many times that family can and will help. My ma was willing to help me out one last time. I could only pray my brother would be as merciful. If I struck out and lost that last hand of mercy, I knew I'd be done for good, one way or another.

"So my ma and pa gave me food and shelter for a week or two while they went around discreetly to all the neighbors, collecting funds to buy me a ticket to America and get all the necessary papers." Walter still found it highly suspicious how his parents knew where to go and who to talk to in order to get papers without questions being asked, but at the time he hadn't bothered to dwell on it. His parents were either helping him or secretly turning him in. "In the meantime, my pa tried to give me a crash course in some basic life skills, which, at that time, were things like basic carpentry, hunting and preparing food, tanning, basic farming from hooking up the horses to the plows to bringing it all in at harvest, and more skills I'd never even considered necessary like smithing or even sewing.

"I'd never had such an appreciation for my parents and brother as I did during those two weeks. More often than not, as a kid, I got sent to bed without supper, but they couldn't not feed me growing up, and even if they did that, I just stole what I wanted or needed with no regard as to the work it took to get it into my greedy little hands."

"Did you and your pa ever make up?" Tommen wondered quietly.

Walter sighed. "Well, we weren't on bad terms, I'll say it that way. He didn't put a bullet in my back as I walked away, and he didn't turn me in to the authorities. But the things I had done...the only way I could ever make it up to him was by truly changing my ways and making a real man out of myself. We could talk and chitchat and do all the apologies we wanted, but until I actually made good on my promise to better myself and turn myself around, we were little more than familiar strangers."

Walter would never forget the day he walked away from that old house for the last time. His pa had given him some words of advice and gone out to plow, almost entirely disinterested in the actions or whereabouts of his older son whom he'd basically disowned. It was a hard thing, to be rejected by his pa knowing it was entirely his fault. No daddy issues here where Walter tried and tried but Daddy didn't care. No, this whole thing was his own fault, the fighting and the drinking and everything else. His fault. And he lost his father long before he died. The worst part was that he couldn't even remember his pa's last piece of advice.

But his ma had seen him off. She'd mended all his clothes and even made him a new coat and pair of socks, something to take with him to America, so she could go with him, too. And she gave him a little stitched cloth, something to show his brother that their parents had sent him and he was as good as his word, which wasn't much considering he needed a cloth from his mother to prove it. It made him feel warm and sick at the same time.

"They gave me the name of the ship and the captain that my ticket was for, emphasizing to approach only that ship and speak only to him. He would get me across the ocean, but there were no guarantees about anyone else. It was probably two weeks to the port, a little dinky place that couldn't be found on any map."

"So a popular place for smugglers?" Tommen asked.

Walter sighed. "Yes. But again, it's not as romantic as Hollywood makes it out to be. The place was dark, dingy, rustic in that it was all but falling apart into the ocean. The people were a rough crowd; it was like walking into a place populated entirely of me when I was an uncaring drunk fighter."

"Why would your parents send you there? Not like nicer ports don't have smugglers."

"It was all they could rustle up for cash to buy a ticket. Five bucks to sleep with a sack of potatoes the whole way across the ocean, or fifty bucks a week to get a decent-sized cabin? Desperation is a terrible thing, especially when you have no choice but to put your life in the hands of someone who is just like you. And if you wouldn't trust yourself with your life, you're pretty desperate."

It was an awful thing to think about, not being able to trust yourself with your own life. When speaking only of yourself, it's called suicide watch. When talking about two or more people, chances are, someone is going to get killed. Walter counted himself lucky that he survived his first five minutes in that place, especially since it was next to impossible to walk half a block without seeing someone dead, dying, or sick with some deadly illness or gaping wounds.

In all reality, it was as though he'd walked into his own history, his own soul, even, looking at the darkness and the filth that was there. At the time, it had been frightening, but looking back, Walter was relieved that he'd been so frightened and repulsed by it. What mayhem would have occurred if he had, at the last minute, slipped back into his old skin and joined that crowd? What if instead of being the cargo, he became one of the smugglers? What if he'd joined a crew and engaged in a little piracy?

Walter credited his ma's stitched cloth for keeping him away from all that, a subtle reminder of the promises he'd made and the future he was trying to make for himself. As long as he kept his mouth shut, even if he had to starve the whole way across the ocean, he was going to make it. This time, he was going to do it right.

"I found the ship and the captain," Walter continued. "It would have been easy to go back to who I'd been, try to bully my way onto the ship or any number of stupid things, but I decided to just go meekly this time. It wasn't easy, and I think the captain only agreed to the arrangement out of amusement. As far as he was concerned, I was a big guy who didn't even realize it. I was no threat to him.

"I had to stay hidden for the first week or so until we were well out of range of the coastal ships patrolling the waters, looking for smugglers and pirates. I slept with the fishes, literally, dozens of barrels of salt fish and pork. I came out on deck two weeks into the voyage smelling like a can of ripe tuna fish." He smiled as Tommen grinned. "That was an awful experience in itself, but I would have taken anything, even that, over the black cells.

"Other than the first couple weeks, the voyage was remarkably forgettable. One day turns into another when the only thing you have to stare at are grouchy sailors and open ocean."

"No women allowed on ship, huh?" Tommen said, grinning.

Walter sighed and shook his head, unable to suppress a grin of his own. "No, no women."

He leaned back in his chair. Fatigue had finally found him. Probably had something to do with the sudden stress he was under, complete with racing heart, high blood pressure, and unwelcome memories. He wanted to go to bed, save chapter two for next time, but he knew there was no stopping now. His thoughts and memories were flowing, and Tommen still appeared very awake, eager for the next little bit.

"I remember asking if I was going to have to hide again as we approached New York. Captain said no. I was not the only person being smuggled across the ocean. There were maybe a dozen or so, mostly teenagers and young children, sent across by their parents to some distant relative whom they'd never met, all in hopes of finding a better life.

"When we arrived at Ellis Island, the captain got us in. I don't know if he bribed his way in or what, but we got in. From what little I heard, we were reportedly the survivors of a wrecked passenger vessel that his ship just happened to come upon. All crew and passenger rosters were lost, and only a handful had any kind of papers. There was an argument, and the captain simply said that he'd done his good deed for the Lord to atone of his past crimes, and he wasn't going to be taking on any more crewmen. He was dropping us off at Ellis Island, and what the Americans did with us was their business.

"I didn't like the idea because I'd had too much experience being at the mercy of the authorities, but what could I do but go along? I think I got through the line a little faster because I did have papers, but considering the conditions of Ellis Island and the long wait already, it didn't mean much. Every so often, we were allowed to send out a short, simple letter to some family telling them where we were and to come get us if possible. That was assuming we knew where they were.

"And suddenly I was faced with the realization that I had no clue where my brother had gone off to. America was not like Wales; you couldn't just ask around by name or affiliation. You certainly couldn't just walk around and trek the whole country in a week, and certainly not at that time with the Civil War right around the corner. The best you could hope for was someone who knew someone who knew someone, or just by asking around where other immigrants went.

"No one knew the Forbes name, but a few suggested I try south, towards Virginia — there was no West Virginia at the time; that didn't happen until after the Civil War, but you know that.

"After a time, with no family to contact and no one at all to claim me, the border guards simply let me loose in New York City. I was given the tiniest sack of change you ever did see, even for that time, and told to go make my fortune, welcome to America.

"My pa had given me a crash course in country life skills, but they didn't help much in New York City. Even living under Balk in London, I felt ill-prepared for it. With Balk, I had been a fairly wealthy man. And when I'd been reduced to begging, I knew my role. Being little better than a beggar on the streets of New York, trying to keep sight of my goal to better myself, I was lost.

"The best I could do with the money I had was get myself a hot meal and a warm bed. The only thing that I had going for me was that I spoke English well, so people were less likely to mistreat me. It only went as far as asking which way Virginia was. Apparently, it pegged me as an obvious outsider. Worse, an immigrant.

"Eventually, the best I got was that it was south. Just keep going and I'll find it eventually, assuming the Southerners or the Indians didn't find me first, of course.

"Like I said, America was not Wales. I thought I could just start walking and put some of my pa's teaching to good use. Catch my own food, sleep under the stars. Spring had arrived, so it was only going to get warmer. But I was sorely ill-prepared for the American wilderness. On the roads, I was liable to get robbed or even killed. In the wilderness, there were bears and bobcats and all manner of animals I'd never seen or even heard of before. And if those didn't get me, then there was always your friendly neighborhood Confederate faction, though they weren't quite as official as they would be some years later. And even if they let me live, no way the local Native tribes would let me pass, not after everything the U.S. Government had put them through. Seemed like everyone had a bone to pick with everyone else, and some lone white guy out walking down the road was an easy outlet for that stewing rage.

"I'd barely made it five days before deciding that I wasn't able to go it alone. It was too dangerous, even though nothing had actually happened to me yet. So I started asking around, looking for a ride, some kind of convoy, strength in numbers.

"First problem, I had no money, so there was no way I was getting any kind of ride, easy or hard. I was going to have to work for it. Initially, I blanched at the thought, but I knew that if I was going to turn myself around, I needed to start doing some honest work. Honest work, honest pay. America, land of opportunity; work hard and achieve your dreams." He chuckled, unable to keep a straight face, and shook his head. "Anyway, that was the general sentiment.

"But the second problem was that I was an immigrant, fresh off the boat, too, unaccustomed to the way things worked in America. Needless to say, I wasn't getting any kind of high-paying job. Decent pay for a full day's labor—loading carts, wagons, boats, running errands for elderly folks—was a bowl of soup and maybe a place to sleep. If I got anything extra, I counted myself fortunate.

"After a while, I got smart. I stopped asking city folks for work. They had labor at their disposal, so they could afford to auction it off to the lowest bidder. Instead, I turned to rural folk, farmers. Poor farmers, anyway, who didn't have the luxury of slaves Overall, they were nicer, more fair, and more willing to help someone down on his luck. Yeah, there were those who looked down on me because, after all, their grandfathers had tamed this American soil and damn it if they were going to ask some immigrant for help. But, whatever."

"Did they never hear of Thanksgiving?" Tommen interrupted. "Nation of immigrants and all that?"

Walter frowned. "That may be true, and I know that argument persists today, but you have to understand that there was so much going on in the country at the time, everyone was afraid of anything new. They wanted something familiar to hang onto. War changes things, and civil war even more. Then here come these huge waves of immigrants with their own traditions and ideas, and it can feel like the world is falling apart."

"So then what did you do?" Tommen pressed.

"I learned how to make better bargains, how to make myself less useless as a laborer. For a day's work, I'd get a ride into town or to the next town, always heading farther south. Eventually I reached Virginia. And again I started asking around for the Forbes family, hoping that maybe someone knew someone who knew someone. I didn't realize just how big Virginia, the whole United States actually was. Bigger than the United Kingdom, say it that way.

"I probably wandered around in circles for a month before I finally heard of a small Welsh settlement somewhere in the Appalachians. If there was any place that could help me find my family, that would be the place to start.

"Problem was, mountains were still a big problem back then. Rail lines through the mountains were few, and there were even few passenger trains; those that did exist were expensive. Wagon roads through the mountains were more numerous, but it was a long and very dangerous trek. Maybe it was the time or maybe it was just the place, but the Civil War always felt like it was hovering over my head. You could feel it; something wasn't right, and it had gotten to a point where it wasn't just going to go away quietly.

"I did my best to avoid discussion of war and rebellion and confederacy. All I wanted was to go into the mountains, far away from civilization, find my brother, and live a good and decent life. Problem was, the way things were getting, only the most remote areas were unaffected by such talk, and even those places were starting to get little drips of the outside world.

"I think my biggest fear was that if and when I did find my brother, he would be somehow wrapped up in the whole thing. He was a lover, not a fighter, your pa, and sometimes it got the best of him. Kind of like you. You're a lover, not a fighter. You believe in something, and you believe it passionately. Unfortunately, your passion isn't enough to give you the physical strength you need to actually do what you want to do. If my brother saw some just cause for choosing a side and going out and fighting in the Civil War, he would do it, no question, all passion and no brains or brawn. He was going to get himself killed, that much I knew. And for the first time, I think I finally felt that protectiveness that a big brother has for a little brother. I wanted to find my little brother, to keep him safe and tell him not to go to war. It wasn't worth it, the fighting. But first I had to reach him.

"But the work I was willing to do only got me as far as the foothills, or within sight of them. Few were daring enough to go farther up without good reason, and taking one man into those peaks wasn't a good enough reason. I considered toughing it out, going on my own. The day before I was planning to leave, there came reports of a band of highwaymen, robbing the rich and killing the poor. So I sat and waited just a little while longer.

"Eventually, my break came, though not in the way I would have wished. It was a band of would-be Confederate soldiers, a sort of misfit band, outcasts of an outcast society, charged with delivering news, reports, tactics, strategies, and arms to various sympathizers in the mountains, delivering the message to be ready. For what? War. It was a-comin' and the more sympathizers the Confederates had behind enemy lines, the better. Take the Unioners right in the ass where they least expected it.

"According to the leader of the group, they'd lost four of their guys to sickness on the road, and they were short-handed to drive the wagons. Any help would be appreciated. The pay now was scarce, but when the Confederates won, I'd have my choice of land and I could do what I wanted with it without the Union government telling me what to do or what taxes to pay or anything else. I would be a real free man. Welcome to America, immigrant. Confederate America, land of opportunity; do what you will and answer only to God and your nosy neighbors.

"I wasn't thrilled with the idea, but I signed on, only because they were set to go right by the Welsh settlement. Apparently they knew it well. Most of them grumbled, calling them 'damn Pacifists' and 'a man who isn't with us is for the Union' and so on and so forth. I told myself that I wasn't going to get too involved. I would drive the wagon and mind my own business. Believe me, that wasn't easy for me because I always had an opinion, always had to have the last say. And I had a temper.

"The first ten days in the mountains were uneventful, just climbing up and up and up, trying to find the best route through. And that wasn't always on the main road. The group was not a little paranoid about being discovered by Unioners so we'd leave the main roads and take small footpaths and deer paths, and sometimes I'm almost certain we were completely off the path and just wandering around in a general direction until we came across some kind of path that would lead us back to the road. But no one ever complained; the men were entirely loyal to their leader.

"The eleventh day, we were assaulted by the band of highwaymen. There were four of them and eight of us, not terrible odds for them considering they had the jump on us, killing one man before we could properly react. It was at that point where I was able to shed my cloak of meek invisibility and go back into fighting mode, pure survival, me or them. And I took two of them down before they decided it was better to leave us alone and cut their losses.

"After that, whatever suspicions or misgivings the group had about me, they were apparently relieved because they seemed to include me a lot more around the campfire and in their conversations on the road, when they dared to have them. They weren't sure whether to consider me a recruit for the Confederates or not, but I was one hell of a bodyguard, and they liked having me around.

"And in all reality, I didn't mind them too much either. There was something...nice about sitting around a campfire with a group of guys that you were on, more or less, equal terms with. It wasn't a rich boys' club where I was the bumbling oaf Welshman. It wasn't a bar or other scene where anyone might kill you over a pint of beer. When they weren't going on about Confederate this and Union that, we were all the same, really. A couple had wives, one was barely older than you, some were wanderers like me."

"So did you tell them all about you and your problems during group therapy?" Tommen smirked.

"No I did not," Walter informed him. "The most I told them was that I had a wife and child who were dead so I came to America to escape the pain and make my fortune, and it wasn't going so well so far. That was all they were going to get out me aside from some fudged details and a few lies. They didn't need to know that a mass murderer sat in their midst. Part of me was afraid they would give me a promotion before they'd even officially recruited me.

"Except for that one incident, our journey was uneventful. Unfortunately, a few days before we were supposed to go by the Welsh settlement, some scout or spy or sympathizer approached our camp and said Unioners were in the area in force. Best to avoid all main roads, byroads, and probably all the known paths, too. Skip right by the settlement and continue north to our destination.

"I protested, saying that was where I needed to go. The group wouldn't let me go. First, for liability because I might snitch on them to the Unioners. Second, I'd signed on for the work, for the whole journey, not just an easy ride to wherever it was I needed to go. I signed up, now I was going to fulfill my obligation. We argued, but I was the one who gave in. I knew that if I didn't, someone was going to get hurt.

"So we continued north, taking hidden trails and a lot more time than I thought was necessary for the whole thing, but paranoia is a strange phenomenon. We never met any Unioners. Or Confederates. Or anyone else for that matter. Sometimes I thought we were wandering around in circles; other times I knew we were wandering around in circles. But I learned to just keep my mouth shut, nod my head like a good little prisoner, and carry on.

"By the time we reached our destination, summer had gone and autumn was well underway. It ended up being a small town just a couple hours north of here; it's actually in Pennsylvania today, I think. Either way, dinky little place. Kind of gives you the same impression as some of the neo-Nazi camps out West. They're big and imposing, but they're pretty much populated only by old people left over from World War II and are slowly dying out, leaving a fully-stocked, heavily-fortified bunker behind. That was what this town was, small, fully-stocked, heavily-armed, but it was pretty much just a small group of crazies who thought they were going to be the force to bite the Union in the ass and ensure victory for the Confederates. I don't know.

"At any rate, we were late. What if the Union had found them? They needed new recruits. They needed food. They needed women. They needed all sorts of things. They couldn't get those things themselves because they had to hold down the fort. They were understaffed; they couldn't afford to let even one person go get them basic supplies. I thought the whole exchange was pretty hilarious, but the guys took it seriously, promising to move faster next time and bring more supplies. Beans were just as important as bullets. Actually, a few of them stayed with the group, leaving four of us to make the trip back.

"We could not have left too soon. But once we found a main road, that's where things went south. I tried to leave very politely, very courteously, with no bad blood. Regardless of whatever I thought about Unioners and Confederates and the whole Civil War bit, the guys had been good to me, and they got me where I needed to go. I thanked them for everything, wished them well on their travels, the whole nine yards, trying to be a decent human being.

"Those guys were not so decent. They had no intention of letting me leave. They had too few men to drive all the wagons back home. I'd seen too much. I knew their names, their faces. I knew their secret trails and their secret town in enemy territory. I was a liability."

"Then why take you at all?" Tommen asked.

Walter shrugged as best he could. "If you want my opinion, they were banking on Stockholm Syndrome, even if they didn't know that's what it was at the time. They were hoping that if I spent enough time with them, ate their food, listened to their sob stories, that I would begin to sympathize with them and want to join them. Or if I didn't join the army proper, then at least be a decent sympathizer. Problem was, my destination was not a Confederate-approved sympathizer settlement; there had been Unioners sneaking around there the last time we went through. And even if they weren't Unioners, they were, at best, Pacifists who didn't care one way or the other. 'If you're not with us, you're against u's type of thing.

"Basically, I had two choices. I would either go with them, or they were going to kill me. To this day, I haven't been able to decide if my actions were justifiable self-defense or excessive force. To make a long story short, I killed them. All three of them. When I realized what I had done, I began destroying their carts and wagons, scattering some possessions, taking a few for myself. I unhitched all but one of the horses and let them run wild. Basically, I tried to make it look like a robbery. Then I took the last horse and rode off.

"I didn't go directly to the settlement. Instead, I meandered back through some of the paths and hidden trails, hoping I could find a different main road and dissociate completely from the incident that had just occurred. I didn't know the trails as well as my traveling companions, and I got lost several times, and I resolved that once I found a main road, I was going to stay on that main road.

"When I did come across a decent road, I actually ended up just east of the settlement, not far from where the spy had come to us and told us that there were Unioners about. So I continued on the road toward the settlement, keeping an eye out for Unioners and Confederates alike, knowing I would be an enemy to both if they found me. To the Unioners, I might be seen as a Confederate, and to the Confederates, I was a traitor who'd murdered three of their own. Maybe it was my own paranoia; after all, no one had seen me do it and come after me, and wherever they'd been heading to, they wouldn't be expected for a while. And on top of that, even as I rode into the hub of the settlement itself, there was no panic or news or anything at all about any kind of robbery or murder in the area. It was like it had never even happened.

"And I intended to keep it that way. The settlers would never have to know what happened. If news came, I knew nothing about it. Highway robbery wasn't uncommon. Attacks by the Native Americans in the area weren't entirely uncommon.

"So I tried to make a good impression on the people in the settlement. And know that by 'settlement' we're talking about a very tiny sort of 'town square' or gathering place that wasn't much bigger than our house. There was a little church, a formal trading post that probably hadn't been used in quite a while, and an abandoned Pony Express stable. Other than that, the actual settlers of the settlement lived scattered far and wide, flung across the mountains haphazardly. A few people milled about, mostly young people escaping their parents on ill-considered love ventures, or children also escaping their parents to play and shirk chores.

"I was viewed suspiciously until I actually began speaking Welsh to them, telling them I'd heard of a fair Welsh settlement in the area. After that, those present were more than willing to help, bringing water for my horse and a bite of food for me. When I asked if anyone knew the Forbes name, I was never so happy as when they all said yes. Teo Forbes Sr. was a wonderful man in the community, helpful and kind. Oh, but be gentle with him; they just suffered a terrible loss recently.

"I didn't ask about the loss, hoping I could use it as a starting point to talk to my brother again and show him that I'd changed, I cared.

"By the time I started off, the first snows were falling. I was afraid that I wasn't going to find your pa's house before dark, and I didn't. I managed to find a sheltered area in a grove of pine trees to wait out the night. Even for first snows, it was a cold night, and I was moving again just when the sky started to turn colors.

"I found the place just before noon. To be more accurate, the farm found me as I was attacked by a rooster before I ever came within sight of the house."

"I remember that rooster," Tommen said, grinning. "I wanted to kill that thing."

"I almost did," Walter laughed. "But on hearing the commotion, your ma came running up the trail and captured the damn bird. She apologized and whatnot, inviting me to the house to get me cleaned up; the chicken had scratched me up pretty good.

"Maisy didn't recognize me, but Teo sure did. She started hollering for him just as we came in sight of the house, telling him they had a visitor. As soon as he came around the corner and saw who it was, he started shouting orders to grab all the kids and get inside the house. Lock the door and don't let nobody in." Walter sighed. "My brother was a lover, not a fighter, but he had a family to protect now, and he would kill his own brother if he had to.

"I stopped in my tracks and let him be king of his own castle. He demanded to know what I wanted, and I held out my ma's stitched cloth, telling him that our parents had sent me. I needed help, and they'd suggested I find him. I was too well-known, too wanted back home, but America was the land of second chances. I was living on the Lord's mercy, and hopefully he would grant me a little mercy as well.

"Your pa was skeptical, but he knew our ma's stitching. He told Maisy and the kids to stay inside, and we were going to take a walk and have a little chat.

"It had been probably fifteen years since I'd seen my little brother, but he wasn't little anymore. Frontier life had hardened him.

He was strong, well-built, calloused from long days of chopping wood, mending harnesses, breaking horses, and general hard labor. He'd gone from a scrawny, starry-eyed newlywed with an infant son to a proper man with a wife, children, a full household and farm, living and dying by the sweat of their backs.

"He asked what had become of me, and I told him. Similarly to how I'm telling you, though I didn't mention the bit about getting mixed up with the Confederates. Otherwise, I had nothing to hide. Yes, I'd been married, beaten my wife and child, lost them to another man and watched them die. Yes, I'd gone back and killed half a dozen men. Yes, I'd escaped from prison. Yes, our parents had helped me to escape the law and smuggle me to America."

Walter sighed. "Your pa was the one who did everything right. Normally it's supposed to be the older brother setting the example for his siblings to model and look up to." He shook his head. "Your pa ended up being that role model for me. I knew it was late in the game for me; I was just past forty years old with nothing to my name. I probably wasn't going to build a farm from scratch. There was every chance that even if I did marry, I wouldn't be having children. I would be living on charity for the rest of my life. And I knew it.

"Something I did or said must have reached your pa, touched his good-natured side, and we began talking more openly than I'd ever talked to anyone, let alone my own brother. He told me about leaving Wales, how hard it was, but he was so sure there was something that could be gotten here. Whatever it was, he looked like he'd found it, a little plot of land to call his own and raise his family. He said that occasionally they would pass letters back and forth with our parents, but they were few and far between. Our ma and pa had never mentioned anything about my marriage or imprisonment; I was simply excluded.

"And then he told me something else. He'd told me all about Teo Jr. and all his daughters and even his next child who was due in just a couple months—" Walter noted Tommen's expression. *Yes, Tommen, your mother was pregnant with another sibling when you disappeared.* "—but now he told me about a second son, whose name was Tommen.

"See, Tommen was eight years old and the most joyful child you'd ever seen. He was lively and curious with the same streak of mischief that plagues all little boys, playing tricks on his brother and pranks on his sisters, shirking duties in order to go play some game or another, living in his own little world. He loved to run around in the forest, and he especially liked to climb. He liked to climb trees and rocks and look out over the valley. He also liked to explore caves."

Walter paused, reading Tommen's expression, the hurt and the sorrow, but also the love. He was trying not to cry or show what he evidently perceived as weakness, but he loved his ma and pa and he missed his family, even now, eight years later. He knew that farm and that house and that rooster. No doubt he remembered the little church and the old trading post and the abandoned stable. Memories so long forgotten, now coming to the surface again. Walter shifted in his chair and went on.

"But there was this one cave, you see. It was an old salt cave not far from the house. There was a big boulder in front of the entrance and there were several warning signs, but there was still a big enough opening to get in—easy for an eight year old, a little snug for an adult. Multiple people had disappeared into that cave over the years without a trace, hence why it was blocked off. Several months ago, Tommen had also disappeared into that cave. He'd wanted to explore it for a while, begging his older brother to go and show him since he was a miner and knew how to properly explore caves. When Teo wouldn't do it, Tommen took it upon himself to go exploring. He hadn't been seen since.

"Your pa issued me an ultimatum. He had no doubt that our ma had stitched that cloth, and that was the only reason that we were talking in the first place. And he could respect that it had taken a lot to find him in his seclusion in the mountains. But if I really wanted to prove that I was worth a second chance, I would go and bring his son back to him. And if I couldn't bring him back alive, then don't come back.

"I agreed, and your pa took me up to the old salt cave where his boy had disappeared. It was evening, and he was kind enough to offer me a place in the barn so I could set out at first light, but I refused. I was determined to find my brother's boy and bring him back so we could all have a second chance."

Walter took a breath. "The last time I saw your pa, I saw a boy who had become a man, a father who was willing to risk his brother's life to save his son's. I wanted to be him. So I managed to squeeze through the opening and enter the cave.

"I didn't stay in there very long. In broad daylight, the light doesn't last very long, especially when there's a huge boulder blocking most of the entrance. When the sun is setting rapidly, the light fades even faster.

"When I came out, it was dark. I chalked it up to being unfamiliar with the area why I had a hard time finding the trail and getting back to your pa's place. But somehow I got myself all turned around and stumbled on the same road you did. I didn't get hit by a car, but I was stunned by the scene before me. It was unlike anything I had ever seen, all the lights and sounds, a city I had never seen before, hidden in the mountains.

"I knew your pa wouldn't let me anywhere near his house without you, so I decided that the city was my next best option for food and lodging."

Walter shook his head and chuckled humorlessly. "I remember once you had a history assignment to write either a letter or a story to someone who lived before the Civil War, explaining to them modern life, a brief overview of things. You weren't the best at English, but I remember you got a perfect score on your paper. Essentially you wrote a story about yourself, the day you walked into modern life."

"I remember," Tommen said. "It was seventh grade and Mr. McIntyre read it in front of the whole class. I was so embarrassed."

"Well, that was me when I walked into Charleston. I'd known

that the city was around, but I never knew it was so big. But I knew something was up when I saw roads, cars, and God Almighty, the clothing. I thought that the city was full of strippers until I realized it was just the fashion of the day, the flappers and whatnot." He shook his head. "It was like walking into a totally different world, even more different than heading to London and becoming a banker. This was totally alien to me.

"I didn't have much money, but I wouldn't have known where to begin to look for food or lodging. That first night I ended up sleeping in an alley, trying to get as far away from everything as possible and hoping I woke up to everything being normal again.

"Actually, I woke up to a couple of guys kicking me. Turned out it was a couple of policemen trying to rid the city of the homeless population, and they wanted me to move along. I tried to explain that I just needed directions to a local inn or a restaurant or something; I was new and terrifyingly lost. They laughed at me, called me a dumb country hick, and mockingly pointed me to a run-down bar of the shady variety.

"Nothing had gone back to normal. I still didn't understand where I was or what was going on. I wasn't even sure how to get out of the city back into the mountains to look for your pa and ask what the hell was going on. So, what did I do? I started drinking. Eventually I ran out of money and got in a fight with the bartender, then a couple other guys at the bar, and next thing I know, I'm being hauled off to jail again.

"When I wake up, I'm alone in my cell but there's a guard at the door. His name was Mark, and he was a Timekeeper. Master only, but apparently he'd heard about me, and I'd been ranting and raving and said enough key words for him to take an interest in me, at least enough to figure out what was going on in my head."

He paused and drummed his fingers on the table once. "There is a certain point when a person goes from being able to comprehend and accept Time and what's been done to him—for example, making a seventy year jump—and when it sends him into a psychotic break. As the years go on and modern science continues to advance, that threshold in the human psyche is slowly increasing. Back then, for someone from 1855, that threshold was about twenty years of age, maybe twenty-five. I was forty-two."

"What happens when someone has a breakdown?" Tommen inquired.

"Most often, the most merciful thing to do is kill them. You should always take the time and try to explain things, but that's usually what ends up happening. Life in a mental hospital is no life at all.

"Maybe it was because I'd lived such a messed up life that I'd learned to roll with it, or that I didn't really have anything tying me to a single place, but I was more receptive to what Mark was telling me than I might have been had I been in the area longer, had a family, had ties, that sort of thing. As it was, my connection to my brother was tenuous at best.

"Once we came to a sort of understanding, and once I was released from jail, Mark let me stay with him. He provided food and shelter and clothing to start out with as he explained that it was 1923 and all the changes that came with it. There had indeed been a Civil War. The Union won. The president had been assassinated. Virginia had split into Virginia and West Virginia, the latter of which I was now a resident of with Charleston being its capital. World War I had happened, though at the time it was simply called the Great War. And now America was in a grand time of prosperity, which was good because it afforded me many opportunities to integrate into society, which ought to be my main focus before even thinking about dealing with Time.

"And we had a nice chat about my life and my shortcomings. I was a wanted criminal, though probably not anymore. I had no skills beyond thievery, lying, fighting, drinking, murder, all the things that described the underbelly of humanity. I wanted to change, I really did, but it seemed like every time I tried, something would happen and I just wasn't strong enough.

"You don't care, but that was the first time I really found God. It was Saturday, after all, and Mark took me to church Sunday morning. That afternoon we went to lunch and by Monday, Mark was training me how to be an effective human being. I wasn't perfect; I had a lot of slip-ups those first few months. But he got me through it. He helped me get a job, a place of my own, and build a real life for myself. I owe a lot to Mark, and I daresay I loved that man."

"Wait," Tommen interrupted. "You weren't like...were you?"

Walter gave him a look. "Tommen, unlike what pop culture wants you to believe, it is entirely possible for two men or two women or a man and a woman to love each other without it needing to be sexual or intimate in nature. There are more kinds of love out there than just familial and sexual. No, we weren't gay, and I'm not gay, or anything like that." He noted the look of relief on Tommen's face. Had his son actually thought he was gay? Because he didn't pursue women?

"Anyway, we were very good friends, maybe I'll say it that way. By the time 1925 rolled around, he'd even begun teaching me about Time and made me a probationary Timekeeper, advancing to Apprentice the next year."

"I thought it was three years to Apprentice?"

"It is if you're talking about the minimum training ages. It's as much about your physical and mental development as your Time abilities. I was already a grown man when I was exposed to Time. More than that, I was starting to get into my declining years. So I was able to advance quickly, making Journeyman a year and a half after that.

"When the Great Depression hit, Mark decided it was time to go dark, for both of us. And that was when he showed me how to both go dark and build a new life for myself—the papers, the licenses, the history; there's a lot more that goes into building an entire life than you think, and it was hard work. But when we were almost done constructing our new lives and ready to rejoin society, that was when I confessed the real story of how I got caught up in 1923. I'd told him that I'd become a miner, got separated, and walked out through a Time trap. Now I told him about finding my brother and having to look for his son.

"We visited the old salt cave where my eyes were opened to the sheer terror that was the Band within that cave. He gave me the strength estimation, saying that if you were as lively and curious as everyone said you were, assuming you didn't die in the cave from some other phenomena, you could be in there for decades, centuries even.

"We couldn't stay in Charleston; that was the whole point of going dark and building a new life. It had to be somewhere we wouldn't be readily known or identified. We were leaving for California, a couple of venture capitalists looking to profit from the poor man's sorrow, maybe get rid of some of the Hoovertowns popping up all over the place.

"Obviously I knew all of this ahead of time; we'd planned for months. But now the time was coming, and I couldn't bear to leave Charleston. I had to be here; I had to find my nephew. I was never going to be able to return you to your pa, but maybe, just maybe, I could take you in as my own son. If Mark was right, you would also be exposed to Time in such a way that you almost had to become a Timekeeper in order to handle it. And each decade you became further and further removed from a time and place that you were familiar with meant you needed someone to guide you and help you make sense of it all.

"I became obsessed with waiting for you, so much so that I almost split with Mark. Eventually he got one of the local Journeymen to keep an eye on the cave from time to time, and he sent word for all Timekeepers to keep an ear out for anything strange coming from Charleston in the realm of missing and exploited children or foster care or anything like that. And if anything came across as a little hinky, send word immediately. I gave him the name to pass along, and we left for California within the week.

"World War II was another point where we went dark, but by

then I was a Master Timekeeper, and Mark and I had grown tired of seeing each other day in and day out. It's just what happens. So once we'd constructed our new lives after going dark, he went one way and I went another. We kept in touch, but I never actually saw him again."

"Do you know where he is now?" Tommen wondered.

"I'm sorry to say he died. He was killed in Vietnam. Too much action, he couldn't control it all. Bomb from the air finally got him, or so I heard.

"As for me, after World War II, I thought about going back to Charleston, then decided that twenty years just wasn't good enough. Too many people would still recognize me, or had the potential to. So instead I did a stint in Detroit, auto capital of the world. Elected to be a manufacturer and build cars. Did that for about twelve years or so. Went dark to avoid the draft. Resurfaced in 1980, did some fishing along the New England coastline, humble work, but I tried to keep a low profile while I trained to become a Timekeeper Lieutenant.

"I went dark again around 1990, popping up in 1995 in Police Academy in Austin, Texas. I did a few years there, chasing drug lords and border hoppers, and advancing into Timekeeper Captain. Then in 2001, I transferred back to Charleston and worked Missing Persons with a special interest in children. I didn't know if you'd show up in my time that I was here, but I was tired of waiting for word. Mostly I was afraid that you'd already come out and been placed with a family. Or maybe you'd died in the cave, and I would be waiting forever for something that would never happen.

"But one day I did get the call I was waiting for. A little boy had just shown up out of nowhere and been hit by a car. He must have had a concussion or something because he swore up and down that he was Tommen Forbes, as in, *the* Tommen Forbes." Walter took a calming breath. "I was never so happy in my life. And you know the rest of the story."

Then they went silent for a long moment, each staring at the other, sizing him up, considering his words and expressions and body language. It was a lot to unload on his son, Walter knew. He'd probably expected some nice, easy story about a grand childhood where he, Walter, and Teo were best friends and they did brotherly things together and it was all just a big misunderstanding. To confess to drinking, fighting, murder, evading and eluding, it was a lot to digest. It had made Walter's throat dry, from the talking itself as much as the content of his tale. He hadn't always been a nice man, putting the good of the public first. At one time he'd been a very dangerous, very selfish man who was on the executioner's block.

"That's a lot," Tommen said finally after probably ten minutes of silence. "That's...wow, that's a lot. That was not what I was expecting."

"I know," Walter sighed. "I'm not proud of some of the things I've done. And I know that even for as many times as I go dark and build new lives for myself, that part, that beginning, that will always stay with me. But yet, if I hadn't gone through all that, who's to say what would have become of me? Would I still have gone through a Time trap and been left to look for you? I don't know. But I do know that since I found you, I wouldn't have had it any other way."

Tommen managed a small smile that eventually turned into a yawn which Walter involuntarily mirrored. He looked at the clock. Damn, it was past five o'clock. Not that he had anywhere particularly important to be, but normally he was already up and on his way to work at this hour.

After a moment, Tommen pushed his chair back and stood slowly. "I'm tired and that's...a lot to take in. I mean, I have a million questions, but I just need to take time and sort it all out first, in my mind."

"I understand," Walter reluctantly conceded as he painfully got to his feet, his leg and shoulders screaming. "Look at me, Tommen." He did so. "I love you. As my son, as my nephew, I love you. I'm sorry it took so long for me to tell you the truth, and if you hold it against me, I understand, but I hope you can forgive me. But know this: no matter what, as long as I have breath, I will protect you, for your sake and mine, as well as for the promise I made your pa.

Okay?"

Tommen stared at him for a minute before breaking into a goofy grin. He shook his head and managed to give him a brief, awkward, lop-sided hug. "You can be such a sap sometimes, you know that?"

"Better a sap than a cold-hearted bastard," Walter told him as he started to walk way.

"Hey now, watch your language," Tommen warned lightly.

Walter sighed dramatically. "Not allowed to be a sap, not allowed to be a cold-hearted bastard, what do you expect from me, Tommen?"

But the teenager just shook his head and disappeared down the hall.

Walter stayed in the kitchen a minute longer. He was still exhausted, but even his mind was reeling from this night's unexpected experience. He picked up the mug of cold hot chocolate, still with some left in it, and went to the sink to wash it. Outside, the neighborhood was quiet except for some gusting winds. No dogs barked, no cars went by. The neighbors across the street had a little candle flickering in the window. Probably the light spilling out through the kitchen window was the brightest thing out there.

Then the light went out, flicked off as he left the kitchen, forcing aching limbs to move and take him where he wanted to go. He was so tired, and yet the exhaustion that came with his burden of a lie was lifted now. He went down the hallway toward his bedroom, but before he could go in and lie down, Tommen's door opened just a bit, and he stood there in the doorway.

"I have a question."

"What?" Walter asked, trying not to sound irritable. He just wanted sleep.

"Did we ever actually come up with a story of what happened to my family, why everything happened?"

"No, I don't think we did."

"Would anything get really messed up if I acknowledged you

as my uncle? I know you said it takes a lot to build a new life."

"I don't know; I guess it depends on the story you want to tell."

"Oh." Tommen ran his tongue over his teeth.

"What did you have in mind?" Walter prompted.

"I'll think it over a little bit and then tell you in the morning or whenever we get up."

Walter had his doubts. He more suspected that Tommen was going to sleep for another twenty-four hours or so before being really, truly, officially awake enough to get back into a regular rhythm. Still, he nodded, wished Tommen good night, and headed for the comfort of his bed.

The sheets were cold, the blanket was cold, and pretty soon, he was cold. The night light offered its comforting glow, and the fan provided its white noise, but still Walter found he couldn't sleep. At first it was just shock and a racing mind, going over everything he'd just told his son, memories so long buried now coming roaring back to life. But pretty soon the specific memories faded into vague concepts and images until it all melded into a single sensation: pain.

And it wasn't even just figurative pain. The coolness of the bed had subsided, and now his body ached again. He couldn't shift, couldn't get comfortable, couldn't find any place where the pain was gone or even just lessened.

Oh, for goodness' sake, it's five in the morning and I haven't slept a wink.

After another five minutes or so of mentally batting the ball back and forth, he sat up, grabbed the script bottle and tapped out a pill. Then he grabbed the glass of water he kept on his nightstand and used it to chase down the painkiller. A minute or two later, the throbbing in his leg and shoulder subsided enough that he was able to find a fairly comfortable position and slip into a restful sleep.

Tommen was actually awake long before his alarm went off. He'd spent pretty much all of Saturday and part of Sunday asleep, his body still trying to work off the drugs and the review. Since then, it had been a battle to get his Circadian rhythm back in order. It had been difficult in that a blizzard had rolled in late Sunday night, stranding everyone and quarantining most people in their homes or wherever they had been at the time of the storm. So it had been a long day of nothing but TV and Internet...when they were working.

Monday had been a snow day from school, which was awesome until he got put on shovel duty, clearing the walkway and the driveway, then getting roped into helping out some of the elderly neighbors. He didn't mind it—it was the right thing to do—but he missed the days when a snow day meant Cheetos for breakfast and playing video games in a dark room for hours on end.

But he figured it could have been worse. He could have been his dad who was not only stranded in his own home, but pretty much unable to do anything to keep himself occupied other than watch TV or read a book. He couldn't shovel, couldn't work, couldn't do much of anything. And for all the neighbors who came by, asking if they could do anything to help him since he was down and out, no, he was fine, Tommen could handle it.

Not that he had anywhere to be, necessarily. He hadn't been able to get to work, and the twins had told him to stay home anyway; the bakery was deader than a door nail.

Of course, as he lay in the darkness on Tuesday morning, he probably would have been okay with another day of having nothing important to do or anywhere important to go. The previous night, Walter had gotten a call from Dr. Polski's office. Despite the storm, Tommen's hearing aids were in. They could pick them up first thing in the morning.

So he lay in bed, waiting for his alarm to go off, contemplating the shadows cast on the ceiling from the bathroom night light. It all seemed so surreal. He'd been kidnapped, held captive, seen his dad shot and left to die—held him in his hands, even—watched his dad die in front of him slowly and painfully, been rejected by the highest known court in the universe for help, gone on an adventure of monumental difficulty, endured one of the cruelest professional reviews he'd ever had, and now he was going to head to the doctor and then to school, followed by work and then back to bed.

Everyone else was going to be talking about the presents they got for Christmas, the vacations they went on, how much they loved or hated this relative or that relative, all the usual stuff that should be talked about after Christmas break. And he was going to be sitting in the corner with nothing to offer. Well, yeah, he got some pretty cool gifts, but compared to everything else, it was so small and insignificant. Yeah, he went on an exotic vacation...to another planet. Yeah, he had people he hated, like the Hands and Rifun. And he had people he loved, like the twins and his dad. And there was that whole part about his dad almost dying which everyone had heard about. So, how was your Christmas?

And...there it was. The alarm of doom. The alarm telling him to wake up and join the real world. Yes, all that had happened, but that was one side of his life he could never share, as Eric's and Varad's reactions had already proved. But now came the other real world, the one that everyone else saw, the one where he had to help his dad during his recovery. The one where he was going to claim his hearing aids before going to school.

Grudgingly, Tommen slapped the alarm off and dragged himself out of bed. He opened the door to see his dad only a few feet away.

"I was just coming to make sure you're awake," he said.

"Oh, I am," Tommen grumbled.

"Been awake?"

"Yeah." He headed to the bathroom and shut the door.

"Well, don't forget we're heading to the hospital this morning."

"I remember."

How could he forget? He'd only spent half the night thinking about it.

He wasn't even sure why he was grumpy about it except maybe he didn't want to go to school with them. He'd gotten pretty used to just walking around the house and stuff. School was a whole different story. It was only fuel for the bullies—and by "bullies," insert "Tyler Freeman and his cronies"—and he knew it.

Still, he wasn't doing himself any favors by stalling; he had to go. Didn't mean he didn't drag a little, slipping into a Fast Band so he could drag as much as he wanted and still have time for breakfast. He picked out the new shirt the twins had gotten him for Christmas. Not beige, but green. It was strange to think about. He could remember what it looked like in its true color, but the beige looked back at him, mocking him.

That was the reason why his selection of pants was pretty limited to jeans, dress pants, and half a dozen pairs of shorts which he was assured were brown or black.

Rifun might be a nutcase, but if there really was a way to fix his eyesight, he would endure half a dozen of his fanatical lessons to learn it.

Tommen shook his head. No. He couldn't let Rifun trap him like that. The carrot wasn't worth the hoops to get there. And just like in basic trapping, as soon as he grabbed that carrot, the latch would give, and he would be caught.

"Are you ready?" his dad asked as he meandered into the kitchen.

"Yeah, just let me grab something for breakfast," Tommen

replied.

"Make it quick because you're driving."

"What?"

"Why wouldn't you be? You need the time if you're going to make it to your next segment. You kind of missed a couple weeks."

So, skip the cereal and go for the toast. Got it. He could have Banded and made himself a gourmet meal, but there was only so much he could do in a Band, so much he could stall, so much he could handle. Sometimes, Banding was boring.

"Wait," Tommen said as he got in the driver's seat. "This means that...are you going to be okay driving home from school?"

"Why not? I can drive with my left foot. And I can move the seat a little more forward to give my shoulders a rest." He sighed when Tommen did nothing. "It will be uncomfortable, but it's not like I'll be doing Indy or anything. And anyway, it's just from school to home. Not that far. Now then, let's get going before you're late."

Tommen obeyed. There was no other way to do it now. The bus had already come and gone, and it was obvious the twins weren't coming, not that he expected them to. He was driving, and then his dad was driving. He didn't like it, but he accepted it, opening the garage door and starting the car. His dad was only injured, not helpless. A flurry of snow gusted into the garage, and he cautiously backed out. Once he was comfortably going down the road, he noted how the majority of the accumulation seemed to be dry snow. It kicked up and whooshed around, but the roads themselves were decent—assuming he could see where they were.

"Did you get all your homework and back-work done for class?" his dad asked.

That was another thing he'd spent most of the previous day doing: homework. None of it had been assigned over break, this was all the stuff he'd missed out on while he was in Rifun's clutches. It had taken at least forever and it sucked, but he got it all done. Okay, okay, that was a lie. He got about eighty or ninety percent done, depending on how much he cared about it. The online work wouldn't let him stop until he had an answer for every question, but he was fairly certain that answering "ketchup and mustard" on a critical thinking question for *Of Mice and Men* was incorrect.

"Yes, I did," Tommen replied. "And I'm sure I'll have more tonight."

"I won't pretend that playing catch-up on two weeks worth of work was fun, but school is still important."

"What does it matter if I have to go dark every ten years anyway?"

"You can make up all the fancy degrees you want, but if you don't actually know the material, it's about as useful as counterfeit money. You'll get found out real quick."

Well, there was that.

Of course, there was also an idea there. Was it possible that he could go to college and pay for it from his Timekeeper salary? Theoretically, he would be a Journeyman by then, and once he reached that stage with more advanced abilities and the ability to arrest and turn in Runners, his pay increased quite a bit, at least enough to be able to take a few years off work and "do some traveling" as it were. He could do a year as an exchange student in one country, then be an exchange student in another country the next year, and so on and so forth. True, he might not actually earn any degrees, but travel and experience was worth ten times a single piece of paper from sitting in the same classrooms of the same school for four or more years.

"So...once I'm done with school and stuff...will I have to go dark?" Tommen wondered.

"You could probably get away with a few years sticking around, but eventually, yes, you would have to leave," his dad answered.

"What about you? When are you going dark?"

His dad shifted uncomfortably. "Well, in a manner of speaking, I'm kind of overstaying my welcome as it is. By the time you get out of school, fifteen years is a long time for me to stay in one place. So I might have to leave pretty soon after you graduate."

Tommen glanced sideways at him. If it was just a matter of moving, he probably wouldn't have much of a problem with it. Maybe he could find a college wherever his dad was moving to. But going dark was about more than just moving; it was erasing himself from society completely for a number of years, living kind of like a fugitive, existing entirely within Time in that anything he needed, he stole. Walks in the park were allowed, but human contact was to be kept to a minimum. A passing word on the street, maybe helping someone in an emergency, but otherwise, he had to live life as a ghost until he was all but forgotten.

"Since you were able to find me and raise me, you did kind of fulfill your promise to my pa," he began cautiously. "What will you do the next time you resurface? What kind of life will you have?"

"I don't know," his dad replied honestly. "It's not like I can exactly retire and go live some quiet life somewhere. Well, I could, but I'd hate myself and go stir crazy before a year was up. I don't know; guess I'll just have to wait and see."

There was a point when every child had to leave the nest and separate from their parents, but this was a different kind of separation. It wasn't even a final separation, like death. It was going their separate ways, each knowing that the other was out there, somewhere, under an assumed name, living an assumed life. Fake.

They rode the rest of the way in silence, pulling into the hospital parking lot and playing musical cars until a spot opened up for them. The lot had been sanded into oblivion, and they crunched their way into the lobby, heading for the elevator. A few people gave them stares or sympathetic looks, probably thinking Walter was the one coming in for something, physical therapy maybe.

"Are you going to need physical therapy?" Tommen wondered as they got on the elevator.

"Oh, it's entirely possible," his dad answered, "but I don't see what good it would do except to stretch and strengthen the muscles. I didn't have any kind of replacement, and there's nothing that can really be done for a couple ribs and shoulder blades. It's all just in the body's timing."

"Just like there's nothing that can be done for color-blindness or deafness?" Tommen asked, maybe more sharply than necessary.

His dad sighed. "Yes, just like there's nothing that can be done for that. In theory."

Tommen could hear the frustration in his dad's voice. He wanted to be able to Band his way out of his injuries, to endure the pain and discomfort and tingling that came with that level of Banding, just suck it up for a good five or ten minutes in exchange for having a fully restored body. Well, as well as could be expected. And not a few times, when his dad had gone in for a work-mandated physical, the doctors had always commented on what great shape he was in for his age, especially given his profession and history. True, Time was only a tool and not medicine, but there were some restorative properties associated with its use in healing. Just not enough to correct color-blindness or deafness.

Rifun's ability to completely cut off Tommen's hearing might be reasonably passed off as coming from the hallucinogen in the waiting room, a phenomenon similar to his being shot. But the ability to correct color-blindness so completely, in a natural and uncontrolled environment, that was presently inexplicable, at least reasonably.

The elevator stopped at a few more floors, picking up and dropping off all number of people, before finally depositing them on the necessary floor. Tommen still preferred the calm quiet of the audiology floor to the twenty-four hour insanity of the ICU floor. There, people ran to and fro, barking orders, grabbing things, and carrying on with every mission like it was life-and-death—which it probably usually was. Here, people, if there were any, walked purposefully but quietly, still having time for a glance and a polite nod. Things weren't crashing down all around them, and even the door was quieter as they opened it and slipped into the office.

This time there was a different receptionist, one of the young pretty ones probably interning or fresh out of college, still bright-eyed and hopeful for the future, thinking she was going to win customer service points by smiling with every word and wearing magazine-class makeup. Still, Tommen would have taken her over the grouch who'd been at the desk the previous week. And then, he would take her later and —

"Forbes, Tommen," his dad said, interrupting his thoughts, and probably for the best. "We're here to pick up his hearing aids."

"Of course," the receptionist replied, smiling with every word, showing off blinding white teeth that could have landed her a toothpaste-spokesperson gig. "If you'll just step this way, I'll take you down to the room, and Dr. Polski will be with you momentarily."

"We can't just pick them up?" Tommen asked.

"Nope, not with a first-time fit."

Reluctantly, Tommen got the door for his dad and followed them down the short hallway to one of the exam rooms where he sat down in a heap.

"Nervous?" his dad asked.

Tommen shrugged.

"I know it's hard. I know it's not fair, and you don't want to do it. But it's necessary."

Tommen didn't reply. He knew that was all true, but that didn't mean he had to like it. People were generally resistant to change, and he was no different. Things were going to change now for him. A lot. It was kind of like the trial hearing aids had been a game, a neat experiment to explore what it was like to be deaf or almost deaf. Today was the day when he finally had to admit that he really was in that category and now he had to own up to it. He himself wasn't changing, personality-wise, but he was going to be different. He was now going to have a disability that, at some points, others were going to have to take into consideration. Just like the little Bible camp he'd gone to where he had to have special meals prepared, he was again going to be "that kid" who got singled out because he was different. And it wasn't always the bullies, but the teachers, too. Could he hear the movie; did he need a quiet space to work and study; did it help by doing this, that, or the other thing? He was going to be different. He was going to be a freak.

Even as he thought it, he knew it wasn't fair to those who had real problems and disabilities, those that couldn't be fixed by such small devices and were devastating to the self or family. As far as what he could have, he figured he had it pretty easy. That he hadn't gotten trampled by the xur or the d'bok, and he didn't get bitten by some venomous snake in the D'Bok jungle and left paralyzed was a small miracle in itself.

But that didn't mean he had to like it. And he most certainly did not like it.

He jumped as the door opened and Dr. Polski walked in, pretty spry for a man who was easily pushing seventy. And way too cheerful for anyone this early in the morning.

"Well, good morning, Tommen," he greeted cheerily. He walked to the desk and set down a box. "How are we doing this morning?"

Tommen shrugged. "Been better, been worse."

"Weathering the blizzard?" Polski glanced at Walter as he opened the box.

"As always," Walter answered. "Probably quite a shock to you coming back from California."

"Well, I won't say the constant warm weather wasn't really nice." After taking out more tissue paper and foam than Tommen thought the box could feasibly handle, never minding its actual contents, Polski pulled out another smaller box and opened that, setting it on the table and turning it around for him to see. It was like one of those ring boxes at the jewelry store, except here the item of value was a pair of very expensive hearing aids with a small charging pad.

"The trial pair worked well for you, I hope?" Polski inquired.

"I guess. I mean, I can hear," Tommen answered. "There was a little rubbing, but no blisters or anything."

"That's good. Hopefully, with this pair, it's like you're not wearing anything at all. Go ahead and take those out for me."

As he removed the trial pair, Tommen had his doubts about the doctor's statement. He might not feel the new pair, but he would always know they were there. And if he forgot, well, there was no shortage of bullies to remind him about it. Or well-meaning teachers or classmates or the local humanitarian on the street. So he figured he had his bases covered pretty well. That was the thing about disabilities: everyone worked so hard to make the disabled feel equal and normal that they ended up overemphasizing the disability.

"Now, go ahead and put these in like normal," Polski said, handing Tommen the new set, "We'll see about the fine-tuning, and then we'll talk a bit about operations and things."

Tommen didn't wear glasses or contacts, but he'd heard from a number of classmates that the first time putting in contact lenses was always the hardest, trying to overcome the eye's natural tendency to blink and protect the eye from a foreign body. After a few days, though, it was just *plop!* in and out as needed with no fighting.

That was how it was with the hearing aids now. The first few days, he'd had to take the earpiece in and out and in and out, wiggling, adjusting, trying to get the behind-the-ear part in a moderately comfortable position, always fussing and probably just making things worse. Now, like that morning, he'd simply grabbed them off the charging stand, fitted them where they'd found a comfy spot, and off he went. No muss, no fuss.

The only difference with the new hearing aids, as he put them in, was that they did exactly what Polski said they would. It was as if they vanished. At least the inner earpiece did. He set it, and it was gone. Whether that was because it was form-fitted to his ear or because his ear felt naked without it, he was unwilling to rule on. The outer piece he had to finagle a bit, but once he found the sweet spot, it was gone. Well, not truly gone, but it was just...comfortable. It was something he could work with instead of fuss with.

"Your expression tells me it's working for you," Polski said, interrupting his thoughts.

"Yeah," Tommen agreed. Then, "Yeah, I mean, it fits better."

Polski leaned back in his chair. "I know, you're trying to play it cool and tough it out. I have a son who was sixteen once, too. He didn't like being told he wasn't invincible. It's okay to acknowledge your hearing aids. Trust me, they're doing you a great service."

"I know. I have to go back to school today, and I usually sit in the back of the room."

It was a blatant lie, but Polski didn't need to know that.

"Operation is basically the same as the trial pair; hearing aids aren't exactly rocket science when it comes to working them. The nice thing about these, though, is that they have a quiet mode. And what I mean by that is if you feel right above the adjuster, yeah, that, you got it, that's just a little switch that will automatically cut the input down to twenty percent, and then back to wherever you had it set, so you don't always have to adjust up and down and try to find your comfortable spot again, it's just flip and go."

"That sounds good," Walter quipped.

"It is good. It's a neat feature of those ones." Polski sat up and looked back and forth between Tommen and his dad. "That being said, these hearing aids are backed by a two-year total service warranty, so if anything goes wrong in two years, you can get them fixed, replaced, refunded, whatever you want. And after that is a three-year upgrade warranty. Anything goes wrong, the company will replace them with a newer model if it's available or give you a fifty-percent discount on repairs." He handed Walter a folded piece of paper that came out of the box. "These are all the terms and limited liability and all the fine print for you to look over."

"Love fine print."

"Makes the world go round." Polski grinned. "And I also have my own six-month guarantee that I do personally out of my office. And that is if something goes wrong or you decide that these just aren't working out for you, then we can have another appointment, another casting, pick a different pair to order, and it is all free to you. No co-pays, no insurance, nothing like that. But it only applies on the first pair."

"So people can't abuse it?" Tommen guessed.

"You got it. And in all my years of practice, I can count on one hand the number of times people have had such a problem."

The man was a nice guy, good at his work, but he knew how to stroke his own ego. Still, Tommen kept his mouth shut.

"Now then, are there any questions before you go?" Polski inquired.

"I have a question," Walter said. "How does he take these to college with him? He might be in before he goes just as a final check-up before he gets sent off, but if he has problems and, say, he's out of state, what should he do?"

"What grade are you in?"

"I'm a sophomore," Tommen answered.

"Okay, so we're still a couple years out from that, and obviously it will be dependent on the circumstances that are present at that time, but speaking generally, it is a good idea to have a thorough check-up before going out. At the same time, however, no matter where you decide to go to school, it's a good idea to find a doctor nearby, someone you trust. Now, you can go out with a fresh pair of hearing aids and just walk in the door to an audiologist and say, 'Here I am! I might be in from time to time or in a couple years,' or you can schedule an appointment, go through the tests and the fitting and have that conversation with your new doctor right from the get-go. Plus having that conversation early will help you find someone you trust, versus simply picking a doctor, and then two years later when you have problems, find out that you don't like who you picked. Does that make sense?"

Tommen nodded.

"As I said, there are a couple years between now and then. And depending on where you decide to go to school, I might be able to recommend an audiologist, and I can write up a formal referral."

"I have a question," Tommen said suddenly. "Does the warranty cover normal wear and tear and unexplained malfunctions, or does it cover damage, too? Like if they get ripped out and stomped on the ground?"

"Are you planning on doing that later today?"

"I'm not, but that doesn't mean it won't happen at school."

Polski glanced at Walter; Tommen didn't see what look, if any, he gave him. Finally, the doctor sighed. "I haven't had anyone ask me that, but I think I understand what you're referring to. Bullies and jerks making fun of you for your hearing loss." Tommen nodded. "In those circumstances, I'm sure an exception can be made on the warranty if that isn't already covered. And if you like, there is a support group that meets—"

"I'm not interested in the support group."

Polski nodded graciously. "I understand." He looked again at Walter. "Were there any other questions?"

Walter glanced at Tommen who shook his head. "No, I think we're set for now."

"Very good. And you have the number here if you do think of any questions. I try to get back to all of them by the end of the working day." He slapped his knees and stood. "If there is nothing else, then I wish you well. Dina will set up your next appointment on your way out."

Polski opened the door for them and headed for the receptionist while Tommen and his dad went back out to the tiny waiting area on the other side of the desk.

"Six months," Polski told the girl. "Otherwise they're good to go."

"Great." Again with the huge smile and the bright red lipstick that would put *Vogue* to shame. She looked up briefly at the two of them standing in front of her and then at her computer screen. "Okay, so, six months would put us in the beginning of June. Because this is your first pair of hearing aids and this is all new, the doctor will want you to set a specific date and time. If we get to May or June and you realize you're not going to make it, we can work around a bit."

Walter let out a breath and looked at Tommen. "Well, you'll be out of school for the summer, so we won't have to worry about that, and the twins are pretty understanding about your work schedule."

"So it sounds like it's all up to you," Tommen told him.

"No guarantees I'll be going back to work, not in the same position anyway, so I guess we'll just have to set a date and time and hope for the best. What do you got?"

So they set up the appointment and the receptionist wished them well, smiling hugely as they left. Tommen could have sworn she winked at him, but maybe that was just him overreacting again.

"How do they feel?" his dad asked once the door was shut and they were on their way to the elevator.

"Good," Tommen answered. "Better than the trial pair." He looked at the box in his hand. Like a ring box, but much more depressing.

"Bullying aside, you're going to have to take good care of them because I don't feel like coming back and going through this whole song and dance again."

"I know, I know."

It was a fatherly warning, like telling Tommen that he had to do his own laundry or else he was going to be wearing dirty clothes around school and girls did not find that very appealing. Not that he didn't think his dad would give him a good talking-to and a list of chores a mile long in order to make up for whatever song and dance they had to go through if he did mishandle his hearing aids. The garage had finally been cleaned, but there were any number of other little projects that could always been done. Remodeling, for instance. His dad had talked a lot about remodeling the house and sprucing it up a bit while he was out of work.

"So, that didn't take as long as I expected," his dad said, looking at his watch. "What do you say we make a detour on the way to school, hm? Official police officer business; you can tell Layman it was all my fault."

Tommen raised a brow, intrigued. "What kind of official police officer business?"

"The kind where I was out for a walk when I saw this starving teenage boy on the side of the road and, being a good public servant, decided that instead of arresting him for disturbing the peace or whatever, I was going to take him to breakfast and listen to his tale of woe and worry."

"Not the bakery, please."

His dad shook his head. "No, I won't force you to suffer there any more than you already do. Actually, I am aware of the existence of other bakeries, restaurants, and one particular little diner that is said to be especially tasty. What do you think?" He grinned.

Tommen managed a smile. "I think that sounds great. Where is it?"

They stepped off the elevator and headed for the door, neither of them particularly enthused about stepping into the whipping winds just beyond the glass. As Walter pulled on his hat and gloves, he answered, "Well, if you're willing to drive, then I guess I'm willing to give you directions. And I might even pay for your meal."

So they walked out into the biting cold and whipping winds, searching for the beat-up old Cadillac, finding it, pretty sure, half a mile farther out from where they'd actually parked. But it was no matter as Tommen got in the driver's seat and his dad began relaying him directions.

Chapter Thirteen
Back to School

Breakfast turned out to be a full platter of eggs, sausage, bacon, and toast for Tommen, and a couple enormous pancakes for his dad. In all reality, it was pretty nice, and a good way to somewhat ease the tension that was gripping Tommen's shoulders in a painful vice. He didn't want to go to school. At the diner, he went to the bathroom twice just to check and see how visible his hearing aids were. With his hair as long as it was now, they were completely invisible. Even when he pushed the longer locks back, they weren't immediately noticeable.

He tried to tell himself to stop being paranoid. As long as he didn't act like anything was amiss and draw attention to himself, no one would notice. Of course, his dad was going to make him get a haircut eventually, but that wouldn't be until long after he'd grown more accustomed to them. Then his classmates would be surprised but he wouldn't be. And everything would work out.

"Tommen," his dad said as he signed the receipt and slid a cash tip under his coffee mug, "it's going to be okay."

"I know," Tommen replied, shrugging.

"You don't need to play the tough guy around me." He grabbed his cane and got himself to his feet. "You don't do it well."

"What good would it do otherwise?"

"Honesty. Self-respect." They headed out the door, the little bell jingling overhead. "And anyway, there's no one around to impress."

Tommen did not reply as they got in the car and he put the key in the ignition. After a moment of pause, he said, "I don't want to be different. I don't want people to look at me differently."

His dad sighed. "I know. I don't want that for you either. If I knew of a way to stop people from looking at you differently or treating you differently, believe me, I would have told you about that a long time ago. But people, once they see your hearing aids, will look at you differently. Most will probably look at you with pity, and all you can do then is shock them with how much you can do in spite of it. And some will look at you with sneers and amusement, and all you can do then is shock them with how much you can do in spite of it. I know you just want to fit in, but maybe that's not the answer in this case. I don't know. I wish I did."

Tommen stayed silent as he turned on the car and began the treacherous drive from the diner to school. It was terrifying, the realization that your parents don't have all the answers and you have to start figuring things out on your own. Eventually, Mommy and Daddy couldn't step in and intervene anymore because some bully made their kid cry. The moral lessons had already been taught and, hopefully, instilled. Eventually, the kids had to work it out on their own.

Tommen would have rathered cross the universe a hundred times than go to school that morning.

The roads weren't as treacherous as they had been only half an hour before, though the gloomy skies promised more snow by day's end. Still, he plodded along in the little Cadillac, his dad not doing much to correct his driving except to occasionally remind him about speed or blinker usage or tell him the lane pattern at intersections that were all but invisible.

They made it to the school in one piece, Tommen pulling toward the drop-off section.

"Might as well park it," his dad said. "I'm going to have to go in and excuse you."

"Right. Official police business," Tommen said, trying to find some humor in his anxiety.

"Absolutely."

Tommen rummaged around in the backseat for his stuff. "Are you going straight home afterwards?"

"Why? Do I need to?" His dad gave him a funny look, as if he hadn't quite processed that his puppy had been kicked.

"I don't know, I was just wondering if it was okay for you to be driving."

Then came the other look, and with it, the one phrase Tommen had heard more in the last week than the last year. "I'm only injured; I'm not helpless. It's not any worse for me out there as it is anyone else. We're all plodding along on the same crappy roads. I can drive with my left foot. Tommen, we went over this this morning."

"I know, I'm just making sure."

"And I appreciate the concern, but we're already here. Come on, let's get you to class."

Reluctantly, Tommen followed his dad inside. Like everything else so far, it was as if no time had passed at all. He knew these halls and these lockers. He knew the classrooms and the students who hurried along on "bathroom breaks" but who would actually sit in a stall for fifteen minutes on Facebook or Youtube. Everything came back to him, perfect muscle memory, just another automaton in a building full of automatons.

They headed for the office, the secretary having a stunned expression as she looked up from her work and saw who it was.

"Tommen," she said, momentarily forgetting herself. Then, "Good morning. How can I help you?"

"He had a doctor's appointment this morning," Walter told her smoothly. "I just came to sign him in so he can get to class."

"Right." She slid a clipboard toward him. "Is everything okay, I hope?"

Translation: What the hell happened? Give me some juicy details so I can be the sensation around the watercooler later today and spread all the gossip around until it comes back to you as something completely wrong from what actually happened.

"Never better," Walter replied, sliding the clipboard back.

Before anyone could say anything more, Layman's office door opened, and the man poked his head out.

"Walter," he said, grinning and coming out of his office. "I thought I heard your voice. My God, how are you doing?"

"Been better, been worse," Walter replied, his answer one he used to try to end a conversation quickly. Layman did not apparently catch on.

"I can imagine. Actually, I called you yesterday and left a message...?" Translation: Did you get it, or are you ignoring me?

"Well, as you can also imagine," Walter said, "I've been getting a lot of calls and messages lately. I haven't really gotten around to all of them yet." Translation: I was ignoring you.

"Of course. Well, since you're here, do you have a minute where we can all sit down?" Translation: You can't possibly have anything else planned for today given the state you're in, so let's have a talk.

"Yes, though I think Tommen has missed enough school for one year." Translation: I don't want to talk to you.

"Ten minutes more won't hurt him then. And that's what I want to talk about. Come on in." Translation: You're not leaving without talking to me first.

So they filed into Layman's office, as spic and span and pristine as ever, straight from boot camp, Tommen was sure. If there ever came a day when faculty was allowed to carry in school, not only would Layman be carrying, but he would probably gladly furnish all the teachers and staff who wanted or needed.

"Tommen missing school was not his fault," Walter began. "If anyone is to blame, it should be me."

"No one is blaming anyone except the madman who took him," Layman assured him. "And while it may be understandable and some work may be excused, he still missed a lot of class time that will need to be made up in some way. It's not just about getting homework done; it's about sitting lecture time. Just like the school has so many 'free' snow days, eventually we have to start making them up at the end of the year."

"You want to keep him for summer school?"

"Hopefully not. With the advent of technology, I think we can get away with having him take some makeup work online. I've seen that you caught up with your English work online—some of it creatively—so that is all accounted for. The rest of your classes, we'll have to work something out."

Tommen grinned. "Well, I'm sure Mr. Robinson would be more than happy to let me borrow his collection of *The Joy of Painting* and watch that for some makeup time."

"You never know," Layman told him.

Tommen had a hard time judging his attitude. Normally the man was on him for one thing or another, usually the fighting, telling him how violence wasn't the answer and if he kept following the path it would only take him to places he wouldn't like and blah, blah, blah. As if getting his ass kicked every other day was always his own fault and not the gang that did it for sport. Now he seemed almost friendly, if his shitty attempt at amiability and humor was any indication. A case of not realizing what you had until it's almost gone?

Even as he thought it, there was a gentle knock on the door and Mrs. Wendell poked her head in. "Am I interrupting?"

"Not at all," Layman told her. "Actually, you're just the person we need."

She stepped in the room and shut the door behind her. "Tommen," she acknowledged. "Doing well, I hope?"

Tommen shrugged. "Sure, I guess."

She handed Layman a few papers, and he laid them out on the desk, turning them so Tommen and his dad could read them.

"Mrs. Wendell has compiled a list of the classes you need to take. It's as simple as logging in to the student portal like how you normally would to get to your English class. The next time you get in, you'll see more classes. I believe most of them are titled Makeup Econ or Makeup Web Design and things like that. There is an expiration date on when you can access them and complete the work. Once that's closed, you forfeit everything you didn't complete."

"If nothing else, you should at least get into each of the lessons or units," Mrs. Wendell went on. "Just going into them and watching the lecture video or reading the material will be makeup for an absence even if you 'fail' everything else in it. I don't think you'll have a problem with any of the work, however."

"And this is something that can be done on any computer?" Walter wondered.

"Any computer, but I don't think all of the material is mobile friendly. You can try it on your phone, but no guarantees."

"That's more in his department, not mine. If there's nothing else...?"

"Actually, there is," Layman said.

Tommen only glimpsed the flash of the Fast Band that his dad slipped into. Had he gotten up and gone somewhere? Had he cursed Layman and his apparent inconsideration? Whatever he did, he still looked disgruntled as he shifted in his chair and nodded for Layman to continue.

"I don't need to rehash what happened," Layman began. "Everyone is coming back from Christmas break, and they're all happy about it. You guys' Christmas break, however, and the weeks leading up to it, were not what anyone would wish to endure. Now you're coming back to school, to normal life, and, quite honestly, normal life is normally less than stellar and stress-free."

So that's what this was all about. Layman knew that he caused Tommen a lot of stress and teeth-grinding, so he was going for the good cop vibe now because he was finally understanding the effects of that stress. It wasn't just something that could be pushed off, not when there's the stress of captivity and a dying father to deal with now.

"You two seem to have a great relationship," Layman blathered on. "And that's wonderful, not everyone does. But we want to make sure that you're okay coming back to normal life. Because you know that everyone will have questions for you. School isn't much fun, but we want this place to be a safe environment where your biggest worries are the next test coming up and who you're going to the dance with, especially since Eric and Varad are both gone, too."

Oh, right, couldn't forget that bit, could you?

"If he does start having problems, what would you suggest?" his dad wondered, his tone hard to judge. Was he just going along with it so they could all move on, or was he actually listening to this bullshit?

"There are any number of options available; you might remember we discussed some of them toward the beginning of the year. We have Art Therapy; Drama Club is taking auditions for the play and gathering up their behind-the-scenes crew; there are any number of religious groups. A lot of the teachers know you write but won't share your stories, but you might consider writing for the school paper."

The same old talk, the same old stupid options. He would never live down Art Therapy; he wasn't an actor; he wasn't religious; and writing for the school paper sounded like English class all over again except he had to actually care about what was going on around the school, and the Powers That Be were a group of drama-loving senior girls who would never respect him for anything.

"And as always, you know my door is always open," Mrs. Wendell chimed in. "Or Mr. Layman, if you'd rather talk to him."

I'd rather go stick my head in a pit of vipers.

Tommen stood. "I'm fine. Life is back to normal, and I'd really rather just move on without having to talk about it over and over again. I'm not an artist or anything like that. Most of the people here don't like me anyway."

"That's not true," Mrs. Wendell said softly. "Lots of people like you."

"Yeah? How many people—besides teachers—have ever stepped in when Tyler Freeman is whaling on me? Who stands up for me then? Only Eric and Varad, and they're gone. No one else has. And no one else will."

"Tommen," his dad began.

Before anyone could say more, the bell rang, ending first period. Within seconds, the muffled sound of students moving through the hallways reached them in Layman's office.

"First period's over, and I'd really like to make it to Economics," Tommen said. "Tuesdays are our investment projects, and I made a lot of money while I was gone."

It was a challenge, and Layman relented, giving him a single, sighing nod. Mrs. Wendell moved wordlessly aside as he pushed past and left the room.

He headed for his locker, his legs taking him instinctively to 371 where his hands knew the combination even if he couldn't actively bring the numbers to mind, which, in retrospect, was a really good thing because there was little more embarrassing than giving his principal and counselor some cold words and then having to go back with his tail between his legs to ask for his locker combo.

Tommen would have given anything for Eric or Varad to be there, to run up to his locker and slam the door shut on him or something, make some sarcastic comment, let him know that everything truly was back to normal. In the end, he couldn't be sure whether it was a blessing or a curse that they were gone. If they were around, they would be just like everyone else, asking questions, spreading rumors, whether maliciously or not. But at least they would be some semblance of normal, something he could look forward to.

It was a terrible thing when he found himself looking forward to Economics and the investment project. He hadn't been lying, though, his stocks had made some good money while he was gone. He'd done the math and the short answer questions that accompanied every week's analysis, that on top of all the class work from the other eight days he'd missed. Eight days? More? He couldn't be sure.

Another strange thing, though, was that for as bad and uncertain and potentially dangerous as his captivity had been, he found that he would have rathered been there than here in school, and it wasn't just the impending bombardment of questions and the rumors that would snake their way from circle to circle. He'd felt alive.

Well, as a lot of returning soldiers and some cops said, you never feel more alive than when you're almost dead. But he'd felt alive. Part of something. Not part of Rifun's group, of course, but part of something bigger.

He'd been part of Time. Finally, it had been more than just some weird secret cult-like training where he had to sit down, keep his mouth shut and try not to get into trouble. He'd been right in the middle of a Time fight, where everything mattered, and because lives were in danger—most notably his—he wasn't told to just sit down and be good. Essentially, he was forced to use his abilities, save his skin, and worry about the ramifications later. Or, at least, that's what it would have been like if Rifun hadn't all but made his pitiful talents null and void and all but Suppressed him completely.

Tommen had just shut his locker and turned to go to class when suddenly he was falling face-first towards the floor, books and papers flying and fluttering through the air. He Banded quickly enough that he was able to make a safe roll to the ground, even if it was still a hard landing that knocked the wind out of him. He barely got his bearings and was able to look around when he saw a huge boot coming toward him. He protected his face and was able to twist around just in time to see Tyler Freeman stepping over him. A couple of his goons did as well, one of them "accidentally" kicking him in the shoulder.

"Welcome back, Tommy," Tyler taunted. "Glad to see you grew a pair and came back. Or is that part of you being a terrorist now? Coming back to exact revenge?"

Before Tommen could say anything, they were already moving away, laughing and mocking him further, their voices growing louder and louder so all could hear, but especially him.

He wanted to run away.

He wanted to cry.

He wanted to die.

He would have taken a year in that cave over the fifteen seconds that had just transpired. He kept his head down as he gathered his books and papers and folders, a few faceless people handing him some of his things that had scattered near and far. He ignored the questions, straightened his back, made his gaze glass over, and headed numbly for class.

It was a trick he'd learned years ago in middle school, to deaden his senses to the world and work solely on muscle memory to get him where he needed to go, and reflexes to keep him from running into things and people. It worked well, on the same principle as looking busy so no one interrupted him. He navigated the halls of the school easily enough, avoiding people and obstacles, arriving at Morrison's room feeling little better than a zombie. But the most important thing had been achieved: He hadn't cried. If he hadn't deadened himself to the world, he knew his mind would have only dwelt on the incident and he probably would have cried like a baby, and he couldn't have that.

He could have Banded and taken the time to collect himself, but it was like Micaiah said, "You can Band as much as you want and get as much work done as you like, but at the end of the day, you only move as fast as your slowest customer, and you are always dependent on Base Time."

"Tommen."

Likely everyone knew that Tommen was safe, his dad had saved the day, almost died, and was now recovering. Charleston was big, but the news had blared the story incessantly from start to finish, and word got around. Why Mr. Morrison would be surprised to see Tommen standing before him was a mystery. Only when Tommen handed him the excused note from Layman did the man seem to remember himself.

"Right," Morrison said. "A little extended vacation, but your dad did come and pick up your homework for you. I expect you had enough time to complete everything?"

Tommen nodded and started handing over papers as Morrison named them, checking them off in his gradebook.

"Some of these I'm just going to mark as complete-incomplete because they're old and, weight-wise, unimportant. What about the Chapter Four quiz, did you get that?" Tommen turned it over. "The quizzes were meant to be pop quizzes, no notes, no book, so the maximum score I'm going to enter for you is a ninety-five." Tommen mused over the fairness and legality of that, then figured there was no way he was going to have a perfect score on it anyway, so it didn't matter. "And how about those tests, I know there were a couple."

"Here's one," Tommen said, handing it over. "The other was online."

"Yes, and I did get that one. You did very well, actually. And how about your investment project?"

"I did all the work, it's all caught up."

"Okay, why don't you give me the weeks you missed and keep the papers for this week; we'll go over them like normal."

"Okay."

"I think that's it. Go ahead and take your seat; I'm just going to take a minute to organize all of these and then we'll get started in class."

Tommen couldn't have heard better words. The man didn't ask, didn't pry, didn't make a scene, didn't give him funny looks once he got over his initial surprise. He was making a lot of exceptions to the missed work rule, but otherwise he treated it like any other student missing a few days of class. This was going to be a normal class.

Well, as far as Morrison was concerned, it would be normal. Tommen didn't miss the looks he got from his classmates. He'd been gone for two weeks, kidnapped and held for ransom. He'd almost lost his dad.

Did his classmates actually think that stuff when they saw him? Had they talked about it at all, and Morrison would have to tell them to be quiet and focus on their work? Or had they noticed him gone the first day or two only to dismiss it after that as nothing unusual? Were they more surprised that he'd come back at all? Had they expected him to go the way of Eric, huddle alone on a computer doing all the work online so as to avoid contact with other human beings? That's what he wanted to do, the more he felt their penetrating stares. He saw a couple girls whispering to each other. He saw a note going around. Even after the bell rang, rendering all incoming students late for class, Morrison sat quietly as his desk, trying to sift through Tommen's late papers as quickly as he could.

He wanted to disappear.

He wanted to cry.

He wanted to die.

Instead, he did his best to ignore the heat reddening his cheeks and pretend to be looking for this week's investment papers.

"Dude, are you okay?"

Tommen looked up, unsure where the sound had come from or if the question was even directed at him. He Banded long enough to look around and see Garret staring at him. Tommen dropped the Band.

"What?" he asked dumbly.

"Are you okay?" the junior repeated. "We heard what happened."

"Fine," Tommen answered quickly, going back to his papers and hoping Morrison would hurry up and start class.

"Is it true you were held captive by the same guy who killed those women?" another classmate, Nick, asked.

"Yeah." Tommen hoped his curt tone would deter them. It didn't.

"Did they really hold you in a cave in the mountains?"

Tommen was ready for a smart reply but Hannah beat him, her tongue dripping acid as she said loud enough for half the class to hear, "Are you sure you're Tommen Forbes? You're not someone else, right? What year is it, anyway? 1855? Or maybe 1903?"

"He probably wishes it was," her partner in crime, Natalya, agreed seamlessly. "Did they molest you in there?"

"Now that's enough," Morrison barked from his desk, eyes like a couple of stones. "That is way out of line. Both of you with me;

we're going to take a little walk down to Mr. Layman's office."

"One for both of us," Hannah snickered only loud enough for those immediately around her to hear.

Tommen rubbed his face. He wanted the earth to open up and swallow him.

He wanted to cry.

He wanted to die.

He wanted to be anywhere in the world but sitting in Economics.

What he wouldn't have given to have his old friendship with Eric and Varad. It wasn't quite on the same level as crossing the universe, risking his life and a civil war in order to get it back, but at the moment, it was pretty darn close.

At the very least, the awkwardness of the bitches' comments was enough to ward off any other questions, and Tommen was free to open his notebook and start writing without interruption while Morrison was gone, which wasn't very long, really. When the middle-aged man returned, he ignored the disorganized pile of Tommen's papers still on his desk and instead grabbed his briefcase that he always used on investment days. At the sight of the briefcase, everyone in the class began packing up and grabbing their papers.

"We lost a day because of the snow, so we're going to have to make this quick," Morrison told them. "Check your investments and get your numbers down. You have about thirty minutes, then we're going to quickly go over yesterday's planned assignment. Then you can get started on your homework or finish your weekly investment. Tommen, stay just a second so we can get the rest of these papers checked off."

So while everyone else moseyed their way out the door and meandered down to the computer lab, Tommen went again to Morrison's desk, fully aware that he had no intention of going over the papers.

"Tommen, what Hannah and Natalya said was entirely inappropriate and way out of line," Morrison began. "I just want you to know that it is being dealt with, but if they or anyone else ever makes similar remarks —"

"I know," Tommen cut in. "Tell someone, get someone involved."

"Your attitude isn't convincing."

"Because I don't appreciate how everyone is just suddenly concerned because I was gone for two weeks, as if it hasn't already been happening over the last, I don't know, ten years?"

Morrison sighed. "I know. And maybe we as staff or just as adults were in the wrong, have been in the wrong. Maybe this is our wake up call. All I'm asking is that if you need help, ask for it."

There had been a meeting, Tommen figured. More than just watercooler gossip, there had been a meeting. It had probably started out as the usual student safety meeting, lockdown drills, stranger danger, drug and violence intervention, the whole nine yards. But inevitably it had turned to a particular sixteen year old sophomore who had recently been kidnapped, then returned. He'd been bullied his entire school career, lost both of his best friends, and very nearly lost his dad, his only living family. Did they know about his hearing loss, too?

He was on suicide watch, he realized suddenly. With good reason, probably, but he found himself a little put off by it. Why now? Why hadn't the bullying and the fighting and the general disdain for school not been enough? Why had it taken all of this for anyone to care? Was "better late than never" really applicable here? Was it sufficient to make up for it all?

"Tommen?" Morrison asked, interrupting his thoughts.

"Huh?" Had he said something?

Morrison leaned back in his chair and folded his arms. "We were also informed, via your dad telling Mr. Layman, that you suffered hearing loss and have hearing aids."

Tommen sighed and pushed back his hair enough that Morrison could see them, just barely visible.

"Are you okay where you're sitting? I can move you if you

need."

"I'm fine," Tommen told him.

Morrison studied him for a moment longer, and Tommen almost expected him to start in on some long lecture about being different and getting help and pretty much restating everything he had just said. In the end, he simply nodded and stood, grabbing his briefcase.

When they reached the computer lab, some students had started in hard on their investment projects, diligently gathering their data and studiously working out the math that went with it. Others were working on homework from other classes, their investments pushed to the side to make room for history, chemistry, English, and so on. And still some were busy playing games and going on social media sites through backdoor URLs and protocols.

When Morrison walked in, the class hurriedly returned to their assigned work. Tommen found a computer with at least one empty seat on either side of him, no easy feat given that there were forty computers in the lab and thirty-five students. But with two in Layman's office, one out sick, and one not back from Christmas vacation, the whole place was just a little roomier.

At the start of the project, they each had $100,000 to "invest" however they chose. Basically it amounted to picking some stocks and just observing them, doing all the applicable math by hand versus the computer doing the investments and making any real money. Or losing it, as Tommen observed most in the class were wont to do. Some had moderate losses, sitting there with $70,000 or so. Others were suffering Great Depression kind of losses, sitting at $20,000 or less.

Tommen, however, was a rich man, or he would be had he actually invested money. When all the math was said and done, he was looking at $160,000 and his stocks were showing no signs of slowing.

Whether it was because he had the best gains or as some attempt at integrating him back into the class, Morrison called him out on it, making him stand and briefly address the class and talk about his investments. He wasn't allowed to say which stocks he chose, but he had to give a reason why he chose a particular sector to invest in—banking, restaurants, and so on. The whole "presentation" only took about five minutes, and when it was done, Morrison announced that they were moving on to the lesson plan from the previous day.

Tommen sat, feeling very conspicuous and trying to focus solely on the lecture, or at least pretend like he was interested. Time was, even though he wasn't fond of public speaking, he would have loved to have gotten up and bragged about making more than the rest of his classmates. *That's right, bitches, I'm just a dumb country hick but I out-invested all of you. So fuck you and your city learning.*

He had no such desire now, to be the best and make sure everyone knew it. Most of it existed only in his head, anyway. He wasn't athletic; he would never beat anyone in anything physical. He wasn't particularly talented at any one thing, or not anything that mattered; no one gave much of a rat's ass that he could tan a hide to top-dollar quality, at least until they realized that the smaller furs that they might get at the outdoor sporting goods store actually came from him. But on the whole, no one cared. He wasn't the best or even close to being the best at any one thing. He was just...average. And that on a good day.

So he waited for Morrison's lecture to end, at which time they were free to work on their investments or homework. Tommen turned quietly back to his computer and went to work.

Chapter Fourteen
Back to Work

Walter couldn't remember the last time he'd waited so long for a wound to heal. Pinpoint Banding was kind of like your pinky toe, you don't know what you've lost until it's gone. Heck, even when he had hurt himself, it was most often stupid cuts and nicks from his own clumsiness—cutting his thumb while slicing potatoes, paper cuts, and so on. He hadn't actually taken a bullet or a knife or even a dog bite on the job, or at all, for probably fifty years or more, easily. Some called him lucky, others God's pet, but the fact remained that Walter Forbes was basically Superman. And now he wasn't.

He put on a good face for Layman for the remainder of the man's speech. Walter knew well that Tommen was doing emotionally what he was doing physically, putting on a brave face so no one could see how the pain was getting to him. The kid had been through a lot. Walter knew that. He wished he knew how to help him. He wished Tommen would be more open to getting help if he could find it. But just like any number of repeat drug offenders, he couldn't help someone who doesn't want to be helped. Tommen was convinced that he could just tough it out and put time and distance between him and everything that had happened and it would all go away, and that was the mindset he would carry until something changed or he finally broke.

Speaking of breaking things, Walter damn near broke his other leg as he slipped on the sidewalk heading back out to the car. Part of him hoped no one saw it, or if they did, they couldn't identify who it was who'd slipped. The other part of him hoped someone did see it and knew who it was so word would get back to whoever it needed to get back to in order to get some salt on this ice.

He made it to the car regardless and got in, forcing himself to be mindful of his movements; he couldn't just slide into his normal comfortable position like he always did and expect everything to go well. For one, even though he normally sat with the seat all the way back, he knew he would have to move up just a little in order to give himself some more forceful leverage since he was driving with his left foot. And it brought him closer to the wheel so he could rest his arms and thereby his shoulders a bit more. That and being slightly scrunched put some pressure on his thigh wound which actually made it feel a little better.

Pinpoint Banding was kind of like your pinky toe, you don't know what you've lost until it's gone.

By the time he'd even started the car, it felt like a short eternity had passed. His right thigh was screaming at him, his left foot felt clumsy and awkward, and his shoulders were tensioning like a couple rubber bands as he forced his arms to stay in position and not simply flop away from the steering wheel. And he still had a long drive ahead of him. No longer than normal, obviously, but it sure felt like it.

Sighing, he leaned back and fingered the script bottle in his pocket.

Don't do it, he told himself. *You can tough it out for a couple more weeks. You know where this goes. You know exactly where this goes. You've arrested people who go there.*

His left foot found the brake, and he shifted into gear. The car lurched forward, Walter's driving almost as bad as Tommen's had been, starting out, that mini-heart attack as your life flashes before your eyes and you're pretty sure you're going to die before you ever get out of the parking lot. He really hoped no one saw that one.

By the time he reached the main road, he'd managed to trick his brain into going back into police mode, thinking he was in a cruiser and he was heading somewhere serious. Reject the pain, reject the aches, reject the fatigue, carry out the mission. It wasn't easy, but it took the edge off even as his body seemed to realize that it had been tricked. He had no lights or siren and was following all basic traffic laws; everything was apparently normal. As soon as the thought crossed his mind, all the pain came roaring back. He seriously considered the script bottle in his pocket, rejected it harshly.

Pinpoint Banding was like your pinkie toe, you don't know what you've lost until it's gone.

The light turned green and he started forward again, this time much more smoothly. The last thing he needed was to get pulled over by one of his own brothers. Wouldn't that just make their day at the office? Hey guys, guess who I pulled over today! Walter! Oh, wow, he's out of the hospital? Yeah, and he didn't even come to say hi yet!

I'm coming, I'm coming, Walter thought ruefully, as he passed up the right-hand turn for the left-hand turn, making his way deeper into the city until he pulled into the packed parking lot in front of the big brick building in the governmental complex. He thought about pulling around back and messing with them a little, but figured he should do things the right way. Just this once.

He turned off the car and slumped in his seat. Damn, but he hurt. That had been a workout in itself. And he still had to go home. Maybe he should have turned right. Well, he was here now. Might as well say hi. But still...

Pinpoint Banding was like your —

Oh, knock it off. Walter shook his head and tapped out a single painkiller. Just one. Just enough to get him through the office and then back home where he could get a nap. Damn, was he that feeble? He was injured, but not helpless.

Grudgingly, Walter grabbed his cane and got out of the car. He was only injured, not helpless. He hurt, and he knew he was going to limp and be stiff and look like hell, but he wasn't going to shuffle with his head down like some frail old man.

His resolve lasted until he got to the door. He probably should have saved his bravado until he actually got among his peers, but at least he looked good crossing the parking lot. Internally, he shook his head and scolded himself.

You sound like Tommen, always have to look good, look impressive, show no weakness. That may have been true at one time, but now it's your time of rest. You don't have to do it all.

Not that he liked admitting such things, and he wasn't about to admit them aloud. But he—

"Walt!"

Walter startled and might have fallen over except that he was still able to Band enough that he caught his balance before anyone knew anything was off. When he released the Band, all his wounds began stinging anew, and he gritted his teeth.

Emily was the receptionist this morning, and she stared at Walter like a deer in headlights for a good ten seconds before getting up and moving out from behind the desk to capture him in a surprise but not-uncharacteristic hug. He let out a small grunt of pain.

"Oh my God, I'm so happy to see you," she said before releasing him. "You...you're the first good news we've had in weeks."

"Well, you know I'm a workaholic and always aim to please," Walter told her.

"I'll call Greg and let him know you're here."

"No need. I think I'll surprise the rest of them and spread the cheer."

"God, we need it."

Walter paused. "What do you mean?"

Emily frowned and took a step back. She looked ready to say one thing, thought better of it, and finally replied, "Well, you'll see. Or maybe you won't. Like you said, spread the cheer."

Walter had been through too much lately to be in the mood for ominous words and cryptic messages from those he knew. He was trying to put all of that behind him for the time being, move on from the disaster that had been Christmas. So he simply thanked Emily and went on his way, through the door to the room behind the bullet-proof glass.

He paused and looked around as the door swung closed. Emily hadn't been exaggerating when she said the place needed a little cheer. Normally the guys couldn't be bothered to take down Christmas decorations until at least April, and the place had been very festive even by Thanksgiving. Now it was dull and gray, devoid of any cheer. Forget taking the decorations down by April, there were always still little tufts of cheap garland and the occasional curse as someone stepped on and crushed a stray glass bulb ornament rolled out from under a desk, lasting all the way until the Fourth of July.

That wasn't to say the guys were messy or left the office in disarray, it's just how it was. Random little mementos of joy and festivity to keep them sane, mixed in with the dust bunnies reminding them to do their work.

Now, though, it was like the whole place had been deep cleaned by General Alfred Hitchcock. The entire office was nearly spotless, probably had been two weeks ago, and everything seemed painted over with a new shade of gray, as if all the color and joy had been sucked out of the place. Not that Walter expected everyone to be smiling—police work was one part heart-stopping pants-pissing action and nine parts office drudgery—but it was just...dull.

"Damn," Walter said aloud. "I'm pretty sure I got out of the hospital, but I think I just walked into a graveyard."

Whether someone actually heard his words or just coincidentally looked up to see him he wasn't sure, but first one person saw him, then another, and a call went up. "Walter's back!"

In no time at all, there were wide-eyed stares and dropped jaws and excited whispers. Then the clapping started.

Walter had never fought in a war. He skipped over the Civil War and the Spanish-American War, went dark during both World Wars, Korea, Vietnam, the Gulf War. But he had been at the airport when those soldiers had come home. He saw the weariness and the haunted looks, the gazes that wondered why these people were clapping, what fantasy were they imagining that clapping would make it all better? What Hollywood heroics did they think they'd done? There had been no heroics, nothing that would win Hollywood gold. Everything they'd seen and done would only make Hollywood sick, and then it would make them rich.

Walter had never fought in a war, and he would not claim that anything he'd done had been close to what the soldiers faced, but now he understood those looks in the airport, the weariness and the haunting. He didn't want their clapping, didn't want the attention, didn't want the praise or the admiration. He didn't want to be pointed out to the new recruits as an example of a fine officer. He didn't want any of it. As much as he loathed the office drudgery, he wished that was all he was in to do, just punch in for his shift and make for his little cubicle.

Even as he thought it, he realized the other half of the equation, why the office seemed so dull: there were decidedly fewer cops, and probably half a dozen of them were normally second-shifters. They'd lost over a dozen officers in a single round; they were strapped for coverage, pulling guys from everywhere — second-shifters, the reserves, even the Academy, it seemed, to cover some of the office work — but it still wasn't enough.

All of this crossed his mind in about three seconds, long enough for him to get a good sweep of the room and then be surprised by Standish coming up on his other side, clapping him on the back so he gasped in pain and tried to cover it up with a cough. When he managed to straighten back up, Standish pulled him into a bro-hug.

"Hey, man, how ya doin?"

"I'm in quite a bit of pain, thank you," Walter managed.

Standish took a step back. "Sorry. Seriously, though, dude, how are you? One minute we hear you're about to die, the next you're out and about just fine and dandy."

"Decidedly less than that, but yeah, getting there. Slowly but surely."

"Very good. Listen, there's some cake in the break room. I can take five minutes, let's have some cake and coffee. How's that sound?"

Sounded like he didn't have much of a choice seeing how they had already started walking toward the break room in the last ten words. But he didn't have much of an objection.

"Where'd the cake come from?" Walter wondered as Standish crossed the room and started fishing for a couple of pieces, of the four tiny ones left.

Standish paused for just a second, which seemed like an eternity. He went back to cutting and serving. "Um, well, Pat's retiring. Actually, he retired officially on December 31st, but we had his retirement party yesterday."

"Why wasn't I invited?" Walter felt hurt. He'd worked with Pat a long time, trusted him, looked up to him even.

"I don't know. Supposedly him and his wife are taking off for Arizona at the end of the month, maybe you can drop by and see him before he goes."

Walter sat at the table and Standish brought out two mugs from the cupboard. "You can have coffee, right?"

"Yeah."

Standish handed him a steaming mug as he sat. "I don't know why you weren't invited. At the same time, yesterday wasn't exactly a great day to be out and about; even some who were invited didn't show if they didn't have to be here." He shrugged. "Maybe he was just trying to look out for you, especially since you just got out of the hospital and all."

That would be just like Pat. At the same time, just an invitation would have been nice, a little Thinking of You card or something.

"But anyway, how are you doing? First we hear that you're going to die and now this. What gives?"

Walter shrugged as best he could. "I wish I knew, but I'm not going to turn my nose up at miracles."

"Miracles is right. Somebody upstairs seems to like you."

He got around having to reply immediately by taking a bite of cake. It tasted like day-old cake, but it was better than hospital food and a relief from what had survived a week without tending at home.

He chewed slowly, trying to come up with some response or even something off-topic, but by the time he came up with something,

Steggmann walked in the room.

"I'm not invited to this party?" he said with fake hurt.

"Two more pieces of cake, chief," Standish pointed out.

"Maybe later if they're still here. Walt, I'd like to talk to you if I could."

Steggmann never asked if he "could" do anything, not like that. Still, Walter nodded, got to his feet, grabbed his coffee, and followed the chief of police out of the break room and down the short hall to his office. Steggmann's Christmas decorations were still up, Walter noted, but he doubted the man even realized they were there still. Probably not until April.

"Have a seat." Steggmann held out a hand as he went behind his desk and sat, leaning back a bit and folding his hands on his belly.

Walter obeyed. "Is everything all right, sir?"

"You tell me. How are you feeling?" He went on before Walter could answer. "I walk in one day, they're getting ready to pull the plug. I walk in the next day, you're ready to walk out the door. What happened?"

My son braved hell, high water, and civil war to cross the universe and bring me a cure from a distant planet populated by human-animal hybrids?

"Well, as Jim said, Somebody upstairs must like me."

Steggmann nodded unconvincingly. "Maybe. Why don't you give me a little better rundown than that?"

Walter nodded once and shifted position. "Three bullets, sir. One severed my femoral artery and passed through. Another hit my sternum, ricocheted, tore through my lung, chipped my shoulder blade, passed through. The other hit me in the chest, did not touch my lung, but it spider-webbed my shoulder blade and got lodged. Anything beyond that was flesh-wound only."

"Any head injury?"

"A few stitches, but nothing to the skull or brain."

"What about the coma?"

"The doctors did a small textbook of tests and scans and exams on me; they say I'm completely fine."

Steggmann nodded slowly. "I'm glad to hear it. Any physical therapy?"

"First session on Friday."

"You don't sound enthusiastic." Steggmann's eyes glittered with amusement.

"I've heard many horror stories about PT; I have little desire to gather some of my own."

"Well, I don't blame you." His amusement faded to dull melancholy of a man who is practiced in hiding his feelings and toughing it out, but having a hard time with something much greater. "There's been too much horror around here lately." He paused and made a small sigh. "Walter, I'm going to be very straightforward. Are you planning on coming back, assuming you were able to get the physical clearance?"

"You're asking about my mental state."

"I am. What you experienced, not just on that day but in the weeks leading up to it, is more than most anyone would bear in a lifetime. And now is a time where you can walk away with honor, with your head held high. I don't want you to come back and have something happen to you because you were too stubborn to quit while you had the chance."

"Is that what Pat did?"

Steggmann paused again. Finally, "Yeah. That's what Pat did."

Walter shifted positions and ran his tongue over his teeth. "How many men?"

"Don't do this to yourself, Walt."

"How many men, Greg?"

For a second, he wasn't sure Steggmann would answer. Then, "Seven from Bravo Team. Three from Alpha Team."

"And?"

"Dan from Bravo Team sustained what should have been a lethal neck wound, but he'll pull through. He's on suicide watch. Sean's been paralyzed from chest down, has use of his arms but that's all. Pat wasn't badly hurt, but he finally conceded that it's a young man's game, and he's not a young man anymore. Everyone was ordered to take time off for psychological evaluation. Miles is set to come back next week, but I don't think Connie will."

Walter leaned back in his seat as best he could. Ten dead. One lost to injury, another to retirement, and one on suicide watch. Plus one that might not come back.

"Don't beat yourself up, Walt," Steggmann said as a warning. "There was nothing you could have done different to make it any better; we went up against a maniac. No one blames you. If anyone is to blame, it's me."

"What for?"

"For not doubling and re-doubling our manpower and resources, budgeting and city powers be damned. We got your son back and Miss Guile is alive, but there is still an armed and dangerous band of fugitives on the run who snub their noses at the cops, killed some of our finest, and ran away laughing. That is unacceptable, and I will take the blame for it."

No doubt there had been dozens of press conferences and interviews and meetings both public and private as people wanted to know what happened, how it happened, why it happened, and how to keep it from happening again. And not only was everyone a critic, but suddenly everyone became an expert in stand-offs, hostage negotiations, and firefights. Suddenly everyone had a piece of advice for them about how they should have done this, or if they could have done that, then disaster could have been avoided. As if any of them had been there and really knew what had happened. As if any of them, even the other officers involved, could have understood the true gravity of the situation.

But they didn't, and they couldn't, and now the entire department had to dig in to weather the long haul of bad press and skewed interviews.

"If you want," Steggmann went on, "I know you missed the memorial service, but the government building wants to put up a plaque commemorating everyone involved. You could help them with that."

Walter let out a breath. "I think I've done enough helping for a while, thank you."

"Walt, don't make me put you on suicide watch, too."

He chuckled. "No worries on that front. I couldn't leave Tommen behind, not after he already almost lost me once."

"I like you, Walter, but I will tell you that I've heard that excuse a number of times from people who still went on to attempt suicide. I've got eyes on you, all of you. And if anything smells out of place—"

"I know, I got it." Walter nodded. "I know."

"Just promise me you're not going to blame yourself."

How could he not blame himself? Ten men died because he'd led them into a slaughter against an enemy they could not hope to understand or fight back against. Heck, he'd been more prepared to fight and he'd still almost died. How anyone had survived that bloodbath was a mystery.

"I can't say I won't blame myself," Walter answered honestly. "But I can tell you that suicide is the furthest thing from my mind right now."

"For now, I'll trust you on your word. You seem to be doing well."

"Well, it's not bad now, but it's only going to get worse as I can do more, everything except come back to work."

"Cabin fever's a bitch," Steggmann agreed. "But that does remind me, the girls in the office have a stack of paperwork for you to fill out and sign. I've already approved everything."

"What kind of paperwork?"

"Medical leave papers. When you were heading downhill, I took the liberty of using up some of your vacation days, that way a full check would still be coming in, for Tommen's sake. Then with your miraculous recovery, it goes into the realm of extended medical leave. But don't worry, from what I understand, your vacation days have been mysteriously recuperated for a job well done."

"Wonder how that happened." Walter managed a dry laugh. "Yeah, I'll grab that on my way out. Thank you, though, for the days, and Tommen said you took him to lunch and you had a little chat."

"I try to do right by my guys and their families. Like I told him, if you need anything, let me know and I'll see what I can do."

"Well, it's very much appreciated."

"How is Tommen doing, anyway? They didn't mistreat him, did they? In captivity, I mean?"

Walter shook his head. "No, not really, or so he says. Malnourished, unshaven, but no worse for wear on that front. But when Rifun tried to shoot him, it damaged his hearing permanently so he's got hearing aids now."

"Shit. That's got to be a blow."

"It is, but there's nothing anyone can do about it. You can't just fix it. He got a trial pair while his were on order and we just picked those up today. You can see it on his face; he is absolutely crushed. His life is over, or it is in his eyes."

"He's sixteen, he's supposed to be invincible and worried about girls and —" Steggmann chuckled. "— going out and binge drinking and smoking with his friends."

"Well, that's the other thing. Varad moved away, and both he and Eric basically abandoned him, so Tommen's got no friends right now at school."

"That's gotta be rough on a kid."

"It is. I wish I could help him, but it's something he's going to have to deal with on his own."

"He still working at the bakery?"

"Yeah, he's working today. Everything back to normal, or trying to be."

"Best thing for him, show him the world didn't end while he was away."

"All I can do at this point."

They stared at each other for a minute or two, each trying to read the other's thoughts. Steggmann broke the silence.

"So, you really are planning on coming back if you get the physical clearance?"

Walter nodded once. "I don't think that will be too much of a problem, getting the clearance."

"Glad to hear it. Either way, I want you to go to meet with a CISM counselor." Steggmann continued before he could protest. "Mandatory for everyone who was there, whether they're returning or not. If you are able to come back, once you get a rough return date, then you're going to be evaluated again. Mandatory. If you or the CISM counselor says you need further help, that can be arranged, but the two I mentioned are mandatory if you want to wear your blues again. Got it?"

"When is the first one?" Walter agreed grudgingly.

He knew why they were required. On any given day, he was a huge advocate for grief, stress, and suicide counseling for police and other responders. But normally he was the one who came out on top, came through the clear; normally he was the one the others came to when they needed unofficial, off-the-record counseling or advice. Well, not always, but most knew he was an open door if they needed an ear. Now it was turning the other way. He wasn't sure how he felt about it.

"The initial CISM counselors already came and left, but we can call one back. If you like, I can see if they'll meet you before or after your physical therapy session," Steggmann offered.

So he could either go to physical therapy depressed, or go to counseling grouchy and irritable. There was no situation where he won, was there?

"Sure, why not?" Walter conceded. "Before might be better."

"Well, how about I get one in, and then I'll give them your phone number and you can hash out the details?"

"Works for me."

"Just remember, this is mandatory."

"I know, I know."

"Think of it this way, Walter. Tommen's been through a lot, too, only he's a lot less likely to want to talk. So you need to make sure you get yourself in order so you can help him like you want and he needs."

Damn Steggmann and his logic. "I understand."

"Good. Now then, I think I've kept you away from your cake long enough. Why don't you go make sure someone didn't swipe it?"

Walter nodded reluctantly as he grabbed his cane and stood slowly. "It's probably gone by now, but I'll check anyway."

"And don't forget to see Emily about your paperwork."

With that, Walter left Steggmann's office, unsure of how he felt about the exchange.

Ten officers dead. Ten officers who had woken up to a perfectly normal day. Ten officers who had husbands, wives, children waiting for them at home, who would sit down to a nice dinner and talk about their day, who would express excitement at Christmas only a couple days away while lamenting that they still had to work. Ten officers who looked to him for leadership in that high-stakes situation. Seven who had died without ever seeing the faces of their killers or having a chance to fight back. Three who had seen the faces of their killers and had been unable to defend themselves or each other. All of them who looked to him for leadership and a plan and answers, who depended on him to be able to go home that night.

Ten officers dead. Because of him. Because he had caved to Rifun's demands that there be a strong police presence. He'd played right into his hands to murder police officers and get away with it. Ten officers who existed now only as the corpses six feet underground and names etched on some plaque. Because plaques were pretty. And cheap. Real life was ugly and messy and utterly priceless.

As expected, his cake was gone, and Walter was momentarily distracted from his mental self-flagellation by the disgust that someone would literally steal food that someone else had been eating off of, not knowing if that person had been sick or had some other transmissible disease. Still, he dumped his coffee and washed out the mug before leaving the break room. He started toward the door leading back out front but made a detour to Standish's cubicle. As usual, the poor guy just couldn't catch a break as he tossed away pen after pen, each one drying up in his hands.

"I'm heading out," Walter said.

Standish looked up, apparently startled in his attempt to find just one working pen. "Yeah? You coming back?"

"Eventually, once I get rid of this thing." He indicated the cane.

Standish stood and took Walter in a much gentler bro-hug. "Hey, man, I'm glad you're okay and your son's okay. You need anything, just let me know. You got that?"

"Yes, sir." Walter gave a mock salute and turned to leave.

He returned to the front desk where Emily did indeed have a small novel's worth of paperwork waiting for him, because apparently huge press and a doctor's note just wasn't enough to prove that he'd been down and out and was going to be down and out still for a time. Thankfully, everything had already been approved, so when he returned the papers to Emily, she was able to file them swiftly away.

"You going to be okay, Walt?" Emily asked as he dropped the pen back in the cup on the desk.

"I expect I will be," he told her, trying to sound as if everything was perfectly inconsequential. "I'm moving slow, but it looks worse than it is."

"Okay." She looked like she wanted to take him at face value but was having a difficult time. "Well, don't be a stranger between now and then. I'm sure there are all sorts of shenanigans you can get into while you're not working."

"Don't tempt me."

With that he departed, feeling pretty good until he got to the car and was faced with the daunting task of getting in and getting comfortable again. It took some doing and more than a few grunts and groans, but he managed to find the position he'd been in earlier, about as comfortable as he was going to get.

Even then he did not leave immediately. He could go home where he would just putter around uselessly until he went to pick up Tommen from work. He could go to the bakery and surprise the twins, but given the weighty conversations he'd just had, he didn't want to risk the chance of having another weighty conversation so soon. Plus the twins knew him too well, they'd see how distracted he was. Then they'd want to know why, and then they'd try to help.

When he did finally pull out of the parking lot, his destination was neither home nor the bakery. It was a road he did not take often, had only been there half a dozen times in ten years, but he knew the way well enough.

No surprise, there was a For Sale sign in the front yard with a picture of a pretty young realtor covering half the brokerage advertisement. The front walk and driveway looked recently shoveled, and at least one vehicle could be seen through the little windows in the garage door.

Walter pulled in the driveway and paused for just a second before gathering his strength and getting out of the car, trying not to wince or flinch or otherwise seem too out of the ordinary. Not that his bravado would matter. Pat had seen it all, done it all; he'd know Walter was fronting. Still, he tried to hobble confidently up to the front door where Avalanche the St. Bernard was woofing in his deep voice. Before Walter could even knock, the door opened and Pat expertly got between the dog and the outside.

"Walter," Pat said, his expression no less than shocked. "Sweet...mother of Moses, Walt, I heard you were near dead."

Patrick Pence was not a swearing kind of guy, though Walter wouldn't have considered that swearing, but Pat was the one who chastised the receptionists for saying, "Oh my God."

"Just about," Walter told him. "Heard you retired. And your party was yesterday."

"Yeah. Party. Storm kept everybody away. Doesn't bother me, though, I suppose."

Patrick Pence was not a public speaker, but he was the epitome of Southern hospitality, and he hadn't immediately ushered Walter into the house.

"Pat, are you okay?" Walter asked severely.

"Well, it's been a little busy, trying to sell the house and get moved to warmer climates and..."

"And...?"

Pat shifted his stance into one that said he was about to be very candid. "Walter, we've worked together a lot of years. We've seen things that should never be spoken of, should never be witnessed by anyone. Christmas was hard. Greg tell you the stats?"

"Yeah."

"I've lost men. You've lost men. We've all lost good guys, and sometimes there is no one to blame but the bad guys. But...I can't shake the feeling that this was different somehow. A whole team wiped out without a shot fired. Rifun's...companions. Walter, I can't speak for the pink girl, but if the rock guy was wearing a costume, it was a pretty darn convincing one. But you weren't fazed by any of it. No wide eyes or confused expression, no second-guessing, not even an off-handed joke. Walter, there's focus and commitment, and then..."

"What are you saying, Pat?" Walter asked, even though he knew exactly where this was going.

"You knew things, Walter. No, you know things. You knew exactly what you were doing, what had to be done, what the likely reactions and results were going to be."

"Wait, are you accusing me of setting the whole thing up? You think I staged my boy being abducted?"

"I don't know. Maybe it was a conspiracy of some sort, it went sour, Rifun tried to kill you to cover it up. I don't think so. I think it goes beyond even that, beyond your ordinary criminal, hostage types. Even beyond the run-of-the-mill terrorist types. I think there is more to the story. The problem is, whether or not you conspired with Rifun, you knew things that you didn't tell the rest of the guys. And ten good officers died because of that."

Walter bit his tongue. "Why did you retire?"

Pat folded his arms. "I'll admit, I took my concerns to Steggmann. He listened to me, said that while my concerns were valid and even logical, he wasn't going to slander a dying man's name. When you had your miraculous recovery, I went back to him but he dismissed me, saying there was no evidence of any sort of conspiracy. He also said that because of my seniority and the respect I garnered from the other officers, that if I went public or even just spread it around as office gossip, it would tear the precinct apart." He sighed. "The problem is, he was right. And we couldn't afford division, not after that kind of tragedy."

"So he offered you a way out."

"He said that I was of an age and time when I could retire if I wanted, and conceding that Christmas had been difficult and it was all a young man's game ensured that all names and reputations were saved."

"Pat..."

"I want to think good of you, Walter. And I do. You're a good officer and a good dad. We've been through a lot together. But I can't ignore what happened or my gut instinct saying that there is more to the story. Maybe just a good guy making a bad decision, I don't know. I just know that it's easier this way for all of us. I get a full pension, get to go someplace warm, and all names and reputations are left in tact."

Walter was at a loss for words. "Pat..."

"Goodbye, Walter. I hope things turn out well for you in the end."

With that, he took half a step back, pushing Avalanche back into the house, and closed the door in Walter's face. Walter stood there for a second, trying to comprehend what just happened. Then, with skin flush with cold and embarrassment, he turned and hobbled his way back to the car.

Chapter Fifteen
Becky

Tommen should have felt heartened when the bell rang, announcing the end of second period. Not only had Economics finally ended, but he was on his way to AP Physics. It was his class after all; Mr. Gillingham had given him the opportunity to get out of the idiot mainstream and into something he loved and wanted to do. He'd fought tooth and nail to get into the class. He was smart; he was one of the best in the class, and it was just his thing. He couldn't wait to be able to dual-enroll his senior year, to do some real work that actually meant something, to have his name on research papers and findings, to make a real difference in the scientific community.

But he found himself no more excited for third period than he had been for second period. If nothing else, he felt a little worse about going there. It was his class after all, but he'd missed several weeks. Sure, he'd gotten all the homework done and made sure to catch up on everything, but he'd still missed class. He'd had to do alternative assignments to group projects and one purely opportunistic field trip. It was nice to be able to get grades in and keep his scores up, but he'd missed class. He was no longer the best. He was going to fail. And all because of Rifun.

About the only thing that pleased him lately was how light his backpack was getting as he took out all the books and folders and papers, class by class. This time he made sure to keep an eye out for Tyler Freeman in case he decided to try another surprise attack. The attack never came, and he headed off to class.

He tried to get excited. He wished he could get excited. But by the time he actually reached the door to his class, he felt no more excited for AP Physics than he had for Economics. It was just another class to plod through, listen to the lecture, do the work, jot down the homework assignment, and then leave.

As he plopped his things down at his seat and began to sort through them, he reflected on his attitude change. He'd been kidnapped. He'd been held hostage. He'd been in a position where Hemingway wasn't going to save him, where Wall Street held no power, where NASA was no more advanced than cavemen, where none of his schooling had mattered. The only thing that had mattered was life and death, who was going to go home to dinner that night.

Then he reflected upon his reflecting. Most people just assumed that sixteen year old boys were shallow, sex-driven Narcissists. And that was largely true, but that wasn't to say they weren't capable of deep thought and reflection. Or had he somehow skipped over thirty years of his life to his midlife crisis?

"Ah, Tommen, you're back."

Mrs. White did not say it in a surprised manner, as if stunned at his existence, thus calling attention to his absence. She said it as though she'd merely summoned him to her desk and had gotten distracted between the time she called him and the time he showed up. She was carrying a box out of the lab supply room. She might have been going to set out materials for something, but seeing him, she just set the box on one of the lab tables and went to her desk, motioning him forward.

Tommen obeyed sullenly, grabbing his stack of papers and making for her desk.

"You got all the online work done, so that's good," she said, taking the papers and setting them to the side where they would likely disappear into the black hole that was her desk. "You didn't miss anything that you couldn't have made up. The field trip I counted as extra credit because of how spontaneous it was, and you weren't the only one who missed it, so don't worry about it. Did you have a nice New Year's?"

He didn't miss the way she skipped Christmas and went

straight to New Year's, but he nodded anyway. "Yeah, it was good."

"That's good. So, I made up a new seating chart because new year, new seats, why not? We got told that you—"

"I don't need help," Tommen cut in, aware that if anyone was paying even half-attention that word would get out and the rumors would fly out the door and circulate through the whole school before they got dismissed to lunch. "You can keep me wherever you put me."

"Okay, I'm just asking. And if you do need to move, just let me know."

"I will."

He returned to his seat, mulling over the likelihood of him actually asking for help or asking to be moved. He didn't wear glasses or contacts, so he couldn't claim he couldn't see the board, and it wasn't at any kind of bad angle where the sun would reflect off it making it difficult to read. And Mrs. White was too diligent about keeping taller and bigger students in places where they wouldn't block the view for shorter students. Not that he was one of those shorter students anymore anyway. So no matter which way he looked at it, there was no conceivable excuse for him to discreetly be moved if he actually needed it.

He didn't foresee needing to move anyway. Morrison's class had gone just fine, even if it was difficult getting used to just hearing words spoken into his ears instead of being able to locate the sounds and keep everything in their relative positions. But that was just part of it, he supposed. Probably in a month he was going to be so used to it that hearing things without his hearing aids was going to be strange.

But for now, the thought put ice in his veins.

The late bell rang, but Mrs. White still plinked away on her computer, hurriedly trying to enter in as many of Tommen's papers as she could before tearing herself away and grabbing her clipboard.

"So, I graded all your tests—well, all except yours, Tommen, yours was online—and I am going to hand them back to you. We'll go over them briefly, talk about a couple of the questions, and then we have a lab we're going to do in order to get us prepared for the next chapter in the book. But first, I made up a new seating chart." There were groans all around as papers were shuffled and stuffed in folders and notebooks and textbooks. "So, grab your things and line up against the wall there."

That was the way Mrs. White did her seating charts—by firing squad. Obediently, the class lined up against the wall, spilling into the lab room, slouching and sulking as White turned her clipboard one way then the other before figuring out which way was up. Then out came the pen and she started pointing.

"Ollie, there." She pointed to the senior, then at his new spot, front row, closest to the door. He went there without a word, but his expression said that it was not his seat of choice.

"Sam, there." A junior who wore enough makeup to put a clown to shame. Her front row spot might have been because she was always whispering and giggling or because she was the shortest one in the class. Either way, she was not happy about the assignment either.

"Noha, there." A senior, she was an Egyptian exchange student who actually loved being in the front row and was always very studious and basically the definition of "teacher's pet" even if it was cultural rather than boastful or spiteful.

And on it went. The arrangement was adjusted several times as White realized she put two troublemakers together or she put a short person behind a tall person. Tommen waited patiently against the wall, fairly certain that he was going to end up in the back row, which was fine with him. He could see. More importantly, he could hear.

"Tommen, there," White said, pointing to a seat in the back.

He went, the last person to be assigned. But before he could put his books down, she shook her head. "Nope, nope, stop. I don't like this."

Tommen's stomach twisted, afraid she was going to point out

his hearing aids and move him to the front.

"Ollie, switch seats with Tommen. Tommen, you missed a lot, and I want to make sure you get everything." *Well-played, Mrs. White. Well-played.* "And Gina, go back there, sit next to Ollie. Sam, come over to Gina's seat." *And I get my own table. Very well-played indeed.*

Once all the shuffling and moving had been done, Mrs. White looked like she was ready to start handing back tests. Before she could get in two words, there was a knock at the door and a pair of eyes peeped in the window. Tommen couldn't remember the classroom doors locking after the second bell. Was that a new thing?

Mrs. White opened the door. At first Tommen thought there was a child standing there. Then she handed the teacher a note.

"Oh, you must be Rebecca," Mrs. White said, stepping back so the girl could come in.

"Becky, please." That was no girl. Well, it was, but it wasn't a young girl. She couldn't have been more than four feet tall. Mrs. White's desk was almost three feet tall and this girl could probably rest her chin on the top of it. A dwarf? For real?

"Becky," Mrs. White acknowledged. "Well, we just got done doing our seating chart dance, so why don't you take a seat there next to Tommen?"

Tommen had no hatred for dwarves or anyone just based on their height, but he still found himself mildly repulsed by the girl as she lifted her notebook onto the table and crawled into the seat, kind of like a six year old joining the adults at the dinner table. She wore no makeup; her face was dotted with freckles and a few pimples. Brown hair that reached just past her shoulders was drawn back in a hastily-arranged ponytail. Thin-rimmed silver glasses sat on a charming little nose over pale pink lips. She wasn't fat, but she had curves to her. An insulin needle was stuck on the back of one arm, the pump clipped to her belt. Tommen might not have noticed her shoes except they were extremely noticeable. And not exactly shoes. They looked more like the padded braces that some people got when they broke their leg but it wasn't that bad, so they got a brace that let them still walk on it carefully.

"This is Becky, and she's new to our school," Mrs. White said needlessly. "Why don't you introduce yourself, where are you from?"

"Actually, I'm not as new as you think." Becky did not sigh or hesitate or stutter. She didn't have the adorable new girl shyness as she looked to carve out her little place in the school. She projected her voice, let everyone know she was in the room, and hers was a take it or leave it kind of attitude. "I was here my kindergarten year, then my family moved to California. Now we came back because my parents wanted to be closer to my brothers and sisters and nieces and nephews and everyone."

"Very cool. What grade are you?"

"I am a junior. I am sixteen. And I am three-foot-nine."

Mrs. White nodded as if she wasn't sure what she should do with that information presently. Was it a challenge, to say a dwarf could do anything normal people could do—which was, fundamentally, a lie? Or was it just one of those things where everyone was thinking it, might as well answer the unspoken question and save a bunch of time down the road? Tommen guessed it was the latter.

"Well, let's get you a textbook, and we'll get started," Mrs. White decided finally, heading back to the supply room to look for a usable textbook.

Becky turned and looked at Tommen. She held out her hand. "Becky Polski."

"Tommen Forbes," he replied uncertainly, taking her hand.

"Exchange student? Where are you from?"

"I'm not an exchange student; my family is from Wales."

"Really? Awesome. Yeah, my mom is Hungarian, and my dad is Polish, hence the last name."

"I know a Polski around here, just moved from California."

"That would probably be my dad; he's an audiologist."

"Wait, that's your dad? Like, your dad-dad?"

"As in, the man who ejaculated semen into my mom's vagina

and got her pregnant with me? Yes, that's my dad."

Tommen wasn't sure how to take her bluntness, though a few people around them seemed to be divided between also being stunned and snickering at his discomfort.

"But he's..." Tommen trailed off.

"Old? Yeah, he is. He's almost seventy. My mom is sixty-five next month. Doctor says that's probably the reason for my dwarfism, because they had me so late."

"Um, right."

Tommen had never learned so much about someone in such a short amount of time, and most of it he didn't care to know at all, or at least not so directly, as if she were answering questions he'd asked intentionally. He was saved by the teacher's return, Mrs. White handing Becky a textbook and quickly recording the number inside the front cover.

"I understand you were in AP Physics in your high school in California, correct?" Mrs. White inquired of Becky.

"Yes, I was," the dwarf replied. Tommen almost expected her to go into a story about whatever project they'd been working on or some trivial, unimportant story from her class back in California. Thankfully, she left it only at the affirmative.

"So you should have little trouble getting up to speed," Mrs. White went on, turning her attention back to the entire class. "Our next chapter is on light. One person from each table, go over to the box there on the lab table and grab one of everything. The other person, come up to the desk and grab two of every worksheet, one for each of you. Once we're all assembled and ready, I'll explain how this is going to work. Hopefully this will be a short experiment and we'll be cleaned up and starting on homework by the end of class. Ready? Go."

"How about you get the stuff from the lab since I can't reach in the box," Becky suggested immediately as everyone began moving. "I can grab the papers from the desk."

"Um, okay, works for me," Tommen replied, feeling woefully

sluggish and unable to keep up with her fast-moving train of thought.

Numbly he got up and headed for the lab where half the class was huddled around the box of stuff, doling out various instruments. Normally, he was the first one to the box, grabbing the things and getting right into the experiment. Now he hung back, feeling very conspicuous, as if someone was going to raise a shout and point out his hearing aids or some other faceless mean thing. No one did, and he wordlessly took things as they were handed to him, gathering the last couple objects once everyone else had cleared and returning to his seat where Becky waited, looking slightly impatient. She did not say anything out loud, and Mrs. White began reading the instructions from the teacher's handbook.

"In this chapter, we're studying light and, to some extent, color. This experiment will be a basic introduction to both."

Tommen rubbed his eyes, suppressing an audible groan. But Mrs. White still caught his reaction, raising a brow and asking, "Something you'd like to add, Tommen?"

He sighed. "I'm red-green color-blind. I can only see blue and yellow."

Now both brows went up. "Really? Well then, I am especially curious to hear your thoughts on the experiment once it's all over."

That was the last thing he wanted to hear, but he nodded and went along with it as she outlined the experiment and its goals before turning the students loose to gather their own results. Supposedly, each experiment was just a little different so they should all get different exact results but come to the same conclusion.

"You're color-blind?" Becky asked as they found an outlet and plugged in the lamps.

"Yeah," Tommen replied glumly.

"Are either of your parents color-blind?"

Tommen felt his face grow hot. "Um, my pa was red-green, too. My uncle is red-only color-blind—well, color-deficient I think is the term—and my grandpa had some form of color-blindness, but they don't know what. Probably red-green."

"So then it's basically useless to ask you to hand me the red paper," Becky stated, reaching for one of the papers which, to Tommen, looked only yellow. He could picture the color red, knew very well what it looked like, but the color before him now, according to his basic sensory input, was yellow.

"Color-blindness, that's on OPN1LW and OPN1MW," Becky said as Tommen did the measurements and math.

He looked up. "Huh?"

"The gene that controls color perception. Your OPN1LW or OPN1MW is deficient."

"Um, right." He returned to his work.

"Sorry, I'm planning on going to college for genetics. You can probably guess why."

"I'm sure I don't know."

He looked up again, unsure whether her expression was true irritation with him or an understanding of the joke but still pretending to be mad.

"Okay, smartie, hand me the green paper," she told him.

"And which one is that?" he wondered innocently.

She sighed, shook her head, and took another sheet of paper which was, to his basic sensory input, blue. There was, theoretically, one sheet of every basic color, not that he could tell.

God, he hated Rifun. Tommen was still determined to undermine him at every turn and eventually get him arrested or his clock broken or something. But at the same time, the man had shown him color, real color, the whole spectrum perceivable by the human eye. Rifun was hardly a god, but it was still a small miracle.

"So if you want to be a geneticist, why are you in AP Physics?" Tommen asked, silently wondering if he was prepared for any sort of conversation.

"Oh, I want to be a geneticist, but I'm a science geek all around. Next year I'll be in AP Chemistry."

Tommen nodded, impressed, but in no mood to show it. Getting back to normal and working through a Physics experiment was helping to bring everything back together for him, but right now he was just trying to get through the day, just one normal day. That's all he wanted, to be able to get back on track and move on with his life.

"So, if you don't mind my asking, are you actually deaf or just hard of hearing?"

Tommen's head shot up, his heart leaping into his throat as he fully expected everyone to stop what they were doing, turn to stare at him, and then start laughing. As it was, there was only Becky staring at him, Mrs. White helping another group across the room, and the group nearest them did not appear to have heard. The whole incident lasted only a second.

"What?" He tried to keep his voice from breaking.

"We literally just moved back from California; we've barely left the house because of all the unpacking and stuff. The only way anyone knows my dad at this point is from his practice." Becky shrugged. "It was just a question. You don't have to answer. You might have noticed, but I tend to be a little nosy."

Really? I had no idea.

He elected to remain silent, but she kept going on. "Although, the surprise you exhibited at the question suggests it's not a lifelong thing, but something actually very recent. So you're embarrassed by it and don't want anyone else to know." She ran her tongue over her teeth. "Huh. I'm sorry, I didn't realize. I mean, I know I'm nosy, but I don't actively try to hurt people."

Tommen sighed. "Are you done?"

She blinked, looking first confused, then hurt, then apologetic. Then it dawned on her that he was talking as much about the experiment as her annoying nosiness. She nodded and switched out the lights and the papers.

Becky was quiet after that, but Tommen could see a million questions running through her eyes without ever passing her lips. She was curious and talkative, probably drove her parents nuts when she was a kid. She seemed like the kind of person who could talk for the entirety of a twenty-hour road trip, then be disappointed when they arrived at their destination and she still hadn't said everything she wanted to say.

"How are we doing?" Mrs. White asked loudly. "Are we close to being finished?"

Her tone suggested that this was supposed to be a short experiment and they were going into overtime. Was it because she'd misjudged the time needed to complete it or because they were stalling so they wouldn't have to sit through a lecture for the remainder of the class?

Three of the groups had finished, one was falling behind, Tommen and Becky and another group were just wrapping up.

"So far I like this class," Becky said conversationally as she and Tommen put the things away and returned to their seats to wait for the last group. "We didn't do too many experiments in my old class. Mostly it was lectures and powerpoints and tests."

"Well, we do plenty of those here, don't worry about that," Tommen told her.

"I mean, there's a time and a place for them, but there's so much more to science than that."

So, basically, she just carried a soapbox around with her. Tommen made a mental note not to engage her on, well, anything, not unless he wanted to hear her opinion on it whether he asked for it or not. He would rather listen to one of his dad's lectures; at least those lectures were practical and intended to correct behavior and make him a better person. Whether or not he agreed with it wasn't the point; it was the intention behind it that he could respect.

He was mercifully saved by the last group hurriedly scribbling down their last findings before haphazardly gathering their things—almost breaking two lights in the process—tossing them back in the box and returning to their seats. One of them was a super science geek who enjoyed all things science and really wanted to be in the class. The other was only in the AP class because his parents forced him to take as many AP classes as he could because they were overachievers and trying to live vicariously through him. Tommen had little doubt who had held up the experiment.

"Now then, are we all finished?" Mrs. White inquired, her tone not a little annoyed. When a sufficient number of the students bobble-headed their acknowledgment, she went on. "I wanted to go around and ask each group about their findings, but instead I'll just ask each group one question about the experiment overall, and I'll look over your sheets individually. We'll start in the back. Britney and Seth. What did you discover about Trial One?"

So they went around the room, discussing different aspects about the experiment. For the most part, Mrs. White seemed pleased that everyone had gotten the same basic results. Tommen and Becky were the last group to be called on, and she went to Becky first.

"I'd say you had an advantage, coming in while we were starting something new," Mrs. White said. "How did you think it went?"

"Very well, I'd say," Becky replied amiably enough. "I guess I'm just happy it was an experiment that I was able to take part in fully."

Mrs. White nodded as if unsure how to reply. "And you, Tommen, what are your thoughts on this? You said you're color-blind, so how did that affect your participation in this experiment?"

"Well, any time we needed to change the colored sheets, she had to do it because I couldn't tell which was which," Tommen answered dully. "As far as I was concerned, we were just swapping one yellow light for another, or one blue light for another."

"Okay. Well, I think you're going to be a fascinating perspective at some points throughout this chapter, and maybe the next one, too. So, keep your head in the game, and we'll move on."

After that, she started in on what the Teacher's Notes said about the experiment and how it related to what they would be learning and other things that Tommen intentionally tuned out. That was another strange thing about the hearing aids; he had to relearn how to ignore sound when it was being pushed into his ears. But he managed to accomplish it long enough to discreetly thumb through the pages of his textbook to look for the next chapter, curious as to the meaning behind her words. No surprise, the next chapter was on sound. Because fuck you.

Before he knew it, Mrs. White had stopped talking and was squeaking out the homework assignment on the board. Pages to read, questions to answer, section quiz to complete.

"You can get started on your homework now," Mrs. White said as she capped the marker. "You've got about...ten minutes. You may talk quietly with your table partners."

Tommen dutifully, if cheerlessly, flipped back to the beginning of the chapter and started in. Any other time he might have Banded, at least to get the reading done. There was little worse than being in the middle of a chapter, just about to understand some concept or principal or formula, and then being interrupted by the bell. It was too difficult to just pick up where he left off at some later time. Right now, though, he didn't care much to Band his reading. His interest level was mediocre at best, and he knew he would probably fall into once of those trances like he did in English where he found that he'd read the same passage four times and still had no idea what it said.

Beside him, he couldn't decide if Becky was confused or a speed reader, the way she seemed to flip pages quickly and go back and forth and jot down notes in tiny, precise lettering. She glanced at him once, and he averted his eyes.

"What?" she wondered.

He shrugged. "Nothing."

"That's okay. I get stares all the time."

It was bait, and he knew it, and he took it. "Couldn't decide if you were confused or a speed reader."

"Oh, neither, really, I just know how to take notes. And actually I'm less confused with these books than I ever was with my old textbooks. I love it."

"It'll wear off fast," Frank said behind her.

She just shook her head and went back to her speed reading or awesome note-taking, whatever she wanted to call it. But after a minute or two, she spoke again to Tommen.

"So is your mom color-blind, too?"

Please, just stop talking. "I don't think so. I don't remember."

"Color-blindness affects males more often, but it's actually passed down through the female. Do you have any sisters?"

A long time ago. "No."

"Female cousins?"

"No."

"Related aunts?"

"No."

"Who is in your family, then?"

The bell rang just then, and he took the cue to sweep his stuff off the desk and be the first one out the door. Yes, he was probably going to have to talk to Mrs. White about the seating arrangement, but it had nothing to do with his hearing. There was no way he could put up with such an annoying little bitch for the rest of the semester. With any luck, he wasn't going to have any more classes with her. The only reason that was likely was that she was one grade ahead of him.

He didn't want to talk about anything that had happened. He didn't want to talk about his captivity; he didn't want to talk about almost losing his dad; he didn't want to talk about his hearing loss. He didn't feel much like talking about anything else either, whether it was the loss of his family or even his color-blindness. All he wanted was to just go about his business and not have anyone call any attention to him. Was that really too much to ask? Apparently it was. And if there was any sort of god up there looking down over creation, he was probably actively pointing at Tommen and laughing.

Chapter Sixteen
A Freak Like Me

Tommen couldn't explain why he felt such relief when he reached his locker except that maybe it felt like a starting point, a reset. He could forget the horrors of last class and just focus on going to lunch. He felt more receptive to the familiarity of ham on rye with a generous portion of mustard as he slammed his locker and headed for the cafeteria.

"Tommen!"

He didn't even have to look to know who was calling for him. He did not look, did not slow down. If nothing else, he deliberately increased his pace, using every inch of stride he could get out of his six-one height. But the throngs of students left little room for maneuverability and speed, and pretty soon, Becky was at his side. A moment later, she was in front of him.

"Tommen, stop."

Not like he had a choice in the matter; the crowd was going nowhere faster.

"Listen, I'm sorry about Physics, whatever I said that embarrassed you," she told him.

"Doesn't matter. Wasn't embarrassed." He tried to get past her but she proved a big obstacle for a little person.

"You're a bad liar, you know that? Either way, if everything is cool between us as you seem to imply, would you be willing to help me with lunch? Generally the trays are too high for me."

Well, he walked into that one, didn't he? Either things were cool between them, in which case he was more or less obliged to help lest he be anything less than the Chivalrous Welshman, or things were not cool between them, in which case he would have to explain why, and all his reasons sounded selfish to his mind. After a minute, he nodded. "Yeah, I'll help you."

She grinned. "Thanks. Normally I pack my own, but it's been crazy with the move and I haven't had time to cook."

"Moves can be like that."

"You move often?" He could see the thoughts start to form in her mind; she thought he was a foster care kid.

"Haven't moved in eight years. Still in the same old bedroom, same old house."

"I actually like moving, to be honest. It's all so exciting, and it's like a fresh start; you have to decide what you want to keep and what you want to sell, how you want to arrange things and it's like a chance to start over. I mean, this isn't much like that since I have a ton of family here, but whatever."

They got in the lunch line, Tommen still clutching his little paper sack in one hand, grabbing a tray for Becky in the other. They'd no sooner approached the entrée table than they were approached by a spindly kid who Tommen figured was a freshman.

"Fancy seeing you here," he said, looking at Becky and ignoring Tommen completely.

"I know, what a coincidence, right?" Becky said sarcastically.

At an annoyed grunt from someone else in line, the freshman simply said, "Absolutely. Hey, I'll see you around."

"Sure thing."

The freshman left and Tommen raised a brow. "Boyfriend?"

Becky laughed. "No, no, that's my nephew."

If there was ever a moment for the slammed brakes sound effect, that was it as Tommen shook his head. "Sorry, maybe I heard you wrong, did you say nephew?"

"Yes."

"Shit. Wait, so, he's, like, adopted, right?"

"No. My oldest sibling is forty-something years old. I have another nephew who is not only graduated, but engaged."

"Shit," Tommen whispered. "What do you want?"

Becky could grab the chicken strips—or what passed as chicken strips—well enough, but when it came to the salad bar, it was all Tommen, like taking a kid to a pizza buffet. They could see, they might even reach, but coordination was limited.

Tommen knew that by the end of the day, rumors would be flying. Anyone who saw him now would probably immediately assume Becky was his girlfriend. Didn't matter that they probably didn't know who she was; didn't matter that he'd been gone for weeks and didn't feel much like having any interaction with any human being whatsoever. By the end of the day, Becky would be his girlfriend, at least according to the rumor mill.

Not that he minded having such a rumor about him. He wasn't interested in Becky at all, but he figured that kind of rumor was better to have going around than anything to do with his fighting or his captivity, or the one Tyler had allegedly started about him being gay with Eric and Varad, or at least Eric. Having a girlfriend was, comparatively, a very minor rumor.

"Well, Tommen, it's been a while since you've been here," Diana the lunch lady observed.

"Oh, I try to eat healthy but the cafeteria just keeps calling my name," Tommen replied semi-sarcastically.

"And what's your name, dear?"

"Becky Polski," Becky introduced herself. "I might not be in the system yet, I'm new."

"Well, that's all right. It'll be three dollars."

Becky dug out a crumpled up five from her pocket and waited patiently for Diana to make change.

"Are you normally a brown-bagger or are you going to be in here a lot?" Diana inquired. "I'm just curious so we know how to help you, so you don't have to go bothering him all the time." *And there goes the rumor mill.*

"No, I normally pack my own lunch, but the last week or so has just been crazy."

"All right, well, if you need anything, just let one of us know, okay?"

"I will. I appreciate it, thanks."

With that, Becky grabbed her tray and headed out into the sea of tables and hungry students. Tommen slipped by her and headed for his normal seat, this time completely alone. He'd been prepared, mentally, for Varad leaving. He still wasn't quite over the total rejection he'd gotten from both him and Eric. Technically, Eric was still in school; he just did most of his work online. But he did sometimes still eat lunch in the cafeteria. Tommen saw him now, a few tables away, talking with some other seniors, other friends of his who'd apparently been promoted from sometimes-weekend-friends to really-close-friends. Tommen was glad for him that he still had friends after the whole homecoming incident, but what explanation did he give for suddenly abandoning his once-best-friend Tommen?

Didn't matter, Tommen figured, as he pulled out his sandwich and stared at it for a second. Maybe he should change things up a little. Routine was nice, but it was just as wearying as everything else that went on. Maybe he could try a turkey and cheese sandwich, or a modified Italian sub. Maybe he could really change it up and go for chili, make a big pot of that Sunday night and be good for the whole week. Maybe he could do like most other people did—from kids in school to adults in the workplace—make a nice dinner the night before and take the leftovers for lunch the next day.

He mulled that over as he mechanically ate his sandwich. He did like to cook, although he would be the only one eating half the time; his dad ate more for the taste of food than being hungry. He claimed that was why he was still a little heavy despite all his exercise, and Banding could take its toll. So basically, Tommen would only be cooking for himself, and that was a depressing thought. There was something wonderful about cooking for someone else and having them appreciate it. Maybe that was why he really didn't mind working at the bakery, even if he was on counter most days.

Despite his brooding and planning, at the end of the day, he was probably just going to stick with his ham on rye with a generous helping of mustard. Most people found it a strange combination, but then, he found most people strange anyway. And furthermore, his weird sandwich was still healthier than most of the cafeteria options—despite whatever healthy kick they promoted. The rye came from the bakery, the leftovers from the day before; the ham he got at the grocery store but it came from a local pig farmer. The mustard? Well, sometimes when he got up the motivation he might try to make his own, but it failed nine times out of ten, and he resorted to just buying the big yellow bottle on the shelf. So two out of three wasn't bad, right?

Some days he wondered what his parents and brother would think about such edible abundance—and as a result, edible waste. When they were starving in the mountains, to even conceive of a future where more food would go in the trash than in someone's mouth. It was almost disgusting to think about really, it—

"You look deep in thought."

Tommen was jerked from his thoughts as Becky sat down across from him. None of her food appeared to have been touched yet, and in three minutes out of the heating light, that meant it was probably grossly cold. Nevertheless, she peeled back the lid of a little cup of...marinara sauce? When had she grabbed that? And she started in.

"What are you doing here?" Tommen wondered, acutely aware that he probably sounded cross and rude, but at this point, he was equal parts curious and annoyed.

"I'm eating my lunch, what's it look like?" Becky countered. "And you looked like you needed a friend."

"Thanks, but I'm good."

"Everyone needs someone. And I'm no idiot; the kid who sits alone only attracts trouble. Usually of the bullying kind. That's why I try to be outgoing. Announce to the world that you're here, force yourself among the peoples, and find safety in numbers."

"So you're a nosy introvert. Right." Tommen went back to his sandwich.

"Sort of. I talk when I'm nervous. And I talk when I like someone and feel comfortable around them. Then you can't get me to shut up."

"Hooray."

"So that brings me to my next question: why are you so miserable?"

Tommen was taken aback by her forthrightness even as his mind was subconsciously drawing up the contrasts between Becky and all the adults he'd talked to this morning. All the teachers patted him on the head and told him to ask someone if he needed help and not to go it alone and not to hurt himself and everything else, or at least that was the implication. Becky just came right out and asked why the fuck he was so fucking miserable.

"It's been really bad the last couple of weeks; I'm really trying to get over it, so I'd rather not talk about it anymore."

"Have you talked about it at all?"

Fuck you. "You know, if you're going to judge me, do it based on who I am here and not who I am compared to who I was."

"Right now I judge you to be a very miserable sophomore who isn't much for company or conversation, and if he wants to be able to pick himself up and make things right, he's going to have to go through another transformation of who he is to who he wants to be."

Fuck. You. Fuck you. Tommen didn't reply, which only seemed to encourage her and she continued, "So what is it? Failing in AP Phys? Girlfriend dump you the day before Christmas? Boyfriend dump you? Totaled your dad's car?"

Tommen slapped his palm on the table. "I almost lost my dad the day before Christmas, all right?! He's the only family I've got! No mom, no grandparents, no aunts or uncles, no brothers or sisters, no cousins, no nothing. It's just me and him."

Becky stared at him, wide-eyed, for a good fifteen seconds before saying quietly, "I'm sorry. What happened?"

Tommen rubbed his face roughly, growling. *Don't do it,*

Tommen. Walk away. Don't go back there. "My dad's a cop, and he got shot and put in a coma. He got bad, to the point where if he stopped breathing on his own, he had orders to pull the plug. And it almost came to that."

"Is he still in the hospital?"

"No." He shook his head. "No, he came home New Year's Day. He's doing great, but...I almost lost my only family."

"I'm sorry," Becky said again. "I didn't know."

"And there's no reason you should if you just moved here."

"But you were hoping to move on from that with me, someone who didn't know you as 'that kid' right?"

"Yeah."

She studied him for a few minutes. "How did you lose your hearing?"

He sighed. *Don't do it. You don't have to go there. You just met her and she's just being nosy. There's no reason to just divulge that kind of hurt to anyone who asks.*

But she doesn't know. It's like talking to strangers online. The strangers don't know you. They're less likely to judge.

Or more likely.

"I'm the reason my dad got shot. You might have heard that there's a lunatic serial killer in Charleston?" He noted her wide-eyed expression. "Well, there is. Or was. They haven't found him yet. But he kidnapped me to get to my dad."

"Then you aren't the reason your dad got shot," Becky interrupted. "You were only an innocent bystander. Whoever that freak serial killer is, he's the one who's responsible."

"He put a gun to my head and pulled the trigger," Tommen continued. "The noise destroyed my hearing, and it's not likely to recover."

"Well you don't know that," Becky interrupted again. "It's only been what, two weeks? Give it a few months. Listen, in World War I, mustard gas blinded thousands of soldiers. Yes, some remained blind, but others regained their sight after a month or so."

"You mean like Hitler?"

She gave him a look. "You never know; it could come back. In the meantime, you make do with what you have, and if that requires a little help from a hearing aid, then so be it. Press on and continue your schooling in your best capacity. Kind of like me with my shoes."

"What do shoes have to do with anything?"

"My ankle and foot bones weren't properly formed at birth. I had to wear these heavy, clunky orthopedic shoes all through my childhood up until I was twelve years old. Didn't matter if I was trudging through snow or walking on the beach; with exception of swimming, showers, and sleeping, I had to wear them. Two pairs, one for inside and one for outside. When I was twelve, I was allowed a short reprieve since I was grown as much as I was going to for the time being. When I hit puberty and started growing again—barely—I had to put them back on. And I probably won't be able to take them off until I'm twenty or so."

"That's gotta suck."

"Oh, like you wouldn't believe. Other girls go to the school dance in heels or at least a cute pair of flats, and here I am clunking along like Frankenstein. Sometimes, if I know I'm going to be standing for a long time, I also have a back brace I'm supposed to wear in order to keep the pressure off my neck and upper back."

"Now all you need is something for your hands and arms."

"Don't give them any ideas. As if I need anything else to add to my morning routine, because these shoes and my insulin pump just aren't enough."

"Type I?"

"Yeah. But I mean, I've gotten so used to it; I can barely remember a time without this thing in my arm or thigh or somewhere."

Tommen didn't reply to that, instead going for the bag of Cheez-Its still in his lunch bag. Becky started on her second chicken finger but pushed it away. "I can't eat cold chicken fingers. Do you want it?"

He shrugged and pulled the tray over to himself. "Well, I'm not going to say no to free food."

"I do my best to feed starving children, especially teenage boys. Now that we're home, all the family members want to come over and say hi, and of course they always want to come over for dinner which means me and my mom have to cook." She shook her head, then got an expression that Tommen wasn't sure how to interpret. "So if you don't mind me asking, how is it just you and your dad? What about your mom?"

Tommen shifted uncomfortably. "I had a ma and pa, even an older brother and some younger sisters. We lived up in the mountains, not too far from here as the crow flies, but far enough on the roads. One night, when I was eight, I sneaked off into the forest because, I don't know, I think I was mad at my brother for something. When I came home the next morning, I found them all dead." Becky gasped. "Police ruled it carbon monoxide poisoning, killed them all in their sleep. I was the only survivor, and a very lucky one at that, otherwise I would have been right there with them."

"So you went into foster care, I assume."

"Yes, I did. But my pa had an older brother. They weren't exactly on great terms, but when he heard what happened, he'd be damned if I left the family. He had to fight tooth and nail since he was unmarried, in a dangerous profession, and there was no other family in case something happened to him, but he won in the end. Obviously."

"So your dad is really your uncle."

"Technically, yes. But he's my dad just as much as my pa was my dad."

Becky managed a small smile though her overall demeanor was still horrified. "That's sweet. I mean, that you don't make that such an obvious distinguishing...feature."

"The whole 'you're not my dad' kind of thing? I tried to pull that one a couple times, but not anymore."

She nodded. "So you're an adopted kid with no other family,

you almost lost your dad, you lost part of your hearing, and you're an awkward sixteen year old."

Tommen blinked. "Um, sure. I guess you could phrase it that way." *Considering you now know more about me than 99% of the people in this entire school, that's how you want to phrase it?*

"Wow." She ran her tongue over her teeth. "Why are you so miserable, though?"

"I'm sorry?"

"You've had a rough time of it, sure, but in the end, you're just a freak. Like me."

"Did you just quote Batman to me?"

"No, I quoted the Joker; get with the program. Okay, I hate my special shoes, but I know I need them and without them, I would probably be in a lot worse shape than I am. I don't like being diabetic, but in the modern world, it's not a death sentence. I'm not overly fond of being three-foot-nine, but again, it's not a death sentence, and nice people like you are more than willing to help me if I need it.

"You want to be judged based on who you are, not who you were. But you're still judging yourself based on who you were. You want to move on. But secretly, you want to move on from where you were, not where you are, so really, you're going nowhere. If you really want to get on with your life, start with where you are. You almost lost your dad. That's terrible, but that's an almost. You say he's doing great. Awesome. Take him as he is, not where he was in the hospital. You lost part of your hearing. I'm sorry, it's terrible, and it takes some adjustment, but we in the twenty-first century have the technology to help you so you can live as normal a life as anyone else here. And believe me when I say I'm sorry for the loss of your family, but as you can see, life has moved on. And if I had to hazard a guess, you were kept alive for a reason."

"And we're done here." Tommen finished off his Cheez-Its and tossed the baggie in his lunch sack before crumpling it up and standing to go throw it away. Becky stood as well, grabbing her tray and following him.

"Do you deny anything I said?" she demanded, catching up to him.

Tommen turned to face her, feeling as though he was about to scold a ten year old. "You know, they say first impressions happen within the first ten seconds of seeing someone and the first two seconds of actually meeting them. My impression of you is that you are annoying, nosy, and have a very big mouth. Like, a thought just pops into your head and before you've had half a second to process it, it comes out. Good intentions are great, but what is it they say about the road to Hell?"

Becky glared up at him. "You didn't answer my question." When he paused, she went on. "And since we're being so candid here, let me tell you my impression of you. You are depressed and miserable, convinced of your might only in your own mind but when it comes to actually showing it, there is nothing to back up your own big mouth. Most days you put on a good face to deter the questions, but on the days when you can't hide, you would rather lash out than be seen in your misery, trying to convince yourself—not anyone else—that everything is just fine. Have I missed anything?"

Tommen sighed. "We're done here."

"You still haven't answered my question."

"And another thing. You're like a leech. I sit next to you in class because I'm assigned there and you're assigned there. We work on one project in class because that is the assignment. And now I can't seem to get rid of you. Like you said, nice people are more than willing to help you. I'm not the only nice person here."

She was still glaring at him as she said, "Fine. I guess I'll see you in Physics tomorrow, partner."

He did not reply, instead turning and heading down the hall to his locker. Damn, but she was annoying. At the start of the day, he'd at least had some hope that he might be able to really get back into Physics and enjoy it again. Becky just killed all that. There was no way he was going to be able to enjoy it now, not with her snide remarks and psychoanalysis. Tomorrow in class he was going to talk to Mrs. White and see if she could assign him to someone—anyone else. He would rather work with the kid who didn't give a shit and was only in the class because his parents made him take it; he could do all the work just fine. He would rather do an entire project by himself than be stuck with a partner he despised, where they would lock horns every step of the way over every minute detail. That was how this was all going to turn out, he just knew it. When fighting Tyler Freeman wasn't an option, the cosmos looked down upon him and decided he was going to get an opponent who would torture him psychologically but against whom he could not fight back.

Reluctantly, Tommen opened his locker and fished out his Web Programming books. He wasn't sure why he bothered to take them to class. Pretty much every lecture started out with, "Your book says to do this, but because of improvements, upgrades, and other fundamental changes between 1999 and today, we're going to do it this way. Except we're not because I'm grading you based on this other method." So the book was basically useless.

But he had time before next class. He wasn't even sure why he'd already come out to get his books. Because he had nothing better to do, that was why. Not like he had any friends to talk to in order to pass the time.

Tommen had just put his books back in his locker when suddenly the metal door slammed shut. He was too slow to whip up a Band, and the door just about completely closed on his hand, which would have locked it in the door between the top and bottom latches. As it was, it merely bounced off his right hand, though not before slicing it open across the back. He sucked in a breath, determined not to cry out as he put his other hand over the blood bubbling up from the wound. He turned his head stiffly to look at Tyler.

"Oh, sorry, Tommen, I didn't see you there. I just saw your locker open and thought to myself, 'Why, it's wide open. He could have some valuable things in there. I better shut the door so no one can just walk up and steal something.' "

"Fuck off, Tyler," Tommen growled, turning and heading for

the bathroom. "I'm not in the mood."

"Not in the mood? You looked pretty 'in the mood' walking around with Happy. Or is she Dopey? I can't be sure."

"Her name is Becky, and I was just helping her." Tommen pulled the lever on the paper towel dispenser and wiped the blood off his hands. It didn't look like a deep cut; it would heal fine without a bandage.

"Ah, yes, the Chivalrous Welshman, defender of women and the weak, the poor and destitute, those who can neither defend themselves, nor even get their own lunch."

Tommen ground his teeth together as he left the bathroom, determined to just wait it out until the bell rang and he could escape to class.

"Well, this is new behavior by the Chivalrous Welshman. He seems to have run out of fight all of a sudden. No futile fisticuffs? No tenuous threats? No wimpy wit? Not even a glare? Has the Chivalrous Welshman given up on chivalry? Has he realized that it's all for naught? Has he finally come to realize that just because you fight for peace and love doesn't mean you're going to win against someone who is clearly bigger and better than you are?"

On the one hand, if he engaged Tyler, he would only be suspended and Tyler would be expelled. On the other hand, Tyler's younger brother and his goons weren't much better, and the torture would only continue, making it a Pyrrhic victory anyway.

"No. I just figure I've missed enough school as it is, and I don't need to add a suspension to my record." Tommen returned to his locker and spun the dial.

"Oh, so it's not giving up." Tyler leaned against the next locker and folded his arms in mock thoughtfulness. "It's bowing down. The Chivalrous Welshman, always doing what Layman tells him, rolling over for him and licking his boots. Do you suck his cock, too? You know, there are rumors going around that he's secretly a pedophile. Have you been victimized, Tommen?"

Tommen grabbed his books and shut the door. "As I said,

Tyler. Fuck off."

He walked away, every instinct telling him to keep one eye looking over his shoulder. Tyler did not surprise him from behind with a body slam or even a knife in the back, but his words were just as bad. "And you're deaf, too, is that what I heard?"

Tommen stopped and turned. Tyler grinned. He had him, and he knew it. With the ease of a lion stalking as close as possible to its prey before springing, the bully approached. "Yeah, that's right. You're deaf now, aren't you?" With the tenderness of a perverted lover, Tyler pushed back the hair around Tommen's ears, exposing the hearing aids. "What happens when we make those disappear?"

Halfway through the word, Tommen threw up a Fast Band, just enough that he would only appear to have quick reflexes as he knocked away Tyler's arm before he could take out the hearing aid.

"Leave me alone, Tyler," Tommen warned.

"Or what? You'll go and tattle to Layman? You know, I hear he moans really loud when a student sucks his cock, not that you'd be able to hear it."

"No, but I would."

Tommen had never been so happy to see Mrs. Righting as when she appeared, seemingly out of nowhere, just out of the teacher's lounge. She wasn't a very big lady, but she seemed to grow six inches with every step as she approached, strides purposeful, gaze almost murderous.

"That was as inappropriate as I have ever heard," she said, and not in a shocked, hand over the mouth in a faux gasp kind of way, but more like Judge Judy. When she spoke, you shut up. "You are very right, we're going to go and 'tattle' to Layman, and you are going to tell him exactly what has transpired just now." Tommen breathed a sigh of relief, but then her gaze turned on him. "You're part of this, too, and whether instigator or victim, you are going to give your account, too. And get a band-aid; you're bleeding on the floor."

Tommen looked down to see his hand wound was not as clotted as he thought it would be. Reluctantly, he followed her and

Tyler to Layman's office. Once Tommen had given his testimony, he was free to leave and let Layman exact whatever punishment he deemed fit. Personally, Tommen hoped that it involved a certain degree of sodomy, to see how much Tyler liked Layman's cock.

There were only a few minutes until the bell rang for next period, and Tommen returned to his locker again, more out of habit than really wanting to go there. He stopped about twenty feet from his locker, however, when he saw Becky waiting there for him. He turned on his heel and walked away, but he heard Becky hurrying to catch him. And catch him she did.

"Hey," she said. "I heard what happened."

"Yeah, so? Everyone will by the end of the day," Tommen growled.

"No, I mean, I heard what was said. I was coming to talk to you, and I heard the exchange between you and...what's his name?"

"Tyler Freeman. Learn it. Stay away from him."

"I intend to, to be sure, but I wanted to thank you."

Tommen stopped. "Thank me?"

"Even though you're super pissed at me, you still defended me."

"Fight's between him and me. You shouldn't get involved."

"What did he call you? The Chivalrous Welshman?"

He shrugged. "It's just something they call me. To insult me or, at best, lightly mock me."

Becky nodded. "I like it."

The bell rang then and she turned, then stopped. "I'll see you tomorrow in Physics. Listen, why don't we forget today and all of its stupidity, and make tomorrow a fresh start, hm?"

He shrugged. "Sure, whatever."

She seemed uncertain, but the halls were filling up quickly with people, and he took the opportunity to get lost in the crowd and slip away. He followed the seemingly endless stream of people until he found the door he needed, moving against the current to get into the room and then zigzagging his way around the computers to get to the one he'd claimed as his own.

Yes, he could use a fresh start. He'd had his fuck-up day, the one where everyone stared because they knew he'd been kidnapped, knew his dad had almost died saving him, and now they knew that he'd lost part of his hearing. He only had to endure the stares for a couple more hours until he could retreat to the relative safety of the bakery, and then head home. Today was the stare-at-me day, the whisper-behind-my-back day, the point-and-laugh-and-me day, all of that.

Well, in truth, it was more likely going to be fuck-up week, especially since he hadn't made his big debut in his English class yet, having missed it that morning. And there were those who had been absent today and those who knew enough not to say anything the first day but would wait for the third or fourth day once the initial shock wore off.

But after that, everything was going to return to normal. It had to, eventually. The novelty of it would wear off. He was just same old Tommen Forbes, a super hothead who just happened to be super smart, who didn't give a damn about school. The hearing aids were just things he wore, no different from any of the other deaf students or the students who had insulin pumps or anything like that. It was just...everything was normal. He was fine. Everything was going to go back to normal.

"Good afternoon, everyone," Mrs. Floyd greeted as she entered the room. "Hope you all had a good lunch, got some brain food, because we are going to do a pop quiz! Or a pop program, whichever you want to call it." Groans around the room. "I am going to give each of you a different website I want you to build. I have the basic requirements listed and then roughly what it should look like when you're done. No books, no notes, no talking. Log onto your computers if you haven't already, and once you're in, come up and grab an assignment from the pile."

The papers were placed face-down so he couldn't pick and choose which one he wanted, not that any of them were terribly difficult. Tommen might have panicked and begged off, citing his two-week absence, but like most of the kids in the room, he was beyond this kiddie stuff. A couple of his classmates designed apps and even made a little money off them. Another group of seniors actually owned a small startup company of some form and built their own shiny website using real programming languages, not the push-button stuff, like using real construction material versus Tinker Toys.

Still, Tommen dutifully read through the requirements—a yellow background with brown text and a table four rows across and two rows down with some information, among other things—and set to work. It wasn't hard in any sense of the word—heck, to call it easy was an understatement—but he did his coding diligently, double-checking it even when he knew it was correct. There was something relaxing about reading the code and knowing what code made what happen and how to manipulate small elements to enact big changes.

He wasn't the last one done, printing off the visual of the page itself as well as the code, so once he turned in the papers, he went back to his seat and started in on his writing, watching the ink spill out onto the page in a similar way. Just changing one word or, sometimes, just one letter, could change the entire meaning of the sentence or even the story. And he had the power to do it, to make those changes. He was the god of his own stories; he told the people what to do. He told the weather what to be. It was all in the power of the pen, fear his might.

Then the last of the quizzes was turned in and they started the next lesson, again with the familiar, "Your book says this, but this is the right way, and this other way is how we're going to do it."

Tommen didn't mind, though, and he was even glad to go to art class. Mr. Robinson—aka, Bob Ross impersonator extraordinaire—was ecstatic to announce that they were beginning the painting unit, and to kick it off, they were going to watch his favorite episode of *The Joy of Painting*. Then he was going to explain a little more about the techniques and how everything worked, and Tommen was fairly certain the man was going to explode from sheer excitement.

By the time Robinson actually got around to putting the tape in the player, he was shaking and almost couldn't do it without help. But he got it in, fiddled with the controls and the TV for a minute, then stood back as his idol—no, his god—came on the screen, welcoming viewers and telling them all about the happy trees they were going to paint that day.

Tommen had had a bad day. Like, a really bad day. He wanted nothing more than for it to be over. But for now, he was okay with listening to the man on the screen and his soft voice talking about happy trees...

Chapter Seventeen
If Looks Could Kill

Walter debated whether to go home after visiting the precinct, but decided against it. News from the precinct had done little to cheer him up, and he knew that if he went home, he was only going to brood on it, and that was a decidedly bad idea. Instead, he sat in the parking lot of a gas station for a short time, concocting a mental list of things he knew he needed to do, things he should do since he had the time, and things he wanted to do since he had nothing better to do.

Of course, there was also the gap between the things he thought he had the strength and energy for, and the things he actually had the strength and energy for. For example, he was more than happy to slow down at the grocery store and consider what he wanted to eat while he was going to be spending so much time at home. He could cook, have a nice sit-down meal if he wanted, even cook for Tommen so the boy wasn't always taking his ham on rye with an ungodly amount of mustard. His body, however, made it through about two aisles before deciding it was done with that shit. He didn't fall or anything like that, but there was a lot of sweat and a lot of gritted teeth even as he cut the trip short and settled on some necessities to make it through the week. Hopefully he would be feeling well enough to make another attempt next week.

Other stops included Kmart, so he could pick up some replacements for his badly worn and torn undershirts; the auto parts store so he could grab the stuff for an oil change—that Tommen was going to do; and the office supply store for some paper and ink for the printer. By the time he got around to to the home improvement store, his body was screaming ten different kinds of profanity at him, dying down to a grumble only when he took a couple more painkillers. He reasoned that he was pushing himself harder today than he had his entire time being down, so it only made sense that he should be in some pain, and he would need relief from that pain.

"Good morning, can I help you find something?" an employee asked as he headed down one of the aisles.

"That depends," Walter told him. "You know much about remodeling?"

"What are you looking to remodel?"

"Well, my entire house is a freak of nature from the sixties. The worst offender is the bathroom; the whole thing has got to go. The living room is overflowing with flower power, but the kitchen is barely big enough for one person, let alone two."

"I see. How were you planning on doing the remodel? In stages or all at once?"

"You may have noticed, I've come into some time off recently." Walter indicated his cane. "But it's not going to last forever. I'm not stupid; I know remodeling takes time and, more importantly, money. I'd like to get as much done as I can as quickly as I can and as...inexpensively as I can."

"Understandable. Why don't we head back to the kitchen and bath guys first?"

So began a long and less than confident cycle of going to one aisle or another, radioing for one employee or another, being shown either a few super expensive options that were all but shoved down his throat for marketing, or a vast array of cheap options that Walter couldn't decide what was cheap-cheap and what was just inexpensive.

He did, however, end up buying a new toilet—white, not yellow—a new vanity—wood, not pink pressboard—and a new light fixture for over the mirror—tasteful brushed nickel, not tarnished brass. The tile and the shower would have to be done at a later date, but at least this way he felt like he actually started the project, and he hated leaving unfinished projects. Never mind that the entire house was, essentially, an unfinished project. Once Tommen's room had been completed, the rest of the house had to follow suit eventually.

He visited a couple other stores looking for ideas on floors and fixtures and walls. Since the house had only one bathroom, he was determined to get everything done at once. Thanks to Banding, he was fairly confident he and Tommen wouldn't be doing any potty dances while waiting for tile to set and grout to dry. He didn't think that the trees in the backyard would complain, but it was cold outside.

By the time he finished up at the last store, it was almost one. Walter didn't get too hungry anymore, but he still enjoyed food. Probably a little more than he should, but hey, weeks in the hospital had helped him to lose a few pounds; he could treat himself a little, right? But it wasn't as though going to the bakery and getting himself a pastry was much of a treat, more like a routine. Well, what the heck? Wasn't like he had anywhere he desperately needed to be; everything he was doing these days was out of boredom.

The drive to the bakery was a cluttered mess of cars all fighting to get back to the office after lunch break, and Walter found himself cooped up painfully in the driver's seat watching the car in front of him play pinball between the lane lines as the driver chatted away aimlessly on her phone and did other things with children in the backseat. Oh, what he wouldn't have given to have his lights on him now.

But he didn't have his lights on him, and the best he could do was plod along fearfully behind her, waiting for the inevitable accident, hoping he would make it to the bakery first. Thankfully, Someone heard his silent pleas, and he gratefully turned off into the parking lot, letting the chatty cathy car loose into the rest of the city.

The bakery wasn't busy as most of the morning crowd had already come and gone. Now that everyone had made it to work, the tables and booths would be empty until the lunch rush came around. Thus, when Walter hobbled in the door, jingling the little overhead bell half a dozen times, it sounded like a cave echo.

"Be right there!" Micah called from the back.

A second later, the younger twin was busily drying his hands with a paper towel, even as Walter noticed he looked like he'd just stepped out of the shower.

"Is your hair wet?" Walter asked.

"Huh?" Micah tossed the paper towel in the trash. "Oh, um, yeah. Got a tip on some Runners and it was...interesting to say the least. Cai's wrapping things up with them, so he'll be back soon."

"How many Runners?"

"Four. Three of them were punk-ass kids—well, I say kids, more like late twenties—and one was just an old man looking for a little extra time on Earth. Honestly, I told Cai to leave him alone. With a warning about catching him again, of course, but not all Runners are sinister."

Walter nodded. "Sometimes mercy goes further than punishment."

Micah leaned on the counter. "So, is this all we have today?"

"What do you mean?"

The younger twin went to the back and returned with a small round cake which, Walter suspected, had literally just been baked. And if it was meant to be any kind of celebratory cake and therefore to his tastes, he would guess that it was a white cake with buttercream frosting and a lot of gooey icing. Indeed, when Micah came around the counter and set it on a table for Walter, it was exactly that.

"All right, I'll bite, what's this?" Walter asked as Micah sat down across from him, handing out little party plates and forks and cutting the cake neatly into exact slices.

"It's your congratulatory, welcome back, thanks for not dying cake."

"Thanks, I'll keep that in mind, but maybe next time I'll just make the cake myself."

Micah grinned and shook his head. "Seriously, though, how are you doing? You don't come in every morning anymore, so we don't know. And don't quote Facebook to me, either. People lie on

Facebook all the time."

"People lie in person all the time, too."

"Are you going to lie to me?"

"No, but your point is irrelevant." Walter took a few bites of cake and leaned back in the chair. "Let's see, I'm mobile enough that I can drive and wipe my own butt. If I'm dying of anything at this point, it's boredom."

Micah snickered. "Mobile enough to want to move, not mobile enough to do anything."

"Well, that's not entirely true. I mean, I did get some chores done today. I even went and got a new toilet and vanity. Figured that while I'm off, it's time to do something about the terrible state of decor in my house."

"Praise the Lord, hallelujah!" Micah shouted flagrantly. "It's about time you did something in there."

Walter shook his head. "Well, when even your color-blind son can tell that it's hideous, there's something wrong."

"So you and Tommen are getting along okay? I mean, since you told him you're his uncle?"

Walter gave him an abbreviated version of the events from the other night, including the story they'd come up with to explain what had happened to the rest of the family. "Ever since then, he's been as normal as I can expect from him, given everything that's happened. Problem is, I don't know what the difference would be if he was troubled by everything that happened or if he was troubled by my confession. Likely it's both."

Micah nodded grimly. "I feel for you, I really do. I can't imagine it's easy for either of you. And you're right to be concerned. I would tell you to think of yourself when you were sixteen, but since you're a special case, I'll tell you about when I was sixteen. Okay, I was invincible. I could do anything, go anywhere, conquer any mountain. If you told me I couldn't do something, get out of my way because I'm about to prove you wrong. It wasn't just about impressing girls, either. I had my ego to maintain. You don't know what it's like to be a twin, but still live in your older brother's shadow."

"Well, I think Tommen has learned very well that he's not invincible and he can't do it all," Walter admitted.

"And therein lies the problem. He feels powerless. Against Tyler Freeman, he's always had a chance at beating him—whether through noble means or not, doesn't matter, the option is still there. Against Rifun..." Micah shook his head. "No. Rifun's got him beat, and beat hard. Rifun took him, took his hearing, almost took you, and to add insult to injury, he's got the poor boy under his thumb. It's a lot for a sixteen year old to take. I've seen stronger men break for less, but he can't go it alone."

"What do you think I should do? I can't exactly do anything right now, the way I am."

"So don't do anything. Another thing about being sixteen is independence. He loves you, crossed the universe to save you, but he doesn't want to be coddled. He wants to be in control. He needs to feel like he's not just a leaf on the winds of fate."

"And you're suggesting...?"

"What are his hobbies? What does he like to do? What is one thing that, last November, you could have asked him about—say, 'Hey, son, what do you want to do today, just name it!'—and he would have told you without a moment's hesitation?"

Walter sighed and searched his memory. "Well, before all this happened, he'd made plans with Eric and Varad to go skiing at Snowshoe, a last hurrah before Varad left for India. I just don't want to really remind him of what could have been."

"Walt, Tommen loves skiing. He's good at it, from what he brags about; I don't know how true it is."

"He is good. Like you said, he will crash a hundred times just to master a run to prove that he can do it. Trees, terrain parks, he likes to be king of the mountain, even if it's in his own head."

"That's all that matters. As long as he thinks he's king of the mountain, Rifun be damned."

"You really think it'll work?"

"Why not take him skiing and find out?" Micah stood. "I'll grab a box for your cake."

Walter sat and mulled over the idea. It was already January, and Tommen hadn't been out skiing yet. That was like sacrilege to him. Some people got up early for Sunday service; Tommen got up early so he could make first tracks on as many runs as he could, always going for speed on the open runs and tight turns and impossible trails through the trees. Then, once the people came out, he took to the terrain park and the face runs just so he could show off. And, to an extent, make Walter feel bad about his puttering ability as he did his pizza-French-fry turns on the easy runs.

The more he thought about it, the more likely it seemed that it would work, at least to some degree. A day where they weren't thinking about how bad he, Walter, was beat up. A day where they weren't being constantly reminded about everything that had happened; God knew the questions Tommen was getting at school about his absence. A day where they could relax and have fun. Well, Walter would be doing some relaxing. He had little doubt that Tommen would be having some fun, but it was quite a workout to achieve that fun.

"I think you're right," Walter said as Micah reappeared with a box and approached the table. "Maybe we just need a day to get away, relax, and have fun."

"That's the spirit," Micah told him as he carefully maneuvered the cake into the box without it crumbling to pieces or smearing frosting all over the box. "And the sooner the better, right? If you want, I can make an executive decision to give him Saturday off."

"Why don't you do that? Routine is good, but too much routine I think would only hurt him."

Micah grinned and winked. "See? I'm not as useless as Micaiah thinks I am sometimes."

"He's your big brother; he's supposed to think you're useless. Otherwise, how is he supposed to be your big brother and look out for you?"

Even as he said it, the entire bakery was suddenly caught in a Fast Band and Micaiah appeared from the kitchen. Behind him was Lily. He looked murderous; she looked terrified. Micaiah scanned the tables briefly before his black gaze settled on Walter and Micah, both with one hand unconsciously on the cake.

"Office. Now."

With that, he and Lily ducked into the office, pulling the Fast Band tight around the four of them. Walter reluctantly got to his feet and followed Micah.

"I don't work for him, and even I'm terrified of getting fired," Walter chuckled, trying to find some humor in a decidedly humorless situation.

"Whatever it is, if it involves Lily, it never ends well," Micah breathed as he opened the door.

Had Micaiah had a knife or a gun or any weapon at all, Walter would have expected him to suddenly leap from his chair in a murderous rage that would drench the office in blood. Not that his physical disposition was much better as he brooded like some evil villain. Lily just sat in a chair, looking lost in her own world. She seemed to come back to herself when she saw Walter, and she gave up her seat for him.

"What is this, Cai?" Micah asked.

"Tell them what you just told me," Micaiah ordered darkly, not moving a muscle but looking like a rubber band ready to either fly or snap.

Lily hesitated for just a moment. "It's not much of a secret that Micaiah and I are...involved—"

"You're fucking," Micah stated flatly.

"Yes, fine, we're sleeping together. No secret there. But...the truth is...it was orchestrated."

Walter shifted in his seat. "What do you mean, 'orchestrated'?"

"I mean...I was hired to kill Micaiah. Actually both of you, but first Micaiah. Didn't matter how it got done as long as it did. It was suggested that we start sleeping together—coming together after tragedy—" She looked at Walter and shrugged. "—and that one day while he was asleep, I kill him."

"Suggested by whom?"

"We all know who," Micah said. "Rifun. Or Cassius. Or both."

"They're most likely the masterminds, but they're not the ones who approached me."

"Why don't you start at the beginning?" Walter suggested.

Lily took a breath. "Okay. So, after the fight in the warehouse, I'm taken to the hospital, get cleared, check up on you, Walt, and I go home to clean myself up. I do that and I head to the Wheel. I don't know why, force of habit maybe. Anyway, I'm heading to the Auctions when I get cornered. They're in Grandfather shrouds, but I have my doubts. To make a long conversation short, I'm out of money and out of influence and they know it. Everyone knows it. Everyone also knows that what I do is very much illegal, but I no longer have the money or influence to just buy or charm or bargain my way out of prosecution.

"They also inform me that I, we, whoever, royally fucked up the elections, especially with our talk of Rifun and Cassius and a False Zero Hour. And if it doesn't get fixed, shit's gonna get real.

"So they offered me a deal. I kill you two—and a few others, but they're not important, and yes, they are still alive to my knowledge—and they pay me enough to buy off everyone and set the elections to right again."

"Why not buy everyone off themselves?" Micah wondered.

"Because I am—or I was—the face of influence. I was the shining example of how to be corrupt and get away with it. It's kind of like being Donald Trump, if you know what I mean. If I did this task, I would be restored to my former rotten glory. And they also promised that when the elections were over, I would not only be safe from prosecution, but I would be given a seat of power. I don't know what seat of power or what it means or any of it, only that's what they told me."

"Anything else?" Walter wondered.

"I wouldn't get the money until after I had killed at least you two and shown proof. I'd get half, and then when I offed the rest of the people on the list, I'd get the other half."

"And what happens if you tell us all of this?"

"I believe the response to that went something like, 'We're only giving you the opportunity to save yourself; there are others more willing to do the job. But you'll be lying there next to them if that's the case.' "

"So either you kill us or someone else kills us and you," Micah stated.

"Right."

"Is there a timeline for when this has to be accomplished?" Walter asked.

"No, just with enough time for them to get me the money and me buy off everyone who's voting, which is about the equivalent of bribing the entire population of Algeria."

"Deadline's coming up quick, then."

"Did they tell you who you had to 'pick' to get elected?" Micaiah inquired, having been silent thus far.

Lily shrugged. "I mean, they told me a few names but they would give me the full list with the money."

"What are you thinking, Cai?" Micah wondered.

"Why would Rifun and Cassius go through so much trouble to try and murder Lily, only to turn around and try to recruit her to kill us and then give her money and a seat of power?"

"It's all psychological," Walter answered. "You give the person what they think is a way out of their predicament only to turn on them. They're going to kill her anyway, but since they don't have the time to come and kill the rest of us because they're trying to clean up our mess, they recruit her to do the dirty work of killing us, make her influential again just long enough to get them elected, and then dispose of her. Stalin and his useful idiots. Classic communism."

"Maybe," Micaiah mused. "But you said they probably weren't Grandfathers despite being in their shrouds or similar ones, right?"

Lily nodded. "If they cornered her in the Wheel, it would be nothing for them to simply 'escort' her away and then kill her, and ditch the shrouds. She's at the low point of her popularity, so no one would miss her like they would if she regained her influence. On top of that, why use someone of questionable loyalty? Cassius and Rifun have already demonstrated that they have friends, those who are, I hate to say it, but they're more powerful than us. And they're obviously unconcerned about being seen by human beings—if these chosen friends are non-human, as it seems likely."

Walter folded his arms, wincing at the pain lancing through his back and shoulders. "Okay, so if it's not Rifun and Cassius, who is it?"

"Should we be doing this?" Micah cut in. "I mean, Cai, you do make some good points, but do we really need to conjure up ghosts when we have an enemy that we know and can see already?"

"The Cult of the Akari isn't the only cult or whackjob group in Time," Micaiah pointed out.

"Okay. Well, what about this. What if they really were Grandfathers?"

"This happened before Tommen's little jaunt across space," Walter said. "And while the Grandfathers have an interest in the elections, their vested interest is limited, and they don't need Lily to buy votes for them. Most often, their interests just happen to coincide so they let Lily do all the leg work of getting their chosen officials elected and they only interfere if interests diverge." He looked at Lily. "Sorry, you're not as all-powerful as you think."

She just shrugged.

"But if it was the Grandfathers, it would make sense as to why they got all riled up when Tommen proposed his 'civil war,' " Micaiah pointed out, bringing out the bunny ear air quotes. "The Grandfathers and the Hands have been feuding for eons; there really isn't anything special about this election. Except, we come in, screw up their rigged results, leave the whole process in shambles, then Tommen comes in and suggests what almost amounts to a hostile takeover by the

Hands. That's nothing new, but if the Grandfathers can't secure their interests because they have no candidates and no votes..."

"Then they risk losing their power," Walter finished. "Except it still doesn't explain why they would use Lily."

"Less leg work for them. Useful idiots, like you said."

Walter shook his head. "I don't know. Something just isn't adding up. It would make perfect sense if it had happened after Tommen went before the Hands. But it happened before. So, going back to the aftermath of the warehouse, where did things stand, and how could it be so influenced by Lily becoming powerful again and you two dying?"

"Well, you can bet that we'll be looking into this," Micaiah promised. "Count on that."

"The question now becomes, what is the threat to us? Lily, have you been contacted again since my supposed miraculous recovery?"

"No." The look on her face suggested that she thought it was strange.

"Why not? I find it hard to believe word of my survival went unnoticed, especially when I myself was called before the Hands. So either your contacts are completely incompetent or else there's another endgame here."

"Walter, you're making my brain hurt," Micah sighed.

"But you've been removed as Captain," Micaiah said.

"What?" Lily wondered.

"Could it be, then, that it's not about the elections at all? Lily, who else were you supposed to kill?"

She rattled off a list of names, five in total, two Timekeepers, two Harvesters, and a Merchant.

"Three of them aren't even able to vote this time around," Micah stated.

"So the elections are a prize but not the motivation," Walter mused.

"I think we need to do some investigating," Micaiah decided.

"Lily, we need to know everything about that conversation, every detail you can remember, no matter how insignificant it may seem."

"What angle are we going for?" Micah wondered. "Rifun and Cassius, the Grandfathers, or some other cult or whackjob group?"

"We'll start investigating the angles we know, Rifun and Cassius as well as the Grandfathers. But remember they're not our only options, just the most likely, and we have to be prepared for the possibility of another player on the field trying to take advantage of the chaos Time is currently in."

"I have quite enough time on my hands," Walter said. "I can start—"

"No." Micaiah cut him off. "Even from this distance, I can see that this is probably going to get violent, and you are in no shape for heroics, not this time. Furthermore, you are no longer a Timekeeper Captain; you are only Acting Captain. As such, I think it would be best if you kept your head low for the time being. Regardless if Rifun and Cassius are involved or not, they're probably just waiting for you to pop your head up so they can take it off. However, since you do have so much time and we don't, what with the shop and all, we'll hand over all the information we find and you can be our conspiracy theorist."

Sitting there, listening to Micaiah doling out instructions and plans of attack, Walter was torn. On the one hand, he was terribly proud of Micaiah, the strong, bold leader not afraid to jump in headfirst and save the day. On the other hand, he was a little annoyed that he was being pushed to the sidelines with a stack of paperwork like a secretary. At the precinct, sure, he was usually stuck at his desk with a pile of paperwork, but in Time he was a Captain. That only further irritated him when he considered that he'd been removed from his position on what the Hands were claiming was a technicality that would be resolved at the elections. And how did that play in, anyway?

"We have seven days until the elections," Micaiah said in a way that indicated he was wrapping up whatever speech he'd been speaking. "We need to bring this home fast. Any questions?"

"Is there any known danger to Tommen?" Walter asked. "Any new danger? Was he specifically targeted or mentioned at all?"

Lily shook her head. "He never came up, directly or indirectly. You didn't even come up. It was all about the twins and the other people on the list."

"That's probably important," Micah said uselessly.

Micaiah just nodded grimly as he scribbled down notes. "We'll brood on it for a little while. Then probably after work we'll make a trip to the Wheel and see what we can't find out."

"Be careful," Lily told them. "It's like you said, whether they're Grandfathers or just dressed like them, it would be nothing for them to 'escort' you away and kill you in some dark corner."

"Duly noted. Any more questions?"

"If whoever this is makes good on their promise to go after Lily because she hasn't killed us, how are we going to protect her?" Micah ventured stiffly. "We don't exactly have the best track record of doing that cleanly." He glanced at Walter.

For a minute or two, they sat in silence, staring at each other, none of them wanting to voice the suggestion that had probably popped into all their minds at the exact same time. Finally, Micaiah broke the silence, saying awkwardly, "If you wanted, we have an extra bedroom."

Micah scoffed. "Oh please, it's not like you and I sleep in the same bed."

"Regardless, the offer is there."

Lily shook her head. "Thank you, but no. I think I've caused enough trouble for and between you three."

"You mean like how you've fucked both of us, both literally and figuratively?" Micah spat.

"Enough!" Walter barked. "You're not teenagers. You're adults. Handle your personal problems like adults. And that only when you find spare time between your everyday lives and this investigation. Seven days is not very long, and that's even assuming we have that long."

"He's right," Micah conceded guiltily.

"We can kill each other later," Micaiah said, standing. "Right now, though, I have to keep both of you alive so I *can* kill you later."

He left the office, the others staring after him. After a moment, Micah shrugged. "Well, I don't know about him, but I have work to do."

Lily nodded sullenly and Walter grabbed his cane and hauled himself to his feet, slipping past Micah who held the office door open.

"Don't forget your cake, Walt," Micah reminded him as he rounded the counter and very nearly walked out the door without it. "Do you need me to carry it for you?"

"I'm only injured; I'm not helpless," Walter replied grouchily.

His leg was throbbing, his shoulders were in pain, his back was in screaming agony, and he was trying to maneuver an icy parking lot with impaired balance, a cane in one hand, and a cake in the other. Yes, there was no possible way this could go horribly, horribly wrong.

But he made it to the car safely, carefully setting the cake in the passenger seat and going through the same song and dance and grunts and groans of trying to get comfortable with the least amount of pain possible. He leaned back, tried to relax, took a pill, waited a minute for it to kick in, then started the car.

He was being pushed to the side and made a secretary! *No, no, you stay out of this. Stay home from school because you're sick and we'll bring your homework to you. Yeah, just stay out of this one. We'll do the dirty work and hand you all the files to sort through.* Because nothing of significance ever happened that wasn't going to be documented. Nothing exciting was ever going to happen first-hand that couldn't be relayed later.

Walter sighed and rubbed his eyes. No, that wasn't fair, at least not to the twins. They were good Timekeepers, hard workers, and damn fine investigators. They would do their best to find the most relevant information, get that to him, and relay anything that they had or that had happened that wasn't on paper. They'd done it when investigating the murders, and they'd done it when they helped Tommen on his little adventure. There was no reason to think that their performance now would be anything less than stellar. And by making him even secretary was their attempt at both acknowledging his physical shortcomings while trying to keep him in the loop of the investigation, even if he didn't appear to be part of it, mysteriously.

But still. They pushed him aside and made him a secretary. They were going off on their own black ops private eye investigation, and he was just supposed to be the cute secretary who met clients at the door and ushered them into the office. Well, cute being a relative term. He preferred ruggedly handsome, but there was always a distinct lack of ruggedly handsome secretaries in old-school private eye novels.

The drive home was unremarkable. Traffic always sucked, but as long as there was a clear path to drive, he could Band and zip through inconsequentially. He made it home in pretty good time, reminding himself that he still had to pick up Tommen from work at seven. He got inside easily enough, cut himself another slice of cake and cranked up the heat for a short spell, enough to get the house toasty warm before turning it back down to a more modest temperature.

How in the world was he going to get the toilet and vanity in the house? His first problem was just getting them out of the car. One of the store associates had been good enough to load them for him. At the time, he'd figured that Tommen could do it when he got home. Physically, that was possible. Then came the problems of first getting the items through the teeny tiny kitchen and, once that was all done, installing them. Walter had little doubt that he would be able to go down. It was getting back up that was going to be the problem, and he wasn't about to be one of those old person frequent fliers on the ambulance who called because they fell off the toilet and needed help getting back up.

Eventually, after finishing his piece of cake, he made his way to his recliner. Any other time, he would have been happy to take a nap, but his mind was working too much to allow that right now.

Considering everything that had happened, why would someone — or a group of someones — go after Micah and Micaiah, but have no interest in him? Yes, he'd been as good as dead at the time Lily was approached, but that they wouldn't go back to her after his recovery and order his death was odd. Why kill them, but not him? And what would killing them accomplish that they couldn't just give Lily the funds to bribe them, especially if the elections were the prize to be won? But then, why target other people, three of whom who wouldn't even be voting in this election cycle?

He mentally ran over the list of names, trying to remember if he'd heard any news of them lately. They were in different states, he knew, and there had been nothing Earth-side on them that he was aware of, and he couldn't think of anything relating to them Time-side. It was as if this group had just picked the twins and then five random names out of a hat.

Or maybe that was the point. Maybe this wasn't about the elections or threats or anything; maybe this was all a test. Maybe the Grandfathers or whoever was testing Lily to see what she'd do under such circumstances. She'd certainly been vulnerable. Like Tommen, everything had spiraled out of control, and regaining her power and influence would be a way to put her back in control of things. Half of the money for the twins, the other half for the other people. Two people she knew well, five people she didn't. How would she react? Would she kill them all, only those she didn't know?

Who stood to gain from such a test? Had Cassius and Rifun reconsidered their position on her? If they couldn't kill her, maybe they could beat her down, manipulate her, and turn her into their puppet. She'd demonstrated considerable strength when it came to resisting them, even though it cost her her little empire. Maybe now they were considering reinstating her influence but only as long as she worked for them.

When a Time King or Queen is installed, will you be the good knight to bend the knee and pledge his sword? Walter thought ruefully, thinking of how she'd tried to bribe him.

Walter turned the theory over and over in his mind. Simple theories were nice and generally very forgiving, but this sounded just too easy. A test. It sounded almost as bad as "it was all a dream" or "sudden *deus ex machina* saved the day" or some such theatrical cliché. If it was the truth, he'd certainly take it. But until he got more evidence, he was just going to put that one on the back burner.

And even if it was all a test, it still didn't answer the question of who. There was a glaring problem through the whole thing, and that was assuming that the people who cornered Lily were not actual Grandfathers. The shrouds used by the Hands and the Grandfathers were, through some oddly specific biotechnology, rigged so that a Hand or a Grandfather was automatically shrouded as they stepped through the portal into the Wheel, in order to maintain absolute anonymity, or as close to anonymity as could be gotten.

Not just any shlump off the street could rig that kind of programming. That level of access was restricted to only five known Time Agents: the Bat and the Day who served the Hands, the Hutch and the Key who served the Grandfathers, and the Relic who was the head secretary in charge of all secretaries everywhere in the Wheel and in Time. If Rifun and Cassius and-or the Hands were behind this, they probably went through the Bat or the Day. If the Grandfathers did it, and they did disguise someone as a false Grandfather, they probably went through the Hutch or the Key. If it was anyone else, their only real option would be the Relic, and to have that kind of access...that was on the same plane as discovering that the Charleston serial killer was a Warden Timekeeper and his partner was a Triage Harvester, a Labrador fighting a wolf-dog, and a rabid one at that.

Worse, that meant that there was a third power party involved, because two just wasn't bad enough.

Walter rubbed his face and leaned back in his recliner. *Don't jump to conclusions. Like Micah said, there's no need to conjure up ghosts when you already have an enemy you know and can see already. Don't go fighting shadows while your real enemy beats you bloody. It's getting close to Election Day, which means secrecy and subterfuge go out the door quickly for more bare bones threats. There's probably a simple explanation for all of this.*

What that was, however, he didn't know right at the moment, because he quickly drifted off to sleep.

Chapter Eighteen
The Bakery

So he'd fallen asleep during Robinson's presentation of *The Joy of Painting*, so what? It wasn't as if he was the first person to ever fall asleep while listening to Bob Ross talk about happy trees and happy clouds and happy everything else. Still, Tommen earned himself a demerit for the day, just one more to add to the list. It didn't help that he nodded off again while Robinson was explaining the different brushes and the techniques and the colors and basically giving the equivalent of a college analysis of *War and Peace*. The only thing that saved him from earning a trip to the office was that one of his classmates actually thought to jab him awake.

He only had to make it through about forty minutes of the lecture before he was saved again, this time by the bell. Rubbing his eyes, Tommen pulled himself out of the room toward his locker. Normally he would have met up with Eric or Varad, and they would exchange jokes and jabs and various complaints about school that day, as well as make plans for the weekend if they could all get off work. Now, his meandering to his locker was relatively silent, the usual game of Frogger as every student in the school criss-crossed their way from classrooms to lockers to either the bus area or the parking lot. There was an art to making it through the madness unscathed.

His only victory, if it could be called that, came from the fact that even if he wasn't chatting with Eric and Varad, Tyler wasn't around to threaten him either, at least not that he could see. Didn't mean much, though. For being such an ape, he sure could sneak up on people unexpectedly. And unwantedly. Was that a word? Unwantedly? Didn't matter, he supposed. It was now.

For some reason, after every major break, the kids on the bus felt the need to shuffle their normal seating arrangement. Tommen wasn't sure if any particular class or group had started the tradition or if it was something that was simply expected, but as he stepped on the bus, the seat that had been his was already taken, mauled by a bunch of freshman girls giggling about something on a phone. So he pressed on until he found the seat near the back that was still relatively close to the heater, at least close enough to feel it blowing.

But he supposed there was something to be said for the shuffling of people. For one, it meant that there was new gossip to be had so he didn't have to listen to the full year's saga of how Sarah was constantly dating and breaking up with Brad and how Emma wished Paul was available but right now he was more concerned about his gay younger brother Nathan. Rather, he just had to put up with each little saga for a few weeks until the next seat shuffle.

Today's saga, however, was not about any love interest good or bad. At least, not all of them. As expected, news of his hearing aids had gotten around, which again brought up his personal drama. And, as usual, no one seemed to think he needed to be consulted on the facts of the matter, which led to several interesting theories about what actually happened while he was gone and over Christmas.

One theory said he ran away from home and tried to join a gang, but the initiation was too much for him to handle. His hearing was damaged in a territory shootout, and when he was taken to the hospital, he was put in a room with his dad and that essentially sobered him up so he returned home.

Another theory went along the lines of him being the serial killer and the terrorist, and he was the one who killed and wounded all the police officers, including his dad. Again, the gunfire damaged his hearing. No explanation on why he was back at school and not rotting in prison.

Still a third theory, probably started and perpetuated by the girls from Economics, said that he was a victim of a child sex-trafficking ring that his dad was part of. When his dad wanted out, the other ringmen kidnapped Tommen in order to make him pay up. And while he was being held captive, he was molested in unspeakable ways so he would be a submissive man for anyone who wanted him.

Even as he thought about the last one, Tommen felt bile in his throat until he was almost certain that he would throw up.

How could anyone honestly be that cruel to someone else? Sure, Tommen got in a few fights and he didn't have much good to say about Tyler Freeman, but he had never in his life said anything even remotely on that level of cruelty and shame to or about someone. It wasn't even about his traditional upbringing; those words were just plain evil, whether 1855 or 2005. And it made him sick.

He hated school. He liked learning, like Physics, liked the concept of school, but he hated the people. He hated his classmates, hated the students in the other grades. He wasn't a huge fan of the teachers either, but he wouldn't necessarily say he hated them. Never mind that even though they talked tough and stepped in on the fights, they never actually did anything about them. No, wait, he hated them too. Maybe it wasn't their fault; maybe their hands were tied by that fine line between interference and abuse. Tyler knew they were bound by that as much as Tommen did. So where was that one superhero teacher who would chew through his ties to enter the ring and put a real end to the fighting instead of just barking from the sidelines?

Well, if he had to hazard a guess, it was because there were no superheroes anymore. No one was coming to save him. Not this time.

He got off the bus, almost slipping on the ice in the parking lot, and plodded inside. It was as if nothing ever happened. Would any customers have noticed that he was gone? Had they assumed he quit? Just another bratty teenager, whining because he isn't making $15 an hour the second he walks into the workforce despite never having worked a day before in his short life and not even graduated from high school yet.

Thankfully, the bakery was currently empty of any customers so he didn't have to wipe off his bitter scowl quite yet. The office door was closed, the blinds down, and Micah wasn't in the kitchen. Private conference, then. He dropped his backpack and punched in, grabbing and apron and heading for the sink.

"*A Thommen.*"

He turned as Micah poked his head out of the office. "*Tar anseo, le do thoil.*" (Come here, please.)

Probably another heartfelt lecture about making sure he was ready to return to work. Did he need any days off? Was he okay to do full duty?

Actually, the likelihood of that conversation was pretty low, considering how much of the twins he'd been seeing lately. They knew him; they'd all had a talk about him returning to work, and they'd let him back in with no question. And since it was his first day back, he couldn't have done anything terribly wrong already, could he?

"What?" he asked cautiously. "I just walked in. Did I do something wrong?"

Micaiah was rarely in a good mood where his good mood showed on his face, but sometimes word choice and body language were enough to know when he was in a good mood, even if he had a hard time showing it. This was not one of those times. This was one of those opposite times, when everything about him spelled displeasure and murder to anyone who challenged him.

"No, you haven't done anything wrong," Micah told him, trying to sound friendly and reassuring, though his tone was straining.

"Threats have been made," Micaiah stated bluntly.

Fear exploded in Tommen like a grenade as his mind jumped from the cave to the warehouse to his dad in the hospital. It felt as if he'd gone through the portal to the Wheel, the way the breath was sucked from his lungs. He Banded so he could catch his breath.

"What kind of threats?" he asked, willing his voice not to break.

"Death threats. So far, the threats have been made against only seven people, myself and Micah included."

"What about —?"

Micaiah held up a hand. "You and your dad were not named or mentioned in any way that we know of."

"Was it Rifun and Cassius?"

"We don't know who it was, but we're investigating every angle that we are able. Rifun and Cassius, the Grandfathers, and any other groups as they make themselves known."

"Why tell me?"

"Just because you weren't named, doesn't mean you are not involved in some way. Maybe you are completely in the clear on this one, but in light of recent events, we're not taking any chances."

Well, it made sense.

Tommen folded his arms. "Does my dad know?"

"He was in here a couple hours ago and we told him, yes," Micah informed him.

"So what can I do?"

Micaiah seemed hesitant. "We know that this is a lot for you, and we don't want to send you off on some dangerous adventure when you're just barely returning from another."

If there was one thing Micaiah was not, it was stupid. He could read Tommen like a book. It was as if he knew his thoughts and feelings even before he himself was able to sort them out. And right now he could tell that Tommen was struggling, and struggling hard. Less like an animal caught in a trap — after all, most animals have teeth or claws or just brute strength — and more like a fish in a net on the beach, wiggling and flopping and not in a good place to be, either in the net or on the beach.

"Is there anything I can do?" Tommen asked again, dialing back the edge in his voice, trying to sound like he was giving in just a little to Micaiah's implied statement.

Micaiah's Band was so short-lived, only because of Tommen's superior ability to perceive Time and feel everything second-by-second and less than a second did he see it. He'd probably given Tommen a good once-over, tried to determine his true level of emotional and mental stability, his readiness to partake in another "dangerous adventure" as he'd called it.

"Rifun's a nutjob, but he's not the only nutjob out there. Did he or Cassius or any of them ever mention anyone else, other people, other groups, competition as it were?"

Tommen thought a moment and shook his head. "No, not that I recall."

"Do you know of or have you come across any other nutjobs or groups like that?"

"No. I wouldn't even know what to look for, I—"

"It's okay, Tommen," Micah said. "We don't expect you to."

Tommen glanced back and forth between the brothers. "Are we playing Good Cop, Bad Cop here, or what? I just wanted to know if I could do anything to help."

Micaiah sighed. "Relax, Tommen. We're only asking a few questions. If you don't know, you don't know."

"Well, maybe I do know something." Tommen shifted his stance. "Sifura once mentioned that after my petition got rejected, she caught a group of Hands after the meeting, whispering about going off and making their own venture, like what we were talking about with the Borelian antidotes and stuff. She couldn't tell who they were, though. Does that help at all?"

"We don't know, but something might come up in our investigation." Micaiah leaned back in his chair. "Like we said, you and your dad could be totally in the clear on this one, but until we can make that determination for certain, keep an eye and ear out for anything suspicious Time-side, all right?"

Tommen nodded. "Okay. Is that all?" He turned to leave.

"Tommen."

"What?"

"It'll be okay. Really it will. All right?"

He hesitated but nodded. "All right."

"It's election season in the Wheel. If not for your previous adventures, we probably wouldn't have bothered you with this. Do you understand?"

"I understand."

"All right. Micah will be out in shortly."

Tommen left the office, closing the door behind him. He wasn't actually too concerned about whether Micah was going to be out shortly or in six hours.

He headed to the sink to wash his hands, all the while brooding over the conversation. He never should have said anything or asked if he could help. It wasn't as if he had anything better to do other than get wrapped up in another series of threats and other shenanigans. It was election season and he was just a proba—Apprentice. He was an Apprentice now. But he was still utterly insignificant when it came to the elections. He wasn't a candidate, and he wasn't a voter; he was barely an informed citizen to know what the hell was going on and try to keep up with it all.

That's all this was: election season hot air. Death threats were probably made all the time. When turns could no longer change minds and buy votes, threats became the new currency. Who could make the worst threat and make it convincing, regardless of how willing the person was to deliver on it?

Mulling it over, Tommen wasn't sure how convinced he was of his little fantasy. He knew the basics of politics in the Wheel, but not enough to keep up with the Who's Who and how it all worked and everything else. For all he knew, he was spot on, and everything would be totally cool after the elections concluded. At the same time, he could be completely wrong, and they should all be on high alert. He tried to take a clue from the twins' demeanor, telling himself that if the threat was there, they wouldn't sugarcoat it. Would they?

Micaiah knew he wasn't himself. Micaiah knew he was still hurting, still recovering. Was this going to be a "lying to someone you love in order to spare them emotional pain" cliché? No, it couldn't be. Micaiah had readily confronted him about his behavior and words while his dad was dying in the hospital; there was no way he was going to sugarcoat something as impersonal as this. Sorry to say,

Micaiah often lacked the tact to deliver his words with such finesse.

"You okay to take the counter?" Micah asked behind him.

Tommen turned. "Um, yeah, sure."

"I won't make you."

"No, it's fine. I got it."

Micah didn't fight him, simply nodded and informed him there was a customer heading for the door.

He was not a regular customer. Tommen couldn't recall ever seeing him before at all. So it was just another guy, walking in for a quiet bite and shelter from the cold. He had no idea that Tommen had been gone for several weeks, or why. He probably wouldn't have asked what happened to the young kid who normally worked the counter. Still, Tommen served him his food and returned to the counter to deal with the inevitable lemming effect. One person walked in, and suddenly everyone else within sight range decided this was the place to be.

The rush lasted all of half an hour before the store was empty again.

"*Conas a tá tú anseo?*" Micah asked, poking his head out briefly. (How are you doing up here?)

"*Go maith,*" Tommen told him, looking over his shoulder. "*Tá an fhidir thart.*" (Fine. The rush is over.)

"*Ceart go leor. Béic má tá aon rud ort.*" (Okay. Holler if you need anything.)

Micah ducked back in the kitchen. As Tommen turned back to his work, he noticed something in his peripheral vision. At first, he was ready to dismiss it as just someone walking by to another store in the plaza. In the next moment, it registered as someone slipping on the ice just off the sidewalk.

"*A Mhicah!*" Tommen called. (Micah!)

"*Cad?*" (What?)

"*Tar anseo!*" (Come here!)

Tommen was halfway across the floor before Micah appeared. He heard the younger twin swear and pick up the pace until they were both pushing to get out the door.

It was a young woman, thirty years old max, dressed in a petite business suit that was now caked with dirty snow and slush, blond hair pulled back in a bun that was now quite ruffled, modest business heels askew on her feet, purse a foot away from her with the contents mercifully still inside.

"Are you all right?" Micah asked as he and Tommen fumbled to get her first to her hands and knees and then to her feet. "Why don't you come inside?"

For a moment, the woman looked too bewildered to argue or resist. Finally she nodded and walked into the bakery mostly under her own power, cheeks burning bright red. Micah and Tommen got her to a table and Micah sent Tommen for the first aid kit. Tommen walked nicely enough to the kitchen, but Banded once he was out of sight of the woman.

"Are you all right?" Micah asked again. "Hit your head or anything? Do you remember what happened?"

"I stepped off the sidewalk and I slipped on the ice," the woman said, her tone going from slightly dazed to almost a low growl. "Who's in charge of the salt? I'm going to sue. That is dangerous out there!"

"Did you hurt yourself at all? Do you want me to call an ambulance?" Micah's tone changed from concern to one that said, "Oh, great, one of those."

"You might as well. And I want a police report. And a bucket of salt because I will salt it myself if I have to."

Micah sighed, glanced at Tommen, gave a small shrug, and, with just a motion, sent him to find the salt bucket and scoop. Technically, they were responsible for the sidewalk alone, and the plow person contracted for the plaza dealt with the lot itself, but might as well just get it done to make Miss Sue Special happy.

When Tommen returned, lugging the bucket of salt, Micah was just hanging up with dispatch, looking none too pleased. As Tommen was heading out the door, Micaiah exited the office, still apparently in a brooding mood. Miss Sue versus Brooding Micaiah, now that would be a match to watch.

And Tommen did watch it as he scooped out heaps of salt and generously scattered the little crystals over the relatively dry sidewalk and a bit on the asphalt. He kept one eye on where he stepped, lest he fall too, and one eye on the inside goings-on as Micaiah spoke to the woman. It didn't look like a standard exchange either, where the frantic shop owner offers any number of discounts, deals, and other goodies in order to avoid being sued. Rather, it looked more like a very unimpressed shop owner informing the sue-happy patron that it was winter, and in winter, there is ice. Not his fault she elected to wear slippery heels instead of shoes with any sort of tread.

Eventually, he couldn't pretend to salt anymore, and it was getting pretty cold, so Tommen went back inside, pretending to just move hurriedly through the store and not totally eavesdrop on the conversation. Before he could hear too much, the talking stopped and the door opened again. When Tommen got back to the front, the ambulance had arrived. Not far behind them, the cop car also pulled in.

"Finally," the woman hissed. "Don't they take these things seriously?"

No, Tommen thought, *they don't. Dispatch is very good at their job and they ask a lot of questions in order to determine your priority. Conscious, breathing, no signs of concussion or major trauma, you are not getting the golden ambulance ticket, lady. And since we're helping and not assaulting you, you're not getting the golden police ticket either.*

He said none of this out loud of course, but he thought it as he fought a smile. The officer walked in first and approached the woman and the twins. Tommen stayed back, figuring he wasn't going to add anything to the conversation. Then the officer called him over.

"Micah says you saw it happen," he said.

"Um, not really. I mean, I just saw something in my peripheral vision. I thought it was someone passing by, then I guess I saw her step off the sidewalk and slip on the asphalt," Tommen answered.

"She slipped stepping off the asphalt or she slipped on the asphalt?"

"Uh, like, she had one foot on the sidewalk, she took one step down, and that foot got away from her, and she fell."

"You're certain of this?"

"Yeah, as much as I can be."

"He called me out of the kitchen, and we went out to help her up," Micah went on. "We got her inside. I called 9-1-1, and Tommen went out to salt just in case."

Tommen crept away after that while the officer filled out his report and the ambulance crew did their thing. It quickly became apparent that Miss Sue Special wasn't going to win her case. The incident had happened outside of the bakery's jurisdiction and, as the general sentiment went, it was winter. While it was reasonable to expect that sidewalks and roads should have some sort of salt or sand on them, she also had a responsibility to keep herself safe. In other words, wear some dang boots! Tennis shoes at least.

Once the officer had finished his report and the ambulance crew declared her healthy and uninjured, everyone gave their signatures, and the officer walked the woman out to her car. More of a courtesy than a requirement, but Tommen figured let him deal with her and leave them in peace.

"You guys get a lot of these?" Micah asked the ambulance crew as they packed up.

One of the medics shrugged. "More than we'd like, not as many as you'd think in a city this size. Ninety-eight percent of the time, it's pretty routine, either nothing wrong or a twisted ankle or something. Unless they slip a fall down a flight of stairs, it's generally nothing too serious."

Micah sighed and shook his head. The medics wished them good night and headed out.

Once more, the bakery was quiet.

"Because we really needed that headache," Micaiah growled, rubbing his face. "Now I'm going to have to keep an eye out for lawsuit papers coming across my desk."

"Don't worry about it right now, Cai," Micah told him. "We have bigger things to worry about. And you could see it on the officer's face that the woman was fishing. If he didn't buy it, chances are, a judge won't either."

Micaiah grunted but said nothing more. Finally he went into the office, returning a moment later with his coat. "I'm heading out. I need to get some sleep or something."

Yeah, he was going to get some, but it wouldn't be sleep, Tommen knew.

"You sure about that?" Micah wondered. "We don't know what's out there waiting for us."

"I'm heading out," Micaiah repeated, and he left, slamming the back door behind him.

Micah looked forlornly at the back door but did not go after his brother, though Tommen could see the conflict on his face. Finally he just shook his head and went back to the kitchen to continue whatever recipe he'd been in the middle of.

"He'll be okay, right?" Tommen wondered cautiously.

"We can only hope," Micah replied grimly. "I may not approve of his particular evening adventures, but at the very least I know where he'll be, or should be."

"So he and Lily are still sleeping together?"

Micah nodded grimly. "Not just them."

Tommen was about to say more when the bell over the door jingled and he returned to the front.

The rest of his shift passed uneventfully. No one slipped on the ice or stubbed their toe or set fire to the entire plaza. People came and people went. No one questioned whether he'd been gone or why. Well, that wasn't entirely true. There was one elderly woman who questioned where he'd been, but she also had severe dementia to the point where her daughter had to drive her everywhere and do most everything for her, so she always asked where Tommen had gone, even if he'd just worked the day before and saw her then as well.

"How are you doing up here?" Micah asked as he stepped out of the kitchen, drying his hands, while Tommen put up the chairs and swept the floor.

Tommen sighed. "I know you're worried about me. And I appreciate it. I do. But it would really help if every time you saw me, you didn't ask that."

"Okay, okay." Micah put his hands up. "Fair enough. My fault. But this time I was actually referring to how you're doing cleaning up, if you needed help. Did you get the garbages yet?"

"No, not yet."

As Micah went for the trash by the door, he looked up. "Your dad's here. Finish sweeping and punch out."

"You sure?"

"Yeah, I'll take these and mop the floor."

"What about your lecture about whatever is waiting for you out there?"

"Sorry to say, Tommen, but you're not exactly a deterrent. I'll be fine. Go home."

Tommen nodded reluctantly and finished sweeping. He was just putting the broom away when his dad walked in.

"Excuse me, sir, are your ovens still going, because I want something fresh," he said mockingly.

"Sir, I'm afraid if you don't leave now, I'm going to have to call the cops," Micah sighed dramatically. He grinned. "Just about cleaned up. I told Tommen to finish sweeping and head out."

"He can finish his work; he's got a minute. Micaiah here?"

"He left. It's been a rough day."

Tommen dumped out the dust pan and went back to start mop water while Micah recounted the tale of the slip and fall. If they were going to be talking for a while, might as well get paid for the time he was going to spend standing around. And it was well-paid, comparatively speaking, as Tommen not only got the floors mopped, but he got the trashes taken out and everything done except locking the front door. When his dad and Micah were finished talking, Micah looked around, slightly confused.

"Everything's done," Tommen told him before Micah could ask.

"Oh." Micah looked down at his apron, still covered in flour and assorted splattered ingredients. "Guess I won't need this, then. Thank you. I think you're working tomorrow."

Tommen nodded. "I am."

"Oh. Okay. See you then."

They parted ways, Tommen following his dad out to the car in the parking lot, Micah locking the door behind them and heading out the back door.

"Sounds like an interesting day at work at least," Walter commented.

"That's putting it nicely," Tommen said, rolling his eyes.

"Did you make it to class this morning?"

"Yeah."

"Everything went well?"

Tommen shrugged. "My backpack's lighter, anyway."

His dad sighed, but it was hesitant. "It's not the end of the world, Tommen. You'll make new friends. You always do."

Not after the rumor mill gets through with me, he thought ruefully.

"At the very least, when we get home, I have a little project for you."

"I find it hard to believe you could have cluttered up the garage that fast," Tommen said.

His dad chuckled. "No, not quite. I ran a few errands, and apparently my enthusiasm ran ahead of my common sense."

"This could be interesting. What did you do?"

"You'll see when we get home."

That left any number of things to the imagination. Well, obviously his dad was okay and the house hadn't burned down, so Tommen counted those as tiny victories. When they pulled into the garage, everything seemed normal, but he'd learned quickly that looking normal and being normal were two very different things.

"Go ahead and put your stuff in your room," his dad said. "Then come back out."

Tommen obeyed, not sure if he should drag his feet because he was a little nervous about this mysterious errand, or if he should hurry up because he was dying to know what it was. He tossed his backpack on his bed and returned to the garage where his dad had popped the trunk of the car.

"Admittedly, the guys at the store loaded them for me," he said. "Never considered how I was going to get them out."

Tommen relaxed and relief swept through him. So he was just moving a few things. Okay, he could live with that. But why the secrecy? Was his dad just embarrassed that he couldn't do it himself or—

"Holy shit."

"Watch your language, Tommen. I shouldn't have to keep reminding you."

It wasn't actually the fact that his dad had finally gone out and bought a new toilet and vanity for the bathroom that shocked him so much as the fact that they both fit in the trunk. The vanity probably needed a little assembly, true, but the toilet was one single unit and somehow it fit in the trunk.

"You can set them just to the side here. With you working and me like I am, we won't get to them until the weekend anyway."

Tommen sighed and carefully started dragging the vanity out, figuring that to be the lighter package. "Considering it took forty years to make it this far, I'm thinking I might just set them in the living room."

With his dad verbally guiding him up steps and around obstacles, Tommen managed to carry, lift, huff, puff, and drag the two large, heavy boxes out of the trunk, around the car, and through the house. By the time he was done, he was exhausted and collapsed on the couch.

"I suppose I'll have to assemble that vanity tomorrow," his

dad mused, staring at the two boxes on either side of the TV. "Should be easy enough as long as I have all my tools with me the first time so I don't have to keep getting up and down."

Tommen nodded blankly and gave a blind thumbs up. "Just don't hurt yourself anymore than you already have."

"All right, Tommen. Thank you for carrying those in. But you've got school in the morning, so you should probably start on your homework. Are you hungry?"

Vacation time spent at home never seemed to agree with his dad. He got...sentimental. Was that the right word? Tommen wasn't sure. But he wasn't going to turn down a dinner that he didn't have to cook, so he agreed and went to his room to start homework while his dad went to the kitchen to start dinner.

Chapter Nineteen
A Matter of Size

Tommen had dreaded going back to school on Tuesday, and it had been every bit a nightmare as he'd expected. But he'd also told himself that once the damage was done, it was done, and it would be over with. He knew he'd do enough on his own to screw things up and make the day miserable, but he hadn't counted on someone being there to help him out.

So Wednesday morning, he was even less excited to go back to school. He tried to tell himself that Tuesday had been a fluke; it was an awkward day for everyone. He'd just come back and made his grand reentry; Becky was brand new to school and trying to carve out her place in the social caste system. They'd just met at the wrong time and rubbed each other the wrong way. He tried to tell himself that today would be better. Now that all the secrets were out there and they had a general understanding of each other, maybe they could, in fact, wipe the slate clean and start over. Hi, my name is Tommen. Hi, my name is Becky. That sort of thing.

He wasn't sure what good it would do. She was a dwarf, and she knew she needed help with things. He just happened to be her table partner. Being tall himself, he was the best candidate for assistance. Otherwise, though, she would find her circle of friends and he would join them, but only in the context of the rumor mill. So, in conclusion, it was probably best to keep information about himself to a minimum in order to cut his losses from the get-go.

"Tommen!" His dad knocked on the door as he went by. "Up and at 'em!"

The next step was a full-blown assault with excessive force, so

Tommen reluctantly dragged himself out of bed and started his day. It was kind of nice, actually, to not have to ride the bus in the morning. He could sleep in a little, plus he got to drive and get his hours, making up for all his lost time and getting him closer to freedom.

"When's your next day off?" his dad asked as he pulled into the parking lot.

"Um...Saturday, I think," Tommen answered; he'd only glanced at the calendar. "Why?"

"Oh, just thinking of something."

"Another project?"

"Maybe. But maybe I'll just cool it on the projects for a while. I think I have enough to keep me busy."

Between the vanity, the toilet, and his condition, Tommen figured his dad was right. He was glad his dad was feeling well enough to do all the projects and get things done; he was less enthusiastic about the moments when his dad realized he wasn't well enough to do all the projects and get things done, and he made Tommen do them.

But that was neither here nor there. His dad wished him a good day at school, and Tommen headed inside, lugging his backpack. He expected Layman to call him into his office so they could have another chat about Tyler's comments the previous day and talk about feelings and stress and all the other shit they normally talked about. But, oddly enough, he didn't even see Layman. He wasn't standing at the door greeting everyone as they walked in, always keeping one eye on Tommen as he went past, like a hawk watching a mouse far beneath him.

Thus started his day of suspicion. True, he wasn't exactly surprised that Tyler wasn't around to taunt him—probably got suspended after yesterday—but none of his cronies were around to give him nasty looks either. None of the teachers or staff came up to him with advice varying from life lessons and stress management to "finish your homework or you'll live under a bridge the rest of your life." He was able to go about his morning in relative peace.

Even Righting didn't get after him like she normally did, and he knew he hadn't done the best on his homework. He'd been moved to a hybrid class in order to get away from the normal class for part of the time, but whenever he was sitting at his desk in the classroom, she never failed to call him out for something. So when he was able to sit quietly at his desk and not listen to her passive-aggressively chastise him for not doing his homework in any of his creative ways of not doing his homework, his suspicion was only heightened further.

Economics was pretty standard. The bitch partners in crime were also nowhere to be seen. Maybe there was a God and He'd finally listened to Tommen's silent pleas for a hole to open up and swallow all of the bullies in his life. More likely, they'd all just been suspended and they would be back, probably by next week.

But it was AP Physics that he was most nervous about, and as he exchanged his textbooks from one class to the next, he thought about the irony in that feeling. He'd been so ecstatic to finally get out of regular classes. He'd been prepared to walk into class like a badass and take his place among the seniors like a badass. Now he wished he could be going to any class but AP Physics. He would take regular Physics. He would take one of Righting's other hell-classes. He would even take a gym class if it meant not going to AP Physics right now.

But here he was, walking in and taking his corner seat, as close to the door as he could physically get. Did he dare hope that today would be a clean slate? Fuck, was he actually hoping for a boring ass lecture that way he could systematically ignore everything and just pretend to care, enough to see him through until lunch? Had he ever been more anticipatory—was that a word? Anticipatory? Well, it was now—had he ever looked forward to Web Programming more than he had right here, right now? Had he ever been more excited to watch Bob Ross in art class?

"Hey."

He was jerked from his thoughts as Becky climbed into her seat. "How are you?"

He shrugged. "Okay." He hesitated for just a second. "You?"

"Still trying to get used to a new school and everything, but that's to be expected."

And that was that. With exception of her asking him a question about the book later in class, they did not speak to each other, didn't even give each other weird or awkward glances, like the time a teacher made him sit next to a girl he'd broken up with only the week before. They'd had to sit together for six weeks. That had been way awkward.

"Do you need help with lunch?" he forced himself to ask as the bell rang and they packed up their things.

"No, I brown-bagged it today," Becky answered politely. "Thank you for asking, though."

And they parted ways. Tommen grabbed his lunch and headed for the cafeteria. He did not see Becky, and she did not seek him out. While he liked not having an annoying little monkey on his back, he did kind of appreciate her kind gesture, and he missed the company at his otherwise lonely table. So the best he could do was finish off his sandwich and make for his locker.

The rest of the day was pretty much more of the same. It was almost as if he were invisible. How many times had he wished he could be invisible, except now that he had it, he didn't want to be? He just wanted someone to acknowledge him. More to the point, he wanted friends again. Maybe it was his fault for only sticking with the two friends he'd had since third grade, but had it really been unrealistic of him to expect to lose them not-in-that-way? They didn't even talk to him online anymore. He sat in Web Programming for over an hour every day, and he couldn't even sneak glances at Facebook because there was no one he wanted to secretly chat with anymore.

Art went by as slowly as it always did, but it wasn't as bad as it normally was, at least in Tommen's mind. There was something to be said about being free to paint whatever he felt like, to put his "happy trees" wherever he felt like and make them look however he wanted them to look. It put him in mind of Art Therapy, but one look at Tyler's girl across the room, and that idea quickly scurried under a rock to hide.

Overall, except for the strangeness of the day piquing his suspicion, the day was fairly forgettable. Thursday was just as forgettable. Friday might have been forgettable except for a test in English that he forgot about, a pop quiz in Economics, and then in Physics, Mrs. White decided that they were going to do group projects again with table partners, due Tuesday that way they could take time on Monday to ask questions and tie up loose ends before turning in the work.

Tommen dreaded the papers as they were handed out. Normally he loved group work. He loved it. He enjoyed doing things with his hands and seeing how things worked and how tweaking tiny variables caused huge consequences. But the last thing he wanted to do right now was work with Becky. Actually, he didn't really feel like working with anyone, but her most of all. They'd been cordial, friendly even, but he just didn't want to work with her. He didn't want to mess up again and get into an awkward conversation and drive away the only person who was willing to talk to him.

"So, we're going to head down to the computer lab," Mrs. White announced. "There's an activity you're going to access online; you can read about it in your book. It is going to give us a springboard into the next chapter. You and your partner can discuss how you're going to do it. I'll be down in a second if you have questions."

While Tommen grabbed his things, Becky went to Mrs. White. Was she requesting a partner change? Secretly, he hoped not. He'd thought their cordial conversations were pretty good. Mostly he just didn't want to be stuck on a project alone, not now. Still, he went down with the rest of the group and found a computer. It took forever to log on and by the time the home screen finally loaded, Becky was pulling up a chair beside him.

"I'm not in the network yet, so I can't log on," she said.

Duh, Tommen, she's only been here three days and the IT guy is not known for his speed at anything except for getting to lunch. She probably won't be in the system until the end of the year if she's lucky.

"Do you have Internet at home?" he asked.

"Oh, yeah, no problem there."

"Okay. So..."

Tommen ducked out of the awkwardness by simply pretending to have log-in problems on the textbook website, enough to take his attention but not enough to have to submit a help ticket.

The activity was boring and a little childish, but it explained the project well enough. Probably better than sitting in the classroom listening to Mrs. White's lecture and watching the clock tick by.

"So why do they actually call you The Chivalrous Welshman?"

Tommen blinked several times before realizing Becky was speaking to him and seriously asking the question.

"Um..." The activity finished and he pretended to be immersed in closing out the program. "Well, I was raised old-school. Opening doors for girls, seating them at the table, and I guess other people just found it amusing."

"Oh." Becky seemed to mull this over for a few minutes. Then, "Well, I guess there are worse things you could be called. Honestly, I think it's funny, but not in a derogatory manner. I think 'charming' is the word I'm looking for." She nodded for emphasis.

"Um, right."

"So your family is pretty old-school?"

He glanced sideways at her. "Yeah. They were."

"Oh my gosh, I'm sorry. I didn't mean—"

"It's fine." He didn't look at her. "I'm a unique case. I wouldn't expect you to remember."

"Is that because everyone else is always reminding you?"

He looked sharply at her, tart reply at the ready. In the end he clamped down and turned his attention back to the screen. "Yeah."

"But your dad is pretty old-school, too, right?" Becky

ventured.

"Let me put it this way, he filed an official police report every time he switched me up until I was thirteen."

"And after you turned thirteen?"

"I learned quick, believe me. And he also took away phone and computer privileges if he needed to."

Becky nodded slowly. "My siblings always tell me I'm spoiled—which is probably true—but I think my parents were just trying to make things as uncomplicated as they could for me."

Tommen was set to make a sarcastic remark when the fire alarms went off. A collective groan went up around the room, and even Mrs. White seemed startled by it. Normally they were warned when there was supposed to be a fire drill; did that mean the school might actually be burning down this time? Could they hope that much?

"All right, leave your things, stay together, we're heading out the south door!" Mrs. White announced, opening the door to the hall where students flooded out of their respective classrooms, making for one exit door or another.

"I'll just stick with you," Becky said, following Tommen so closely she was almost stepping on his heels and causing him to trip.

They joined the throng of people in the hall. Some were complaining about being interrupted during a test while others were rejoicing over getting out of a boring lecture or stupid video or just their most hated class ever. But the overall question that seemed to prevail amid these complaints or praises was, "Was this a planned drill?"

In the end, the generally accepted conclusion was no, this wasn't planned. None of the teachers seemed to know what was going on; no one had even heard of a drill being scheduled this week or this month. Even the office staff looked a little perplexed as they, too, stood outside, shivering in the cold with the rest of them. Once class counts were done and everyone was accounted for, Mr. Layman took the teachers and staff aside for some private conference.

"So this isn't a normal thing?" Becky asked.

Tommen shook his head. "Not really. We have drills, but this is the first time it's even been remotely possibly real."

It didn't take long for the fire trucks to arrive. Mr. Layman went and met with the chief while a dozen or so men in bulky turnout gear clown-carred out of the trucks and went to work. Tommen was nowhere near their little meeting that seemed to go on forever as firemen went in and out of the school, but from the classes that were within earshot, word spread quickly.

Of course, the story was expected to change, but the overall truth seemed to remain the same: one of the ovens in the kitchen caught fire, and now the kitchen was basically toast. The cafeteria was fine, but there would be no lunch today, kiddos.

"So now what happens?" Becky wondered.

Tommen shrugged. "I pack my own lunch usually. I guess everyone else is just going to have to order out."

They stood outside a while longer as the firemen packed up their things. Before they left, however, Layman borrowed one of their megaphones.

"Attention students!" he called. "As you have probably heard, the kitchen was the culprit of today's excitement, which means that lunch today will be...limited. If anyone finds themselves without a lunch, we will be calling around to some of the local shops to bring in some more food so you have something to eat. Parents are also being contacted to inform them of today's events. However, we will continue as normal." He glanced at his watch. "You will return to your third period class where your teacher will give you further instructions."

With that, it was all over. Layman might have expected that everyone would just file into the building as calmly as they had filed out of the building, but such was not the case. It was cold outside, man! There was a small rush for the doors as everyone clambered to get warm again.

According to the clock, they'd already missed the rest of third period and part of lunch. Still, they dutifully returned to their classrooms. Most did what they were told and stayed put. Others didn't give a fuck, grabbed their books, and left the room. Mrs. White was the last one in.

"Okay, so this is what is going to happen," she said, picking up a marker. She started writing on the board behind her. "You guys are going to get your full lunch, which means this is when it's going to end. Your fourth and fifth period classes are going to be equal times, but they will be shortened; your teachers will dismiss you. Any questions?"

"Is our project still due on Tuesday?" someone asked.

"Yes, it is; you have the whole weekend to work on it."

A few groans and whispers, but no one said anything else. Mrs. White nodded once. "Okay then. Go to lunch."

The cafeteria was much more crowded than usual as some students wanted to get their share of what little food there was, others wanted to see the blackened kitchen, and a few just wanted to take advantage of the chaos to get a free lunch by slipping in and out stealthily. From what Tommen could see, most of the food had actually already made it out to the tables and the salad bar was fully intact. Didn't matter much to him, though, even if the thought of taking advantage of the chaos held a certain appeal, an alternative to ham on rye with a generous helping of mustard.

"Well, it's certainly been an interesting first week for me," Becky commented as she sat down across from Tommen, steaming plastic dish in hand.

"You brought salmon?" he asked incredulously when he saw what was in the dish.

She blinked. "Um, yes? Is there a problem with me bringing salmon?"

"No, it's just..." He shook his head. "Nothing."

"What?"

"Nothing. Doesn't matter."

"Tell me."

He set down his sandwich. "Your family must be rich."

Becky blinked again. "My dad's an audiologist, and my mom's a nurse. We're not exactly loaded, but yeah, we have money. Why does that matter? Can't be friends with me now?"

Tommen laughed. "I don't know any rich people." *Let's see, Lily, Micah, Micaiah...* "I've never been friends with a rich person." *Micah and Micaiah are uber rich, even if they don't brag about it.* "Mostly, rich people don't want to be friends with me." *Once again, Micah and Micaiah.*

"Well then, most rich people are stupid."

"Yeah, well, you say that now. Wait until the rest of the school hears that you're friends with me. Then I'll be your only friend."

Becky grinned. "Empty threats, believe me. I've had my fair share of friend troubles. And if the rest of the school hates you that much that they'll ostracize someone for just sitting with you at lunch, why would I want to be friends with the rest of them anyway?"

He raised a brow and saved himself from having to respond by taking a bite of his sandwich.

"And actually, I figured that if nothing else, we could decide who's doing what on the Physics project? Since we were kind of interrupted by exploding ovens and all."

Project, right. That thing that they were somehow supposed to do together. Because most people were friends or friendly enough to be comfortable with going over to other people's houses and working with them on said projects. But that was most people. Tommen would be okay with that, too, if it was another guy or else a girl he was dating. But this was a girl, and he was not dating her. He was not even remotely interested. So that meant that either of them going over to the other's house was going to be awkward. At least for him.

"I'm really good at models and building things, but math isn't really my strong suit. I know it sounds weird since I love science, but it's not. Like, I'm good if I have a formula and variables, but asking me to derive numbers from an experiment and put them together and figure things out freehand, I can do it, but not very fast. I've seen you do it, though, and you're good at it."

That's because I cheat. "Okay, so I can do the math and you can build the model," Tommen said. "I can give you my number, and you can text me the results and stuff."

Becky gave him a funny look. "Um, okay. I thought you might want to drop by my house or something and we could work on it together and stuff. I'd come over to your house, but I can tell you right now, that wouldn't go over well with my parents."

"No, no, it's just...I have to work." *You have Saturday off, dipshit.*

"Really? Where do you work?"

"Bakery na hÉireann. Mostly I'm on the front counter." *Better hope she doesn't stop by to check on you tomorrow. You know, when you're not working?*

"Oh, cool. Yeah, I actually have my own business. Well, I did. In California."

"What did you do?"

"Sewing. Tailoring, costuming, custom products, whatever you want. I could hem your pants or make you a full suit. Actually, I'm thinking about signing up for the school play and making the costumes. Yesterday I took a peek at the ones they currently have and they're in sorry shape."

"Sounds like a good business. For California. I don't know how much of that kind of clientèle you'll find around here."

"I know," Becky admitted grudgingly. "I had a good client base, too. Like, I was almost making enough that I could live on my own, if I wasn't saving up to get through school."

Tommen shrugged. "Priorities."

"I don't know what I'm going to do now. The good news is that I have a little over a year to get that client base back up, but Charleston isn't exactly L.A., if you know what I mean." Tommen nodded, suppressing a grin. "I need to adapt to my market. What do you think? Thousand-dollar suits and spur-of-the-moment my-Halloween-costume-cost-more-than-your-car types aren't exactly all the rage here. What could I do?"

"Oh, there's a market for suits and Halloween costumes, but think more in the hundred dollar range, less in the thousand dollar range."

She nodded, frowning. "I took a little walk down the strip and through downtown and stuff, just trying to get a look and a feel. And I was thinking, you know, what about furs? Hunting and trapping is big here, and as we just found out, it gets blastedly cold. But add fur to any piece of clothing and the price automatically doubles."

Tommen swallowed his bite and leaned back in his chair. "Well, that depends. Where do you expect to buy the furs to use? You don't look like a trapper or hunter to me."

"I'm not, believe me. The sporting goods stores seemed a little overpriced but those were just gorgeous furs...why are you smiling?"

"Because a lot of those, at least the smaller ones, those are mine. I don't have a business, per se, but I sell furs to the stores."

"What do they give you for them?"

He shrugged. "Enough to cover the time for fleshing and cost of tanning and a little extra."

"Oh my gosh, can I buy a couple off you? I mean, I'll give you at least whatever the store gives you."

Tommen ran his tongue over his teeth and folded his arms. "Well technically, I haven't renewed my contract with them yet; it's on a year-to-year basis. I have until the end of the month to renew it."

"What are you saying? I mean, can you not sell them to me or what are you saying?"

"With the stores, I have a guaranteed sale. They will buy the fur and how much I make depends on how many furs I have. How many furs are you going to buy from me? Do I have a guaranteed sale from you?"

There were a few things in life Tommen couldn't bear to look at. One of them was the heart-wrenching rejection that crossed a girl's face. Normally it came from a breakup. Now he saw it again as the light went out of Becky's eyes. He didn't like to see it, but that was how business worked.

"Well," she said after a moment's hesitation. "How about this? I buy three furs off of you. If you have them. If my business doesn't go well, it's no loss to you. If my business does go well, then...what the store doesn't know won't hurt them?"

"I'll agree to the three furs. That I do have; I'll bring them Monday. I'll have to think about the rest of your proposal; maybe there's a way I can...renegotiate with the stores. How does that sound?"

"All I can ask. And I know it'll take time to get my business up and running again. Believe me, I was not a happy camper when my parents told me that we were moving. It wasn't even about changing schools; I just didn't want to lose my business. But I guess if I stayed in the area...I have enough saved to get me through my first year of college. In two or three years, I can probably have enough to keep myself going."

"So then why become a geneticist? Why not stick with your tailoring business? It sounds like you'd do really well at it."

"Because that's not what I really want to do. I mean, maybe in my spare time — if I ever have any — but genetics is what I love."

Tommen nodded. "Hey, go for it."

"What about you? What are you doing after you graduate?"

"Uh..." *Traveling the universe, meeting aliens, defeating bad guys, further expanding the empire of a corrupt government that's currently trying to kill me, my dad, and everyone I love?* "I don't know. Probably do some traveling. See what's out there."

"That's nice. Anywhere in particular you want to visit?"

"I don't know. Maybe go to Wales, see if I have any family left there."

"That would be good. Do you know if you have any family left? Like, has your dad ever told you about anyone?"

"He doesn't think there's anyone left. Both sets of grandparents are gone, and he's not sure about the rest of the kids. He wasn't really on good terms with the family, so he didn't get told much."

"Too bad."

Tommen shrugged. "It is what it is, but the Internet is a wonderful thing."

"Very true," Becky said, nodding. "Found anything good there?"

"Nothing. Listen, I didn't even enter the school system until I was eight. My family had no electricity or running water. I didn't even see a car until I was eight. My family wasn't exactly plastered all over Facebook for everyone to see and talk to."

"Oh. That might make it difficult. But it gives you a great excuse to go to Wales and do some traveling and old-school research, right?"

"Yeah, I suppose."

"My family is pretty easy to trace, well, relatively easy. My ancestors always kept meticulous records, so we have a four hundred year family tree."

"Where were they from?"

"My dad's family was from Poland. He's from Poland, by technicality, but he was only a baby. Fled during World War II, smuggled out by Jewish sympathizers. Mom's family is Hungarian, but she came over by herself when she turned eighteen. She was an exchange student to the U.S. in high school, and she decided to move here."

"So you speak Hungarian?"

"And Polish. And Hebrew. It gets a little crazy around my house at Christmastime or Hanukkah or Thanksgiving or any huge family get-together. Family reunions are pretty messed up, too."

"Huh."

Becky shifted in her seat. "So you're not going to do it?"

"Do...what?"

"Ask me to say something in Hungarian or teach you swear words or something?"

Tommen shook his head. "No. I hate it when people do that to me."

"Oh, good, because I do, too."

Then why ask me about it? But he didn't say that out loud, just finished his lunch peacefully, slightly confused at how she had managed to get so much information out of him so quickly. And why he had been so eager to volunteer the information and continue the conversation.

The day being messed up, the bell didn't ring to signal the end of lunch. Rather, Layman walked in the cafeteria and, using his best Drill Sargent voice, informed everyone that lunch was over and to head to their fourth period classes. Within sixty seconds, the stampede began. Although it was less like a stampede of elephants and more like the slow plodding of a herd of turtles through peanut butter.

"So, I'll see about a model and stuff, and I'll get you the numbers, right?" Becky said as they reached their point of divergence.

"Yeah. Um..." He took out his phone. "What's your number?"

They exchanged phone numbers and headed for their respective lockers and classrooms.

Tommen felt giddy in the same way he felt giddy whenever he got a girl's phone number, even if he couldn't explain why he got giddy this time. They were just working on a project together, right? She still freaked him out a little, more from her forthrightness and the incident on Tuesday than anything. And yet, she still managed to get more information out of him in a couple days than most people could get out of him in months or years.

He shook his head as if it might work to clear it. He was just working with her on a project for AP Physics. She was going to build the model and get him the numbers so he could do the math. He also had to remember to bring in some furs on Monday. If she was half as good as she was portraying herself to be, then she might be a good source to sell to. If her stuff sold as well as she was hoping, maybe he could up the price just a little rather than continue on with the paltry drippings the stores gave him.

His attention was caught by the poster—one of many—for the school play coming up later in the spring. *Alice in Wonderland* was the theme. Maybe she was going to use the furs for that. What in the world was she going to come up with?

Well, maybe you should sign up for the play and find out.

Yeah, because nothing stupid or dangerous or embarrassing ever came out of a boy's curiosity for a girl. And a girl that I don't even really like.

Now you don't really believe that, do you? Like she said, you're both freaks. And you know more about each other than you and Emily ever knew about one another. Physics project aside, you two seem to just fit together just well.

We've known each other for four days. That's almost as bad as two people meeting in a Las Vegas bar and getting hitched by some drive-through preacher.

Because high school is definitely Las Vegas.

He walked into Web Programming feeling a certain sense of déjà vú. Maybe it was just because he was walking into a computer lab. But as he crossed the threshold, he felt the hair on the back of his neck stand up. Immediately, he threw up a Band and looked around.

Everything was still and silent. In the classroom, some students were working diligently, looking through their textbooks and notes. Others were chatting with friends or surfing the web on their phones. In the hallway, students headed to and fro, on their way to one class or another or their lockers or their friends' lockers or the bathroom. One couple was kissing, another having an argument, another saying goodbye as they parted ways, never to see each other again. Or at least, not for another forty minutes or so.

But as near as Tommen could tell, nothing was out of the ordinary. No one was heading toward him or even looking at him. More to the point, he saw no evidence of Time—no Bands, no wakes, and certainly no one trying to break into his Band as it stood. Maybe he was just paranoid. But it was only paranoia until it was true.

Eventually, he released the Band and went to his seat, trying to tell himself that everything was fine. By the time Mrs. Floyd walked in and tried to cram an entire class period into half a class period, his greater sense of being watched had gone, but he couldn't shake the lingering doubt that somehow the fire in the kitchen hadn't been entirely an accident.

Was Rifun behind it? Was that the supposed "sign" that Tommen was supposed to look for? But Rifun had said the sign wouldn't come until after the elections. Had something changed? Was he supposed to meet Rifun somewhere now? What was the procedure here?

Or was this the work of another group, the one that was targeting the twins? Like Micaiah said, just because he hadn't been named explicitly didn't mean he wasn't involved. Was this their work? Was it a threat? Could it be a warning? Layman had said that parents were being contacted after the fire, so Walter would easily know about it; he might have known about it even beforehand over the scanner. Would he investigate the fire from that angle? Should Tommen tell him his thoughts? Or would he just be seen as being paranoid? Did he really want to get his dad all hyped up over something they couldn't prove or do anything about?

It was all too much to think about. Thankfully he only had to work today and then he was off tomorrow. Then he could take a day to just sleep in, stay home, and relax. Well, there was that AP Physics project. Which meant texting Becky. Which meant possibly explaining to his dad why he was texting a girl. Which opened up a whole new can of worms.

Fuck, he just wanted the day to be over with. At the very least, having shortened classes made the day feel like it was going by faster. Not that Bob Ross was something he normally looked forward to anyway. But they skipped the video for today, instead being told to practice their techniques freehand for the duration of the class, ask for help if needed.

Five minutes in, Tommen figured he would have rathered watch the video. He wasn't much of a painter, but he likened painting alongside the videos to kind of a paint-by-number or a traceable picture or something easy of that sort. He could copy an image or a video no problem. Being told to run wild and let his mind and paintbrush go where it wanted? Yeah, that wasn't happening. He even seriously tried to make some masterpiece flow from brain to brush—the cabin where he grew up, the view from the mountain the day he entered the old salt cave, anything at all. But his rocks and mountains more closely resembled piles of poop, and his snow was little better than white paint haphazardly flung on by Picasso as a toddler. The only thing he figured looked moderately correct were his trees. His happy trees.

Robinson's call to clean up couldn't have come any sooner as Tommen's quaint little cabin in the woods with the thin spiral of smoke coming out of the chimney turned into a lopsided, dilapidated pile of rocks and old lumber threatening to catch fire from whatever fire had been started in an old fireplace by some desperate lost hiker looking for shelter. Unfortunately, the fascinating narrative he conjured up in his head still couldn't rescue the terrible paint job he'd laid out on his canvas.

"You are free to take these home if you want them," Robinson said in the chaos of cleanup. "Show them to me on your way out, and I'll enter them as extra credit."

Tommen did not want his painting. He did want extra credit. He would take all the extra credit he could get in order to pass this infernal class. Maybe he could throw it in the dumpster on his way out of school, Band, slip over there, toss it in, and leave like nothing ever happened.

Just as Tommen returned to his seat, waiting the last sixty seconds for the bell to ring, he heard a voice.

"Hi. Are you Mr. Robinson?"

Becky approached Robinson's desk where he sat, grading a couple paintings as students brought them to him. Once the last one had gone, he turned. "Yes, I am. How can I help you?"

Tommen couldn't hear every word that was said, but from what he could hear, Mr. Robinson was the one in charge of set design and costuming for the upcoming play, and Becky was inquiring about offering her skills and making some new costumes for the play.

The bell rang, and all hell broke loose.

Tommen merged with the stampede as they filed out of the classroom, spilling out into the halls and racing for lockers. He got to his without incident, his fingers numbly twisting the combination while his mind raced. The day was over. Only a few hours of work now, but the day was over, and he was free. He didn't even have a ton of homework, and his backpack felt light. He paused for a second to run through things in his mind and make sure he hadn't forgotten anything. Nope, the only thing he really had to do was the Physics project.

He'd no sooner thought it than he turned and very nearly ran over Becky.

"Sorry, I didn't mean to scare you," she said apologetically.

"No, it's fine," he told her.

"Just wanted to make sure we're good on the project for the weekend."

"You've got the model and I've got the math," he said, not a little irritated that they were going over this yet again. "Just text me the numbers."

"Okay, I'll do that. And don't forget the furs on Monday. I'll buy them from you right there if I like them."

"Well, if you liked the ones in the store, you'll like these, too. Listen, I have to go and catch my bus."

"Right." She stepped to the side. "Sorry. See you Monday."

"Yeah. See ya."

He left her then, making for the bus and finding his seat before it got taken. For a moment, he wondered if he should feel guilty for being so curt with Becky. He was always supposed to be polite towards women and not just cut them off and leave them hanging. He mulled it over for a second before deciding that it might have been a smidge rude, but he really did have a bus to catch. Nothing said "grounded" like having to call his dad and tell him that he missed the bus and needed a ride to work. Worse, he would have to explain why he missed the bus which meant admitting that he'd been talking to a girl. Then he'd have to tell his dad all about the girl, especially the part where they were supposed to be working on a project together and he'd effectively sidestepped part of the responsibility.

That would not go over well, Tommen knew. If he told his dad that, he knew that his dad would find out where Becky lived and then take Tommen—on his day off—over to her house so he could help her with the project. Tommen wasn't against working together on a project, it was just...she was a girl. He just didn't do that kind of thing, not really. He wasn't dating her or anything. He didn't have a problem with her, just...she was a girl. Maybe it was the curse of being raised old-school. Don't get caught going over to a girl's house because rumors will fly. Not that he thought that his dad and her parents would be making marriage arrangements, but still...

Tommen sighed and rubbed his eyes. He just needed a day off.

Chapter Twenty
Alone on a Mountain

From the moment Tommen opened his eyes, he knew he'd woken up way earlier than he'd intended. He'd hoped to sleep in until noon at least, maybe just sleep the whole day away. But that was the problem with waking up before the sun every fucking morning; his body got used to it until it panicked when it wasn't awake before the sun. Looking outside, the sky was changing colors, but the sun hadn't broken the horizon yet. Not that it meant much considering the mountains could hide the sun for quite a while before it ever showed its face.

Eight o'clock his clock read. Well, damn. On the one hand, he could just Fast Band until he got tired again, but wasting a whole day just so he could go back to sleep so he could waste another day just didn't seem sensible. On the other hand, he could Slow Band and skip ahead a few hours when he'd originally planned to get up. But again, that wasting part of a day thing...it didn't feel right. There was a lot he could get done in four hours.

Like what? Your Physics project?

Tommen rolled over and groaned. What a way to ruin a day within the first five minutes of waking up. He didn't want to think about that Physics project. Becky had texted him a few preliminary numbers but said she'd have more of them today. Obviously he'd had to acknowledge and agree, even if he had every intention of not doing the math until he absolutely had to, either late tomorrow night or even right before class on Monday, when he could Band and get it all done when he had sneaky access to the teacher's book with the answers, or some of them anyway. He hadn't told his dad about the project either in order to ensure that he wouldn't have to do the math right away.

He pulled the blankets up as far as he could and pulled the pillow down over his face. Go to sleep. Get back to sleep. Stop thinking about the stupid shit you have to do and just go back to sleep. *Sleep. Dream.*

To die, to sleep; to sleep, to dream...

No, fuck you. Stop fucking thinking. Clear your mind. Think sleep. Go back to sleep. Where the fuck did that come from anyway? You aren't even studying MacBeth...or is that Hamlet? Let's see...Yeah, that's Hamlet. To be or not to be and all that. How do you even know that soliloquy? How do you even know what a soliloquy is? You don't give a fuck about English. Must have picked up something somewhere. But I thought that sort of stupid shit we didn't get around to until, like, senior year when we have to pretend to know stuff in order to get into college where they're just going to teach us that stuff all over again anyway. Except this time they'll charge you for it.

Tommen flung the pillow from his face. It hit the footboard of his bed and rolled off onto the floor. Nope, there would be no sleeping now; his brain would make sure of that. He hated it when that happened. Well, at least he would have a second chance tomorrow since the twins had seen fit to give him the whole weekend off.

Grudgingly, Tommen pulled himself out of bed. Was sleeping in really too much to ask today? Apparently it was. He stared at his bed for a second before deciding to actually make it up. It would probably be the only time he did it this month, one of a couple times this year. He didn't usually see the point in it, and his dad had stopped making him once he turned thirteen. He'd figured that either Tommen would have the discipline to do it himself, or else it would just be a bone of contention that wasn't worth fighting over.

When he was done with that, he looked around his room. His dad had made it spotless, as if he had been expecting the Sargent to come by with white gloves brand a measuring tape. There was still evidence of how clean it had been a couple weeks ago, but most of that was gone as things had been moved, shuffled, arranged, rearranged, piled, and dust and dirt had settled in once again. He really should keep his room a little cleaner. A huge yawn reminding him of his morning plight interrupted his thoughts. Hell with that. He'd clean his room some other time.

When that other time was, he wasn't sure. Not like he had anything pressing to do today. Didn't have to work. Wasn't going to do his schoolwork. Didn't have anyone to hang out with. The worst that was probably going to happen was his dad might have him assemble and install the new vanity and toilet in the bathroom and haul the old ones out to the curb. He'd seen his dad's valiant attempt at assembling the vanity, but he hadn't gotten too far before the pain got to him, and he stiffened up. Or at least that was his excuse. Tommen knew better; his dad was not so shy to a little pain. More likely he'd gotten hungry or tired or had some show he wanted to watch and got distracted by. Whatever the case, the half-assembled vanity still sat in the middle of the living room, waiting to be finished and moved into its new resting spot.

And it would be a welcome change, Tommen knew as he trudged his way from his bedroom to the bathroom. The psychedelic paint monster that had slept in the bathroom for the last forty years just had to go.

As Tommen finished up in the bathroom and started back toward his bedroom, he heard water running in the kitchen and the banging around of a few pots and pans. So he wasn't the only one so accustomed to waking up early that sleeping in was a foreign concept.

Tommen got dressed and did a little to tidy up his room. Okay, he picked up a few pieces of clothing that had migrated across the floor and got them into the hamper. He might do a load of laundry a little later if he got really bored. But he wasn't to that point yet. He stared at the hamper a minute longer before leaving his room and heading out to the kitchen.

"You're up early," his dad observed as he plopped a small scoop of butter into a frying pan, the sizzle making Tommen's stomach growl.

"So are you," Tommen replied.

His dad shrugged. "I gave up on sleeping in a long time ago."

Tommen folded his arms. "Have you ever thought about working the night shift? So you wouldn't have to sleep with a night light?"

"It did occur to me. But I didn't like the thought of leaving you alone at night."

"Well, I mean, that's great, but I'm not ten anymore."

"That's true. But I still don't like the thought of leaving you alone at night. And I'm not talking about cat burglars."

Physical condition aside, Tommen wanted to ask what he thought the difference would be if Rifun broke in when Walter wasn't around versus if he broke in when Walter was asleep, but he bit his tongue. The man had his pride, and Tommen knew he would do anything to protect him, even if it was moderately ineffective.

While Tommen was thinking, he realized his dad had been saying something. He hadn't put his hearing aids in yet. He'd hoped for a day off from them, too, but apparently not. "Sorry, what?"

His dad regarded him for just a second. Then, "I asked if you wanted some eggs."

"Oh, um, yeah, sure."

"Go put your hearing aids in. How do you want your eggs?"

"Over easy."

Tommen slunk away to his bedroom and put his hearing aids in. He hadn't quite nailed down the routine for off-days yet, even though it was probably the first thing he ought to do every morning. By the time he meandered his way back out to the kitchen, his dad already had his eggs on a plate with buttered toast and was working on a second batch.

"Cabin fever, huh?" Tommen said, breaking the yolk of one egg and sopping up the mess with the toast.

"So I'm not allowed to do something nice for my son after what he did for me?" his dad replied, not looking at him.

Tommen nodded. "Yup. Definitely cabin fever."

"Maybe a little."

"I don't blame you."

"Getting tired of sitting at home with your old man already?"

"I didn't say that. Wasn't even thinking it."

And, really, he didn't mind his dad being home. He was glad he still had a dad. But Tommen knew that six weeks out was going to drive his dad crazy. If his first round of physical therapy had been any indication, he'd be looking to get back to the precinct by next week.

"Well, anyway, we're both feeling a little cabin feverish." He slid the eggs onto a plate and hobbled his way to the tiny chair at the tiny table. "So, what do you say I pack me a few things, you pack you a few things, grab your skis, and we head over to Snowshoe?"

Tommen blinked and stopped, dripping toast halfway to his mouth. Finally he lowered the toast. "What?"

"You heard me. Grab your things, and I'll take you skiing. Or, to be more precise, you're driving, I'm just your responsible driver."

"Why?"

"I'm surprised. Normally if you're not out on the slopes within the first week of the season opening I have to hear about it for a month. Now it sounds like you don't want to go at all."

Tommen shrugged. "No one to go with."

His dad sighed. "Tommen, you're a good kid and a great skier. You scare me to death every time you go into the terrain park. But I also know that even when you went with Eric and Varad that you always managed to make some friends or acquaintances while you were busy showing off. I don't see why you can't make some friends today and make it a little less boring as you go flying by every one of us slowpokes who cling to the safe runs."

His dad was needling him, and they both knew it. Tommen knew very well that he probably gave his dad a small heart attack every time he went off a jump or hit a rail, and probably a slightly larger heart attack every time he wiped out. He also knew his dad was egging him on just a little with a sideswipe not only about his speed, but his propensity to poach runs and get in trouble with Ski Patrol.

Nothing huge, just ducking lines and causing a little mischief.

"So does that mean you're going to be skiing, too?" Tommen wondered, deciding to return the needling.

"Aw no. You want me to break my neck?" His dad shook his head. "No, I think I'll just stay at the lodge for the time being. Maybe by the end of the season, I'll be out again, but not right now. As much as I want to..."

It was difficult to judge whether he was being sarcastic and he wasn't thrilled about the prospect of going skiing — which he only did about once or twice a season anyway — or whether he really would have taken skiing and the chance of breaking his neck over his current predicament.

"What do you say? We can go skiing, in which case we'd have to leave now, or we can stay home, and you can assemble the bathroom fixtures, install them, and haul the old ones out to the curb. And then you can work on your homework and your room could probably stand to be cleaned."

Well, when you put it like that...

"Okay, I'm in," Tommen told him. "Can I at least finish my breakfast first?"

"I don't think it will take you that long," his dad replied smartly.

Tommen emphasized the point by Banding and finishing his breakfast in about the space of half a second. He gave his dad a knowing look as he showed off his empty plate before taking it to the sink to give it a quick wash. When he turned around, his dad had done the same thing and now stood behind him with his empty plate held out. Tommen suppressed a groan as he took the plate and fork and washed those, too. That was the thing about being a cheeky bastard; it seemed to run in the family. Not only that, but his dad had a few decades more of experience in it. Not that he was going to admit defeat or anything. He was simply acknowledging his opponent's strengths. That was it.

That was the magic of Banding, though. Once the dishes got

finished, it was as though no time passed at all as Tommen rounded up his gear, bringing his snow pants out of the closet, checking to make sure his goggles weren't scratched and his gloves didn't have holes in them, dusting off his helmet and making sure all the zippers on his coat still worked. His coat had about one more season left in it, he figured. The main zipper was still good, but most of the others were broken and useless.

He stuffed all of his clothing in the backseat before bringing his skis out of the garage rafters. In all reality, since his growth spurt, they were probably a little short for him now. Problem was, they were only a couple years old; they were the first thing he'd bought with his first ever paycheck—okay, so it had been more like four or five paychecks, but he'd saved every penny for these babies. Black and green Völkl skis, perfectly balanced for downhill and terrain park, able to withstand the beating from smacking a jump landing or sliding a rail while maintaining the speed and balance necessary for icy slopes.

"Your boots still fit?" his dad asked as he got down the garage steps and headed for the passenger side of the car.

"Um..."

That was a good question. Tommen loaded his skis in the backseat and dug out his boots. They'd fit the last time he wore them, but again, that had been before his growth spurt. He took off one shoe and started wiggling his foot into the boot. It took a lot of wiggling, some pulling and adjusting of the boot, but he managed to squeeze his foot in there. It was a little tight even for ski boots, but he could make it work for the day.

"Waiting on you, kiddo," his dad said as he fought to get the boot off. Maybe he should get a new pair, even just rent a pair until he could buy a pair.

Eventually, though, he got the boot off and tossed them in the backseat with everything else before getting in the driver's seat. Snowshoe Ski Resort was a couple hours east of Charleston. Tommen might have asked if he could Band while driving, but not only did he know his dad would say no, but it would do them no good as the hill didn't open for another hour anyway.

Conversation was limited to commands and warnings as it related to driving, at least until they got outside the city and civilization quickly gave way to open mountain country.

"So, I heard through the grapevine that Tyler Freeman was expelled," his dad said conversationally.

"Really?" Tommen wondered. "Cool. Finally. Maybe I can get through the rest of the year in peace, then."

Walter raised a brow and shifted in his seat. "I'm surprised you didn't know. I would have expected you to come home singing or something if that happened."

"Didn't know he was expelled. Figured he was suspended, but that was it. And anyway, I've been busy."

"Too busy to notice when the kid who's been bullying you for over five years suddenly disappears?"

Tommen shrugged. "I guess. I mean, after a couple years it just becomes background noise. Besides, since having to deal with Becky, I guess—"

"Who's Becky?"

Fuck.

"She's a girl in my AP Physics class."

"Okay. And what do you mean 'having to deal with' her?"

"We got new table assignments and we sit together and she's really annoying. Like she won't shut up. And she's a dwarf."

"What does that have to do with anything?"

"I don't know. It's just...I don't know, it's kind of weird."

"Yeah, and so are you. But being bullied for being who you are is no excuse to bully others for being who they are."

"I don't bully her. Good grief, I have to help her in the lunch line."

"And it's just a terrible thing to have to help someone who can't help themselves."

"Well, no."

"What don't you like about her? Just because she talks a lot?"

He made it sound so petty. Problem was, when Tommen thought about it, it did sound petty. It wasn't as if Becky was one of those girls who just talked and talked and talked and talked without ceasing and never let anyone else get a word in. She was able to hold a conversation.

"Maybe she doesn't talk a lot, but she's very...forceful in her conversations," Tommen decided.

"Forceful," his dad echoed. "Interesting choice of word. So she holds you at knifepoint and demands that you talk to her and answer her questions?"

"What? No."

His dad laughed.

"What's so funny?" Tommen demanded.

"Tommen, you've stood up to police-level scrutiny. But you crack under the pressure of talking to a girl. That you like."

"I told you, I don't like her. You haven't even met her; you don't know who she is."

"I don't have to, but I suspect that I will soon enough." His dad was smiling the whole time now.

Tommen snorted indignantly and clenched his fists on the steering wheel. He was not going to give his dad the satisfaction of a reply. Well, okay, maybe one little reply.

"She's Dr. Polski's daughter," Tommen informed him.

"Oh really?" His dad raised a brow. "He seems a little old to be doing that sort of thing."

"Guess she was a surprise baby. She has nieces and nephews who are already graduated."

"Huh. Well, that is interesting."

Tommen wasn't sure what he expected to get out of that little addition to the conversation. His dad already thought he liked Becky; telling him that she was the daughter of his super elderly audiologist wasn't going to change that. It might make him pause for a second the next time they had to go visit him, but the whole bit had been pretty meaningless.

Tommen figured his best chance at a peaceful drive and ski time was to just keep his mouth shut. No more talking about Becky, especially since he already let slip about her; he didn't want to risk telling his dad about the project that he was now, in effect, completely blowing off.

They made good time to the resort but it was already swarming with people. It was a beautiful day, hardly a cloud in the sky — a rarity for January — and people were certainly taking advantage of it. The parking lot was packed full of cars, its occupants ranging from veteran skiers to thrill seekers, families with tons of kids, cute couples, various school and race groups, and Tommen's usual attractive group — the park rats and misfits.

"You want to ski first or get something to eat first?" his dad asked, grabbing his cane and getting out of the car.

"I'm still full from breakfast," Tommen told him, pulling his snow pants on over his jeans. Hm...a little short. Well, he should have expected that. Oh well, no one would ever know once he got them down around his boots.

Oh, right, the boots. He gritted and ground his teeth, pushed and finagled and forced, but he got those boots on, even if he was fairly certain that his feet were probably going to resemble Chinese foot binding by the end of the day. Maybe he should rent a pair.

"I think I should have gotten you some new snow gear for Christmas," his dad observed casually as Tommen pulled on his coat. It was a little snug, but the length was still okay, at least around the waist. The sleeves were a tad short, but his gloves would cover that up easily enough he figured.

"No, it'll be fine. For today at least," Tommen told him.

"Uh-huh. For today. Do your boots actually fit?"

"Mm...they're a little tight."

His dad sighed. "I'll rent you a pair of boots for the day. That'll probably affect your bindings, won't it?"

"I can ride fine for today."

"No, I'll pay for it. I'd rather make sure everything fits and is comfortable than see you get hurt because you cut off circulation to your feet."

Well, there was that. Tommen was pretty sure his toes were just a little cold, though. It was only a few degrees above zero after all. Well, it was a relief to know his head hadn't gotten any bigger lately anyway. It seemed like the only thing that actually still fit well and worked well were his helmet, his goggles, and his gloves. Nope, wait, what was that breeze? He searched his gloves until he found the small hole between his thumb and forefinger, right along the seam. It wasn't big, but that would be where the snow would get in. Maybe he could talk his dad into getting him a couple hand warmers.

It was kind of a strange thing to think about, going skiing with his dad. Especially since it had been his dad's idea and his dad who was offering to pay for all of it. Normally Tommen had to beg and plead, and even then he still had to buy his own lift ticket and his own lunch and whatever he needed or wanted. To add to that, they didn't even do stuff together that often, not anything big like this.

He grabbed his gear and followed his dad toward the main building that housed Ski School, Rental, the Pro Shop, and a myriad of other little goodie stores, including Ski Tech, the less-touristy and far less expensive alternative to the Pro Shop for those who knew it existed. Their first stop was Rental.

"Good morning, how can I help you?" the rental tech inquired, his voice strained as if he was trying to be happy and punctual like his boss told him to be, but it was just another day of helping another customer.

"I need boots," Tommen told him. "I seem to have outgrown mine."

The tech nodded. "Okay, we'll get you set up. What size are those?"

So Tommen spent the next ten minutes trying on boots. It wasn't that they didn't have the size he needed, it was the adjustment aspect of it, coming to terms with the fact that no, the rental boots would not look or feel quite like his regular boots. They would not be conformed to his feet, they would not have the same little nuances, and they would not react the same way to the tiniest movements as he compensated for varying terrain and conditions, the minute muscle movements being calculated at the billionth of a second by sheer muscle memory.

Mostly, he just didn't want to be caught in rental gear if and when he wiped out. There was nothing worse than being called a tourist or a bunny hill idiot who decided he was going to try and ride with the big dogs. Any real skier who was worthy of riding anything more difficult than a green run had his own equipment, from top to bottom. It didn't have to be state-of-the-art high performance Olympic-worthy kind of equipment, but no self-respecting skier would be caught dead in rental shit.

But soon enough, Tommen walked out of the Rental shop with rental boots on. It was pretty obvious that they were rentals—the flat, dull gray color with the tarnished, slightly rusty latches—but he still pulled his pant legs down as far as he could in order to cover them up as best he could.

"I don't think anyone is going to notice," his dad said when they stopped for probably the tenth time so he could stretch his pant legs just a little farther down. "If you're that worried, then go get yourself another pair of boots. And a pair of snow pants while you're at it."

Tommen sighed. "I don't have my wallet on me."

"Why not?"

"Because I don't want to lose it out there."

His dad regarded him for a second. "And maybe add a coat to that list, one with zipped pockets that actually zip."

Tommen grudgingly agreed as he straightened and followed his dad again, this time to Ski Tech.

"Hey, about time you came in!"

Thankfully, Tommen was well-known by the guys at Ski Tech as he always went to them for pre-season adjustments, post-season summerizing, and a number of waxes and sharpenings throughout the season.

"I was getting worried, dude," Justin said, slapping hands with Tommen who set his skis on the counter. "Thought maybe something happened to you."

"Not quite," Tommen replied evasively. "Late start is all."

"So, the usual adjustments, tightenings, all that jazz?"

"Well, unfortunately, I outgrew my boots. So I had to rent." He was pretty sure his expression mirrored Justin's, that look of disgust and revulsion. "Anyway, hopefully, it's only temporary, but they are bigger, and I need my bindings adjusted for them."

Justin shook his head. "Okay, I'll see what I can do."

"Thanks, dude. I need a whole new set of gear, really."

"No kidding. You look like you grew a couple inches."

Tommen shrugged.

"Well, you can get away with it for this season, today at least, but man, your skis look short, your poles are obviously short, and it kind of looks like you're trying to stuff yourself into clothes that are just a couple sizes too small."

Tommen sighed. "Gee, thanks a lot. I know everything is short and small, but I didn't bring my wallet, and I don't have quite that much money even if I did."

In his peripheral vision, Tommen saw his dad, who was looking at the used skis, pause in his browsing and give him a sideways glance. His expression was two-fold, first wondering how it was that he claimed not to have any money when he worked at the bakery and had his fur ventures, and second telling him that if that was the case, don't expect him to volunteer to buy him any of the gear he might need.

In actuality, he did have the money he needed to buy himself a complete set of gear, from helmet to skis. He could just be a cheap bastard sometimes. That, and he was trying to be a little more responsible with his money, save for college, a car, an apartment, all the things he would really need in life. Assuming he actually wanted to do any of that normal stuff. At the same time, if he did become a

Scout, he would need a pair of skis even less.

"There," Justin said finally. "How does that feel?"

He set the skis on the ground and Tommen stepped into them, feeling the bindings lock with a satisfying click.

What was he saying about not needing skis?

"Feels great," Tommen told him, moving his foot around to make sure the boots and bindings fit correctly and stayed together. "Thanks."

"Hey, next time I see you, you better be doing better than those ugly things," Justin told him severely, indicating the rental boots.

"I'll do my best."

"Do better than that. Do it."

His dad paid the adjustment fee, and they left the shop.

"So, is there anything else you're missing or need adjusted?" he asked. His tone made it difficult to judge how sarcastic he was being.

"Well, if I ever want to come back, I'm going to need a ticket," Tommen said.

"Besides that. Your helmet still fit?"

"Yes, it does."

"Good. Wear it. So it sounds like you just need your ticket."

Normally the ticket line wasn't very long, but it was not a normal day. The weather brought out people by the van-load, and the line promised a wait, especially when the person at the very front was presently arguing with the poor ticket person that they had booked a package with the hotel through some travel website and blah, blah, blah, I want to speak to a manager.

As they waited in line, Tommen's phone went off. He knew with almost complete certainty who it was and what it was about. Problem was, he didn't want to acknowledge it with his dad standing there because then he would ask about it. But if he didn't acknowledge it, he would get suspicious and ask about it anyway. He didn't dare lie about it either; since his dad had discovered his addiction and Internet activities, he'd been watching his history like a hawk and randomly asking to see his phone, perusing his Internet history and texts.

He took out his phone.

Yup, it was Becky with the numbers and labels and a nice big note saying that she was done with her part of the project and she wanted to look at the math on Monday to see if she could understand it and maybe have him explain it to her.

"Somebody important?" his dad asked as they moved up one spot in line, the cranky lady being taken aside politely by management.

"Um...kind of. Not really," Tommen said haltingly.

"Is it Becky?"

Was there any way he could get out of this? If he said yes, his dad would definitely want to read the text. If he said no, there was about a seventy percent chance he would still want to read the text. Either way, he felt his cheeks grow hot, which must have been enough of a confirmation for his dad to hold out his hand. Reluctantly, Tommen surrendered the phone.

He watched his dad's expression go from cheeky to confused. Then came the realization and the silent anger as he went back through the last day or two of texts. Finally, he held out the phone like he was giving it back, only to snatch it away when Tommen reached for it.

"So what project is she referring to?" he asked.

Tommen wasn't sure how much redder his ears could get. "Um...just a little Physics project."

"What kind of Physics project?"

Briefly, he explained the project, trying to play it down as much as possible. Just a little project, something to keep them busy over the weekend, no big deal. Besides, she didn't want to do the math part, and he didn't want to do the model part, so it worked out fine.

"Tommen, I'm less concerned that you decided to withhold this information from me, and more concerned with why you left her alone to do it while you went skiing." His dad finally returned the cell phone. "And on top of that, you also lied to her and said you were working."

"I couldn't—"

"Tommen. I'm not happy. You lied to her, and you deceived me. Tell me why we shouldn't leave this line right now and go home."

"Because we already spent the time and gas to get here, you already paid for the rentals and binding adjustments, and because we both need a serious vacation from work and school?" Tommen answered quickly.

His dad gave him a hard regard for what felt like forever; Tommen thought he caught a glimpse of a Band, probably he was being scrutinized heavily. He felt his stomach twist as he was almost sure his dad was going to say no, march him out of the line and back to the car and lecture him the whole way back.

They moved up another spot in line. Only two more to go.

Finally his dad spoke.

"All right. I told you I'd bring you skiing, and you're right that we both need a vacation. But when we get back, you're going to do exactly what you told Becky you were going to do, and you're going to work. And if the twins can't or won't give you any extra hours, there is plenty to do around the house. Got it?"

"Yes, sir," Tommen murmured as relief washed through him like a tidal wave followed hard by a wave of dread. His skiing was feeling less and less like a vacation and more like a calm before the storm. Every run was going to bring him closer to being put to work, grounded for his deception.

In a way, he knew it was exactly what he deserved. He did kind of leave Becky to do the hard work, hadn't even told his dad about the project, and instead took advantage of his kindness and willingness to take him skiing. On the other hand, he figured that they had delegated responsibility fairly, and there was nothing to have been gained by doing it together. Lying to her and saying he was working when he wasn't, well, okay, he guessed he kind of deserved it. But still, what was he expected to do? Get all hyped up over a stupid little project that wasn't even worth much?

They stepped up to the window where his dad grudgingly paid for an all day ticket. The place was only open until four-thirty and time was ticking. Tommen could use all the Time and Band all he wanted, but there was no good way to speed up the lifts without raising a few eyebrows and potentially causing harm.

"Are you heading over to Silver Creek at all today do you think?" his dad asked as he slipped the ticket through his zipper.

"I might, if there's time, but I don't think so," Tommen replied. "Right now I'm thinking Western Territory is calling my name."

His dad frowned. "All right. As always, be careful."

"When am I not?"

"I'm choosing not to answer that. Have fun, kiddo."

His tone was light, but his gaze was still hard, a warning that he could have fun but don't forget the punishment that awaited him at home. Tommen nodded, trying to be cheerful. Then he picked up his skis and started toward the bus stop. About halfway there, he stopped. He could take the bus over to Western Territory. Or he could spend a little extra time and just ride there.

He turned back around and stared out over the valley to the lake below. Then he let his skis fall to the snow, stepped into them, and started off with a nice, easy black diamond.

Chapter Twenty-One
The Rail

The wind whipped by him as he slid around the first corner of Cupp Run, keeping to the left and skipping into the Sunset Glades, snaking around trees and over fallen logs, hitting the small jump at the end and going airborne, bursting out of the trees, narrowly missing another skier as they cut across from Shay's Revenge. Ignoring their shouting, he tucked in and rode the treeline of Lower Cupp Run, sliding into the first corner, then the next, staying in the center of the narrowing run, sliding left and right around other patrons as if they were slalom gates. The bottom of the lift came into view. Tucking in tighter, he rode it until it seemed as though he would go flying into the bar there at the bottom. At the last second, he stood and twisted, spraying snow everywhere and coming into the line like an Olympic champion.

Western Territory, on a normal day, was like a little private piece of heaven for advanced skiers who didn't like to be slowed down by beginner skiers on the main slopes. Problem was, on a nice day like today, the place quickly became packed with advanced skiers, and it was just as bad as the main slopes. Then there were the really good, really fast skiers and the really good, not-so-fast skiers, usually older skiers who were more concerned with making the perfect turn rather than setting world speed records. Tommen didn't mind those skiers, except when they insisted on taking up the whole damn run, having to go all the way as far to the left as possible, turn, meander across the run all the way as far right as possible, turn, meander back across the run—and doing none of this particularly fast, mind you. And Tommen, more often than not, just came on these guys out of nowhere, completely surprised, and because he was going fast and they were going slow, they were going back and forth and he was going more or less straight, it was almost impossible to predict potential collision patterns.

Basically, slow skiers made his runs halfway to miserable. Unsatisfying at best.

He got on the lift.

Last year he'd been asked if he wanted to join the high school ski team. He had, excited at first. He thought he'd finally found a sport he was good at, something he could excel in and make friends and find his place in high school. The coach had seen him on the slopes multiple times and complimented him on his speed, agility, and fearlessness. Thus, the invitation. He'd blown them all out of the water during practices and even did well at several meets.

The end of the fairy tale came during regionals, when all the schools were competing for the right to run for the state championship. Tommen was so sure that he was going to be the one to lead their team to victory, or the finals anyway. Before the meet, the coach took him aside. Tommen thought he was going to get a pep talk, a rousing speech on how he was the one they were counting on, how he was their anchor.

Instead, the coach told him to lay off and let a couple other members of the team overtake him. Let them win. He didn't need to crash or miss a gate or anything, just slow it down. They'd chalk it up to nerves, to stress, to whatever, but let the other guys win. Let them qualify and go to the finals.

When Tommen asked for a reason, the coach was very diplomatic and told him that they were seniors, and this was their last shot at a state title. Tommen was dejected and had a sneaking suspicion that the coach was lying, but he meekly accepted the answer and went to take his spot among his teammates. Then they proceeded to tell him their version of events. First, as the coach said, he was making them all look bad, and this was their last shot at a state title. Second, he was a fucking freshman and an idiot anyway. And third, how would it look to have some derpy kid with a dumb accent who barely spoke English walk away with that title? They needed someone with real school pride and real American pride to be the winner.

Needless to say, Tommen hitting a kid in the face with a ski pole did not go over well. Thankfully, he was still allowed to race. And race he did. He disobeyed the coach and did not let the other boys win. In fact, he ended up walking away with the highest score for the day and a personal best in all fields. In his anger, he used Time to give himself an advantage and even sabotage the other skiers until he was the only one left on the team who made it to state finals.

His coach reluctantly admitted that he was their only hope at winning the title that year and to do his best, but the pep talk was far below what one might expect from a coach having only one skier representing his entire team and school. Still, Tommen sarcastically promised the coach that he would do his best.

There was no real reason that he couldn't have taken home that title. In hindsight, he probably should have taken that title and cemented his name in history just to snub the coach and spite his asshole teammates. But he didn't. As a hotheaded fifteen year old boy, he was more concerned with the revenge of the moment. So he took his first run and, as expected, he came out on top, easily the favorite to win; his name had become huge in the high school ski sports world.

The second run, he took his revenge. He Banded so he could do it safely yet dramatically, and he wiped out. He wiped out hard. He hit the first two or three gates, but as he made the next turn, he leaned just a little bit forward and there he went, tumbling head over ass probably three-quarters of the way down the hill, yard-saling his equipment all over the slope.

Even though he Banded so he could make the tumbles a little safer and more dramatic, it still knocked the wind out of him pretty good. So aside from being disqualified for both losing his equipment and missing a gate or ten, he was also taken to the first aid tent. Ski

Patrol assessed him and gave him the all clear, citing how lucky he was. Then his coach walked in.

There were words. There were many words. Even better, there were many witnesses.

It wasn't illegal or anything to pad a team with shitty skiers in order to make the stars look better, but when Tommen had become that well-known and people found out the coach and the entire team had tried to keep him out, there was some severe backlash, and the coach resigned after that. He still gave Tommen hateful looks when they saw each other in the halls after school or in the grocery store or some such thing.

As far as Tommen knew, the ski team this year was a sorry sight to behold and had no chance whatsoever at gaining any titles. But the new coach hadn't approached him at all. Whether that was because he'd been told not to or because he was afraid to, Tommen didn't know. And he had no intention of going to them and asking to join them again.

By the time he got to the top of the lift and considered everything, the last thing he felt like doing was racing down the hill again. At least not this one, which he'd been on for the better part of an hour now. And he could only ride the same two or three runs so many times, especially when he was constantly dodging slow skiers.

Not that he expected the main hill to be any better as he stepped out of his skis and crossed the road to Powder Monkey Lift. There were more children and families here. Honestly, he hated child skiers more than the slow adult skiers, mostly because he was terrified that if he hit them, he would crush them. To say nothing of how frail old people could be, but still. He didn't have to worry about spastic parents if he collided with an old person.

He took a few turns on the main slopes and headed over to the south mountain. It was kind of like Western Territory, but more accessible; it didn't involve having to venture forth into unknown territory and cross a busy road. By the time he'd tracked out all the trails there, it was almost noon.

He got on the lift one last time, watching the little skiers below him. Some were speed demons like him, others the old skiers who felt the need to go from edge to edge, and still others were skiers who were working up the nerve to graduate from the intermediate runs to the black runs. A group of snowboarders also zipped by under-chair.

Strictly speaking, Tommen knew how to snowboard, and he could get down a green run without falling, but he was unnerved by having everything in a single line. As the lift crested the hill and he could see the unloading ramp, he saw a group of three Ski Patrollers take off down Sawmill, two skiers and one boarder. Another pair of boarders went sliding down Flume.

Tommen followed the pair, keeping a polite distance behind them even if it meant sacrificing speed. When he finally got down to the bottom of the hill and back up to the top of Powderidge Lift, he paused and waited. He could easily head back to the main lodge, find his dad, and get something to eat, take a break before coming back out. But that would cost him time. Plus he wasn't sure he wanted to face his dad again just yet.

On the other hand, there was a terrain park calling his name. Evolution Park wasn't the biggest park in the basin, but it was the longest, perfect for seeing how many tricks he could string together before getting too disoriented or tired.

He set off down Camp 4, keeping to the left side until he saw the starting platform come into view. The park was packed with skiers and snowboarders. Being a Medium-difficulty park, it should have been populated exclusively with those who had good knowledge of jumps and rails and how to be safe and navigate the park. Obviously, it wasn't.

Some people just didn't understand the concept of a terrain park. Whether they misjudged the size of a jump or the angle of a rail, there was a reason a Patroller was almost permanently stationed at the top of the park, and it wasn't for people ducking lines. Well, not exclusively. Other people didn't seem to understand that a terrain park meant that casual riders were not supposed to be allowed in. But there they always were, making their turns, riding the funnel that ran between the features, completely oblivious to the people going off jumps and riding rails and exploiting other park features.

This park had five standard decks with alternating jumps and rails on either side. After the fifth deck, one side continued on with two more half-decks and the other side became a quarterpipe with an additional jump at the start and a rail on top. The turn at the bottom of the run was a strange misfit collection of a couple C-rails, a steeple, and what looked like a failed attempted at a bowl.

For as often as he rode the park and did his stunts, Tommen was always terrified in the moment when he went from standing on the platform to turning and starting down the hill. Something about that little motion, that decision to be the daredevil and take his life into his own hands, it terrified him. That terror was quickly replaced by exhilaration when he approached the first jump. It was a small jump, since he didn't have a lot of speed, and the best he could do was a 360. He made a hard turn to the right and went for the rail on the second deck, hopping off the approach and sliding sideways along the rail, landing flawlessly and tucking down to gain more speed as he approached the next jump.

This was where Time came in handy to help him show off, to let him appear to get through his flips faster. Problem was, Time couldn't save him if he approached wrong or didn't actually have enough speed or any of the things that really mattered when executing a jump and a flip — or any trick for that matter. Here, Time was just a party trick to draw attention to himself.

Nevertheless, he landed the flip and hit the rails on the last two decks, making for the jump on the half-deck, executing another flip, and tucking for the last jump. The last jump was actually in the shape of a pyramid, but the top had been leveled and a bonk stuck out of the top maybe a foot or foot and a half. This was where talent came in, the ability to get up to speed to clear the jump while maintaining enough control to skim or even land on the bonk.

Tommen scolded himself as he went high of the bonk, hitting

the landing and riding down toward the park builders' last attempt at making this park more interesting than the other parks. He went for the steeple, another test of skill and talent, to reach the top without going over—which was decidedly more dangerous than clearing the bonk—and without going off either of the increasingly narrow sides. This he was able to execute better than the bonk, but it, too, was less than perfect as he couldn't quite ring the bell that had been placed just over the top.

Frustrated, he slid back into the bowl and headed out of the park, riding the last rail as a show for the lift running overhead before riding the last little ways to the bottom of the lift.

Well, it hadn't been his worst run, anyway. Actually, it had probably been one of his better runs. Certainly he'd done well considering it was his first time out for the season. Muscle memory worked in his favor sometimes.

He got on the lift and tried to relax, figure out what he was going to do next.

When Tommen had first been introduced to skiing and snowboarding and had to pick which one he wanted to learn, he'd originally leaned toward snowboarding. As most boarders had told him, they couldn't stand the thought of either crossing skis or having one slip out or just keeping track of all the equipment. But while he was weighing the pros and cons of both skiing and snowboarding, there happened to be an advertisement—he thought it had been some kind of sports drink or something that just happened to use snowsports as its medium that go round—featuring skiers and snowboarders in a terrain park. Both were very impressive, but the skiers had caught his attention. The best way he could describe it was the optical illusion of moving faster and doing more just by the angles. Like watching a karate master swing and flip and whale on invisible bad guys with a bowstaff; it looked fast and tricky and impressive, but it was primarily working smarter, not harder, and relying on the optical illusion as much as brute force.

That was also the reason Tommen took his poles with him into the park. He didn't wear the wrist straps, obviously, but it was another set of angles that added to the optical illusion that the trick he was doing was cool and difficult, when it really wasn't much more than a basic twist or flip.

He took his place at the starting platform, waiting for the people in front of him. General rule was that one waited until the first deck was clear before starting. Did everyone obey that unwritten rule? No, not really.

Still, he waited patiently for his turn, his stomach twisting in dread as he eeked over the edge, his heart soaring as he began picking up speed. And he was off again. First jump, second jump, three rails in a row, head down, tight turn and launch off the quarterpipe. Well, maybe not launch necessarily, but he got enough air to do a flip. Then down and tuck in as he approached the bowl. Hit the approach on a C-rail and slide around effortlessly. Feel the physics and the forces at work. Jump off, tuck in again, hit the last rail, do a 180 on it, land backwards and ski down to the bottom of the lift backwards.

And for his next trick, he would do it all again but make it look easy. Tommen waited to get in line for just a second as he caught his breath. Pulling off all those tricks in a row was no walk—or ski—in the park. Most of the others in the terrain park, if they hit every deck, they usually did it at a slower speed. Those who went full speed might only do every other deck.

Just as he was about to get in line, he heard a voice.

"Hey!"

He Banded and looked around, trying to determine if that was meant for him and where it was coming from. Unfortunately, with everyone all bundled up, it was almost impossible to tell. He dropped the Band and got in line. He jumped as a skier and a snowboarder slid up beside him and got on the lift with him.

"Hey, we're riding with you," the snowboarder told him. He kicked the snow off his board and put an arm around his girl who was the skier. Both appeared to be in their late teens, early twenties. "You're pretty good in the terrain park."

"Um, thanks," Tommen answered.

"You got like a GoPro or something on you, filming all that?"

"No, I don't."

"Dude, I bet that would be a hit on YouTube. Hey, listen, we run a YouTube channel showcasing local ski and snowboard talent, everything from sheer speed to slalom and obstacles to glades and heli-skiing and terrain parks. It's not anything paid, it's not like an official channel; we're not owned by some corporation or magazine or anything like that. We just go out, film people who are really talented, do some editing, and put it online for everyone to see and marvel at. Kind of a vanity thing."

"Sometimes our work will get picked up and used, though," the girl told him. "Like some of the tourism bureaus have used our stuff, things like that. If that happens, we keep record of everything and you will get paid for it, but just being on the channel you don't."

"Wait, so what are you saying?" Tommen wondered. "You want to film me?"

"If that's okay with you," the man said. "You know, we'll put a GoPro on you. Then Vicki will go ahead of you, I'll come behind you, and then we just take and edit all the footage into something awesome. We send you the link when it's finished and uploaded, and you can show off to all your friends."

Yeah, well, the only friends he'd want to show off to who would give a damn had abandoned him.

"Is there anything I need to sign or anything?"

"Nope. It's kind of a spur of the moment thing."

Tommen was skeptical, but if all they were doing was putting it on YouTube, then so what? Wasn't like he hadn't posted his own videos, so he was already out there on the Internet. And even if they did do something bad with it, they didn't have a contract saying he agreed to it, so he could always request, petition, or sue to get it taken down, right? What was the harm?

"Okay," he told them. "Just tell me what I need to do."

"Anything you want," the man said. "Oh, I'm Dan by the way.

And Vicki, obviously. What's your name?"

"Tommen."

"Where you from, Tommen?"

"Charleston."

"Great." They got off the lift. "We'll meet you down at Evolution Park, then."

Tommen nodded and headed down the hill, mind spinning. He wasn't sure what to think. They wanted to film him as local ski talent? It was almost too good to be true, and not in a weird way either. How many times had he gone through his trick routine, pretending as though there was a crowd of adoring fans cheering him on? How many times had silent commentary played in his head, almost distracting him from the moment and almost causing—or actually causing—an accident?

Okay, so this didn't sound like the big time where he was going to be on ESPN or in a magazine or even on the local news channel, but it was nice to be discovered and recognized for his talents.

Dan and Vicki skied up to him where he waited on the starting platform.

"So, what are you thinking?" Dan asked. "Let's say we do three runs. That should be enough." He looked at Vicki. "Yeah, three's good. We won't tell you what to do or how to do it, but what's your intended plan of action?"

Usually he just went where he felt like. He looked out over the park. "Well, I guess I'll do a mixed run first. I'll hit the first rail here, then head over to the jump and see how I'm doing from there."

"Lead the way," Dan said.

It took half a second for Tommen to realize that he was actually talking to Vicki who turned around on her skis and started down the hill. Once she was a good distance away, not quite off the first deck, Tommen started down the run.

The feeling was different this time as he aimed for the approach and slid over the rail. Like, this was actually happening.

Someone—who wasn't one of his friends making some derpy amateur video—was filming him. As in, someone saw his talent and approached him. They came to him. They asked to film him. Somehow, that made him feel like a real skier, a real athlete.

He tucked in and started toward the jump, momentarily distracted by Vicki who, despite going backwards and going slower, still managed to ride the jump safely, even though she had to slide off one side of the landing in order to make room for him as he went flying by. He thought about slowing down and letting her get back in front of him, then figured that they told him to just do his thing, so that's what he would do. He couldn't do his thing if he had to stop and wait for them; he had to get up to speed if he wanted to keep going and do anything worthwhile on the last three decks plus the rest.

Tommen did two more rails and a jump to finish out the standard decks, then had to make a split-second decision whether he wanted to hit the half-decks or make for the quarterpipe. He decided to go the safe route for the first run and leave the more complicated tricks for the last run.

He landed the last jump and tucked in, speeding toward the steeple, intent on ringing that damn bell. He made the approach and jumped, swinging for the bell as he turned, trying to keep his skis perpendicular to the narrow top rather than risking a rather unpleasant groin strike.

The bell jingled, and he cheered, almost losing balance but saving it as he hopped off the top and hit snow again. Vicki was again in front of him, continuing to film as he went for the last rail, hopping on facing forward and hopping off facing backward. He skied the rest of the way backwards, just like before, reaching the bottom and sliding dramatically, spraying snow, much to the dismay of a couple other patrons. Dan wasn't far behind, doing his own dramatic slide as he fiddled with something on his little camera.

"Was that good?" Tommen asked. "I wasn't sure since I kind of got in front of you." He looked at Vicki.

"Oh, no worries," Dan said, bending over to unstrap his one binding. "Not our first rodeo. But yeah, it was excellent."

They got on the lift again.

"So, yeah, that was a good run," Dan repeated. "Two more runs. Like I said before, you know, this is your thing so do what you want, but I think it would be cool if you did something on everything. Like the quarterpipe would be great. We saw what you did there."

"Okay," Tommen said.

"Think you could do something like that again? It's okay if you don't. I mean, it's all edited, but safety first, definitely."

"No, no, I can do it."

"Great. We'll do it the same way as before. Vicki will go in front, and I'll come up behind. You do what you gotta do."

"Okay. So, what did you say your YouTube channel is called? I want to see some of the other things you guys have produced."

"Yeah, no problem. It's — "

"Hey, hey, he's coming around. There he is. Hey, buddy, welcome back."

The first image that came to mind was some kind of Yeti. Or maybe a mountain goat. Then he realized it was a Ski Patroller looking down over him. He was an older man with more hair than face, mostly gray, long ponytail, glasses.

He coughed, and shockwaves of pain went shooting all up and down his right side. He cried out involuntarily.

"Whoa, whoa, hey, easy now," the Yeti told him. "I know it hurts, but we have to get you splinted and up to the patrol room, okay? Do you know your name?"

Name? Right, name. "Tommen."

"Tommen? Tommen what?"

"Forbes."

"Okay, Tommen Forbes. I'm Ian. This is Tom, and that's Butch. We're going to take good care of you. What's the last thing you remember?"

He looked around. It was daytime, but there was a shadow over him. He was looking up at a snow wall. No, not a snow wall. It was the thing. The quarterpipe. A spotty trail of blood coming down the wall led...right to him actually. Huh. Interesting.

"Tommen. Tommen, look at me." He turned his gaze back toward the Yeti. Ian. Ian the Yeti. "What's the last thing you remember?"

"On i'n reidio'r lifft efa Dan a Vicki. Maent yn ffilmio fi." (I was riding up the lift with Dan and Vicki. They were filming me.)

"Do you speak English, Tommen?" another Patroller asked. Tom, that was his name. He had a yellow helmet and a blond goatee. Maybe. Either of them could have been any number of colors, really. He handed something to Ian the Yeti.

"Uh..." Yes. Yes, he did. But for the life of him, he couldn't think of anything right now. He could understand them well enough, but he couldn't bring to mind anything that might help him formulate an answer.

"Where's Brooke when you need her?" Ian the Yeti mused.

"It's her day off," Yellow Goat sighed.

"Okay, Tommen, we got your arm splinted. Do you hurt anywhere else? Head, neck, back? Can you feel me tapping?" Ian the Yeti tapped on the bottom of his boots. The ugly rental boots. Tommen nodded. "Good. Does your neck hurt?" He gently ran his fingers along the back of his neck. "Okay, good. Listen, buddy, we're going to take your helmet off and put a really uncomfortable collar on you. It's just a precaution, okay?"

Not like he had much choice as Ian the Yeti gently took his chin and neck in his hands while Yellow Goat slid the helmet off. A third Patroller approached, bearing some kind of plastic collar. For a moment, Tommen had an image of a cottontail rabbit, the way the Patroller's man bun stuck out of his helmet. What was his name? Butch? Butch Cottontail.

"Tommen? Buddy, does your back hurt at all? And I mean at all, like the slightest bit of discomfort or anything?"

"Dim," Tommen replied stiffly. (No.) He made a weak thumbs down with his left hand.

"Okay, that's great. Are you experiencing any nausea or dizziness or light sensitivity?"

"Bendro." (Dizzy.) He made a sort of swirling motion with his hand.

"Well, listen, we have to get you in this toboggan so we can get you to our patrol room. If you're feeling dizzy, we're just going to have you lay right out flat in there, all right? Hey, where are you from?"

"Charleston."

"Yeah? What language are you speaking now?"

"Cymraeg." (Welsh.)

Ian the Yeti glanced at Yellow Goat and Butch Cottontail who both shrugged.

"Ready when you are," Butch Cottontail said.

"Okay, Tommen, we're going to put you on this sheet, and then we're going to lift you into the toboggan on the back of sled and strap you in. Tommy's going to ride tail to make sure you're okay. If you start feeling real dizzy—like super dizzy, feel like you're going to pass out—or if you feel nauseous like you need to throw up, let him know, okay? We'll help if we can, but we need to get you to our patrol room."

"Bus is on the way," Tommy Yellow Goat reported.

"Good. Let's roll him up. Head has the count."

Only when they were lifting him into the toboggan did Tommen really become aware of his injuries. Everything from his right elbow down was screaming in agony, and he could hardly breathe for the pain in his right side. His face felt like he'd gone a few rounds with Tyler Freeman, too.

He wasn't sure what was worse: being lifted into the toboggan and being coddled and squished in the sheet, or being placed in the toboggan and allowed to relax completely. Didn't matter, he supposed, seeing how there was no way he could get comfortable.

"These are your skis and poles?" Tommy Yellow Goat asked, holding up the equipment.

"*Maen ndw,*" Tommen answered, managing a thumbs up with his left hand. (They are.)

"I'll bring his helmet," Butch Cottontail told them. He looked away at something else. "You two said you witnessed it?"

"Yeah." Dan's voice could be heard. "I mean, actually we filmed it, if you need to see it or something."

"Come up to the patrol room with me; we'll need to get your statement."

"Yeah, sure," Vicki said. "Absolutely."

"Okay, here we go," Ian the Yeti said on the snowmobile. "Tail on?"

"Tail on," Tommy Yellow Goat confirmed.

Tommen blacked out for a minute as the snowmobile jerked forward. The next thing he knew, they'd gone from the quarterpipe to just leaving the park, going uphill. They went fast where possible, but were just as limited as anyone else, having to watch out for skiers and other hill patrons. They used a maintenance trail cut-across to get to Heisler Way, and from there it was a straight shot to the main lodge.

"How was that, Tommen?" Ian the Yeti asked as they came to a stop. "Still feel dizzy?" Yes. "Nauseous?" A little.

A set of double doors was flung open and a canvas stretcher brought out to them. The toboggan straps were taken off and a new Patroller squatted down beside him.

"Tommen, this is Doug," Ian introduced, then looked at Doug. "Sixteen, took a full body blow off a jump into a rail, down the quarterpipe. He was unconscious for about five minutes. Knows his name and where he's from, understands what we're telling him—we think—but doesn't speak English."

"Okay," Doug the Squirrel said. He had the appearance of always needing to go, do, like a squirrel. Sitting around didn't sit well with him. He leaned over Tommen. "How ya feelin', Tommen? How'd the ride up treat ya?"

"*Gwell na'r daith i lawr,*" Tommen replied, finding a little humor in him. (Better than the ride down.)

"We're going to put you on this stretcher and get you inside on a bed. I see Ian's already got your arm splinted. We'll have to take your coat off to look at that, okay?"

Again, not like he had a choice. They lifted him out of the toboggan onto the stretcher and quickly had him inside where it was considerably warmer.

"Tommen, do you have any friends or family with you today?" Tommy Yellow Goat asked as they got him on a bed and, mercifully, removed the collar. "Is there anyone we can contact?"

Shit. His dad was going to murder him. Still, he had to know. Cautiously, Tommen used his left hand to try and reach for his phone. Doug the Squirrel jumped in and got it to him. He dialed his dad.

"Hello?" his dad wondered.

"*Tad, mae o fi,*" Tommen said, emotion suddenly overwhelming him, threatening to choke him. "*Dw i...uh...Dw i yn ffordd ddrwg.*" (Dad, it's me. I'm, uh, I'm in a bad way.)

"*Beth ddigwyddodd?*" (What happened?) It was tough to gauge if he was worried or irritated.

"*Nes i...syrthio. Dw i ar batrôl sgïo rŵan.*" (I...fell. I'm at Ski Patrol right now.)

"*Dw i ar fi ffordd.*" (I'm on my way.)

And he hung up.

"Is that a parent?" Doug the Squirrel asked.

Tommen nodded.

"Hey, it's okay, buddy," Ian the Yeti told him. "These things happen. What matters right now is that you're awake and talking to us, right?"

Tommen took a breath and nodded, flinching as a bright light was suddenly shined in his eyes.

"Pupils are unequal," Doug the Squirrel reported. "Left is smaller. Both are pretty sluggish."

"Okay, Tommen, we have to get your coat and gloves off so

we can get a look at your arm," Ian the Yeti said, cutting off the makeshift work he'd done on the hill. "Now we can either cut your coat off and your arm can stay in place, or we can pull it off like normal, and we'll do our best to keep your arm supported and not jostle it around."

Neither option sounded particularly appealing. But if he needed a new coat, he needed a new coat. Sighing, he made a snipping motion with his left hand.

"Cut it off?" Ian confirmed. "Okay, we'll cut it. Left side first, though."

The left side wasn't the problem, and that glove and sleeve came off easily without the need to cut.

"Just breathe, Tommen," Ian coaxed. "Let us do the work, and you just breathe."

They'd just started cutting when the doors opened again, but it was just Butch Cottontail, along with Dan and Vicki.

"Hey, how's he doing?" the Patroller asked.

"He's a trooper, Butchie," Ian told him.

"Do we have Mom or Dad on the way?"

"Yeah, we do," Tom confirmed.

"Excellent." Butch turned to the couple. "Why don't we go in the office here? I'll get your statements, and then you can go back out."

Dan and Vicki agreed wordlessly as they followed Butch into another room. Not ten seconds after they disappeared into the office, the doors opened a third time, and Tommen's dad walked in.

"*Tad!*" Tommen said. (Dad!)

He jerked, winced in pain, sucked in a breath, felt hot tears streak down his cheeks. The last cut on his coat was made and the layers were peeled away.

"*Beth ddigwyddodd?*" his dad asked. "*Wyd ti o'r gore?*" (What happened? Are you okay?)

"Are you dad?" Doug ventured.

"Yes, I am. What happened?"

"An accident in the terrain park," Ian informed him. "Hit a jump, hit a rail. Supposedly it was all caught on camera."

"Whose camera?"

"They're in giving their witness statement to Butch right now," Tom explained calmly. "When they're done, you can probably ask them for the footage."

"What about Tommen? Is he okay?"

"Well, he was unconscious for about five minutes. Has not been able to speak any English, though he understands us perfectly fine from what we can tell. Pain and deformity to the right arm. We just cut it off as you can see so we can get a better look."

"Is there an ambulance coming?"

"Yes, there is."

"*Tommen, beth brifo?*" his dad asked. (Tommen, what hurts?)

"*Popeth o dan y penelin. A mae o'n brifo anadlu,*" Tommen reported. (Everything below the elbow. And it hurts to breathe.)

His dad relayed the information to the Patrollers.

"Do you want us to cut your shirt sleeve or do you just want us to pull it up?" Doug asked.

"*Tynnwch hi i fyny.*" (Pull it up.)

When they did so, Tommen was less than encouraged by their expressions. He tried to look down at them, but moving his head just made the vertigo worse.

"Yeah, that's obvious deformity," Ian said.

"*Beth sydd wedi'i dorri?*" Tommen asked. (What's broken?)

His dad let out a breath. "*Dy fraich. Dy arddwrn. O bosib cwpl bysedd.*" (Your arm. Your wrist. Possibly a couple fingers.)

Doug did a gentle tapping up and down his right side, noting where he winced and groaned. "And you've got some broken ribs."

Before anyone could say more, Butch, Dan and Vicki peeked back in the room.

"Feel better, Tommen, okay?" Vicki said.

"You're the ones who got it on film?" Walter asked.

"Um, yeah. Are you his dad?"

"Yes, and I'd like to see it. If you haven't already deleted it."

"Um, no, not yet. Um, okay. Here."

The whole group of them went into some private conference, leaving Tommen to stare at the ceiling. Fuck. Fuck, fuck, fuck. He hurt. This sucked. And he couldn't even remember how he'd fucked up.

Eventually, he assumed Dan and Vicki left because the rest of them came back around him, pointing and speaking.

"So, yeah, given the mechanism of injury, there could very well be more internal damage," Doug explained. "We're talking lung, possibly liver. And given his concussion-like symptoms, especially since he hasn't come back around to speaking English, he really needs to see a doctor."

"Oh, I'm not disputing that," Walter assured him. "How long until the ambulance arrives?"

"It shouldn't be too long yet," Tom answered. "We called them from the hill. In the meantime, if we could just get some information from you, it would make things that much faster when they do arrive."

So while his dad and Tom did the paperwork, Doug and Ian sat on either side of him.

"So what are you going to tell the girls at school?" Ian teased. "Wrestling bears? Racing down icy slopes to escape a yeti?"

"I wouldn't worry about what he's going to tell the girls," Doug said. "How about what he's going to tell his mom?"

"There's no mom," Walter said, looking up from the paperwork. "Not for eight years."

"Oh," Doug said, his face turning red with embarrassment "I'm sorry."

"Just me and him." And back to the paperwork.

Thankfully, the awkward situation was saved as Butch announced the arrival of the ambulance and opened the doors wide, propping them open and letting in a chill wind. A couple medics walked in the room, one leading, the other hauling the bag. A moment later, another medic walked in, dragging the cot.

"This is Tommen," Ian introduced. "He's sixteen. Wiped out in the terrain park. Unconscious for about five minutes. Knows who he is and can understand us, but for some reason, he can't speak English. Dad and everyone else says he knows it very well, but right now it's just not coming to him. Reportedly very dizzy, a little nauseous. Obvious deformity to the arm, wrist, pain in the fingers and ribs. No neck or back pain."

Even though Tommen knew that it was probably just protocol, he always wondered if maybe the medics didn't believe him or thought his assessment wasn't accurate because they did their own assessment on him. Not surprisingly, they found basically the exact same thing. He knew English, confirmed by his dad, but it wasn't coming to him. He felt dizzy, but his head didn't hurt per se. No neck or back pain. Yup, his arm and wrist hurt like they were broken. Jury was out on the fingers because the arm and wrist were the greater pains. And the ribs. Because pain while breathing was pretty noticeable, too.

"Okay, and he's basically been maintaining, getting better from there to here?" the lead medic, her nametag read Valerie P., asked.

"Yeah," Tom replied. "I mean, he's talking, answering us as best he can, holding conversations with Dad. It's just the unconsciousness and all that which got us concerned."

"Oh, absolutely. So. Dad."

"Walter."

"Walter. He needs to go to the hospital."

"I'm not arguing that. Where are you taking him?"

She told him the name of the hospital. "They'll probably want to do an MRI, just to rule out any major head and brain trauma, but you'll probably be back home tonight. Maybe tomorrow morning."

"All right."

"You guys are from Charleston, you said?"

"That's right."

"Yeah, you'll probably be home tonight, barring catastrophe.

So, Tommen, let's get you loaded up. Walter, are you able to come with us so you can translate?"

"Only if you can give me a ride back so I can get my car."

"We should be okay," the second medic told her. "Once we get an IV started, he won't be making much sense anyway because he'll be feeling real good. And it's not that far."

"He understands you just fine," Walter told them. "Yes or no questions should suffice, right?"

"Yeah. Okay, up and at 'em."

So Tommen was moved again, this time onto the ambulance stretcher. They buried him under blankets and rolled him outside. Before they loaded him into the ambulance, his dad came beside him.

"Byddaf yn dilyn 'chti i'r ysbyty, o'r gore? Bydd yn iawn i gyd. Byddwn ni'n gartref heno. O'r gore?" (I'll follow you to the hospital, okay? It's going to be all right. We'll be home tonight. Okay?"

Tommen nodded uncertainly. Then he was hoisted up, and the stretcher locked in place. A minute later, both medics got in the back with him. One started rummaging around for drugs while the other cleaned the crook of his arm for an IV.

"See, this isn't so bad," she said. "We've just got a short ride to the hospital where they'll fix you up nice and tight. Okay?"

Sure, whatever that meant. He bit his tongue as she slipped the needle.

"Here you go," the second medic said, handing her the end of the line.

Carefully, the line was attached to the needle and the medic fiddled with the drip monitor...regulator...thing. Drops of clear liquid began dripping down and in half a second, his vein felt like ice. And then, all of a sudden, it didn't matter.

Chapter Twenty-Two
Just a Few More Broken Bones

Tommen couldn't say exactly what switch flipped in his head that one moment he couldn't speak English and the next he was conversing perfectly fine, but he could see the relief it brought to the medics when they handed him off to the ER nurses.

"So, now that we can finally talk to each other, what language were you speaking?" Valerie inquired once they transferred him to the trauma bed.

"Welsh," Tommen answered, still feeling pretty good from the pain meds they gave him.

"Really? I never would have guessed. Your dad speaks it pretty good, too, then?"

"Yeah, our family is from Wales. He decided to lose his accent; I didn't."

"Cool. Well, I hope you get better and get out of here quick."

He barely had time to thank her before the doctor walked in and began his assault, barraging Tommen with questions, demanding answers, and harassing the nurses for tools and tests. They took X-rays and then had him rushed to CT first followed by MRI. It all happened so fast, Tommen wasn't sure what to make of it.

The good news, his figured, was that aside from his language coming back, his dizziness had mostly subsided except for when he made quick movements.

Eventually, his dad was let in to see him, at least when the doctor appeared to finally give the verdict on his injuries.

"The good news is, it's not as bad as it first might have seemed," the doctor told them. "You sustained a moderate concussion which has been improving rapidly even in just the time that you've been here. Still, we want to keep you for a while for observation. Dad, if you are able to stay with him, you know him well enough to let us know if there are any severe changes in mood or behavior, things like that, any deviation from normal."

"That's assuming he's normal in the first place," Walter said, smirking, giving Tommen a knowing look.

"Well, I think you'd know what abnormal looks like."

"What about my arm?" Tommen wondered. It felt like forever ago that they'd taken X-rays, and the most he'd gotten for it was a cold pack to keep the swelling down. He was no doctor, but he was pretty sure his arm and wrist wasn't supposed to look like that.

The doctor whipped the films onto the lightbox and switched it on. "You suffered multiple breaks. Your elbow was sprained, but you broke your arm in two places, your wrist, these two bones in your hand, and these four bones in your ring and pinkie fingers. We'll cast up to here. For your elbow, we'll put a brace on it for a couple weeks. You also broke these three ribs, but there's nothing we can do for that. Just take it easy. I would recommend that you see your regular doctor when you get home."

"Speaking of which, when can we go home?" Walter wondered. "I know you said you want to keep him for observation, but how long will that be?"

"Just for a few hours, until we're sure that he can safely go home and rest."

"Now, I'm not a doctor, obviously, but I seem to recall vaguely that with concussions, there should be limits on exposure to TV, phones, computers, video games, things like that."

"Correct." The doctor looked at Tommen. "Sorry, kiddo, but you're going to be bored out of your mind for a few hours. No TV, no phones, none of that. And I'd say stay away from them as much as possible for at least a week, or until your doctor tells you. And if at any time you develop any sort of light sensitivity, definitely get it checked out, okay?"

Tommen nodded reluctantly. That was not going to make his day any easier, that was for sure. Well, at least he still had his Banding. It wasn't medicine, but it was a tool he could use to make the time go by a little faster. Maybe he could get his dad to Band him to heal his head and his ribs, just skip over that bit and say screw it about the things the doctors couldn't do anything about. He could probably Band his arm, too, but if he was going to be in a cast for six weeks, there was no point to healing himself.

"You said there's nothing you can do for his ribs," his dad said. "They don't even tape them anymore?"

The doctor shook his head. "Nope. Studies were showing that it was doing more harm than good, if it did anything at all. Your ribs move when you breathe, and you can't just stop breathing, so they just have to heal as they are."

Walter nodded solemnly. He Banded and looked at Tommen. "What do you think?"

"They've been Band-healed once; I don't see why they couldn't be a second time," Tommen pointed out.

His dad dropped the Band and looked at the doctor. "So what's the best position for him to be in so they can heal correctly?"

The doctor looked at the X-rays. "With the breaks where they are, probably upright. If it's sleeping you're worried about, he might fare best in a chair or recliner, but we all toss and turn; there's no getting around it."

"I understand."

He Banded again. Tommen sat up as much as he could, trying to keep the compress on his arm and gritting his teeth against the pain in his ribs. When the pain finally was reduced to a dull throb, he looked at his dad and nodded.

Band-healing hurt only in the sense that it was weeks of healing compressed into a few minutes or even a few seconds, which meant that all the repaired bone and scar tissue, all the blood and bruising and healing that went on, it would all come as a sudden rush of pain once the Band was dropped.

And Tommen felt it most certainly. He groaned and sucked in a breath and held it. When the aching subsided, he forced himself to relax. His side felt kind of funny, like pins and needles, as if he wore a metal plate against his ribs, but it went away quickly.

"How's that feel?" his dad inquired.

"Strange," Tommen admitted. "But I think they're all healed up."

"Kind of tingly and stuff?"

"Yeah, but it's going away."

His dad nodded and dropped the Band. Everything went back to normal, and the doctor had no idea what had just transpired, the veritable miracle that had just happened in his office.

"If there are no more questions right away, we'll get started on that cast," he said. "Any preference on color?"

Tommen shrugged. "Blue or green."

The doctor picked green, apparently, because he came back with yellow. Tommen would have picked blue because he knew what blue looked like, and he liked it; it was different than the yellow-ness of everything else, but he picked green because, having seen it, he decided that was his favorite color, even if he couldn't normally see it. Maybe one day, if he ever learned how to fix his eyes, or if he just got his eyes fixed. Someday. Apart from Rifun, that is.

When his arm was cast and home care papers delivered, the doctor left, and Tommen was left alone in the room with his dad for an indeterminate amount of time, just to be observed. It was kind of like being in a goldfish bowl, he figured, always being watched but never doing anything of interest.

"Can you Band me and heal my head, too?" Tommen whined after about ten minutes of sitting in bed. No TV, no phone, not even any good magazines. His dad sat in a chair reading some article in a magazine a child had apparently gotten hold of with crayon scribbles on most of the pages.

"The mind is a delicate thing," his dad replied, not looking up from his article. "As is the brain. Some Timekeepers can do such things. Physically, I could do it, too. In the same way that I can open up someone's head and poke around in their brain, but I'm no brain surgeon."

"So...that's a no?"

"If I was going to do it, I would have already done it. You might still be in trouble for your antics earlier, but I don't like to see you suffer, though suffering from boredom is the least traumatic, I think, in this case."

"I'm still in trouble?! Karma didn't kick my ass hard enough?"

"Cuss again and you'll be in even deeper trouble. Yes, you're still in trouble for that. Taking advantage of my ignorance, I'd say that's paid well enough. Karma, as you put it. But you still lied to Becky, and you're still going to make up for that. Got it?"

Tommen sighed. "Yes, sir."

"How are you feeling?"

"Bored."

"Besides that."

Tommen shrugged. "Okay, I guess."

"Still dizzy?"

"Only if I like turn my head quickly or something. Otherwise, no. My arm's starting to really ache, though."

His dad nodded. "It will. It'll ache and it'll hurt and it'll itch. Good Lord, it will itch. But that means it's getting better."

"So you're not even going to Band my arm to heal?"

"What for? Whether or not I heal it or you heal it, you're still stuck in that cast."

Tommen grunted. He'd figured as much, but he was hoping his dad might know some way around it. He didn't know how, but somehow. Then he came up with another idea.

"When are you going to take me to the Wheel, to the Arena, for training?"

"I'd initially planned to wait until after the elections when all the craziness died down a little. That's even more certain now since I'm reluctant to take you to the Wheel, your head the way it is. Why do you ask?"

"Maybe when I'm about halfway through this cast and stuff, you can show me how to Pinpoint Band so I can heal my arm, or try to."

His dad mulled that over. "It's possible, I suppose. But that will be after I show you how to Pinpoint Band. I won't let you use yourself as your own guinea pig for that. Maybe you can do that for your test. All right?"

"Okay," Tommen conceded. It made sense, he supposed. Pinpoint Banding wasn't just about smaller Banding; there was art and finesse involved; he didn't need to screw up his arm forever just because he got a little overeager and decided to start experimenting. He'd tried to do that on Sifura; he'd gotten lucky that he hadn't hurt her, but he certainly could have.

"And I want you to limit your Banding for a couple days," his dad went on. "I know that Banding a lot can cause headaches—I know it causes you headaches—and I don't want you to overexert yourself. Fair?"

"Fair. Can I at least Slow Band now just so I can get through this boring part a little quicker?"

His dad looked ready to say no. Finally, "I'll Slow Band you. That way I can keep an eye out for nurses if they decide to come in and ask after you."

Tommen reluctantly agreed. As the Band overtook him, he decided he hated concussions. They just ruined everything. No TV, no phone, no Banding, everything that was fun in life just got taken away. He knew why there were such restrictions, and he knew that there were certainly times when a concussion could be not only debilitating, but life-threatening. This didn't feel like one of those times. This felt like one of those times when something bad happened, he suffered consequences, now he just needed to be left alone for a short time to recover and then move on.

The Band dropped suddenly as a nurse walked in.

"How are we doing in here, guys?" he asked, looking first at

Walter, then at Tommen.

"I'm all right," Walter said.

"Just bored," Tommen told him.

"Okay. Do you still feel dizzy at all?" The nurse brought out a pen light and checked his pupils.

"Only when I make sudden movements."

"All right. Well, your pupils are still a little slow, but the good news is that they're equal now. Can I get you a glass of water or something?"

"No, I'm okay."

"Let me know if there's anything I can get you," the nurse told them as he stepped out.

"I know I've Banded you a few times," Walter said once the nurse was gone. "That doesn't hurt or make you disoriented or anything, does it?"

Tommen shook his head, then decided that was a bad idea. "No more than when you usually do it."

"And what's that supposed to mean?"

"Nothing, just that you Band a little stronger than I do."

His dad nodded. "I'll keep it in mind."

The Slow Band that enveloped Tommen a second time was a little gentler, less of a strong wind that threatened to knock him down and more of a fierce summer breeze.

The thing about Slow Bands was that unless one was really proficient in reading Band strengths, their strength was impossible to tell from the inside because of how quickly they seemed to come and go. So for Tommen, it seemed as though the Band had no more overtaken him than suddenly it was gone as another nurse came in. She, too, quizzed Tommen, checked his pupils, and asked if there was anything she could get for them, which they declined. Before the Band could go back up, however, Tommen pushed against it, and it went away.

"What?" his dad wondered.

"I remember something," Tommen said. "Dan and Vicki

should have gotten the whole thing on video."

"They did. Although I'm curious to know how that all came about, but go ahead with your train of thought."

"Can I see it? Is there a way?"

"That would fall under the category of electronic use which you are presently not allowed to do, so no, you can't see the video."

"But you saw it, didn't you?"

"Yes, I did. And I had them email me the videos."

"So if I can't watch them, can you at least tell me what happened?"

His dad shifted in his seat. "I can try, but I don't know all your fancy technical terrain park feature trick whatever terms."

"Just tell me; I can see the videos later, I'm sure."

"Dan said it was your third run—"

"My third run?" Tommen interrupted. "But we were just getting on the lift after the first run." Shit, how much had he missed?

"Be that as it may, he said it was your third run. You were speeding down the hill toward the halfpipe-looking thing—"

"The quarterpipe."

"Whatever, the halfpipe-looking thing, quarterpipe. But you instead diverted to the jump that went up the side of it. You tried to do a backflip and land on the rail, but instead you hit the rail and went rolling down the half—quarterpipe."

Tommen let out a breath. He didn't remember any of it. It was like it never even happened. Except it did. Obviously. Because he was here, in the hospital. It certainly sounded like something he would do. Actually, it sounded like one of his more famous signature tricks that he liked to do, when conditions permitted. He just couldn't remember doing it. He remembered the first run and getting on the lift after the first run. And suddenly he was on the ground in the snow with Ski Patrol hovering over him, asking him questions and fixing him up and stuff.

The fuck happened to him out there?

He couldn't remember. He looked at his dad for some kind of

comfort and reassurance, but instead he found only grim contemplation, the same look he got when he was on a case that wasn't going well.

"What's wrong?" Tommen wondered. "What are you thinking? Am I still in trouble?"

"Oh, you're still in trouble, but not for this," his dad said.

"Then what is it?"

"Normally I wouldn't have any interest in the videos, at least not enough to want them emailed to me so I can rewatch my son crashing into a rail like a lunatic." He spoke the words with love, Tommen told himself. "But there was something about it that caught my attention, struck me as being off."

"What do you mean?"

"It's impossible to see Bands on video and in pictures, the strength and wake and so forth, but if you know what to look for, you can tell when they are being used."

Tommen flushed bright red. "I sometimes use Bands to make it look like I'm going faster."

"I know. That much I saw. And then I saw what I think was a second Band, a Fast Band. You used a Slow Band so you had time to complete your flip and make it look dramatic. The Fast Band cut into that and you essentially were unable to complete the flip, so you crashed."

"Wait, so someone else was there who could Band and intentionally tried to hurt me?"

"Like I said, it's coming only from a few seconds of video where the Bands themselves are invisible, but it looked like a definite possibility."

"Could it be Rifun?"

"It is very probable. Do you remember seeing anyone at all while you were skiing who looked like Rifun or one of his associates? With everyone bundled up, it would be easier for non-human humanoid associates to hide." He was talking about Isthim.

Tommen scoured his memory, but it was sketchy. He didn't

normally commit people to memory on the ski hill; there were just too many. "No, not that I can remember."

"All right."

"Do you think whoever it was actually tried to kill me?"

His dad folded his arms. "I don't know. Rifun is definitely not one to shy away from carrying out his threats, and you did tell me and the Durvins about his hold on you, which he ordered you not to do. It could be his way of telling you that he can make good on his threats. Whether his intent was to kill or to scare, I don't know."

"What about this other group that Micaiah told me about, the one that threatened him and Micah?"

"That's still under investigation, but I don't believe them—if it is a separate group—to be connected to this. First, they made no threats against you, and with Rifun already over you, it gives them no advantage to harm you in secrecy. Second, if they decided to use you to get to the twins, it would make more sense to do so in such a way where they are rendered helpless and they know it."

Like Rifun did to me. But he didn't say that out loud and Tommen didn't bring it up.

"So it was probably Rifun," Tommen concluded.

"Probably," his dad admitted. "That's how I'm going to investigate it anyway; that's going to be my starting point."

"You're going to investigate it?"

"Why shouldn't I? Micah and Micaiah are busy with their own threats."

"But you're..."

"Injured. Not helpless. And getting better every day."

Tommen still wasn't sure, but he knew he wasn't going to persuade him otherwise.

If it was Rifun, that was some scary shit. Tommen wasn't sure how to take it. Had Rifun actually tried to kill him, or was this his way of reminding Tommen who currently had the upper hand? Would he try to contact Tommen and have another "chat" with him? Or would he just keep hurting him until he gave in? Worse, was this

his only warning before Rifun decided to move on to other things? Maybe he would try again, next time reversing the situation and taking his dad hostage, forcing Tommen to risk everything.

All of this passed through his mind in the space of only a few seconds. Before he could quite sort them out and voice his concerns, the door opened, and the doctor walked in.

"So, Tommen, how are we feeling? Still dizzy?"

Tommen shrugged. "A little. Not really."

"Well, you haven't gotten worse, which is important. You've already been given your home care papers. Do you have any questions for me before you leave?" Neither of them did. "Excellent. I will let you get on your way then, but just be sure to check in with your regular doctor. As always, don't hesitate to call with any questions—" He looked at Walter. "—and if he gets worse, starts deteriorating or just gets weird on you, definitely take him in."

"Will do, thank you," Walter affirmed, nodding politely.

They exchanged departing pleasantries for a minute or two before the doctor finally left, and Tommen was able to get redressed before heading out.

"Well, now you have an excuse to get a new coat," his dad told him. "And gloves. And whatever else they had to cut off."

"I just need new gear all around," Tommen said. "It's going to cost a small fortune."

"I don't think you're as strapped for cash as you told the ski tech."

"Maybe not, but if I'm only going to be using them for a couple more years...I mean, what's the point?"

His dad sighed and shook his head. "Tommen, you have more years left in you than you think. And there are a few things you have yet to learn about going dark. But I'll tell you something: you don't have to give up everything. Get your new gear and whatever else you need; don't assume that time is ticking down and you have to give up everything." He chuckled. "It's not like you're getting married."

They went to the desk and checked out, or tried to anyway.

First they had to wait for the person in front of them in line. Once they were gone, then the girl behind the counter had to make a phone call. Then there was some issue with the insurance and this, that, and the other thing. It took the better part of an hour for everything to go through and play nice, and by the time they actually left the hospital, it was almost eight o'clock at night.

Tommen shivered against the cold as they crossed the parking lot. "I think I might have to get me a new coat sooner rather than later."

"Ah, I probably should have come out and started the car, picked you up at the door," his dad said apologetically. "Oh well, it'll warm up soon enough."

"Did you grab my stuff?" Tommen looked in the back seat where his skis and assorted gear lay across the seat.

"Yeah, I got everything. Ski Patrol said they'd return the boots, so we're good there."

"Oh, okay." He leaned back his seat a little and blew on his good hand to warm it up. His dad turned the heater fan on full blast but it was a few minutes before it was blowing out anything but cold air.

"You got everything you need? Didn't forget anything?"

Tommen patted down his pockets. "Yeah, I got everything. Including a phone I can't use."

"It's for your own good."

"I'm only injured, not helpless." Tommen gave him a smart look.

"Sorry, kiddo, it's too soon for you to be pulling that line on me."

Tommen shook his head and looked out the window. They should have been home already, really. He was supposed to be one of those people whom Ski Patrol had to shoo off the hill, warning him about how close he was cutting to closing time on the hill. They weren't supposed to have stayed a few more hours at the hospital, leaving at shit o'clock at night and not getting home until even later.

"You hungry?" his dad asked suddenly.

He shrugged. "Sure, I could eat."

"You're a teenage boy, of course you can eat. The meds are messing with you."

There wasn't much open late at night, but they found a small mom n' pop pizza joint willing to stay open for just a little longer for them.

"What kind of teenager doesn't get everyone he knows to sign his cast?" the waitress inquired, indicating Tommen's cast.

"The kind who just got it today," Tommen told her.

"Really? I'm sorry. What happened, if you don't mind my asking?"

"Skiing accident," Walter told her.

"Oh. You a terrain park junkie?" Tommen nodded and so did she. "Yup, yup, I know how that goes. My boys were, too. Every year it was something. An arm, a leg, a collarbone, a shoulder. One year my eldest broke both his legs. He was out for the season, but he still goes back every year. Teaching his kids the same bad habits." She shook her head. "Anyway, what can I get for you?"

Nothing short of a large meat lovers, obviously. They ate and made small talk with the waitress who was also the owner. By the time they got out of there, it was nearly ten o'clock.

"My vote is for sleeping in tomorrow," Tommen said, yawning and leaning his seat back.

"Hey now, you can't do that yet," his dad told him. "How am I supposed to stay awake?"

"The same way you do when you have to go out in the middle of the night to deal with some idiot. Very carefully, with a lot of vengeance in mind for the idiot who woke you up, and with a little help from Banding and Time."

His dad sighed dramatically and shook his head, but said nothing more.

Tommen wasn't sure if his dad did actually Band, but he figured he must have fallen asleep at some point because the next thing he knew, they were just coming in sight of Charleston.

"Are we back already?" he mumbled, sitting his seat up and looking around.

He wasn't quite used to the cast yet, how big and bulky it felt and how very...inconvenient it was overall. He couldn't rub his eyes or his face, couldn't do much other than use it as a club, though he was loathe to do anything with it given how much his arm was aching right now. He could feel his pulse in his arm. Was that possible? He decided it was.

"Almost home, kiddo," his dad said. "Then we can both get some sleep."

Tommen sighed. "I don't know how much sleep I'm going to get with this thing on."

"I imagine in six weeks you'll get some sleep. But it's a good thing that it's the weekend still, so you can sleep in. Especially since you don't have to work tomorrow."

"I'm still in trouble."

"Yes, you are."

"How do I get out of trouble?"

"I haven't decided yet. If it was just your arm, that would be one thing, but I don't want to hurt you more with your concussion. So it might be a week or two before I come up with something. But don't worry, it'll happen."

That was what Tommen was afraid of. Delayed punishment. His arm and head bought him time, but that wasn't a good thing in this case. It was like Rifun hanging over his head. Problem was, Rifun was a direct and obvious threat. Lingering punishment from his dad was a lot more dodgy and a lot more scary. Scarier. More scary. Whatever. It spooked him.

Either way, he probably deserved it. He lied to a girl, and the universe got its karma revenge. Yes, yes, the Chivalrous Welshman wasn't all chivalrous all the time, so sue him. He wanted to have some fun now and again, too.

They arrived home fairly late, both of them exhausted.

Tommen couldn't decide if his fatigue was from the excitement of the day or the meds they'd given him in the hospital. Either way, his body felt heavy, his arm felt like lead, and he actually felt sick to his stomach. Probably the pizza mixed with the meds. He told himself to keep it down unless he really wanted to go back to the hospital because his dad thought it was from the concussion.

They pulled in the garage and sat there for a second, the car still warm. Tommen was the first to move, pulling himself out of the car and making for the backseat.

"Leave your stuff," his dad said as he got out of the driver's seat. "You can grab it in the morning. We're both tired."

Tommen nodded wordlessly and followed his dad in the house, noticing how his dad didn't seem to rely as much on the cane anymore. He still used it, but he no longer leaned heavily on it like some frail old man. How long had it been since the warehouse? Three weeks, maybe? He was doing well. He'd be going back to work soon.

"I'm going to bed," his dad announced. "You can stay up if you want, but no TV or anything like that, like the doctor said. Okay? Read a book, do your homework, or go to bed, whatever. Got it?"

"Got it," Tommen agreed grudgingly.

With that, his dad wished him a good night and headed to bed. Tommen saw only the wake of his Band before the door to his bedroom shut and all that could be seen was the faint glow of the night light within.

Tommen headed to his bedroom and looked around, suddenly very aware that there was little he was able to do that didn't involve electronics in some fashion. Even his homework was dubious considering he used his phone as a basic calculator anyway. To say nothing of the research he did on his phone.

But his big calculator was probably exempt from the electronics warnings, and he'd need that to do his AP Physics project work. Maybe he could work on that for a while and pretend like he'd done something worthwhile and hadn't totally blown off his partner. Reluctantly, he dug out the math and other paperwork as well as his calculator.

Well, fuck. All the variables he needed were in the texts on his phone. But then, he'd only have to look at his phone for a minute or two, just long enough to get the numbers, right? No harm in that. Not any worse than using his phone earlier in the Ski Patrol room to call his dad.

It proved more difficult than anticipated considering the decided lack of function in his right hand. Then it was only exacerbated when he actually tried to write down the numbers and variables. Writing with only three fingers produced something that landed between chickenscratch and intelligent primate copying letters initially written by a kindergartener on the first day of school.

After a while, he gave up. He'd probably have to type it out, which was only going to be more painful—to his pride, anyway—since he would have to plink it out key by key. But Mrs. White was almost as bad as Mrs. Righting when it came to handwriting, because anything was done by hand anymore. Still, being deprived of his ability to write badly only made it more frustrating when that was the only thing he could do.

He was tired, but by the time he got ready for bed and ready to turn out the lights, he was suddenly wide awake. Fucking Time abilities, already messing with him.

He turned off the lights and got in bed, hoping that by doing so, he might reawaken the fatigue—no pun intended. It didn't happen. He sat there in the dark. He didn't know how much time passed before he just couldn't take it anymore; he had to do something. He couldn't write, didn't want to do his homework, and didn't really feel like reading either. He looked at his stand where he knew his phone would be. He shouldn't. He might pass his dad off as a worrywart sometimes, but even he knew the value of listening to a doctor.

Don't do it. Go to sleep, Tommen. Use your concussion as an excuse not to go back there. You're better than that. Don't dishonor your pa or your dad. Listen to the doctor. Just go to bed...

Chapter Twenty-Three
Behind the Scenes

Truthfully, Walter lay in bed for quite a while after officially going to bed. Sometimes, in the past, he would Band until he got tired enough to actually fall asleep. He did that for a while, but there was something depressing about watching the clock and not seeing it tick. Eventually, he just let the Band drop and did his best to clear his mind and drift off.

He must have slept at some point because the next thing he knew, he was opening his eyes to a room bathed in dim light, probably the sun hidden behind thick clouds. He tried to roll over and go back to sleep, but wakefulness took hold of him and drove him to the window. Six inches of powder lay fresh on the fence between houses and more was coming down in tiny, dry flakes.

He glanced at the clock. A little after eight. Theoretically, he still had time to go to church, something he rarely did these days. But now he had decidedly more time on his hands to do so. It was a good thing to do every so often, when he could. Refresh the soul, find penance for the sins he'd committed between the last time he'd gone to church and now. Tommen wouldn't go, wouldn't care—would probably sneer and make some snide remark—but eventually there came a time when everyone had to make his own decision. Tommen wasn't yet legally an adult, but he was a human being with free will, and there was nothing to be gained by trying to force him, so Walter would have to go alone. Assuming he went at all. There was something to be said for using the brains God gave him and not going out when the weather was as bad as it was, or could be.

At the same time, it seemed a poor excuse when he knew he

was going to go out anyway. He had to talk to the twins and inform them of Rifun's latest attack and see if they'd uncovered anything about the group that had made threats against them. So to take the time and risk to drive to the bakery but not to any of the churches along that same route seemed oddly selfish. Maybe he was just sentimental.

Tommen was not yet awake when he stepped out of the bedroom and headed for the bathroom on his morning routine. Terrible things, habits; he very nearly put on his blues. And to think he'd been off the job for three weeks. Three weeks? Already? Considering that one of those weeks had been spent in a coma, and he was going to be off the job for another five weeks at a minimum, he was going to go stir-crazy. At this rate, he was going to have the whole house remodeled by the time he went back to work. Which wouldn't be a bad thing, in all reality.

Walter headed to the kitchen to make coffee and get the paper while waiting for it to brew. As he sat down with the newspaper, he heard the bathroom door squeak close. A minute later, Tommen walked drearily out to the kitchen.

"Good morning, Sunshine," Walter greeted. "You feeling all right?"

"Didn't get to sleep right away," Tommen mumbled. He reached into the cupboard for a mug. "Slept like crap when I did." The coffeemaker finished brewing, and he poured himself a cup. "Feel like I haven't slept at all." He grabbed another mug and poured coffee for Walter. He looked at him. "Where are you going?"

"Who says I'm going anywhere?" Walter took a drink of the coffee.

"Because the only thing you're missing are coat and shoes."

"Habit is a terrible thing."

Tommen shook his head. "No, you're going somewhere. I can tell."

Walter sighed. Knowing a person well worked both ways sometimes. And sometimes it was very annoying. "Yes. I'm heading to the bakery to inform the twins what happened yesterday. Then I thought I'd go to church."

"Church?" Tommen said the word like it was foreign.

"I'm not going to force you if you don't want, but yes, I'm going. I'm rather grateful to be alive, and figured I should thank God for it. For you."

Tommen shrugged. "Whatever. Make yourself feel better, I guess. But I'm the one who traveled across the universe. Not Him."

Walter shook his head and took another drink. "Whatever. Like I said, you don't have to go. You're going to stay here. You still have a Physics project to work on, as I recall? Are you able to do it without too much screen time?"

"Yeah, my calculator isn't that kind of screen."

"Good. You can work on that. When I get home, I'll help you move the vanity and the toilet and we'll switch out the old for the new, clean out the living room, and finally get rid of some of that sixties disaster in there. Sound good?"

"Sure."

"How's your head?"

"I'm not dizzy anymore, but I've got a headache like a hangover."

"And your arm?"

"Throbbing, aching. Nothing I can do about it." He shrugged.

"All right. Well, I'm going to have my phone on me, so don't hesitate to call me if you need something, okay?"

Tommen nodded blankly and took another drink of coffee. "All right, I guess I should get motivated to do something."

Walter watched him get up and drag himself back down to his bedroom. Any other time, he might have shaken his head and, while he would always feel bad for the accident and his injuries, dismiss it largely as he got what was coming to him for lying to Becky and him about the project. But this time, there was that old, familiar, inner rage, deep down, one he'd learned to channel away from drunken brawling into a kind of mother bear defense, one that said, "Something attacked my cub, now I'm going to kill it."

He thought about this as he pulled on his shoes and grabbed his coat. He held his cane, leaned on it, considered.

Don't do it. You're doing fine, healing fine. It's been three weeks and you're practically walking on your own. Don't do it; you don't need it. You know where this came from and you know where it's leading. Leave it alone.

At least until you're in the car where Tommen is less likely to surprise you.

He headed out to the car, pressed the garage door button, and started the car. Taking a breath, he closed his eyes and leaned back just a little.

Don't do it. Don't do it. You're better than this. What would everyone think?

Don't get caught unawares and don't get caught groveling in pain.

Pain is a measure of wellness. You can't measure yourself accurately if you blot out the units. It's as useful as scratching out the marks on a ruler. Don't do it.

He sighed, the war raging back and forth in his mind. He knew where this ended. He knew how he should end it.

He opened the bottle, tapped out a pill, and swallowed it before backing the car out of the garage.

The roads weren't as bad as he had feared, but it might have had something to do with the fact that he was out later than he might normally be, after the trucks had sanded and salted the roads. That wasn't to say they were perfect as he did slip and slide a little, but he made it to the bakery no worse for wear.

"Morning, Walt," Micah greeted as he walked in. "A little late for you, isn't it? I think retirement is starting to suit you."

"Retirement, yeah right," Walter said, shaking his head. "I don't think it's quite my lifestyle. Just the precinct or just the District, either of those I might welcome as a vacation from the other, but not doing either? This is just boring as all get out."

"So you've made it your mission to bother the average hard-working American with your powers of grumpiness rather than your powers of police work, is that it?" Micaiah asked teasingly as he brought a tray of donuts up to the front counter and set them in the display case, the glass fogging momentarily.

"Absolutely. That is my new goal in life."

"Well, maybe we can stave off the grumpiness with a pastry, hm?" Micah suggested, grabbing one with wax paper and setting it on a napkin. "What do you say, Captain?"

"I'd say you're trying to fatten me up and make even more lazy in my retirement." He took the pastry anyway and headed to a booth next to one of the large windows.

The bakery was part of a plaza with six other businesses all crowding around a poorly-planned parking lot, but the window at least showed some of the road beyond where the morning rush to get to work was now replaced by the leisure crew who were out running errands to the grocery store, the pharmacy, the doctor, or wherever.

"So, did you take Tommen skiing?" Micah asked once the next wave of people had come and gone.

"I did," Walter confirmed, wiping crumbs from his mustache.

"How was it? Is he king of the mountain again?"

"Well, apparently a small film crew caught up to him and filmed him for some project they were doing."

"Because that's not going to stroke his ego a little. Is he going to be famous? Should I roll out the red carpet next time he comes in to work?"

"No, but you can probably hand him a hospital gown instead of an apron."

"Oh, shit, what happened?"

"That's actually the real reason I came in to see you guys."

Micaiah appeared with another tray of baked goodies. "Good grief, Walter, you always come in wanting something. Can't you ever drop in just to say hi and enjoy the pleasure of our company?"

"As pleasurable as your company is, I need to pick your brains on something."

"All right, all right. Give me five minutes to get the rest of this stuff out."

"What's this about?" Micah asked. "What happened?"

"To put it simply, Tommen crashed hard. Moderate concussion, broken arm, broken wrist, couple broken fingers. Sprained elbow. I Band-healed his broken ribs."

"Ouch. Is he all right? Like, he's not conked out on pain meds at home, is he?"

"No, he's doing fine, all things considering."

"But it's the rest of it that you want our help with."

Walter nodded, and Micah stepped aside as Micaiah started bringing out multiple trays of food. According to every foodie, reporter, and sneaky undercover investigator from the Health Department, there was no possible way that just the two of them should be able to turn out as much food as they did. But that was the magic of Time, being able to condense twenty minutes of baking time into only a few seconds, to say nothing of the prep and mixing time.

"All right, so we're meeting in the office?" Micaiah said as he delivered the last tray and took off the oven mitts.

"Unless you've recently added on a conference room to your store," Walter told him.

The elder twin shook his head and Banded them, a Fast Band so they could have their meeting without losing any time at all. Walter moved around the counter and followed them into the office. It wasn't a huge office, but big enough that they could all sit comfortably. The largest window was split between watching the kitchen and watching the front, with separate blinds for each. The door also had a window, and the front-facing wall had a TV mounted on the dining room side, usually turned to the weather channel or sometimes the nightly news. The desk was almost always buried under a mountain of papers, loosely organized into incoming and outgoing. Even the computer seemed to disappear sometimes. Under the desk, the one-ton safe that was bolted to the floor, if you didn't know it was a one-ton safe bolted to the floor, seemed no more harmless than an old filing cabinet picked up from some yard sale.

Beside the desk, a Pepsi mini-fridge hummed.

There was also a round table in the corner opposite the main desk. It, too, was littered with papers, a small section cleared as a place to eat without getting condiments on invoices. Walter and Micah pulled chairs from this table while Micaiah opted for his usual captain's chair at the desk. Micaiah was the twin who worked out, and the way he folded his arms definitely showed it. It was almost a shame that he didn't have any tattoos to show off. But then, he was a baker, not a biker. Well, no, he was that, actually. But whatever his attitude and general disposition said, he was a lover at heart.

"You look like you're doing better," Micaiah observed, as if to prove Walter's thoughts. "Injuries healing up all right?"

"Oh, they ache and throb, but I'm better than I was," Walter told him. "I don't know how I'm going to survive another five weeks being off."

"If you really want, you can take a job here for a while," Micah teased, punching him in the shoulder gently. "We can't work Tommen more than a certain number of hours per week, but we could work you to death if we wanted."

"Sure, I'll be the kid who sweeps the floor then goes and hides in the corner for a few hours to text my girlfriend and chat on Facebook and whine about how hard my job is."

"Amen to that, but thankfully Tommen isn't that bad," Micaiah said. "I don't know if it was his pa's upbringing or his fear of what you'd do to him if we told you that he was slacking off."

"Probably a little bit of both." Walter nodded.

"So, now that we're done shooting the breeze, I assume there was something that you wanted to talk about. Otherwise, I have a lot of stuff to get done out there, and a lot more stuff to get done in here."

"Yes, there is." Down to business. "I took Tommen skiing yesterday, went down to Snowshoe. You both know he's a good skier, and he also loves the terrain park." They nodded wordlessly. "Well, yesterday he had an accident in the terrain park, and I don't think it was because he misjudged the jump, if you get what I'm saying."

"What exactly happened?" Micah asked.

"Better to show you." Walter pulled out his phone and, after several mishaps with the wifi, finally got his email to show up. "I had the film crew send me the videos of what happened."

He hit play.

The video started out with Tommen approaching the quarterpipe, tucking in and going at the side jump at full speed. Even from the approach, it was obvious that there was a rail on top of the quarterpipe, with the markings on the jump showing exactly where it was, everything fairly standard as far as Walter was concerned.

As soon as Tommen went into a direct approach on the jump, he switched up the Bands. First, he Fast Banded, for no other reason than to make it look like he was going faster than he really was. Then, just as his skis left the jump and he popped into the air, he switched to a Slow Band. To Walter, it was an obvious Band, but that was because he knew that Bands existed, and he knew what to look for even if the Band itself was not visible.

Tommen did a backflip, just getting into the twist that would allow him to land on the rail, when suddenly the Slow Band released and was replaced by a Fast Band. Tommen lost control and smacked hard into the rail, his right arm folding up unnaturally under him, his head clanging against the rail. When he hit the snow, his poles and skis sprung away, and he was completely limp as he flopped and rolled down the hill and came to a stop, a trail of blood following him where his nose had started to bleed.

"Holy shit," Micah said as Walter stopped the video and put his phone away. "Seriously, is he okay?"

"He is," Walter assured him. "He's fine. Or he will be."

"Should he come to work tomorrow?"

"If he makes it through school, I think he can work. He thinks he can work. So I won't stop him. If you think he's a little weird and shouldn't, I'll leave that up to you. Just call me."

"Okay." Micah nodded.

"But the bigger question is, did you see what I saw?"

"You mean the Slow Band being ripped apart and replaced by a Fast Band?" Micaiah wondered. "Yeah, I saw it."

"I just have one question, though," Micah said. "Tommen is good for a probie—or, you know, an Apprentice. He's very good. But he hasn't developed his reflexive Banding. Not that he necessarily should, but how can he be so bad—or maybe 'less skilled' is how I should say it—at standard Banding and yet he can change that fast when going down the ski hill?"

"Because reflexes are not the same as muscle memory," Walter informed him. "If I throw something at you and you hit it away, those are reflexes, designed to protect you. Being able to ride a bike after years or ski a mountain after six months, that's muscle memory. Tommen developed those Banding abilities as muscle memory specifically for the ski hill, Fast Bands to make him look faster, Slow Bands to make him look cooler."

The younger twin nodded. "Makes sense."

"So we're thinking this was Rifun?" Micaiah wondered.

"That's what I'm thinking, in retaliation for snitching and telling us about his hold over Tommen. The question now becomes, was it simply a warning, or was he actually trying to kill him? If it was a warning, we might be able to consider it lesson learned. If he was actually trying to kill him, we can expect him to try again."

"We also have to consider whether this was Rifun himself or one of his cohorts," Micah pointed out. "I believe Tadashi used to be a Timekeeper, so he could have done it even if he was just a Journeyman or a Master. And I don't believe that the friends we saw are Rifun's only friends. If he and Cassius are planning to sweep the elections and essentially launch a coup, they're going to need more than just four friends. And on a ski hill, with the right gear, any humanoid could be passed off."

"That's what I was thinking," Walter mused. "Much as I don't like to admit it."

"So let's say that this was Rifun or on his orders," Micaiah said. "What are we going to do about it? For one, we can't prove it.

Personally, I think that even if it was Rifun, he wasn't the one who did it."

"How do you figure?" Micah asked.

"Rifun likes to make a show of things. He would have let Tommen know, somehow, that he did what he did. He's already gone up against cops, revealed his face, and gotten away. He's not shy. I'd say it was one of his minions."

"Makes sense."

"But again, what are we going to do about it? He's too powerful, and the Hands have already demonstrated that they don't care and they won't act. Ignorance and apathy."

Walter sighed. "I don't know. Suggestions?"

"A lot of it is going to depend on the elections," Micah said. "And just how powerful Rifun and Cassius are going to become."

"All the more reason to hit them now," Micaiah suggested. "If we fail and they lose power, we have the option to try again. If we fail and they win, then what's one more charge on top of everything they're already going to hit us with? And if we win, then we've managed to stop a catastrophe before it starts."

"Which brings us back to, how do we plan to win?" Walter growled. "We've already hit him with dozens of men and some pretty good firepower. Ten people died because of that."

"Then maybe it's not about force, but finesse," Micah offered.

"Micah, the counter on the bomb is ticking down," Micaiah informed him. "We don't have time to play twenty questions and try to finesse our way out of blowing up."

"True, but we already almost blew ourselves up with the red wire, force," Walter said. "At the same time, I don't know how finesse would work, especially since, as you said, the clock is ticking down. We have less than a week before the elections."

"Oh, we haven't forgotten."

Walter sighed and rubbed his face. "You know, it's one thing when you're being threatened. It's another thing when your kid is being threatened. Especially when you can't do anything about it."

"Don't beat yourself up, Walt," Micaiah told him. "That's what we're trying to do, figure out how we can help and put this to an end."

They sat in silence for a minute or two, all brooding. It was Micah who spoke first.

"Maybe we can't force Rifun. Maybe we can't even finesse him. But what if we finesse everything around him?"

"I don't follow," Walter said.

"Right now, Rifun and Cassius have no legitimate power; they're running on false and perceived power. They're holding Tommen hostage under perceived power that they can simply order him to be taken away and it'll happen. What if we took away that power? What if, even if they did win the Zero Hour, they still had no power?"

"You're saying that instead of us four attacking Rifun and Cassius directly, we get everyone else on our side to attack them for us?" Micaiah summarized.

"Something like that, yes. Right now, none of the Hands or Grandfathers will touch them, so it wouldn't matter if we were able to arrest him and bring him under our custody because nothing would happen. Rifun and Cassius aren't afraid of the law. To an extent, they are the law. Maybe we should make them afraid."

"Interesting theory, but you're forgetting a few things. First, Rifun and Cassius have vast influence in power and money. Maybe you forgot, but we kind of went through all our credibility and all our money the first go round. We have nothing to barter that they can't match and raise us on."

"He's right," Walter agreed reluctantly. "It's a fine theory, but we're not dealing with humans; there is no common sense of morality that inherently governs the Wheel and its citizens. The only morality there is greed, and for that we have no currency to bargain with."

"They've been preparing for this a long time," Micaiah sighed. "We probably would have been completely oblivious to the whole thing if not for those women they murdered."

"So we're giving up?" Micah asked incredulously. "I don't

believe this. We're seriously just going to let these two psychopaths threaten us, hurt Tommen, take over the Wheel, and do unspeakable evil, all without at least trying to stop them?"

"Once again," Walter said, "if you have a feasible plan, I'm all ears."

"And in all reality," Micaiah said thoughtfully, "it might not be as bad as we're making it out to be. I mean, yes, Rifun and Cassius are evil psychopaths who need to be drawn and quartered, but right now they're operating in the dark, under shadows and cloaks. Whatever their plan is for the elections and taking over, they're going to have to do it publicly. They will have to show their hand. When they do, then we can really start to plan."

"But would it be better to already have a plan—?" Micah began.

"Agreed." Walter leaned back in his chair and looked at Micaiah. "Until then, our primary concern is ourselves and each other, keeping each other safe and riding this out. Have you two been able to find anything on the person or group who threatened you, hired Lily to kill you? How is she, by the way?"

Micaiah shrugged. "She's still upset I imagine. We haven't seen each other since then, actually. As far as the person or group, we haven't been able to do much looking."

"Not much to go on?"

"Nope. We've tried tracking down the person who contacted Lily and essentially hired her or played the middle man, but when half the people who are out to get you are shrouded anyway, without more to go on, it's like looking for a hay in a haystack. A particular strand of hay."

Walter sighed. "I can understand that."

Micah scoffed. "I still don't like the idea of giving up."

"We're not giving up," Micaiah told him. "We're biding our time and picking our battles. If we run off recklessly and fight everything that moves, half of them will be shadows, the other half will be our friends and allies, and we'll not only have worn ourselves out but we will have provided endless entertainment for our real adversary."

Micah shook his head and said something under his breath, but otherwise remained silent.

After a moment of sullen silence, Walter grabbed his cane and hauled himself to his feet. He was getting better, but he was still stiffening up something fierce whenever he sat for too long.

"So, I guess that's the plan," he said, not wanting to admit that he also felt like they were declaring defeat. "Watch out for yourselves and keep each other safe. And don't forget to do your patriotic duty and vote on Friday."

"Whatever, man," Micaiah told him, shaking his head and grinning. "That's like telling me to vote for our next president when our only options are Hitler and Stalin."

Walter wished them good day and left the office once the Band was dropped. He still didn't like the conclusion they had come to. It really did feel like admitting defeat, cowing under the pressure, bowing their heads and submitting to a tyrannical regime. At the same time, there was no point at yelling your defiance at an incoming tsunami. You might disapprove of it, protest it until Hell froze over, but the tsunami was coming nevertheless. It was smarter to take shelter, ride out the storm, and plan the clean-up instead.

Not that he enjoyed admitting that Rifun and Cassius had that much power either. But then, maybe he'd lived in America a little too long. People thought that if they chanted enough slogans and painted enough signs and inconvenienced enough people that something would happen. Sometimes it did. Sometimes the ruling powers caved, and anarchy ruled, as Rifun and Cassius would demonstrate. Sometimes the ruling powers catered and encouraged the slogans and signs, as Rifun and Cassius would demonstrate. Once the present powers caved and were overthrown, Rifun and Cassius would turn on their own, the very ones who put them in power. They would destroy the world to be kings of the ashes.

The problem then became who was controlling whom. Cassius

was the psychopath who got a kick out of ripping people's throats out, and he was the one who was going to be voted into power. Rifun, though, he really seemed to be the one calling the shots. He was the brains of the operation, the one who worked out plans and schemes, whom to blackmail and how, whom to punish and how, whom to reward and how.

So their only option, then, was to take them both out. Didn't matter who was alpha, they both had to go.

Walter got in his car and sat there a second. Life went on around him. Cars zipped by on the numerous streets criss-crossing through Charleston. Grown children took their aging parents out to breakfast. A young mom pushing a stroller took her elementary-aged daughter to one of the clothing stores in the plaza. None of them had any idea what was about to transpire. They had no idea of the secret war that was going on. They saw only that a kid got hurt in the terrain park. Walter saw an attempt on his kid's life.

Sometimes Walter wondered if it wouldn't be better to simply expose the entire human race to Time and bring them into the larger universe. Once they got past the political and religious scandals, not to mention the swath of suicides that would likely sweep the globe, it couldn't be all bad, right?

Yes, it could. Humans were greedy, selfish bastards, and they'd want to dominate the industry just as much as anyone else. Professional politicians would see the Hands of Time and the Zero Hour as just another Congress and just another president, but with far greater power, just as Rifun and Cassius did now.

More than that, humans were small and weak, and once they were brought into the larger universe as Actively Engaged, they'd be easy pickings for slavers and other ne'er-do-wells. Oh, the occasional abduction happened, but generally, the Accordia Agreement (yes, it was redundant, but it was mild compared to the normal punny names and titles floating around Time) of the Laws of Time was observed, that Unengaged civilizations were to be left alone to fight amongst themselves.

Would Rifun and Cassius seek to change that? Would they abolish the Accordia Agreement and sell Earth to the highest bidder? Or was Earth just the crumbs on the plate of their feast? Would they suffer Earth just so they could have access to the real major players in Time, like Greg, home of the Grunjor, or Brelix, home of the Borelians?

Never had retirement looked so good. Maybe he should throw a curveball at Rifun and drop out of the race for Captain in the District. Ha! Wouldn't that be a surprise. What would happen if he sent in his letter of resignation and just walked away? He was too old for this stuff anyway. The only things he had going for him were his gun and his Time abilities. He was too old to do any real fighting anymore; his strengths came from gadgets and party tricks. And once Tommen left home, then what would he do? Live and go dark, live and go dark, in an endless cycle until the inevitable insanity came upon him like it did all who were cursed with an extended lifespan?

Sighing, he started the car and backed out of his parking space. When he got to the main drive, he paused and considered his destination. Some things he couldn't reason into an answer, and some things had no answers; he wasn't so arrogant as to think every question had an answer or that he could come up with answers to every question that did have one.

He turned right instead of left, then, and pushed into the growing traffic. It was the church crowd traffic, almost as busy and almost as rude as the normal morning commute. But Walter told himself that they were going to church to ask for forgiveness for some of the stupid things they did on the road. That had to be it, right?

Walter was still undecided on the role of religion in Time. On the one hand, he had a firm belief in God; he'd been through too much to say that there wasn't some Guy in the Sky watching over everyone and everything everywhere. On the other hand, did Jesus die just for humans or for literally the entire universe? Were there mirror religions elsewhere? Was it a bit like Judaism where everyone was human but the Jews were special? Were humans like intergalactic Jews, special because they were created in the image of God? Was there some intergalactic Jesus on the way? What were the rules here? Who decided them? And who informed the rest of the universe what they were?

Walter pulled into the church parking lot and waited a minute before getting out. It wasn't one of the mega massive Roman Catholic cathedrals that could be seen from space, but neither was it the wasting away, dilapidated thing with ten members that was doomed to become just a museum or maybe some city office within the next year. He didn't go to church often—a couple times a year—and he doubted they'd remember who he was, but that was okay. Going someplace where he wasn't casually known and where he wouldn't stand out as a police officer was fine with him.

"Good morning," the greeter said with a huge smile. "May God speak to your heart today."

"Thank you," Walter replied, even though he was really thinking, *He could do a little less speaking to my heart and little more speaking to my ears. I need a plan of action, not a Sunday school story.*

But, as anticipated, the worship and sermon had very little to do with aliens, intergalactic wars, tyrannical governments, and invisible assassins. It did have something to do with persecution for doing right. Walter mulled this over for a bit. Was it still persecution if it was political and not religious? Was every "underdog" really persecuted? Did every underdog have a right to overthrow the big dog and become the big dog, come into power? Was every underdog the bearer of a noble cause?

He decided no on all accounts.

So then who decided what was good and evil and had a right to be in power? Why was his and the twins' cause to overthrow Rifun and Cassius just that noble? Why were they working to overthrow him even though they had so far done nothing to infiltrate, overthrow, and rework the current system which was just as corrupt? The only difference was the nameplates on the office doors. Was it because they'd allowed the corruption to spread so far and so deep that they didn't notice it until it finally hit them at home? Like

Micaiah said, they wouldn't have known or probably even cared about any of it until those women were murdered.

Rifun wants you to know. He wants to draw you in. He wants you to see and understand his might and your helplessness. Whatever he's going to do for the elections, it wouldn't be enough to just show you there; he wants you to have that element of psychological torture, too. You're already submitting to him now; just wait until he's king.

The service ended, and the congregation was dismissed, but Walter did not get up right away. After a minute or two, the pastor walked up to him and greeted him with a firm handshake.

"Is there something I can do for you?" he wondered politely.

"Well, maybe you can answer a question," Walter said. "A hypothetical."

"All right." The pastor sat down in the chair in front of him and turned around. "What is this 'hypothetical'?"

"Let's call it a workplace hypothetical. Every department in the business, in the office is corrupt. Like, Soviet Union, Venezuela kind of corrupt. The people in the mail room, your hourlies, they know it, but they are generally unaffected because they are unimportant; the mail just passes through their hands. Follow?"

"I follow."

"In the middle of this corruption, the board is planning a hostile takeover, get rid of the CEO and whatnot, shake up the power structure, so on and so forth. But the VP has his own plan to get rid of the whole board and basically just crown himself king of the company. One day, the VP looks down at his company and realizes that the people in the mail room aren't even going to really notice or care when this coup happens because they're unimportant. So the VP decides to one day come down to the mail room and kill one of the mail people in front of the rest, basically informing them that things are going to change, he's going to be in charge, et cetera, and if they don't play nice or if they try to just leave, they're going to end up just as dead."

"Has someone threatened you?" the pastor asked cautiously.

"To make matters worse, building security is corrupt, saying that they'll be the ones to carry out the deed if ordered, and even the police are reluctant because this VP has the power and influence to take out whoever he pleases. Think mobster, godfather kind of thing."

The pastor let out a breath. "That's quite a, um...hypothetical image you've got going there. Again I ask, has someone threatened you?"

"Only a hypothetical."

"If something is happening or going to happen, I am obligated—morally, if not ethically or legally—to report such a crime."

"Once again, only a hypothetical. Maybe a bit extreme, but still. What can the boys in the mail room do to both get out from under the evil company and see that the company gets its due?"

The pastor nodded. "Hypothetically speaking? Notifying the police would release them of any legal liability to report the crime, though I do believe that would be considered duress." *Not quite, but thanks for playing.* "Otherwise, there isn't a lot that the mail people can do. Action heroes in movies always have a way out, but those adventures are scripted. Our lives are not, at least not in a way that is known to us. In such a situation, I think the best course of action would be to just sit tight and pray. You can't take on the storm by yourself, but you can weather it and let God fight the tide for you."

Walter knew he was going to say that. He wasn't against praying and asking for a little help, but David still had to physically go out onto the battlefield to defeat Goliath. God guided the stone, but David still had to throw it.

Nevertheless, he thanked the pastor, once again assuring him it was only a hypothetical, and stood to leave. As he did, he saw someone kneeling at the altar. He might not have given much thought to it except he knew when he saw a Band, or the wake of one. It was only for a moment, but it was there.

Instantly, Walter threw up a Band around himself and the praying person. The person caught on and turned around to look.

Upon seeing Walter, he tried to run, but a few manipulations in the Band and a few other party tricks and he was rendered immobile.

"I don't recognize you," Walter said. "Walter Forbes, Captain of District Four."

It was a young man, somewhere between eighteen and twenty-one, having the appearance of a couch-surfer from California or some such thing. At Walter's words, he burst into tears.

"Please don't turn me in," he wailed.

"Name, Rank, District."

"Kyle Malargos. I was an Apprentice from District Eight."

Couch-surfer from California.

"You're a Runner," Walter stated.

The young man sniffed hard. "Please, I only Band just to get around town and stuff. I don't hurt anyone. I don't even steal Time and try to use it illegally or anything. I just wanted to get out and see the world a little bit, away from my mentor."

"How long are you in the area?"

"I'll leave right now if you want me to." He nodded vigorously for emphasis.

"Actually...I want you to stay. If it's possible."

"Huh?" Kyle wiped his eyes and nose.

"How long has it been since you've been to the Wheel?"

"Um...my Apprentice promotion, about three years ago."

"Have you had any training?"

"Not really. I mean, I've picked up a few things, but I've never been to the Arena or anything. Why do you want me to stay?"

"First, I want you to stay away from the Wheel. Bad things are happening there in the elections, and I don't want to see anyone hurt. Second, I want you to stay in the area. And if you want me to not turn you in after the elections are over, or just Suppress you right now, I have a little job for you."

Chapter Twenty-Four
Over the Shoulder

Tommen groaned as he rolled over and slapped off his alarm. He was feeling better, he really was, but the thought of having to get up and face another day of school was more than he wanted to think about right now. Was one more day really too much to ask? A snow day? The school mysteriously burning down over the weekend?

"Tommen?" His dad knocked on the door before opening it a little more. "How are you feeling this morning?"

He sighed and answered honestly, "Not very good, but not bad enough to stay home. Not like school is anything particularly exciting or physically strenuous."

"Your arm is pretty obvious, I'd say. Your head, less so."

Grudgingly he sat up and looked at his arm. At least he'd learned not to roll over on it at night. And he could sleep all night again finally. "No, I'll be fine."

"What about your Web Programming class?"

"I mean, I've got the doctor's note and stuff. I'll just have to make it up or do something else."

"All right. Last chance. I don't want you hurting yourself more."

Tommen sighed and considered the offer. Hadn't he literally just been wishing for another day off? Well, he'd do about as much good today as he had yesterday: none whatsoever. He had tried to get away with just a little phone time, but two minutes in and his world was spinning, eyes exploding from a migraine, and he could barely remember his own name. A nap had taken the edge off the worst of the pain, but he hadn't felt right the rest of the day. Truthfully, he was still feeling it.

"I'll be okay," he decided finally and pushed the blankets back.

Actually, he got more sleep now than he might have normally since his dad was taking him—well, chaperoning him, basically—to school instead of having to ride the bus for an extra half hour or so. And there was that whole thing about being able to Band and sleep in even more. But that was out of the question for the time being since he was supposed to be limiting that, too. Of course, he'd had to try it just to see what would happen. It was almost as bad as when he'd first learned to Band, as far as the severity of the headaches and the length of time it took for them to come on—that is, ultra severe, and not long at all.

So he plodded along, getting ready at a snail's pace and having to take his breakfast to go, eating it tiredly on the way to school.

"You look any worse, and I'll turn this car around," his dad warned, looking at him.

"I'm fine," Tommen told him. "I'm never excited for school."

"I've seen you have more enthusiasm for school on days when you have a cold and still go in. If you're not feeling right, it's okay. I'm not going to punish you. I'd rather see you stay home and get better."

"And I'd rather go to school and feel like I've done something with myself today." He paused. "Did I seriously just say that out loud?"

"Why, yes, yes you did."

Well, fuck. Whatever, didn't matter, it was true. And it wasn't that he wanted to go to school, more that he just didn't want to stay home.

"Are you going to be okay to work tonight?" his dad asked.

Fuck. "Yeah, I'll be fine."

"Okay. If you say so, because here we are."

They pulled into the school parking lot. For a Monday, it was pretty busy. Usually Mondays were the days that people claimed as sick days or icy road days or something to excuse them from being late or absent completely.

"If you need to come home, you know how to reach me," his dad told him as he pulled himself out of the car and grabbed his backpack. Instinctively, he reached with the right hand. Then he checked himself and went with the left hand, feeling his ears turn red as he turned and went inside.

Well, he had one good thing to look forward to, anyway. With Tyler Freeman expelled, he didn't have to worry about the taunts and teases that would come from him, as well as the supposed unspoken challenge to break his other arm in mirror fashion. So that little piece of worrying was off his shoulders.

To say nothing of the stares he garnered just walking down the hall. Mostly they were double-takes and stolen glances. Everyone saw, a few whispered, no one actually wanted to comment out loud. More to the point, no one was very eager to sign his cast, either.

His dad had wanted to sign it, but Tommen didn't want that to be the only signature he got, like some cutesy little lunchbox message that Mommy sent with her darling little angel to make sure they had a good day. Once he got a few other signatures on his cast, then he would let his dad sign it. But no sooner.

Oh fuck.

He slammed his locker shut as it hit him. Being unable to use the computer, that meant he was going to have to sit in Righting's class. Like the actual class, in the classroom with the other students and her at the head. Fuck. He should have just taken the day off. He really should have just taken the day off.

Reluctantly, when the bell rang, he gathered his things and went to her class.

"Tommen," she greeted, surprised. "Isn't today your online day? Are you having problems logging in?"

He shook his head and handed her the doctor's note, making a point of using his right arm. At the sight of the cast, she dropped the note and it went fluttering to the floor.

"Oh my goodness, what happened?" she asked, bending to

pick up the note.

"Skiing accident," he told her.

She read over the note and nodded. "Okay. I understand. Well, better safe than sorry, and we don't need you hurting yourself anymore. Go ahead and take your seat."

There were whispers and questions as the other students filed in and noticed his injury, but the most he gave them was that it was a skiing accident.

He dreaded the thought of having to suffer through a week or two weeks of this class; he'd gotten used to only doing a day or two in class and spending the rest of the time doing the online work. It worked for him. How awful this seemed now. It was like all eyes were on him, watching him. The hair on the back of his neck stood up. He told himself that it was silly. Not only was he at the back of the class, but it wasn't that interesting. He was just being paranoid.

Still, it felt like everyone was staring at him as he moved from class to class. It was like they all pointed and whispered and giggled behind his back. What were they saying? He honestly told everyone it was a skiing accident, but that wasn't going to be the only story going around. Fight with Tyler Freeman? His dad abusing him? Some other stupid story?

Second period passed much the same as the first. Mr. Morrison read over the note and nodded, saying he would help him with his investment project the following day.

Tommen's hackles were prickling all that morning as he was sure someone was always watching him, but his stomach didn't really twist until the bell rang and they filed out of second period, heading for third. He was heading for AP Physics. Fuck. What would Becky say about it? Did she know that he'd blown her off? Yeah, he got the work done eventually, but not quite in the manner he'd intended, nor had he apparently done his duty to physically be there to help her, as his dad seemed to think.

He walked into the classroom unmolested and handed Mrs. White the note.

"Are you okay?" she asked. "What happened?"

"Skiing accident," he told her simply.

"What happened?"

He sighed. "I don't remember. Supposedly I hit a jump and crashed into a rail. I don't know."

"Okay. Well, if you need to step out for a minute, go ahead."

Tommen nodded and headed to his seat. Just as he sat down, Becky entered the room. As soon as she looked at him and didn't say anything, he knew he was in for it. She greeted Mrs. White politely and took her seat.

"So what happened?" she asked, looking at his cast.

"Skiing accident." He didn't meet her gaze.

"Was this before or after you were not working at the bakery?"

Tommen felt his whole face and neck turn red, and the rest of his body felt pretty warm, too.

"About halfway through the project on Saturday, I thought, 'Gee, I'm kind of hungry. Maybe I'll head down to the bakery and see Tommen at work. Food service generally sucks, so maybe I can brighten his day. Get there and the place is empty with some banging around in the kitchen. One guy comes out and probably does his standard greeting. I ask if you're working. He tells me no, you have the weekend off. More than that, he heard you were going skiing at some point. Apparently he saw that I was getting mad because he told me you'd be back Monday. I told him not to worry because I was going to see you before then."

Somehow, Tommen was less frightened by her tone and more amused because he knew exactly what Micah's expression would be during the whole latter part of the exchange.

"My dad offered to take me skiing on Saturday," he admitted. "I didn't tell him about the project because I really needed some time to get away and just...destress."

"Yeah? And how's that working out for you?"

She tapped the cast and he jerked his arm out of reach. "It's fine. Nothing major."

"So what happened?"

"Skiing accident. I hit a jump and ended up crashing into a rail."

"Oh, come on, you can tell a better story than that. Or can't you, because you don't remember and therefore have a concussion?"

Tommen rubbed his face with his left hand. "Fine, yes, I got a concussion. So what? At least I got the math for the project done anyway."

Becky smiled mischievously. "Some people call your accident karma. But just in case, I made my own karma."

"What...do you mean?" He was afraid to ask.

"I wasn't done with the project when I went to not visit you at work, so I was a little mad when I got home. I thought, 'Hm, how can I get back at him in a way that isn't mean but will show just how pissed I am?' So I came up with an ingenious plan. Want to hear it?"

"Um...I have a feeling that you're — "

"I sent you the wrong variables."

Tommen felt his blood run cold. "What?"

"Oh, I kept all the results and all the variables and stuff, but I texted you all the wrong numbers. By definition, they are feasible answers, which is why you probably didn't even catch on, but they are not the precise numbers."

Tommen swallowed, feeling more embarrassed than anything. Not to say that he wasn't also a little pissed that she did that to him, wasted his time with bogus results, but he figured he probably deserved it. He sighed. "I assume there's a price to be had if I want to get the real results."

"I'm glad you asked and that you're so willing to negotiate."

"You know, this is as much your grade as mine."

"I only said the math would take me longer," she pointed out. "I didn't say it was impossible. And besides, the grade is divided into the work I did, the work you did, and the project overall. So, theoretically, even if you did nothing, I could still get a 75% while you would only walk away with a 25%. Might as well have not done it at all than waste the time, am I right?"

Oh, she was a spiteful bitch.

"Fine," he conceded. "What's your price?"

"I'll tell you at lunch since class is about to start, and I have a few questions about the project."

Spite. Full. Bitch.

Fuck, but she was so...awesome about it, too. Something about the way she concocted such simple yet such evil little schemes was just...awesome. It was something more than just a cute face but mashed potatoes for brains. She was straightforward and blunt, and she spoke her mind and weaseled information out of people that way she could keep it in her armory to shoot those people in the ass later. She didn't rely on revealing clothes and a cute face to get through life. It was kind of a turn on, actually.

Despite being told not to, he found himself having to Band, at least long enough to make a quick trip to the bathroom. Because apparently it was too much to ask to just be turned on by a girl's intellect and cunning without having to deal with other things, too, even more awkward that he had to use his left hand.

But, fuck, she had him in a bind. He wasn't sure what she was going to ask in return for the proper variables, but his best guess was that it wasn't anything he would part with easily or willingly. He was going to have to weigh his options. First, he could go through with the blackmail, give in to her demands, whatever they were. Second, he could guess at the proper variables; she'd said they were close enough to the real thing. Third, he could really fast rebuild the model at home and do the whole experiment himself just to show her up.

Problems with the first option, first and foremost, he was giving in. It was a loss of pride. There might not be any monetary loss, and probably no one else would know about it, but he would know, and that was all that mattered.

Problems with the second option were obvious. He didn't know exactly which variables were off, and he didn't want to trash more of the math than he needed to in an effort to find out.

Problems with the third option included the model being incorrectly done and too far from her original model that it negated the whole experiment and they both failed the project. He was pissed at her as much as she was pissed at him, but he wasn't going to fail her on a project, especially since all of her grades would be weighted more heavily this late in the semester; he wasn't going to compromise her academic standing because of some petty argument.

And all of this was assuming that she was telling the truth and not just looking to exploit him, extort some money out of him, maybe. There would be little worse than giving in, giving up something he didn't want to give up, only to find out that she'd conned him and he'd done everything correctly in the first place.

Somehow she didn't seem like that type of person. But then, her dad was Jewish.

Now, that isn't fair, is it? Actually it's racist. People bully you all the time because you're different, but that doesn't give you the right to bully someone else. It might not be fair what she's doing or going to do to you, but that doesn't mean that you didn't bring it on yourself in some way. You lied to her and left her out to dry, and this is your just dessert. You made your bed, now sleep in it.

He returned to class and dropped the Band, rubbing his eyes and willing away the headache that was blooming behind his eyes. Maybe he should evade Becky and slip out at lunchtime, just go home.

As if on cue, the bell rang. Tommen gathered his things and headed for his locker. As he walked through the halls, he almost could have sworn that someone was following him. Not as in, just through the halls in the same direction, but literally following him, tracking him. He Banded and looked around, looked at every face, looked at every window and door, looking for anyone unwelcomingly familiar. After a long minute or not spotting anything, he released the Band, almost hitting the floor at the headache that crashed into him.

Lunch. That was all he needed. Some food in his stomach and just make it through two more classes. One class he was probably going to have a do-nothing day and, well, Art was pretty much a do-nothing class as far as he was concerned. Fuck, maybe good ol' Bob Ross was exactly what he needed today.

He grabbed his lunch bag and the second plastic bag. At least he hadn't forgotten the furs that he was going to show Becky. He wasn't opposed to making money. Maybe that would help him a little, too, knowing he wasn't scraping dirt this month. Yeah, because he was just so poor. He wasn't poor; he was cheap.

Becky was already waiting for him at their usual table. Interesting. Their table. They actually sat together. Well, depending on how this deal went, they might not be sitting together for very long, at lunch or in class. Still, he tried not to seem nervous as he approached, plopping the bag of furs on the table half a second before sitting down with his lunch bag.

"Oh, are those the furs?" Becky wondered, putting down her fork.

"Yeah, but I'm not going to take them out until after the food is cleared," Tommen told her. "If you don't want them, I can still get a good price for them, but only if they're clean."

"Hey, I totally understand. And all things depending, you might be taking them elsewhere for a good price."

"What do you mean?"

"Well, that's part of my deal."

He didn't like where this was going. "Okay, I'll bite. What's the deal?"

"In exchange for the proper variables, you give me the furs. No charge."

Tommen almost choked on his sandwich. "Are you insane?! Do you know how much—No." He shook his head. "Nope. Not going to happen."

Becky raised a brow. "So...having fifty bucks today is more important than a successful academic career which will land you a better job in the future and a good ten, twenty, thirty grand more per year in your adult life?"

Oh, if only you knew what my adult life is going to be like. "One failed project is not going to kill me."

"Oh, I'm sure it won't, at least where your overall grades and GPA are concerned. But, if I recall correctly, all teachers are required to report when a student adamantly refuses to participate in or complete a project, test, something of graded significance in class. That'll go on your permanent record, so everyone will know that Tommen doesn't do the projects he doesn't like with people he doesn't like, not when skiing is at stake."

Tommen held his arm up. *"Dw i'n anafus, cariad, cyn medra'i cana y cerdyn 'na am ychydig diwrnod. Mae Bns. Gwyn ddim gofal os o'n i'n gweithio o's o'n i'n sgio. Es i sgio ar ddydd Sadwrn. O'n i'n gynllunio gweithio ar y prosiect yn dydd Sul. O heno, cwedy o'n ychydig cwestiynau hateb."* (I'm injured, sweetheart, so I can play that card for a few days. Mrs. White doesn't care if I was working working or if I went skiing. I went skiing on Saturday. I was planning on working on the project on Sunday. Or tonight, after I got a few questions answered.)

Becky glared at him. *"Nem te vagy az egyetlen, aki sértheti valaki tudta nélkül. De a válaszom van. Jó tárgyaini veled."* (You're not the only one who can insult people without their knowledge. But I understand. Nice negotiating with you.)

"Paid ag sarhau fi heb fy ngwybodaeth am o," Tommen told her. (Don't insult me without me knowing about it.)

"Good negotiating with you," Becky finished. Tommen expected her to stand up and move away to a different table to gossip, but she stayed where she was and finished her food.

"Sy ni da drafod?" (Are we done negotiating?)

"You can stop now, okay, we both had our measuring contest; we can both insult each other without the other knowing what we're saying."

"Dw i...Dw i'n feddylia..." (I am...I mean...)

Tommen leaned back in his seat. Becky gave him a hard regard. "Are you okay?"

He looked at her. *"Dw i ddim yn gwybod."* (I don't know.) He stood. *"Dw i'n meddwl bo' fi angen mynd i'r swyddfa."* (I think I need to go to the office.)

Actually he just went to his locker. His dad had sent him with a bottle of Ibuprofen, per the doctor's instructions. Technically, he was supposed to go to the office because if someone caught him, he could be taken to the office, suspended, even arrested for distribution of drugs on school property. But what the Powers That Be didn't know wouldn't hurt them. Besides, it was fucking Ibuprofen. It wasn't even Norco or some shit; he didn't swipe his dad's pills to try to make a quick buck. He needed this for his migraine, for his concussion.

He rested his forehead on his locker. Fuck, he had a headache. He was ready to go to the office and ask for help, call his dad, call an ambulance, do something, when he felt the pain relax.

"Hey."

He jumped and looked to see Becky staring at him. She handed him his lunch bag—still half full—and the bag of furs. He took them. *"Diolch.* Thanks."

"You okay?"

He nodded. "I will be. Concussions aren't the easy recovery the movies make them out to be."

"Well, it isn't exactly the charming, romantic road they seem to think dwarfism is, either."

"So, do dwarves—"

"Dwarfs," she cut in. "I don't live in Middle-Earth, and I don't work in the mines of Moria."

"Um, okay, whatever, do you drive?"

"No. I can't even ride in the front seat because of the air bag."

"How did you get to the bakery, then?"

Becky shrugged like the answer should be obvious. "I had my mom drive me."

"Oh. Makes sense."

"Seriously, though. Are you okay? Should I get you to the office or something? You're kind of weirding me out."

"Clearly you haven't known me long enough, then. I'm always

weird. That's why you'll notice that the lunch table is otherwise empty."

"Oh, don't worry about that. I can fix that. I tend to bring out the freaks in people. Pretty soon, we'll be the Island of Misfit Highschoolers."

Tommen was fairly certain she meant it to be encouraging. Actually it sounded like the name of some demented insane asylum that was the center stage of some freak show circus act or horror movie or play. It did not sound like anyplace he wanted to be, say it that way.

"Listen," Becky said calmly, "I'm sorry you got hurt, especially in the head. I really am. But I'm not going to back down on my offer."

"How do I know that you aren't just trying to get me to give you free furs and that the variables you gave me and the ones you claim to have aren't the same?" Tommen asked.

"You don't. And you won't until you give me an answer."

Spite. Full. Bitch.

"Businesswoman to the last."

Becky gave him the same mischievous grin she'd given him earlier. "Well, my dad is Jewish. He taught me a thing or two."

The bell rang then, and Becky wished him well before heading for her locker.

Tommen wanted to Band so he could finish his lunch before heading to class, but he didn't want to risk anymore than he already had. As it was, he'd almost turned himself back into the idiot he'd been with Ski Patrol, understanding everything fine but seeming to lose his grasp on all other aspects of language, that is, speaking English, which he normally did very well.

As he swapped out lunch bag for textbook and notebook and everything else, he got that feeling again that someone was watching him. Actually, he'd had that feeling the whole time he was talking to Becky, like some Peeping Tom was secretly taking photos of him, him and her, the whole deal.

Eventually there came a point when paranoia turned into true gut instinct, when you knew something was wrong and ignoring it or constantly dismissing it as paranoia was not only not going to make it go away, but was probably going to make it worse. That was probably the point when Tommen decided that his paranoia about being followed wasn't just his ego or his paranoia, but a true gut reaction to some imminent danger.

The best thing, he decided, was to carry on as normal. Or at least act like it. Carrying on and acting normal was different than ignoring the problem. Carrying on was making the problem think he was ignoring it while secretly trying to come up with a plan to deal with the problem. Second problem, though, was that he wasn't entirely sure what the problem was.

Well, he had a pretty good guess. Rifun was following him. Probably waiting for him, waiting to pounce. Tommen found himself smiling ruefully. Rifun and Voldemort, he and Harry Potter. Overall, Voldemort had to be admired. He really cared about Harry's education; he never attacked him until the end of the year. Similarly, it seemed as though Rifun wouldn't attack him until the end of the day. How quaint.

Stop. You're being an idiot again. You have to stay on your toes, think rationally, and not give in to the concussion.

Tommen might have shaken his head to clear it, but was too afraid of what that motion might do. So he settled for a small sigh as he entered his fourth period and handed the doctor's note to Mrs. Floyd. As usual, she asked what happened, and he gave her the same bland answer he gave everyone else.

"Well, this kind of makes this class totally moot for you, doesn't it?" she said once she'd signed the paper and handed it back to him. "At least for a few days. The good news, though, is that you are caught up and have done a little work ahead, so you won't miss too much."

"Is there some kind of alternate assignment I can do or can I get other class work from my locker?" he asked.

"I don't have any alternate assignments I can give for this unit.

And as much as I know that all the books are outdated and most of you are far beyond what we're doing, I don't want to jump you ahead just yet. Go ahead and get some other class work if you have it."

Tommen did so, acutely aware that he felt more watched than a goldfish. At any moment, he expected to turn his head and see Rifun standing there, whether by himself or with his goons, or even taking pictures, just there, present in some fashion. But it never happened. Tommen reached his locker, grabbed out some English assignment or another, and returned to fourth period where Mrs. Floyd was just handing out the day's assignment.

"Find something?" she asked.

Tommen nodded and sat down to start working.

The class dragged by as his pencil was scratching away to the tune of a couple dozen keyboards clicking away. There was an occasional page turn, some whispering, and, every so often, a chair sliding across the carpet.

He sighed inwardly. After all the excitement he'd been through in the last month, he should be grateful for some mediocrity. Even if that mediocrity was punctuated with occasional death threats to his friends, attempts on his life at the terrain park, and being stalked by an insane serial killer who fancied himself Tommen's mentor in some freakish occult.

Art had never looked more exciting and enticing.

"Can I get something from my locker?" Tommen asked suddenly.

"Sure," Mrs. Floyd said, writing him up a hall pass.

He wasn't actually going to his locker, though he passed it on the way. Actually he headed for the main lobby where the gym and the cafeteria met, where all the sports trophies were displayed in huge glass cases, dating back to whenever the fuck they started caring that much to display them. Past all of these gross displays of athleticism, however, was a spot for all the other school clubs. Most of the tables were empty now; signups only occurred at the beginning of each semester. With one exception: the school play.

He couldn't say exactly what made him sign up. Maybe it was boredom, that he was tired of the mundane reality that was his life. Maybe it was stress, the need to escape from the roaring, death-defying excitement that was his life.

Or maybe it has something to do with that girl that you seem to have a love-hate relationship with right now?

Oh, fuck off.

And go where? Who are you talking to? Your conscience? Yourself?

I don't care. Fuck off.

I thought we made a promise not to do anymore fucking.

That was different; that was embarrassing in the middle of class.

So rather than Band and make it go away, you Banded and satisfied it.

Who the fuck are you, anyway? My pa? What do you care?

I don't know. What do you? You made the promise even though, as you said, you have no moral grounds to tell yourself to do or not do.

But I'm better than that.

Apparently not, if AP Physics was any indication. And the other night in bed when you tried to get on your phone. The concussion saved you there.

Tommen rubbed his face vigorously. Fuck, he hated mental conversations with himself. Fucking conscience.

He headed back to class, stopping by his locker to grab something from Economics to make it look like he'd done what he said he wanted to do. Not that it mattered since he no sooner got started on it than the bell rang anyway.

"I don't think this matters as much in this class, but here," Tommen said, walking into the art room and handing Robinson the doctor's note to sign.

He looked at Tommen, looked at his arm, looked at the note, looked at Tommen again. "What happened?"

"Skiing accident."

"Too bad." He took a pen and signed the paper. "Well, I guess I'll have to show you all today's technique instead of letting Bob do the talking for me. That's okay, though, I think we can manage. And if you need to step out for a few minutes, that's fine; I know the lighting in here can be pretty harsh."

At least he was honest. The lighting in the art room was very harsh; it was known to give even the strongest willed people headaches. Supposedly it was set to be replaced by LED fixtures soon. Supposedly it had been on the list of things to do for almost five years now.

There were several times when Tommen considered stepping out of the room for a few minutes, but he never did. His paranoia sense had gone from tingling to full red alert. And, honestly, it made him afraid. He didn't want to go anywhere alone. Not in the sense that Daddy had to hold his hand, but he wanted there to be people around him, witnesses in case he suddenly dropped dead. He knew, even without seeing him, that Rifun was watching him. It was like being out in the middle of a field in the middle of a huge windstorm. Couldn't see the wind, but no one was going to dispute that it was there.

Of course, being in a crowd, like the one that filled the school when the final bell rang, wasn't particularly advantageous either. Too many people and no one would notice if he suddenly dropped dead. It was just a fact of life. Or death. Whichever. And Rifun could just as easily slip in and out and no one would be the wiser.

It was not a comforting thought, but Tommen got on the bus with no incident.

He should tell the twins when he got to work.

Tell them what, that you think Rifun is following you? Everyone already knows that. You already told them about the deal and how Rifun is trying to control you. What revelation is there is telling them that he's following you? And what do you expect them to do, anyway? He hasn't said anything to you, hasn't made any threats or moves to harm you. Heck, he went up against two dozen police officers and won. Okay, there is nothing you can do anyway.

Still, there wasn't any harm in telling them anyway, right?

Rifun already knew he'd snitched on their little "deal" so it wasn't like telling them that, ooh, Rifun was following him, was any skin off his back, any wrench in his plans, whatever they were.

He got off the bus, still a little dizzy, still debating. So he did something stupid; he did a stupid mental coin toss. Well, mental eeny-meeny-miney-mo. If the store was busy when he walked in, he wouldn't tell them. Chances were, he'd forget anyway. If the store wasn't busy, he'd tell them. Assuming he didn't forget between the back door and the office door.

"Hey, Tommen!" Micah greeted as he walked in the door. "How are you this mor...today?"

Tommen shrugged. "Been better."

"Well, obviously. Hey, let me and Cai sign your cast."

"Okay, hang on. While you're doing that, I...guess I have something to report."

Micah nodded seriously. "All right. Step into our office."

Micaiah was on the phone when Micah opened the door. The elder twin whirled in his chair, looking ready with a sharp word, but whatever the person said on the other end of the line was enough to distract him.

"Uh-huh. Right. Right. I understand that. Well, that's not your problem, is it? Uh-huh. Sure. Yeah, Thursday is fine. Nine a.m.? Yup. Talk to you then."

"*Cé bhí sin?*" Micah asked. (Who was that?)

"*Éigin gamal cé táim ag iarraidh a fhógairt le. Ní sé ag téigh go maith,*" Micaiah stated obviously. (Some asshole I've been trying to do some advertising with. It's not going well.)

"*Is léir go.*" (Clearly.)

"So, what can I do for you, Tommen? How are you feeling? That's a nice looking cast you've got there."

"I told him we should sign it," Micah said before Tommen could speak. "He also says he has something to report."

"I think," Tommen clarified.

"You think?" Micaiah leaned back to grab a couple markers.

"Okay, what do you think you have to report?"

"I think Rifun's been following me today. Like, around school and stuff. I mean, I haven't actually seen him, but I just have had this gut instinct all day that if I just turn around fast enough, I'll be able to catch him before he Bands and gets away."

"Who's Becky?" Micah asked as he signed.

"What?"

Tommen twisted his arm and looked. Sure enough, Becky had, somehow someway at sometime managed to sign his cast. "Becky" with a smiley face.

"Doesn't matter," he grumbled. "Anyway, I didn't actually see him, but—"

"In this matter, I'd trust your instincts," Micaiah said, scooting over in his chair to sign the cast also. "You'll never be able to move fast enough to catch Rifun like that, but your intuition will react as swiftly as it needs to in order to warn you. Has he sent any signs, made any threats?"

"Nothing out of the ordinary that I saw."

"Rifun isn't subtle," Micah stated. "So if you didn't see anything, there probably wasn't anything to see."

"Why would he be following me, though? Usually when he follows me, he's trying to hurt me or hurt someone I know."

"He could be trying to judge your reaction to the accident on the ski hill," Micaiah told him. "If he wasn't trying to kill you there, he was certainly trying to send a message. Did you get it? Are you fearful enough? Do you cede power to him? That sort of thing."

"And if he judges that I'm not afraid enough?"

Micah sighed. "We don't know. We're still trying to figure out our own problems, the person or people who are after us. We suspect it could be Rifun, but we don't know. There's just too much uncertainty with the elections coming up. We're kind of hoping that once the elections are over, everyone will show their hand, at least enough to give us a good lead on them."

Micaiah finished signing. "Keep your eyes and ears open,

Tommen. It's good that you reported this to us. Keep it up. Really, it's good. Now then, why don't you take counter tonight and let Micah handle the kitchen."

Not that it was any different from any other night he worked. He was on counter probably eighty percent of the time. He knew why: he didn't have the same abilities that the twins did, to keep up to twenty different Bands going at the same time, knowing which was which and what went where and which oven went off and everything else. So he managed the counter, catering to the people as they came in, demanding one thing or another.

His paranoia still prickled all that night, but it wasn't screaming at him like it had been at school, and he made it through work relatively uneventfully. Mostly because it had been pretty dead.

That left him plenty of time to consider his Physics situation. He could buy himself all the time in the world, theoretically, but he just didn't have that Banding ability at the moment, and he didn't want to bring his dad in to help, or anyone else for that matter. So he could just suck it up, Band, do the project and suffer the consequences and potentially end up back in the hospital. Or...

"I can't use my phone because of the screen," Tommen said, walking back to the kitchen. "Can I use the phone here?"

"Sure," Micah told him.

"I just need you to read me a number."

Thankfully, Tommen hadn't actually entered Becky as one of his contacts, so Micah was just reading a plain old phone number. Fewer questions that way.

The call went to voicemail, but at the end of the automatic message, Becky included her home phone number, which Tommen wrote down and dialed.

"Polski residence," Dr. Polski answered.

Fuck fuck fuck fuck fuck... "Is Becky there?"

"She is, may I ask who's calling?"

"Um, this is Tommen." He swallowed hard. "We're working on a Physics project together at school, and I need to ask her something."

"Ah." The way he said it told Tommen that Becky had told him all the details of their little fiasco. "Just a moment."

Tommen danced on the balls of his feet for a few seconds before Becky came on the line. "I knew you'd call sooner or later."

Spite. Full. Bitch.

"So, have you thought about my offer?" she wondered.

He sighed. "Yes. But I'm not going to take that offer. I propose a counteroffer."

"I'm listening."

"If you want the furs for free, you do the math but give me the credit. If you want me to do the math, you give me the variables and you get the furs at half-price."

There was a moment of silence and Tommen was afraid she'd reject both proposals. Finally she said, "All right. I'll agree to half-price. You got a pen and paper handy or are you okay to text?"

Chapter Twenty-Five
Treading Water

Any other day, Walter was at work, lamenting how much stuff he could be getting done at home. Rather than responding to yet another noisy neighbor complaint from Mrs. Wilson, which always turned out to be nothing, he could be home ripping down old wallpaper. Instead of dealing with Mr. Yale's little Jack Russell and another trip to Animal Control, he could be ripping up old carpet. And who could forget the thrill of chasing down "the little heathens"—also known as the neighbor's cats—that always terrorized Mrs. Ericson's flower garden—even though it was actually rabbits who had the sense to run away when the cats didn't. Because that was always more fun than watching a new coat of paint dry.

He'd made a promise not to bother the twins at the bakery any more than he absolutely had to, instead spending his time at various hardware and home improvement stores. But now that he actually had the time and was regaining the strength to do so, Walter found himself at a stalemate on the remodel. He knew what he wanted, but ultimately he was faced with the same thing most humans feared: change.

The living room carpet was ugly and probably twenty shades more brown than the day it was installed. It probably had all manner of dust mites and flea carcasses and all sorts of gross things stained into the fibers. But that was the carpet that had been there when he moved in; it was the carpet he knew. He wasn't sure how well he could handle new carpet, and God help him if some salesman talked him into something like hardwood or laminate flooring. He'd have a heart attack.

The living room wallpaper with all its faded metallic paisley power probably would have been considered hideous even at the peak of paisley. And yet, it gave the walls character, a sort of faded look while still providing depth, something that a solid coat of paint really couldn't do. Not to mention the work it would take just to get all the old wallpaper torn down. It was one thing to have a few little pieces left over when putting up new wallpaper, but paint was flat and any pieces left on the wall would be noticed. And that meant using some toxic chemicals to remove all those stubborn little pieces. Or he could go through all the effort of tearing down one wallpaper and then the hassle of putting up new wallpaper. He wasn't sure he was ready for that yet, and the last thing he wanted to do was leave bare walls that were uglier than papered walls. And all of this wasn't even including the time and muscle it would take to move the furniture around, assuming he didn't just get rid of the furniture and replace it completely.

It was pretty much the same story throughout the house, the projects he wanted to get done and the excuses he came up with to not do them. Once during the week, in a fit of frustration at himself and a surge of productivity, the need to just do something and quit making excuses, he had actually gone out and gotten paint, enough to do his bedroom. It was only a beige color, but he figured it was better than the pink-ish...kind of orange-y stuff that was on the walls now. He couldn't really tell.

Then he realized that he was kind of stuck with the project now that he'd started it. Yet another one. But painting wasn't hard. It had been the easiest thing about redoing Tommen's room. He just needed some painter's plastic, a few trays, some rollers. He could do it. He could probably even do it while Tommen was at school, surprise him when he got home.

The nice thing about his room was that even though the carpet was as old as the living room carpet, it had weathered much better. It had probably been a brilliant shag white at one point, but the sort of dull off-white sort of gray wasn't all that bad, he figured. At any rate, it wasn't as high on the list as anything in the living room. Or the walls and floor of the bathroom. Either of which he still hadn't figured out. He and Tommen had gotten the vanity and the toilet in over the weekend. Problem was, the contrasting styles were almost uglier than the single ugly style it had been, and only exacerbated the need to finish the whole bathroom remodel.

Walter sighed as he sat down and made a list of things he needed, things he wanted, how he wanted to do them. It looked like a disorganized set of scribbles—and, admittedly, it was a disorganized set of scribbles—but he understood it—or pretended to—and it helped him get his thoughts together and on anything but the elections.

It was Thursday. The elections were in less than twenty-four Earth-side hours. So even though the two events were entirely unrelated, he was using that timeline as a motivation to get things done. He had less than twenty-four hours to go to the hardware store, get the supplies he needed, and get home to paint his bedroom. And if he had a little extra time, he might pick out a color for the bathroom walls and kill two birds with one stone.

His list settled, he grabbed his cane and stood. He was on the verge of not needing it at all, but there was still one thing glaring at him, and that was the pain pills. If not for them, he probably wouldn't even need the cane, but he knew that as long as his body still inflicted pain on itself, he would still obey the urge to take a pill.

It was addiction, plain and simple. He tried to keep it to a minimum, tried to count his pills and plan it out so that by the time he ran out, he wouldn't need them anymore, but it was hard. It was as if there was a second consciousness in his brain, reading his thoughts, knowing that he was trying to cut off the supply, and fighting all the harder to keep it.

With that thought in mind, Walter intentionally ignored the spasming in his leg and chest and headed out to the car. The weather had been pretty hit and miss all week, whether it was just cloudy or cloudy with a good dump of snow. Today was starting out just cloudy, but it certainly had the potential to turn real quick, especially the way those bigger, darker clouds were coming in. Best to get his supplies now and do the work inside where it was warm while it snowed outside.

He did a quick calculation. Assuming he was allowed back the Monday after his official eight weeks was up, that meant that he would be going back to work about the middle to last part of February. He ran his tongue over his teeth. Maybe he could weasel out just a couple more weeks, at least until the first week of March. No driving in the snow and slush and whatever weather Mother Nature decided to churn out, no trudging through knee-deep snow on search and rescue, no need to dig four feet to find evidence around a crime scene. Sure, they still got plenty of snow in March, but January and February were just miserable months, the heart of winter when all seemed hopeless; March was when hope and light started coming back as the snow started going away.

It sounded like a terrible thing, as if he hated his job. He didn't. Actually, he quite enjoyed his job. Not that he enjoyed dead bodies or anything, but it was the mystery, the puzzle. Most cases went unsolved, true, or they ended up being more gruesome than anyone dared imagine, but those few cases where everything came together, everything made sense, and justice was done, those were what made his job worth it.

And then there were those cases that were secretly directed at you and your friends as warnings to watch your backs or end up like the dead women and subsequently the dead cops. Those were fun, too.

He pulled into the hardware store parking lot and got out just as a chill wind blasted him in the face. Yes, there was definitely a system moving in, and this one was going to dump a hefty amount of snow, he could tell. Damn. He was becoming one of those people who could use their joints to predict the weather. He needed to move to a tropical island or something if that was the case. Maybe the next time he went dark, he'd resurface in the Virgin Islands, or maybe Tahiti. Fiji sounded pretty nice, too.   Except then he had to contend with hurricanes and typhoons.

"Good morning, sir, can I help you find something?" the cashier inquired as he walked in, the bell over the door tinkling almost inaudibly.

"Paint things. Rollers, plastic sheets, that sort of thing," Walter told her.

"That'll be aisle ten. Do you need an associate to mix you up a gallon or two?"

"No, no, already got that, thank you. I'm just not one for fingerpainting."

"Okay, well just let someone know if you need help."

It was probably the most friendly anyone have ever been to him in this store. Not to say that they were normally unfriendly, but on any ordinary day, he got the ordinary treatment. Sometimes he got special (skeptical) treatment if he walked in wearing his blues. Today, though, everyone was very friendly and helpful. *Must be the cane,* he decided. *They've come to the conclusion that I'm old and infirm and need extra assistance.*

He found the supplies he needed, momentarily overwhelmed by all the different options there were. Two-inch rollers, six-inch rollers, plastic pans, metal pans, a vast array of paintbrushes. He just wanted to paint his wall; why did this feel more like trying to get fitted for SWAT gear?

His phone rang and he dug it out, not looking at the number before answering, "Forbes."

"Durvin," Micaiah replied sarcastically.

"You know, I'm trying to stay away from you guys for a few days, give you a break from my presence. Do you really miss me that much?"

"That's okay, because you might be going on a road trip, Captain."

"Why is that?"

"We got a deader."

"Shit. Why are you the one telling me, though? What's going on?"

"Because it's not in our area. Actually it's in Massachusetts."

"Do you guys even leave your office?"

"Believe me, we'll be here."

Walter hung up and stared at the hooks and shelves of painting supplies. He glanced outside. It was getting mighty windy out there.

Why wasn't he rushing outside and driving like a maniac to get to the bakery and find out what was going on? Maybe...because it wasn't in his legal police jurisdiction so he would have no power over that investigation. Maybe...because he wasn't even sure of his Captain status in the District, so he wasn't entirely sure how his investigation would go over, especially since he could lose all Captain powers in the next forty-eight hours. Still, why not rush into the action?

He pondered this as he picked up the things he needed. Maybe this forced retirement was exactly what he needed. It game him some perspective. That, and the situation which had brought about his retirement. Family was important. Tommen was important. Work was important, too, true, but maybe he should make it less of a driving force in his life. Something he did rather than something he was.

"Perfect day for it," the cashier commented as she rung him up. "It's supposed to get pretty snowy and windy today. Stay inside where it's warm."

"I have every intention. You stay safe yourself if it gets bad when you go home," Walter told her.

He reflected on his words as he paid, gathered his things, and headed outside. He honestly sounded like a kindly old grandfather imparting wisdom to a cute young cashier.

He needed to get out of this retirement bullshit, and fast.

He made good time to the bakery where an unusual midmorning rush put a delay on their meeting. Actually, he could have just Banded, gone in, and they could have had their meeting in the middle of the midmorning rush. But Walter elected to sit in his car and wait until it was all over, or mostly over. He wasn't going to wait until the dining room was completely devoid of people, just until the last person in line had been served.

As he sat and waited, Walter noted how his leg had stopped spasming, but now the chest and back muscles around the bullet wounds were starting to throb and spasm. Had they been itches, it wouldn't have been like a little tickle of hair; this would have been like an army of mosquitoes from Hell coupled with the worst case of allergic dermatitis ever witnessed. Had he been the type of man who couldn't control himself and maintain composure under strain, stress, or pain, he might have been curled up in a fetal position, grabbing at his chest, making onlookers think he was having a heart attack.

He focused on the line inside, the last two people at the register. When it was down to one person, he got out of the car and started walking toward the door. When he got inside, the last person in line took his goodies and left, nodding amiably to Walter as he held the door.

Even before he reached the counter, he was swept up in a Band with the twins and all but hurried into the office.

"All right," Walter said, sitting down. "Talk to me."

"At about four o'clock this morning, Ron Patrick was found dead in his backyard," Micaiah reported. "He has to be to work at the wonderful hour of three a.m. He's a good worker, reliable, so when he didn't show up, someone went snooping. And by someone, I mean his mentor, Amy Rowlings. He's an Apprentice Timekeeper, she's a Master. She snapped a couple pictures before calling the cops, and she sent them to me."

Micaiah dug out his phone and tapped away until he got to the aforementioned pictures. They were decent pictures, but Walter could tell they were taken with the intention of being kept secret, probably trying not to alert the neighbors with bright flash or obvious camera set-up and poses for specific angles and whatnot.

"She's been keeping me updated, but the cops are pretty tight-lipped since she's not any kind of family or relative, just considered a close friend."

"What does she know?" Walter wondered, still looking through the pictures.

"From what they could tell on scene, he was strangled first, shot second."

"Well, he's no bodybuilder, but he's no lightweight either. In order to be effective at strangling him, the attacker would not only have to get the jump on him, but be physically strong enough to hold him in position. Or..." He let out a breath. "Get creative with Bands."

"As an Apprentice, very nearly a Journeyman, the only way anyone could get that kind of jump on him would be with Time," Micah stated. "I'm sorry, but if some idiot petty criminal tries anything on me, damn the rules about not being seen; I'm defending myself first. They can spend ten to fifteen in a mental asylum."

"What else did she say?"

"Nothing immensely helpful. It looked like he'd been on his way out the door to his car in the alley. No weapons were found, no shell-casings."

"No shells means the guy is either meticulous or using a revolver."

"Rifun uses a revolver," Micah pointed out.

"What caliber, does she know? I wouldn't think so." Walter handed Micaiah back his phone.

Micaiah shook his head as he took it. "Didn't say." He leaned back and sighed. "Ron was one of the people Lily was supposed to kill, along with me and Micah."

Walter frowned. "More to the point, she was supposed to kill you before the elections, which are tomorrow."

"Which means we could be looking at a killing spree today," Micaiah finished.

"Get me the names and phone numbers of everyone else on that list."

"Already on it."

"Were you able to find any kind of connection between the

people on that list? I mean, why you and them? What makes you guys special?"

Micaiah looked at him briefly. "I don't know. I mean, I've met Ron and Amy. Jake Orrin was the other Timekeeper on the list; I've met him, too. The others I've heard of, maybe seen briefly, but that's about it." He started scribbling on a piece of notebook paper and tore it out to hand to Walter. "Here you go, names and numbers. I looked them up when this all first started."

"Have they been warned?" Walter asked.

"They were warned the first go round, which is why Amy knew to contact me—aside from being Lieutenant. But I don't know that any of them have heard about this."

"Well, they need to. Here, write down Amy's number, too."

Once all the names and numbers were taken down, they headed out of the office to resume their charade. Micaiah dropped the Band and they went through a small routine of Walter getting his pastry and heading back out to the car. He dialed the first number, a Harvester named Greg Fields.

"Hello?" came a husky male voice.

"Greg Fields?"

"Last I checked."

"Walter Forbes, Timekeeper Captain, District Four."

There was a pause. Then, "Greg Fields, Master Harvester, District Four. I assume you're calling in regards to whomever has threatened my life?"

"Sort of. I'm calling in regards to the man who is now dead at the hands of whoever has threatened your life."

"Yes, your Lieutenant said there were several people on this list, though the connection I don't see."

"We're still working on it, but the threat was to kill everyone on the list before the elections. You might know that tomorrow is Election Day."

"So we're looking at a killing spree, is that it?"

"It's certainly possible, yes."

"Huh. Well, today shall be interesting to say the least. Thank you for the warning, Captain. Good day."

Oh, for goodness' sake, were all Harvesters jerks?

He held a similar conversation with everyone else on the list, saving Amy for last.

"Hello?" a female voice choked. She sounded like she'd been crying for a while.

"Walter Forbes, Captain, District Four."

"Oh, yes, good. Micaiah said you'd call. This isn't related to the killings that you had, is it? I read something about the Charleston killings online."

"We don't know. But it is related to a different threat. Ron was on a kill list of some unknown person. Micaiah, Micah, and several others are also on it."

"But why? If it's about the elections, Ron couldn't even vote yet."

"We don't know. Micaiah showed me the pictures you sent, and I'm not entirely convinced that it's related to the Charleston killings either."

"Because his throat wasn't ripped out."

"Right. But in order for us to get anywhere, I need to know everything you know."

Unfortunately, she knew very little. Until recently, Cassius and Rifun were little more than Timekeeper bedtime stories to scare kids into behaving; she had no idea the extent of their treachery and Walter was reluctant to tell her about it. But every question he asked and every detail she gave indicated a person or group other than those two. Finally he decided he'd put her through enough stress and wished her a calm day.

"Sometimes, walking away seems like a pretty nice option," Amy lamented.

"I know the feeling," Walter agreed reluctantly.

He hung up and was ready for go back inside when he decided to call Lily. She'd been threatened as well, that if she didn't carry out the murders, she would be lying there right alongside the rest of them. Best to keep her in the loop since she and Micaiah didn't seem to be sharing information anymore, genetic or otherwise.

Her phone rang and rang and rang and finally went to voicemail.

"Lily, it's Walt. Call me or the twins, have them fill you in."

After another minute or two, he went inside the bakery. A few people still ate leisurely at a booth or a table.

"Well?" Micah asked.

"Little and less, nothing of real interest except to say that I don't think this was Rifun and Cassius. It's all wrong for them."

"Wonderful. So we might be shadowboxing after all."

"Something else. I tried to call Lily, since she'd been threatened as well if she didn't carry it out, but I couldn't reach her."

Micah shrugged. "So? She has a day job."

"I know, which is why I'm not panicking yet. I'm going to head to the hospital and let her know what we know, just to keep her in the loop. I'll call you if there's anything unusual."

"Suit yourself."

Walter regarded him for a moment. "I guess I won't be calling on you to deliver a eulogy if something does happen."

"Do I want her to die? No. I'm not that cruel. But I would appreciate it if she could make up her damn mind whether she's a kind and considerate person or a cutthroat bitch. Tell me you don't feel the same way."

"Sometimes," Walter admitted. "But in my experience, such people have underlying issues."

Micah shrugged again. "Can't help someone who doesn't want to be helped. At the very least, I'm glad I have my brother back."

"So there you go."

"All right, be safe out there, Walt. I don't want to have to save your ass every time something happens."

Walter shook his head and returned to his car, trying to ignore the pain in his leg and chest. He did share Micah's sentiments about

Lily, but he wasn't going to blatantly agree with him like a couple guys around the water cooler gossiping. Right now, they had bigger problems than one person who could be a pain sometimes; they were dealing with a person or group of people who were set to begin a murderous rampage.

He tried calling her cell phone again, and again it went to voicemail. He tried her office phone but also got nowhere. That was more worrying. As he started the car and backed out of his parking spot, he tried to tell himself that she just wasn't in the office at that moment. She was on lunch break. She was in the bathroom. She was on the floor assisting in the care of a critical patient. She was on the floor Harvesting a patient because there was just no chance to save them. Any number of reasons why she wouldn't pick up her phone. The murder was making him slightly hysterical, and right now, he had to think clearly.

His mind slipped into police mode even as he told himself he couldn't drive as though he was in police mode. He was taking information he had, more or less, illegally obtained, and acting on it based on information he'd obtained through otherworldly sources. That would not be easy to explain to Steggmann, so he had to play it cool in more ways than one. Overall, as far as any ordinary person knew, he was also just an ordinary person paying a visit to his friend at work. The term "friend" could be interpreted many different ways, and he used it loosely, but no one who didn't know her didn't need to know anything was amiss.

When not in his blues, Walter figured it would be a little more difficult to just waltz into a children's hospital. The access wasn't necessarily restricted, but the whole place was very protective of the little hearts and minds housed within. Those who knew him wouldn't have a problem. Those who didn't might find it strange that he was there with no apparent relative to visit. So it was time to recreate the scene in the hardware store and play the kindly old man who imparted sagely advice to cute young cashiers.

It was impossible to gauge how effective his ploy was as he

leaned just a little more into his cane and really turned up the old man charm, smiling and greeting people along the way to the elevator. By the time he punched in the number and the doors closed, his leg was screaming. He told himself to ignore it, but it was like Julius Caesar trying to ignore the onslaught of knives being driven into his body repeatedly.

The elevator stopped at the NICU floor, and the doors opened. Immediately it was like leaving a shopping mall at the lobby and stepping into a sterile lab environment—which, essentially, it was—where everything had to be mask, gloves, gown, decon, the works. The halls looked fairly standard for a hospital, and a couple people roamed around, most of them appearing to be wary, nervous parents. A nurse left a room, as dressed up as Walter expected.

He dropped the kindly grandpa routine as he headed for Lily's office. He turned the corner and saw her inside, looking over some paperwork. She did not see him. Curious, Walter backed up back around the corner and retreated to a small waiting area that was currently empty. He called her office phone again. She didn't answer but in the quiet of the floor, he could hear it ringing on her desk.

Maybe he would need to keep up the kindly grandpa routine. He Banded quickly and looked around. A nurse worked in one unit. A father watched through the windows of another unit. In a third unit, a mother and older child looked on over the crib of another neonate. Otherwise, everything looked clear.

Walter pretended to look at a map for a second before turning and heading back toward Lily's office. He got there, knocked on the door, and let himself in, quite rudely but, he suspected, necessarily.

"Can I help you?" Lily asked politely, looking up. Her expression was one of faked interest straining to cover up sheer terror. "Please, make it as fast as you can, I have a meeting to go to."

Taking the hint, Walter threw up the fastest, tightest Band he could manage. Where Tommen's best Band was like putting on a straightjacket, this was like being vacuum-sealed, shrink-wrapped, and then wrapped in fine wire followed by a layer of tight gold leaf.

"Thank God, I never thought you'd come," Lily hissed.

"What's wrong?"

"To put it mildly, I'm being held hostage."

"Start at the beginning."

"Well, you already know that I was hired to kill Cai and Micah and if I didn't, I'd end up dead."

"That's why I came. One of the people on the list turned up dead this morning. We were thinking that whoever is behind it is planning a killing spree today."

"Yeah, that's pretty obvious, isn't it? I was supposed to volunteer for a late shift, or so says my captor."

"Who is it?"

"He's pretending to be a dad here. In the interest of not getting anyone else killed, I haven't told any of the other nurses."

"The room is bugged," Walter stated.

She nodded. "And the phones, which is why I wasn't able to pick up."

"Lily, do you know anything about this group? Are they in league with Rifun and Cassius?"

Lily leaned back in her chair. "See, that's something I've been trying to figure out. The group doing the killing today is not the same one that approached me."

"What? That makes no sense."

"That's what I said. The group today is part of Rifun's gang of cronies."

"How do you figure?"

"Because when the guy initially confronted me, I asked if he was the one who'd been under the shroud and why they were holding me here instead of in the Wheel like the first time we spoke. The guy was like a deer in headlights. I probably could have run right then, but I was scared. He tried to play it off, but I could see that I'd caught him in something he had no knowledge about and that he'd be reporting it later. After laying out the framework for my captivity, he thanked me for being most helpful in tracking down a particularly malicious band of Runners, and that for my own safety I had to stay in my office, or at least on the floor, while their group cleaned up the mess." She scoffed and shook her head. "I'm not an idiot."

"Wait, wait, wait, so Group A approaches you and tells you to kill this list of people including Micah and Micaiah. Group B is also tracking this list of people and somehow Group A's contacting you gives them the information they need to go out and kill them which they hired you to do anyway?"

"But without the money," Lily pointed out. "Group A wanted them dead and then they'd pay me. Group B wants them dead and me with them."

Walter folded his arms and mulled it over. "I wonder..."

"Wonder what?"

"What if Group A telling you that you'd be dead if you didn't kill them wasn't a threat, but a warning? What if they were trying to protect you?"

"Who'd want to protect me? I mean, they could have bribed literally anyone with that sort of money to buy the votes they wanted; they wouldn't need specifically me."

"What if they did?"

"But who?"

"I don't know. Your captor didn't happen to give any names or details, did he? About this other group that initially approached you?"

Lily shook her head. "No. Honestly, I didn't ask. Like I said, he was caught completely by surprise, but I could tell that he'd report it to whatever person is over him in the group pecking order."

"Has he harmed you in any way?"

"No. He's only come back once to 'bring me my lunch as a small gesture of gratitude for my help and all the work I've done for him and his family.' " She shuddered. "I almost threw up." She rolled her eyes. "Otherwise, he keeps tabs on me from his phone for the bugs in the room, and he'll make regular passes, about every ten to fifteen minutes."

"Do you know what he is in Time?"

"Nope. I don't see Bands, and I haven't seen him Harvest or anything. Your guess is as good as mine."

"Well, as powerful as Rifun and Cassius are, we should assume that whatever he is—and the rest of the group for that matter—that they have some decent ability."

"I wouldn't go that far."

"What do you mean?"

Lily shifted in her chair. "I don't know how much you remember about the warehouse, but you might remember that Rifun basically declared me dead. Obviously, I wasn't. I used a trick that the Harvesters kind of stole from Timekeepers and modified it. I took all my years and stored them deep inside myself in a kind of pre-Time Capsule. Then I pushed a disease to the surface so that when Isthim went to Harvest me, she'd find brain cancer or some shit. Anyway, not worth Harvesting."

"I don't follow. I mean, I get the trick, but I don't see what that has to do with—"

"It's a dirty trick, Walter. But it's also a very common one. It's a method of self-defense that most Journeyman Harvesters will learn to some degree. So either Isthim was just one of those rare Journeyman who never learned it, or she's not that powerful of a Harvester."

Walter searched his memory. "Ron was only an Apprentice Timekeeper, so it's feasible that a Journeyman Timekeeper might be able to restrain him long enough to kill him. The others on the list were all Masters or above, though."

"What are you suggesting?" Lily wondered.

"I think we've stepped into the middle of a turf war."

"Like, gang kind of turf war?"

"Yes, but Time style. Group A wants their list of people dead. They know how powerful they are, that they can't do it on their own, so they hire you to seduce the twins and do what you have to with the rest. Group B wants those same people dead, but doesn't understand how powerful they are."

"Or maybe they do," Lily suggested. "Maybe Ron was an exception. Maybe Rifun's trying to clean house of his own guys before the elections."

"A common gang initiation ritual is murder," Walter stated. "If Rifun wanted to get rid of those with questionable loyalty, one way to do it would be to put them to the test of loyalty, knowing they won't be able to pass."

"That's great and all, but we're still sitting here with the first group of people who hired me in the first place who still want those people on the list dead."

"I've already contacted the others on the list, and everyone's on high alert."

"Okay...And now they need to know that there could be a second group going on a killing spree."

"Maybe, but right now my concern is the enemy I know, and he's the one who's close to hand. Come on. You're going to show me which one of these things is not like the other."

Lily stood from her desk and followed Walter out of the office. They were still in a Band, and everything around them still appeared frozen.

A few nurses worked in one unit while nervous parents looked on. There was the mother and older child, watching the tiny baby in another unit. The elevator doors were just opening but too narrow to see who was inside. They made another turn and Lily stopped.

"That's him," she said.

It was the man who had appeared to be a single father, observing some newborn who was, in reality, a total stranger to him. His gaze was pleasant, but had no love in it. Concerned, but more in the way that one worries about what to cook for dinner, rather than about the infant fighting for life amid the tubes and wires.

"Did he give you a name?" Walter wondered.

"No."

"So he's not dumb. Not completely anyway." Without looking

at her, he told Lily, "Go back to your office. For the time being, continue to be a good little captive until myself or one of the twins comes to get you."

"He's all yours," Lily told him, taking a few steps back before turning and walking away. Walter gave her a couple minutes to get back to her office before releasing her from the Band. Then he moved forward toward the man and brought him into it.

The man sucked in a breath and assumed the posture of a teenager who has just tried his first cigarette. He wants to cough, but doesn't dare for fear of looking like a wimp in front of his friends. So the man sucked in a few breaths, cleared his throat, tried not to cough, and then sighed.

"So," he said, not looking at Walter. "She managed to get a word out. I wondered how long it would take her."

"Actually, she didn't get a word out," Walter told him. "Call it clever deduction."

"At any rate, you know who I am and why I'm here."

"You're here to kill Lily."

"That's just one small part of it."

"Here's what I don't understand, though. Your hit list includes Micah and Micaiah, but not me. Did Rifun give up after his last attempt failed?"

The man chuckled. "You? You were an amusement, a side show, a little experiment Rifun carried out in order to test your son, who, by the way, might have also been on the list today except Rifun seems to have taken him on as a pet project."

Walter folded his arms. "Does this particular hit list have anything to do with the elections?"

"Mm...yes and no. It wasn't, originally, until Lily mentioned that another group was involved. Once we figured out who they were, well, call it more of an opportunity than a plan."

"What are you talking about? Who is the other group?"

The man grinned. "Maybe you ought to ask your trusted Lieutenants. After all, why would they keep secrets from you?"

"I don't play games with murderers. I ask questions, and I get answers."

"Why, because you're a cop?" He shook his head. "I've dealt with you on both ends of the universal spectrum. Timekeepers, police, doesn't matter. And as far as you're concerned, I'm just here spreading good cheer to the poor patients of the NICU. I haven't actually done anything."

"You're holding Lily hostage."

"Be hard to prove it. And I haven't committed any other crimes."

Walter took a breath. "See, that's one of the advantages of being a Timekeeper. I don't need to meet that burden of proof for the Grandfathers like I do before the district attorney. All I have to do is haul you in. Even if they release you, it won't be before the elections."

"Maybe, but is that really how you want to waste your time today? When there is so much else you could be doing?"

"It'll only take a minute."

"And my, how they tick by."

"All right. I'll bite. What are you talking about?"

The man smiled now, like a man who's just reeled in the big one. "Rifun is eliminating his enemies. Some of them, anyway. You know who's on the list. As I said earlier, your son would be on the list, too, if Rifun hadn't made him his pet. Or his bitch, whichever you prefer. Problem is, not everyone got the memo. See, after the fight at the warehouse, one of his guys dissented, and he's got a real bone to pick with Tommen."

Walter felt his stomach turn but he refused to give anything away to this man.

"What better way for Tadashi to win back his master's favor by killing two enemies with one stone? Or by holding one hostage—again—and forcing the vote of the other?"

Walter dropped the Band. Life returned to normal as nurses and doctors worked in their units with parents looking on. He brought out his phone and dialed the twins.

"What you got for me, Walter?" Micaiah asked.

"Go to the high school and check on Tommen for me," Walter ordered, keeping his voice level. "Keep an eye out for Tadashi or any of Rifun's minions."

"On my way."

"I'll join you in a few minutes. I have to take out the garbage first."

Chapter Twenty-Six
We Meet Again

Good job on your projects," Mrs. White said, handing back the graded papers. "I think you are all more than ready for the chapter test tomorrow, but we're going to use today as a review."

"Nice work on that math," Becky said, elbowing Tommen in the ribs. "You'll have to show me how you do that sometime."

"Shut up," he told her, still feeling disgusted by how she'd managed to con him. It wasn't even disgust at her or anything, just disgust in general, directed more at himself and the situation overall.

Still, she grinned. " 'Vengeance is mine' says the Lord, right?"

"Hell hath no fury like a woman's scorn is more like it."

"I choose to take that as a compliment."

"Suit yourself."

"I do, usually."

Fuck, he hated how her sharp wit was so aggravating and yet so sexy at the same time. She wasn't one to giggle, except when it was a maniacal little laugh that said she was scheming something. She wasn't one to do cutesy little movements and hip swaying and hair flipping and whatnot, except to knock you off balance, swipe something right out of your hands, and flip her hair when she knew she was right and wanted to emphasize it. She was a spiteful, conniving little bitch and Tommen loved her for that. Well, not *love*-love, but it was fun and interesting and sexy. Except for the times she used it on him, but even then...

Lunch had become a group affair as Becky made friends in other classes and invited them to sit with her. Most of them made a point of sitting with her and not with him, but it was kind of nice to have group conversation again, instead of just staring forlornly at his sandwich.

"I noticed you signed up for the play," Becky observed as she and Tommen walked to lunch together. "What made you change your mind?"

"I don't know," he lied. "Guess I just wanted to do something other than school and work."

"Obviously, since skiing is out of the question."

"Only for a couple months. I'll be able to get some more runs in at the end of the season."

"I've only been skiing a couple times."

"You can ski? Like, you're allowed?"

"Yeah. Actually, it's encouraged since the boots are so tight. I mean, it's not a replacement for these clunkers, but they're okay for an hour or two. Not that it matters since I'm terrible anyway."

"Maybe you just need some instruction."

"And you can instruct me?" She gave him a look.

Tommen felt his cheeks grow red, and she laughed. They entered the cafeteria and made for their usual table.

"So, who's got plans for this weekend?" Becky asked as she took her seat.

While the others at the table erupted in conversation, Tommen stayed silent. He didn't really have plans other than working—for real this time—and probably helping his dad with more remodeling. So far, it was limited to easy fixes like paint, small fixtures, switchplates and so on, and there wasn't anything major happening, like new floors, new shower, anything like that. Tommen wondered how high his dad's cabin fever was going to get before that sort of stuff started happening.

At any rate, that probably wouldn't be happening this weekend, not with the Time elections coming up in less than twenty-four hours. His dad and the twins had been careful not to get him too involved since he couldn't vote anyway, and they wanted to keep him out of the line of fire if something did happen, but he could see the stress and strain on their faces. Since his dad was off, he visited the twins during the day, meaning Tommen wasn't exactly privy to their conversations or their immediate reactions. He saw them hours after whatever news had come across had sunk in.

Tommen asked for details, but tried to do so casually, trying not to seem super interested, even though he was, hoping that a relaxed question more than a demanding one would elicit more answers. Really, he was interested inasmuch as his fate was as much tied to Rifun coming to power as any of the normal Time and Wheel operations. Rifun seemed pretty confident that Cassius would be made Zero Hour and he could have some seat of power, too, thus having absolute authority over everyone and everything, including Tommen. What would happen if somehow they weren't voted into power? What if none of his dreams of grandeur came to pass?

Somehow, entertaining that thought felt like a lie, wishful thinking for an idiotic optimist who couldn't see right where they were heading.

So it seemed strange, then, to even call them elections. If the results were already predetermined, did that just make them motions? Just going through the motions? What if no one voted? What would happen to the rigged results then? Would the system somehow collapse? Would things stay the same? Would it make any difference at all?

Tommen rubbed his face. Questions that were far above his pay grade. Greater men than he were probably asking themselves those same questions and coming up with no good answers.

"What are you doing this weekend, Tommen?" Becky wondered, taking a bite of her food.

"Huh? Oh, working."

"Really?"

"Yeah, I really am this time. Working Sunday. Other than that, probably just helping my dad remodel the house. Well, it's just easy stuff right now like paint and fixtures. Nothing big yet."

"Oh my gosh," Amber interupted at the end of the table, "so

we were looking at old pictures in our family's photo album and we looked at pictures of my old room when I was a kid..."

Tommen tuned her out as best he could. The hearing aids forced sound into his ears, and he was still having to re-learn how to filter out what was necessary and unnecessary. It was a strange thing, to have to re-learn something that he, everyone learned from a very young age, before they were even consciously aware of such an ability. He tried to tell himself it wasn't any different than having earphones in and listening to music; sometimes he zoned out and couldn't "hear" the music.

"Okay, so I have to ask," Ollie said, pointing first at Becky, then at Tommen. "Are you two going out? Seriously, like, are you?"

"No," they both answered, looking at each other.

"Really? Because you sit together at lunch, you walk together in the halls, you talk at each other's lockers before class. And Tommen, who is probably the most cynical of everyone here, just spontaneously signed up for the school play. It seems like there's something going on here."

Extortion, Tommen thought, but figured it best not to say it out loud.

"No," Becky repeated. "We're not going out. Just friends."

"Oh, okay, just friends," Ollie said, exaggerating a nod. Then he laughed and shook his head. "They're dating."

Becky tried to refute it, but Tommen knew there was no point. If they were asking, it was because the rumor had already made its way around the school and that was what people were saying. They were dating because obviously it was impossible for a boy and a girl to be just friends without one of them being homosexual which they both denied.

Never mind that Tommen happened to like this female friend really, really a lot and found her very interesting.

The bell rang, signaling the end of lunch. Tommen threw away his garbage and headed for his locker, grabbing his Web Programming textbook as well as a few other items from other classes.

Over the last couple days, he'd been okay to look at a screen for a few minutes, long enough that he could send a quick text message or watch the weather on the evening news or something without being slammed with a sudden, debilitating migraine and being reduced to mumbling gibberish in Welsh. He'd also been okay to Band for a few seconds at a time, long enough to occasionally look over his shoulder whenever his paranoia prickled. It hadn't been too bad the last day or two, but he'd never lost the feeling that he was being watched.

Tommen was able to get a little work done in Web Programming, looking at the screen long enough first to get logged in, then to bring up the program, then to write a few lines of code, then a few more and a few more. He wasn't nearly as productive as he might normally be, but it was better than falling behind and certainly better than just sitting doing work from other classes. He still wasn't able to go back to his online English class until at least next Monday.

Art passed without incident, except for the part where Robinson sorrowfully announced that Friday was going to be the last Bob Ross day as they moved on to another unit. Tommen honestly thought the man was going to cry, as in, break down bawling like a baby in front of the class. As much as dear Bob had grown on Tommen—his soothing voice and, really, relatively simple techniques—he was ready to move on and do something, anything else.

Before the last bell rang, the PA buzzed and someone—probably some Student Council member—came over the speakers.

"Attention everyone who signed up for the school play. The first meeting will be Monday after school in the auditorium. This is for everyone who signed up or is still interested in joining, no matter your part. Thank you."

She'd barely gotten off the PA when the bell rang. Tommen bolted out the door with everyone else into the bustling, crowded hallways. People pushed and shoved, called to their friends, slammed locker doors, raced to the parking lot or the bus line. Briefly, Tommen had a vague, stupid expectation that he would find Eric and Varad waiting for him at his locker. As expected, they weren't there. Even Becky wasn't there.

At least having an art class in the mix meant that was one less class to lug homework around in his backpack. Having Web Programming was an added bonus, since most all the book work was so outdated that they skipped over it almost entirely—the homework portions of it anyway. So he really had just three classes to worry about, and Physics could be counted as two classes sometimes.

He slammed his locker door shut and rejoined the throng of students flowing out into the outside world, toward the bus line. Layman was there at the doors, wishing everyone a good day. He and Tommen locked eyes for a moment. For a second, Tommen was sure that Layman was going to call him aside for some lecture. Instead, the man simply nodded and wished him a good day as well. Tommen did not reply, just shifted his pack and walked out the door.

As soon as he got outside, the noise stopped. The movement stopped. It was as if he'd suddenly walked into a painting or, more accurately, a 3D landscape. All around him, students were frozen in the act of walking, running, tripping and falling with papers flying out of backpacks, talking, kissing, texting. Everything, all of life, just stopped. Except him. And, if his suspicions were correct, one other person.

"Okay, Rifun," he said aloud. "Where are you?"

"Rifun isn't here," a familiar voice said. "But don't worry, you'll see him again soon. Maybe."

Amid the forest of still life, it took but a moment for Tommen to pinpoint the source of the voice. Tadashi came strolling up the sidewalk, kicking up some of the new fallen snow not yet shoveled away. He appeared completely at ease just in jeans and a light spring jacket, hands shoved in his pockets. He didn't even wear a hat or scarf.

"What are you doing here?" Tommen asked cautiously.

Tadashi did not answer right away, not until he'd gotten within thirty feet of Tommen. "Isn't it obvious? I've come to see you."

"Send a postcard next time. Or an email." Tommen gave him a hard regard. "I thought you said you gave up Banding?"

"And you believed me? The same way you believed that story I told you about a wife and daughter and faking my own death? I thought I taught you better than that; I thought we had a real connection going and you might begin to listen to me. In the world — no, in the universe we live in, the truth doesn't matter. It's all about the story we tell. No one alive today is going to remember your story fifty years from now, when they've grown old and you haven't. Your dear daddy might have already told you about the concept of going dark and resurfacing. It's all about stories, building a carefully-crafted lie so that no one goes digging."

"So then what story do you tell people who do live in our universe, who do understand what we go through?"

Tadashi smiled. "Whatever I want."

Tommen sighed. "Why are you here? I have to go to work."

Again, Tadashi approached him, completely at ease. "You see, Rifun promised a lot of things in the beginning when I started working for him. Power, money, all that fun stuff. As you can no doubt remember, there was nothing particularly empowering about being cooped up in that cave. During the fight at the warehouse, well, your dad's guys are certainly worth their salt and they managed to capture me. Obviously, I could have escaped, but I figured that I was done with Rifun and his shtick. I'd use the cops as my getaway and then, well, get away.

"That didn't go so well. Isthim caught up to me later and sprung me. She called me all sorts of names, including a dead man because apparently Rifun was not pleased with how things turned out. Between you and me, it was all his fault anyway." By now he was right in front of Tommen as if they were having a casual conversation.

"Is this going somewhere?" Tommen interrupted, hoping his childish arrogance could mask the sound of his heart thudding against his chest.

Tadashi paused for just a second, like a storyteller being

interrupted right before the good part, or a comedian interrupted right before the punchline. "Isthim took me before Rifun, where he'd gone to lick his wounds. He'd been chewed out by Cassius and, as they say, shit rolls downhill. He called me a bunch of names, too. However, because he felt that he should bear the brunt of the responsibility for things going the way they did, he was going to let me go free and not kill me outright. Just as long as he never saw me again and blah, blah, blah, you can guess whatever other threats he made."

"So you're not working for Rifun, is that it?"

"I haven't decided, actually. See, a good portion of my time with Rifun was spent hunting you down—well, you and your dad. Therefore, essentially, you took part of my life away from me—"

Tommen took a step back and put his hands up. "Hey, don't go blaming this on me."

"And that's why I'm having trouble deciding whether or not I'm working for Rifun. On the one hand, I could blame you, fight you, kill you, and I would have my revenge on you, your dad, and Rifun. Unfortunately, that would put me in a pretty bad spot with Rifun and Cassius, and with them poised to take control of Time tomorrow, well, things don't look good for me.

"On the other hand, I could still blame you, fight you, subdue you, and turn you over to Rifun. Think of it as kind of a make-up present. Make-up sex if you want. I turn you over to him, grovel a little bit, take the blame for everything, swear my fealty and the fealty of the others I run with, blah, blah, blah, you get the gist, and I get my job back, but with a few more perks."

"I don't see how that would work," Tommen admitted cautiously. "For you, that is. I mean, it's not like Rifun doesn't know where I am. Pft, I'm at school, not exactly hiding. And he's more powerful than you; he wouldn't really have to break a sweat to capture me, never mind have to fight me. It's kind of like taking a book to someone as a peace offering, except it's a book off that person's bookshelf. It's like, so what? The person knew where it was and could go get it at any time. I just...I'm not sure how this...I don't know."

Tadashi blinked, stunned as if he'd never considered any of that before. Tommen guessed he'd been hiding somewhere other than Earth or the Wheel, conjuring up his plan in some dark cave.

Tommen shrugged apologetically. "Sorry, man. I feel for you, but like I said, I have to get to work."

He politely moved past Tadashi and continued on his way, feeling the Band that Tadashi had him in. It was strong, that much was for sure, but a stone shield held lightly can be easily knocked away. Tommen did knock it away, and life went back to normal. Sound momentarily overwhelmed him as people resumed walking, running, tripping and falling with papers flying out of backpacks, talking, kissing, texting, and everything else. He did not look back.

In a way, he really did feel sorry for Tadashi. Poor guy had probably been duped the same way most impressionable people are, with promises of the things they think they desire. Power, money, fame, freedom. Half the time, a good salesman didn't sell have to sell a product, but ideas and dreams. That was why most SUV commercials were set in the mountains or desert. Ninety percent of the people who bought the SUV wouldn't go mountain climbing or desert-trekking. They weren't sold on the product; they were sold on the idea of rugged freedom and survival. Most car commercials were set up for speed, despite the fact that ninety percent of people were still going to be stuck in the same traffic jams they always were.

And then there was the romantic idea of the power and money and freedom that came from rigging an election, murdering the competition, and intimidating the voters. The idea of power and revolution and *viva la resistance* was so tempting, it was easy to forget that the means that catapulted you into that power would probably be the same means used to depose you as well. Tadashi was willing to fight and kill in order to gain favor with Rifun and get in power, never considering that someone might fight and kill him in order to keep him out of power.

It was all very sad, really. Of course, Tommen had no wish to harm Tadashi, but he would defend himself if he had to, just like he would have at the warehouse. Had he been more able to defend himself. But that was another matter.

He continued down the line of buses until he found his bus. He didn't recognize the driver. Substitute, then. Great. That meant that he was going to have to explain to him where he got off and how to pull in, making sure that they hit the right driveway and—

Tommen was alerted to the presence of mischief only in the half-second it took him to realize that all sound had vanished again. He turned his head and just caught the gleam of an eye as Tadashi crashed into him, full kilter.

Tommen was almost launched into the air, but as it was, he was knocked back several feet, falling hard onto the sidewalk with Tadashi on top of him. Tommen recovered first and managed to wiggle out from under the slender man and roll away a couple feet. He could feel Tadashi playing with Bands, trying to manipulate one that would immobilize him in such a way that he would be able to see Tadashi and still hold a conversation but have virtually no control over his body.

Time and Bands were only slightly fucked up.

But as long as Tommen could feel the Bands and stay ahead of them and get out of them before they could take hold, he could keep moving.

The only true experience he had with Time-fighting was his fight with the Bat, which had ended very poorly, and the Bat hadn't even been Banding. Tommen had no experience whatsoever in true Time-to-Time combat, how to use Bands for entrapment or to escape them or any of the numerous little tricks that he was sure would help him if he knew what they were. He was only just an Apprentice; he only knew the bare bones Banding 101 version of how to protect his own Bands, something he was sure Tadashi could break through in an instant.

But then, how many instants made up a moment? And how many moments made up just enough time? Well, okay, so it sounded better in his head. But clever thinking was useless until he turned it into clever action.

In truth, Band fighting was not the stuff of kung fu Jackie Chan legend. It was more like a glaring contest, but with mind powers that affected the fabric of reality. So aside from the initial tackle, there was decidedly very little physical danger involved here. And just like the last fight with Tyler Freeman, the best thing to do was establish a pattern and then suddenly deviate from it.

Tommen began to feel out Tadashi's Bands, letting them touch him just enough that he could see and understand their strengths, their forms. He let them strengthen as much as he dared before peeling them away and dissolving them. Judging from Tadashi's expression, the man thought he was winning, wearing him out, ready to go in for the kill. Then just as Tommen felt Tadashi's strongest Band yet, the one meant to hold him down and bind him up, he threw all of his energy into breaking through it.

As he broke through the Band mentally, he also launched himself at Tadashi, taking him by surprise much the same way he had just a second ago, and driving him to the ground. Within Tadashi's Band, he also threw up another Band of his own making, his own Fast Band that allowed him to get in several good blows before they both hit the ground. The impact broke Tommen's concentration, and he lost the Band, but he was in decidedly better control of himself in the tackle and managed to keep Tadashi on the ground.

"You're right," Tadashi laughed. "Rifun knows where you are, and me bringing you to him will make no difference. So why diminish myself by groveling at his feet? Let the Cult and the Akarin fight their petty battles. I'll kill you myself for my own revenge and satisfaction. If Rifun wants you, he can come and get you himself. Won't that be ironic?"

Great, so they'd gone from Tadashi merely capturing Tommen and turning him over to a captor he already knew the consequences of, to simply killing him outright. Fuck. Too bad that Time didn't seem to allow for travel or else he'd probably go back and take the first option.

In his moment of distraction, Tadashi took the opportunity to grab a fistful of nasty, brown, slushy snow and throw it at him. It exploded across his face but the brunt of the impact hit his hearing aid, sending a boom pulsing through his skull. He reflexively cried out, and as he did, Tadashi heaved himself up in a motion that Tommen was almost sure should have been impossible for a man his size. Nevertheless, Tommen was again dumped into the snow on his back.

This time, Tadashi's Band came down like an iron vice. Tommen could feel his body, but there was a separation of the nerves across Time, where his signals to struggle against the restraints would not reach the rest of his body until the Band was let up.

Tadashi stood over him, one hand bloody, the same as the collar of his jacket. He'd apparently sustained some sort of head injury when they hit the pavement, but it did not appear to slow him down any. He brandished a knife.

"That's...that's a nice knife," Tommen said, his voice breaking. "I've got one kind of like it at home. I, uh, I use it for...for uh..."

"For gutting the animals that you legally and illegally trap?" Tadashi finished. "Huh. What a coincidence. That's what I use this one for, too."

Tommen wasn't sure if Tadashi meant to cut his throat first or gut him alive. Then again, it probably didn't matter; dead was dead. He closed his eyes and waited for the plunge.

It never came. Instead, there was a grunt of impact, the sound of something hitting the ground, and a cry of pain. Two cries, actually. Tommen felt the Band release. His body involuntarily twitched for a second or two as disconnected signals suddenly came together, but when he managed to roll over, he found a very different scene from the one he was expecting.

There was another Timekeeper. He was probably five-foot-ten, one-sixty, twenty-five years old at a maximum. He was white and blond, but sported some major dreadlocks and a failed attempt at a sixties soul patch. "SoCal surfer dude" was the first thing that came to mind at the sight of him, and Tommen could easily imagine he was more comfortable in board shorts than the jeans and jacket he wore.

He was bleeding from his arm where Tadashi's knife had gone through, but Tadashi was also bleeding from one side just below the ribcage. They were facing off like a couple of angry dogs.

"This isn't your fight!" Tadashi snapped.

"It is because his dad says it is," the new guy informed him.

"Fine. He's nothing but a glorified probie. I'll take you down first."

The man had gone completely insane, Tommen realized. Time abilities or not, two against one, while not impossible, was not working in Tadashi's favor. And, really, Tommen didn't think the fight was all that worth it. Tadashi was no longer fighting for revenge; he was fighting because he wanted blood.

Not that Tommen enjoyed being called a glorified probie. Hell, he'd spent almost twice as much time as a probie as most normal people. He'd picked up a few things, thank you.

So while he wasn't sure about SoCal being on "his side" per se, he certainly wasn't going to attack the guy who'd just saved him from certain death. Instead, he turned his attention toward Tadashi. Using SoCal's Bands, he was able to feel where he penetrated Tadashi's Bands, and then lend his own strength to breaking them apart. It wasn't much, more like a ten year old "helping" a couple of much stronger men to lift a tree or something, but something was better than nothing he figured.

Tadashi refused to give up, throwing out every trick he knew. Tommen wasn't sure about SoCal, but he knew that he himself wasn't feeling too great as the war of will went on. He'd been doing well so far this week, but his head still wasn't fully recovered. It started around his ear, where the majority of his concussion was reported to be and where the snow had hit him. It began as a low-level ache, and then a pulsing, like his heart was in his brain. Soon the pain went from a deep throb to a knife stabbing through his head over and over again, a constant tide of aching and sharp pain.

Reluctantly, he dropped his Band. Whatever mental strength he had suddenly abandoned him so that even a first-day brand new probationary Timekeeper could have overpowered him. As it was, he felt his knees turn to jelly, and he could barely stand. With a gentle sigh, he dropped to his knees. And still the pain...he couldn't tell if it was just the headache or if Tadashi was actually stabbing him in the head right now.

He opened his eyes, his only saving grace being that it was a cloudy day and not a blinding sunny day. He saw Tadashi's expression, one of bloodthirsty glee as a predator realizes that his prey has given up. He probably would have pounced on him and ripped him open if not for SoCal's continued efforts at restraining him while simultaneously defending Tommen.

Tommen closed his eyes again and took a breath, telling himself that it wasn't that bad. He couldn't give up now, not when he was so close. Close to what, he didn't know. But he'd be another second closer to death if he didn't get up and try to help SoCal some more. He had to get up, had to try.

It was nothing for Tadashi to put him back on his knees even as he tried to stand.

"How do you like that, huh?" Tadashi taunted. "Maybe I ought to break your other arm before I kill you."

Well, how was that for irony? Tommen thought dumbly. After all, it wasn't as if Tadashi had anything better to do, like win an election that's already rigged. It made sense, then, he supposed, that Tadashi would have been the one to try and kill him in the terrain park. Well, it seemed pretty obvious now, whether it had been a warning or a true attempt on his life.

Tommen did not try to stand again, but he did try to muster up some strength to help SoCal who almost looked like he was starting to struggle. The element of surprise was gone, and his bag of tricks was much smaller than Tadashi's. Tommen gave it all he had, but it was like the woman who gave only two bits. Sure, the heart might be in the right place, but it still wouldn't buy anything, and soon Tommen had given all he had.

He sat on his heels. When he closed his eyes, there was the stabbing pain and a low-frequency pulse ringing in his brain. When he opened his eyes, it was as though there were a couple more knives looking to skewer his eyeballs, to say nothing of the dark spots that danced and moved every time he blinked.

As he closed his eyes, he felt a wave of vertigo wash over him, and he felt himself falling to one side. Or at least, he thought he was falling to one side. It might have been all in his head. Most things were, after all.

Suddenly he felt warm splatters on his face. Then the sound of the gunshot reached him. Even as that was still echoing in his skull, he felt an arm come under him and gently guide him onto a lap. He let out a breath and opened his eyes.

If he could have gasped in surprise and scrambled away, he might have, as he saw Rifun's face looming over him. As it was, the best he could do was give a little sigh and cry on the inside. He closed his eyes and wished it all away. Today just sucked.

"Now, now, Tommen, you're safe," Rifun cooed.

Rifun stroked his cheek and moved his hair back behind his ears as best he could. Tommen wanted to throw up.

"How do you feel?"

"*Dw i ddim yn teimlo'n dda,*" Tommen whispered. (I don't feel so good.)

"No, I wouldn't expect so after the hell Tadashi put you through."

"*Merdu chi siarad.*" (You can talk.) Tommen lifted his arm that felt like a block of lead and tapped his hearing aid.

"Perhaps, and yet, here I am, saving your life. You know I would never let any harm come to you, at least, not knowingly or intentionally. Lucky for you I just happened to be passing by or poor Kyle wouldn't have lasted much longer and you'd both be dead."

But something else, probably silly, had caught his attention.

"Ydy'chi siarad Cymraeg?" (You speak Welsh?)

"Ydw." (I do.) He paused. "How often do men wish for more time to pursue something? More time to travel the world or learn a skill or do anything at all? We have the time, Tommen. And I use it to my advantage. With you and your father-uncle on equal terms now, I figured that there ought to be no secrets among us. *Agus labhraim Gaeilge, má cheap tú aon smaointe cliste.*" (And I speak Irish, in case you got any clever ideas.)

An idea passed through Tommen's mind, then, that maybe he ought to learn Hungarian or Polish or Hebrew and one day surprise Becky with it. That would make an impression, wouldn't it?

Then, like fog lifting from the snow, the window of Tommen's mind was suddenly clear. Or clearer, anyway. Grudgingly, he sat up, every muscle aching and groaning even as the cold from the snow started to register in his mind and he began shivering. With movements like a snail, he got himself around and together and stood, Rifun on his arm until he was steady on his feet.

Tadashi lay dead in the snow, half his head gone. Tommen looked and found Rifun's massive revolver safely on his hip.

"Why did you help me?" Tommen asked, speaking his words deliberately and trying to keep the roiling in his stomach to a minimum, intentionally not looking at the gory scene.

"After all I went through to keep you alive and make sure you passed your Apprentice review, you think I was going to let this idiot kill you?" Rifun kicked Tadashi's shoe. "After he made his grand departure, he went and joined some other political group, thought he was going to use them to outwit me at my own game. As I said, I take care of my own."

"Why were you here? Really?"

"Just checking up on some things, making sure everything is in order for the elections tomorrow."

"Handing out Uncle Sam fliers, I'm sure."

"You never know. And he got my interest, too."

Rifun indicated SoCal. He'd been removed from Tadashi's

Band and now stood frozen, still in a fight posture, suggesting he hadn't seen or registered Tadashi's sudden demise.

"Who is he?" Tommen wondered.

"Name is Kyle Malargos, from District Eight." Rifun folded his arms. "Apprentice who decided he wanted to take a few years to himself and use Time to couch-surf and see the world from a homeless person's point of view, I suppose."

"What is he to you?"

"Nothing. I was curious to know what interest your dad had in him. They were in church together. At first I thought maybe your dad had mercy on him because they were in a church, and because with the elections so heated, ordinary business can be suspended. Then I quickly realized he'd sent Kyle to keep an eye on you, watch your movements, keep you safe, report to him and the twins if something happened, like Tadashi showing up and trying to kill you."

So had it been Kyle watching him all week, making Tommen's paranoia superpowers come out in all their glory? Or had it been Kyle and Tadashi, both scoping him out for different reasons?

"What are you going to do to him?" Tommen asked.

"You think I'm going to kill him? The person who intervened and saved my young pupil's life from the knife of my estranged former companion? Absolutely not! If your dad wants to put a bodyguard on you, he is more than welcome to."

"As long as it doesn't interfere with your interests."

"Well, there is that." Rifun shrugged. "At any rate, we should probably get this mess cleaned up before releasing the Band. Having a body suddenly appear on school property, well, we both know how that one goes, don't we?"

It was a sick joke, but there was a point to it. Even more so since not only would the body appear in a huge throng of people, but it was a rather gory scene with a fairly obvious gunshot wound. There would be a lockdown and cops called and all sorts of precautionary nonsense — well, nonsense only in this case. But it would just be easier to dispose of the body and cover up the blood. As Banding did not affect air or most weather, the snow that was still falling would help to cover up all signs of any sort of scuffle.

Tommen did not relish the idea of helping Rifun dispose of the body. For one thing, it was disposing of a body and every part of him that was his dad's son screamed at him to stop and call the cops and do the right thing. For another thing, he was helping Rifun. He was *helping* Rifun, not because the man held a gun to his head, but because he agreed with him. There was something just sickening about going from being taken hostage to being a willing accomplice. Wasn't that considered Stockholm Syndrome? He was going to need therapy.

And why not just walk away, and either let Rifun do it himself or let the body suddenly appear? It wasn't as if he could be implicated in any way, not feasibly. He glanced down at his clothes. Only a little blood on them, not enough to really be noticed. He hoped. Damn color-blindness anyway.

At any rate, he really just helped with the minor clean-up; Rifun did all the heavy lifting. Tommen did not ask where he stashed the body, nor did he want to know. He just swept the snow around as much as he could to hide the remaining blood and stepped off the grass back onto the sidewalk. All around him, life was still frozen, the end of the school day. As if a murder hadn't just occurred.

When he was finished, Rifun went and stood beside Tommen, staring at the empty space. Tommen suppressed a shudder as Rifun put a hand on his shoulder.

"I know that was probably tiring and difficult for you," Rifun said gently. "Your dad is on his way. Get some good sleep tonight, and don't worry about tomorrow. Except for that part where you have an Economics test. You can fake all the degrees you want, but it's a good idea to have some smarts to back them up."

With that friendly advice, Rifun turned and started walking away.

"Where are you going?" Tommen asked after him.

Rifun turned but just continued to walk backwards. "As I said,

I was just passing by. I have other things to do today, as I'm sure you do. You go to work or go home, and I plan for election victories. Everyone has their priorities."

He turned back around but waited until he got to the sidewalk on the main street before releasing the Band.

Everything roared back to life once more. Walking, talking, texting, and whatever, none of it seemed to matter anymore. Probably two Base Seconds had passed since Tommen walked out of the school the first time to the point where he was standing there now, having survived an assassination attempt on his life and helping with the disposal of the body of the man who tried to kill him.

"Tommen!"

He whirled to see SoCal, er, Kyle, jogging toward him, looking tired and frazzled.

"Shit, Tommen, are you okay?" he gasped, the weariness catching up him as he bent over and put his hands on his knees.

"Yeah, I'm okay," Tommen answered numbly. He felt like he was going to be sick.

"What happened?"

"I'll tell you later."

"Well, your dad's on the way. So are his Lieutenants."

Kyle cried out as Tommen kicked his shin, then immediately Banded them. "Do you know how crazy we look and sound? We can't just be talking about that shit in front of everyone. You think no one here is paying attention? They're all paying attention. All of them, all the time. Got it?"

"Ow, yes, fine. Shit, that hurt."

Tommen sighed and folded his arms as best he could, dropping the Band. "Sorry. You're sure my dad's on his way? I've got about twenty seconds to get on the bus before they pull out."

"Yeah. I saw Tadashi and took, like, just a couple seconds to find him and tell him. I guess he was already on his way because something happened at the hospital and then something about Massachusetts, I don't know. Bad stuff is all I know, and they're all on their way here to get you."

"Okay."

Tommen waved to the bus driver and walked away, heading back around the school to the main parking lot.

"I'm Kyle."

Tommen almost said, I know, then caught himself at the last second and said, "Well, you know who I am, obviously."

"I wasn't sure if your dad would tell you about me, but judging by your reaction, I'm guessing not."

"No, he didn't."

"Well, I'm actually a Runner. Your dad caught me and said he'd spare me if I did a job for him. All I had to do was keep an eye on you, keep you safe if I had to, and report any and all strange goings-on to him or his Lieutenants."

"Where are you staying?"

"He put me up in a small hotel for the time being. Said I had two choices after the elections, either stay here and get a job and he'd take care of the legalities with my Master, or else I return to my Master. Or, you know, he'd turn me in."

"What are you going to do?"

"I don't know. I mean, I like Banding just as a cool party trick to get me from one place to another, but I don't really want to do anything with it, you know? And if I had to choose between being normal again and getting a job and stuff, and going higher and furthering my education and having to deal with that crazy shit on a regular basis...I think I'd choose normal."

Tommen wished he could tell him that the crazy shit didn't happen on a regular basis, but he didn't want to have to make a promise he wasn't sure was true, or would be true after tomorrow.

"There he is," Tommen said, spying the old Cadillac as it pulled onto the street and then into the parking lot.

He could see the look of relief on his dad's face when he spotted Tommen standing coolly at the front step. Instead of pulling in quickly and sliding up to the steps like a lunatic, he instead slowed down and took half a second to pull into a parking spot, considerably easier to find now that most of the seniors had gone.

"Are you okay?" his dad demanded, crossing the parking lot, using his cane but not really using it.

Tommen shrugged. "I guess."

"What happened?"

"I really think that's something we should discuss in private. Where are the twins?"

"Micaiah's coming; I told Micah to stay where he was; we have other problems this morning."

"Like what?"

So, once Micaiah got there, the four of them all turned around and headed back to the bakery, and in the space of about an hour, they filled him in on the details of all that had happened that day, from the murdered Apprentice in Massachusetts to Lily being held hostage. Well, it was highly likely that they omitted a ton of information and just gave him the CliffNotes version just so he was aware of the day's dangers.

In return, he gave them a detailed account of Tadashi's attack, including Kyle's involvement and Rifun's interference.

"Rifun killed Tadashi," Micaiah stated. "You're absolutely sure about that?"

"I know that Time can heal a lot of wounds, but there's no coming back from missing half a head," Tommen said, hoping it wasn't obvious how sick he was feeling just retelling the tale.

"Useless idiots," his dad muttered. "What happened after that?"

"He...well, we...disposed of the body. We didn't want it to just suddenly show up on school grounds in the middle of a crowd of people."

"Both of you did this?"

Tommen felt his cheeks turn red. "I didn't have a choice."

"Where did you dispose of it?"

"I don't know, and I didn't want to ask. I just did minor cleanup like in the snow and stuff; I couldn't do much heavy lifting." He indicated his arm. "After that, he said that he would be hanging around the neighborhood for a while before going back for the elections. Then everything went back to normal, and me and Kyle went to wait for you."

For a moment there was silence, as everyone mulled over the information, having their own thoughts. Walter was the first to break the silence.

"Are you okay?"

"Yeah," Tommen answered. "I still have a little headache from the Banding and the fighting and everything, but he never got me. He did get Kyle, though."

They looked at Kyle who took off his coat and rolled up his sleeve; all that was left was a scar. "I learned Pinpoint on my own; I'm fine."

"Tommen, I'm asking if you are okay," his dad clarified. "Seeing a guy lose half his head is not something to take lightly; even some soldiers returning home have problems with what we might consider less than that."

Tommen scoffed. "Does it matter?" He stood. "We're all going to see a lot more of it before this is all over."

He left the bakery office and headed to the back to punch in. He was just tying an apron around him when he looked and saw his dad blocking the doorway.

"It does matter," Walter said calmly. "Because you are not the tough guy you think you are, and you are not equipped to process things like that. Truthfully, no one is. I don't expect an answer right now, but I want you to think about what you've seen. If you want, I can find counselors who are also in Time who you can talk to without sounding crazy. At this point, I'm not going to force you because I want you to recognize your limits and go willingly. But I will force you if I have to, if I think you need it. Got it?"

Tommen sighed. "Why is all this happening?"

"I wish I knew. But I can tell you two things for sure—"

"Death and taxes?"

"Besides that. First, there is nothing new under the sun. Whether it's a local Earth-side government or the Hands of Time, this has all happened before. Which means that, secondly, it can't last forever."

"So then what do we do now?"

"You sit tight and focus on whatever homework or tests you've got coming up. Or think about how you can talk to or about Becky without blushing."

Just at the mention, Tommen felt his ears grow red and his dad laughed. "What about you? What are you going to do?"

"The only thing I can do, I suppose." He dug in his back pocket and handed him a folded piece of paper. Opening it up, it was an Uncle Sam poster, slightly modified, reading, "The Hands of Time Need You!" Walter chuckled. "I'm going to vote."

Chapter Twenty-Seven
Voting Day

Walter always wondered how Americans would react if voting was made compulsory, and whether that would have a positive or negative effect on things. On the one hand, it would ensure that everyone who could vote and wanted to vote got to vote. On the other hand, for all those people who didn't give a rip about politics or voting, they'd probably treat the ballot as a game to be played, a test to be taken and passed, likely resulting in thousands of invalid ballots and cases of voter fraud. And he wasn't talking about the choice between voting and a fine, but between voting and fifteen years in prison, or voting and potentially the death penalty. That kind of motivation would certainly shake things up.

That was the kind of compulsory voting that governed the Wheel of Time. The only thing that would have been able to get him out of voting would have been his coma and possibly a handful of other medical ailments, all of which would have had to be reviewed by the Hands or the Grandfathers or the secretaries or whomever.

The only nice thing, if it could be called nice, was that voting was open all day. And by all day, the times roughly corresponded from eleven at night on Thursday to about three in the morning on Saturday, Eastern Standard Time and all that. Therefore, it was easier to simply say, go vote on Friday.

So after a long night of waiting for terrible news from the other Time Agents on the mysterious hit list that never came, Walter had finally gotten to bed about two in the morning. He supposed he could have gone and voted before going to bed, but if there was going to be a fight—and every indication said that it was going to be impossible to get in and out unscathed—it was better to do it well-rested and with a full stomach.

He was startled awake by a knock on his door.

"Walter? Are you okay?" Micaiah asked from the other side.

He stretched and looked at his clock. Half past eleven. Damn, he'd slept in, hadn't he? He'd grudgingly gotten up early to take Tommen to school, then come back and only intended to sleep in just a couple more hours, not half the day. Still, he felt pretty good having been able to just sleep in.

"Walt?"

"I'm awake," he told him sleepily, breaking into a yawn. "I'm coming."

After a minute or two of consideration, he pulled himself upright. Of course, on the other hand, it could be the pills that made him sleep so heavily. He'd been ignoring his body's demands for the most part, but with all the stress of the elections and Ron's death and especially the attack on Tommen, well, he'd had the ability to put himself quite a bit under, put it that way. Was it the smartest thing to do? No, seeing how he could have slept through another attack. Had it helped? That remained to be seen.

He Banded and went through his morning routine, maybe a little slower than normal but he got it done. Shower, shave, dress, and head out to the kitchen where Micaiah was reading his morning newspaper. When he appeared, able to get around the house without his cane, Micaiah looked up and stood.

"Don't scare us like that," Micaiah told him sternly.

"Why, what happened?" Walter wondered.

"We've been calling you for the last hour or more."

"Well, don't wait too long to come check on me." Walter poured himself a cup of coffee.

"Honestly, we texted Tommen first to see if you were up to something. He said you probably went back to bed since you had a late night. But eventually..." Micaiah shrugged. "I had to check, just to be sure."

"I thank you for your concern. And for checking up on Tommen." He collapsed into the chair and started flipping through the large pages. "So, what were your plans for voting today?"

"We thought about going this morning, figured maybe wait until Tommen gets off the bus, then we all go together."

"You want to take Tommen to the Wheel on Election Day? After what happened yesterday?"

"Yes, I do. Because we don't know who else could be waiting for him. Kyle's watching over him right now, but what if something happened in that moment that we were gone? Who is going to come and get us? What damage could be done in that split second?"

"It's Election Day, Cai. One of the few days where threats mean virtually nothing. Yesterday was the day to threaten Tommen Earth-side. Today, in the Wheel, that's where the threats are going to be."

"Threats are going to be everywhere. Difference is, he's an Apprentice now. The next Election Day that rolls around, he'll be at least a Master, if not an officer, which means he'll be voting. You want to throw him into that unprepared?"

Problem was, he had a point. Not every Timekeeper got to see an election from the relative safety of not-being-able-to-vote. Still, the thought of taking him into that was far less than appealing.

"Listen, we can all go together. You go in to vote first, and we'll watch over him. When you get done, we go vote, you take him, give him whatever speech you need to give him, and you can leave without worrying about us, okay?"

After a moment of thought, Walter nodded. "All right. Sounds like that's going to be our best bet."

"Okay. Do you want a ride or are you going to drive?"

"I'll be a few minutes; you can head back to work."

The elder Durvin seemed uncertain but finally nodded and headed out. Walter took his time musing over his coffee and newspaper, though he tasted nothing and read nothing. The Wheel was the last place he wanted to go right now, never mind where he wanted to take Tommen. The phrase, "where angels fear to tread" came to mind. On the one hand, Rifun and Cassius were going to be in the Wheel somewhere, lurking about. On the other hand, they could have minions Earth-side, ready to snap up unsuspecting victims who were left unguarded. Maybe he was just being paranoid. When the threats came from all directions, there was no use in picking one direction as inherently safer than another.

Walter spent the morning moving at his own pace before driving to the bakery, arriving only minutes before the bus and walking in the front door about the same time as Tommen It was a short wait until Micah got the line cleared and he could Band and get them all in the office.

"Is there news?" Tommen wondered, shutting the door behind him.

"Yes," Micah told him. "It's Election Day in the Wheel. So far as we know, there have been no further reported deaths or hostage situations related to the elections or any other nasty things that have been going around lately."

"That's good. Are you guys all going to vote, then?"

"We are," Walter told him. "And you're coming with us."

He blinked. "But, I can't vote."

"Doesn't matter. You're safer with us there. And you'll get to see what the elections really look like."

Micaiah sat up in his chair. "What's going to happen is that we're all going to the Wheel together. The voting takes place in the Judgment Wing. We'll head down that way. Your dad will go and vote first, so you'll stay with me and Micah. When he's done, we'll go vote, and he can take you wherever he wants to go. He'll show you around a little, give you his Election Day speech, and you can return home without worrying about us."

"Oh," Tommen said. "Okay, cool. I'm assuming there's no dress code?"

"No, there's no dress code," Micah said. He was normally the less serious of the two brothers and even he sounded exasperated, as if just thinking about the elections was exhausting and he just wanted it to be over with. Walter could relate.

"Well then," Walter said, preparing himself. "No time like the present to go and do our part to bring chaos into the universe."

"Amen to that," Micaiah agreed sarcastically, just a moment before he and Micah ripped open a hole between dimensions and they stepped into the portal room of the Wheel.

Walter had a considerably easier time getting through now than he had two weeks prior, though it was still no walk in the park. Thankfully, his cane helped keep him upright even as both twins went to one knee and Tommen went face-first into the floor.

"Tommen?" he asked. "Are you okay?"

Tommen groaned and did not move, instead mumbling into the floor, "I feel like my head's been sliced in half."

"Get up, kiddo, Time and her elections wait for no one, and I don't want to see you trampled."

Still, he wasn't very fast getting up, even with a twin on either side.

"You're here now, so let's get moving," Micah told him, sounding more like his cynical older brother with each passing moment.

After a few steps, Tommen was able to walk on his own; Walter went up to walk beside him.

"Okay, even I can tell that we're a lot farther out that we normally are," Tommen observed as he looked down the row of portals.

"Yup," Walter confirmed. "There are probably ten times the number of portals open right now as there normally are. It's about the difference between parking in the parking lot at the bakery and walking to the bakery from our house."

"Just to get to the main Wheel?"

"Mm-hm."

And the rows of portals weren't empty, either. Rather, they were swarming with creatures of all shapes and sizes going both directions. It was like taking a standard two-lane two-way road, that had light to moderate traffic on it for 364 days a year, and then on that 365th day, shoving the five o'clock rush hour from Los Angeles down it, assuming all the vehicles ranged in size from tree-crunching front end loaders to a child's toy car. There was no passing or moving faster, but there was plenty of pushing and shoving and cursing in all manner of languages and other communications.

"Are we even going to be able to get translators?" Tommen wondered.

"We will," Walter assured him. "That's actually probably what this line is."

"Oh."

Once again, it was like taking a single ATM machine that saw light to moderate traffic on any given day, but for one day out of the whole year it was the only ATM machine in the entire world and everyone was forced to use it. Walter considered it poor planning, but who would listen to him? After all, elections only came around every seventeen years, so it wasn't as though there was a huge demand for change. At least, not until they got in this infernal line.

But the line moved swiftly enough, faster than most retail lines of comparable length, anyway. The four of them held up the line only inasmuch as Tommen had problems getting the machine to read his hearing aid and dispense an appropriately modified translator. There were grunts and growls and curses behind them, but they were on their way soon enough.

"It's almost like normal," Tommen observed once they got out of the portal room and into the main Wheel. "Where did they all go?"

"The Judgment Wing," Micaiah answered. "It's bigger than it looks and better equipped to handle the crowds, more so than the portal room anyway."

"Oh. So that's where we're heading?"

"Unless you know of another place where we can cast our predetermined votes?"

Tommen shook his head meekly. "What happens after the day

is over? Do they count them in real time or what? When do the results come in?"

"The responses are made and counted in real time," Walter explained. "You'll see once we get there, but you can watch as the numbers come in. Once the last person has voted or the polls close, the results are analyzed a second time and the results are published within one hour. After that, it's up to the Gatekeepers and other Planetary Time Agents to send word of the results."

"Oh. Can someone concede, like, drop out if they're losing hard core during the voting?"

"No. All the names in the hat when polls open are going to stay up, regardless of how much they're ahead or behind."

"So everyone can share in the shame," Micah said cynically.

"What happens when the results come in, then, and the winners are declared?"

Walter was starting to have second thoughts about bringing Tommen along, but told himself it was for his safety and education. The comfort was minimal. "Once all the winners have been notified—which only takes a couple hours anyway—then preparations are made for the relinquishment of power and inauguration of the new Hands of Time."

"Basically that means we'll be back tomorrow," Micaiah summarized curtly. Had he been wearing all black and had his hair slicked back with dark sunglasses, he would have looked every bit the grouchy bodyguard his demeanor betrayed him as. "It'll be a good idea for you to just keep your translator with you when you leave. You think it's crazy now? Just wait until the inauguration."

"Where is that held?" Tommen wondered.

"Coliseum, where else?" Micah replied.

"All the people who voted go to the Seat," Walter expounded. "That's as mandatory as the voting. Anyone else who wants to come and try to watch stays outside the Seat. You'll have all three tracks just packed with people, to say nothing of everyone who will still be waiting outside. If you want to come, I won't stop you; it'll certainly be educational and interesting to watch. But know that you won't be able to come in, and we won't be able to stay out."

"How long is the inauguration?"

"You know the phrase, 'a day like a thousand years and a thousand years like a day'?"

"Yeah...?"

"Think more like the first part."

"Oh."

Well, it shut him up anyway. Normally, Walter wouldn't have any problem answering his questions and giving him some insight; he'd even be happy that Tommen was interested at all and wanted to participate. But right now, the stakes were too high, his stress level was through the roof, and he couldn't shake the feeling that something bad was going to happen. Hopefully it was just paranoia and the stress of the day, and it would all go away once they were out of there.

They reached the Judgment Wing in good time and no worse for wear; the closer they got, the more people milled about, waiting to get in. The line did not appear to be as treacherous as the one in the portal room, though.

"Where do you want us to wait?" Micaiah asked as Walter told Tommen to stay with them and wait for him.

"I'll look for you either out here or in the Food Court," Walter said, "otherwise I'm going to assume something happened to you."

"Understood."

He was in no mood to play games, especially not hide-and-seek. He wanted to get in and get this over with, so he turned and followed the line into the Judgment Wing.

The initial entry into the Judgment Wing was more reminisce of an enormous bank vault. Everything looked like solid steel, the walls, floor, ceiling, and really that was all it was: walls, a floor, and a ceiling. There was no furniture, no desks, not even an office plant dying in the corner. If not for the huge bank vault-like door taking up almost the entirety of one thirty-foot wall, Walter might have actually compared it to solitary confinement, or an insane asylum. Some days it certainly felt like an insane asylum.

The live results were projected on one wall of the room. Like everywhere else in the Wheel, actual writing was minimal, using only the Commonly Accepted Symbols depicting the Hands, as well as numbers up to 5,235,906,317,400,312,778. No one knew why the numbers stopped there, but apparently that number had never been approached and was deemed sufficient. As for the races themselves, instead of names, there were pictures. Some races were so close the pictures were constantly sliding back and forth in the lead; others stayed where they were as the race was a runaway.

The Zero Hour election was listed at the top, much like a presidential election put the president first. Shockingly, though, Cassius' picture was nowhere to be seen. Neither was Rifun's. What the...hell?

The secretaries were in charge of preliminaries, taking down name, title, rank, all the fun stuff. Currently, the secretary on duty somewhat resembled a giant hamster. Or gerbil, as it had a tail. If Walter remembered correctly, this was the Hutch, like the Day for the Grandfathers.

Walter often wondered how the secretaries got their jobs. He couldn't recall ever voting for them, and it always seemed to be the same ones in the same positions. He knew it shouldn't have bothered them too much, but Time secretaries were not the low-lifes that most humans mistook them for. A housekeeping secretary in the Wheel had more power than most Earth-side CEOs, to say nothing of those who oversaw the Archives, the Judgment Wing, all the major functions of the Wheel. And if someone had that much power, Walter wanted to know where it came form. Certainly not from the people. The secretaries were appointed, likely for life. And as the old adage proved time and again, "the maid knows everything."

Walter felt his blood pressure go even higher.

The line moved along and even though it was still faster than the portal room, Walter found himself wishing he could Band and make it feel like it was going just a little faster. His leg was stiffening up, after all, and he still had physical therapy to go to. But that was the rule in the Judgment Wing, as in the Coliseum. No Time abilities of any form. So not only could Timekeepers not Band, but Harvesters couldn't Harvest, and Scouts couldn't do...whatever it was they did.

Even as he thought it, a couple Scouts exited the vault door and left the Judgment Wing. Walter knew they were scouts only because they wore the Scouting pin, a relic of an older Wheel and a way that Scouts often thumbed their noses at the system. They labeled themselves as free spirits, rebels, outlaws, like the romantic view of the Wild, Wild West, cowboys and highwaymen and whatnot. They had no formal hierarchy, more of a pecking order, and it was the Hand of the Scouts who determined which Scouts would vote in the elections, thus basically securing his own position as long as they liked him. Or her.

Walter inwardly shook his head. He knew why Tommen wanted to be a Scout; it was the same wanderlust that afflicted most people and drove them to go globetrotting, if they had the resources. He wanted to get out of his mundane life—if it could be called anything even remotely synonymous with mundane—and go see what was out there. For most humans, that translated to India, Thailand, China, South Africa, those sorts of places. Walter was even hesitant about that, but he would take that over his son becoming a Scout.

Scouting wasn't like vacationing, globetrotting, or even humanitarian work somewhere deep in remote African villages. Scouting was about going out to planets who were untouched by Time and bringing them into the fold, the kind, non-Crusading, non-Inquisition, non-ISIS way of expanding the empire. In a way, it was almost worse than Crusading, Inquiring, and mass terrorism because the people willingly accepted their fate.

Walter sighed. Truthfully, some days he wished that he and Tommen could just have a normal life. But they didn't have one, and this was their world, their universe. They were going to make decisions based on the universe they lived in. Walter might be able to keep Tommen from going out for a time, but eventually, he would have to become his own man.

So he probably looked less than enthused when he finally stepped up to the Hutch to give his information. At the same time, he also had the advantage that most races didn't understand human body language outside the obvious, overly-exaggerated gestures. Basically, unless Walter had been openly weeping, this hamster, gerbil rather, had no clue how awful and dejected he was feeling.

"Walter Forbes, Quadrant One, Parsec Eleven, Sector Five, System Four, Planet Thirty-Eight, Region Four, District Four, Timekeeper, Captain," he recited blandly.

The secretary took a small blood sample on its machine, not unlike some of the diabetic meters found Earth-side. After a moment, the gerbil looked at him, looked at its machine, looked back at him.

"Is there a problem?" Walter wondered. If his blood pressure went any higher, he was going to have an aneurysm.

"My report says you were removed from your position," the gerbil told him. "It says you died."

"No, that's not quite true, not entirely. I was going to die, so a new Captain was appointed, and then I didn't die, so now my position is being voted on. The Zero Hour himself ruled that way. Officially, I'm listed as an Acting Captain."

The gerbil's nose twitched. Then, "I will ask. Step aside."

Walter did so, feeling very conspicuous, like the person pulled aside at the airport to be taken into a small room, and everyone looks on like he must have done something wrong. The gerbil called for another secretary, a messenger, and sent them on a mission to discover the truth behind Walter's title crisis.

As he sat there, he looked around at the line for a moment, then at the results. Cassius and Rifun still weren't pictured, and he couldn't figure out why. Their whole bid was for the Zero Hour, absolute control, king of the hill, et cetera. Why wouldn't they be running the very elections they helped to sabotage and rig? A chill crept down Walter's spine as he considered what that could mean.

The messenger secretary returned and spoke to the gerbil who motioned for Walter to approach. Damn, his leg was stiff.

"Your position has been confirmed," the gerbil informed him. "Apologies for the confusion and the delay. You may enter to vote."

The gerbil stamped his hand and moved on, completely uninterested, to the next person in line. The stamp didn't seem like much, kind of like the ones used at county fairs to make sure you paid your ticket, but this one was actually technologically infused to get him through the force field — yes, force field — that shielded the vault door opening from those who would try to jump the line and get in to vote. Walter had never tried it, but apparently the force field was strong. Really strong. Stronger than an electric wire to keep cattle corralled, put it that way. Stronger than the electric chair, supposedly. The stamp he'd gotten was a two-way stamp so he could pass in and out again; the stamp that the Runners got when he brought them in was a one-way stamp, so they could go in, but, if they escaped his custody, couldn't get back out.

Walter entered without incident. Immediately behind the vault door was a hallway reminisce of the front room: all steel everywhere. The hall itself was probably two hundred and fifty feet long, maybe closer to three hundred. At the other end was another vault door, same size as the main one, also open specially for this day. This one was also guarded by a force field, but the hand stamp allowed Walter to pass through.

Behind that vault door was a mirror room of the front room, but with three slightly smaller vault doors. The first, he knew from experience, led to what he referred to as Booking but was actually called Initial Processing. He took Runners through that door to be seen by the Processor who took down the Runner's information and records and decided where and how to send them through to be judged by the Grandfathers. There were holding cells there and more vault doors and so on, but that was as far as Walter had ever been through that door.

The second door led to the prison itself, the deeper corners called the asylum. If a Runner had his clock broken, should anyone care to claim him, he was released to the custody of such a caregiver. If no one claimed him, or if he was to serve a true prison sentence, he was sent there. Walter had been in there only once when he was a Journeyman, when Mark took him on a tour and showed him what happened to the Runners they turned in.

Even now, Walter didn't like to think about what lay behind that door; it was too similar to Beaumaris Gaol. Every room and corridor in the Judgment Wing was soundproof, except the asylum. The wailing and the screaming and the shouting was like the stuff of nightmares. It, too, was solid steel in the main corridors, but the cells were specially crafted for the prisoner. If a human was going to be housed in a cell, why take the extra time and resources to make it strong enough to hold a Taryian? Why make the door big enough so an Egeli could get through? If the cell was for a human, design it for a human.

The prison did not have any guards per se, as the force field at the vault door was enough for that. And even if every prisoner did somehow escape and were out roaming the halls, they'd eat each other alive before working together to come up with a solution to the force field problem. The most luxury the prisoners got was an occasional meal, enough to keep them from starving too quickly, but not enough to keep them alive for very long after the point of starvation. It was a cruel and lonely way to die, but they had to keep cells open; they weren't going to pull a twenty-five to life schtick and keep what they perceived to be the enemies of Time alive.

Walter took a breath and turned his gaze to the third door which was open. Behind it was a tiny room—well, comparatively tiny—with a portal gate much like the ones found in the portal room, but there was no portal in it at the moment. Unlike the open portals of the Wheel which were set to a fixed location, portal gates allowed portals to be opened from the gate to anywhere. In the case of the elections, Walter had only to walk through the small vault door for the portal to open.

When he stepped through, he found himself in a box room. He'd been terrified of the asylum, but the voting rooms weren't much better, in all reality. For him, it was like stepping into one of those old-fashioned telephone booths on the street corner, except the whole thing was made of solid steel and instead of a phone, there was a computer screen.

It wasn't like any computer screen currently found on Earth, but the technology wasn't far off. It wasn't a screen made of glass, but a combined projection from the four metal corners which were movable and could make the screen as big or as small as desired with no loss of clarity. That was the beauty of fluid coding, Walter supposed...whatever fluid coding was. Bah, that was for the techies and nerds. He was just here to vote.

The big difference between American voting and Time voting was that there was no second-guessing. Once he made his decision, the result went straight to the main computer, and he was just one more number on the results screen at the main entrance.

The only thing that really held him up was his being stunned that Cassius was not on the list for the Zero Hour. Of all the humans vying for the position—all one of them—the candidate did not resemble him in any way, shape, or form, the most obvious difference being that the candidate was white. Cassius was a Harvester, true, but like all genetic bleed that occurred, it took a lot of one genetic feature for it to actually effect a change in the Harvester. In the couple months since Walter had last seen Cassius, the man would have had to do a lot of Harvesting to have that kind of change in such a short amount of time. Even if Rifun Banded him to give him more time to do so, it just seemed highly unlikely.

Or could it have been the other way around? Could Cassius have done what Lily called a bad copy and paste of features onto Rifun? It would disguise both of them to minimize panic, but to what end? Did they want to cause panic and chaos or not?

Besides, Walter was pretty sure he'd met the candidate. He

couldn't actually think of where, but probably in one of the many excursions he'd made to the Wheel just for the sake of being bribed by all the candidates. He couldn't remember a lot of the candidates, actually, but he knew he'd met quite a few of them. It would have been only natural for him to gravitate toward human candidates, after all.

Problem was, his impression of man was not a pleasant vibe. Maybe the guy had said something, done something while they were interacting, Walter couldn't remember precisely, but it just really turned him off, saying that he wasn't the guy fit for the Zero Hour position.

He looked through the other candidates. Unlike American democracy where there were parties and primaries and a narrowing down of the candidates, here there were no parties and no limit to the number of candidates for a single position, and no way to narrow it down except by candidates dropping out before the deadline, that is, the start of voting day. The good news, though, was that on the screen it was possible to "dump" candidates, push them aside so he could view only the ones he was considering. Any that Walter had never met or even seen got dumped. Ones he'd never met but seen got dumped. It was kind of like reading a stack of resumes, looking for any reason to dump a candidate. It might not have been very fair—the best candidate of the bunch who might have brought true universal peace to the Time industry might be dumped for the simple fact that he didn't get his name out there enough. But then, it wasn't Walter's job to manage publicity. He was just here to vote.

There was still an element of trepidation as he finally selected his Zero Hour pick. Why wasn't Cassius in there? Or Rifun, even? Maybe they had a falling out. Tommen had said that Rifun was just "in the neighborhood" and "taking care of election things." What sort of "election things?" What was going on?

His blood pressure wasn't sure whether to go up or down. Down, because Cassius and Rifun weren't in the system as Zero Hour candidates. Up, because there was something awfully strange about that. Still, he was mandated to vote, so vote he did.

After the Zero Hour came the remaining Hands. Some Walter was fairly unconcerned about—such as the Hand of That Which Lies Beneath, whatever that meant—and he simply picked one that he'd seen before, if he'd seen one before. Others he considered more carefully, such as the Hand of the Timekeepers. Still, none stirred up the same anxiety that the Zero Hour vote had. And, as he got down to the last few elections, he found that his blood pressure and heart rate had gone down. Oddly enough, he found something relaxing about choosing the fate of the universe—ha ha ha.

Normally, the Hands were the only positions to vote for; everything under the Hands was dealt with by the Hands or other internal politics. The Hand of the Timekeepers promoted and appointed the Dominion Timekeepers and Wardens who appointed the Gatekeepers and on down the line it went. It would be like voting for the president who then appointed the governors who appointed the county governments who appointed the city governments and so on and so forth. Maybe things were different for Engaged Civilizations, but as far as Earth was concerned, only the Hands mattered in the elections.

This time, however, there was an extra ballot for consideration, and that was the Region Four, District Four Captain. Walter paused for a moment, wondering if this election was visible to everyone else in the universe who was voting, or if it was only for humans, or maybe just for those from the Region. Either way, his picture showed up among the others who were in the Region who were Captain-trained. On the one hand, it would only make sense that he vote for himself and keep his position. On the other hand, maybe it was his chance to retire. Not that it would matter if he was the only one who voted against himself.

He sighed and tapped on his picture. Might as well get this over with.

As soon as his last vote was cast, the screen in front of him shut down and the portal behind him opened. He gripped his cane and headed out of the tiny voting booth.

The instant he exited the booth and made it to the room with the three doors, a wave of nausea and panic swept over him and it was as if the breath was sucked from his lungs. As much from surprise as the sudden symptoms, he stumbled and figured it safer to just slide to the floor for a moment rather than fight it and hurt himself. He closed his eyes for just a moment and took a breath. Of all the aliens and creatures passing by on their way to and from voting, hardly any of them gave him a moment's regard.

He knew what it was and he knew where it had come from, but that didn't make it any less embarrassing or shameful. God help him if he ever ended up in prison for some reason with no means of escape; he'd probably kill himself. The severity of the situation had covered it up, but now that it was over and he was done, one anxiety was exchanged for another. His blood pressure was through the roof, and his racing heart could be felt everywhere in his body.

After a minute or two, he managed to get himself under control enough to pull himself back to a standing position and limp his way back down the main corridor. As embarrassing as it had been, better to do it there among strangers than in front of his son. He didn't know what he would do if he ever had such a panic attack in front of Tommen. Bad enough he knew, not only about the night light, but the reason behind it, afraid of the dark like a frightened child, still afraid of the demons that he'd left over a century in the past. In some respects, he was one of those demons now, delivering criminals into their own personal hell.

He stopped for a second and took another breath, trying to calm himself. There was no doubt that he'd deserved every second of his time in prison, but he was tired of living in this secondary hell, like some retribution for his escape.

As he stepped back into the front room of the Judgment Wing, another secretary was waiting to check him out, removing the stamp from his hand and preventing him from walking back into the vault. Then, once his information was again confirmed, he was free to go.

Walter did not immediately spot Tommen or the twins, but he wouldn't have blamed them for heading to the Food Court. In just the short time he'd spent in the Judgment Wing voting, the line had lengthened, and the remaining, meandering crowd looked as though it had doubled in size. He pushed and shouldered his way through the crowd until he got to a spot where he could breathe. He disliked oversized crowds almost as much as small, dark, empty rooms.

He made his way through the Wheel and all its idiosyncrasies, fearing that, as the crowds first thinned and then expanded, the Food Court was going to be just as busy as the Judgment Wing.

The nice thing about the Food Court, however, was that it was not just one area where everyone conglomerated, much like the Judgment Wing was now. The Food Court was divided into a variety of realms, each suited to the general diet of thousands of different species. Sometimes things were as familiar as a burger with all the fixings; other times there were dishes that Walter was pretty sure did not originate in China.

The Food Court, or their part of it, was not as crowded as the Judgment Wing, but still more than on a normal busy day. A slow day was like the mall on a Monday morning, busy was like the mall on a Saturday night. This was more like a Saturday night plus Black Friday.

His first thought was to look for Tommen. His second thought was that the Food Court was a smörgåsbord of free prepared food. So not only did he not have to pay or tip, but he also didn't have to cook. He sometimes took advantage of this fact on long shifts at the precinct, and it saved a hell of a lot of money on the grocery bill; it was hell trying to raise a teenage boy with a black hole where his stomach ought to have been.

In the center of the Food Court was the world's—no, the *universe's* largest salad bar. There was no possible way even a frugal person would make it through the entire maze and still walk out with only one plate. Well, maybe if they took the Irigin-sized plates, but that was another matter. Walter was guilty of ending up with a three-plate salad from time to time, but today he forced himself to stop once he'd filled up one plate. As soon as he turned around, he spotted his entourage.

"Thought you'd never come out of there," Micaiah said, his voice straining to make it sound like a jest.

"I thought I'd never get in," Walter replied and told them briefly about the snafu where he'd been apparently removed from power.

"Do you think that was deliberate?" Micah asked. "The secretaries are usually pretty on top of things, sometimes even before an official ruling has come down."

"I don't know. I still got in."

"But by sending a secretary to verify, if they had to verify with the Hands or the Bat or whoever, it would alert Cassius to our presence," Micaiah mused, his expression turning darker than ever.

"I thought it was mandatory voting," Tommen wondered. "What does it matter if they know exactly when we're here?"

Walter and the twins glanced at each other uncertainly. On a day that was, indeed, mandatory, there was only one good reason to find out exactly when someone arrived and, also, when they left. Immediately they began scarfing as much food as possible before standing.

"We'll head in to vote," Micaiah said. "You get yourself and Tommen home. We'll catch up with you."

"Be safe," Walter told them.

With that, they left the Food Court and parted ways, the twins heading purposefully toward the Judgment Wing while Walter and Tommen turned to go back to the portal room.

"You really think Cassius would try something in the middle of all this?" Tommen asked, looking around at the crowds.

"Anonymity is crime's best friend," Walter said gravely. "And what better cloak to use than the Wheel, where everything and nothing is out of the ordinary?"

They made it to the portal room with no more incident than

the expected pushing and shoving and name-calling.

"Keep your translator," Walter reminded Tommen. "It'll let us bypass this line at the inauguration."

"How long are we going to wait for them?" Tommen inquired. "You took almost two hours."

"We can wait here for a time," Walter decided after a moment of consideration. "If anyone does come after us, we can simply step through the portal, and I'll close it."

"But you'd trap Micah and Micaiah."

"And when they saw it, they'd know something happened. They're resourceful. They'd get back."

"What if something happens to them?"

Walter didn't really want to consider that option, especially since Micaiah was still on that hit list. As far as he knew, everyone else who had been on it was still alive, Ron notwithstanding. He hadn't seen Lily yet, but with the crowds, he would have been more surprised to see her without intentionally searching for her.

"Did you get enough to eat?" Walter asked Tommen who was watching the people and aliens go by. "Tommen?"

"What?" Tommen turned.

"I asked if you got enough to eat."

"Oh, yeah, I was already done before you got there." He went back to people-watching.

"How are your hearing aids holding up?"

He saw Tommen's ears turn bright red even as the rest of his face turned a shade or two pinker. "They're fine. They work. Translator works well with them."

"And?" Walter pressed.

Tommen shrugged. "And what?"

"How are you holding up? How are things at school?"

"Good. My arm itches like crazy. At least I can get back on the computer to do my schoolwork."

"That's good, but I meant in reference to the hearing aids."

"I'm fine, why?"

"Because I've asked you the same question three times."

"What?" His eyes got wide as he snapped his attention on Walter who shook his head.

"Not true. Answer the question."

Tommen scoffed, rolled his eyes, folded his arms as best he could, looked away. "I'm fine. Sometimes I just have problems telling sounds and voices apart in crowds. Like, the hallways at school can get irritating, but I can generally tune it out. Sometimes if it gets loud at work, I have issues."

"It'll take time to get used to them," Walter told him.

He rolled his eyes again. "I know, okay? I don't like them but I know I need them. They help, they really do. Just...leave it alone."

"I just want to make sure you're okay."

"I'm fine." Tommen shuffled his feet. "Thanks."

Walter decided to leave it at that and let Tommen have his pride. He was only injured, not dying. It was appropriate to ask if he was okay; it was inappropriate to assume he was always not okay and insist on helping. Or at least, that was what Walter told himself because that was usually how he felt about his own injuries.

It could be difficult to keep track of time in the Wheel, surprisingly, but Walter figured they had waited at least two hours before he stood from where he'd sat beside Tommen and stretched as much as he could, feeling the muscles in his leg come alive and protest vehemently. For a moment, he thought he was going to be taken down by a charliehorse.

"Are we leaving?" Tommen wondered, standing and stretching also.

"I expected that they'd take a little longer," Walter said, "but this is a little too long for my comfort."

"Oh, I see how it is."

They turned and looked to see Micaiah shouldering his way back through the crowd toward them, the much smaller Micah struggling to keep up.

"Leaving us for dead, huh?" Micaiah said when he reached

them. "I see how it is."

"As I recall," Walter told him, "you were ready to leave me for dead if not for my son."

"Ouch," Tommen chuckled nervously. "I call that a burn."

"Make a few more sarcastic remarks, and I'll break your other arm," Micaiah told him, his tone making it difficult to judge how serious he was being. Only because Walter knew him so well did he know that he was only fifty percent joking.

"Went well with you two?"

"Well is a relative term," Micah said, finally making it to the group. "But if you're asking if we made it in and out without being assaulted by a group of Grandfathers, Hands, or other bandits, then yes, everything went well."

"And you saw what I saw, right?"

"About the Zero Hour? Yeah, we saw it. Probably better to talk when we're not in such questionable company."

They all agreed to that and stepped through the portal back to the safety of the bakery. Walter's leg cramped up then as they went through and he hobbled to a chair and sat down.

"What was wrong with the Zero Hour?" Tommen wondered.

"Neither Cassius nor Rifun was listed as a candidate," Micaiah told him. "There was only one human running, and it wasn't either of them."

"But that makes no sense. I mean, it's one thing if they'd talked abut some military coup and take out the Hands by force, but they've been obsessing over these elections."

"Believe us, we know," Micah said.

"There's nothing else that Rifun told you yesterday about his plans, what he was doing around here, who he might be seeing, anything like that?" Walter asked.

Tommen was silent for a minute as he thought. Finally he shook his head. "No, I told you guys everything I can remember."

Micaiah leaned back in his chair. "What if it was someone on the inside who deleted them at the last moment, made it look like they pulled out?"

"What, you mean like a mole?" Micah wondered. "One of the secretaries, maybe?"

"If it is, remind me to thank them if we ever figure out who it is or was," Walter commented. He sighed. "Problem is, we won't really know until the results come in."

Micaiah stood. "Well, better get back to work. I'd hate to be caught slacking if the Thought Police come knocking on my door."

Chapter Twenty-Eight
Overnight

Tommen stayed to work his normal shift. While it was feasible that Walter could stay for a few hours, he elected to go home and do something, anything else to get his mind off the impending doom. He went out to the parking lot and got in his car, but it was a minute or two before he actually turned it on and went anywhere.

It still bothered him that Cassius and Rifun hadn't been listed. He highly doubted, after the warehouse, that they would go through so much trouble to buy off the candidates, kill off competition and dissenters, and terrorize the voters, only to suddenly drop out at the eleventh hour. Something else was going on. Did he dare hope that there was a mole on the inside who erased them from the ballot? Was it a conscientious secretary, perhaps, one who knew who the two men were and the devastating consequences they would bring to the Time industry? Or could it be a secret dissenter among their own ranks? Maybe there had been a falling out, and the same secretary who put them into the system also took them out as a means of some retaliation. Could there be some connection to the hit list and the groups or individuals trying to kill Micah and Micaiah?

Walter drove slowly as the snow began to come down harder, going from a gentle winter wonderland to nightmare blizzard in only a few minutes. Fitting, he supposed, for how this whole thing was about to turn out. Deep in his gut, he had a suspicion that even if he hadn't seen Cassius' picture among the candidates, he was still in there somehow.

Maybe he should have voted against himself in the Captain vote. Lose the vote, retire from Time, settle down into a normal life.

Even as he thought it, he knew he couldn't do that. Not now. Not while Tommen was still an Apprentice and the object of desire for an intergalactic cult-based psychopath. Tommen might have his pride, but he had squat for defensive capabilities, and he would need all the help he could get, even if all the help had comparatively shoddy abilities against the psychopath, too.

He arrived home in a grim mood overall, but was more than grateful for a clean garage and warm house. As he stepped out of the car, his senses were immediately overwhelmed by the stench of vinegar and decay, both of which came from several buckets of furs lined up against one wall. A little table stood next to the buckets on which a container of minced brains sat, hence the smell of decay. Walter did his best to just not breathe while he limped up the steps to the door and entered the house. He was going to have to talk to Tommen about that. He did not need that smell permeating the entire garage permanently. To say nothing of how most of his trapping was illegally done anyway.

Walter sighed and shook his head. It wasn't as if he was going to be much better about it, considering he had a lot of painting to do yet. He figured to do his bedroom first, get a feel for this whole painting business and how well it was going to work when he was still slightly crippled.

He set aside his cane as he went back out to the garage and hauled in all the painting supplies he'd so far been hoarding. Rollers, pans, brushes, plastic, and, of course, the paint itself. He moved what furniture he could, like the night stand and the chest, the mirror, and assorted things that had collected over the years; the burlap board of patches he removed from the wall and took out to his recliner. Looking over all the things he brought out, he figured that maybe some of it could go out to the garage and he could have a spring garage sale. Maybe he should ask Tommen if he wanted his room repainted and then go through and sort out his stuff.

He managed to scoot the bed out a couple feet from the wall, but once he did that, he all but collapsed onto it, breathing heavily.

How was it that he'd weakened so much in just, what, a month? Not even? Yeah, it was smart to work out several days a week, do it regularly, and slacking would do him no good, but this...this was ridiculous. It was like Hercules being sapped of his strength or something. Maybe it was some evil side effect of the Borelian poison. Maybe he'd never been that strong to begin with, always relying on his Banding to cut corners and make it look like he was more than he was. Maybe he should go beyond physical therapy and get to the gym.

Groaning, he sat up. He'd already done his physical therapy for the day, but those were just exercises. He hiked up his pant leg until he could see the bullet wound. By now the torn flesh was almost twisted into a proper scar; he had an appointment next week to go in and get the stitches removed. But damn that still hurt. Even if the femur itself hadn't been damaged, the muscle damage alone was more trouble than he figured it was worth.

And he had not yet begun to paint. This was going to be harder than he thought. Maybe he should look around for professional painters, get quotes. No, he was going to do this himself. He was doing it in the first place because he was bored, and he had the time to do it. Hiring someone wasn't going to help his situation of being bored and having an ample amount of time. Besides, he knew he could do it, and he wasn't going to let a little thing like a sore leg stop him from doing it.

Still, he took a couple pills before actually getting down to the nitty gritty, laying down the plastic and making sure it covered every inch of carpeting, taping off windows and the door, even managing to get up and tape the perimeter of the ceiling. He opened the new rollers and brushes, laid out some pans, and finally pried open the lids of the paint cans and began mixing them.

All of that he did on the ground or from the comfort of a chair. Once everything was prepared, he looked dauntingly at the wall, then at his cane, leaning against the bed. He shook his head and forced himself to stand. He was just about to pick up the first can and pour it into a pan when his gaze hit the alarm clock, resting haphazardly next to his cane. Shoot, he had to pick up Tommen.

Groaning, he hammered the paint can lids back on, grabbed his cane, and hobbled out to the kitchen for his coat and shoes. He thought about taking a couple more pills, then decided against it. Best wait until he got back and was ready to start again on the painting project, otherwise he was just wasting his relief time. Without the pills, he still had to use the cane, but he'd save it until he got back. With a last mental check to make sure everything was ready, he headed out the door.

The snow had since stopped, but the roads were treacherous. He drove as fast as he dared, even Banded a little bit, but he still didn't make it to the bakery quite as fast as he'd hoped. Micah was just flipping the lights off when Walter rolled into the parking lot. The younger twin saw him and disappeared for a second. A moment later, Tommen appeared and went out the front door, Micah locking it behind him again.

"You could have called," Tommen said, shaking off the cold as he got in the car.

"I lost track of time," Walter told him. "And I figured I could Band my way here just fine. Roads are a little more slippery than I first thought."

"Oh. Heard anything about the elections yet?"

"Nope, not until tomorrow morning. Why, have you?"

"No, but I don't expect to, really."

"Well, you hear more about it than most probies and Apprentices, and you're more involved than most."

"Eighth grade state capital trip has nothing on this, that's for sure."

Walter chuckled. "That is very true. And how was school?"

Tommen shrugged. "Same as every other day. Oh, I'm not working on Monday, and I'll need a ride home."

"What for?"

"I have to stay after school."

"Did you get a detention?"

"No, it's kind of for the..." His words slid off into an incomprehensible mumble.

"For the what?" Walter asked.

"For the school..." Mumble, mumble.

"Tommen, just tell me."

"I kind of signed up for the school play. There's a meeting Monday after school."

"Oh really? What did you sign up for?"

"I don't know, backstage work. Not an actor or any speaking parts or anything, you know, just something to do without being seen."

"No shame in that; there's more to acting than just the actors. But I'm thinking this didn't come about from any suggestion that I or the school counselor has given you. Maybe this has something to do with a particular girl?"

"No!"

Walter laughed. "And in your denial, you just admitted to it. Is it Becky or someone else?"

Tommen shifted in his seat. "Becky's doing the costuming since she says most of them are pretty well in shambles. I guess in California she had a tailoring business or something and a lot of hoity-toity clients."

"I see. So then why aren't you an actor? You'd get costumed by her."

"Because I'm not an idiot; I know I'd still have to, you know, actually go out on stage and act. Besides, I guess you could say I'm kind of helping with the costuming anyway."

"Tommen, you can't sew. At least no more than to fix a pair of pants."

"Well, no."

"Does this have something to do with the increase in furs that are stinking up the garage?"

"Yeah, Becky's been buying them from me so she can use

them for the costumes; she's hoping the exposure will help her build a client base here so she can reopen her business."

"I see. Well, if that's the case, and you've got more furs coming in, you need to find somewhere to put them other than the garage. The carbon monoxide detector's going to go off, I swear."

Tommen reluctantly agreed. "So what have you been doing all afternoon?"

"Well, when we get home, you'll see," Walter told him. "And since you're home, you can help. Unless, of course, you have another Physics project that you need to tell me about?"

"No," Tommen answered guiltily.

"How's your head doing?"

He shrugged. "Okay. I can do some work on the computer, but sometimes I'll get a really bad headache and I have a hard time speaking or remembering things."

"Hard time speaking English or hard time speaking period?"

"Usually just a hard time speaking English. Once I almost couldn't speak at all."

"Did you tell anyone?"

"I just told you."

"I'm being serious, Tommen. I need to know if you need to go back in for more tests. Your arm is one thing, but I don't want to see you hurt. The brain is a delicate thing, and I don't want you to have problems for the rest of your life. Okay?"

"I'm fine; it's better than it was before."

Walter studied him, trying to gauge what was stubborn pride at not admitting weakness, and what was irritation at the "injured but not helpless" level. Tommen hadn't gotten weird on him at home yet, and neither twin had called to tell him about problems at the bakery. So far, it just seemed to be a school thing. So if it was a stress thing—which school had plenty of to go around—then it was probably a blood pressure thing. Blood pressure got too high, caused swelling in the brain, Tommen became incapacitated. Of course, that was just a theory. Question then became, was this going to go away normally, or was this a permanent thing?

He sighed. In a matter of a month, Tommen had lost his hearing and, now, it seemed, his mind, with no guarantees that either would ever return completely. Walter tried to think of ways to help him, but the last time he'd tried to help—taking him skiing to make him feel better about his hearing loss—Tommen had only been injured more. Was there anything he could do that was safe that would help?

Well, maybe the school play and his completely-not-interested pursuit of this girl would help him out some. Love—even puppy love—could do wonders for a teenage boy's self-esteem. Even if she rejected him in the end, it would be something normal. Besides, after everything he'd been through, all of his near-death experiences, the most recent of which just happened in the last twenty-four hours, what were a few cold words? It would be life; it would be high school; it would be completely and utterly normal.

Sometimes Walter wondered if he'd done the right thing, bringing Tommen into Time. There must have been some way to both acknowledge what had happened without bringing him into the understanding of how and why it happened. It was like trying to explain that "God needed Grandma in Heaven," but instead of leaving it at that and working through the pain and grief, taking the poor kid down to the morgue to see her cold, dead body, and the cold, dead bodies of a dozen other people, some of whom had been cut open for autopsy. It just wasn't right.

Tommen said something that Walter, in his own cloud of thoughts, didn't catch.

"What?" he asked dumbly.

"Dad..." Tommen sighed. He shook his head and looked out the window.

For a second, Walter was lost. Then he realized Tommen probably thought he'd been insulting him and his hearing problems. He took a level breath. "I wasn't trying to insult you, Tommen, I was thinking something else. What did you say?"

At first it didn't appear that he was going to answer. Then, "I said that if it doesn't get better over the weekend or something that I'll go in. I don't want to be afraid that a stupid headache is going to incapacitate me."

Walter nodded. "Okay. That sounds good to me. But if you get weird on me over the weekend, you're going in immediately. Deal?"

Tommen reluctantly agreed. "Deal."

Although it seemed more likely that Walter would get weird on Tommen, as high as his blood pressure was, given all the events and suspicion surrounding the elections. At this point, he was more likely to have a heart attack than Tommen was a concussive episode. So it then became a race to see who was going to end up in the hospital first over the weekend.

Walter sighed internally. Wasn't vacation and retirement supposed to be about relaxing, taking time to yourself, doing all the little things you always said you'd do but never got around to? This was not feeling very much like a vacation so far, and if he did end up having a heart attack or otherwise went into the hospital, chances were that Steggmann wouldn't let him back on the police force, at least not in his present position. He'd end up being a meter maid or something. He'd have to get a job with campus police. Worse, he'd end up having to teach them.

He shook his head. No, he was being silly. And a little paranoid. It's not over until it's over, he told himself. Tommen didn't give up on him, wouldn't have given up on him until he was six feet under; the best he could do was try to match that attitude. It was a Forbes attitude, one that they learned from their father and his father and all the Forbes men before them. It's not over until it's over.

They arrived home to the stench of vinegar and brains. Walter gave his son a look, and Tommen promised he'd move them in the morning.

The house was warm, though. As Walter sat to take his shoes off, Tommen just slipped his off and headed to his bedroom. A minute later, "Dad?"

"Yes?"

"Your project today wouldn't happen to be painting, would it?"

"It could be."

Pause. Then, "Okay."

Walter pulled off his shoes and went down to where Tommen was unpacking his backpack. "You got painting clothes?"

Tommen did not look at him, just kept unloading book after book. "Um...yeah, somewhere. You want to paint it now?"

"Why not?"

"I have homework to do."

Walter shrugged. "Okay, so do your homework. I'm not going to be Banding, if that's what you're wondering. I'm too awake to get to sleep, and it'll kill time until the results come in. What homework do you have?"

"English. I have to write an essay."

Walter folded his arms. "By 'write,' you mean 'type on the computer.' "

"Yeah."

"Are you okay to do that?"

"Yeah, if I do it in little pieces at a time. You know, one paragraph at a time or something."

"Don't strain yourself. Remember what I said about getting weird on me."

"Oh, I know."

"If you need a break, you know where I'll be."

Walter headed to his bedroom where everything was as he'd left it, all the plastic and brushes and paint. He got down on the ground and pried the lids off a second time. He was no painter, but he was pretty sure that one hour wasn't going to hurt the paint any, and he poured it into a pain.

He looked at the wall and sighed. *Don't do it. Mind over matter.*

Still, he extended his good leg and reached for his pill bottle, popped a couple, then managed to get to a standing position. He grabbed a roller, bent over to get some paint, wished he had his cane, straightened again, took a breath, and slapped the new color on the wall. No going back now.

Walter considered himself to be a pretty savvy shopper, at least in the realm of studying his options and not getting duped by hype. He wasn't immune to hype, but he figured he was better than most about it. Generally, he figured that cheap was cheap and the ultra brand names that used fancy words only found in the thesaurus were more reminisce of the guy who bought an apple for a penny, shined it up and made it look nice in order to sell it for a nickel. Walter generally tried to pick the happy medium.

Paint was not his strong suit. As far as he was concerned, there was watercolor that kindergarteners used, acrylics and stuff that artsy-crafty people used, car paint, specialized paint for road signs and lines, and everything else, by which he meant, wall paint. He was not well-versed in matte, gloss, eggshell, semi-gloss with a tilestone texture or whatever the latest fad was. He had a general idea of what such terms referred to — gloss was gloss, right? — but mostly he just looked at the little sample cards hanging on the shelves in the store, picked the one he liked, and tried to find a gallon to match.

Today was a day when he found himself wishing he had done a little more research or asked a few more questions. The color itself was correct; he liked the color. He did not like that the color beneath still showed through and that he'd apparently grabbed the gloss paint when he'd originally wanted matte. Good news, he'd only bought one gallon to start with. Bad news, he still had that whole gallon left, and he wasn't about to waste a forty-dollar investment.

After a short time, Tommen poked his head in the room. Walter had finished what he grudgingly conceded to be the first of many coats on the first wall and had started on the second wall.

"How's it going?" Tommen asked.

"Not as well as I thought," Walter replied evenly. "I might be here a while."

"Oh. Want some help?"

"Rollers are right there."

Walter heard Tommen rustling around in the package of rollers. After a second, "Oh."

"Oh, what?" He was afraid to look.

"You do know you need primer with this paint, right?"

"The wall is already painted."

"Yeah, but this is cheap paint."

"It wasn't the cheapest there; I went with the middle-priced product."

"Dad, it even says on the instructions, 'Make sure there is a layer of primer, even if the wall is already painted.' "

Walter felt like beating his head against the wall, paint be damned. Seriously, who reads the instructions on paint? It was one thing to tell a child not to drink the red-colored water or lick their fingers, but this was paint. It should be simple. Why wasn't this simple?

"And I assume you know how to fix this, too," he sighed, finally looking at his son.

Tommen gave him sort of a half-smirk. "Band it so it's dry, first of all. Then we can go out and get a can of primer and more paint."

Walter sighed again, looked at the paint on the wall, looked at the roller in his hand, looked at the paint still in the pan. Finally he shook his head. "No, not tonight. Maybe tomorrow after the inauguration."

"Need time to salvage your pride?" Tommen guessed.

"Something like that."

Tommen helped him clean up, gathering the unused materials and tossing them in one corner of the room while Walter poured the paint from the pan back into the can, scraping as much as he could and figuring that a little dried paint wasn't going to hurt anything. He'd already wasted enough paint, what was a little more?

"Are you going to sleep in here tonight?" Tommen wondered.

"Assuming I sleep at all, which isn't too likely," Walter told him. "Why?"

"I guess I just thought the fumes would be too overwhelming."

Walter paused and considered it. He'd been working with the paint long enough that he didn't even notice the smell anymore, but that wasn't to say that it was good for him. He probably should have picked up a mask or something to wear, but he hadn't even thought about it.

He let out a breath. "I can take the couch for a night, I guess. Like I said, that's assuming I sleep at all."

"Why wouldn't you sleep?" Tommen asked. "I mean, if Cassius wins — somehow — then he wins. You staying up or sleeping in isn't going to change it at that point. Better to rest and save your energy for when you really need it."

Walter folded his arms and shifted his stance, trying to take weight off his right leg. "When did you start spouting sagely wisdom? First the paint and now this."

Tommen shrugged and sighed. "When I finally woke up on the ski hill, I was pretty much just looking straight up at the sky. You know what I saw?"

"No, what?"

"Two eagles and a sunrise."

Walter sighed dramatically as Tommen broke out in a grin. "All right, sage boy, back to your essay."

Tommen shook his head. "I have to take a break. Between the computer screen and now these fumes, I don't think I'll be working on it much more tonight."

"Headache?" He nodded. "All right. Well, how about some food, at least?"

"Sounds good."

They headed out to the kitchen and, after brief deliberation, decided on a pizza. Start with a basic cheese pizza and it was a build-your-own free for all from there. Truthfully, either one of them could have eaten an entire pizza by himself on a normal day, but as it was, they decided just to split a single one this time.

"You keep asking about my head," Tommen stated as he closed the oven door and started the timer, "but what about your leg and chest and back and everything else? How are you feeling?"

Well, if I had to answer that honestly, I don't know because I can't distinguish between real pain and the pain my body fabricates in order to get more drugs. Yes, I know that I'm on the fast track to dangerous addiction, but I need to heal and I need to not be in pain so if some bad stuff happens in the next day or two, I'm not being held back by these injuries.

"The good days are starting to outnumber the bad days," Walter answered. "If I can get my leg to stop cramping up all the time, I'd probably be free of this cane already."

"The muscle relaxers don't help?"

"They do, but I'm loathe to take them more than I really need to." *Because one addiction is bad enough; I don't need two.* "I'm already skeptical about the painkillers."

Tommen studied him, and, for a moment, Walter was actually honestly afraid that his son could read his mind and knew what was going on. He didn't say anything about it directly, but he did ask, "Is there any way I can help? What can I do?"

He was a good kid. He had his faults and his shortcomings, but he was a good kid at heart. Walter almost breathed a sigh of relief as he dug into his pocket for the pill bottle. He held it up. "I get one more refill on this, and it's coming up next week. And that's it, that's the last refill, the last of the pills. You know these are opiates. Once these are gone, you take this bottle and throw it away. Not just in the little trash can there, but completely away, even if you have to hand it to the garbage man himself. Do you understand?"

Tommen nodded. "I understand. I'll do it."

"You're a good kid. A good son." Walter eased himself into the chair at the kitchen table. "Your pa would be proud of you."

Tommen claimed the other chair at the tiny table. "Tell me more about him."

Walter felt his heart skip a beat even as he sighed. "Sorry to say I didn't know a whole lot about him; I was too selfish and caught up in my own exploits and misadventures to care much about anyone else. But I remember that he liked to sing."

"Sing?"

"Mm-hm. Looking back, he had a wonderful voice, and he and our sisters would sing together. It was the most amazing thing you'd ever heard, just listening to them walking up the street, all in perfect harmony, singing any old song they knew. I think that was how he met your ma, or got her attention anyway. I'm not entirely sure."

"Can you sing?"

"No, are you kidding me? I count myself fortunate that I can whistle a tune, but I could never sing."

"But you can play the harmonica, right?"

Walter shook his head. "Nope, never learned that one."

"Do you not like it when I ask about your time in prison?"

He shifted in his seat. "I'm not proud of what I did and how I got there. I have no fond memories of that place, and it still haunts me to this day, as you now know. But I don't want you to think that you can't ask me about it. I'll tell you when to stop."

Tommen nodded. "Understood."

"That said, was there something you wanted to ask me about it?"

"No, it's just...I guess it's been on my mind a little bit lately. Just trying to reconcile who I know you as versus who you say you used to be. I don't know, I just have a hard time trying to make them fit together."

"If that's intended as a compliment, I'll take it."

The pizza finished cooking, and they both claimed a half, sliding the slices onto plates and heading to the living room to eat and watch some TV.

"So, assuming I ever get this painting thing figured out, did you want to repaint your room?" Walter asked.

Tommen shrugged and shook his head. "What for? I can only see two colors anyway. Doesn't matter to me."

"Just thought I'd ask."

"How far are you taking this remodeling project, anyway? Am I going to come home from school one day and find that you've smashed out a couple of walls or what?"

"We don't have any walls to smash like that, but no, I hadn't planned on anything like that. For now I'm sticking to walls, and I haven't yet decided on floors."

"How about you wait and see how the walls turn out?"

"So far, that's looking more and more like the plan."

It was still early in the night yet, so they stayed up watching a movie, using the commercial breaks to take their dishes to the kitchen to wash. Or rather, for Tommen to take the dishes to the kitchen to wash and rest his eyes and head.

"I'm going to bed," he announced when he returned from the last trip to the sink.

"Don't feel good?" Walter guessed.

"Not really."

"Okay. Well, get some rest and let me know how you feel in the morning."

"Why, you going to offer to take me skiing again?"

"No, but it'll tell me whether I'm taking you to the inauguration or not."

"Oh, I'm going to that no matter what."

Walter raised a brow. "If you're not feeling good, and it gets dangerous, I don't want you caught in the middle and unable to defend yourself because you're suffering from a migraine."

"I'll be fine, really."

"We'll see. Go to bed."

Walter watched Tommen walk away, mildly amused at his son's attempts to walk straight and keep his head held high rather than hunch over and stumble down to the bathroom. True, he might be perfectly fine in the morning, but Walter didn't want to put him in any more danger than he had to. Taking him to the inauguration where Cassius was set to be crowned king and Rifun installed as his right-hand, there was a certain level of danger in that.

Of course, watching Tommen only brought to mind Walter's growing fatigue. He'd promised himself that he wasn't going to sleep until he got the call and heard the results, but realistically, that wouldn't be until morning, and there was a point, in that he could do nothing about the results so he ought to save his strength for whatever became of those results, whether Cassius won and all hell broke loose, or if he didn't win and the transfer of power was a peaceful one.

There were too many variables, too many factors to consider. It was like looking at an enormous math problem, being given none of the variables, and having to work through it piece by piece using a thousand smaller equations to finally get back to the main equation. And Walter was no math whiz, that was for sure. Thank God for tax preparers.

He looked back at the TV as the movie returned from commercial break. He wasn't particularly interested in it, but Tommen seemed to think it was pretty good. Well, with Tommen off to bed, there was no real reason to keep watching it, and at this time of night there was nothing on anyway. With a sigh, he turned off the TV and hauled himself to his feet.

When he stepped in his room, he was immediately struck by the smell of paint. Tommen was right; this was not good for him, and he would never get to sleep. Well, the couch was as good as any place, he supposed. He kicked off his clothes and grabbed a blanket. By the time he was done in the bathroom and got comfortable on the couch, it was past midnight. Voting wouldn't be done until two, then the votes had to be sent back through the system and re-counted. After that, all the Dominion Timekeepers—and other Time Agents of equal-standing—would be notified, and they would notify the Wardens and on down the line it went until it reached Walter, the lowly little Captain from District Four.

Or would he be notified? His status was in limbo as it was. If he didn't win the local election, would he be notified so he could notify the person taking his place, or would the Manager pass right over him and go straight to the new guy? Was it really possible that after today, he would be answering to the twins instead of the other way around? He didn't know how he felt about that. It meant that they wouldn't be able to have their secretive little chats in the bakery office anymore. He'd be out of the loop.

As he lay there on the couch, pondering all of this, he realized another thing. He had no night light. The living room was dark, and the only light came from the little red lights on the electronics and the glow of the clock on the oven. Maybe that would be enough. He didn't want to go back in and grab his light. For one, it still felt foolish, like a child going to grab his stuffed animal that he couldn't sleep without. And secondly, he just got warm and comfortable on the couch under the blanket.

He wasn't sure how long he lay there in the dark, telling himself that the oven clock was enough and to just go to sleep. But every time he closed his eyes, something would move. He'd hear a noise and see something move that he couldn't identify. This was why he didn't travel well.

Eventually, he did get up and go back down to his room to grab the night light. Before he went back to the living room, he went to Tommen's door and pushed it open just a touch. As usual, he was sprawled out every which way, still in his clothes from the day, broken arm kept far away from the rest of his body, blankets pulled up tight around his front while leaving his back bare. He was a good kid. He had his faults, as everyone did, but he was a good kid.

Walter returned to the living room and plugged in his night light. Then, shivering only slightly, he slipped back into the warm blankets. Maybe he ought to knock down a few walls and put in some new insulation. Middle of January and this sucked.

That was his last thought before he drifted off. It was a strange sensation he sometimes got, knowing exactly when he fell asleep. And yet, he was surprised when he woke up. For a second, he couldn't comprehend what had happened or why his state of mind seemed to change. Then he realized he'd been sleeping and was just now waking up. It took him another second to figure out what had woken him up until he spotted his cell phone on the coffee table.

He glanced at the clock as he reached for his phone. Almost seven. He didn't recognize the number, but there was only one reason anyone would be calling him this early. Well, okay, there could be any number of reasons someone would be calling him this early, but only one was he expecting.

"Walter Forbes," he answered sleepily.

"Good morning, Captain," Paul, the Regional Manager, greeted grimly.

"That depends, am I?"

"You are. The vote was nearly unanimous. Honestly, I think part of it had to do with that it was such an unusual and unprecedented election, everyone just decided to go with what was already in place."

"And here I thought people really liked me."

"Well, I'm thinking that after today, it won't really matter."

Walter took a breath. Time to ask the question. "So, who won the Zero Hour?"

"I know we all saw the candidates yesterday, and most were pretty certain that Rifun and Cassius weren't on the ballot. But somehow, someway, they managed to do it. And actually, I was able to get answers on how they did it."

"Would it really make a difference?"

Paul sighed. "No, it wouldn't. But all the same, the results are in. Cassius is officially the Zero Hour. Again."

Chapter Twenty-Nine
Inauguration Day

Walter was less than thrilled about calling the twins with the news, and as soon as they heard, they all but closed up shop and came to visit. Walter stopped them from doing that, and instead told them to stay put and he would meet them at the bakery, as usual. And to think, for a while, there had actually been a possibility of not being able to just go over on a whim and have officer meetings.

He was in the middle of making breakfast when he heard the toilet flush and the sink sputter to life in the bathroom. A minute or two later, Tommen sleepily walked out to the kitchen.

"Morning, Sunshine," Walter greeted, trying to sound cool and not let on about his worries.

"What's for breakfast?" Tommen mumbled.

"You all right? Sleep okay?"

He shrugged and deliberately sat in one of the chairs at the table. "Slept okay. Kind of a headache, though. Probably from watching TV last night."

"Don't push yourself too hard to heal. Let your body do its thing on its own."

"Yeah. So who won?"

"Well, it appears I get to keep my position as District Captain. Manager said it was almost unanimous."

"Who's the dissenter?"

Walter shrugged. "Don't know. Doesn't really matter, I guess."

"What about the Zero Hour?"

He hesitated for a moment. Then, "Cassius won."

"I thought you said he wasn't—"

"I know. I know, and I already called the twins and told them the news. I even know how it happened, or what the Manager told me how it happened. So I'm heading over to the bakery, we'll discuss it, and then head to the inauguration."

Tommen shifted in his seat. "What about me?"

Walter scraped the scrambled eggs out of the pan onto two plates, then moved on to the toast. "If you're not feeling good, you're not going."

"I'm fine, I can go. I want to go."

"No, Tommen." He handed Tommen one of the plates and took the other seat, both of them trying to fit around the tiny table without spilling their sausage, eggs, bacon, and toast.

"It's not that bad," Tommen insisted. "I can take some Ibuprofen, and I'll be fine."

"No."

"Dad, I want to go. I'll be fine. Rifun won't let anything happen to me."

Walter stopped and looked at his son. "Rifun won't let anything happen to you? On what evidence do you base your conclusion? That he keeps saying he won't because he believes you're some part of a crackpot religious cult? That he appears to have saved your life the other day when one of his own men attacked you?" He went on before Tommen could protest. "Tommen, *I* won't let anything happen to you. And I'm your dad."

"Sorry," Tommen mumbled.

"I don't think you understand just how many people are going to be at the inauguration. If something bad happens and the crowd starts moving, it'll be like getting caught up in a stampeding cattle herd. Sure, Rifun might want to protect you, and even though I definitely want to protect you, there is something called friendly fire. No one may intend to hurt you if something happens, but in a blind panic, someone always gets hurt."

"I'm sorry," Tommen repeated.

Walter sighed. "I know. It's not your fault. And I wish the

circumstances were different, that I didn't have such reservations about even going myself except that it's unofficially mandated, and I want to see and know what's going to happen. But I'm not going to put you at risk."

"But if I didn't have this concussion and headache, you'd let me go?"

"Maybe. You'd at least have better chances of it."

They ate in silence for a few minutes. Then, "I don't see what difference it makes since the Coliseum has that dampening field or whatever that we can't Band anyway."

"You're not going."

"I was only saying that—"

"I know what you were saying. But I'm not changing my answer."

Tommen grumpily finished his breakfast and washed his plate. "Guess I'll just go finish my essay then."

"Don't hurt yourself," Walter called after him. "Remember what we agreed on about going to the hospital!"

"I know!"

Walter shook his head and finished his breakfast. He knew and understood why Tommen was upset. He'd be upset, too, if the situation were reversed. It was another seventeen years until the next election and inauguration. But Tommen didn't understand just how big and how busy and how dangerous the inauguration was. Even being at peak health at the top of his game with all the best training did not guarantee a smooth or pleasant experience.

The inauguration was not set to begin until about six-thirty, so Walter puttered around the house for a while. This time he decided to actually read the label and the instructions for painting before going out and buying whatever else he apparently needed. Why couldn't paint be simple, really?

About the time six o'clock rolled around, he gathered his things and made for the door. "Tommen, I'm heading out!"

"Okay!" came the reply from Tommen's bedroom, the tone

still grudging and grouchy. He hadn't come out all day.

Walter considered his cane. On the one hand, it would only add more mass to try and squeeze through the crowds, and it was liable to get lost or broken. On the other hand, he could use it to force his way through, and, if worse came to worse, use it to beat people and move them out of his way or fend them off. Eventually, he decided to take it. Worst case, he just left it in the car or in the office.

The weather outside seemed as gloomy and uncertain as Walter felt. Big, gray, ominous clouds hung low in the sky, promising snow overnight, at least a few inches. Already the roads were becoming slick, and they would be no better on the drive back. Once over the bridge and into the city, they weren't as bad, the mad six o'clock rush keeping the road warmed and the slush from turning to ice. Walter made it to the bakery without a problem, noting how several cars in the lot looked like they'd had a run of bad luck over the winter so far with missing headlights and crinkled front ends.

Inside, the store was decently busy with people grabbing a warm bite to eat on their way home. No one appeared to be in line, and Micaiah was on the counter. As soon as he looked up and saw Walter, he threw up a Band and motioned for him to come inside.

The parking lot was a minefield of alternating dry asphalt and black ice, and Walter was more than grateful to have his cane with him. He was glad to reach the safety of the sidewalk and enter the bakery which was a balmy seventy degrees or so.

"It's nice in here," he commented, shedding his jacket and following the twins into the office.

"It is," Micaiah confirmed. "Except when inconsiderate pedestrians open the door and let in a cold draft. Have a seat and tell us what happened. Sorry for the mess. I'll clean this chair off for you, Tommen."

Walter whirled to see Tommen was standing right behind him.

"Where did you come from?" he demanded.

"I Banded and hid out in the car for a couple hours," Tommen answered. He shrugged. "I knew you'd be looking for me right as you were leaving, so I decided to wait it out for a while."

"But...when I told you that I was leaving..."

"Um. Yeah. About that. I wasn't actually working on my essay in my room. I kind of discovered or developed a little trick, I think, that I want to go over with you when we get back."

Walter sighed heavily. "You're still not going."

"Why?" Micah asked. "If he managed to dupe you, I think he'd be all right."

"Besides," Micaiah went on, "what happens if we don't come back? So then, how did Cassius manage to pull off this party trick?"

Walter sighed again. He didn't like the answer, and he didn't want to repeat the answer. "The human who was pictured as a candidate was Cassius."

"Wait, what?" Micah blurted. "But that guy, I mean, he was white. And he didn't look anything like Cassius. Not nose or eyes or anything at all."

"It was his picture when he first became the Zero Hour, back when he was a gaoler at Beaumaris Gaol."

That was why Walter had gotten a bad feeling from the guy, and why he didn't immediately recognize the modern Cassius as the old Cassius, or whatever his name had been back then.

"Okay, I'm officially lost," Micah said, slumping in his seat. "Start at the beginning?"

"We're not the only ones interested in Cassius and how he got to be where he is. Mi Chin and others have been investigating him, too. The only name they have on him is Cassius, but they suspect there could be other aliases. Apparently, he was a Negro slave back in the day. He wasn't particularly submissive, so his master beat him to within an inch of his life and, long story short, he became a Harvester. He sought revenge and, over a long enough period, Harvested enough white people to alter his appearance that dramatically to become the man we saw in the picture.

"Obsessed with power, he became a gaoler. He also advanced as a Harvester until he was elected Hand of the Harvesters and, ultimately, Zero Hour of Time. At some point, he got mixed up with the Cult of the Akari, came over to America, and got stuck in the same Time trap that claimed myself and Tommen. Hence the discrepancies in the leadership and succession of powers and the whole False Zero Hour business. That's as much as the Manager was able to give me. At the same time, it could be as much of a ploy as finding false records of his Timekeeper training. No one could really figure out a timeline for how or when he changed from white to black again, but it wasn't as if he didn't have the time, if he buddied up with Rifun somewhere in there."

"Fuck," Micaiah hissed and shook his head. "Unbelievable."

"That explains the picture," Micah said, "but what about the votes? I mean, if the picture was from eons ago, he couldn't have campaigned as that person. Generally, if your voters never see you, they're not going to vote for you."

"That's the other part of this whole thing," Walter said levelly. "We assumed that because we didn't see Cassius or Rifun that it meant something happened. Maybe they had a falling out, or maybe there was a mole. Well, there was a mole. But the mole didn't operate to take Cassius out, but to put him in and rig the system so that a majority of the votes were automatically cast for him during the recount when the data got recycled through the computer."

"So what's being done about it? I mean, if they found that out before the inauguration—"

"The Hands of Time must have a Zero Hour. They're not going to postpone the inauguration because of this, however horrifying it is."

"Then what are they going to do?" Tommen wondered. "What can they do?"

Walter let out a breath. "Under normal circumstances, they could call for a special session of the Hands, where the Hands would look at the top three alternate candidates and vote on one of them. Problem is, I don't foresee Cassius letting it get to that."

"The only way we're going to know for sure," Micaiah said,

standing, "is by going and seeing for ourselves."

Walter reluctantly agreed and stood, electing to take his cane, if for no other reason than to have a weapon. He glanced at Tommen. "You can come. But you're not helping yourself. Whatever I come up with as your punishment for lying to Becky about skiing, consider it doubled."

Tommen perked up at the mention of going to the inauguration, but he faltered when Walter mentioned he was still in trouble.

"Shall we?" Walter said.

The twins opened a portal to the Wheel, shouldering the weight equally so it was more bearable for them to go through. That wasn't to say the ride wasn't still arduous and nauseating, especially for the rest of them who just simply walked through. Walter felt his chest wounds tighten where he'd thought they were almost completely healed. When he tried to move and get himself situated, his leg cramped up, and he almost cried out in pain. While the others recovered, he dug out his pills and took one. Really, he should have taken one of the muscle relaxers, but the painkillers had become a habit.

"Everyone okay?" he asked.

"Fantastic," Micaiah growled, using his little brother as a push-off point to get to a standing position, then turning and helping both Walter and Micah up. Tommen was already standing, but he was bent over with his hands on his knees like he was about to get sick. Micaiah offered him a bag but he declined.

"You feeling okay, Tommen?" Walter asked.

"*Dw i ddim yn teimlo'n dda,*" Tommen replied. "*Ond fe fydda i'n braf.*" He straightened. (I don't feel good. But I'll be fine.)

Well, sending him back through the portal would only make it worse, but Walter still didn't like it. Finally he nodded. "All right. Fine. If you start feeling sick or something during the inauguration, you can always come back and go home. Got it?"

Tommen agreed wordlessly.

"So, did everyone remember their translators?" Micah wondered, bringing his out of his pocket.

That started the awkward pat-down search of every pocket until each man found his translator and had it inserted or installed. Then they started down the row of portals. It wasn't as terrible as it had been on voting day in the same way that the five o'clock rush on Monday wasn't as bad as the five o'clock rush on Friday. Both sucked, just one a little less so.

They were saved about a half hour or more of waiting just by being able to bypass the translator dispenser, but that meant very little compared to the pushing and shoving and waiting they were going to be doing once inside the Wheel proper.

The first thing Walter noticed was that security was everywhere. And by security, he meant Grandfathers. Everywhere. It was like having a cop on every block corner plus at every doorway to every business, and some windows, too.

"How many Grandfathers are there?" Tommen wondered quietly.

"Go to the New York sewers and count the rats," Micaiah told him. "You'll have an easier time of it."

It was not a comforting thought, but probably as accurate as anything Walter had ever heard. Once, he'd been on a murder case that turned into some international serial killer fiasco. In the end, it involved the FBI, CIA, even the Secret Service; it was like something out of a spy thriller. Walter remembered being called on, early on in the investigation, to meet with the head honchos of the respective agencies and fill them in on everything CPD knew and what had been done so far and so forth. Even though he was just supposed to relay information and was in no real danger himself, he still felt like a kindergartener being sent to the principal's office on the first day of school.

Comparatively speaking, that event now felt like a wonderful flower-filled trip to grandma's house. Here, now, even though he was just passing through to get to a place, he felt as though he were going to be beheaded if he walked through the wrong door or something. He felt as if he was being silently paraded to his own death sentence, and not something gentle like lethal injection, either. More like electric chair. Or hanging but with a rope too short. Or any number of awful medieval tortures. Walter felt his gut turn and his breakfast turn with it. Maybe he should have gone with a little lighter fare, like cereal.

"When we get to the Coliseum, you have to stay outside," Walter reminded Tommen as they approached the portal. "If anything happens, don't wait for us, you just run."

"The portal can't close without us anyway," Micaiah told him, trying to sound reassuring.

"But—" Tommen began.

"Tommen, there is nothing you can do in there to help," Micah interrupted. "Everyone that's going to be in the Coliseum, in the Seat, is more highly trained than you, in both Time and combat. Something happens, you run. Got it?"

"But—"

"Run, Tommen," Walter ordered sternly. "Don't make me tell you twice."

Tommen sighed. "Okay. Something happens, I run."

"Good lad."

There was no such thing as getting to the Coliseum "early" in Inauguration Day. It was possible to be early for Black Friday. It was possible to be early for the Superbowl. It was not possible to be early for the inauguration. There were some who camped out for the voting and then just moved over to the Coliseum once the last of the sessions was held and the place cleared out of normal business. That was as "early" as it could get, but the Coliseum was never so empty that a person could ever have his pick of front row seats.

As they stepped through the portal into the Coliseum, Walter shivering internally as he felt the Suppression field settle over him, it became apparent that they might not have their choice of back row seats either.

"All voting officers have to be in the Seat?" Tommen

wondered. "How are you supposed to get in?"

"Very carefully and with a lot of pushing and shoving," Walter told him, not relishing the idea. "You remember what I told you?"

Tommen rolled his eyes. "Yes. If something happens, I run, and don't wait for you."

"Just making sure. You can get as close as the first track, I think, but it might be safer if you stayed here in back near the portal."

"I'll find a spot."

Tommen turned to go off and stake out his square foot of space, but Walter called him back. "Tommen." He looked back. "I love you. Stay safe."

Tommen grinned. "It's only inauguration, not a death sentence."

The words were meant to be cheerful and reassuring, but Walter could see that even Tommen was having a hard time convincing himself of that. He managed a lopsided grin. "Love you, too, Dad."

Then he was gone. After a second, Micah and Micaiah prodded Walter to keep moving toward the Coliseum.

"He's a good kid," Micah told him. "He might be an idiot sometimes, but he's smart when he has to be. Resourceful. If something happens, I'm not too worried about him making it out."

Walter glanced at him. "Have you ever thought about kids?"

The younger twin quickly averted his gaze. "Maybe once, a long time ago. You and Tommen are a special case, but we all know that it's not really an option for us."

"What about you, Micaiah?"

The elder twin also avoided eye contact. "Like he said, maybe a long time ago. These days, I don't think I'd want to raise a kid in this world."

That didn't really help Walter any as those were the exact fears and doubts he was currently having. Did he do the right thing, raising Tommen in this world? And setting aside Time and all its chaos, what about just Earth? Good God, the shit that was happening around the world right now? No place for a child. True, Tommen was sixteen, but still, just a child. He was having a tough time as it was with school and bullies and girls and work. Why did Walter ever think a teenager would be able to do all that plus balance a secret double-life?

Well, what was done was done. He'd tried to teach Tommen some tricks and some common sense. Now, if something happened, they'd both see just how much of an effect it had and if he'd really learned anything. Because if something happened, chances were, Walter wasn't going to make it in time to save him.

With a heavy heart, worried mind, and blood pressure high enough that he expected to keel over at any second, they entered the Coliseum. The guard slots at each entrance were just a little more visible today, as were the guards themselves, a tripled and quadrupled security force roaming the tracks and scrutinizing everyone who was present. It was kind of like going through airport security and being scanned and frisked and everything else, except the guards here actually made a difference in the services they provided. They actually had on record all the times they stopped lunatics and bad guys and Time terrorists.

"Ever wonder how those guys get their jobs?" Walter hissed, nodding slightly toward the nearest guard.

"Sometimes," Micaiah admitted. "I figure it involves either sex, blood, or money. Probably a combination of the three."

"How do you figure sex into it when pretty much all of them are different species?" Micah wondered dumbly.

Walter wasn't sure he wanted to know the answer to that, and hoped Micaiah would leave the question as a rhetorical. But his expression indicated he was ready with a smarmy reply. "Hey, if it's got a mouth..." He made a gesture.

Micah's expression contorted into something between disgust and shock that his brother actually said it out loud. Walter pinched the bridge of his nose and shook his head. "Thank you, Micaiah, that was more than I needed to think about right now."

"He asked," Micaiah defended.

"And you answered. Unnecessarily." Walter sighed. "Come on. Might as well see if we can get in and get some decent seats anyway."

The twins agreed, and they started their slow trek to the Seat of the Hands.

The crowd filed in through the enormous iron gates that served as a direct line from the outer track to the Seat, the gates that were only opened for this one occasion, and, for as big as they were, just didn't seem quite big enough.

"Do you think it's wise to sit together?" Micaiah asked as they approached the inner track. "Or would it be better to separate?"

"Where are our exits?" Walter wondered. "The main gates, obviously, but they're too obvious."

"The only other option is the gate on the floor that the Bat or the Day opens, but that's likely to be closed," Micah said. "Other than that, there's no way in or out."

Walter didn't believe that for a second, but an emergency was not the time to go snooping around for secret panels and switches. At the same time, there was never a time to look for said panels and switches when no one was watching, because someone was always watching.

"I don't think there's any advantage to splitting up," he decided finally. "Something happens, we need to run, and not fight unless we absolutely have to. We'll just have to stay as close to the exits as possible."

On any normal day, when the Hands were in session for petitions, reviews, and so forth, the Hands sat in the stands and their victims stayed down on the floor. For the inauguration, it was the other way around. The voting public would crowd the stands and look down upon the Hands.

The path to the stands was, as could be expected, a very steep set of stairs. There was no ADA compliance here, and Walter looked upon them with dread. Micah got in front of him and Micaiah behind, coaxing him up as if he were a stubborn mule or something. Still, he bit his tongue and swallowed his pride, accepting the help and telling himself there were bigger fights to be had today.

"I think the last time I was at an event this big, it was a soccer match in Brazil," Micaiah commented.

It was almost impossible to hear, even sitting next to each other. The air was filled with chatter and grunts and groans and all manner of animal noises that passed as language to one culture or another. There was pushing and shoving and a thousand different kinds of name-calling. Walter and the twins got jostled quite a bit as they fought to maintain their position as close to the stairs as they could get and stay together. It was like sitting in the end seats of a prime row at some event or concert. Everyone wanted to get through, had to get through. And if they had to get out, then back they came, bumping and jostling some more.

There were some fundamental differences between the inauguration and other major events, like sporting events. For one, there were no hot dog or T-shirt vendors, no sponsors doing crazy raffles and giveaways to the fans who screamed the loudest, no radio or TV hosts interviewing people and sweeping cameras around to show just how huge the crowd was. Really, it was more like going to a lecture at a university. Walk in, sit down, wait to be amazed.

The biggest difference, however, was the fact that there were no bathrooms. None whatsoever. And given what day it was, there wasn't even a quiet place to be found just to piss in a bucket. And of course, what should happen as soon as Walter sat down than his need to pee should make itself known. But he had no desire to go back down the stairs only to come back up the stairs, give up his seat, probably be reduced to peeing behind a bush or something and still be in full view of anyone who noticed, and so humiliate himself and be late for the start of the procession. He shifted position and told himself to think about something, anything else. Where was Tommen? Was he okay? Did he find a spot to stand and watch and be safe? Did he still have a headache?

"You okay, Walt?" Micah asked next to him. "Someone put

tacks on your seat?"

Walter groaned. "I...probably should have gone before we left the bakery."

On his other side, Micaiah shook his head. "Go now while you still have time. We'll save your seat."

Walter thanked them, grabbed his cane, and started on the treacherous journey back down to the floor of the Seat. His reason for going was actually two-fold. Ninety percent of it was so he could find somewhere to relieve himself. The other ten percent was so he could quickly scope out another exit, one they hadn't seen yet. The majority of the crowd had filtered in, making it easier to see across the floor where secretaries ran to and fro, getting who knew what done and ready. He couldn't imagine them fighting their way through the throngs, so there had to be another way in and out.

Unfortunately, there were no neon signs marked, "Secret Exit," and his bladder was about ready to burst.

By the time he returned, he was surprised he hadn't missed the start of the procession. Everyone appeared to be situated, but nothing was currently happening.

"They were having security issues," Micah told him. "You missed some alien just losing it and running down and across the floor there. Guards took him down and hauled him off to the Judgment Wing. It was terrifying but also pretty funny. So they're not starting until everything's been cleared."

"There was something happening, and I missed it?" Walter whined, only half-joking. A lot could be told by one little incident like that, not only about the perpetrator himself, but whether there might be others. Equally as important was the reaction of the crowd. Were they afraid? Were they amused? Did they try to join in?

He didn't get to consider it for much longer before the floor cleared and the lone little gate, where all of them had gone to face the Hands at one time or another, began opening. In a stadium of untold thousands, maybe even millions, it was possible to hear the scuffle of the Bat's claws as he walked through the tunnel and out onto the floor.

Sometimes Walter wondered if all the introductions and formalities that they went through for every little thing had been invented by some failed horror movie director who liked his suspense so much that he literally forgot to add in the actual horror or action that was supposed to come at the end. So what was supposed to be a masterful suspense thriller just turned into some Absurdist comedy.

"Timekeepers!" the Bat thundered in an uncommon and yet terrifying voice. "Harvesters! Merchants!"

Still, it was the way things were, and there was something to be said for familiarity. When something became familiar, it became easier to spot that which was unfamiliar.

"You have endured eleven years—" Because it was only eleven years in the Wheel, but seventeen on Earth. "—of submission to the same Hands of Time."

The good news was that it allowed Walter time to look around and consider the scene as a whole. The crowd was too tense, too eager to listen to the Bat. Whatever had happened while Walter was gone, whoever it had been and for whatever reason, it was unlikely to be an isolated incident, not once the news was made official and Cassius was crowned the Zero Hour.

"You have cast your votes and let your voices be heard, whom you want as your Hands and your leaders."

There was a nervous ripple that went through the crowd just then. So, word had gotten to everyone that the votes had been re-cast in Cassius' favor. Would that be mentioned here? Would it be acknowledged? Would it be reconciled and put to rights in a special session of the Hands? So many questions went unspoken around the Seat.

"We begin today by shedding the old leadership to make way for those whom you have chosen to take their place."

The hair on the back of Walter's neck prickled. He'd been to his fair share of inaugurations, and he had a general idea of how the intros and formalities worked and how they were worded. But something was off about the way the Bat kept referencing the choices of the voters, how they chose their leaders, how they voted and made their voices heard. The Time industry held elections, but its version of democracy was only a faint echo of how true democracy worked. The bribery was obvious and everyone knew that, to some extent, yes, the elections were rigged. But to have such a blatant hacking of the system, that was the shock here.

The Bat took a step back, wings shifting. The small gate opened again, and fifty-one shrouded figures filed into the Seat. They came in pairs, two by two walking dutifully into the ark, the pure white shroud of the Zero Hour bringing up the rear. As they hit the center of the floor, the pairs parted and went opposite directions until they all stood in a single line in the middle of the Seat.

There was movement in the crowd again. Nervous shifting, talking, whispering, pointing. The Hands did not move, and in fact stood very much like statues there on the floor. The Bat took another step back, his wings fluttering as he looked around, possibly trying to identify some threat.

What would happen if suddenly someone — or a lot of someones — jumped the wall and tried to attack them?

"Hands of Time!" the Bat bellowed.

The crowd quieted and waited in breathless anticipation, though far from the romantic kind.

"We shall begin the oath of leaving office."

The Hands maintained their stony formation as the Bat led them in the end of term oath. It was one of the few things that Walter actually really liked about Time politics and wished he could somehow bring it to Earth-side politics. The basic gist was that the Hand would recognize all actions as of their own will and volition, that they would accept all responsibility for them and could not deny them. All actions, all words, all votes were set in stone, and they would have to stand by them forevermore.

The idea was that if, for some reason, an action was done under duress and it was not reported, then the person was a coward and would have to stand by his cowardice. In addition, it prevented them from backpedaling later if they were questioned. There was no, "Well, what I meant was..." or "You have to read between the lines and think abstractly..." A man's word was his word, nothing more, nothing less. And finally, even if someone changed his mind later and disagreed with a stance he once supported, he would have to acknowledge that, at one time, he did agree. No wishy-washy pandering, all set in stone.

Obviously, there were flaws and loopholes and, occasionally, someone could get burned by their own words or deeds. But Walter honestly thought it was one of the smarter and more decent things that the Time industry brought to the political table.

As the Bat brought the oath to a close, Walter took another survey of the crowd. Some were beginning to relax. The Bat hadn't announced a hostile takeover, and everything was going as planned. The Hands and Zero Hour took their oath, and nothing spontaneously combusted. Others in the crowd were still on edge, wondering if there was some cue they should be listening for, something that would let them know when it was time to run.

Nothing of the kind happened. Instead, it moved into the second phase of the oath, when the Bat went and met with each Hand for a private word. It was a tradition, part of the inauguration, but no one knew what the Bat or the Hands said as they only spoke for a couple seconds at the most. Not even former Hands would tell, either explicitly or in some sagely non-answer like, "He tells you exactly what you need to hear."

But what had been originally meant as some private word as the current Council of Hands prepared to give up their power, now turned into the object of suspicion and whispering. Walter had turned down the range on his translator, but he could still hear them as they wafted around the room. Giving the Hands instructions, directions, threats, promises. All manner of conspiracy theories came from this, too, none of which Walter wanted to consider.

"You think Tommen's okay?" Walter asked, not looking at either Micah or Micaiah.

"You want my honest opinion?" Micaiah wondered rhetorically. "I think he's more okay than we are."

It was not a comforting thought in that it only made Walter's gut twist more at the thought of impending doom, but it was a scraggly reassurance that no matter what, Tommen had the best chance of making it out if and when something happened. What that something was, he didn't know, and they all waited for it.

The Bat finished speaking to the last Hand and returned to his normal spot. "And now! We begin the unshrouding!"

He went to one end of the line and walked behind the Hands. Approaching the first Hand, he said, "The Hand of Scientifically Superior and Openly Engaged Civilizations!"

The Bat lowered the hood of the Hand's shroud. Humanoid with kind of gray-lavender skin, enormous eyes, and that was where the similarities ended. The Bat moved on to the next Hand.

"The Hand of Scientifically Superior and Engaged Privilege Civilizations!"

The difference between Openly Engaged and Engaged Privilege, also just called simply Engaged or Reserved, was that Openly Engaged allowed average citizens to enter the Wheel, to buy Time, to sell wares, and so on. Engaged Privilege Civilizations may or may not tell their public about the use of Time, but its use was restricted to business only.

"The Hand of Scientifically Superior and Unengaged Civilizations!"

They were generally considered the snobs of the universe, those who were, clearly, scientifically superior, but had no interest in being part of Time because, well, they were superior. What use did they have for the Time industry when they were already so wealthy and civilized without it?

"The Hand of Scientifically Advanced and Openly Engaged Civilizations!"

Scientifically Superior Civilizations were those who had advanced space travel capabilities, had a forceful presence in the universe, and were always on the cutting edge of technology in pretty much all fields. Scientifically Advanced societies were capable of extended space travel but weren't exactly a force to be reckoned with and might lag behind in other developments.

"The Hand of Scientifically Advanced and Engaged Privilege Civilizations!"

And on and on it went, through Scientifically Advanced, Advancing, Modest, and Primitive, all of them Openly Engaged, Engaged Privilege or Unengaged. Earth was Scientifically Advancing because humans had space travel capabilities to get to the moon, to Mars, to send probes and gather data about the universe, but it had no sustainable capabilities as of yet and often lagged far behind in other advancements such as eco-stability, energy efficiency, medicines, and other scientific fields. Scientifically Modest Civilizations were more in the Renaissance era, or maybe the Industrial Revolution, an explosion of new inventions and thoughts and a drive to become bigger and better as a whole society, but there was still the gap between the drive and the realization.

"The Hand of Scientifically Primitive and Unengaged Civilizations!"

"She's alive!" Micaiah blurted as the Bat removed the hood to reveal a stunning humanoid tigress.

"What happened to her?" Micah wondered. "I thought Cassius killed her?"

"You'll have to ask her later," Walter told them.

So that was the mysterious Sifura who took his son across the universe, across a desert, through a jungle, and up a mountain to find the cure for the Borelian poison. Pretty thing. She certainly looked capable. Oddly—or perhaps not so—Walter began to question his son's sexually active status.

Once the Civilization Hands were over with, the titles turned into specific alien types.

"The Hand of Flora!"

Because apparently it was just a bigger deal on some worlds

where, Walter had heard, it was possible but illegal to Harvest trees and flowers.

"The Hand of Fauna!"

Again, because it was a huge deal to some people.

This continued for the Hand of Rocks and Pebbles, Oceans and Water, Sky and Cloud, That Which Lies Beneath, even Energy and Waves. Yes, there was a Hand who was in charge of all issues as they pertained both to Time and to the energies and waves and other non-particulate matter of a planet or civilization. Walter wasn't sure how that worked exactly, but it must be a big deal to someone.

After that, they turned to the titles of the Hands governing the Time Agents.

"The Hand of Timekeepers!"

Give the Bat credit for one thing, he never faltered on any of the names when he gave them with the titles.

He lowered the hood of the Hand of Timekeepers, a centaur-kind of thing in that it was a quadruped but with half a humanoid body. Well, sort of. His exact appearance was difficult to describe other than very big, and Walter would hate to get caught under those enormous hooves.

"The Hand of Harvesters!"

Walter leaned over to Micaiah. "I haven't seen Lily at all lately, have you?"

Micaiah shook his head. "No. But if she doesn't want to be found, she won't be found."

"I have a hard time believing that, or that it works well."

The older twin just shrugged and said nothing more. The Bat went to the next Hand.

"The Hand of Merchants!"

Merchants were a bit sketchy as far as their role in Time. About half of them, if not more, had no real Time abilities to speak of. They didn't Harvest, couldn't Band. All they did was buy Time from the Harvesters and sell it in the various marketplaces. Not a few of them stole on a regular basis, and the profession was almost considered the legal wing of the Runners, like a storefront that acted as a disguise for the mafia dealings in the office. Like a bakery that served as a front for the two Timekeeper Lieutenants who ran it, and their Captain who couldn't stop pestering them.

"The Hand of Scouts!"

The Scouts were easily the sketchiest bunch of all. Except for the Hand and the probationaries — or Underdogs as Walter had heard them called — the Scouts did not have an official hierarchy, just a pecking order. They were like the wild motorcycle gang who showed up in the bar occasionally. They didn't really cause a lot of fights, didn't bring out the guns and knives, and brought in a lot of business, but the bartenders were usually left in the morning, wondering if their business was worth the trouble.

"The Hand of New Blood!"

He was the Hand who represented all probationaries across all fields of work, whether Timekeeper or Harvester or Scout. Anyone who was a probationary was covered under his jurisdiction.

"The Hand of Secretaries!"

Well, maybe Walter had been a bit hasty, calling the Scouts the sketchiest group. Of the Time Agents, they certainly were. But if the secretaries were included in that group, then they were easily the shadiest bunch. The secretaries knew everyone and everything, and Walter generally tried to watch himself whenever he was in the presence of a secretary. And sometimes, even when he was alone in a room, he still didn't trust that he was completely alone.

The unshrouding continued on, and Walter quickly grew bored. There were titles relating to the lifespan of various races, relating to various communications of races, hierarchical style, and all sorts of things that Walter never would have guessed to be so important that they warranted a Hand to oversee them. Some of them, he was pretty sure, weren't actually as important as people or the Hands thought they were; it was more just that eons ago when the first Council of Hands was being constructed and they decided to have fifty-one flipping Hands, they ran out of actually important titles and just started making them up as they went along.

"Ever wonder what it would be like if we all walked in, they brought out the new Hands, said, 'These are your new Hands' and then left? Like, that was the whole inauguration?" Micah said, stifling a yawn. "I mean, seriously, this is just boring."

"Good thing it only comes every seventeen years," Walter agreed.

"These Hands!" the Bat went on. "These are the Hands who have served you for the last eleven years! They have taken their ending oath of office, and now they will turn over their power to the new Hands whom you have chosen!"

Again with the emphasis on the elections and choosing the new leaders. Walter shifted in his seat, taking in the reaction of the crowd. The monotony of the unshrouding had lulled everyone almost to sleep and produced a familiar sense of security, as if everything was progressing well with no further incidents. Now they were back awake again, whispering, pointing, looking, moving and fidgeting.

The only one who had not had his hood removed was the Zero Hour, but that ceremony was done separately, once the Hands had changed over. Still, it was more than a little disquieting to see fifty Hands standing there exposed, their identities and so their deeds open for all scrutiny, while the Zero Hour remained covered, anonymous.

"If Cassius has been masquerading as the Zero Hour," Micah began, "and yet he was elected Zero Hour, what happens when the newly-elected Hands make their grand entrance onto the floor?"

"Then I suggest you start stretching your legs and get ready to make a mad dash for the exit," Walter told him grimly.

He didn't say that he'd been wondering the same thing. No Hand could serve consecutive terms; there always had to be a resting period, a total change of leadership. The only exception to this might be if a position ran unopposed as a few were wont to do, such as the Hand of Scientifically Primitive and Unengaged civilizations, like Sifura. This go around, with Cassius not one to play by the rules, clearly, this could get real interesting, real fast.

The gate on the floor opened again and more people and aliens filed onto the floor. They were not shrouded, but they also walked in pairs, splitting off as the first group had until the old Hands faced their new counterparts.

There were fifty-one of them out there, fifty Hand- and one Zero Hour- elect. But the man standing in for the Zero Hour was not Cassius, either as Walter knew him today or in Beaumaris. Rather, that man was Rifun Ndolo. He wore blue jeans and work boots as well as a bland gray sweatshirt, long hair tied back.

To anyone who wasn't familiar with humans—which was probably ninety-eight percent of those in attendance—they probably wouldn't have been able to tell the real different between the man in the picture from the day before and the man who stood out there now. A picture didn't give height or weight or anything like that, only the face. They wouldn't have known that Rifun was a good six inches taller than Cassius and maybe twenty pounds lighter.

At the same time, it was a near-perfect decoy. If anyone intended to make a move and kill Cassius, they would take Rifun out instead. And Walter highly doubted that Rifun would go down easy if he had any chance at all.

"The Hand of Scientifically Superior and Openly Engaged Civilizations!" the Bat announced.

The Hand, already with his hood removed, unclasped his cloak and put it around the new Hand, saying, "I, Turio Kalu, Warden Timekeeper, Quadrant Three, Parsec One, Sector Twelve, System Eight, Planet Ninety-Three, Region Three, District Eleven, bestow this shroud and its accompanying responsibilities upon you, Edes, Quadrant Five, Parsec Nine, Sector Nine, System Two, Planet Eighteen, Region Two, District Five. May you govern with wisdom, to lead your charge well with truth and justice, to rule not with favoritism but according to the Laws of Time, passed down from Hand to Hand. And may the universe be a better place for it."

The Hand-elect dipped his head. "I, Edes, Quadrant Five, Parsec Nine, Sector Nine, System Two, Planet Eighteen, Region Two,

District Five, accept the appointment as the Hand of Scientifically Superior and Openly Engaged Civilizations, as well as its shroud and all accompanying responsibilities. I promise to govern with wisdom, to lead my charge well with truth and justice, to rule not with favoritism but according to the Laws of Time, passed down from Hand to Hand. I hope to make the universe a better place for it."

And so it went, each Hand passing their shrouds to the next generation of leaders with a lot of pomp and circumstances, filler speech, flowery words, and a lot more bullshit than Walter thought he would be able to stomach. The wisdom the Hands governed with was not King Solomon kind of wisdom, more like the cunning and scheming of a very vengeful cat. Truth was whatever money said it was, as well as justice. Bribery and favoritism was rampant. The whole speech was hypocritical and offensive, and it was going to be repeated fifty times.

"You look about as sick as I do," Micaiah growled beside him.

"False hope," Walter said. "As long as the Hands keep spouting these nice, safe images—as hollow as they are—it lets everyone know that things are going to stay exactly as they are. No one likes the corruption, but I don't think anyone can imagine things any other way. I certainly can't."

"That's what happens when you try to connect things that won't be joined. There are too many races, too many cultures, too many conflicting values and laws and virtues. Try to make everything play nice with everything else and you get this. An implosion."

"With Cassius as both arsonist and king of the ashes."

Again, the procession of handing over the shrouds skipped over the Zero Hour who simply waited patiently. Walter wasn't at a particularly advantageous viewpoint, but he was almost sure that Rifun and Cassius were communicating in some way. Small hand gestures, facial expressions, some weirdly acquired telepathy. Somehow, they were coordinating and planning everything, even now, in front of everyone in the Seat.

"Start planning your escape now," Walter hissed as they got

down to the last ten Hands.

"We go with you, Cap—" Micah began.

Walter cut him off. "No. Don't worry about me. Do as I told Tommen and just run, get out. The portal will close for you and keep you safe. I'll open and close my own if I have to. Jut get yourselves to safety."

The twins exchanged an uncertain glance over his head but they did not argue. They weren't in the planning stages anymore; now they were getting down to the real action part of this. No encounter with Rifun didn't end in some kind of violence. Put him and Cassius together, and it was about to hit the fan.

The last shroud was handed over, and the Bat stepped up again.

"The power of the Hands has been transferred!" he confirmed. "Look upon your new Council of Hands!"

Not that there was much to see, really. After three seconds, all the Hands pulled up their shrouds and then they were gone, not to be seen again for eleven-slash-seventeen years. When they did that, all the former Hands were dismissed, and they filed off the floor, back through the gate from which they emerged.

This left only the new Hands and both Zero Hours, or the Zero Hours as most in attendance understood them to be. Walter felt his leg cramp up. On one side of him, Micah gripped his seat hard. On the other side, Micaiah clenched and relaxed his fists in his lap, gaze fixed on the floor like a hawk on a mouse.

"The final transfer of power," the Bat announced, "is that of the Zero Hour! The Zero Hour is the leader of leaders, the Hand whose only job is to oversee the Hands and govern without bias! The Zero Hour is the final voice in votes and matters of state, voting only when the Hands are unable to reach their own conclusions! The Zero Hour is the ultimate and final authority figure, the champion of Time and its interests, bearing upon his shoulders the awesome weight of the universe!"

"Gee, don't forget about the part where he invented the

Internet, brought world peace, and died on a cross," Micah hissed under his breath.

Walter grunted in agreement. He might have had some witty remark to add, but he was too focused now. It all came down to this. All around him, people and aliens fidgeted in their seats, looking, watching, listening, waiting to see what would happen next. Would everything go as normal? Would they live to see the end of the day?

"And now we begin the final transfer of power!" the Bat went on, moving to take his place behind the Zero Hour. Walter thought he saw Rifun grin fiendishly. "Behold, your Zero Hour who has governed you for the last eleven years!"

The Bat reached up to remove the Zero Hour's hood, but the Zero Hour stepped out of his reach. Rifun moved to the side as he did so. Then the Zero Hour stopped and removed his own hood. It was Cassius.

Time felt suspended there in the Seat of the Hands. This was not how it was supposed to go. There was an order, a tradition. Yes, the formalities were boring as hell, but they were there for a reason. It was to make sure everything went smoothly, gave people comfort in uncertain times like this. Those traditions and formalities had just been broken, and no one knew quite what to do. Did they panic and run away? Did they attack the fiend who dared to break said traditions? Did they do anything at all? In the end, no one moved. Except Cassius, who took center stage and seemed to fill the whole Seat.

"Many of you were expecting to see a familiar transition of power," he said. "Many of you were expecting to hear the same familiar words that have been spoken from one Zero Hour to the next as he hands over his cloak."

Immediately, alarms were going off in Walter's mind. He leaned over to Micah who was the closest to the stairs. "We need to go."

"What?" Micah wondered, looking at him.

"He only said that many of us were expecting the old

traditions. Which means that there are those here who were not expecting it, and they're the ones who are going to kill us if they catch us. We have to go."

Walter turned to Micaiah and said the same thing. The elder twin simply nodded, almost imperceptibly.

"I know that you were told—by your Lieutenants, by your Physicians, whoever told you today that the elections for the Zero Hour had been rigged in such a way that it didn't matter how you voted because they got rearranged anyway," Cassius continued. "For many of you, this came as a shock. And now you sit here wondering what's going to happen. Was it done with the Zero Hour-elect's knowledge? Was it a scheme, a scam, a ploy? What fiendish powers are behind this? Could there be some truth behind the rumors of a Flase Zero Hour?"

"He's getting too ominous for my tastes," Walter murmured. He elbowed Micah. "Go."

"We can't all go at once," Micaiah said, grabbing his arm as he tried to slide out with the younger twin. "It's too obvious. He's the smallest of us; he can slip out easier than all three of us. Let him go, wait a minute, then you go, and I'll follow suit."

Walter hesitated. Somewhere in his gut, he knew there wasn't going to be time to pull off something like that. But Micaiah was right; Micah could get out by himself easier than the three of them trying to make a break for it. After a moment, he nodded and relayed the plan to Micah.

"You sure you'll be okay?" Micah wondered.

"No, I'm not," Walter confessed. "But one of us has to make it at least. Find Tommen and go home. Don't stop for anything."

Micah looked at them, wide-eyed and fearful, but with the quiet determination that said he'd do anything for them. He nodded, gave them a searching glance, then turned and slipped down to the stairs, vanishing in an instant.

"All during the elections, you heard about a False Zero Hour, one who was masquerading as the highest authority in the land with no one to rein him in." Cassius was still talking. Say one thing, he'd probably practiced this dramatic monologue for a while. And it wasn't half-bad, either, as far as evil, psychopathic, villainous monologues went. "You heard tales of Calis Cutthroat being this enemy, this False Zero Hour." He looked around at the gathered crowd. "I. Am. He."

"I think that's our cue," Walter said, sliding out of his seat and making for the stairs, Micaiah right behind him.

They weren't the only ones with that idea as the crowd as a whole seemed to shift. But like any sporting event, moving massive crowds of people took time, and no one went anywhere faster. Walter got pushed and shoved, almost lost his footing several times on the steps; in fact he might have if not for Micaiah's quick reflexes and strong arms. As they moved, Cassius kept talking, his voice rising above the growing din of the crowd.

"I am Cassius, and I am your Zero Hour!"

"We've officially entered into the Twilight Zone," Walter said, turning the corner and starting down the last flight of stairs. "Time to get out of Nutjob Town with Mayor Crackpot."

"I second that motion," Micaiah said behind him.

They reached the ground floor and turned to head out the main gates. Walter didn't want to because it was too obvious, but there was still nowhere else to go that he knew of.

As it turned out, there was nowhere to go at all. The crowd began clogging up the passage. There were roars and screams and gurgles of blood coming from up ahead, and the crowd began backing up. Walter couldn't see well, but from what he could tell, the Coliseum guards were blocking the exit and pushing the crowd back into the Seat, killing anyone who tried to slip through the line. The guards did not move especially fast, and pretty soon, Walter and Micaiah were hemmed in on all sides by terrified people and aliens trying to escape.

"Do you think Micah got out?" Walter wondered, hanging onto Micaiah's arm so they wouldn't be separated.

"I don't know," Micaiah admitted, and Walter heard fear in his voice. Fear that his brother hadn't made it, that he'd been killed, that he was lost forever and they might not even know it. He shook his head. "Hang on to me."

"Believe me, I can't think of any better alternative," Walter said, trying to find some sort of humor in the situation but finding only grim reality.

Micaiah turned and began bulldozing his way through the crowd, going against the grain and making for the little gate, the one where they normally entered and exited the Seat. No surprise, the gate was down.

"Get to the center," Walter ordered. "Whatever Cassius is planning to do, his goons will have to work from the outside in."

"Makes sense to me," Micaiah said, turning and doing as he was instructed, using his broad shoulders to push his way through the throngs one more until they got about as close to center as Walter figured they could manage. But he also noticed something else.

"Where is Cassius?"

They looked around, but the madman was nowhere to be seen. Then Walter spotted him and Rifun heading up the stairs into the stands. They'd effectively traded places. Where the crowd was typically supposed to be seated above the Hands to scrutinize them, now Cassius and Rifun stood over them. Opposite them, also in the stands, were the newly-elected Hands. Some looked as uncertain as the crowd, while other were more resolute in their posture, or what could be seen of it with the shrouds in place.

Cassius still overlooked them with his hood down, but he did not speak anymore. The panic of the crowd was simply too loud to even attempt it. But Walter did see that he and Rifun exchanged words, looking here, looking there, pointing. Then they became still for a moment. Then Cassius said a word.

Walter did not hear it, but he did not need to. He didn't need to know Cassius' exact command to understand what was going on when Grandfathers began flooding into the stands. A panicked roar went up collectively from the crowd and Walter felt himself being jostled and pushed around again. He held tighter to Micaiah's arm.

"It's been nice knowing you, Micaiah," Walter said. "Maybe we'll see each other again in some other life."

"Maybe," Micaiah agreed.

"I guess I'm just glad I got to tell Tommen one last time that I love him."

"He knows. He always knew."

The frightened crowd seemed to hush then. Walter and Micaiah turned to look at Cassius who was commanding attention.

"You all came here today expecting—hoping that you could hear some fancy, familiar, empty, lying words that would let you know that everything was going to be okay; everything was going to stay exactly the same," he began, sneering. "Well, things are not going to stay the same. Things are going to change, and we're going to start doing things my way. But if you're going to clean house, first you have to...clean house."

That was the cue everyone had been waiting for. On the other side of the Seat, in the stands, even the Hands turned on each other. Some went down quickly as easily with a knife or a claw or some other means, spraying blood on the stands and even onto the crowd immediately below them. Others were not so easily subdued and fought back. Walter watched one pair of Hands wrestle fervently until they both ended up falling off the wall into the crowd. The crowd, confused and scared, descended mercilessly upon them both.

At the main gates, the Coliseum guards continued to push the crowd back until there were none in the center passageways. Behind them, in front of them, bodies lay strewn across the floor, those who died trying to escape. A few in the crowd got clever, taking advantage of larger aliens to have them throw them over the line of guards. A few even made it to the other side and took off running. Walter watched them go, hoping they would be able to make it. But another line of guards appeared suddenly and cut them down. After taking care of them, the guards then started lowering the gates. First the outer gates, then the middle, and finally the inner gates. The guards pushed into the Seat and spread out a little more, cutting down those who were too slow to move.

The smaller gate opened, but no one rushed toward it. Rather, they tried to run away from it as Grandfathers poured through it, striking down any who were too slow to move, fanning out until the entire crowd was completely surrounded by either guards or Grandfathers. After a moment of nervous shuffling and a few late attacks that only resulted in death, the crowd quieted.

The small gate opened again, and a small legion of secretaries came through. They did not strike anyone down or lift a hand to anyone but the dead. They did not say a word as they worked to remove all of the bodies from the floor. They were scary in their efficiency. Walter tried to judge whether they were also part of this coup or if they were simply foot soldiers doing as they were told in order to live.

When they were all done, there was a surprising amount of breathing room that had opened up, though no one really wanted to think about how and why it got that way. Once everyone had shuffled and adjusted themselves to where they wanted to be, they all faced Cassius expectantly. Expecting to live, expecting to die, it all seemed the same now.

"We're still not done," Cassius said coolly. "That was just the easiest and fastest way to weed some of you out. The second way is going to take some time, but it is not productive to keep you here. Therefore, I am implementing martial law within the Wheel of Time and across the entire Time industry, to all civilizations, from Scientifically Superior and Openly Engaged, to Scientifically Primitive and Unengaged. I am the final authority in Time. Rifun may also speak with my name and my power. But from now until this mess is cleaned up and I have instituted a new order, only the Grandfathers and the chosen Hands have authoritarian power. The Merchants do not. The Scouts do not. The Harvesters do not. And the Timekeepers especially do not have power.

"And so, I, Cassius the Zero Hour, shall send you all to the Judgment Wing, to the prison to be held until your trials where the

Grandfathers will determine your loyalty and your usefulness to me. Take them away."

At the mention of being taken to the Judgment Wing, to the asylum prison, Walter's legs turned to jelly and he collapsed. Micaiah got him to sit up, lightheaded though he was.

"I know," Micaiah said softly. "I know. It's hard. But if we stay here, we're going to be trampled."

"I can't go there, Cai," Walter said, feeling like a child telling his mama that he couldn't go back to bed because there were monsters in the closet.

"Do it for Tommen. You're no good to anyone if you're dead."

"I'll die in prison, Micaiah. You know I will."

"No, you won't. Because in prison you will still be alive, and you can still plan on how to get out and get back to your kid. He's counting on you, Walt. Now get up!"

Walter stumbled to his feet. Then, with a sigh, he followed the rest of the crowd to prison, like a flock of sheep being led to slaughter.

Epilogue

Rifun stood beside Cassius as they watched the massive crowd get led off to the Judgment Wing where probably ninety percent of them would ultimately be sentenced to death.

"That's how you do it, Rifun," Cassius said. "That's how you win."

"Only day one," Rifun cautioned. "Winning is something you have to do every day."

"So now that you're my adviser, I can expect more of these sagely tidbits of wisdom."

"I expect so."

Cassius regarded him for a moment. "So, how's your pet project coming?"

"Better than I expected, given the circumstances," Rifun answered. "Tadashi going off the deep end certainly didn't help things, but the situation was salvaged."

"I don't see why you want to pursue this. We have the journal. We have the power. It's not smart to take on pupils in the middle of this. How many of them have officers in this mess? Tommen alone, his father and Lieutenants are here. Sentencing them to death is not going to win his heart. And he's already defied you multiple times. Cut your losses, and get rid of him."

"Is that an order?"

"Do I need to make it one? You can't kill them and keep Tommen, but you can't let them live either. You've created a no-win situation."

Rifun ran his tongue over his teeth. "Oh, I can think of a few ways to make this a win-win scenario for everyone involved. I just won't be able to prosecute them as fast as the others; they may have to be held a while."

Cassius snorted indignantly. "Your games got you in trouble last time; why do you think you'll fare any better a second time?"

"Because I've made some modifications to my game. And if it doesn't work, I still have the option to kill them all."

That was assuming they didn't kill themselves first. It was a fine line with Walter, after all. The man could run into a shootout or a domestic abuse situation, and it didn't seem to faze him one bit. But get him in a dark room with virtually no light, and the man turned into little more than a fearful child. Unlike fearful children, however, fearful adults were capable of seeing reason, as long as the end goal was not only freedom, but freedom of their own choosing.

What would Walter give so he could see the light of day again? Rifun had no interest in his house, his car, his turns, or any other worldly goods. Would Walter be willing to give up his free will? His soul? Would he be willing to give up his son in exchange for the one thing he held most dear? He'd already proven that he would die for his son, but that had been in a heat of the moment situation, when they'd both been in danger. Now it was time to test those limits. Just how selfish was Walter Forbes?

Keep reading for a preview of

Stopwatch

the next exciting installment of
The Chivalrous Welshman

Chapter One
Aftermath

Inauguration Day was supposed to be a day of excitement and anticipation, as eleven-slash-seventeen years of the same leadership came to a close and a new crowd of faces—or shrouds, anyway—assumed the mantel of leadership. Sure, there would always be grumbling about a particular candidate who didn't get elected, and trepidation that the new leaders would be terrible, but that was normal. That was to be expected.

But the atmosphere in the Wheel, surrounding the Coliseum, it was not one of excitement and anticipation with a few pockets of grumbling and trepidation. Rather, the entire Coliseum, inside and out, seemed to be an atmosphere of grumbling and trepidation with a few pockets of excitement and anticipation.

Tommen had heard several stories from his dad about policing protests on the college campus. Most often, they were peaceful and eventually everyone got bored and went home. But sometimes, his dad described a scene that it was like watching the crowd become a collective tiger, poised to strike. Just the right flutter of movement, indicating prey, and all hell would break loose. And that was when the peaceful crowd became an angry mob, a collective tiger, mob mentality.

He was pretty sure that this was such a scene. Just the right word or movement, and all hell would break loose.

Tommen was torn between wanting to be as close as possible to hear and see what was going on—an impossibility anyway considering the crowds—and wanting to stay as close to the portal as possible in order to make a quick exit. It wasn't a matter of if he would have to run, but when. He debated just leaving early and saving himself the trouble of potentially getting caught up in the running of the bulls. At the same time, from what he could hear and from what news got passed around through the crowd, everything was going as planned. The Hands handed over their shrouds without incident and all seemed well. Had they imagined the whole thing? Was it possible that this collective tiger would not strike?

The break came when the Coliseum guards started moving. Tommen saw it coming, though he couldn't quite say how. Maybe it came from understanding basic police tactics and how to move in such a way so as it round up as many as possible and gently herd them into an area. Maybe his paranoia superpowers were kicking in. Either way, once he saw the guards moving, he made sure to make himself as small and possible and just melt back into the crowd beyond the line of guards.

As the crowd quieted, Tommen heard a voice coming from inside the Seat, one he knew too well, one he'd hoped never to hear again.

"All during the elections, you heard about a False Zero Hour, one who was masquerading as the highest authority in the land with no one to rein him in." Cassius' voice carried over the crowd so even Tommen could hear him clearly. "You heard tales of Calis Cutthroat being this enemy, this False Zero Hour." Beat. "I. Am. He."

That was apparently some cue that the guards were waiting for because they turned from stealth mode to actively trying to push and shove as many people into the Seat as possible. That was also when the killing began. Any who tried to slip through the lines were struck down, whether by knife, fist, or some other means. Panic gripped the crowd, which only made it worse. Those who were not killed at the line were trampled by others, driven by instinct to escape.

Tommen took a few steps back, watching it all unfold, wanting to run but not wanting to look away. His dad was still in there!

There is nothing you can do in there, and there are Timekeepers much more powerful than you trapped in there.

Even as he thought it, the enormous gates started coming

down. And still the guards pushed, killing anyone within striking distance. He looked behind him. Several had made it through the lines, or had been outside the lines to begin with. He jumped as someone grabbed his shoulder. Once the mini heart attack subsided, he looked to see Micah nose-to-nose with him.

"We have to go. Now!"

They got about three steps into a run, when Tommen pulled them to a stop. "What about my dad?"

"We couldn't leave together," Micah told him. "Too obvious. But they were right behind me. Come on!"

Tommen allowed himself a small measure of relief and kept pace with Micah, making a beeline for the portal. Some other alien beat them to it, but it was just as well. As soon as it stepped through, it was attacked and killed, nearly beheaded in fact.

"How are we going to get through?" Tommen wondered breathlessly.

"Very carefully," Micah said, not slowing. "Stay close to me."

The only thing left was trust and hope. Trust that Micah knew what he was doing and hope that it would work. Tommen stayed hard on Micah's heels, following him through the portal. They were not attacked or impaled, but on either side of the portal lay two dead Grandfathers.

"What did you do?" Tommen asked.

"Tell you later," Micah said, pushing back the Grandfathers' cloaks, taking a knife for himself and handing one to Tommen. Well, to call them knives was a severe underestimation. Tommen had seen full swords shorter than these knives. Still, he gripped it hard and followed Micah through the Wheel.

The situation was not unique to the portal leading to the Coliseum. In fact, every portal had Grandfathers, waiting and ready to murder any who stepped through. But they were out of the Coliseum now and they could Band once again, moving into a Fast Band so it was as if everything else was standing still. A couple times, one or two Grandfathers would recognize the Bands and break in. But Micah was no amateur. Rather than letting his Band be shredded and opening them up to an attack by several dozen Grandfathers, he would instead restructure the Band and absorb the attacking Grandfathers, to make it a more even fight.

Most often the fight did not involve the knives so much as Micah simply using his Bands in such a way so as to confuse the hell out of the Grandfathers and ultimately kick them out of the Band so they could continue on.

The Wheel proper was largely devoid of life, but not empty. It looked like everyone everywhere had been taken by surprise. Most of the strewn dead were average Time Agents from all disciplines, but here and there, Tommen spotted a couple secretaries. He managed a grim smile of satisfaction whenever he saw a Grandfather among them.

"You're sure my dad and Micaiah are close behind us?" Tommen wondered as they slipped through the last portal door before heading for the portal room.

"That's the last I knew of them, Tommen, I'm sorry," Micah said. "Believe me, I wish I knew more and I wish I knew what the hell is going on. But we can't figure it out here where everyone in a black cloak wants to kill us. We need to get home."

When they got to the portal room, they found it completely empty. Not just of pedestrians or Grandfathers, but of portals, too. The whole room, where normally there were rows and rows of portals going to all corners of the universe, had been reduced to what amounted to a big, empty warehouse.

"All the portals have been closed," Tommen stated dumbly.

"Yes, I see that," Micah said. "Makes this easy, then."

He went up to the nearest row, put a hand on the metal bar, and, with some effort, opened a portal to the bakery office. Sweat dripped down his forehead as he said, "Go!"

Tommen did not hesitate, but he jumped through the portal as if a T. rex was after him. It was kind of like doing a dive off the tall diving board and not exactly getting into perfect form at the entry. He hit the portal hard and it reverberated through his body, rattling his teeth, squeezing the air from his lungs, and slamming into his arm, making it feel as if it had been rebroken. Then he took the real physical hit as he stumbled into the office and over half a dozen objects in his way, like a table, a chair, and finally a door, instinctively putting his hands out and catching his injured arm once more, the fingers to be more precise. It was as though someone sent an electric shock up his arm, and it was all he could do to bite his tongue.

Micah was right behind him, though he was slightly more graceful, stepping through and more collapsing into a chair than tripping over it. He was breathing hard and sweating as if he'd run twenty miles through the desert. Tommen gathered himself and calmly stepped out of the office to retrieve a glass of water which he accepted gratefully and drank in two gulps.

"Thank you," he breathed, setting the empty glass on the table. He used his shirt to wipe his face. "Are you hurt?"

"I don't think so," Tommen replied, checking himself and trying to ignore the throbbing in his arm. "No, I think I'm okay. You?"

Micah nodded. "I'm fine."

"Why are you sweating so much?"

"I'm assuming it was the Grandfathers; they put a dampening field over the portal room. It closes all currently open portals and makes it nearly impossible to open a new one."

"But you did."

"I only said nearly impossible."

"Micaiah can do the same thing, too, right? He can open a portal through the dampening field?"

"He's better at it than I am."

Tommen found his own chair to slump into, feeling suddenly very weary. "Are we safe now?"

Micah sighed. "That remains to be seen."

"What happened in there?"

"Oh, I wish I knew exactly. The previous Hands were named and unshrouded, all according to plan, the usual bullshit from every inauguration that's more pomp than practical. Then they brought out the newly elected Hands, as well as the Zero Hour. Except the supposedly elected Zero Hour turned out to be Rifun."

"Rifun?" Tommen wondered.

"Yup. Think about it, though. Everyone had heard about Cassius and the False Zero Hour and the whole scandal. If someone was going to try something, stop Cassius from becoming Zero Hour, they'd only take out Rifun instead." He shrugged. "I don't know, it's only my theory. Anyway, the Hands transfer power like they're supposed to. The Zero Hour is always saved for last because...drama, I guess. But when the Bat goes to remove the Zero Hour shroud, the Zero Hour steps away and takes it off himself. And that was Cassius."

"That was when the guards started moving."

"Right. That was when your dad also said that it was time to go. We couldn't go all three together because it would be too easy to get caught, but we weren't going to be waiting around if you know what I mean. I went first because I was the smallest. Your dad would come next and Micaiah would generally stay with him to help if needed. Last I knew, they were almost right behind me. I slipped through the line of guards and went to find you and get you out of there."

"So there's no real way to know if they actually made it out. I mean, they'd be here already, wouldn't they?"

Micah sighed. "I don't know. Maybe. Maybe not. I wouldn't count them out just yet."

"Micah, we both saw the guards killing everyone, the Grandfathers, too."

"Tommen, it does Cassius no good to kill absolutely everyone. He might use those events to make a point and make the rest of those inside bend to his authority, but he didn't go through all the trouble of these elections just to murder everyone. He could have murdered everyone without needing to become the Zero Hour." He went on before Tommen could speak. "I don't know what his plans are. But I do believe that your dad and my brother are smart enough and resourceful enough to stay alive as long as they can and figure out a way to get home. Okay?"

Tommen nodded grimly, trying to hold it together. But as soon as Micah touched his shoulder, he lost it. Micah drew him gently to his chest, letting him cry on his already sweaty shirt. "I don't want to lose my dad again," he bawled.

"I know," Micah whispered. "It's frightening and unfair, and I don't want to lose them either. But the important thing is that you're safe, which was what your dad wanted most, whatever happened. He wanted you to be safe. Okay?"

After a second, Tommen nodded and pulled away, feeling like a stupid child. He took a tissue from a box on Micaiah's desk. "I'm sorry, I'm an idiot."

"No, you're not. You love your dad, just like I love my brother."

"Yeah, well, you're not the one sobbing like a child."

"Who says I don't want to? There's a time to weep and a time to be strong."

Tommen sighed and tossed the tissue in the trash. Micah went on, "Just like you said when your dad was in the hospital: I'm not giving up until they're six feet under. When they're six feet under, then I'll mourn. But it's not over until it's over. All right?"

It sounded silly, like a word salad of pithy little motivational quotes that might normally be found on the walls of yoga and karate studios. At the same time, half of it was directly quoting him. He sighed. A time to weep and a time to be strong. Just like last time, he supposed. Until his dad and Micaiah were six feet under, he wasn't going to give up. And this time, he had Micah beside him to help. He grabbed another tissue from the box and tried to clean himself up and make himself at least a little presentable to the public, still sitting out there at various tables and booths, completely ignorant of the massacre that had just occurred inside another dimension. How quaint to be immensely concerned with the affairs of Hollywood and its idiot celebrities.

Tommen sniffed and wiped his eyes. "Okay, so what do we do?"

Micah leaned back in his chair. "I haven't actually figured that out yet, as far as a rescue plan goes. However, I do have an obligation to warn anyone and everyone who is still here on Earth to not go or even attempt to go to the Wheel. Who knows, maybe we'll get a bite as to a plan of action. In the meantime, you think you can run the store?"

"Um...Like, the whole thing?"

"Yeah." Micah glanced at the clock. "It's getting to be about closing time, once the dinner crowd leaves, so you don't have to do a lot of baking."

Tommen scoffed and shook his head. They'd just survived a massacre and been separated from those they loved most. And now they were talking about closing up the bakery like it was any ordinary Saturday. It made Tommen's stomach churn. It felt disrespectful, cowardly even. He'd done as his dad said and gotten out of the thick of things, but now he felt the need to use his vantage point on the sidelines to figure out a way to rescue them.

And they sat here talking about baking.

"I know what you're thinking, Tommen," Micah said. "I understand. But if I can't do anything right now, neither can you. And actually, you're going to be more help to me here. I'm officially promoting you to the temporary position of Sub-Lieutenant."

"Is that a position?" Tommen wondered.

"No, I just made it up, but I still need you. Go out and manage the store, and I'll call you when I need you, okay?"

After a second of hesitant consideration, he nodded and stood. He made it to the door when he stopped and turned. "Wait, so you said that you made up the Sub-Lieutenant position, but...that bit about managing the store...is that a promotion, too?"

Micah raised a brow. "Weren't you just feeling guilty about working while Walter and Micaiah are still trapped in the Wheel?" Tommen felt his cheeks turn red. Micah managed a half-smile. "Prove you can do this, and we'll talk later. All three of us. And don't forget to take your translator off." Even as he spoke, he removed the one still in his ear.

Tommen had completely forgotten about the translator. He'd thought it was strange that he could hear Micah speaking English and Welsh at the same time. As he went to the back to punch in and grab an apron, he removed the translator and stuffed it in his pocket. The sounds around him became clearer as he first went to the counter to make sure no one was waiting, then retreated to the kitchen to see if anything was waiting for him in the ovens.

So Cassius had really done it. He'd not only won the elections and become the Zero Hour, but he'd launched a full military coup in the Wheel, murdering hundreds, if not thousands, and assumed total authoritarian control of Time. Had all four of them made it out of the Wheel, Tommen would probably be less concerned, but as long as his dad was a captive of that maniac, he felt rage burning in his gut and spreading throughout his entire body.

There were several pans still in ovens that he worked on, all the while coming up with dozens of different ways he wanted to torture and kill Cassius and Rifun. From a firing squad, to being drawn and quartered, to any number of obscene and obscure medieval tortures. Taking the two and taping them together with a bomb between them wasn't off limits either, as far as he was concerned, but he really felt his calling more toward the slow, painful deaths. Just as every second that passed by where Tommen wasn't sure whether his dad was alive or dead was agonizing, so he wanted those two to suffer. Just as Cassius had murdered those women so precisely, so he wanted those two to feel torturous pain.

Supposedly, people who were always cynical and angry and held every grudge since kindergarten were more likely to die young and with few friends. Tommen was certainly feeling that way now, as though his rage would make his blood pressure go so high that he would spontaneously combust. But, the way he figured it, there was no point in dancing around the kitchen whistling some cutesy little tune while baking a humble apple pie. He was angry, he was scared, and he wanted to pummel Cassius' face until it was puffy and bloated like the dough beneath his fists. He wanted to—

His thoughts were interrupted by a ding from the service bell on the counter. Clapping the flour dust from his hands, he went up front, nodding to the lady at the counter and quickly washing his hands.

"What can I get for you?" he asked, trying to sound courteous and not ready to rip someone's head off.

"Do you do custom cakes?" she wondered.

Tommen sized her up. Pretty thing, early twenties, blond, probably went to yoga every morning at sunrise and ran a marathon every other weekend. Probably had a salad for lunch with extra kale and drank a chocolate protein shake as her way of indulging. This cake would not be for her.

"Yes, we do, what's the occasion?" He reached under the counter and found the custom order slip and a pen. "Birthday, anniversary? Something off the wall?"

"I'll take C, final answer. It's kind of unusual, so I hope you don't mind." Tommen didn't mind the uncommonness of the cake so much as the way she hesitated and wouldn't get to the point. "It's for my sister. It's a congratulations cake; she just adopted two kids. We're having a party for her."

If there was a God, He certainly enjoyed sticking his little Tommen voodoo doll with needles. Most often they went straight through the heart, it seemed.

"Okay," Tommen told her. "Actually, it's not as unusual as you think. What are you thinking?"

She gave him the parameters and requirements and he calculated the total, ringing her up when she decided to pay in full upfront.

"So, if you don't mind me asking, what kind of kids?" he wondered, knowing he was willfully jumping into a pool of sharks. "Boys, girls?"

"A boy and a girl," she replied. "Brother and sister. From China, to be precise. We're all pretty excited, actually."

If she would have said "from Wales" he probably would have run to the back of the store and beat his head against the back door, which was solid metal. He nodded pleasantly, saying, "Congratulations."

She thanked him, grabbed her receipt, and headed out. The dining room was beginning to clear as the dinner crowd finished up their more civilized meals and prepared to head out to the club or the bar or someplace where they didn't necessarily have to be civilized, where the whole point was to become uncivilized on a Saturday night. Tommen sighed as he thought about Micaiah who usually was one of those people, going out every other Friday or Saturday. He almost missed hearing him announce that he was leaving, and Micah chastising him for leaving him alone.

He turned, ready to go back to his dough, when Micah opened the office door. "A second?"

Tommen tried to tell himself that it was because he was the unofficial, temporary Sub-Lieutenant, as well as a candidate for manager, and not because he was in some kind of trouble. Problem was, generally whenever he got called into the office, it was because he was in trouble, and the feeling of dread was hard to shake.

"Good news?" he wondered, looking around the office. Obviously their missing persons were not back.

"Good and bad news," Micah replied. "I called around the District, to Timekeepers, Harvesters, Merchants, every Time Agent in the District. The good news is that about seventy percent of them are still around. The rest I couldn't reach. I don't know if it was because they're sitting under Cassius' thumb right now or they just stepped out of the office for a minute, but I'm counting them as being missing.

"Bad news is that upper management is in chaos. The only District Captain I was able to raise was District Three. As for Managers, I actually got a call from Region Nine Manager; he's the only one left of the Managers. Mi Chin the Gatekeeper is gone. There are a handful of Captains and Lieutenants left around the world, but they're mostly gone. A majority of the layfolk are still around, though."

Tommen folded his arms. "What does that mean for us? What do we do?"

"That means that for the time being, we report to the District Three Captain and he reports to the Region Nine Manager. I'm currently going through my list of others around the world who are at least Gatekeeper-trained." He indicated a file open on the computer. "If I can do that, we'll be in pretty good shape."

"What about Wardens or Dominions?"

"Acting as Gatekeepers, yes. But with the state of the Time industry and the Wheel, it does us no good to have such high-ranking officers. In fact, it's more likely to make us a target. Right now, we have to focus more on planetary needs and filling the gaps, figuring out who we have and who we don't have. When in chaos, establish order. Then you can work out your plan of attack."

"And what is our plan of attack?"

"I don't know yet," Micah admitted.

"What do you want me to do?"

"Right now, I just wanted to let you know what's going on, what's being done. You are a Sub-Lieutenant and even though it is unofficial and temporary, you still need to be kept in the loop as much as possible."

"Oh. Okay." Tommen looked at his feet.

Micah chuckled nervously, humorlessly. "Believe me, I know you want to go back and murder every one of those black-clad bastards, but it's not going to happen at this moment."

Even as he spoke, the office phone rang. He picked it up. "Bakery na hÉireann, Micah speaking." Pause. "Uh-huh. Yeah. Okay, thanks for keeping me updated."

"Who was that?" Tommen dared ask as Micah hung up.

"District One has an Acting Captain."

"That's good."

"It is. It's even an old friend of ours. Assim Foyez."

Foyez had helped Tommen escape the Grandfathers when he returned from Sifura's world with the cure to his dad's illness. Tommen thought for sure that he'd been killed or had his clock broken or any number of horrible punishments.

"That reminds me," Micah went on. "Sifura is alive and well, also. Or she was. She was present at the inauguration at least."

Sifura had been the one to take Tommen to get the cure in the first place, crossing desert and jungle and facing off against some of the ugliest creatures in the universe. She'd been injured in their quest and sent Tommen home early in order to not waste anymore time. But there had been a spy among the rescue party, and Tommen had been so sure that he'd done her in.

It was too strange, too convenient. When the Grandfathers had chased Tommen with murder in their eyes, why had they spared his accomplices? It made no sense.

"What's the likelihood that the Grandfathers would actively chase us here?" Tommen wondered. "Would they actually, like, come to Earth and kill us all?"

"Well, they can try," Micah said, "but it's unlikely. Well, for you. Me, I'm not so sure. But Earth is Unengaged and unimportant; we contribute about as much to the Time industry as Guam contributes to the U.S. economy. Some participants are outliers — Lily, for example — but if they do come after us, it's because they've already desecrated the rest of the universe and are just mopping up the rest."

Tommen wasn't sure if he intended his words to be encouraging or not, and decided it was better to just take them at face value. They were safe for the time being. How long they were safe was unsure, but for the moment, they could take a break.

The phone rang several more times over the next minute or two. District Seven had an Acting Captain. Region Three had an Acting Manager. A couple people within District Four had returned to their phones and were now informed as to the recent tragedy.

Tommen folded his arms. "How long do we wait before

declaring our chain of command as good as it's going to get?"

"Probably not until tomorrow morning," Micah told him. "People need to know what's going on, and it's going to take time to tell them the truth as well as sort out who's here and who's not."

"But that's at least an eternity in the Wheel! What if they're already dead?!"

"Keep your voice down, Tommen, there are still guests in the dining room. If they're already dead, then it won't matter if we went now or waited a day. But if they're alive, we do them no good if we go in there with an ill-conceived plan and get caught ourselves. Do you understand what I am saying?"

Tommen sighed. "Yes."

"I know, Tommen. I know. I do. You want to go in there and murder the Grandfathers and free everyone. Part the Red Sea and deliver everyone to the Promised Land. I get it. But it's not happening right this second. Now, I either need you with me as a Sub-Lieutenant who can handle slow and uncomfortable information and make rational decisions, or you can just be an Apprentice and I'll do this myself."

Part of him wanted to just say, "Fuck it," throw his hands up, and let Uncle Micah do his thing, do all the work. He felt like a small child facing big problems, and he wanted the grown-ups to take care of it and make it go away. Like when he'd first come into the twenty-first century at eight years old, alone and afraid. His dad had done all the work to help him make sense of it all, explain it to him, and help him adjust to his new life. How Tommen wished he could have that again in this situation, surrender it all to Micah and just make it go away. Go to bed tonight and by morning his dad would be back, smiling and saying that it was all just a little misunderstanding and everything was going to be okay.

The other part of him knew better. The other part of him was his pa's son, his dad's son, the part that said that he was a man now and he had to face things like a man. No more hiding behind ma's skirts like a frightened child. It was time to bury his feelings, take the information—no matter how sad, how disturbing, how angering—and come up with a rational plan of action that saved more lives than it sacrificed, even if the only life he sacrificed was his own.

He took a breath and nodded, saying quietly, "I can do it. I can be your Sub-Lieutenant."

Micah nodded slowly. "Good. I was hoping you'd say that."

"What do you need me to do?"

"Your first priority right now is managing the bakery while we're open and making sure that no one notices anything amiss." He raised a brow and Tommen flushed. "And when you get time, I want you to make up a list of all the Regions and Districts with the current Acting or True Managers and Captains. I'll scribble them down on paper; I just need you to write it up so it's more organized. Can you do that for me?"

Tommen nodded. "Yes, sir."

"Good man." The phone rang. "I'll get back to you."

Tommen turned and left the office just as a customer walked up to the counter. He put on a good face and hoped it looked convincing. From his experience, there were only two acceptable options when it came to greeting customers and not letting on that something was wrong. The first was the nice face that everyone expected, the one that said, "Hi! How are you today? How's the wife and kids? Isn't little Johnny getting big!" The second option was the face that everyone expected from a teenager, the one that said, "I don't give a fuck about you or what you want because I hate my job, I'm just here for the paycheck, and I think that you should actually be catering to me." No one wanted to see the sad face and hear the sob story because that made everything awkward, and the mad face and the whiny story just left everyone feeling miserable.

The order was simple enough, and once the customer was gone, Tommen was faced with the task of doing full store shutdown alone. That meant going back and finishing his baking project, then working on condensing all the trays in the display case. It also meant cleaning the kitchen from top to bottom as well as the normal dining room duties—wiping down tables, sweeping and mopping, trashes, cleaning the display case once everything was empty, cleaning the coffeemaker...

Yeesh. And to think that Micah normally had to do it all by himself on the days Tommen didn't work, or mostly by himself; Micaiah didn't always leave early. Still, it almost seemed cruel of Micaiah to leave his brother alone to do all the cleanup.

As the last of the customers filtered through, Tommen tried to make up silly little scenarios about what Micaiah really did when he left early. He always said that he went out to bars and clubs and got laid—maybe not explicitly, but hey, when it's just three dudes in a bakery, talk happens—but even if he did do that occasionally, what if it was really just a cover-up for something else?

While his less serious scenarios involved Micaiah secretly being Batman and the like, he also considered the possibility that maybe he really did have another job. Probably not the normal kind, moonlighting as a bartender or a saxophone player on various street corners, but as a true Timekeeper? He had a day job and couldn't just up and leave on a whim to go chase down some Runner in Vermont who'd stolen six minutes' worth of Time from some low-level Merchant. Maybe he worked a night shift, unofficial, unpaid, but it was his eight hours where he would respond to all things Runner, and other assorted Time shenanigans.

Tommen dumped a bit of bleach in a bucket and started filling the final cleaning bucket. It was kind of like when his dad had still worked Missing Persons, doing that for about six months after the adoption. It wasn't always about hunting down international terrorists who kidnapped the pretty daughter of some secretive ex-FBI agent. Most of the time it was a parent or relative doing the kidnapping. And sometimes, it was all about getting a vehicle description and direction of travel. His dad would be out at three in the morning, hiding on a side road or behind a bush, waiting for the kidnapper to try and make the crossing into Tennessee. He might sit there for ten minutes or six hours, only to learn that they'd gone north to Ohio instead.

Tommen told himself that it was just the stink of bleach that got him all teary now. *Fuck, but you're an idiot. What are you, a child? A girl? What would your dad say if he saw you like this, if you and him and escaped and it was Micah and Micaiah trapped in the Wheel? He'd probably say the same thing Micah did. A time to weep and a time to be strong, but not until they're six feet under. Not over until it's over.* To say nothing of the fact that if those had been the circumstances, he probably wouldn't be so torn up over it. Did that make him a bad person?

He rubbed his eyes on his shirt sleeve, feeling his sinuses burn as he turned off the water and hauled the bucket out to the dining room. Dipping a wash rag in, he quickly found several small cuts on his hand and wrist and he sucked in a breath through his teeth. Trying to work around a cast sucked. Couldn't get it wet, so washing his hands was difficult and that only made it harder to do his job seeing how he had to contend with frosting and icing and glaze and sprinkles that somehow, someway, managed to slip in under the wrappings and cause him to itch and scratch something fierce. Luckily he was able to dig them out with only moderate difficulty, like trying to lick a piece of silk out of your teeth after eating corn on the cob.

After he wiped down the tables and put away the bleach bucket, he started on trashes. He'd just opened up a new box of large bags when the bell on the counter dinged. He glanced at the clock. Well, technically they were still open. For another fifteen minutes.

It was a group of college students, as evidenced by age, school pride sweatshirts, and general drunken demeanor, suggesting that whatever they were up to tonight, it wasn't going to be studying—not the book kind anyway. As it was, of the ten people in the group, seven of them—yes, seven—appeared to be unable to keep their hands off their significant other, or others. Tommen didn't even want to think about why they decided they needed the last eight unsold donuts of the day. Not to say that his mind didn't go there, but something about present circumstances just didn't make it seem like much fun.

"How's it going out here?" Micah asked, standing in the office door and stretching, looking about as grouchy as Micaiah normally did after being cooped up in the office for too long.

"Just about ready to take these pans back to wash and lock the door," Tommen reported, trying to sound responsible, a polite balance of eagerness to be promoted in some fashion, without seeming to completely neglect why he was in that position in the first place.

"Is the kitchen clean?"

"Aside from a few last dishes, yeah."

"Damn. I was hoping for a distraction."

"Sorry...I think?"

Micah shook his head. "No, you're doing good." He rubbed his eyes. "Micaiah makes this job look easy. And I'm not even talking about the bakery stuff."

Somehow it just suddenly occurred to Tommen that Micaiah did as many Timekeeping duties as baking duties as he sat in that office for hours on end. He was the one who did all the leg work while Micah ran the bakery and Walter raised Tommen. He wasn't a baker who did a little Timekeeping on the side; he was a Timekeeper who did a little baking on the side, probably as a hobby just to keep him sane.

"You okay?" Micah asked, cutting into Tommen's thoughts.

"Yeah," Tommen answered, probably a little too quickly.

"Hang in there just a little while longer. We'll get them back."

The elections have come and gone, and I don't think it's quite what anyone expected, to say the least. Personally, I imagine two very different reactions to the ending of this book. The first is that terrible, awful, love-hate frustration of a tense climax and cliffhanger ending. Our heroes are separated and no one knows what could happen now that Cassius and Rifun are in charge.

The second reaction I expect is a bit of resentment. The last two books, all twelve hundred pages, have encompassed a time span of about three weeks. The second book may be excused as it was an adventure to a new world and new culture that required detail and backstory in order to fill it out and be believable. But what about this one? Couldn't she have skipped or maybe glossed over some of it, like all the school drama? The workplace drama was pretty expected, but that could have been shortened, too, right?

Well, yes, I certainly could have glossed over it a bit, condensed a majority of the middle portion between the review and the elections and cut the chapter count in half. Problem is, I had already done that by the publication of this book. In the coming books, there is going to be a lot of information and a lot of action that builds off of what you read here, bringing together several plot threads and unearthing a number of little Easter eggs hidden throughout.

To that end, there was a ton of information that couldn't be contained here because it would turn into its own story. A bit of exposition would turn into a novel within a novel. Walter's story is an example of this. A small sample of it has been provided here, and I would advise you to keep an eye out for it in the future. It is not required reading for the *Chivalrous Welshman* series. While it will provide greater backstory and depth of understanding for Walter's history and character, there is nothing in there that you must know in order to make sense of future events here.

Such is my goal for all future series within the *Timekeeper Chronicles*. I know that if I say too much, I'm only going to dig my own grave, but the world of the *Chivalrous Welshman* is about to explode, and you, Reader, are about to go on a wild ride across the universe. If you want to explore certain aspects of this universe further, I intend to make them available to you in due time. Until then, for any information regarding the *Timekeeper Chronicles*, you can visit the website listed on the back flap or back cover.

I'm excited for you, Reader. Hang on tight, because its about to get real.

The Prisoner and the Priest

He shuffled into the tiny chapel, feeling very conspicuous, but, more than that, very weak. His body was starved and wounded. Worse than that, though, his soul was heavy, crushed under the weight of his sins. The distance between him and the priest seemed to stretch on forever until he sat in the front pew.

The priest was perhaps fifty-five years of age, maybe closer to sixty. He had blond hair that was quickly turning white and falling out almost in clumps. His build remain large and strong, though his back was bent and he moved with the obvious pain of arthritis. He nodded once to the gaoler who moved back a pace. Then the priest pulled up a chair and sat down in a heap.

"What's your name?" the priest inquired.

"Walter Forbes," the man answered, studying his feet.

"Is it? If I recall correctly, your given name is Owain, named for our ancient king."

"My wife called me Walter. It was a more proper, more British name, but still slightly exotic."

"Your ex-wife, whom you beat and murdered."

Owain-called-Walter glared at the priest. "I don't deny that I beat her, but I did not murder her."

"Yet you murdered her father."

"And five of his associates, including the man who killed Paige and our daughter."

The priest leaned back in his seat as comfortably as he could manage. "Mr. Forbes, Owain, the Church is in the business of mercy. Often we advocate for the prisoners here for reduced sentences or even clemency. You are here on very serious charges, and you are a known drunkard, brawler, thief--quite frankly, you are a criminal.

The Lord extends the hand of justice just as readily as the hand of mercy." He sighed. "It is unlikely that we can exonerate you of your crimes, but we may be able to keep you from swinging."

"For what purpose? So I can rot in my cell?"

"Saint Paul made good use of his time in prison."

"If I recall correctly, he was still executed."

"What I am saying, Owain, is that even if you were to spend the remainder of your days here, I am sure that, with the help of the Church and good behavior, you could make it worthwhile. Perhaps, in time, you could earn privileges. But it has to start here. Today. You have to talk to me."

"I didn't ask for this."

"Did any of us ask for salvation? The light came into the darkness, and the darkness did not understand it. I am offering you a chance to make the right choice. You are sentenced to hang in two weeks. Seeing you walk in here, I can sense your heart is heavy and your soul is suffering. Perhaps the Church cannot dissuade the courts, but perhaps you can walk up there with a clear conscience."

Owain let out a breath and studied his hands for a moment. His fingernails needed trimming, but he was not permitted any sharp tools. If he didn't kill someone else, it would be himself. Besides, did it matter whether a dead man had trim fingernails? Finally, he nodded.

"All right. I'll talk. I don't think you're going to keep me from swinging, but I think you're the only person who has ever cared to listen."

The priest dipped his head. "Why don't we start at the beginning?"